SHOWDOWN AT THE TOP!

"Tony, you're vulnerable," said David Battle. "Believe it."

Tony shook his head. "I'm not nearly as far as vulnerable as you. Suppose it were true. If I ever told the ... ... men's mind ... ... believe it, they'd ... ... you —you ... ... with just one girl. The ... ... man can comprehend that. That ... ... ing they'd do themselves if they had the opportunity or the nerve. They'll hate you for it. Add that to an alcoholic wife and an odd-ball mother, and I think you're in worse shape than I am."

David Battle's eyes narrowed. The battle lines were beginning to be drawn. The next president of National Motors just might be selected by the standards of a scandal-mongering gossip columnist.

THE HARD WINNERS

JOHN QUIRK

AN AVON BOOK

AVON BOOKS
A division of
The Hearst Corporation
959 Eighth Avenue
New York, New York 10019

First Printing, August, 1966
Third Printing, June, 1968

Cover illustration by Hector Garrido

Printed in the U.S.A.

To Detroit:

We have the biggest, most powerful and perhaps most important single industry in the world. What is done here affects the economy of America more directly, with more impact, than anything that can be done outside of government. What is good for Detroit is good for America. We've learned to say it the other way around, too. What is good for America, what's good for New York, and Jacksonville, and Bangor, St. Louis, Seattle and La Jolla is good for Detroit.

To some friends among the men who make the automotive industry great:

Bob Anderson, Bill Bogan, Chuck Brethen, Rine Bright, Ed Cole, John DeLorean, Bob Den Uyl, Bud Goodman, George Goodwin, Jack Gordon, Bill Hankins, Leon Hart, Ernie Jones, Ted Lindsay, Tom Morrow, Urban Rice, Dick Steding, Lynn Townsend, and George Webb.

And to Ethel Lucinda Hall from the Kanawha Valley.

BOOK
I

1

ON NOVEMBER 22, 1963, President John Fitzgerald Kennedy and Jacqueline Bouvier Kennedy disembarked from *Air Force One* at the Dallas County Airport. She was given a bouquet. Their faces were unusually bright. There was between them an evident, noteworthy conjugal harmony. This may have been a day, such as comes now and then to husband and wife, when the warmth that brought them together in the first place is rekindled to burn as brightly, or brighter, for a while. It could also have been a day of presentiment, when something warned them to know again the best in one another while there was still a little time.

The sun was bright, the sky blue after the morning rain. The President's party took it as an auspicious omen. This was a political trip—to show Texans that the Catholic, liberal President who sent troops to bend Southerners to the will of the Federal Government was not a carpet-bagger-nigger-lover but a strong, warm, charming, vigorous man of principle who thought well of Texans and wanted to go to great lengths to woo Texans back into his fold.

The President shook hands with Governor Connolly and the other welcoming dignitaries. He was led toward the black presidential Continental which would parade him through downtown Dallas. From the crowd of ordinary people come to greet him, men stretched their arms out to him. Kennedy could not resist. He darted to them to give his hand and warm smile. The Secret Service men fluttered back and forth to interpose themselves, but the President deliberately foiled them. He was at his best. He was on top of the world, in love with the world. John Kennedy had not long to live.

At exactly the moment John Kennedy disembarked in Dallas, James Lee Parker climbed the ramp of the National Motors flagship at the Detroit City Airport. He took one last upward glance at the gray clouds that covered Michigan from horizon to horizon. This sky was not appropriate. The cloudless, sun-filled Dallas day would surely have been more fitting for Jim Parker's November 22. There was no smile on his strong, square face, but he was filled with elation. He was on top of the world, in love with the world. James Parker had not long to live.

He entered the doorway of the executive Convair, made his way down the aisle and seated himself in the armchair across from Carl Pearson, President and Chairman of the Board of National Motors Corporation. Pearson looked up from the *Detroit News*.

Parker asked, "Nobody else riding with us?"

"They're on Albright's plane. I thought maybe we could talk some."

Parker said, "Good."

Pearson held up the paper. "It says here a major announcement is expected to come out of a special board meeting to be held this afternoon. Who do you suppose leaked that information?"

"Probably me. Did they spell my name right?"

"No names. But they know, of course. We made sure. Always make sure your PR men get the full story to the key reporters in advance. That way they can write their stories ahead of the press conference and do a better job. Do you have an acceptance speech, Jim?"

"Your secretary gave me yours. She said you got it from Warren Court when you took over."

Pearson grunted. He looked up at the No Smoking sign and deliberately and defiantly lighted a blunt cigar. The steward came back to check the seat belts, looked at the cigar, and then looked quickly away.

The turbine engines whirred to life and whined loud.

The senior pilot of the National Motors air fleet taxied out to the end of the runway and took off almost at once, veering right to avoid the Consolidated gas tank, climbed to a thousand, came back over the field, then headed east for New York City, leveling off at thirteen thousand.

Jim Parker said, "Carl, I've got to ask a stupid question. Do I make an acceptance speech?"

Pearson smiled. "You wouldn't think a man would have to ask a question like that."

"You wouldn't think so, but I do."

"I had to ask Warren Court the same question. I'd never been at a board meeting when a new president was installed. Maybe this will teach you the same humility it taught me. We don't know quite everything we think we know. And it's the littlest things that can throw you."

"What's the answer?"

"No speech. Just give us a routine couple of sentences about recognizing the honor and responsibility involved. And how you expect continued co-operation. Say you'll rely heavily on the board's advice. And a couple other things you may or may not mean. No speech."

They flew awhile in silence. Jim Parker asked, "When are you planning on coming back, Carl?"

"Tomorrow morning. Early."

"Good. Maybe you can drop me off at East Lansing."

"Tomorrow morning it will be your plane. Stop where you want."

"I've got two tickets. Want to watch State make it to the Rose Bowl?"

"Jim, I couldn't care less. The older I get the more anxious I am to be a participant, not a spectator. Did I tell you I've got a new swing?"

"Which new swing is this? One of the old new swings, or a new new swing?"

Pearson said seriously, "Listen to this. Graham had me believing a man my age should swing more with the arms, but he's wrong. Now I'm putting turn into it, and getting my drives out there two hundred and fifty yards. I haven't hit them that far for twenty years."

Parker smiled and let the gross exaggeration pass without comment.

"Try it, Jim. More turn on the backswing. It's a motion like the twist."

"Carl, up until now I've believed you could do anything you put your mind to. But not the twist, not the twist."

"Just when I was about to get it, my daughters informed me that between the twist and now, something called the bird and another one called the hully gully have come and gone. I don't even know the name of the thing they're doing now."

"Whatever it is, on daughters it looks good. Got a game Sunday?"

"I do now. Bring money."

"If it's above freezing, I'll play. And if you promise to use your new swing, I'll send a cab for you."

Carl Pearson regarded the younger man. He said, "There's a subtle change."

"In what?"

"In your attitude toward me. Up until today you wouldn't ever really josh me."

Jim Parker said earnestly, "Carl, you know how I've always thought about you."

"I wasn't objecting. It's the natural change. It's got to be. The moment you finally get your hands on those reins, you'll know for sure you're your own man." He took out a second cigar and lighted it. He blew a puff of blue smoke and said, "I've given up smoking. Mayo's says a man my age has to cut it out." Despite himself, an almost rueful look crossed his face. "A natural change. What year did I meet you, Jim?"

"Nineteen thirty-four. The Parker Special Packard."

"Did you really build that car, Jim?"

"From scratch. By myself."

"It impressed me. I wasn't sure you did it all by yourself."

"It got me my job." Then he said, "Carl, if I haven't said it before, I'll say it now. I appreciate it. The job in the beginning, and this job."

"Don't be too appreciative. I'm running a business. You were the logical choice, the only choice, and it's as simple as that."

"I just wanted you to know." Parker leaned back into the armchair. "The Parker Special Packard! I must have been the greenest hillbilly in Dee-troit." He waved his arm at the plane's executive conformation. "This is a long, long way from Sweet Water."

12

Pearson followed the motion of the arm. He said, "And from Fond du Lac."

The two giants of American industry settled again in their own thoughts.

Jim Parker said in his own sequitur, "It must be one helluva ride, in a rocket. I think I'll get NM in the rocket business so I can drive one."

Pearson said, "You might build one, but you won't drive it."

"Too old? I'm only ten years older than John Glenn. I'll make it to the moon before I'm done."

"Not now you won't. Now you ain't going nowhere, no time. You'll find out, Jim. You've got a price to pay, that maybe you haven't prepared yourself for quite enough. All of a sudden you're too important to do anything important."

Jim smiled. "I'll change that. I'll just change that."

Pearson said with a sudden tinge of asperity, "You'll change a lot of things I've done, I'm sure, but that's one thing's out of your hands. You've had it, boy. You don't fly your own airplane any more. No more hot-rodding down Telegraph. Now you're old and valuable, Father William."

After a long minute, Jim Parker said, "Carl, you know damn well I'm going to run my own show. But you know damn well, too, I'm not going to change the good things you've done."

There was another long pause before Pearson said, "Don't pay any attention to me, Jim. Either I'm going through the menopause, or it's coming home that I'm through with it all. This has been a tough week preparing myself, and I haven't quite made it yet. After forty-one years, that's a long time, to come to the end of it." Before Parker could answer, he went on. "It's the only way. You got to get out of the way of the young men. You get past sixty, you don't get new ideas any more. You know how to make the old ones work better, but you don't get new ones. I think we ought to make sixty the age to get the hell out of the way, not wait those last four sclerosis years."

Parker said, smiling, "I haven't noticed any particular senility in Pearson, Albright and Williams. You guys tore into me like a schoolyard fight."

"The Embassy plant? You were wrong, Jim."

13

"Maybe so. Maybe not. Anyhow, as far as age, I think it's going the other way. Kids are getting bigger sooner, and men are living longer and working longer *better*."

Pearson shook his head emphatically no. "We'll live longer, but not do things any better. You wait and see. You get to be sixty, you just sit there polishing your same old ideas. But you *were* wrong on the Embassy plant."

"Maybe so. Maybe not." Parker smiled. "You'll still outrank me on the board. Maybe I was wrong."

The retiring president and chairman of the board grinned. "Don't con me at this late date. You already got the bit in your teeth." He leaned forward and swung an armchair around and rested his feet. "Let's talk about your successor. Who gets it? I assume we're agreed."

"Carl, I have a feeling we're not at all agreed."

Pearson turned his head. "It is Bud Volk, isn't it?"

"No, it's not."

"Do you think Cleary is more qualified? I don't."

"It's not Cleary, either. Or Tony Campbell. It's David Battle."

Pearson let his feet fall to the deck. He twisted to face his successor. "You pulling my leg, Jim?"

"Of course not."

"Then it's a good thing I brought it up. You'll want to make the announcements on the other promotions in maybe two weeks, so we better talk this out now."

"I'm listening, Carl."

"Jim, the Group VP has got to be the logical man to succeed you as president. But even that isn't as important right now as the day-to-day running of the automotive divisions. You've got to have your best man there. That position is no place for sentimentality."

"Do you still think that's the case between me and Davey? Evidently you do."

"Jim, I think you've brought him along for old times' sake, and okay, he's worked out better than I thought he would."

Jim interrupted. "He's worked out better than you know, that's more accurate."

"But the Automotive Group has got to be your best man. Jim, I don't understand your thinking on this. It's not like you. The man with the best background and ability, that's Volk. He's had every right job, just like you

14

had, just like I had. Jim, Davey's a helluva nice guy, and all that, but he's a football player."

"He's an automotive man."

"No, he's a football player. And if you require my further elaboration of what I think of him, he's an opportunist. He's a man who married for advantage. You've got a blind spot where he's concerned. Jim, I can't let you make a major mistake like this. Your loyalty has given you a blind spot."

Jim Parker set his jaw. "Carl, I know better than you what gives among the vice-presidents. I've grown up on the job with all of them. I know which one can do what. I knew you were going to kick up a fuss about Battle, but I know what I'm doing. David Battle succeeds me."

"If you want to give him more money, go ahead. Raise him twenty-five thousand. Give him a new title. But I won't let you put the wrong man in the key spot."

Jim Parker leaned forward in his chair. "David Battle will succeed me as Group Vice-President Automotive."

"Well, sir, the board will do the voting, not just the two of us."

"Just how much of a threat is that, Carl? Are you going to fight me on it?"

Carl Pearson set his own jaw. Then he puffed three times, blowing the smoke at the cabin ceiling. He said in a mollifying, casual voice, "Let's find some agreement before we find disagreement. Let's talk about the things that make a man get to the top of this business. How would you list the requirements?"

Jim Parker said, "Pull. A sponsor. That's first."

"Are you serious?"

"I'm not sure. All right, I'd say ambition is number one. Not just the wish for success, there's expectation of success, the winning complex."

Pearson nodded thoughtfully.

Parker said, smiling, "And then there's pull."

Pearson said, "Pull is when somebody recognizes in you the ingredients of success and helps you along, because that's his duty, and his instinct, and to his own personal advantage to have you on his team, that's what pull is. When you pull somebody, he pushes you ahead even faster than you can pull him. Ambition and confidence, we've all got that in common, I agree with that. I don't think it's the number-one particular. I'll tell you another re-

15

markable thing we have in common. We all have small-town backgrounds. Did that ever occur to you? Plainview, Texas. Or Richmond, Indiana. Or Fond du Lac, Wisconsin. Or Sweet Water, West Virginia. Then you go to college, get the automotive bug, and come to Dee-troit to knock the spots off the city slickers. That's the recurrent theme. Small-town hunger, small-town shrewdness, and small-town self-reliance."

Parker asked, "Brains?"

"There are ten thousand men in the Corporation smart enough to run it, half of them smarter than you and me. You take David, him and some men down on the production line know some things out of books you and me never heard of. Brains isn't number one, either. You should have just the right amount of brains, like Bud Volk.

"The most important thing, the final thing that separates the men from the boys, is stamina, pure stamina. Other smart guys, other ambitious guys, can't take the grind. A sixteen-hour day, they think that makes no sense at all, that's no way for a man to live his life. They want to go home. They don't want to put in a double workday and then go to the Boy Scouts, the United Foundation and a couple dealer meetings. They can't do it. They just plain don't have the physical and mental stamina for the rat race. You and me, we don't even think it is a rat race, and we're just as ready as ever for the next day, and we're ready for nine thousand rat-race days in succession. It takes physical strength. And dedication. You've got to be single-minded. You've got to go to work for the Corporation right out of school, get completely and totally absorbed in it, and stay that way for the rest of your life. Do we agree?"

"We agree, Carl."

"Then who are we talking about? We're talking about Bud Volk."

"We are. We're talking about you, and about me, and about Bud, and about David Battle. You've just described David. He meets all your requirements." Jim smiled a little. "The only indictment you have of him is that he's a little too smart."

"All right, all right," Carl Pearson said, again testy. "For the sake of argument, we'll say he does. I know better. I don't see it in him to the required degree. But I'll say he has it. He still doesn't have it as much as Bud

16

Volk has it. And Bud's got the direct line of experience that we went through, you and me. He's prepared. I can think of ten or twelve men who are better prepared than your home-town friend."

Jim Parker said stiffly, "Carl, maybe you think you could stop me from taking over. I don't think you can at this late date. The board will vote me in this afternoon even if you suddenly have a change of heart. You aren't running things any more. I am. You picked your team when you ran the show, and I appreciate it that you picked me on it. I told you that. Now I'm picking my own team. David Battle will be Group Vice-President Automotive. As soon as it's feasible, I'll make him executive vice-president and move Bud in behind him. And that's the order of succession as I see it. Do you want to fight me on it, or let me run my own show?"

Carl Pearson bit deeply into his cigar. He said, "I don't know, Jim. I'll have to make up my mind."

At two-seventeen, Eastern Standard Time, the white-faced steward burst from the cockpit and said loudly, "Sir, President Kennedy has been shot. They think he's dead."

Carl Pearson said, "Oh, my God!"

But James Lee Parker did not hear the steward. At two-seventeen a leaden hand gripped his heart and constricted it until his chest burst, and he slumped in speechless agony, flooded with dread, until unconsciousness spared him more. The steward clapped an oxygen mask on his face. The plane landed in Pittsburgh to waiting doctors. It was too late for the blue-faced man. It was too late for the man from Sweet Water, West Virginia, who had ambition and expectation of success, and brains. It was too late for the man who had dedication and pull. It was too late for the man who had stamina. The President of the United States was dead, and the next president of National Motors, the sponsor of David Battle, was dead.

2

THE DEATH of James Parker should have been headline news in the Motor City. Now he rated only the left-hand column. The lead paragraphs said:

In the wake of the tragedy that has struck the whole nation, another tragic death has taken from Detroit an outstanding citizen. James Lee Parker, Group Vice-President of National Motors, was stricken this afternoon with a fatal heart attack within minutes of the assassination of President John Kennedy. The Detroit business community is reeling under the twin blows.

At the time of his death, the fifty-two-year-old executive headed the automotive operations of the giant corporation. He was a member of the Board of Directors, the Finance Committee, the Operating Committee, the Administrative Committee and the Policy Committee. It was widely believed that he was to have been named on this date to succeed the retiring Carl Pearson as president, and that when he succumbed in the company plane, he was en route to New York to a special board meeting and press conference which would have made the announcement. Thus he died on the threshold of his greatest achievement in a life filled with the high regard and respect of his associates and competitors alike. . . .

Ben Cowell, the automotive editor of the *Ledger*, enjoyed his rare front-page by-line. He reread his account with the pleasure of knowing he'd done it well. Then on the second page he reread the James Parker obituary, long since prepared and stashed in the morgue. "James Lee Parker was born June 12, 1911, in Sweet Water, West Virginia . . ."

The city editor winked as he passed Cowell's desk. Then he turned and came back.

Cowell said, "I hope one of them dies every month. This is living."

The city editor said, "But not Presidents of the United States."

Cowell said, "I don't want to talk about that. It makes me sick at my stomach."

"I thought you lunatic-fringers would be pleased about it. Have you ever seen this place in such chaos?"

"No. It's unbelievable. Just unbelievable. I wonder if it was like this with McKinley and Lincoln. What can you say? What can you do? I don't want to talk about it. I'll stick to Jim Parker. Do we follow up on it? Or wait until we get over Kennedy?"

"We're still running a sports page. And the comic strips. I guess we're still in business. That's a good story you wrote."

"Ain't it jist?"

"You missed one thing. No speculation on the possible successors. The king is dead, long live the king."

Cowell swore softly, "Damn!"

"Fortuitous oversight. Now you'll have a good follow-on for tomorrow. I like your tie-in of Kennedy. You could expand that now. Johnson takes over for Kennedy, but who takes over for Parker? Who does?"

"You tell me. Tell the National Motors board. They weren't thinking about anybody but Parker. He's had it wrapped up for years."

"They'll have somebody. They never leave anything to chance. My guess is they've got a list of next-in-lines as long as for JFK."

Cowell shook his head. "They're starting from scratch, that's my guess. It's wide open."

"Then we're king-makers. We'll decide for them. Who are the candidates?"

"Depends. On whether or not they decide to put in an interim president. Why don't you cover the funeral with me? We'll look over the possibilities and make our choice."

"You're on. By Monday I'll be glad to get out of this house of gloom."

3

THROUGH THE STREETS of the capital they came in measured panoply, like pagans burying a great chief, civilized
human beings finding some sort of comfort, and stability,
and expiation in the pomp and the magic rites, in the
muffled drums and the creak of caisson and leather, in
the braided, pious kings, princes and ministers, in the
ruffles and flourishes and the dirge, in the bagpipes of the
Black Watch, their wild, stirring, eerie shrill, in the slap
and crack of the Irish Guard, in the presented arms and
the gloved military hands smartly to the visors, salute to
the Commander in Chief, and in the black horse, the
riderless black horse, stepping and prancing and shying
and dancing, as full of life as the vigorous young man
was now full of death.

Down Long Lake Road they came—in Cadillacs, Im-
perials, Embassies and Continentals—to Kirk in the Hills
for the burial of the strong man who had almost become a great chief. The automotive writer and the city
editor of the *Ledger* waited for them at a good vantage
point. There was no awe in them.

The city editor asked, "Where would you rank the Kirk
among churches?"

"In prestige? Probably a tie for first with Christ Church Cranbrook."

"I'll make you a bet. James Lee Parker was not a Presbyterian when he came to Detroit."

"From Sweet Water? No bet." Cowell pointed his arm to the first car to reach the parking area. "Dana Albright. If the board decides to go with an interim president, they'd take one of the executive vice-presidents, and I'd say Albright. I'd get an argument. Most people would say Marion Williams because he's Finance. That's the most important thing in business. Taxes, pensions, unions, all the Government things . . ."

The city editor said, "I like your quaint Birch way of putting things. Are you saying that the CIO is an instrumentality of the United States Government?"

"Are you saying they're not part and parcel of the same liberal movement? Are the aims of the union and big government distinguishable in any way?"

The city editor smiled. "Lunatic J. Fringe." He lost his smile. "Are you a Bircher, Ben?"

"Are you a communist?"

"Go to hell."

"You must be, to have got so high up on our Red sheet."

"We're a middle-of-the-road newspaper, old friend."

"Thirty years ago. And before that it was reactionary. Now you can count on one finger the employee on this newspaper who is right of center. Me."

"I think we're going to have an argument. Why don't we talk about pleasant things, like Kennedy getting shot. Like Dana Albright."

They watched Albright walk to the church door, preceding his wife by half a step.

The city editor said, "He even looks like a hatchet man."

"Williams should get it. But he won't. Carl Pearson doesn't trust pencil-pushers. Albright is an operating man. If they go for an interim president, Pearson will take Albright."

"With his Lizzie Borden reputation? Would they make Bobby Kennedy President? Albright's public image is too cold."

"The PR men can fix that up. I could make Profumo look like Albert Schweitzer, you give me enough space. You Pinks have made Khrushchev more popular with the

22

American public than Governor Wallace. In one week we'll have Albright planted in the public mind as a man of engaging, sincere warmth and charm underneath that forbidding exterior."

"You slay me," the city editor said in a voice half amused and half sarcastic. Then he said brightly, "All right, we'll choose Albright. Let's announce him as the favorite, and see how much we can sway the board."

Cowell smiled broadly. "I think we really can influence them. It would frost their agates if they knew we thought so, but I think we can."

"What's the other depends?"

"If they pick the long-term man now, instead of an interim man. Then we've got a mittful of candidates. Five, six, seven."

"Too many. Narrow it down. Let's concentrate on two, that would be good journalism. Cleary? He's a hot shot. And you'll be running that feature on him this Sunday."

Cowell shook his head. He pointed to the swelling groups making their way to the church. "There's Cleary now. I don't like him. He made me cool my heels for the interview, like he was God-Almighty-Automotive doing the press a favor. I'll give you a clue. Him and his turbine engine don't come off so goddam important in my story as he's thinking he will. I think he's a communist. We'll start with Bud Volk and Tony Campbell." He pointed to arriving Cadillacs and the disembarking men. "The General Motors contingent. Jack Gordon, Bud Goodman, Goad, Cole. That's Bunky Knudsen and his wife going in with the Russells." He gestured again. "Chrysler. Townsend, Anderson. Bright. Do you see Ford anywhere?"

The city editor said, "We'll have as much brass as Kennedy after all. Volk and Campbell are young. Too young?"

"It would be a long jump for Volk. All the way from division manager. But the word was he'd succeed Parker as Group Vice-President Automotive, which would put him right in line."

"He a Bircher?"

"Like most conservatives, and unlike liberals, I don't base my decisions on a man's politics as long as he agrees with me politically. I'm mainly for Tony Campbell." He pointed.

The two men watched the very handsome Anthony

Campbell and his extremely attractive wife walk purposefully into the church.

Cowell said, "I'm really for Wendy Campbell, that's who I'm really for. She makes Madame Nhu look like Liz Taylor or some other slob. Tony and Wendy would do for National Motors what Jack and Jackie did for the country, sex things up. I hope our Tony doesn't get shot. Getting out of somebody else's bed."

"Any truth to that talk?"

"I wouldn't bet there was. But what would you do if you looked like him and had that much money?"

"Die before I reached puberty. That would be just my luck."

"We'll start the campaign for Tony and Wendy. They'd sure be a welcome switch from the Calvinists in the Corporation. A thing gets this big, it's too impersonal. A cabbie in New York told me that up in that room they had all these charts, and some guy named Carl Pearson and another one named Avery Winston went around with big pointers and every once in a while when they saw a thing on the chart they didn't like, they said fire that man. I think NM is run by communists and bureaucrats. We need Wendy. So we've got Volk and Campbell, and there's one more guy I want to promote. For the fun of it, if nothing else. One of the pallbearers."

The two newspapermen left their car and walked closer to the arriving funeral procession proper. The widow and children walked firmly, numbly into the church. The pallbearers formed.

The automotive writer said, "Interesting selection. You sure got to be somebody to make that list."

The city editor said, "I recognize the automotive presidents. Who are the rest?"

"Three executive vice-presidents and two ordinary vice-presidents. One sore thumb, a whore at a tea party. The white-haired, ruddy-faced guy, that's King Smith. He's a peddler, a manufacturers' agent. Maybe he ranks pretty high up moneywise, but he's a peddler. He's a member at Bloomfield Hills Country Club, but he must have got in through the side door. I didn't know he was a big enough buddy of Jim Parker to be a pallbearer. I knew David Battle was."

"I thought that's who that was. He sure doesn't change much, does he?"

24

Who would you say was the best, Jon Arnett or David Battle?"

After a moment, Dipper asked, "Who's going to be president of National Motors, Volk or Campbell?"

"Did you really have a running feud with the Little Dipper?"

"No. We were out there to win football games. We were pros. Does that answer your questions?"

"Yes. I'm glad to hear that."

"Football had nothing to do with it."

Jack asked with curiosity, "With what?"

King Smith said, "With nothing."

"You started it. I mean, as soon as I m[...] tle's name, it was like I broke wind in [...] between you and Battle? I never hea[...] there was supposed to be the feud [...] players."

There was silence.

Jack said, "I thought y[...] Parker too, Dipper."

"I'd say I was."

"How come you[...] was."

The sile[...]

King said, "I'm sorry to hear that, Jack. I guess you know."

"I'll cry on my own time. That's all I was saying. How far, Dipper? I got a bet."

Dipper Coogan said, "This neighbor kid run out for a pass yesterday, maybe forty-five yards, and I couldn't hit him. My arm went further than the ball."

"When you were playing, how far?"

"Maybe sixty yards. The ball was fatter then, harder to ip. I think maybe I could throw the new one maybe yards. But we could dropkick the old one better. dropkick the new one. It doesn't bounce right."

"opkick?"

asser there ever was? Baugh? Luck-

Sarazen says he expected to
ed. When he lost, he sat
t the hell went wrong,
the Yankees, they

arms out
ayers.

"He's my other choice. I'll include him among the favorites. We can get a hell of a lot of mileage out of David Battle."

"Would people take you seriously?"

"Who cares? They'd enjoy hell out of it. Who's the most popular guy in Detroit?"

"David Battle, if you're as old as we are. Before him it was Dipper Coogan and Joe Louis and Charlie Gehringer. And now it's Al Kaline and Joe Schmidt and Gordie Howe. I talked to a young girl the other day who didn't know who Gar Wood was."

"The readers would still eat Davey up. The Little Dipper running through a broken field with a Cutlass under his arm, sidestepping Ford and stiff-arming General Motors, great stuff. And he might fool us. He might just be a real dark horse."

"Get serious. Horse around with your readers, but not old Dad. Battle would be refreshing, but I got the idea NM ain't quite as interested in being refreshing as they are in making a few billion dollars."

"He's a helluva smart guy."

"For a ballplayer?"

"For anybody. He's got some things going for him. He married Warren Court's daughter, for what good that will do. Mainly, he was Jim Parker's boy. They both came from Sweet Water, I guess you know."

"Suit yourself. Write up all four. Dana Albright, Bud Volk, Tony Campbell and Davey Battle. Sounds good."

"Front page tomorrow?"

The city editor pondered as they trailed into the church. "Let's let it ride until next week. No use competing with the Kennedy news." He smiled just a little. "It might even be in good taste to wait." He turned his head. "Does David Battle suit you politically?"

"Now, who knows what the hell a ballplayer thinks politically?"

4

KING SMITH, the sworn enemy of David Battle, slipped into the leather horseshoe seat on the bar side of Frank Gagen's. The waitress leaned over with some intimacy, with the pleasant intimation that she would brush his face with her handsome bosoms. She said, "I brought you the two martinis you ordered before twelve o'clock."

King nodded absent-mindedly. Then he asked, "What's with twelve?"

"Governor Romney said no booze between twelve and two. Kennedy's funeral."

Jack Stowe, the purchasing agent from National Motors, said, "I thought sure he'd rate twelve to three, like Jesus." He raised his glass to King. "Cheers. You should have seen it in here. Teetotalers were ordering drinks as fast as they could before the curfew. People are just naturally stubborn."

King raised his glass. "I need this. Boy, I need this. The next time I'm a pallbearer, I hope it's my own funeral."

Dipper Coogan, the all-time great quarterback, King Smith's partner, the second sworn enemy of David Battle, asked in his high-pitched rasp. "How's Coby taking it?"

"Who knows how anybody takes it?" Then King said, "I think she's taking it hard. Where does a woman like that go when her husband dies?"

Jack Stowe said, "Just like Jackie Kennedy, to the solace of all that money."

King sighed deeply. He drank, then sighed deeply again. "I'm beat."

Stowe asked with real curiosity, "Is the casket heavy? A couple times it looked like one of those jokers on TV was going to drop Kennedy's casket. Boy, wouldn't that be a show-stopper?"

King said, "I don't remember if it was heavy or not. Do you know which one hit me the hardest? Kennedy, not Jim. When I heard that news, it was just like a cannon ball hit me right in the chest. I was shaking. You know what I did? I started smiling. I asked myself what the hell I was doing smiling. And then I figured out it was a shock reaction."

Stowe said, "It's the President. If he can get it, anybody can get it. I think it makes everybody feel insecure."

King beckoned the waitress. "How's to turn that thing off?"

She walked to the bar and turned down the volume of the television coverage of the President's funeral.

Jack Stowe said, "I'm getting hypnotized by those goddam drums. I'm getting so I still hear them, even when I can't hear them any more. My gut is beginning to keep time."

Dipper said, "This country's got to stop itself right now and put some rock and roll back on the air and drink some drinks and start thinking about pussy or something else."

Stowe said, "The goddam television, it's drowning us in crocodile tears. They love it, the television people."

King said, "Well, they're paying for their fun. Think how many millions of dollars this is costing."

Stowe said, "Don't worry. Starting tomorrow they're going to run three days of solid commercials. Did everybody show up for Parker's funeral?"

"Everybody that isn't at Kennedy's."

"I'll bet you one thing. I'll bet Coby Parker didn't walk in front of the parade, like Jackie."

The waitress with the handsome bosoms said, "I think that was a good thing for her to do, a brave thing. She's acting the part of the President's wife."

Stowe asked speculatively, "Is she? Or is she hogging the TV cameras?"

"That's a terrible thing to say!"

"Maybe it is, but the thought has occurred to me. It seems to me like somebody wrote a bad script for her. And I can't help wondering what Ethel is thinking about Bobby and Jackie holding hands for three days. And how come Jackie's the one suggesting all these memorials, like the permanent flame?"

"It's terrible to talk like that. The poor woman is burying her husband."

King said, "Well, turn the TV down some more. I've got my fill of funerals for one day."

Stowe asked with friendly malice, "You get five per cent on Parker's funeral?"

Dipper Coogan said, "We get ten per cent on one-shot deals."

Stowe said, "You know, if you asked me who was the least likely candidate for a coronary, I'd of said Jim Parker."

King said, "He was just up at Mayo's. Getting the check-out to be president. They told him he'd live to be three hundred."

Stowe said, "That figures. Osculation la mort. That must be some language for kiss of death. Helen, come around here and I'll give you the kiss of death."

The waitress said, "Big talk."

Stowe asked, "What did you make of Jack and Jackie being together in Dallas? Do you think they decided to get married or something?"

The waitress said, "Those are terrible things to say."

King Smith said, "I guess I agree with Helen. Aren't you ever serious about anything?"

Stowe replied in a flat voice, "I just finished my own checkup at Ford Hospital. This guy that looked like Boris Karloff asked me how many cigarettes I smoked, and I said three packs except when I was drinking or under tension, and he said he was going to sell all his tobacco stock, because I was going to die of lung cancer in six months and leave just a hell of a void in the industry. So I've got it made. The doctors are always wrong. Like sports writers. You hope they pick your team to lose. I hope they're wrong about my wife. They just found inoperable cancer and gave her a year at the outside. I hope they're wrong." In the same breath, he asked, "Dipper, how far could you throw the ball?"

gr[...]
eighty [...]
You can't [...]

"What's a d[...]

"Go to hell."

"Who's the best p[...] man? Unitas?"

Dipper said, "Coogan."

King said, "He means it. [...] win every National Open he ente[...] in the hotel room and wondered wh[...] how he could miss. Palmer, Nicklaus, [...] expect to win. That's Dipper."

Dipper said, "They got a lot of strong brow[...] there now. Golf and football both. A lot of good p[...] We were as good as the good ones now, only now there[...] are a lot more good ones. It was a cinch to make Hall of Fame if you were good when there weren't as many good ones around."

Stowe said, "I remember you when I was a kid. You were probably the worst passer in the history of the game. The unlovely passer. All you did was complete passes and win ball games."

Dipper Coogan said seriously, "Go to hell."

"I think Hugh McIlhenny and Jimmy Brown could run circles around Red Grange and Bronco Nagurski. Stands to reason. In every sport where there's a direct comparison, like track, the new generation is a hell of a lot faster and stronger. It must be true in football and baseball, too. Somebody like Staubach would run circles around your generation."

King said, "You may not survive this lunch, Jack."

"As a matter of fact, I'm not ragging Dipper, I'm serious. I believe it, the ones now just got to be better.

entioned Bat-
church. What's
rd anything except
when you were ball-

ou were good friends with Jim

weren't a pallbearer? David Battle

nce was heavier.

Stowe said, "As for who takes Jim Parker's place, I'm going to volunteer."

King said, "They'll be delighted to hear that."

"No shout. I could sit in that office as easy as the next guy and let the committees tell me what's going to happen next. Besides, I need the money."

Dipper Coogan said, "Cleary or Volk."

"Why?"

"Engineers. It's still the engineer's turn."

Stowe asked, "Do you think they run it in turns? Maybe so."

King Smith said, "Cycles. Finance. Then Manufacturing. Then Engineering. Then maybe Sales."

"Then it's time for a buyer. I'll volunteer right after lunch."

King said, "My bet is Tony Campbell. They must have been thinking of him for after Parker. He's too young, but they might just go ahead and jump him now, with the emergency."

Stowe said, "I ran into him in New York last week,

and he forgot all about rank when he saw the two broads I was talking to."

Dipper said, "He as much a cocksman as people say?"

Jack Stowe said carefully, "Not so anybody could prove. They just know they'd be cocksmen if they had everything Tony Campbell's got, that's all."

"And your two broads?"

"We all just had a couple of drinks."

King said, "I get the feeling you're suddenly circumspect."

"Anthony and me are buddies, now, that's all. No, I'll tell you the truth. I think he might have gone, except he'd never do it in front of me. I'm for him for president, only next to just one other guy."

King asked, "Who?"

"David Battle. And I'm serious. Wouldn't be a guy works for him, wouldn't want to see him get it. I don't know what the goddam mystery is between you guys and him. You must have a hard-on for him for something, but I can't imagine what he'd do to you. There's one guy without an enemy in the world. And in case you don't know it, he's done more for you guys in Purchasing than you can ever add up. Don't you know that?"

King said, "We don't know anything of the kind. What we've gotten has been through people like you and Quince."

"And Jim Parker? Don't fool yourself about that, Parker wasn't that kind of guy. He'd give you the glad hand and be your friend, but I swear he'd help an enemy before he would a friend. David Battle, he'd help you without letting you know. Believe me, he did a lot for you. What's between you and Battle?"

"Forget it, Jack."

"No, damn it, I want to know."

"Well, we're not going to tell it. I'm sorry we can't keep a straight face when his name comes up, but we're not going to talk about it."

Jack Stowe said with forced humor, "If I was you guys, I'd be browning up to me. With Parker dead, I don't have to kiss your ass any more."

Equally forced, King Smith said, "I've got every one of your boys in my hip pocket, and you know it."

"How come I never get any?"

"Because you're stupid. The smart ones work for you."

"But I am for Battle. When he had Purchasing, that

31

was when Kelly got caught on the take, and they wanted to investigate all the buyers, and morale got low in a hurry, but Battle wouldn't let them do it. You got to admit he's an honest, likable guy, and I say he's got a hell of a lot more ability than people give him credit for. He's one smart ballplayer."

Dipper Coogan said, "I'll tell you what I'll admit. He did more with what he had on the football field than anybody I ever knew. He had more guts than was good for any one man. I tried to beat his ass, and I don't know if I did. What King and me think about him now, you just got to let it go, we got our own reasons. Doesn't make any difference, anyhow, what we think. Ballplayer wouldn't ever make it that high, to president. You think people look up to ballplayers? Hero worship? They do, and I know it, because I been through it. And I'm not knocking it. It's opened a lot of doors for me. That's how I got in with King in the first place, and everybody knows it. But when big chips are down, they still look at you like a ballplayer, and never do get around to seeing you as a businessman. They'd still call him the Little Dipper. He couldn't ever be president of a company like National Motors."

"Can I ask you just one question? Where did you know Battle besides with the Lions?"

King Smith said, "I'll tell you that much. He worked for us for two years, 1946 and '47, just before he went with the Corporation."

"Well, whatever it was, it must have been pretty serious, to last all this time."

"It was."

"I'd sure never have thought it. Not from anything he's said or done about you two. And I still think he's going to surprise everybody and get the job. My five against your ten."

King said, "You're on. I'd have given a thousand to one."

Jack grinned. "But if you try to collect from me, I'll cancel every order you've got."

After a few moments, Dipper Coogan looked at King Smith and said, "Wouldn't that be a bitch if he made it?"

5

THE *Ledger* story of speculation said, halfway down:

While Volk and Campbell are the names most frequently mentioned, the name of David Battle contin-
ues to arise as a dark horse possibility. Battle, the for-
mer Detroit Lion great, started with National Motors
in 1948 and is now Vice-President Administration.
In this capacity he has been intimately involved in
corporate decisions, both operations and policy.

By coincidence, Battle is from Sweet Water, West
Virginia, the same coal mining town that sent James
Parker to success in the automotive industry. Though
Parker was six years Battle's senior, they were friends
as youths and continued the friendship as the Little
Dipper made his spectacular mark as an all-pro half-
back for the Lions, and later within National Motors
as each climbed to positions of eminence.

Battle would be a popular choice. He is held in
highest regard at all levels of the Corporation. . . .

Avery Winston, eighty-two-year-old chairman emeritus,
closeted himself with Carl Pearson. "Do you think this
country is ready to go back to work?"

"No."

"Nonetheless, it's time we got cracking. We have a decision to reach."

Carl said, "If we delay just a little longer, the newspaper will have the job done for us."

"That's a temptation we must ignore."

"Who will be the nominating committee, Mr. Winston?"

"You, myself, Dankworth and Williams."

"Williams?"

"You wouldn't have selected him?"

"I assume that you have decided that we will not have an interim president."

"I have. I think we have enough good men to choose from, and there would be no point in delaying the decision. I'll want your concurrence. Do I have it?"

"Yes, sir, I concur. I'm not sure Albright and Williams will concur."

"As far as I'm concerned, between the two of them it would be Hobson's choice. Do you know why?"

"I know they're both capable. As capable as I."

"No, not quite. Or they'd have gotten it instead of you. And that's the point. When they knew they'd lost out, their attitude had to change. Inevitably they would be put in the frame of mind of riding out the last years." He shook his sandy-haired head. "This is no time to retread some ambitions and outlooks. Will you concur?"

Pearson thought of the ambition that had burst into hot fire again in Albright, the hatchet man. He thought of disagreeing with the old man who had made National Motors great. He thought better of it. He said, "Yes, sir, I will concur."

"We'll set ourselves a deadline of one month. Where do we start?"

"Volk? Campbell?"

The old man nodded his strong head on his firm neck. Then he smiled. "And David Battle?"

Pearson smiled, too. "Our friends in the press are enjoying themselves. He makes good copy."

"Shall we do them the honor of considering their dark horse?"

"Mr. Winston, I think very highly of him. Not as presidential material, of course, but he's done an exceptional job in positions I wouldn't have given him."

"If Jim Parker thought a great deal of him, he must be

a worth-while man. Let's have him up to a board meeting to make a report."

"Yes, sir, I'll arrange it."

"Carl, did Jim Parker ever make a recommendation as to his successor? I'd respect his judgment. It would certainly weigh on my own decision. Did he indicate to you who he would have for the Automotive Group?"

Carl Pearson looked the old man square in the eye. He lied firmly. "No, we were just going to get into that conversation when he died. His previous indications, and that's all they were, were that he would choose either Volk or Campbell."

"Then we'll consider Volk, Cleary and Campbell. Let's get in with the rest of them. We'll get you extended as president, then we'll select the nominating committee."

Carl Pearson walked deferentially just a quarter-step behind the old tiger.

At the door of the Board Room, Winston turned and asked, "Were you ever in Sweet Water, West Virginia?"

"Good heavens, no!"

"But it must be like your Fond du Lac and my Brattleboro. Only more so. If it turns out men like Parker and Battle, it must be quite a town. Tell me something about our young Mr. Tony Campbell. I'm not presenting it as a reservation, but I do have some serious curiosity."

"Yes, sir. To answer your question, it's just inevitable rumor. Campbell understands the responsibility of his position. He's been pointed for the presidency since he was a boy. I'll personally vouch for his conduct. The rumors are unfounded."

6

UNTIL there was seventeen-year-old Jeanie Templeton, there was no one who knew Anthony Campbell. He was outside normal comprehension. There was a paradox. Men did not know him at all, precisely because they knew him entirely.

David Battle was as many different men as the number of men who knew him. Like almost all men, David Battle had thousands of identities as he reacted to each new person and was then seen in the light of that person's own identity and environment. Not so Anthony Campbell. Tony Campbell was the same man in the eyes of all the different men who beheld him. He did not respond and vary for them individually. Every man who knew Tony Campbell, knew the same golden robot. Inevitably they refused to accept the simplicity of him. Inevitably the beholder went on to read his own emotions and predilections into the strange one, and since ordinary processes did not apply to Tony Campbell, they ended up not knowing him at all.

In truth, then, he was not human at all in an ordinary sense. He did not have an identity, a reality, an entity of his own which could modify with circumstances. He was a reflection. He was a parody of a paragon of virtues. All men thought well of the reflection that was Tony Campbell.

There was no place to grab hold of him and think poorly of him. He was golden. He did everything well. He was a mirror of nobility. The things he did well, he did with enthusiasm but without inspiration. His accomplishments and his smile were equally dazzling, equally warmly mechanical. He loved the world in a strange and wonderful way, half with the unfeeling acceptance of an automaton, and half with the uncomplicated, unemotional lust of a satyr. Those closest ones held quicksilver in their hands when they thought they held Tony Campbell.

He was the product of both uncommon environment and uncommon circumstance within that environment. His father was rich as Croesus. Tony grew up in a block-granite house on Chicago Boulevard in the solid, insular, high-society section near downtown Detroit. He was the only son, the only offspring, of Roger Campbell, the second president of National Motors. In 1935 he consummated affairs with four young women. This was a noteworthy accomplishment. He was fifteen at the time.

There were some parents of daughters on Chicago, Boston, Edison and Longfellow boulevards who thought Tony Campbell might be a little on the wild side. They didn't have much to go on. Tony was a model student. He was a fine, modest athlete. He combined refreshing forthrightness with pleasing deference to his elders. Certainly his family was impeccable. The retired Roger Campbell may have come penniless from Scotland, but in only seventeen years he had risen to succeed Avery Winston as president of the Corporation, and therefore he was, by virtue of present money and past deeds, a most acceptable Detroiter. But the parents of daughters were still a little uneasy about Tony Campbell. He was too good to be true. They looked at him and searched for a flaw, they listened to him as though listening to a symphony for a discord that they couldn't quite pinpoint. The most glaring evidence against him was his white Cord convertible with tan leather seats.

His own father was tolerantly indignant. "You should be driving a National Motors car."

Tony said, "It could be worse. I could be driving a La Salle." He smiled disarmingly and disarmed his father.

Roger Campbell said, "Keep the Cord. Anything rather than General Motors."

When Tony came calling on the daughters and blasted

his air horn from the curb, the mothers said, "Honey, make him come to the door," but the daughters didn't make him come to the door. The fathers said, "A fifteen-year-old boy's got no business driving a car," but the daughters replied, "Oh, Daddy, he's never even been stopped by the cops," so the fathers fretted and stewed and wondered why seventeen- and eighteen-year-old girls would go with a fifteen-year-old boy, and they harbored vague suspicions that Tony was a little on the wild side but were reluctant to put a foot down because the son of Roger Campbell's money would make an excellent son-in-law.

Tony drove his beautiful Cord through Detroit streets with circumspection. He never exceeded city speed limits, because he had no driver's license. None of the parents, including his own parents, knew that once he reached open highway, the pedal hit the floor-board, and he went roaring off into the night at one hundred miles an hour, because he loved the deep thrill of speed and because he learned quickly that the young women who tensed beside him and put their feet against the firewall, then relaxed trembling with excitement, were surrendering themselves to adventure. Tony Campbell was not wild. The parents of the daughters had nothing to go on. He never drank or talked loudly, he was the personification of youthful manliness, he attended church services of his own volition, and all he did was drive like a maniac and seduce four of the girls of the neighborhood on a quite regular basis. He lived a charmed life, because the police were never around on the highways when he was around, and because no one knew of his seductions. He didn't talk about them to anybody, and the underage girls didn't talk about them to anybody, and each girl thought that she was the only girl.

Tony liked Chicago Boulevard. He liked the sense of the twenty-room, block-granite respectability. The families were here more Brahmin, even, than those in the bigger mansions in Grosse Pointe. The four streets were an island, and the residents were self-contained. Outsiders might feel themselves borne down by the heavy, stuffy Bostonianism, but to Tony Campbell, who reacted to the world with his skin, the granite homes were the warm sun on his skin, his father's money was the spring wind on his skin, and the young women he seduced were a refreshing clear pool which set his skin to tingling each time he dove in. The fathers of the daughters would have come closer to under-standing Tony Campbell if they had visualized him not as a remarkable and somehow mysterious young man cutting a wide swath through the world, but as a thoroughly re-markable and not at all mysterious young lion luxuriating in the warm suns, cool winds and refreshing pools of his wonderful life.

Tony knew that he was being raised to become president of National Motors when his turn could come in the far distant future. He responded to the challenge with patent enthusiasm and prepared himself with vigor from the very beginning. But in truth he accepted this great charge only with his instincts, in exactly the way the young lion would prepare himself some day to play his male role in the pride. When and if the time came for Tony Campbell to become president of the Corporation, he would be faultlessly prepared. Tony's sense of values was fundamental and sound, because it was uncomplicated. He enjoyed his father's money for the practicality of it, even more than for the stature it purchased. If he con-fined himself to young women of similar circumstances, it was not so much snobbery as it was a matter of con-venience. These girls were at hand. He understood these girls. Besides, they wore better, prettier clothes than the girls from Highland Park down the way, and this appealed to him esthetically. By ordinary measurements, Tony was not a hedonist. He was a hard-working, sober, athletic young man with a friendly, outgoing manner, who thought he had seduced the girl next door, when in fact he had been seduced, and enjoyed the event so thoroughly that he cried, "Ever more!" and dedicated him-self from that moment on to the ultimate body contact sport.

Beginning with that first beguiling success, he pursued all the pretty girls and most of the not so pretty girls on the four streets. The results struck him as symbolic. Of the thirty-four young women to whom he made some de-gree of representation, the four who succumbed lived one to each of the four streets—Chicago, Boston, Longfellow, Edison. That had to be some bold and brilliant symbolism. Tony Campbell was superstitious. He knew that the ordi-nary superstitions were tomfoolery, but he still wouldn't step on a crack or walk under a ladder. He was deadly in earnest in his superstitions about himself and the strange path of his life. He didn't understand himself any further than other people understood him. He couldn't find a real person inside himself, any more than strangers could find the real person. It was, then, at least partly in self-defense that he began to view himself, mystically, as a child of the gods. He saw symbolism in the most minute details of his pleasant life. Sex became instantly almost a ritual symbolism in itself. Four girls from four streets. From 1935 until 1939 he made love to his four with a nonchalant enthusiasm that baffled, intrigued and delighted his partners. In those growing-up years, Tony understood perfectly the physical things he and his harem did. He did not at all clearly understand the metaphysical relationship. The young women remained always an esoteric mystery to him. When he was with them, he was in a lion's Nirvana. He had been admitted to great and wonderful mysteries. Even when he had acquired the skill of a venerable prelate, he was consumed still with the reverential awe of a novitiate, and in addition to the delicate mysteries of women's bodies, there was the mystery of the pattern of numerology, destiny or foreordainment. The gods had selected him, from among all the young men on Chicago, Boston, Edison and Longfellow, to dwell in Shangri-La, and in their own mysterious way, the gods had selected for him the mystic number four, four young women, one from each street, and this had to have meaning. He was grateful to the gods for the great, mysterious revealment of sex. In his superstition, he was almost as grateful to the gods as he was to the four young women who accommodated him.

In 1939 Roger Campbell surrendered to the new elements encroaching like inexorable lava upon his beloved Chicago Boulevard. He built a thirty-room home on Long Lake Road in Bloomfield Township, fronting on the beautiful lake. Anthony Campbell made no protest at being uprooted. The gods must now want him on Long Lake. He was adjusted to his new environment from the instant he drove his Auburn Speedster past the gatehouse and up the curving driveway. Then it took him just as long as it took him to drive the Speedster from Long Lake into Birmingham to forget forever his four inamoratas from Chicago, Boston, Longfellow and Edison.

As he set himself to the stern task of rebuilding his life, which was to say, procuring a new coterie of bed

40

partners, the magic number four was very much in his mind. Now he had not only to think of the huge Birmingham-Bloomfield complex, but also of Yale and New Haven. The responsibility of choosing the four best over such a far-flung territory was more than men of lesser dedication could have faced.

Tony Campbell drove himself unmercifully. In his summer vacation, he pursued the daughters of his neighbors unrelentingly. A volume program of trial and error was the logical procedure. He tested and probed at nearly fifty girls in the first month alone. He dated as many of them as he could. He placed every girl he met at parties under intense verbal and intuitive scrutiny. By now his acuity was well developed, and most of the girls he dropped like hot potatoes before they had the least suspicion of his investigation. To those girls, and to their unsuspecting boy friends, he was that terrific new Tony Campbell, just the greatest. Of the fifty, he found ten prime possibilities. Of the ten, he was able to seduce three and skillfully permit himself to be seduced by two others. He would have preferred a broader sampling before making his decision, but he wasn't a man to rely on wishful thinking, and he accommodated himself to the realities of his busy life, stepped up forthrightly and made the final, irrevocable choice of the home grounds twosome.

The first was from Cranbrook Road in upper-upper-middle class Bloomfield Village near Birmingham. She was the daughter of a Michigan Trust man. She was tall and somewhat angular and not at all as attractive as some others, but when she taught him sheer sexual ardor, she evoked his unstinting admiration and approval.

He said, "I don't know what it is about you, but sex springs out of you when I touch you, and you're wonderful."

She said, "Yes, men say that to me, and I don't know what it is, but I like to do things that excite them, and then I forget about them and think about me."

For the next three years she occupied the larger share of his vigor while he was home. She took the place of the Chicago Boulevard girl.

When he replaced the Longfellow girl, he wasn't sure he hadn't gone suddenly soft-headed. From every standpoint, this new girl was the least deserving of the ten, of the

41

honor he conferred upon her. She had not, in fact, even qualified as a finalist by act of submission in that first trial month. Her name was Wendy Barrett. She was the daughter of the executive vice-president of National Motors. The Barretts lived near Cranbrook School in Bloomfield Hills. Wendy Barrett was the undisputed queen of Kingswood Girls School and of all the young group from Birmingham to Bloomfield and as far away as Orchard Lake. She was talented and reasonably intelligent. She was lively and self-possessed. She was the most beautiful girl that Tony had ever met. He liked the pride he felt when she was with him. Even more, he liked her beauty for its own sake, in the same way he liked the beauty of his Auburn with its chromium supercharger tubes on the sides of the hood, its clean, functional cockpit, and its graceful boat tail. But none of these were sufficient reason to pass over four bona-fide bed girls and settle on a girl who was not quite ready to experiment.

For the first two months that he knew her and dated her, he did not molest her. This was no particular mark of chivalry or high regard. Such motivations did not occur to Tony Campbell. He was religiously, ascetically convinced that sex was an entity that didn't quite have any relationship to any other emotion or morality. He was quite aware that only a handful of the other young men in the group had even rudimentary sexual experience. He was quite aware that they would be confounded, and that all the parents would be dismayed and outraged, if they knew of his assiduous practice. The attitudes and customs of others were simply of no consequence at all to him. The others could, or they couldn't, they did, or they didn't, this was no more than a matter of intellectual curiosity. Tony Campbell knew what he himself liked and wanted to do. He had no wish to harm any man, harm any woman. In the successive sequences of his life, he wanted to make love to four women; there were women who were looking for someone with the gumption to lead them into amorality or immorality, it didn't really matter which; and he was too pleased with the mutual accommodation to concern himself with any serious moral aspects of his behavior, or even to relate his sexual activity in any way at all to the normal activities of the busy, productive life which did, indeed, take the bulk of his time and require the larger portion of his energy and drive. He approached

42

Wendy Barrett with no compunctions at all. He was disconcerted only because he knew he was not choosing intelligently. If he didn't assault Wendy Barrett on the first dates, it was because with each girl he planned a campaign, and he was experienced enough to be a fairly good judge of when the time was right.

The time was right with Wendy Barrett when he took a walk with her through the wilderness around Island Lake very late at night in the last week before he returned to Yale. At the moment when Wendy was consuming herself with wonder that the handsome Tony Campbell did not pursue her, all avidity, like some other young men, he turned on her, pulled her close, kissed her with the skill acquired from kissing skillful girls, and pulled her down to the soft earth and caressed her. The deed was done before she quite knew that the deed was imminent.

Wendy didn't cry. She wasn't dramatic at all. As they walked back, she said, almost contemplatively, "I think some day I will want to marry you, Tony."

They swung their hands as they walked on. Then he said, "It takes a while for that alien thought to penetrate. If I get married, I think it will be to you." When they had walked further, he said, "I think I like you a great deal. Will we do this again?"

She stopped and looked at him in the light of the stars. She said, "I don't know. I'm not sure."

He smiled, and she could see the flash of his teeth. He kissed her cheek, holding both her hands. "I liked the feeling of lying close to you."

She turned and led them further. She stopped and said, "I'm not sure I enjoyed it. It was a shock and it hurt me."

"Hurt your feelings? Your emotions?"

"No, just me. I wondered what it would be like. I thought it would be some big trauma. It was really matter-of-fact."

He was stunned. He said, "I'm sorry."

Now she smiled. "Don't be so stricken. I just don't remember what it was like, how I felt, or anything about it. I think we will do it again, and then I'll know the things I thought I'd know this time."

"When?"

"Sometime when I've thought about it some more."

He was frustrated by her calm, matter-of-fact manner.

He had known more than one girl who experimented for the sake of the experiment, but this was the first girl who turned the tables on him and left him wanting her specifically even more than he wanted sex in general.

Wendy Barrett frustrated Anthony Campbell, and she intrigued him.

Before his vacation ended, she let him love her just once more, and he felt the same degree of dissatisfaction with himself, and he knew more than ever that he was not choosing well, and he was more grateful than ever for the wonderful Michigan Trust girl whose sweet wildness drove all other considerations from his life when they were together into the nights.

To round out his foursome, he took on a town girl from New Haven and a twenty-six-year-old model from New York to while away his time when he was at Yale.

7

TONY CAMPBELL started World War II as a shavetail co-pilot, spent three years in the Eighth Air Force, and rose all the way to bird colonel as the officers ahead of him were depleted. He said, "Vive l'attrition."

He flew seventy-two missions without a flak mark on his aircraft. He flew all the most dangerous missions. His bombardiers and crew, supremely confident in the luck of Tony Campbell, had the highest order of success. He was awarded a bucketful of Air Medals and Distinguished Flying Crosses. There was talk of a Congressional Medal of Honor, because Tony was so heedlessly brave and outstandingly capable. Unfortunately there was no single act of conspicuous valor which Fate permitted him to perform.

His commanding general said, "Tony, if you weren't so damn lucky, and would just get a hunk of shrapnel in your butt, we could go all the way with you. This way, the best I can get you is the Silver Star."

This was quite sufficient for Tony Campbell. He had performed well and bravely; he succeeded because it was a pleasant thing to do. He was pleased that the general appreciated his efforts, and a Silver Star was quite sufficient accolade. He did not have the passion to require

45

always the blue ribbon. He would settle for the red ribbon of second place.

Tony enjoyed the war. He was a little bit sorry to see it end. But, then, he enjoyed the peace. In war or peace, Chicago Boulevard, Long Lake, Yale, the air over Germany, women, he enjoyed them all, and he performed, always, well and bravely. In 1945 he went to work for the Corporation. The Vice-President Sales started Tony high in his organization. Tony was only twenty-six, but he had been an eagle colonel. That was one excuse. The other excuse was Tony's National Motors stock. Roger Campbell died two weeks after his son came home from the war. Tony Campbell and his mother were the sole heirs of the man who held the second largest individual block of NM stock, more than Avery Winston himself, who had long since passed most of his holdings to a trust, and second only to old Dankworth in Grand Rapids, who had merged his wagon works in NM when it was formed in 1912. The stock went half to the widow and half to the son, diminished remarkably little by taxes because of the canny Scot's fiscal foresight. Tony Campbell, the man they made assistant to the Detroit district sales manager, was a millionaire fourteen times over.

He liked the ease of his life. He liked the extraordinary opportunity his stock arranged for him in NM. His associates required no perspicacity at all to see that he would go to the top, and if he did not go out of his way to be high and mighty, neither did he go out of his way to avoid the inevitable deference of men who saw the gathering express train and wanted aboard. The stock was a great comfort. It was a great bait.

He loved the young women who now came to him with matrimony at least subconsciously in their hearts. He was kind and friendly to them. He tried out every single one of them who was willing to go that far to prove their affection for his good looks, his charm and his stock. His average of success improved appreciably. Where once he considered himself fortunate to make love to one in ten, he now bestirred himself to more assiduous attention if the average fell below one in three.

He was ready to select his traditional four partners. He had felt uneasy during the war because of the insurmountable difficulties in settling down with a constant coterie. In the three years he had rotated girls almost as rapidly as the Army Air Force rotated live pilots into the group to replace the dead. Now he had purpose and direction to his sex life again. Now he embarked on a leisurely program of selection, being in no hurry so long as he was pointed in the right direction. He rode carefully through the list of aspirants, and from time to time added a few of his own selection. He afforded thorough, unhasty attention to almost all of them. A few he did cut from his list after only one test. Most lasted through an extended trial. The four who survived the grueling three-year tournament were outstanding.

There was the daughter of a Ford man. She was a tall, angular girl, almost a duplicate of the Michigan Trust girl, and, if possible, her superior in the ability to plunge herself wantonly and singlemindedly into the business at hand, demanding the utmost of him physically and nothing at all of him emotionally or spiritually.

The second was the daughter of a paint man from Grosse Pointe. She had not proven a clear superiority over Birmingham girls, but in making his final decision, he gave considerable weight to the variety of location. It seemed appropriate to have a girl from the Pointe, lest he be thought a Birmingham provincial. Hers was the least secure position on the roster, but he did enjoy the divertissement of chasing clear across town to sleep with her.

There was Wendy Barrett. She was his folly. She wasn't worth all the trouble she put him to, all the nights she left him unfulfilled, just for those very few evenings of consummation in which she left him always unsure of himself. As the fourth, he kept the model in New York, who was no longer a model, because she was in her early thirties and tired of the make-up and lights, but was now fashion editor of a prominent women's publication. But for sheer, free, professional sex, he liked her best of all.

When he had established the foursome, he settled down in a remarkable display of fidelity. For five years he was completely true to the four. In that time he did flirt mildly, out of habit, with most of the attractive women who crossed his path, but he was quite content to be just an ordinary homebody with just four women. He was the wonder of the men with whom he associated. They said, "If I had his looks and money, I'd be strapping half the good-looking dollies of the world. This guy doesn't even chase. I'm not sure he even has many dates. He just keeps his nose to the grindstone." When one man asked him about it, Tony said, "I haven't got time for women right now. I've got a job to do." His superiors approved whole-heartedly and relievedly of the job performance of the young man with the huge block of stock.

Wendy Barrett altered his idyllic existence. She asked her father, "What would you say if I married Tony Campbell?"

"I'd say it was about time. I'd say it was just fine."

"I have a strange question. What's he like?"

"That's not such a strange question. At the moment of truth, I think all of us realize we don't even know the person we're going to marry."

"I think that's more true with Tony than with most people. If you asked anybody about Tony, they'd all know everything there is to know about him. The greatest guy in the world. The friendliest. The nicest. The best. And I'm not so sure I know him at all. I get the feeling I'm looking at a picture, that he's two-dimensional."

"You'll know him, honey, when you're married."

"What's he like at work?"

"I don't know what he's like. I don't see him at work. I hear he works hard, he's enthusiastic, he has a sort of genius for organization. He accomplishes more than could be expected of him and hardly seems to work up a sweat doing it. I know one thing, he's a typical son of an ex-president. He's got National Motors in his blood. He's been trained for the Corporation since he was a boy, and he's got more dedication than most of the young men who come to us through the normal channels. Another thing, he never throws his power around. He's well liked. He has men a lot older than he is working for him, and there's no resentment. Quite the contrary, they're his biggest boosters. I'd say that at National Motors, Tony is a remarkable young man."

"How far will he go?"

Now Will Barrett smiled. "That's my practical girl. Honey, nobody knows these things for sure. Particularly this long in advance. If I tell you some things, I'm sure they will be between you and me. So that there's no misunderstanding, it's not to be discussed with your mother, or with Tony, and not with me after this. I'll be retiring next year. Warren Court will be the next president, that's for sure. After him will come Carl Pearson or Marion Williams.

48

I think it will be Pearson. And off in the future, about 1963, it will be Jim Parker. Of that I am sure. Parker's got to be the brightest hope this company ever had, the near-perfect executive for the automotive business, and you can tell it this soon. And after Parker, your hero, honey—that's his chance. His timing is all right. He'll be at the most eligible age just when Parker retires. Tony has everything going for him if he stays on his track." He smiled. "I guess a father is supposed to think no young man is good enough for his daughter. This is one time I can't say it. I think Tony is good enough for the best." His smile widened. "Besides, I'll take anything at your advanced age. I was afraid you'd be a spinster." Now he grinned. "And finally, Miss Practicality, when you get my stock and Tony gets his mother's, the two of you will have more than Old Man Dankworth himself."

"Who's Mr. Dankworth?"

"Just a man in Grand Rapids. He's on our board. So will Tony be on the board, just as soon as he's old enough so that it isn't ridiculous. You marry your hero. Send him around to get my permission."

"Do you do that sort of thing, Daddy?"

"I guess not any more. Tell him for me, he's got my permission to steal you from me just at the moment I'd resigned myself to having you on my hands forever."

She went to Tony Campbell and said, "Anthony, I'm going to propose to you. I'm twenty-six, and I'm ready to get married. I'm in love with you, but I'll only ask you once, and then I'll marry somebody else before I wait for you to make up your mind."

He said, "Sure, Wendy." He didn't know what else to say.

The day that Wendy and Tony set to be married in Christ Church Cranbrook was the day that Sarajean Court and David Battle set to be married in St. Hugo of the Hills.

8

A HUNDRED black-necked, buff-and-white-bodied Canadian honkers came into Upper Straits Lake, graceful, spilled the air from their wings, extended their feet and skidded across the water to a halt. They moved smoothly to the shoreline, like decoys on a string, leaving wakes in the still surface of the lake. Sounding unlovely honks, they emerged painfully from the water and waddled pompously and proudly up the beach.

On the far shore, the thousands of fall trees lost their brilliant colors and gradually became a low mountain against the horizon. Far beyond, in the southeast, the lights of Detroit came up in a gray-yellow glow. The red light of a thousand-foot television tower, fifteen miles away, flashed on and off, like Arcturus just above the tree line. The Detroit lights and the tower light were poor reflections of the magentas, violets, roses and pinks left behind by the sun at the other horizon over the Orchard Lake Country Club golf course. No breath of wind stirred the needles on the forty-foot-high pine trees planted so many years before by Willis Ward. The evening was warm enough that the last frogs of the season sang. When the full moon came above the tree line, huge and orange, and, rising higher, turned white and reflected itself in a fifteen-foot-wide walkway across the lake, the succession of beautiful things had become unbearably sweet.

Sarajean Court, the daughter of the next president of National Motors, said, "David, I'd like to build a home right here. We'd have it all glass front, so we could see it all, all the time."

"And so people could see in at us?"

"Honey, isn't this the perfect place?"

He didn't answer.

"Wouldn't you like this lot, David?"

"Sure. But I'm not sure I wouldn't rather be over at Bloomfield."

"Honey, it's so stuffy. It's getting as bad as Grosse Pointe. Honestly, honey, Daddy says he can remember when people in Bloomfield didn't take the society pages seriously. And when they didn't check the list of big names in the congregation before they joined the church."

"Your dad is cynical."

"David, I've decided. I think I'll turn Catholic."

He didn't answer.

She asked, "Isn't that what you wanted?"

"It isn't necessary, Sarajean."

"I think it would be more exciting to have a Mass, and center altar, and all the rest of it. Is that a good reason?"

David watched the geese in silence. He stood up on the hillside, and seeing him for the first time, the geese ran cumbersomely to the water and skidded, paddling, in.

He said, "They're sure beautiful. I don't remember ever seeing any geese in Sweet Water. If there were any, they probably had so much coal dust on them I thought they were big crows."

"David, you haven't changed your mind about things, have you?"

"Of course not."

"I wonder, sometimes. David, I understand."

"Understand what?"

"About you and me. At least I think I understand. I think I'm not exactly what you had in mind. That's all right. I think I can understand where all the things I am add up to something almost what you want."

"I asked you to marry me."

"I know. Honey, I've been afraid to say it, but I think I will say it. I'm perfectly aware that you could get most any girl you want. I think I have a lot to offer, but

51

maybe not that much. I guess you know what they'll say."

"What will they say, Sarajean?"

"That there's more than one way to skin a cat at National Motors."

"Is that your feeling?"

"I don't know. All I'm saying, David, if you do change your mind about me, it would be better to tell me before, instead of after."

"I won't change my mind." He took her hand and pulled her standing. "I'm sorry, Sarajean, I don't mean to get moody. I'll make you a deal. We'll buy this property, and when we get enough money we'll build a house here."

"And in the meantime?"

"In the meantime, I assume we'll be sensible and let your dad build the house next door."

"I'm just afraid."

"Of what?"

"Not really about what people might say. I mean, who doesn't? I mean, how many young people do you think there are in the whole of Birmingham and Grosse Pointe, and every place else in the whole country, that live in big houses that their parents don't own or didn't give them? Not many, I'll tell you that."

"You're the one that keeps bringing this up as a matter of concern."

"What I was really afraid about is living next door to them. Getting married, I think the best thing about it will be getting to stay up as late at night as I want to. Mama will be right across, telling me to put out the light and get to sleep." She smiled and squeezed his hand. "It's different with you. A man as old as you, you probably want to go to bed."

"I like going to bed with you."

She waited for him to kiss her. He didn't.

She said, "Well, there's one place twelve years' experience isn't going to help you much. I'm going to catch up quick."

He pulled her in the direction of the car. She took a last look at Willis Ward's pine trees and the golf course Willis Ward gave to the country club.

"This has got to be the most beautiful place in Michigan. I just love it."

He said decisively, "We've agreed. To begin with, we'll move in where the other automotive people are. That's what we are, automotive people." He put her in the car and climbed into the driver's seat. "One thing, I'll be the only purchasing agent who lives in Bloomfield. I'm not sure whether that will remove me from the list of possible buyable buyers, or make me a primer suspect."

He drove down the gravel lane and stopped between the tremendous elm trees that guarded the entrance to Cruise Shores.

He said, "I wonder if I should reassure you, or just let it go. I don't need your father's help. I've got Jim Parker. Mainly, I'm going to get to the top because I'm doing the job. Okay?"

"Okay, David. Daddy will do his best to help, I guess you know."

"That's up to him. The second thing, I want you to call and ask my mother to come to the wedding. I talked to her last night. She's still putting on the Camille act."

"I'll call her, honey. She'll come, I know she will."

"I wish she'd come back and live here. Sweet Water's not a good place for her. She's holed up all alone in the white house like a bitter old woman in a book. No friends. They're all gone, except the bitter old, broken-down ones. All the people that count have gone off. There's no more coal. Sarajean, it would break your heart to see what can happen to your town when it's dead. All the houses that used to be so bright, they're mostly empty and falling down, and Sweet Water's not old enough to look romantic like a ghost town, it just looks filthy dirty. And Mama just sits there in the white house, and I think she enjoys seeing the town fallen down and dirty around her, and her being the only clean spot in the whole world. It's a problem, Sarajean. She's the only virtue, the only clean thing in the world, and everybody else is dirty and full of sin. I hope she'll come back up here and live with us."

Sarajean Court was silent.

David said, "You're right, she can't live with us. She'd make a mess out of us, too. But maybe she'll live somewhere close enough that we can see her once in a while."

"David, you do what you have to do. Just don't let it get off on us."

He pulled out onto Old Orchard Trail, which went winding away from the country club.

He said, "Did you know that Tony Campbell and

53

Wendy Barrett are getting married the same day as us? We'll be overshadowed by quite some."

"Want to bet? More people in Detroit know David Battle than know Tony Campbell."

"Well, we'll get the sports pages, they can have the society section." In a moment he said, "National Motors is getting inbred. We're beginning to intermarry, like royalty or like the underworld, I don't know which."

"Our children will be idiots. That's nice. They won't overshadow me so much."

He said with some asperity, "Don't always run yourself down."

She said humbly, "I was just kidding."

"No, you weren't."

When they had driven onto Pontiac Trail she said, "I love you, David."

As though it had been on his mind, he asked abruptly, "Sarajean, do you want to hear about Kelly Brand?"

She hesitated. She said, "No, or I'd have to tell you about my own past." She smiled nervously.

He said, "Well, then that's good. Sarajean, I'm moving to Cutlass next week. Jim Parker's getting the Division. He's taking me over as purchasing agent. I think inside a year I'll be his Director of Purchases."

She took his hand. "That's marvelous, David."

"Yes, it is."

"David, where will you go in the Corporation? How high will you get? Will you be president?"

He squeezed her hand. "Not quite. After Jim gets it, there's a little matter of Volk, Cleary or Campbell." He let go of her hand. "On the other hand, there's no reason why a man who lives on Bloomfield Hills Country Club shouldn't be a pretty high vice-president before he's done, wouldn't you say that?"

"If the man was David Battle, I'd say that."

9

WHEN WENDY BARRETT and Anthony Campbell were married in Christ Church Cranbrook, the first families came. They came from Birmingham, Bloomfield, Grosse Pointe and Grosse Isle. They came from Dearborn and Detroit. They came from New York, Palm Beach and San Francisco. They came from wherever they were, to attend this wedding of consequence. The society sections of the *New York Times*, the *Miami Herald* and the *San Francisco Chronicle* gave nearly as much coverage as the Detroit papers, the *News*, *Free Press*, *Times* and *Ledger*. The handsome face of Tony Campbell and the beautiful face of Wendy Barrett were on the cover of *Life* magazine. *Time* said: "A merger of NM stock was consecrated Saturday in Birmingham, Michigan's Christ Church Cranbrook."

The reception filled the ballroom of the Bloomfield Hills Country Club and spilled down onto the first level. Guy Lombardo played sweetly for the guests, and he was relieved by Louis Armstrong. The young people, the older people and the old people drank champagne until the glow of good health was upon all of them, and the older people and the old people congratulated the mother of the bride for the exquisite wedding gown and for the exquisite expenditure of thirty thousand dollars for the redecoration of the country club, and for the waiters and bands and buckets of champagne, and the young people outlasted the older people and the old people and took off their shoes when they were at last alone and danced and enjoyed themselves as they had been dying to do.

Anthony Campbell enjoyed himself as much as his wife. He forgot any tentative misgivings at this bizarre turn in his life. When he took his wife to the airport and set off on the month-long honeymoon through Europe, Africa and the Far East, he looked forward to being with her in the adventure and was so overcome with the realization of what a lovely girl she was, that he swore a mighty vow that from this day forward, Wendy Barrett would always be one of the four girls to whom he made love on a regular basis.

The day that Wendy and Tony were married was not the day that Sarajean Court and David Battle were married. Sarajean's mother, as practical as she was proud, had the foresight to eliminate the conflict in which her social presentation would come off second best. The wedding of the daughter of Warren Court to the Little Dipper of Sweet Water, West Virginia, was moved back two weeks. Thus they had their own impressive guest list and their own considerable national attention, half of it, as David had predicted, in the sports pages. Sarajean and her mother were quite satisfied.

10

THERE WAS ONE THING that Tony hadn't counted on when he acceded to marriage. His home territory became, overnight, a strait jacket. Philandering in the same town where his wife lived was quite considerably more complicated than he had ever imagined. Reporting home most nights made proper pursuit of Detroit's single girls nearly impossible, and most young women did require formal wooing, even from Tony Campbell. Despite all his marvelous inventiveness and ingenuity, he still couldn't find enough excuses for enough evenings to wine and dine and woo and love enough women to satisfy his satyr's promiscuous soul.

He tried the logical expedient of making love to his own lovely wife as often as four or five nights a week, but his dissatisfaction only heightened. He craved the endless delight of endless variety, but even this he might have forgone if only she would find at last in marriage the abandonment, the wantonness that the other women found with him. She could not bring surging in him the pleasant, heedless lust that was his deep, churning, invigorating wellspring. She was not skilled, not graceful, not urgently compliant in molding her motions to his. There was no ballet. There was no luxuriance. There was dissonance. There was no sweet dance. He told her only once of her shortcomings, and she was so wounded that she stayed away from him for three weeks, and when she finally returned, it was with no intention at all of learning from him, because her feminist pride was better developed than her femininity. It probably would not have mattered. She could have been the perfect lover, and he would still have required other lovers. He needed one each from Longfellow, Chicago, Boston and Edison.

At one point, he considered approaching her with some sort of intelligent bargain of mutual promiscuity for two mature people. The words choked in his teeth. Peaceful, easygoing Tony Campbell had developed a healthy fear of his purposeful, lovely wife. He couldn't bring himself to offer himself and his monstrous proposal of adultery red-handed to her violent repercussions. Anthony Campbell, the satyr who had known no emotions except wonderful love of the world, now knew the appalling weight of the unhappiness that crushes caged animals.

Reluctantly he turned to married women, because they needed less wooing and were, in fact, more often than not the aggressors. Here there was involved a matter of scruples. Married life in Bloomfield Hills funneled inevitably into small groups of friends in comparable financial circumstances. He knew the husbands. He knew them well. His rudimentary conscience troubled him when he made love to the wives of two men he knew so well. It required the utmost of his self-control to look his friends in the eye on the evenings of the afternoons he had made love to their wives. He wanted desperately to shout to the room of people that he and Jo Courtney had clung close not three hours since. He couldn't bear the surreptitious, warm looks she sent to him, the sly handclasp or brushing touch when she passed close to him. What had this crafty, childlike, conspiratorial touch of hands to do with the full-bodied joy of love-making? Jo Courtney was a silly goose, playing games, now, with their guilty knowledge. He didn't want to play games. He wanted to make love to women. Tony Campbell's life had closed in on him. He was smothered. His wife had smothered him. Detroit had smothered him.

Carl Pearson said of him, "He's getting maturity, now. That's good. You can see it in his face, not quite so much of a college kid any more. That's good."

Jim Parker said, "I wonder if the rumors are true. I wonder if Tony's got his mind on women."

Carl Pearson drew his head up. "Tony Campbell? Why would he look at anybody else when he's got Wendy Barrett?"

Then began, in Tony's sales careeer, the years of extensive travel. They came just at the moment when he had in desperation determined to make a more violent separation from Detroit and his wife. Now he was suddenly free again. He flung himself anew, sighing and bursting, into the wild love which alone gave his world purpose. He fully intended to resume the patterns of his youth. He would find four girls, three and Wendy, and sing such songs of sweet love that the whole world would glow in song with him. But having once been smothered, he now enjoyed his freedom so assiduously and raced off, so full of life, in all directions, that the members of his revolving commission of four jumped on and whirled off as on the spinning platter of an amusement park fun house. His long fast was broken. He now gorged himself.

Through trial and error, he set practical rules to which he adhered stringently. He had thought to forswear married women. Then he learned that this would be to cut off his nose to spite his face. Not all married women came into alliances like silly geese looking for what was not in their husbands. There were some married women who loved their husbands and yet wanted, for this night, and for another night, and for a few other nights, to fill themselves up with Tony Campbell, but wanted no more of him than his tremendous vigor, wanted no emotion from him, wanted to spend their accomplishments of body upon him and lie shuddering under him in heedless climaxes so far below degradation that there came again heaven and godliness. These were the married women he now loved.

With single women, who occupied the bulk of his attention, he disclosed his married status as rapidly as he could, not only because this eliminated the possibility of subsequent recriminations, but even more pertinently because the single women who loved sex and loved adventure preferred a thoroughly married man, not for any legendary technical superiority, but precisely because the single girl was no more interested than he in an entangling alliance. These single girls Tony Campbell knew and possessed

59

rarely permitted single men to possess them, since this was a nearly sure way to lose a prospective husband. These single girls plied single men with virtue, while they plied Anthony Campbell, and were plied by him, with the sheer joy of sex. The new Elizabethan generation of American girls came running and dancing, all swelling breasts, and warm thighs, and throbbing stomachs, and enfolding arms and legs, to Tony Campbell, and he took them, and gave himself to them, and it was a cannibal feast for all of them, and Tony Campbell was once more in love with the world, and more in love with the world than he had been before, because now he knew what it was to be smothered. The year he was forty began the best years. This was the year he became Vice-President Sales, the youngest vice-president in the history of National Motors. It was the year he made love to a Playboy Bunny.

He did this because they said he couldn't do it. The Chicago Embassy dealer said, "A Gaslight girl, maybe, if you spend some time at it, because they're human. But you're dead with the Bunnies, because Hefner drains the blood out of them and puts in embalming fluid before they put on those white bunny tails. The rules are too tough. You can't even touch them, not even shake hands. You just don't even think about getting smart. They're not allowed to talk to you, just take your order, and the worst part is, they couldn't care less. You could drop dead in the Playboy Club, and the Bunnies would step right over you on their way to deliver a drink. You know what they are? They're bosomy zombies, and that's all they are. That's the way they're supposed to be, and that's the way they are."

Tony said, "You sound bitter. Personal experience?" He smiled. "Can't hardly blame them. I think I'd hate to have guys coming in thinking they could lay me at the drop of a hat. I don't suppose Hefner's got any choice. If he relaxed the rules any, somebody would probably try to get him for running a bawdy house."

"Well, there should be a happy medium. Just how many guys do you think come in here thinking about laying a Bunny?"

"I'd say most."

"Seriously."

"Okay, seriously. Most."

"Well, maybe you're right, but it ain't going to do any of

them any good. If I was some cocksman's wife, this is the place I'd want him to spend his evenings out of town."

"Buy me another drink, Perc. And try to convince me that isn't real, live blood flowing through our Bunny's veins."

As far as Percoll knew, this was completely idle conversation. Nothing could have been more serious to Anthony Campbell. He had been challenged, and he was thoroughly intrigued.

He came back the next day for lunch. He estimated correctly that there would be more opportunity to be noticed at noon than at night in the rush of businessmen and their friends. He showed his key at the door and looked over the hostesses in the reception lounge. He discarded them quickly, deciding that they were likely self-important because they were high in the pecking order. He wandered through the floors until he found the one he wanted, a black-haired girl with an alert, intelligent expression.

He sat at her table.

She came to him and said, like a tape recording, "I'm Bunny Kerry. May I see your key, please, sir? May I have your name, sir?" She said, "Thank you, Mr. Campbell. How may I serve you?"

He said politely, "I'd like a Scotch and water, please, miss. If you have it, I'd like Rennell Scotch."

She looked at him for the first time. "Rennell Scotch, sir?"

"Yes, if you please." He was perfectly straight-faced.

When she came back, she said, "Sir, I'm sorry, but we don't have any Rennell Scotch. Are you sure it isn't Chivas Regal?"

"No. Rennell. I like it best. But that's quite all right. I'll take Old Rarity."

When she brought the drink, he said, "Bunny Kerry, I'm awfully sorry to have put you to all that trouble. I'll have some lunch, too, if you please. And nothing more exotic than a ham sandwich."

He smiled at her, most polite.

She smiled back, right through him.

He tipped her just a little bit more than normal, just enough that she would be pleased but not enough to let her think poorly of him.

The next noon he sat at the same table. She didn't recognize him. She said, "Good morning, sir. I'm Bunny Kerry. May I see your key, please, sir?"

He said, "I'll have a Scotch and water, please. Should I ask you for Rennell's?" He smiled at her.

She said, "You were in here yesterday, weren't you?"

"Yes. I'll have Old Rarity, please, Bunny Kerry."

He tipped her just right, just a little bit more than average. And his tour in Chicago was up, and that was all he did those opening days.

The following week, to the surprise of the Chicago District Office, he showed up again, and once more he was unavailable during the noon hours. His Bunny was on a different floor, but he found her and said, most politely, "Hello, Bunny Kerry, nice to see you again."

She asked for his key and his name and address, like an automaton. Then she said, "I remember you. You're the man that wanted that funny Scotch."

"Yes, I'm the one."

When she brought his drink, he said, "I wonder if I could ask you a question?"

She said suspectingly, "What?"

"I don't know much about Chicago. I have a date tonight, and I haven't the least idea where to take her. What's a good place? Some place real nice."

She busied herself at the table and said with her lips not moving, "Try the Kon Tiki Ports. It's in some hotel. She'll like it."

He said nothing else to Bunny Kerry. He did go to Kon Tiki Ports. He took the stewardess of the plane that had brought him to Chicago.

The following noon, Bunny Kerry said, "I'm Bunny Kerry. May I have your key and name, please?"

He said, "I took your advice. She liked it very much."

She stopped looking through him and said, "You're the one I told about Kon Tiki Ports. I went there last week."

He said, "My name is Anthony Campbell. I'm a vice-president of National Motors. I'm married and have three children. Sometimes when I'm out of town I have dates, if I like a girl's looks. I like your looks. I know you're not allowed to date me. I know there is always a way. I will be in town one week from today, and I will come to this table and ask you where I can meet you. I hope you will meet me."

She asked, "What would you like to drink, Mr. Campbell?"

When he left, he tipped her just the right amount.

On the following Tuesday he came at noon. He sat at the table. When she came, he said, "I'm Anthony Campbell, a vice-president of National Motors. I know you can't make a date with me. So I won't ask you. I'll ask you this. Sometimes when one of you girls decides to have a drink when you get off, where would you go?"

She asked, "What may I serve you, Mr. Campbell?"

When she returned with the drink, she said, her lips not moving, a most unconcerned expression on her attractive face, "You should make the Scene. It starts swinging about midnight."

He made the Scene. When midnight came, he thought he had missed, and he thought Percoll was right, you couldn't make a Bunny. But she came at ten past midnight and sat at the bar, and he moved over, smiling, and said, "We've met. I'm Anthony Campbell. May I buy you a drink?"

She said, "Maybe one drink." And as she sipped her drink, she said, "My name is Mary Woodworth. I'm from Milwaukee."

He said, "I hope you'll have more than one drink with me tonight. I'll have to leave you a little bit early. By one-thirty. I have a meeting in the morning. At one-thirty I'll put you in a cab, or drop you where you want."

She looked at him, puzzling over him.

He said, "I'd like to see you again. What is your day off?"

She hesitated. "I don't think I should tell you."

He smiled his great smile. "As long as you don't tell me where I can reach you, you're safe. Now I'll tell you what I want. I may not have a chance to come to Chicago again for a while. But next week I'll be in New York. And I don't imagine it's against the rules for you to date me in New York. Particularly if I just happened to run into you. I want you to come to New York next Tuesday afternoon and stay through Wednesday night. You don't have to promise me anything. I'll put you up in an adjoining room at the hotel. I think I'm going to want very much to make love to you, but I don't know for sure yet, because we don't know each other. If you open the door, it will be because we decided we like each other that much."

She said, "You're very direct."

"Yes."

"I'm nobody's easy mark."

"If I thought you were, you wouldn't interest me."

"I might go. I'd like to see New York. But I think you'd be in for a disappointment."

"Then I better explain myself just a little further. If you don't want me, then I don't want you, because it's no good unless it's a mutual thing." He smiled. "I wish I could meet you here and take you on the plane. I can't. When I leave you tonight, I'm going to give you an envelope. Your round-trip plane fare is in it. Your flight number is on the paper inside. I'll make the reservations for you. All you have to do is show up. I'll meet your plane in New York."

She knew she wouldn't show up. As the days passed, she was ever more sure that she wouldn't go to New York with a strange man. But she was faced with a dilemma. She didn't really want to take his money and make a sucker out of him, and on the other hand she didn't want to mail it to Anthony Campbell at National Motors, because that might get him in trouble. When she realized that she could just hold the money until he accosted her in Chicago to find out why she hadn't come, she put that logical thought out of her mind, and then she knew she wanted very much to see New York, and there could be no better escort than the handsome, rich Anthony Campbell. But she would keep the door locked between their rooms, that she would do.

He took her for first cocktails to Kenny's. He took her to Le Bistro for dinner, so that Robert Allembert could melt her with his Gallic charm. He took her to Chateau Madrid to see the Spaniards in their bright suits-of-lights dance flamenco and blow wild, sweet Moorish strains into her. He took her to Chez Vito, and when the beautiful violins played, she asked him to have them play for her, and they played "Sorrento," and when the great, beautiful opera voices burst into the lush room from the center table, when they sang from *La Gioconda,* and from *Kiss Me, Kate,* when they sang "Wunderbar," she put her hand on top of his on top of the table, and he made no move to take advantage of her. And he took her to hear the Rumanian guitarist play Spanish music on his guitar, and this time he squeezed her hand, and then he took her back to the hotel and let her in her room and closed the door behind them, and took her face and kissed her long and sweetly, and then kissed her with a burst of half passion and let her go, and he said, "Good night, Mary, I've enjoyed you very much."

She locked and bolted the door to the hall. She went to the mirror and brushed her hair. She thought she might call him on the phone to say good night again, but she wasn't accustomed to this sort of thing and didn't know what consternation this might raise below, so she went to the connecting door and opened her side and rapped on his side, and he let her in.

She said, "I wanted a cigarette."

He gave her one and lit it.

She said, "You know, my roommate and me were talking about what it would be like to be great adventuresses. Courtesans. I wonder what kind of life that would be."

He wondered if it was a serious pitch. "Would you like to be somebody's mistress?"

"That might be very nice. For the right man."

"How about for more than one man?"

"I wonder if that would be interesting. Do girls in New York really get one hundred dollars a night?"

Was she just a hooker?

He smiled. "I'd bet a girl like you could get it. It might be interesting, if you didn't mind the kind of men that buy girls."

She studied him. She said, "I don't think I'd have the nerve. It must take a lot of nerve."

Behind his calm, handsome face, his mind ran fast. A hooker? No, she was toying with the idea, the way all working girls toyed with the idea sooner or later. Sometime in the future, she might come to that. But not yet. Now she was a young girl who had gone to Chicago to make a great deal of money as a Bunny, and she was no different from a few thousand other beautiful young girls in the world.

He said, "Now."

He took her by the hand and led her back to her room. Then suddenly she stopped, turned to him and said, "I think it will be more exciting to come to your room. I've never done anything like this before. It makes me feel funny to think about it, sort of scared, but sort of excited, too."

Anthony Campbell accomplished the impossible. He made love to a Playboy Bunny. He made love to her through the night, and through the next night, and he liked her so much, that at long last the New York model-turned-businesswoman was stricken from his list of four and replaced by Bunny Kerry; but when Tony was on the airplane flying home, he was assailed by great loneliness, and he made his way to the washroom, slid home the bolt and stood looking at himself in the mirror, and he said aloud, "Because of the savour of my good ointments, my name is as ointment poured forth, therefore do the virgins love me. Let me kiss you with the kisses of my mouth, for my love is better than wine." He stared deeply into the mirror, but his reflection was a man he did not know in any degree, but was the reflection of a reflection, and he felt suddenly so forlorn that he stopped off in the galley and flirted with the stewardess, and his smile was nearly as bright as it usually was.

11

Werner Bud Volk joined the Bund in 1936. He didn't make any formal application for membership or consummate any formal enrollment. But one summer he did attend songfests at Beyer's beer hall, and he did attend Bund picnics at the farm of Gerhardt Otto, thirty miles west of Detroit. Bud was joined in this participation by four other nineteen- and twenty-year-old young men from his neighborhood, two other Germans, an Irishman and a Czech. As far as Bud knew, the German-American Bund was a social organization, like Sons of St. Patrick, or such.

Bud was born in Constantine, Michigan, in 1915, a year after his parents arrived from Germany. His father had been a well-to-do furniture manufacturer. He watched the war come on, wanted no part of it and bribed his way out of Germany. He arrived in America with a suitcase full of marks. He meant to settle in Grand Rapids and start up a furniture factory. He bought a small farm in Constantine to use as a base of operations while he studied the Grand Rapids possibilities. He paid for his farm out of his hoard of American dollars. This was of no consequence. He believed that Germany would win the war, or at least would force a settlement, leaving them more sound than when they began their martial adventure. Why should he have any concern for the future?

67

In 1920, when his suitcase of money would have mailed a letter from Hamburg to Berlin, he built a fire in the field behind his home and tossed the valueless bills one after another into the flames. The ceremony lasted two hours. Then he sold the farm, packed up his family and moved into a new home in the flourishing German community on Detroit's east side. He still had fifty thousand dollars in American money. This he invested in the stock market, and not only provided well for his family on the income, but watched, with pipe-smoking pleasure, the pyramiding of a small fortune. But in 1930, when his last dollar was called to meet his short position, he walked out onto the Belle Isle Bridge, folded his coat neatly and left it beside the railing, stepped off into twenty feet of water and did not struggle in the two minutes before he was dead. The harbor masters fished him out three days later, two miles down river, his body lodged against a pier, bloated, thumping and flopping sickeningly in the waves from passing freighters. This pipe-smoking man who considered himself calm and brave and had been disdainful of the lesser men around him, this man left his widow and young son to shift for themselves in America's Great Depression.

Gertha Volk rode it out. She earned what she could, sent her son to earn what he could, and accepted city welfare when there was no other recourse. She held the worthless stock. Slowly the value returned. By 1940 she had a five-thousand-dollar income, owned her home free and clear, and owed no man.

Bud Volk missed his father. He was accustomed to stern paternal discipline. He was lost without it. For a few years he was aimless. Though at times he was a brilliant student, at other times he deliberately did poorly to manifest his secret rebellion and disillusionment. At nineteen he was ready for Kurt Beier, a Brown Shirt.

Kurt and Bud hated Jews. Bud had never seen a Jew, as far as he knew. Kurt must have seen Jews in Germany, but certainly none that he could recall specifically. Nonetheless, they hated Jews.

Kurt said, "They're into everything. They're running this country. They control all the money. They lie, cheat and steal. They help each other, and they rob you every chance they get. And the worst ones, they're the ones that pretend they're not Jews. They pretend they're English,

68

or Germans, or something else. Boy, you don't even know when the guy you're talking to might be a Jew. And Jewesses, they'd marry you if they could, and never let you know. Can you think of anything worse? What would you do if you married somebody and then found out she was a Jew?"

Bud replied, "Shoot her. I'd shoot her, then defy any jury in the world to convict me."

Kurt laughed sharply, triumphantly.

Bud asked, "Right?"

Kurt replied, "Right," only he said, "Wight," with the rolling "w."

Bud said, "They sure do have a hold on America. Hollywood, that's where they are."

Kurt said, "But mainly the Government."

Bud was surprised. "How's that?"

"Roosevelt."

"Is he a Jew?"

"Didn't you know that? His real name is Rosenveld. Frankfurter, Baruch, Morgenthau, and the rest of them. It's all part of the world-wide Jewish conspiracy."

Bud said, "Boy, why do we let them get away with it?"

"One man's going to do something about it."

"Hitler?"

"The only man in the world with courage to do something about it. You just watch Rosenveld try to stir up America against Hitler."

"You in favor of a dictator?"

"What else are you going to do? That's what it takes to get rid of them. The Jews are too strong."

"I guess that's right."

"Hitler will do it, if he gets the chance. I mean, if other countries let him alone to get the job done. The Jews will holler their heads off. They'll want England and America to fight him. But if we let him alone, he'll get the job done for everybody, not just for Germany."

Bud said, "I hope we let him alone."

So Kurt Beier invited Bud Volk to attend the Liederfest at Beyer's, and they took Bill Vogel along, and also Joe Quinn and Pete Maznick, the Czech. They enjoyed it, because the Germans let them drink beer without drivers' licenses. They enjoyed the singing. They enjoyed the Bund because it was ego-bolstering to hate Jews in concert, and though there was no formal talk at the gatherings on any controversial subjects, the whole atmosphere bristled with anti-Semitism and with justice-in-the-world through collaboration of the United States and Adolf Hitler's Nazi Germany. Four of the young men exercised themselves at prejudice, played at it. They didn't really give a damn for Adolf Hitler or give a damn if Jews were rich or poor. Not even Bud Volk gave the whole pleasant thing more than intrigued lip-service. But Kurt Beier thought he had at least one firm convert. Bud's indiscretions with Kurt came home to roost.

On December 10, 1941, Germany declared war on the United States. On the same day the FBI rounded up Kurt Beier and two dozen other known Nazis in Detroit and carted them off to internment. Bud Volk, graduated from Cornell and a second lieutenant in the Army Reserve through his ROTC, was already on active duty, having reported to Fort Benning on the ninth. On the twenty-seventh he was sent to the Detroit Arsenal so that they could take advantage of his automotive engineering education. He was assigned to Research & Development, Engine Section. On January 3 he was called into the office of Major Wickersham, security officer of the Ordnance Tank Automotive Command.

Wickersham said, "Lieutenant, we're suspending you from duty."

Bud Volk turned white. It took a full minute before he could manage "What for?"

"The FBI has listed you as a possible subversive. You will have an opportunity to defend yourself."

Bud could barely breathe. He asked, "What for!"

"I'll run down the essentials of the report. 'Lieutenant Werner Volk, son of a German emigrant. Married this year to Marianne Donner, daughter of German emigrant known to have pro-German sympathies . . .' "

Bud burst out, "That's not true!"

"What isn't true?"

"My wife has no pro-Nazi sympathies."

"The report refers to her father."

"That hasn't got anything to do with us. This is ridiculous."

"I'll continue the report. 'Subject speaks German fluently. German spoken exclusively in the home.' "

"My mother speaks very little English."

" 'Close associate of a Kurt Beier, known Nazi, active

member of German-American Bund. Subject frequent attender of Bund social affairs, though not known as official member of the Bund.'" Major Wickersham put the paper on his desk. "You see that it makes no direct accusation. You're listed only as a possible subversive. And you will have every opportunity to defend yourself."

Bud couldn't answer. He was horrified.

"Lieutenant Volk, were you a member of the Bund?"

"No. No, I was not. I only went there to sing and drink beer. So did Joe Quinn, and Pete Maznick, and a lot of other guys."

"They're going through the same thing. You left out William Vogel. He was one of your group, is that correct?"

Is there something wrong with him?"

"As a matter of fact, he's been thoroughly checked, and he's been cleared of all suspicion. The FBI is not worried about Maznick. After all, he's a Czech. That Quinn, what do you know about him?"

"Nothing. He's a hell of a good guy."

"I'm sure a lot of good guys are for Adolf Hitler. How about you?"

"I'm in the Army."

"So are some pro-Hitler people. You've been quoted as saying that we should stay out of the war. Let Hitler get his job done."

"Who told you I said that?"

"One of your classmates at Cornell."

"That was a bull session."

"Did it represent your true convictions?"

Bud hesitated. Then he said, "Yes, it did."

"Does it represent your present convictions?"

"Look, Major, overnight people forget that maybe half the people in the United States thought we shouldn't get in the war. Half the people thought we shouldn't pull England's chestnuts out of the fire again. And that we should let Germany and Russia alone and they'd knock each other's brains out. Lindbergh. A lot of people."

"Wouldn't you say Lindbergh has been discredited?"

"Do you want to argue that, Major, or find out where I stand?"

Major Wickersham was discomfited by the sharp reply. "We want to find out where you stand."

71

"I'm an officer in the Army. I took my oath. That's where I stand."

"You're quoted as being intensely anti-Semitic."

"If you kill everybody in the United States who's been anti-Semitic in bull sessions, you'll kill most of the people. My father was German. He left Germany because he didn't approve of the First World War. What my wife's father thinks has nothing to do with what my wife thinks, or I think. As far as that goes, I don't have any idea whether he's a Nazi or not. Personally, I never heard him say anything stronger than I've heard a few dozen Irishmen and other people say about maybe it would be a good thing if we let Hitler alone, as long as he's trying to avoid war with us. And you can include some English-Americans in that, too. A hell of a lot of people have been neutral or even a little bit pro-German until we got into the war ourselves. But if it comes to choosing between America and Germany, that's a different thing. And you know damn well it is. And the FBI knows it, too."

"Are you telling me you're a loyal American?"

"I'm telling you I'm an officer in the Army, and I took my oath. And I'm beginning to wonder just who the hell you are, Major, to sit behind that desk and rake up all this horseshit and make me defend myself."

Major Wickersham said icily, "I'm a major in the United States Army in charge of security in the Detroit area. I will discharge my responsibilities with my best efforts. Lieutenant, we have made a preliminary decision in your case. We have determined that there is no conclusive evidence of treasonable activities or tendency. Nevertheless there are sufficient grounds to warrant caution. We have determined to release you from active duty, pending long-range observation of your position. We will still wish to avail the nation of your qualifications. We will arrange to have you employed by industry in a non-critical position. We will go so far as to permit your employment in direct defense production provided you do not have direct access to classified information. You will be assigned to Embassy Division of National Motors in their tank production facilities. You will be assigned as a project engineer. If you concur and agree to this disposition of your case, we will arrange your release to inactive status permitting you to retain your Reserve commission. No one except the manager of the tank plant and the chief engineer will ever know that you are under suspicion. They will be apprised that this is a matter of circumstances and suspicion, not of conclusive evidence of any kind. This will not be a unique position for you. Others are in the same category. It is felt that those of them who are loyal will recognize the difficulty the Government faces in situations like yours, will know that we can make no other decision in these hectic first days, and will go on in a loyal and effective contribution to their nation. You will be under surveillance, but it will not be evident, nor will it be constant or in any way harassing. In due time a final decision will be made and perhaps a new disposition directed. This is our decision. Will you abide by it?"

Bud Volk was drained. He asked, barely audible, "What is my alternative?"

"You can ask for formal proceedings and a thorough investigation. I can only warn you that things are moving so swiftly that there might not be enough time to give you, and that the decision may well go against you since it would be based on the same evidence and reasoning on which we have made our preliminary decision. However, that is your choice. You may accept this and go on to prove that we are wrong, or you may ask for a formal inquiry and adjudication."

Bud rose and put both hands on the desk, finally saying in a strangled voice, "I have no choice." It was a decision he would regret. It would return to haunt him when the chips were down at National Motors.

12

BUD VOLK did well at Embassy's tank plant during World War II. He impressed his young superior, Jim Parker, chief engineer and ascending star of National Motors. There was never a hint that Volk wore a bar sinister. There was no evidence of surveillance. He was accepted as an engineer. Indeed, at the end of two years, not having heard further from Army Security, Bud contacted Major Wickersham and said, "Major, I've expected to hear from you. What has your Gestapo determined about me?"

The major said, "To tell you the truth, Volk, we forgot about you. You were never a critical enough case that we could afford to put men on you. We had more important fish to fry."

"You stated, I recall, Major, that you would either hang me or clear me."

"Sorry, Volk. We haven't been able to get around to it. I think you can safely assume you are cleared."

"Just like that?"

"That's what you wanted."

"And how about my record?"

"Well, we should get around to doing something about your record. How are things going for you at Embassy?"

"How about my record, Major?"

"We'll get into it. Within the next few weeks. You have my word."

Bud said, "That's a great comfort, Major."

"There's a war on, Volk."

"How would you know, Major?"

"I'll brook no such disrespect. You are still considered a lieutenant in the United States Army."

"Then why don't you do something about it, Major? Why don't you haul me up for court-martial? I think I'd like to bring this whole stupid affair to somebody's attention."

The major hung up.

Bud did not let his bitterness interfere with his good work at Embassy. Instead it spurred him on. Because he felt dirty, sullied and frustrated, he buried himself in his work and developed that capacity for punishment which marked all those who stood a chance for high success in the Corporation. At the end of the war, Parker brought him to the automotive business as his assistant chief engineer. He was known as Parker's protégé, just as Parker was known as the protégé of Carl Pearson. He followed Jim Parker through the Corporation Indian-style, placing his feet in each footprint left by the man ahead. He succeeded Jim as chief engineer at Embassy. He succeeded him as chief engineer of Cutlass. Then he succeeded him as general manager of Cutlass and became a vice-president of the Corporation and member of the Board of Directors.

He said to his wife, "I'll tell you, all my life I've had a little bit of the feeling that the afflictions of Job have been heaped upon me. But I must have the patience of Job, because things are working out, they're working out."

His wife said, "It's more fortitude than patience. I'm proud of you, Bud."

When Jim Parker was struck down, Bud Volk was horrified. He had lost a man he admired and for whom he had as much affection as he was capable of giving any man. Moreover, he had lost a patron just when the time had come that the patron could give him another big boost toward the top. Bud Volk had every reason to believe that he would succeed Jim Parker as Group Vice-President Automotive. He was utterly dismayed at Parker's untimely death.

Then he was struck with a burst of optimism. He

looked around him at the Corporation and asked himself, "Who can they pick?"

Would they pick Marion Williams? Williams had lost his guts.

Would they pick Dana Albright? Surely they'd never put the hatchet man at the top.

Would they pick Cleary? Cleary was a brilliant engineer, but he just plain lacked the concept of running this awesomely complex industrial giant.

Would they pick Tony Campbell? They might, they just might. He had the stock, and he was basically sound, and he did keep his mind solely on business, instead of running frivolously off as lesser men might have done in his circumstances. Tony Campbell was a threat.

But Tony Campbell didn't have the one great advantage that belonged to Bud Volk. Tony had never run a division. Bud Volk was general manager of Cutlass, the backbone of the Corporation. Surely this would outweigh all other considerations. Upon analysis, it was as clear as day. Bud Volk was the logical choice to step into the shoes of Carl Pearson, where James Lee Parker had been about to step!

In a pleasant daydream, Bud began to select his principal assistants. He would give Dana Albright expanded authority, because the hatchet man was the shrewdest of all the vice-presidents. Tony Campbell, as a sop and also because he deserved it, he'd get the Cutlass Division, which would then prepare him for the broader corporate responsibilities of an operating vice-president. For Group Vice-President Automotive, there was only one possible choice, David Battle. Bud Volk wondered if this selection would surprise the Board of Directors. He wondered if there were others who knew what he knew about David Battle.

13

THE NOMINATING COMMITTEE of the National Motors Board of Directors was in substantial agreement with Bud Volk's basic reasoning. In the first session of the committee, Carl Pearson, the chairman, said in a voice that was at once genial and businesslike, "I had felt that we should give fuller consideration to Mr. Cleary. It appears from the strong sentiment for Mr. Volk and Mr. Campbell that this would serve no purpose. We will hold another brief session prior to the board meeting one month from today. Please be prepared to reach a decision, so that our recommendation can be presented to the board and acted upon at that meeting. Mr. Winston, do you have any remarks?"

Old Avery Winston, the guiding genius of National Motors through fifty years of success and storm, always exercised his options, particularly his prerogative to offer remarks. He rose and said, "I like the idea of men as young as these men taking over. I think we're coming to another turning point in the life of the Corporation. We face new situations. A better way of stating it is that there is a new urgency to meeting situations which have grown more dangerous in the past few years. I think it is going to require every bit of strength, vigor and imagination our younger men can give us, to meet these situations. We're fortunate to have young men the caliber of Mr. Volk and Mr. Campbell ready to take over. It was an unintentional but dramatic indication of how strong we are at the top, that we passed so lightly over a man of the high caliber of Mr. Cleary."

Pearson asked, "Sir, what specific situations do you have in mind?"

The old man looked as though he would smile. "I'm going to chastise your generation, Carl, because you have to ask that question."

Carl Pearson said stiffly, "I'm sure I don't have to apologize for my administration. It has given the stockholders the highest earnings in history. I would say this Corporation is the soundest it's ever been."

"Would you, Carl? I'm sure the auditors would agree with you. The question is not how sound we are, but how sound is the footing on which we rest. The question is not how well we are doing with our stockholders, but how well we are doing with the country."

"I'm not immediately prepared to admit dereliction by this administration in corporate responsibility, either."

"Carl, I'm sure you're aware that this is dispassionate observation on my part and not personal. You have been responsible to the stockholders in that you have earned money for them. But what happens to all your past performance, if the Government of the United States now breaks us up and scatters us to the four winds? Gentlemen, this is the area of greatest responsibility for the new managers of this Corporation. National Motors must be preserved intact. Sound young men of the caliber of Mr. Volk and Mr. Campbell will face this challenge. I think we can help them win. I'd like a preliminary expression. Marion, which of our two prime suspects do you think will best meet this specific need?"

Marion Williams, the executive vice-president who had once thought he would be president, leaned back in his chair. "Mr. Winston, my preliminary opinion is that Tony Campbell is best suited to do the job we need done. He doesn't have Bud's background, but he's been living the Corporation all his life. I think his personal appearance is a very important factor. Everything about him is calculated to inspire public confidence. He's the perfect image of a dynamic, young corporation president, and I think this alone tips the scales in his favor, in view of the over-riding concern as just expressed by Mr. Winston."

Avery Winston said, pleased, "We're not running a beauty contest, but there's merit in your premise. Carl?"

Carl Pearson said, "As of this moment, between the two, I lean to Bud Volk. He's got the solid background that will be needed. Campbell's experience has been too narrow." He smiled. "I'm inclined to prefer the experience of an engineer."

Marion Williams, the financial man, said drily, "There's a surprise development."

Carl asked, "Mr. Dankworth? You haven't expressed an opinion yet."

Old Dankworth, the man who held the largest block of stock in the Corporation, raised his head from a mock nap. He looked at the ceiling and said, "You haven't found your man yet. I can tell by listening to you, your man is neither of these two. Mr. Winston, I'd like to restate your premise."

Avery Winston said patiently, "That's not exactly a surprise development, either."

Old Dankworth looked off at the wall of the subsidiary meeting room of the Board Room. Avery Winston's picture in oil hung there alongside an oil of Roger Campbell by the same artist. Dankworth waved his arm at the paintings of the first two presidents. "That is the point. We don't seem to hear or see anything different or startling around here of late. We have the same old thoughts, and we all sit up and look attentive as though we had brand-new thoughts. What was that latest new thought? Get along with the Government? Don't let them break us up?"

Dankworth waved his arm again at the paintings.

"Gentlemen, I think I'm going to have something to say in the days to come about corporate responsibility in a different sense from what's popular these days. The broad mass of people makes demands upon us simply because we are a giant corporation. We meet those demands, because that is indeed our responsibility. We have, all along, been doing those institutional things which discharge that responsibility. I'm going to suggest that we've been derelict in another direction. Our late administrations have been so preoccupied with stockholders on one hand, and public image on the other, that we have forgotten that

79

our true function above and beyond conduct of our daily business is to be leaders in the community and the country."

A third time he gestured at the paintings.

"Those two gentlemen, whether they knew it or not, were leaders. They created. They didn't give quarter to the competitors. Nor did they toady to Government. When you talk about Mr. Volk and Mr. Campbell, you talk about their soundness. You don't want anybody who might rock the boat. I think we're going to need a boat rocker. I'm afraid neither of these two sound young men you're proposing will meet the true requirements of this position between now and 1975."

Avery Winston waited to be sure the largest stockholder had finished. He said, clearly miffed, "Upon conclusion of that morality play, shall we now adjourn to the board meeting?"

14

DANA ALBRIGHT stood in one corner of the Board Room, his shoulders touching the wall. It was caveman instinct. This way his back was protected from assault. He watched the faces of the other members of the Board of Directors as they greeted the members of the nominating committee, and he watched the faces of the committee members. There might be a clue there. Carl Pearson appeared especially attentive to Bud Volk. That could be the clue.

Volk felt the cold eyes on his back. He turned for a swift look. Albright smiled and winked at the younger man. He could afford to smile. He knew about Volk. He knew the thing about Volk that Volk didn't want anybody to know. Some would have said that it was a stroke of coincident fortune, that the hatchet man came into his knowledge of the other horse's weakness just as they drove down the stretch, but Dana Albright didn't recognize the existence of mere chance. You went out and found the weakness.

Bud Volk smiled back. He was at ease. His confidence had grown every night as he lay awake and went over the possibilities. It had to be. They would consider Tony Campbell, and then they would choose Bud Volk.

Albright turned to Cleary. The Vice-President Engineering was in painfully eager conversation with Marion Williams. That wasn't like the dedicated engineer. The presidential fever had gotten to him. Albright smiled again. Cleary was spinning his wheels. They'd never choose Cleary, that was a foregone conclusion, even if Volk and Campbell were eliminated. But just in case . . .

Cleary felt the eyes. He came to the executive vice-president and said, "I understand we're going to elect Tony Campbell to the board today. Do you see any significance in that?"

Dana Albright said, "There just might be." He smiled. That would worry Cleary. But Dana Albright was not worried about Tony Campbell. Of all of them, Tony Campbell was in his hip pocket. A seventeen-year-old girl! The smile left. This one bothered the conscience of the hatchet man. It didn't seem right, to use this kind of thing on a man. A seventeen-year-old girl? Did you use that, even in extremity? The smile came back. It was such a huge joke on all the men who had wondered for so many years why Tony Campbell didn't do to several dozen women what they themselves would have done, if only they looked like Tony Campbell and had the National Motors stock of Tony Campbell. It was such a huge joke. He'd been doing it all the time, right under their noses, and for all of it, none of them ever knew! Again the smile left. He asked himself, "Will I go that far?"

Carl Pearson asked, "What are you doing over here, smiling to yourself?"

Albright said in the pleasant voice that came softly out of his Lincolnesque face, "Private joke, Carl."

"We're voting Tony Campbell on the Board today. I'm sure you'll go along with it."

"Of course."

"Did Battle come with you?"

"Yes. He's prepared. Give him a workout."

"How's that? What do you mean?"

"Question him on a wide range of subjects."

"What for?"

"He might surprise you."

Carl Pearson said, "We're short on time for surprises today."

Dana Albright leaned back against the mahogany wall. The smile twitched at the corner of his wide mouth in his narrow, craggy face as he calmly surveyed the man who had been made president when it should have been Dana Albright. Carl Pearson had no idea of the magnitude of the surprises ahead. They wouldn't know what hit them. Within two months the president of National Motors would be Dana Albright, that's who would be president. And his key man? David Battle would be his executive vice-president. That had to be, particularly with Volk eliminated. Battle, he might be the greatest surprise of all to them. Albright was convinced that they didn't know the things about David Battle that he knew.

David Battle. The Sweet Water Flash. David Battle. Could it get out of hand? This would have to be handled forcefully, but with great delicacy, too. Otherwise they might take David and run with him. He might even take the bit in his teeth himself. That was the kind of thing about David Battle the rest of them didn't know. They didn't know his implacable ambition. To them he was the football player. David Battle got over that a long time ago, but they never did. Would he cut and run on his own if Dana Albright showed him daylight? The smile came back and stayed. How do you get what you need on David Battle? Where do you look? Was Kelly Brand enough? A lot of men had a Kelly Brand. Even Avery Winston had had a Kelly Brand. Where do you find something really wrong in the life of an all-American boy? Jack Armstrong! What about Sweet Water? If there was nothing to hang on David Battle, what about his family? Catholic, yes. Right now that was a severe handicap to be overcome in dealing with the fundamentalists on the board. If it came to it, Dana could turn around and assault Rome himself. What else? Unionism? Bastardy? Horse stealing? What was in Sweet Water? This project required instant attention. Sweet Water, West Virginia. Was it a town like Dana Albright's Blue Rock, Ohio? What was it about America's small towns? What was it in Sweet Water that could put out men like James Lee Parker and David Battle?

BOOK

II

1

WILLARD PARKER named the town Sweet Water because the sulphur in the first well stunk to high heaven.

Sweet Water sat, company-red and coal-dust-black, on the deep-green Kanawha, upstream from Charleston, Chelyan, Cabin Creek, Coalburg and East Bank. Murder Creek split Sweet Water and ran, a muddy-tan trickle, into the Kanawha. The mountains rose steeply from the narrow river flat and disappeared into a dense wilderness of beeches, hickories, oaks and sumacs. Far up the hollow, at the source of Murder Creek, there dwelt fierce, taciturn descendants of pioneers, the Culpeppers, the Childresses, the Hatfields. In Sweet Water lived coal miners.

Red company houses stood in ranks on both sides of the C & O tracks. There were only sparse weeds on the river side of the tracks, where the great, rumbling, clanking tipple fed six thousand tons of bituminous coal a day to the black barges and the black C & O coal cars. The women of the miners daily swept their hard dirt lawns. The senior miners on the mountain side of the tracks lived among elm trees, hemlock, holly and wild flowers. But the coal dust blew across the tracks, too, and fell in gentle, invisible, perpetual black rain.

In splendor, on the first shelf in the slope, stood the

white houses, which were New England and Virginia in West Virginia. Vincent Carstairs lived in the big white house with the high ceilings, the flowered wallpaper, the stately furniture, the heavy-framed oval photographs of unsmiling forebears, the indoor plumbing, the telephone, the long, long porch, the flower garden, the grass lawn. Vincent Carstairs was a wealthy young man. He owned the Red Flash Mines of Sweet Water, West Virginia.

Next to him, next in size, was the home of Caleb Parker, the mine superintendent. His wife was India Missouri Culpepper Parker. His daughter was Ethel Parker. His sons were Wilbur and Franklin.

Then came Dr. Black, the bachelor, and his young housekeeper. The miners stood at the railroad tracks and hollered up the hill, "My wife is sick!"

"Got any money?"

"I can pay."

"Then I'll come."

It was a joke. Each miner paid a dollar a month, sick or well. There were five hundred miners. That was five hundred dollars a month for young Dr. Black and his young housekeeper.

In the fourth white house of Sweet Water lived Mike Foley. He had no proper claim on a white house. He was only the manager of the C & O passenger and freight station, the bright yellow and brown, bustling building a half mile from the suffusing tipple. But three of his unmarried sons worked in the mines, and the fourth in the company store, and they jointly afforded their white house. Beautiful black-haired, blue-eyed Ellen Foley worked part time for Vincent Carstairs in the big white house. This was a source of considerable embarrassment to her proud brothers. Ellen Foley had a mind of her own. The future mother of David Battle wanted money of her own. She had specific ambitions.

Those were the white houses of Sweet Water. Those were the quality folk. Vincent Carstairs and Caleb Parker ruled Sweet Water. The Carstairs were Johnny-come-latelies. Parkers came west with Daniel Boone, dropped off to form Parker County and provide a succession of logging superintendents, mine superintendents, and Church of Christ ministers in Knee Bone, Fool, Frogsburg, Black Betty and Sweet Water. Roger Carstairs, an ambitious man, came down from Pennsylvania to construct locks and dams for the great logging companies. He found the coal, leased sixty thousand acres for ten cents a ton from the mighty Cole & Crane who had bought the land from the Hatfields for twenty-five cents an acre in 1850, and Sweet Water became coal-dust, company-red on the green-black Kanawha and the muddy-tan Murder.

There was hard toil in Sweet Water. There was prosperity in Sweet Water. The Hunkies, the Polacks and Micks came, Papists all, with their strong backs and their superstitious, pagan, evil religion. They lived in company homes for one dollar a month a room. They bought from the company store at moderately inflated prices. They were rich beyond their dreams. Sweet Water gleamed. Even in coal dust, Sweet Water glistened. Red Flash company homes were painted new bright-red every three years. Only Sweet Water company homes, in all the Kanawha Valley, were supplied electricity from the company generators and then hooked in when Appalachian Power took over. There was no more popular man in the world than Roger Carstairs, and in turn his son, Vincent, in their kingdom in West by God Virginia.

But stubbornly, in this American prosperity, the Polacks still fought the Czar and the Micks still thought Irish Republican Army. In great content, Sweet Water seethed still with great discontent. *Escape! Escape the mines!* When the fetuses of Sweet Water would have floated serene in their warm water, the instincts of their rebellious, restless progenitors called hollowly to them: *Escape, escape from the Czar! Escape from the British! Escape, a better life lies beyond in Akron!*

David Battle should have been born David Dankowski. He was born David Battle. His genesis shouted: *Exodus!*

2

___

CASIMAR DANKOWSKI, the paternal grandfather of David Battle, emigrated to America in 1881 because his own parents were peasants and his new wife's father was unbearably well educated. From the day that Dankowski first dug coal in the Red Flash Mines of Sweet Water, West Virginia, there was in his slow Slavic imagination a dream of further escape. It was a long time coming.

For thirty years he worked on his knees in the deepest reaches of the mine slopes, chopping into the rich black veins with his miner's pickaxe. A lesser man, who shared the Stygian, dank room, loaded handcars with the fruits of Casimar's tremendous labor; the mule boss drove his beasts plodding like accustomed blind men to the adit; and the conveyor ran the coal swiftly down the incline to the giant tipple on the river bank. Carstairs admired his record-holding digger and paid him well. No amount of money, no amount of honest respect for an honest workman was enough to stifle the plodding dream of escape from the dark, choking, frightening tunnels in the hills of Sweet Water. A thousand times Casimar Dankowski said to Stella Dankowski, "When we get enough money, we go on. We go on to Akron."

On the afternoon of June 12, 1911, the impossible occurred. West Virginia mines were wet mines, and there was no gas. But on this impossible day a digger in a branch room struck dry structure and a pocket of methane, and the carbide lamp on his helmet set it off instantly. The men in the room died with the air sucked from their lungs even before they were buried by the cave-in. The dreadful *boommm* spread reverberating through the passageways. The tunnels shuddered. Timbers began to pop like scattered rifle shots. Miners sprang from their rooms with their hearts in their mouths and raced down the main slope, with the world a mile away. Ten men were crushed and died unable even to gasp. Two more were pinned by timbers, and they yelled hoarsely as coal sifted quickly over them, and then they were silent when the dust filled their mouths and nostrils. Casimar sprang at the blockade of coal and timbers, hewing furiously with his pick. He tugged vainly at the protruding legs of his loader. In half an hour he had the body free. He bent his head to shine his lamp on the black face. Again he attacked the cave-in. After three hours he sat down with his back against the wall of coal and blew out his lamp to conserve air. With Slavic stoicism he crossed his arms and went to sleep. This was Wednesday.

On Friday the haggard rescue crew, led by Caleb Parker and Walter Dankowski, shoring as they went, found and brought out the first of the bodies. In the next six hours they discovered the other eleven dead men and sent them, all disheveled, with the mules to the adit and then by jury rig down the slope to the families who had waited numbly those long two days. By then there were no tears. Each family in turn trailed behind the wagon that carried the husband-father to the mine office, where the formal identification was made. Then the bereft made their way to their red company homes with a great wonderment in them.

The rescuers burst through to Casimar. They found him leaning against the wall, idly scratching the hair on his great chest. They let out a hoarse cheer, reverberating in the tunnel, and Raymond Foley at the entrance shouted down the news that Dankowski lived. His wife and sons accepted his miraculous delivery with the same fortitude they had accorded his loss. Only Pete, the youngest son, joined the new cheer when Casimar emerged to daylight, blinking his eyes until his pupils

91

narrowed, and climbed stiffly into the cart for the ride down the slope.

Young Vincent Carstairs handed Casimar a pint of bonded bourbon. Casimar drank deeply, wiped his mouth with the back of his hand and drank again. Vincent said almost to himself, "Thank God, we got at least one of you back."

The reporter from the Columbus newspaper thrust close, eager-eyed. His straw hat was knocked from his head in the crush. When he had retrieved it, now black with coal dust, he had been pushed to the fringe of the crowd, and he called out, "What was it like in there, Dankowski? What was it like? Give us a statement on safety precautions."

The rescuers turned to him. There was hostility in them. There was sudden, sullen silence. Caleb Parker, worn, his white hair blackened, came close to the reporter and jabbed him in the chest with his strong forefinger. "Rourke, it will take you a hour by train to get to Charleston, all night by the Kanawha."

Rourke smiled ingratiatingly at Vincent and the three West Virginia reporters. "Mr. Carstairs, I'm just trying to do a job. A mine disaster, they want to know about it all over the country."

Vincent said in his soft, almost gentle voice, "Rourke, you don't get the message. We got no use for you in Sweet Water."

Rourke lost his smile. "Well, you don't scare me. If you're smart, you won't push me around. What I'll write about this goes to the whole damn country. You cooperate with me, I'll take it in account. You threaten me, I'll tell the whole world."

Instantly Walter Dankowski, Casimar's oldest son, struck Rourke backhanded across the face and sent him flying in the coal dust. Rourke picked himself up slowly, wiping futilely at the smears on his seersucker suit. His lip was cut and bleeding. He said defiantly, "If anything happens to me, my editor will get the whole damn Army down here."

Walter Dankowski, his face black and tired and angry, said, "The Army can come, they won't go back."

Rourke looked at him, greatly perplexed. "What's the matter with you? Carstairs and Parker, I can understand it. But that was your father, nearly died in there. Don't

92

you understand, he nearly died because Carstairs was too goddam greedy to take the safety precautions? I'm trying to help you." When Walter took him by the coat front, Rourke said quickly, "Give me a minute. One minute to ask you a question. You know what I'm doing for you, don't you? My stories are the best hope you've got. Before I'm done, public opinion will force the owners to install proper safety precautions, so disasters like this won't happen. And they'll be forced to pay you more than animal wages. Don't you know that? And most of all, public opinion will force the owners to recognize the IWW. I'm the owner's enemy. I'm the miners' friend. Don't you know that?"

Walter said, "All right, mister, we read what you got to say about the dumb Hunkies in the mine. Now I want to tell you something. We might be Hunkies, but we're not dumb. I don't know how much you make writing that Wobbly stuff for that paper of yours, but I'll tell you right now, you don't make as much as Casimar Dankowski makes digging coal, so don't you come around here talking about animal wages. You git, you goddam foreigner. You git while you can. We're just plain not interested in what a goddam rabble-rousing anarchist has to say about our business."

Rourke said hotly, "You got no right calling me an anarchist. Anybody that's for social justice, you call him an anarchist, and you got no call to do that. And I'm no more goddam foreigner than you are. I was born in Coalburg."

Still holding the coat front, Walter slapped Rourke sharply. "I say you're a Wobbly. I say you're an anarchist. I say you're a goddam socialist."

Rourke yelled defiantly, "Casimar, what were you thinking in there? Did you think about the safety precautions they didn't take? Did you think about Carstairs sitting safe in his big house?" Casimar heaved his big shoulders and didn't answer. Rourke rushed on. "I need a story. For New York and the rest of the country. Not a milksop story like the rest of them will write. They might get bribed by Carstairs, but not me. Did you pray? What did you think, in there in the dark? Did you think you were going to die for Carstairs' greed?"

Casimar raised the bottle and drank again, then extended it to his employer. Vincent said, "Yours, Casimar.

93

And take as much time off as you need. You'll be paid."

Rourke shouted hoarsely, "Bow down, Dankowski, and thank your master."

Casimar said in Polish to his oldest son, "Let him go, Walter. Don't get any more of his dirt on your hands." He walked away from the mine office, his family trailing behind him. Rourke made a move to follow. He was brought up short by a strong hand at the scruff of his neck. He turned slowly and looked into a mine guard's revolver. The guard said in a deadly flat voice, "Wobbly, reckon you're about to get your head blowed off your shoulders. You got five seconds to git."

Rourke shouted to the three other reporters, "You're witnesses!"

Templeton, from Huntington, smiled ominously and said, "It's amazing, sometimes, how little I see."

Tuohy, from Logan, said, "Shoot the Wobbly bastard."

Smith, from Charleston, said, "We'll swear it was an accident."

Rourke said, "All right, all right, all of you, but I'll be back."

The guard said, "You come back, you're dead."

"I'll fix you. I'll fix you all."

Two miners from the rescue party took him by the arms and the seat of his pants and sent him sprawling into the coal dust. He rose to his feet, glaring and breathing hard. Another miner joined the sport, hooked his leg and sent him down. Two miners jerked him erect.

The guard said, "I say you're a Wobbly, *I Won't Work* bastard. I want to hear you say it."

Rourke drew a deep breath of defiance. He watched the gun level on his stomach. He said, "I'm a Wobbly."

"Louder. An anarchist bastard. Tell us loud."

The miners wrenched his arms. He shouted, "I'm an anarchist bastard!"

"Not near loud enough. I want them to hear you up the holler."

With his arms forced up his back, Rourke yelled at the top of his lungs, "I'm an anarchist bastard!"

Vincent Carstairs said, "It's enough. Let him go."

The guard turned the reporter in the direction of the bright-yellow and brown C & O station. He kicked him mightily in the seat of the pants, and Rourke went stumbling a final time on his hands and knees.

94

Caleb Parker, the father of James Lee Parker, said, "Wobbly, you got off lucky. Now when you git back to Ohio and think about what you're going to write about Sweet Water, I advise you to think one thing, and that's that no distance is safe enough, we don't like what you say. And the next time you bring your *I Won't Work* ideas down here, you're dead. Now git."

Rourke walked fast to the station, his lips and hands bleeding, his seersucker suit ripped and coal-dust smeared, his straw hat left behind, his hot thoughts of revenge consuming him.

3

THIS WAS no red company house, this was a gray house, the fifth of the six non-company houses in Sweet Water. Casimar Dankowski's gray house stood on its own hill above Murder Creek. This house was stature. This was the only house in Sweet Water owned by a miner. This was the only house in Sweet Water owned by a Polack. This was a house to savor, this was a house to let a man forget every lost dream, except the final, stolid, inexplicit dream of escape.

At the foot of Casimar Dankowski's rude, sparse hill, a spur track ran in one direction two hundred yards to the main C & O line, and in the other direction ran four miles further into the hollow to Red Flash Number Three. Along the unfenced track ran the wagon road which began at the Charleston Road and ended fourteen miles back in the mountains where Murder Creek sourced and where lived the Slaughters, the Forsyths, the Culpeppers, and some of the Hatfields but no McCoys.

From the rutted wagon road a narrow path ran straight up the hillside to the six front steps of Casimar Dankowski's house on the acre of ground that had cost him six hard-earned dollars, without mineral rights, in 1888, seven years after he brought his gentle, educated wife to Sweet Water and began plotting his next escape. The gray house did not cling precariously to the hillside like the neighboring cabins clung on their steep banks. It was sturdy. It was a two-story house with four bedrooms. This was a house. It was a castle. David Battle's paternal grandfather was the liege lord.

Stella Dankowski boiled water in two pots and a teakettle, the stove lids glowing red from the big coal fire in the black-iron maw. From the cistern Pete Dankowski drew enough cold rain water to half-fill a galvanized washtub on the back porch, recessed into one corner of the house. Stella added boiling water, lovingly checking the temperature until she was satisfied. Casimar slipped his straps and let his overalls fall around his feet. Starting from the top, he unbuttoned the seventeen white buttons of his long underwear, shrugged his arms out and then laboriously tugged the legs over his bulging calves. He stretched and breathed in sweet air. He stepped gingerly into the hot water, lowered himself painfully until the water splashed at his huge belly. Stella handed him a bar of laundry soap, picked up the coal-blackened, sweat-stained clothes and retired respectfully to the kitchen. Casimar scrubbed away with the hard brush until the worst of the grime was abraded from his pale, oddly smooth skin. Then he sat luxuriating.

He gazed with ever prime approval at the gray walls of his home. Then he looked along the winding path through the straw-littered, nearly barren ground up the hill to the hen house and the duck wallow. He approved of his chickens and ducks, clucking and quacking and flying abortively. To the left of the duck wallow was the grand three-holer. To the right was his cow shack, with unpainted boards sagging and warped from twelve years' exposure. He listened to Pete lulling the hard-bitten cow, "Whoa, Bossy," and he could hear the milk squirt hissing-pinging into the pail. It occurred to him that the cow had probably not been milked in those two days he'd sat entombed in the mine's black bowels. It could have appealed to his sense of humor to think of the cow bursting with its milk of life while the rescuers dug for the dead. But Casimar had no humor, not even a grim humor. He had not smiled since the day in Poland he first knew his station in life and then determined to rise. He'd damn well make an issue of it, if his cow had been left unmilked.

He splashed the dirty water once more over his great chest and tremendous arms. He stood up, dripping. Two days in the grave, and he was still strong as an ox. His strength pleased him greatly. He expanded his shoulders to feel the good, strong tension in his back muscles. It was good to be alive. It was good not to be dead with the coal dust sucked frantically up his nostrils. It was good to have strength, eight sons, and the gray house.

He snorted and said aloud, "Foley."

Always he came back to Foley, because Foley had a *white* house. Foley had a cow, chickens and ducks, and a vegetable garden and flower garden to boot. Foley had a *white* house, just as though he were *somebody,* when he was just a Catholic.

Casimar snorted and reassured himself for the thousandth time, "It isn't the same. He rents it. I own mine. I could paint mine white, if I thought I was somebody. Can you imagine that? Casimar Dankowski in a white house?"

Then came the sigh in his unsmiling soul. Proud of himself? Proud of his gray house? For the thousandth time he berated himself for succumbing to his pride and the beguiling flush of well-being, because in the end came always the frustration, the gnawing bitterness, the coal-dust-black resentment of his lot in life. Who was Casimar Dankowski to be proud, when in Sweet Water there were Carstairs, and Parkers, and Halls, and Culpeppers? Casimar Dankowski. No matter how high he might rise above the other Polacks, the Hunkies, the Micks, he was still a Catholic in Protestant America, still a foreigner in pioneer West by God Virginia, and though the Protestants praised his strong back, and proclaimed him king of diggers, and accepted his counsel in the Red Flash, which was nearly the totality of Sweet Water, he must accept their high regard as dispensation, rather than as approbation from peers, because above every other thing in Sweet Water came pioneer English descent, came Parkers so proud of their heritage that they would not kowtow to Vincent Carstairs himself. Casimar Dankowski, strongest man in the mines? A gray house? The lowest Parker took precedence.

Stella Dankowski handed her husband fresh-laundered denims. He grunted acknowledgment. While he dressed, a revelation made its way through his slow thought processes. For two days he'd faced hideous death alone and unafraid. Fate had chosen not to take him. He had thought he would be prepared to go on to further days unchanged from the other days. But the revelation came that it would never be the same. The endless contemplation in the River Styx had wrought a shattering knowledge for him. Now he was in the sun again, but he was facing life as inevitable as death. His struggles these long, long years had been those of an impaled insect. Gaze upon my works, oh, ye mighty, and despair!

On the back porch, struggling to get his great limbs into his laundered trousers, proud one moment for rising so high, frustrated then that he could never be highest, never, never be a Parker, he capitulated at long last to his predestination.

Casimar convoked his eight sons. He said without ceremony, "Now it is your turn. The seven, you will now put in ten dollars a month. Peter, you will start at the mine tomorrow. You keep ten, put in thirty for room and board."

The sons regarded him with a mixture of astonishment and perplexity. Finally thirty-year-old Walter asked, "What's the matter with you, Papa?"

Casimar did not think explanation was required of him, but in this extraordinary situation he was constrained to repeat, "Now it is your turn." When still they stared their incomprehension, he said with some impatience, "I put the bread in your mouths. I put you to grow up in the gray house. I am done with it. Now it is your turn to repay."

The room was sucked as by the mine explosion. Finally Walter said, "You're telling us you're not going back in the mine." When his father didn't answer, he said, "Papa, if you got hurt, you should tell us. It will make a difference."

Casimar asked scornfully, "Do I look hurt?" Then he asked, "What is this, this make a difference?"

Stella Dankowski asked fearfully, "Papa, is there something wrong? Is it the TBs?"

Casimar contemplated the presumption of his wife's interjection. Finally he said with growing annoyance, "Do I look like the TBs?"

Walter set down his pipe. He took out a Cubeb and

lighted it carefully. The other sons watched him hope-fully. Walter screwed up his courage and said, "Papa, you're telling us you're not going back in the mines and you want us to support you. You're only fifty-three years old."

Casimar asked, "What is this? What is this?"

"Papa, fifty-three, that isn't very old."

Casimar waved his arm to dismiss the subject summarily. "I've said what will be done."

But Walter persisted. "Papa, is it the explosion? That couldn't happen again. They had their chance and didn't get you."

The father pointed his big finger at his oldest son. "Are you asking Casimar Dankowski if he is afraid?"

Walter said quickly, "No, Papa," and looked at his mother. All the sons looked at their mother.

Casimar asked, "Why do you look at Mama? What has she to do with this?"

Walter said, "Papa, ten dollars a month is a lot of money. We don't make your money. We owe the store, all of us."

The seventh son, twenty-year-old George, who had a year-old daughter and another seed well-sprouted in his wife's belly, said nervously, "Papa, ten dollars a month . . ."

Casimar said, "Ten dollars out of sixty is not much, for all the bread I put in your mouth."

Peter Dankowski looked pleadingly at his mother. He was filled with numbing shock. In one sweeping pronouncement his father had crushed his great, sustaining dream. In the long silence that now filled the kitchen, he couldn't bring himself to speak up to the father who, in the old tradition, could not be questioned. Finally he began, "Mama . . ." but he couldn't get any more out.

Stella Dankowski said to her husband, "Papa, Pete should tell you about Carnegie Tech. First we should talk about Carnegie Tech, then we talk about the other boys."

Casimar said, "I want to hear nothing about Carnegie Tech."

Pete said with a rush, "Papa, the man from Tech, Mr. Carstairs told him about me. He's a friend of Mr. Carstairs. He says they'll give me a scholarship."

"I want to hear nothing about it."

Walter said, "You should listen, Papa. They'll pay his way and pay him some extra to play football. They all

100

say Pete can be one of the best football players in the country."

Casimar said loudly, waving his big arm, "Enough football. Enough talk about college. I know all about it. You play two years high school, that is enough. Two years you got to go to high school, that is enough. Nobody else but you gets two years high school, Peter. Now that is enough."

Stella said gently, "Papa, there was no high school for the other boys. Now there is a high school in time for Peter, and he does so well . . ."

Walter interrupted. "Papa, you should go to the games. Everybody in Sweet Water and miles around, they go to the games. Pete's the hero, Papa. They've won every game, and you've got to take it in account. Next year you ought to go watch Pete play."

Stella said, "Peter studies hard, Papa. What a good, strong boy we have here. For the one boy there is the wonderful opportunity. The boy should have his chance."

Casimar roared, "What is this?"

Walter said, "Papa, if you're bound and determined to quit, maybe we can see about the rest of us putting in some money. Or maybe after a few days you'll decide you want to keep working some more until we're better fixed. But Pete, he's got the chance to go to college. Papa, that's why Mr. Carstairs put in the high school, so some could get out of Sweet Water. And Pete, he's got the best chance of anybody." He realized he was getting nowhere. He crushed out his cigarette and said softly, "Papa, there is one in the family who got a high school education. Just because you didn't, it's no reason to take it out on Pete."

It stung. Casimar burst out, "What has the reading all the books got Mama, except hard work like everybody else?" Then he said as calmly as he could, "Peter, you have the two years high school, that is more than the rest of the boys. That is good. Maybe Mr. Carstairs will put you in the office or the store. Now it is time for you to grow up. Football and school, that is for boys. Now it is time for you to be a man like your father and your brothers." He couldn't help adding, his voice rising again, "The education, we will leave that to the women."

Stella Dankowski, the dark-haired, dark-eyed Polish woman with the romanticism of the Jewish blood in her,

101

spoke gently in her rich voice. "Papa, such a wonderful life we have. We come from Poland, where there was nothing for us, to America where we have so much that we cannot count it. My husband makes one hundred dollars a month, think of that! Ah, I remember in Warsaw, we dreamed the great dreams, we took the train for Vienna, the wonderful music, and we spent all the money, and we went back to my father and he gave us enough all over again to get to America. Walter, you came three years after we were in Sweet Water, such a wonderful name, Walter, in all the coal dust, and your father was strong and handsome, young like you, Stephen, with strong arms like all of you . . ."

Casimar asked, "What is this history you are giving?"

"And Mr. Carstairs' father, he looked at Papa and said: *With those arms you don't have to understand everything I'm saying to you, but if you want to work hard, I've got a good job for you.* And Papa was the strongest and the best. Like Peter, Papa was, the strongest and handsomest and best. And the boys came, so fast after you, Walter, the wonderful boys, and Papa and I, we would count you over and over . . ."

"Who are you talking to, that doesn't know this?"

"And the gray house came, and only Papa, of the miners, had his gray house, and who is it to say what is the dream come true? If it cannot come true in the books we said we would get, or in the fine carriages, or a stone house, it will come true as best it can. Such wonderful dreams, come true as best they can." She clasped her hands and rocked ecstatically in the gesture of the Jewess in her that Casimar denied so vehemently. "Papa, we have a son who sees the books in his hand. The books we dreamed about in Warsaw. And the dream in Sweet Water, the wonderful dream of going away from the mines, it is here with the books in Peter's hands. And it will be all of us going away from the coal dust. Not just Peter. But also the mother, the father and the other sons, all going away in Peter. This wonderful dream must come true."

Walter said firmly, "Amen, we agree."

Casimar stood up. He struggled with himself and lost to his bitterness and resentments. He smashed his big hand on the kitchen table. "Enough! Enough of this talk! There is no more argument. He goes to work at the mine to-morrow."

Pete Dankowski clenched his fists. He was afraid, but he stepped forward and said resolutely, "I'm going to Carnegie Tech."

Casimar lunged and smashed his open hand across his youngest son's cheek with a resounding crack. There was deathly silence. The finger marks on Peter's cheek were white, then deep red. Pete raised his right fist in great rage. But he hesitated a fatal moment. His father's hand cracked again on his cheek, harder, stunning him, shocking him physically and destroying his resolve in the very moment of its birth. The rage drained out of him. The sorrow consumed him. His hands dropped at his sides. Walter took a step forward. Stella Dankowski put her hand on Walter's arm, and he stopped.

Casimar said, "You will go to the mine in the morn-ing."

Pete couldn't answer.

"You will go to the mine in the morning. Answer me."

"Yes, Papa."

Casimar glared into the seething resentment surrounding him. "Who else wants to stand up to the father?"

Walter said carefully, "Don't try it with me. You are not the strongest any more. I am."

Casimar raised his hand in new violent rage. His oldest son waited. Casimar looked into the face of his strongest son. He held back the blow. He said, "The father will get respect. You will each put in ten dollars a month. You will act like sons, with respect for the father."

Stella said softly, "Respect for the father comes first above all else."

The hatred dissipated and was replaced with the old inbred absolute respect for authority. One by one the strong sons said, "Yes, Papa."

Then Stella Dankowski said, "We prayed for you, Papa, when you were in the mine. We lit the candle and prayed, because the father is everything to us. The won-derful dream, it would end with you, but the prayers brought you out, and the dream, it is still ours for the future."

Casimar Dankowski thereupon, at the ripe old age of fifty-three, retired to the rocking chair on the front porch of his gray house. From there he would look down the sweep of the hollow to the red houses of Sweet Water and to the deep-green Kanawha. In the mornings he watched the miners head for the slopes in their clean overalls, the big black lunch pails in their hands, the lamps on their billed caps or metal helmets. In the afternoons he watched the miners' women sweep scrupulously clean the bare dirt lawns around the red houses. He listened to the grinding, clanking tipple. He listened to the trains chugging in, empty, and away, full. When the boys from Murder rode the coal cars into Sweet Water and shied lumps of coal at his gray house, he took down his rifle and shot at them with intent to kill. Each Wednesday and Saturday night, he walked to the Kanawha and took the pole-ferry to Shawnee to drink hard whiskey at Green Billy's Saloon. These were his divertissements. They were not quite sufficient to drown his dissatisfaction with himself that he had taken from his youngest son the grand opportunity and had done so in sheer spitefulness because of his half-Jewess wife's knowledge of books. On the June night in 1911, Casimar embarked on the self-recriminatory, stubborn retirement that would last for thirty years until his death from stomach cancer in Detroit in 1941, and Peter Dankowski, who would become the father of David Battle, was started on the road to destruction.

4

VINCENT CARSTAIRS had a happy faculty for doing the right thing. He brought back from his British Isles tour a piece of the Old Sod as a gift to Sweet Water's hundred Catholic families, who could not have been more pleased. Only an elaborate planting ceremony could do justice to Vincent's thoughtfulness.

It wasn't easy, in Sweet Water, to find a suitable site for the green-grass monument to Irish sentimentality. Two homes had lawns. One was the old Carstairs home, which Caleb Parker bought for two thousand dollars when Vincent built the big white house for his cold wife. The other was the stately big house itself, with its grand garden and great green lawn commanding wonder and admiration, untouchable within the cold wife's formidable black-iron fence. Neither of these common-sense possibilities was acceptable as a repository of the sacred soil.

Certainly Parker land was out of the question. Reverend Davis Parker, the splendid orator of Sweet Water's Church of Christ, lived with his brother in that second-best white house. The Church of Christ, this was the congregation of men whose blood shouted against King George and then the federalists. This was the church of men who would not be told by others. This was the church of Americans. This was the congregation of West by God Virginians, and no Irish icon was going to be set in Parker soil.

Like all the current-generation Protestants in the close-knit Red Flash commune, the Parkers were friendly enough to the Catholics on a workaday basis, but inevitably they harbored ingrained distrust at best, and at worst downright revulsion for anything to do with the Church and formal Catholicism. They half believed what their immediate forebears believed implicitly, that the Pope was the devil incarnate. It distressed them that obviously intelligent men like the Foleys and the Dankowskis were so misguided when the fate of their immortal souls and of Americans' America was at stake. Pastor Davis Parker prayed deep into many nights that he be given the power to exorcise the papist devil from these otherwise decent, hard-working foreigners, so that they might be given their ultimate acceptance as Americans and full comrades in the deadly struggle of God-fearing, independent men against those debilitating foreign influences epitomized by federalists and by radical Wobblies with their imported doctrines of class warfare that could lead only to that most desolate, desperate subjugation, the namelessness of collectivism.

Of course, only the kids believed that the Catholics ate blood pudding at Mass. But even the enlightened Caleb Parker was not unconvinced that the Catholic churches from one end of America to the other hid arsenals in their basements waiting for Rome to signal the day of take-over. Not even Caleb could turn his back on the Casimar Dankowski he esteemed for accomplishment, without feeling a prickle of uncertainty. Even Caleb accepted his Catholic neighbors with vastest, deepest reservations. No, the Old Sod, with its automatic Catholic implications, could not be planted on Parker soil.

Nor did it seem appropriate for Vincent to bequeath any portion of his own property for the shrine. In the first place, this would carry a too obvious sense of paternalism, a relationship between Vincent and his employees tacitly accepted but overtly denied by both sides. In the second place, it was one thing for Vincent to manifest his friendliness to his Catholic miners, but it would be carrying things a bit far if he let himself be intimately involved in Catholic formalities, and Mike Foley had immediately timed the grand ceremony for the once-a-month visit of the

106

priest who traveled on horseback out of Cabin Creek. Vincent might correctly be considered non-fundamental in his Church of Christ adherence. It might even be safely assumed that he gazed vacantly through the terrible two hours of Davis Parker's fire-and-brimstone sermons because religion could not distract him from his eternal dedication to his mine and his town. If it could be granted that a cold wife either drove a man deep into religion, for the relief of flagellation, or away from religion, cynical, it could readily be discerned that Vincent in church smiled ruefully, just a little, at the pomposity of any religion that promised peace of mind to its adherents, when it was clear to all that the twin albatrosses of mines and wife hung heavy around his neck. But this most moderate, most cynical of Protestants in Sweet Water still had his ample share of abhorrence of Rome. All knew this much about him. Only as a last recourse could the sacred sod of Erin be planted on Carstairs land.

Then where? Oh, it was a thorny problem, what to do with that square foot of Ireland resting uneasy and impatient for delivery from Vincent's nursery to its own Catholic hallowed ground. There was no lack of volunteers from among the Catholics. But in no event did it seem appropriate to set it in the ground of a company red house. That seemed even more degrading than the thought of the big white house grounds. Mike Foley assumed they would accept his offer, because he could set aside a fine park at his white house. But, Mike, too, lived on company land. Who among the Catholics did not live on company land? Only Casimar Dankowski.

The Dankowskis, the Dvoraks, the Wrobleskis, the Beltzes, all the Polacks and Hunkies took as much interest in the project as the Micks. Indiscriminately they felt the sod was as much a gift to them as to the Irishmen themselves, and indeed the non-discrimination had been in Vincent's mind. He had brought no gifts to the Poles and Hungarians. He had lumped them all together with the Foleys, the Daughertys, the Bryans, and those ninety-per cent Irish-blooded Cardozas, and without stopping to think about it, equated Catholicism with Ireland. No matter, the Dankowskis, the Dvoraks and the rest of them understood, accepted and joined in with first-hand enthusiasm. Now, suddenly, there was bitterness in Sweet Water.

Sweet Water had been different. Sweet Water had been

a melting pot for the diverse Catholics. When the Poles came and would have kept to themselves, as they always did, there weren't enough of them. When the Hungarians and Ukrainians would have kept to themselves, as they always did, there weren't enough of them. They were thrown into the community and learned to speak English. More precisely, they were thrown into one pot of Catholics, banded together for moral support against the Protestant pioneers who were still the great majority up and down the Kanawha. This was nearly a unique town in America. For once Polacks, Micks and Hunkies were joined together simply as Catholics. It was a noble experiment that flourished. Now it wilted and sagged.

Casimar said in his heavy voice, "I will give the land at the front of my property."

The jealousy surged. Mike Foley said, "Now I must object."

"Why would you object, Foley? I own my land. I am the only Catholic who owns land."

Mike Foley chewed his pipe awhile, then using it as a pointer, said, "All of us are well aware that you own your own land. I would say that not many days go by that you do not find some way to remind us. Sure, and it's no mean accomplishment." His expression stated very clearly that he considered it an entirely mean accomplishment. "But I'm afraid we must refuse your well-meaning offer."

Casimar roared, "Who is we, that refuses?"

Foley said blandly, "The Sons of Erin, Dankowski, to whom this precious sod has been bequeathed."

Walter Dankowski stood out and said, "In a pig's ass, Mike Foley. Mr. Carstairs brought the sod for the Catholics."

Raymond Foley, the first son of Mike, moved out and said, "Mr. Carstairs brought it for the Irish, and who else would it be for?"

"Who says?"

"I say, you dumb Polack."

Walter moaned, "Oh, sweet Jesus!" He tore into Ray Foley. The two strong young men went crashing to the hard ground by the C & O station, Walter on top, his steel fingers clutching at Foley's bulging-muscled throat. Foley reached back and found coal chips. He ground them in the contorted face above him, the skin abraded, the blood flowed, Walter released his grip, and the two of them rolled over like cats. Francis Daugherty called, "Hoo, boy!" and threw his knife to Ray Foley. Foley advanced purposefully, the knife gleaming. Dvorak sprang out and handed his knife to Walter. He gripped it, the eight-inch blade circling in the air, and the young men crept warily, legs wide, waists bent, ready to kill.

Ellen Foley emerged from her hiding place. She sauntered slowly through the men, swishing, so that her skirt swirled around the ankles of her button shoes, and she flipped the neckerchief of her middy blouse nonchalantly.

Mike Foley said, "You get home arunnin', Ellen Foley."

She tossed her black hair. Her blue eyes sparkled. "Now why would I want to leave when the killing is about to begin?" She walked straight to the combatants. She planted herself, fist on hips. "Look at you! Foley and Dankowski, like a couple of hillbillies from Murder, now aren't you a pretty sight?"

Ray Foley said to his sister, "Get home, honey. This isn't for you."

"I think you're right. Catholics in Sweet Water fighting with knives just like Snakes up the holler. That isn't for me." She tossed her hair again. She walked slowly away a few steps, turned and said, "Good grief!" and then continued slowly up the Charleston Road.

Ray Foley and Walter Dankowski straightened up, nonplused. Walter looked at the knife in his hand. He threw it down, point-first in the ground. Ray Foley followed suit, the hafts quivering side by side. They turned and walked away with their own groups, but there was no handshake and the bad taste hung in them all.

For three days the Catholic Polacks and Hunkies did not speak to the Catholic Micks, except in the mine tunnels in the line of duty. There no importance transcended the importance of official communications between men risking their lives in the black shafts. On the third day Stella Dankowski made the overture of peace for which all the stubborn men longed. She proposed that the plot lying between the Sweet Water Station and the Carstairs Community House be purchased from the C & O and be dedicated, consecrated, nourished and tended into communal gleaming green evidence of eternal Catholic truth in the barren wasteland of Protestant clay, and that for such a sacred project Poles and Hungarians were as much Catholics as Irishmen. Of course!

Mike Foley, the station manager, negotiated the transaction. He said, "It will be no mean feat, since the C & O parts with property less readily than a lion with his teeth or a virgin with her virtue." With the excitement and the fervor of the project full in him, Foley was at his maudlin, glib-tongued best, and in a wonderful afternoon melted into submission the rail-track hearts in the Huntington District office, and the bargain was struck. Foley took himself to Casimar's house and said sheepishly, still a little stubborn, "Sure and we'll consider you a black Irishman with the rest of us, if you'll be after collecting the funds for the purchase."

Casimar said gruffly, "I've been thinking, we should have a church. There's enough of us to have a church."

Not having thought of it, Mike asked, "And what is wrong with the Community House?" But then he relented and said, "It would warm the cockles of Father Hannigan's heart."

Casimar collected two dollars each from the hundred Catholic families, and Vincent added an anonymous donation to reach the specified three-hundred-dollar starting fund. Vincent's attorney in Charleston drew up the necessary non-profit corporation articles. Among the provisions, Mike Foley, Casimar Dankowski and Carl Dvorak were officially installed as co-trustees. Thus the hurdle was cleared, the breach mended, and Old Sod Square, Inc., came into being.

The beginnings were modest. First the sod plot was outlined with whitewashed stones. Across the Kanawha, in the more fertile ground beyond Shawnee, the Dankowski brothers and Tom Foley found a patch of black soil to sustain the sanctified life and brought back enough to cover the hard ground six inches deep where the sod could flourish and spread. Though the beginnings were modest, there was nothing modest about the ceremony itself.

On September 11, three months from the day of Casimir Dankowski's retirement, Father Hannigan rode in, unsuspecting, from Cabin Creek and was led by his proud flock to the ground they wished to hallow. Father Hannigan was instantly enthused. When Mike Foley accepted the foot-square patch of sod from Vincent and lovingly set it in place in the center of the plot, the priest glowed with Irish nostalgic emotion, and he outdid himself in reverence and enthusiastic energy as he sprinkled holy water from his

110

scepter, and he said in his high-pitched voice, "In the Name of the Father, and of the Son, and of the Holy Ghost, Amen. Dearly Beloved, God and Ireland are always with us. Let this Old Sod serve as a tangible expression of our eternal love of God and Home. In this sod are memories of the past and dreams of the future. Let us tend it well. Let this holy water speed its growth. Let it spread and make bright green this plot of ground, and as it shines amidst coal and clay, let it remind everyone that our spirits also shine brightly amidst coal and clay.

"I propose that a suitable statue be added to grace this place. And that the Sodality take this project as their important work in the days ahead. A holy white statue as an outdoor shrine to our beliefs, in this greenness of our dreams in America, for where we go, goes Ireland." Then, in a further outburst of enthusiasm, he added, "Soon we will have God's holy house on this site. Today we will hold Mass here, under the blue skies, and we will do honor to nature, which is God manifest."

This was a noble thought, but the Catholics of Sweet Water were uneasy. They were not the only citizens of Sweet Water present at the ceremony. They were outnumbered four to one by the unbelievers, for wild horses could not have kept the Protestants from the carnival excitement of such an unusual doing as a sod-planting complete with such cabalistic rites as the sprinkling of holy water. They had turned out en masse to enjoy the lively show before entering their drab Church of Christ for another drab two hours of Davis Parker. They ringed the plot and the Catholics and accepted the strange goings-on with friendly tolerance and no more than nudges and winks at the holy-water sprinkling. But Mass was something else. Would they stand still for that? The Catholics had good reason to feel uneasy and to wish devoutly that they could go as usual inside the Community Hall, where a Protestant would not dare follow when the devil was in session.

Ellen Foley whispered to Pete Dankowski, "I hope the good father knows what he's doing."

"You should worry. I'm serving Mass today."

Ellen's blue eyes sparkled. "When this is over, they'll burn us all as witches, and you upside down. Sure and you're going to have to fight somebody before this day is over."

111

But Father Hannigan was oblivious of the consternation in his flock. In the first place, he had no inhibitions in his religion. In the second place, this was to him a God-given opportunity to speak out to a great host of Protestants and perhaps strike a spark in one of them that would bring another soul to Truth. The priest had no way of knowing that he was embarrassing his people, that the mortally pious congregation was mortally ashamed of its beliefs before the ascendant Protestant hillbillies.

The Protestants folded their arms and watched the Mass with huge curiosity and no little disconcertion. Some of them now expected the devil to leap out among the celebrants in a puff of incense smoke. They were fascinated with the priest's vestments and with the Latin liturgy, but to them the Latin was Druid chant or the chilling mutterings of cabalism. To them the vestments were as weirdly wonderful as a witch doctor's mask. These fundamentalists of the Church of Christ stood there at Mass at the new Old Sod Square and congratulated themselves that they were at last seeing, in the safety of open air, the strange and dreadful carryings-on, and though the very marrow of their bones crawled with the dread of it all, not a one turned to flee.

Father Hannigan was possessed, this day, of rare restraint. Instead of his normal forty-minute sermon delivered with the sternness of a Roman Catholic priest to a small captive audience he saw but once a month, he spoke briefly and with, for him, remarkable tolerance.

"Dearly Beloved, the Blessed Savior has enjoined us above all else to love our neighbors as ourselves, to judge not lest we be judged ourselves, and to do unto others as we would have others do unto us. These things above all else.

"There is a oneness in Christianity. All of us in Sweet Water believe in the same True God, Jesus Christ. This is a unity that defies all the differences that would put us apart one from the other.

"We in this congregation believe in our Church. We believe that we are fortunate that we were born to this True Church or have been converted to it. This, we believe, is our greatest blessing on this earth. It is also a great challenge and responsibility to us who believe in the Holy Mother Church. If a man is a Roman Catholic, then always must he be a Roman Catholic, for spurning his opportunity for Grace, once it has been given him, he will surely suffer eternal damnation. The Catholic has been given the opportunity of belonging to God's Church. He must not fail.

"But if a man be born a Protestant, or a Buddhist, or a Mohammedan, then if that man lives his religion and believes in his religion, will merciful God gather him unto His bosom. The good that is in man lies not in church, but in the good of God Himself.

"We are united in Christ. We are united in this community in the toil with which we earn our daily bread, but we are more truly and more surely united in Christ. We would like our friends to know more about us. The Catholic Church invites investigation from anyone who would like to know what we believe and why we believe as we do."

This was fine. Caleb Parker whispered to his brother Wilbur, "Damn white of him to let us go to Heaven," but he was as impressed as the other onlookers with the priest's civilized reasonability that was in such marked contrast to his pagan conduct. The Catholics sighed inwardly with sudden relief. They even dared hope that not only would they not be made fools of before the Protestants, they would indeed gain wonderful new respect from the assumptors apparent. As a result, the sudden denouement was the more cruel.

Pete Dankowski knelt behind the priest, held up the vestments and rang the bell for Consecration. Young J. B. Stubbs, Pete's close friend from the Sweet Water High football team, said more loudly than he intended in the dead silence, "Ding-aling-aling, ring a little bell, hold up a priest's coal tail, go to— heaven!"

A laugh was smothered. Another could not be stifled. The tittering spread, and as the jingle was repeated for those who had not caught it, the laughing swelled until the words of the Mass were drowned out, and J. B., pleased with himself, said, "Ding-aling-aling, next boat leaving for Rome!" and Ben Hall gripped his thighs and said, "Sweet Jesus!" and the small kids laughed and searched their parents' faces for approval that they were laughing in the right places.

Father Hannigan turned, his neck flushed, and said with a strained voice, "Do unto others as you would have them do unto you," and the laughing stopped, but the spell of

113

amity and mutual respect was gone, and as the priest served Communion to his faithful, the Protestants knew it for exactly what it was, a pagan rite, an invention of the devil to divert man from the simplicity of the true God, a blood ceremony to hypnotize men and nourish the evil, revolutionary designs of the monstrously evil papists.

When Pete Dankowski knelt for Communion he could scarcely open his mouth. He knew that if he accepted his Creator, he committed mortal sin, for he was as far as a person could be from a state of Grace. On this September Sunday morning, with the sun shining warmly and white cumulus clouds in the blue, breathless sky, he hated. He hated his friend who had mocked him and caused all of Sweet Water to laugh at him. He hated the mud and coal dust. He hated the shafts in the hills. With sudden renewed ferocity he hated the father who had smashed his dream of escape. He hated. There was no love in him. There was not even belief. There was only bitterness and hatred in him, and he struggled a long time to swallow the bread, and his hugely muscled arms felt weak as with ague, and he felt strangely giddy, as a man feels when he has held his breath too long.

5

FROM WAY OFF in the mountains, the train whistle came, a high hoarse wail of loneliness, mournful, ever more mournful, slowly caroming off the mountainsides, crying its this-world other-world, strangled, shivering lament down the hollows, mournful, ever more mournful, hoo-hoo-ahoooooo, and Ellen Foley stiffened and said tremulously, "I don't think we ought to do it," and his hand was already run up under her skirt, stroking clumsily on her thigh. "Pete, I don't think we ought to do it. Oh, please, Pete, please don't."

He took his hand away abruptly.

After a moment, knowing that he was offended, she asked tentatively, "Pete?"

He didn't answer.

"It's the train whistle, Pete. It makes me feel all sort of funny. Mama says it's the sound of a dead dog hunting for his lost dead owner."

He sat up and looked off into the darkness. "It's a train whistle."

"Mama says it's a dead dog. You know what it says to me? Mortal sin. I can't help it. I keep hearing it. Mortal sin, all kind of drawn out and unhappy for us, mortal sin, all crying across the valley at us."

"Sweet Jesus! Dead dogs, mortal sins and leprechauns

115

be jumping out any minute! You've heard the train a million times. That's what Sweet Water is. Hunh! A jail with train whistles, that's what Sweet Water is. And the whistle don't say nothing about mortal sin. It says get out of jail, boy, and get on me and git to Akron. The only good sound in Sweet Water, that's what that whistle is."

"Pete, don't be up there all by yourself. Lie close to me and kiss me, and don't let me be scared."

"Dead dog!" He snorted again. "Hunh!"

"It's making you feel lonely, too. I can tell."

He burst out, "What call you got not to let me?"

After a moment she asked, "What do you mean, what call?"

"Ain't as if it was something so all-fired important."

"A mortal sin is all-fired important, isn't it?" She pulled him down beside her on the cushioning weed-grass. She kissed his cheek. "You're getting so you talk more like the hillbillies every day."

"Just because I want to do it to you?"

"I mean you *talk* like them. The words. The accent. It sure is strange. I mean, it's sort of sad, talking like hillbillies, wishing we were hillbillies. We're the ones got the true church. It's us that have some culture. I'll sure bet the Dankowskis and the Foleys have got more books than the Parkers put together. And for sure more than the Culpeppers. But you end up trying to be like them, just because they were here before we got here. It's strange and sort of sad."

"What do you want me to talk like? My Polack old man? My half-Jew mama?"

"Is your mama really half-Jew? Is she really?" He didn't answer. "You better not let anybody else hear you say that. Bad enough being a Catholic in Sweet Water." He could see the flash of her smile. "Wasn't that something today? I thought Father Hannigan was going to throw a conniption fit. That J.B. is the funniest boy in Parker County."

"He don't think he's so funny right now."

"Pete, you didn't have a fight with J.B.?"

"Fight! I wiped up the coal dust with him."

"He was just making a joke. He didn't mean all that harm. And you've got to admit, it was funny."

"Well, he'll think twicet before he makes the next joke on me. How come you're sticking up for him? I don't get it. You think it's funny when a guy makes cracks like that at Mass, when it's blasphemy and sacrilege, and then you turn right around and practical have a Holy Roller fit on account of just some plain, ordinary doing it, like the whole world does."

"Don't talk about doing it, Pete. It makes me feel sort of sick inside. It is a mortal sin. You know it is, Pete."

"Maybe if I was Wilbur Parker, you might feel different. If you're not satisfied with me, why don't you just say so?"

"Don't say things like that, Pete, you're so bitter all of a sudden. Don't be so bitter about everything. It's your own fault you're going in the mine. Don't take it out on everybody else."

"My fault!"

"You're full-grown. If you want school as bad as you say, then why don't you just do it? He can't really stop you if you go back to school, he can't really stop you."

Rather than face that truth, he said again, "If you're not satisfied, get Wilbur Parker. I notice he's sucking around your house all the time."

She was tempted to be pleased and chide him for jealousy. But she said, "You ought to march right out of that mine and march right into school, and you just tell Casimar you're going to Carnegie Tech no matter what he says."

"Sure."

"I mean it. I wouldn't let him push me around, if I were you."

"So I'm a Polack. So Polacks get pushed around. That's the real difference between us and the Parkers. When the English go somewhere, you know, Africa, or India, or some place like that, or Sweet Water, they don't try to act like the people there, they make the people there act like them, and they get away with it. But the Hunkies, and the Micks, the Polacks, we know we're second-class citizens. I guess it's just a difference of natural-born attitudes, and ain't nobody or no thing going to change it no time, now or ever. Did you know there was a nigger in Sweet Water today?"

"What was he doing?"

"Just walking down the track. Going somewhere, I guess. Who's really worst off, a Catholic, a Jew or a nigger? I'd say a Catholic, because the Catholic, he's almost there, and that's worse than not even being close."

"Did they do anything to him?"

"I flung a hunk of coal at him."

After a moment she said, "That doesn't seem like much of a thing to do. Was he hurting anybody?"

"No, he was just walkin' down the track. In his clean work clothes, wagging a little poke over his shoulder, with his head sort of down, not looking right or left. So when they started stonin' him, I flung a hunk of coal at him and hit him right in the back. Right between the shoulder blades. And he didn't even let out a yelp. Didn't even touch where it hit him. Just kept awalkin'. Hunh! Reckon it hurt." He was silent before he said, "I kind of wished I hadn't flung it at him. Everybody else was flinging' at him. And J.B. and me had just got done knocking ourselves around, and I got him to say he wished he hadn't said that about the bells, and we didn't know what to say after that. Then there came the nigger, and I flung that big ole piece of coal and it hit him smack in the back, clunk, and he just kept on walkin', only then his head was up in the air and his eyes still straight ahead, and everybody hollering nigger at him, and I reckon it will be a blue moon before he comes back thisaway."

Ellen would have spoken, but the train whistle called closer, looking. Hoo-hoo-ahooooooo. She turned her head toward it.

Pete said, "It's a train whistle."

"It's a terrible lonesome sound. When I was a little girl, it made me all sort of shivery and lonesome, and I'd wish somebody else was awake."

"Some day I'm going to be something besides a Polack."

"Are you, now? Just how are you going to change your spots?"

"I will. I'll change my spots."

"Not unless the leopard can. You could go off to Carnegie Tech and be all-American, and be somebody, but you'd still be Pete Dankowski, ringing his little bell and going to heaven, if you knew you just had new spots on the outside of the same old inside."

"Are you all that satisfied with what you are?"

"I'm satisfied being a pretty girl."

"I'll bet you are."

"I like it when I swish past the station and they whistle, and I act like I'm provoked, but they know better."

"I bet they do."

"I know what I bet, Pete. I bet not many people have as good a life as us. I bet their folks don't love them like ours love us. I bet you can go a week without seeing somebody unhappy in Sweet Water. You just don't see people scowling. Even when they're fighting!"

"Especially when they're fighting. Or maybe only when they're fighting. You shouldn't have broke up the fight."

"Wouldn't that be nice? My brother cutting up my beau's brother?"

"Only it would have been the other way around."

Her Irish pride flared. She caught herself. She smiled. "My brother can lick your brother any day of the week and twice on Sunday." And she added quickly, to forestall his own temper, "And my old man can talk your old man to death, and you can't argue that. And you got to admit, this is the best town in the valley. Not one person that doesn't have a job. And we've got electricity. I bet there isn't a happier place in the whole world than right here. Everybody happy with the coal dust on 'em. Everybody with plenty to eat. I'll bet not many towns have somebody like Mr. Carstairs. Do you know what I think of when I think of Sweet Water? I think of the dolls Mama made for me. And the one Papa bought in Charleston. And the one my brothers brought back that time they went to Wheeling. And the train ride down to Charleston. And Dr. Black on his big black horse. And Mama reading Shakespeare, and Papa asking her what for she wants to read that Englishman, but he can talk about it right along with her. And me reading *Comfort* magazine in the kitchen after Papa goes to bed, and getting scared out of ten years' growth when he almost caught me. And the showboat. And *East Lynne*. And the wagons meeting the barge, they never get to see that in Charleston. And chicken and dumplings, I don't think anybody anywhere ever gets anything better to eat than chicken and dumplings. And corn bread. And biscuits at breakfast. And bacon and salt pork. And fried chicken for Christmas breakfast, do you have that, too? And turkey Christmas night? What do you Polacks eat, sausage? And all those pecks and pecks of oranges and nuts and candy. And the hair ribbons. And popcorn and cranberries. Everything ex-

119

cept that grapefruit. Did you ever taste anything as terrible as grapefruit? And everybody here lives in a house. And that Rourke, he's got the nerve to say we've got a terrible life, and I'll bet a pretty they've got people starving in Columbus and Wheeling and New York, and everybody here is living like a king. You know that. Wasn't a single miner would raise his hand to agree with Rourke. Not one. When it comes right down to it, everybody in this town knows how good it is here. And everybody happy. That's really *something*, Pete, everybody is happy!"

"Boy, you're as big a windbag as your old man."

"Pete, don't you agree?"

"Then how come everybody wants out?"

"I don't know. That's what I'm saying. I don't think they really do. I think everybody says it just because everybody else says it. But when they really think about other pastures, they're not really all that greener after all."

"Try me."

"Just don't be so glum and bitter, Pete. You used to be so much fun."

"You got your choice. Take Wilbur if you want him."

"Maybe I'll just do that. If you're going to be such a sour face. Pete, didn't you tell Casimar about the scholarship?"

"We all told him. Might as well tell the coal in the mine."

"You've just got to do it. Get him down to see you play football, and when he sees people come all the way down the holler just to see you play, he's bound to change his mind."

"They can cheer me in the mine now. Guess I'll break Papa's record for digging coal, that's the record I'll break. But some day, some day, sweet Jesus, I'll get out of here."

"Will you take me with you, Pete?"

"I thought you were so all-fired happy here."

"Might not be so happy with you gone."

"Then why don't you act like it?"

She didn't answer. They both fell to brooding.

Then he asked, "What's it like up there in Vincent's house?"

"Like our house. Except bigger. And the pictures on the walls are scarier. And there I get paid for doing the same work I do for free at home."

"Does he treat you nice?"

"He treats everybody nice, you know that."

"I mean, does he treat you special nice?"

Now she smiled with pleasure at his jealousy. "Only when she's up at Pittsburgh or New York or some place."

"I believe it. That's what people say."

She asked stiffly, "What do people say?"

"You know."

"No, I don't know."

"Well, why would you want to work up there in the first place? You don't have to work."

"I like the money. I'm saving money." She smiled against his face. "Not all Micks are improvident. I can be as close with money as Dankowskis any day in the week." She put her lips on his cheek. "Should I confess the great secret? You really want to know why I'm working there? To get enough money so when you get your scholarship to college, I can go too."

He said gruffly, "Well, now you can forget it. And what I'm saying is, everybody knows how cold she is and bets he hasn't had any you-know-what since his wedding night, if he got it then, so maybe people are wondering if he's getting it somewhere else. You won't let me do it, but how about somebody else that can give you all that money for college?"

She rose without a word and began walking toward the slope down to Murder Creek. He sprang after her and caught her arm, but she broke loose and walked faster.

"You don't have to be sore, Ellen."

"Pete, I'll never forgive you. Never." She was on the verge of tears.

"Well," he said defensively, "I just wondered, that's all. You're supposed to be my girl, and all the fellows saying things, like how come you're working up there, when your daddy and brothers got good jobs, and you live in your own white house, and don't need the money. And J.B. says he's got it figured out, Vincent's going to heave her out on her cold fanny, and you'll be right there and don't even have to move in, now you'll just spend the nights, too. You can't blame me for just wondering, when you're supposed to be my girl, and you won't let me do it."

She stopped. Suddenly she slumped down, sitting on the ground, and buried her face in her hands.

He said clumsily, "I didn't mean it like it sounds. I guess I didn't mean that."

"Did you have a fist fight with J.B. when he said that?"

"No. But I didn't like it, you can bet."

"But you had a fight when he made fun of you? That was more important?"

"Well, that was different. That was in front of people."

"What he said about me, did he say that in front of people?"

"Well, just some of the fellows on the team. And you know how that is. You know how guys talk about things like that. If you went around hitting everybody in West Virginia that said things about women, you'd hit till your arms were plumb wore off into stumps."

Then she burst out laughing, and he wasn't sure that wasn't worse, until she said, "My Irish sense of humor to the rescue. It is pretty funny, when you think of it. Now you see here, Mr. Peter Dankowski, Vincent Carstairs has never so much as laid a hand on me. Lord knows, I wouldn't blame him, married to her. But he's a man the likes Poland and Ireland and Sweet Water never saw, and if you don't get over being so gloomy, and if you don't keep on your toes, I think I'll just go up to Pennsylvania and find me another one like that." Once more she pulled him down to her. "And you can tell Mr. J. B. Stubbs, the reason I'm working for Mr. Carstairs is so I can go to college when my beau goes. And if you were just a little bit brighter, you'd have it figured out how I feel about you."

"I wish I hadn't said it, Ellen, I guess. I guess I wish a lot of things. I wish I knew how to stand up to a Polish old man. I wish I hadn't flung that lump of coal at the nigger. How come people do things they wish right away they didn't do? It's sometimes like things swell up in you. And you hit around you. Like if you hit a nigger, that'll make up for not going to Carnegie Tech, and if you hit your best friend, that'll make up for you being a Polack Catholic. And maybe you even say something you don't feel like saying to a girl who . . . well, you know what I mean."

"No. Tell me."

"You know, a girl, you think things about. I mean

you think about her. Even when she's not around. Like last winter, when I was out on the hill hunting rabbits, and the snow was so deep, and all white and kind of pure, like nobody ever touched it before, and I got to thinking about the time I saw you without any clothes on . . ."

"Pete Dankowski, just when did you see me without any clothes on?"

"I won't give that away. It might happen again sometime."

"Now I know I'll never forgive you."

"But you're not mad this time."

They sat close awhile.

He said, "All white, and you looked so good, your legs, and the . . . the curves . . . you know. You looked so good, and when I was out there in the snow, just thinking about it, I got to feeling warm all over, like warm soup was running through my arms and legs. Sweet Jesus, I wanted to do it to you!"

They were silent a long, long time.

He said, "Last week I was down swimming in the crick at night. The water was so cold it made goose pimples all over me, but not the shivery kind. The strong kind, like you were bustin' to do something, because you felt so strong. And when I got out of the water and laid down on the ground and looked up through the tree at the moon and the stars, first I thought about Tech and everybody hollering their fool heads off for me, old Pete, and being an engineer, and maybe I'd come back and see how you felt about me . . . and things . . . but then I got to thinking about just you, and how you were that time when I saw you, because you're getting so built and look so good, and how it would be right then if you were lying right beside me looking up through the tree, and both of us without any clothes on, and there was that hot soup running all through me again. You don't know, Ellen, you don't know, and it's running through me right now, and burning me up, when you're so close to me, and I could bust wide open just wanting you, you don't know . . ."

He could feel her lips opening against his cheek. He thought the tempo of her breathing had changed.

"You don't know . . ."

123

She said softly, with a new voice, a woman's voice, "Yes, I know, Pete."

She stood up. Resolutely she undid the black neckerchief. She slipped the white middy blouse over her head. She turned away, though he couldn't really see her, and unbuttoned the black shoes and took them off, and the stockings, and the skirt. She turned and faced him in her white chemise with the gathered top.

"Was it like this I looked, Pete?"

He touched her and said, "No." He took the chemise from her. "Like this." He threw his own clothes away. His brain reeled. He felt as though he were drunk and dizzy. He pulled her close and kissed her open mouth and felt her against him.

She pushed his face away with a hand on each side of his head. "Is the want in you now?"

"Yes. I'm scared and I want you all at once." His own voice sounded a thousand miles away.

She pulled him down with her onto the pile of her clothes, and she said in a vibrating voice he'd never heard, "You can do anything you want to me. Anything you want," and while life opened itself to them, the train chugged gasping to the top of a long grade, hung poised on a curve where the engineer could almost reach out and touch the caboose, chug-a-chug, a little faster, picking up speed, chug chug chug chug chug, the long, agonizing struggle ended, and then as Ellen Foley gave a glad, hot, short cry and thrust herself to be impaled, the whistle drowned her out, hooooo—hooooooo—hoooahhhhhhhhhh, not a shriek of gladness, but the same mournful wail through the hollows, and the hot tears of dreadful regret came drowning her eyes. Though she subsided, he wouldn't relent for a long, long time, and finally she put her arm over her eyes and said ever so softly, "Oh, Pete, it's a mortal sin, and we'll be punished for it."

6

ELLEN FOLEY was three months pregnant the day she married Pete Dankowski. It took that long for Pete to be convinced, and even when she'd begun to swell a little, it still took Dr. Black's corroborative testimony.

"She's pregnant, Pete. Take my word for it."

"From just one time?"

"It only takes one time. The hundredth time, or the first time, it just takes one time. She's got your baby in there."

Pete asked sullenly, "How do I know it's mine? You know what they say, if a girl will do it with one man, she'll do it with somebody else."

Dr. Black said icily, "That's between you and Ellen. If you want my advice, I wouldn't bring that up with her. For myself, I don't care to hear that kind of talk."

"Well, I don't know. I guess the thing is, I never had any idea of getting married."

"I never met a man who did. My own opinion, you're damn lucky. Not a man in fifty miles wouldn't give his eyeteeth for Ellen Foley, and for some indiscretion on her part, you get her on a silver platter."

"That include you?"

"Does what include me?"

"You like to have her? Why don't you take her, you're so bent on protecting her honor and good name." Pete grinned. "Can you get permission from your housekeeper?"

Dr. Black held himself in check with great effort, until finally he said flatly, "I've got nothing more to say to you. Get out of my house."

Pete couldn't afford to be turned away in these straits. He was floundering hopelessly in the mud he and the girl had stirred up. He needed a man to talk to, a professional man. He struggled to apologize, and he managed, "I shouldn't have said that. I thought it was going to be funny, but I'm not thinking too good."

"Then you better start thinking good. You better straighten up. I've been watching you. Along with everybody else, I thought you were the greatest thing in this town. Now I'm not so sure you weren't just a gutless wonder all along."

"Just what is that supposed to mean?"

"You had the world by the tail, and then you threw it away because you didn't have the guts to stand up to your old man. Now you're in here weaseling and crawling and trying to think how you can avoid your responsibility with this girl, and there's nothing lower than a man that would make such slurs on a woman like Ellen Foley. When you do that, you smell."

Pete Dankowski said evenly, "Now I reckon you're going to have to take that back, or you're going to answer."

"You just listen to me say it again. You're a gutless wonder, and you smell. That girl's too good for you. I'd just as soon see her brothers shoot you dead. But she wants to marry you. Lord help her, that's what she wants, and you're in here talking about her like she might be some whore. I'll tell you, if you don't do what's right by her, I'll help her brothers shoot you dead. Can I make it any plainer than that?"

Pete stared at him incredulously.

Dr. Black then relented a little. He said, "Pete, you deserve that, every bit of it. Okay, you're bound to be upset, I'll take that in account. Now, for the next few days just try for once to be something beside a big, dumb, heavy-handed Polack."

"Okay, I asked for it. But you just take it easy yourself. I don't like it when somebody calls me Polack."

"You'll take it from me. I'll tell you why. And why I'm so whizzed off with you, I can't see straight." Dr. Black wrestled with himself, pondered the ramifications. Then

126

he said decisively, "In Elbow, I was Steve Kowalski's boy. At Pitt, I was Joe Kowalski. Only now I'm Joe Black."

"You got to be kidding. Joe Kowalski the tackle?"

"Yes. Only now I'm Joe Black."

"Are you kidding me?"

"I said it."

Pete whistled. "How about that? Dr. Black on his big black horse!"

Dr. Black smiled sardonically. It wasn't a smile at all. "I don't think you're worth it, but Joe Kowalski is going to give you some advice. You listen to me, and you listen good. You think you're the be-all and end-all around here. The big hero. Well, I been rooting for you, just like everybody else, only probably more than anybody else, because I remember me over in Elbow fifteen years ago. Do you know who put Carnegie Tech on you? Not just Vincent. Joe Kowalski, in there fighting for another big dumb Polack tackle. And you let me down. Boy, how you let me down. And let Vincent down."

Pete interrupted eagerly, "How good a ballplayer were you? As good as me?"

Doctor Black contemplated him. "Good as you? All you've played against is other high school teams, where you're the strongest man on the field. You don't know about a ballplayer until he gets on the field with men."

"The man from Tech said I'd of been all-American."

"I don't think you'd of made the grade at Tech. I think you're a gutless wonder."

Pete grinned. "I got you figured out. You're sticking the harpoon in, thinking I'll get mad enough to show you you're wrong."

"You going to prove I'm wrong?"

"Which do you want me to do, do the right thing by Ellen, or go play ball?"

"Both. Why not?"

"It's too late. Papa, you know." He spread his hands.

"You're letting Ellen down. Do you know why she was working?"

"Yes, I know. But that's stupid. It's sure stupid now."

"Look, you got her pregnant and in a mess. And let me tell you about that. She tried to talk me into an abortion, because she didn't want to put the shotgun on you."

"Well, why didn't you?"

"I'll tell you why. Maybe I changed my name in med

127

school, and maybe I don't go to Mass with the rest of you, or I wouldn't be the Sweet Water doctor, but no abortions come from these hands. So she's got her choice of marrying you or having an illegitimate child. She's decided, Lord help her. Pete, I started to say, for her sake, do something worthwhile with yourself."

"What I want to know, how do you change your name? I mean, where do you do it?"

Dr. Black smiled cynically. "Did I strike a nerve? I changed it at the county courthouse back home. Changing names didn't change quite as much as I thought it might. If you get the temptation, think long and hard. That's advice from one who knows."

"How's it hurt you?"

"It has. The successful Dr. Black on his big black horse."

"Boy, I'm going to do it. I'm going to change my name and go to Akron."

"Try Kowalski. There's a vacancy."

"You got Black, maybe I'll be White. Or Green. Sweet Jesus! Or Purple, that tickles my risibilities." He grinned. "It's amazing what a different attitude I got toward you all of a sudden, Dr. Kowalski."

Black's jaw firmed. "I meant to be an object lesson to you. Pete, do something for yourself and that girl."

"I'm thinking how you and me should be buddies from now on. Wouldn't it turn this town upside down, they was to find out you were Joe Kowalski all the time?"

Black jerked his thumb. "Out."

"Don't worry, I won't tell anybody."

"I'm sure you won't."

"What makes you so sure?"

"Because there are only two people in town who know it. I told Casimar in an exchange of confidences."

"You mean Papa told you Mama was part Jew? That doesn't make it true. He says that just to get even with her for being so smart."

"And I'll give you one more reason you're going to keep your mouth shut. Because I might have some things to say to the people of this town about what a gutless wonder you are. I think they might start seeing you in a different light."

"Well, that's just stupid talk. That doesn't impress me."

"No? Then I'll give you a third reason. Because I'll take you on in front of this town and kick your ass from one

128

end to the other and throw you in the Kanawha. Now if you got any doubts I can do that, this might be just as good a time as any for you to call me down."

Pete Dankowski was white. He was in a turmoil. He knew he could take on this man. He knew it. He knew this man was calling his bluff hoping the challenge would be accepted. Why couldn't he take him up on it? It would be so easy, just to say it. He wasn't a coward. He wasn't. Why couldn't he just step up and prove it?

Dr. Kowalski said, "Before this day is over, you will ask Ellen Foley to marry you. And for the time being, you and me, we'll keep our secrets."

7

PETE sat beside Ellen on the front steps of Mike Foley's house. He said casually, "Reckon we better get Father Hannigan to do the thing."

Ellen said with forced naturalness and cheerfulness, "It'll scare me half to death, talking to him. I haven't been to Confession since it happened. What's he going to say to us?"

"Thankee kindly for making another Catholic."

"Don't joke, Pete."

"He won't be hearing anything he hasn't heard before. 'Mongst the fish-eaters up the hollers, babies pop out of the ground. I reckon Hannigan just accepts all of us baby makers like the God-fearing tithers we is."

"We have to face him sometime. We have to go to Communion when we get married."

"Do we? Not if we go off somewhere, maybe not even get married by a priest."

After a moment, she said, "Maybe you're right. I don't think I could bear standing there in front of people, all swelling out." Then she said, "But we've got to go to Confession sometime. We've got to get the sin off us, or it will just get bigger and bigger."

"Mortal-er and mortal-er."

"Don't make fun about it."

"Just for doing it one time, do you really think it's all that serious?" He looked off over her shoulder. "Leastways, *I* only did it one time."

"Pete . . ."

"What?"

"I know what you're driving at."

He didn't answer, just smiled a little.

"Pete, I've made up my mind. I'm going to have an abortion, then you've got no obligation."

"Doc Black won't do it."

"You talked about it? I just bet you did."

"We just sort of mentioned it."

"He's not the only doctor in the world. You don't have to worry. You don't have to marry me."

"Who could you get to do it? The abortion I mean."

Then her dam burst, and all the hurt, shame and fear came flooding out and covered him in a torrent of hot Irish abuse, until she started crying and couldn't talk any more and went after him scratching and flailing futilely against his huge warding arms.

He said in panic, "You *know* I'm going to do the right thing by you."

Abruptly she was icy calm. "I'm going to do the right thing. I'm going to Charleston and have them take this evil thing out of my stomach and kill it. That's what I'm going to do, kill it."

Pete thought about Ellen Foley's brothers. He said uneasily, "It's just that I wasn't thinking about getting married. It takes some getting used to." He added quickly, "I guess I don't have to tell you, if it was somebody else than you, I'd be out of town on the next coal train. I guess that counts for something."

She smiled ruefully. "Maybe the real mortal sin was being uppity. Us going to college. Now you've got coal in your fingernails, and me, I've got a coal-dust thing inside me. What happened to us, Pete? We had the whole world in front of us. What happened to us? It's the devil. He put those things in Casimar to hurt you. And put those words in you to make me all sort of empty and hurting and full of lust all down deep in my stomach, and then that awful sound, that mortal sin sound came blowing its coal dust all over us, and I'm swelling up with this thing, and I want to get it out of me, because even this isn't the end of it, God's going to punish us even worse than he has already, Pete. Oh, Pete, what happened to us?"

He thought he should do something, take her in his arms and reassure her, tell her that he loved her, and that the world would still be theirs. He had known how to tell her that he wanted her. He had put the passion in her. Why didn't he now know how to tell her that he loved her? Why couldn't he put peace in her?

Caleb Parker came from Dr. Black's house, walking fast. "You see Doc Black anywhere?"

"Other way. He just went in to see the cold one. Somebody sick, Caleb?"

"India's time."

"Well, he's with the cold one. She sent for him just when I was leaving."

Caleb said grimly, "Reckon a new baby will take precedence over *her* ailments."

Ellen said, "I hope you get another boy, Caleb."

"Thank you, honey."

"Have you got a name? James would be good. Jim Parker, that sounds like a good name."

"It does that, honey. We were thinking Lee. Maybe we'll just try James Lee; and you give up being Catholic, we'll make you godmother, honey." Caleb set off at a half-run to the big white house.

Pete asked, "What do you want, Ellen, a boy or a girl?" She bit her lip.

He looked her over carefully, as though he'd never seen her before. How had he felt about her before this monstrous turn of events? Want of her, that's what he'd felt. Want of the body that had burst into glowing, fresh, mounded excitement in the six months since she was eighteen, so that every man from fifteen to sixty looked at her with longing. That was it. The want of her body and the want of the pride that would be his in possessing this most beautiful girl ever born in Parker County. Lust and pride? What more reason did he need? Lust, pride, and very real concern for what her brothers would do to him if he failed to do what was expected!

He said more softly, "Wouldn't be so bad having our own baby. I bet we sure would have one good-looking baby. Best-looking girl, handsomest guy in Sweet Water, that baby ought to be really something."

He forced himself to take her hand. She squeezed his

132

hand almost with gratitude. "Pete, will you do one thing for me?"

"I reckon."

"Will you ask me? Will you come right out and ask me?"

"Marry up with me, will you, Ellen Foley?" He was grinning.

She smiled. "I guess that will do, coming from a hillbilly. I accept."

"I reckon it's what I had in mind all along, anyhow, and it doesn't make that much difference what way it happens, just so it happens."

"I'll be a good wife, Pete. I'm a good cook. I really did cook for you, it wasn't Mama."

She moved closer to him on the porch and took his hand in her lap, and when Dr. Black came from the big white house with Caleb Parker striding purposefully ahead of him, Pete called cheerfully, "Hey, you all, going to be a wedding around here."

But the cloud of their mutual recriminations hung over the ceremony. There were additional repercussions. Not from Father Hannigan. Pete was right about him. He clucked mildly at each of them when they confessed their mortal sin, and took it all in a day's work. To him the crucial point was their return to Grace and to his flock through the Sacrament of Holy Matrimony.

Pete's brothers ragged him unmercifully. They did it with such ribald good humor that it wasn't too hard to take. Nor were the disappointment of Stella Dankowski and the pointed disapproval of Casimar Dankowski unbearable. A man expecting a six-month first child could concurrently expect a reasonable amount of pious acceptance, lusty torment, tear-stained disappointment and father-imperious disapproval. None of these things hurt the newlyweds beyond repair. The additional cross was placed on the shoulders of the sinners by Mike Foley, father of the bride.

Mike was alternately outraged and maudlin over the despoiling of his daughter. Not even the wedding ceremony ended his poetically vituperative discourses on the perfidy of the wrongdoers. Rather, the security of the irrevocable Catholic bond spurred him to ever greater heights of sarcasm and indignation, until Pete cringed each night that Foley mounted the hill to the Dankowski

133

house with a new collection of spite. Those first months of the marriage were so painful that Pete dreaded leaving the black solitude of the mine shaft to face the sunny world.

In time, most of the wounds healed. The coal miners respected the comeliest couple in Parker County, their football hero and their black-haired sweetheart, and eventually left off their torment, accepting the new couple warmly and vying with one another for the favor of a dance with Ellen Dankowski at the Community Hall, friendly and good-humored about the great stomach that buffered them from her charms as they danced. The Catholic and Protestant citizens of Sweet Water now accepted the young couple as warmly as they had intended all along.

Stella Dankowski ended her mourning for her lost youngest son as soon as she was sure the newlyweds would stay in the gray house until something better could be worked out, which had to mean months, or years, or even forever, and for this same reason Casimar Dankowski decided that the wisdom of keeping the paying boarders outweighed the valor of turning the sinners out, and he was particularly gratified that Vincent Carstairs gave the husband of his favorite girl a twenty-dollar raise, which was ample to pay the costs of the new mouths to be fed in the Dankowski home.

Even Mike Foley abruptly ended his morality lectures. He ended them reluctantly, because these had been golden months exercising his silver tongue, a lively diversion in his Sweet Water life of train schedules, a grand excuse to drink a little more than his budget permitted. He deserved no credit at all for the surcease. He had no choice. His own wife blackmailed him with the reminder that had it not been for the fortuitous miscarriage, down this same path of advertised sin had walked they themselves.

Said Mike Foley, "Which is the very reason I understand the gravity of their offense."

"Which is the very reason, Mr. Foley," said Katherine Foley, "that you are a hypocrite. Not another word to them."

"And just what might you do about it? It would be you yourself you were telling about."

"Oh, I've already told Ellen. It's a great comfort to her to know."

134

"Sure and you wouldn't," he said hollowly.

"Sure I did. And once more, just once more if you torment those two, she'll be after telling Pete, and Pete will be after knocking your hypocritical tongue, and your teeth with it, down your hypocritical throat, and serve you right."

Thus was finally sanctified the marriage of Peter Dankowski and Ellen Foley, from whom came David Battle. They were accepted in Sweet Water. They dwelt in the Dankowski gray house of stature and respectability. They were nearly happy. There remained only the cloud of their own guilt, spread over them like soot from the mines. Each time the train whistle caromed down the valley, Ellen Foley Dankowski shivered involuntarily.

8

THE TRAIN WHISTLE blew and the locomotive labored the night Ellen labored with Theodore Dankowski in March, 1912. The two grandmothers attended the delivery, because Dr. Black was up Murder Creek watching Henry Forsyth spew the bright blood of his life out of his tubercular lungs. Ellen delivered with great difficulty, a breech birth. The baby came out with the umbilical cord wrapped around his neck. He turned quickly blue. Katherine Foley baptized him frantically, "I christen thee Theodore, in the Name of the Father, and of the Son, and of the Holy Ghost, Amen," and she trembled helplessly and was of no help. But Stella Dankowski cut the cord with a carving knife and untwined it from the scrawny neck, held the blue baby by the heels and thumped its rump and back for a long minute before it gasped in its first breath and slowly turned red.

Dr. Black arrived on his big black horse and pronounced the baby fit. "I'm glad the grandmothers were here. Next time let me know sooner. Deaths, I don't like to attend. Births, I like to attend." He closed his black bag. "A man dies tonight, a man is born tonight." He shook it off and smiled. "From his conception, this boy has been in a hurry to get into this world." He lost his smile under the reproving looks of the grandmothers. He continued lamely, "Anyway, I'm glad you were here. That was a close one."

Katherine Foley held up her rosary beads and said, "It was a miracle of God's saving power. We'll have a Mass for the thanksgiving."

Pete said, "God's power, hooey. It was cutting the cord that saved him. You could have baptized him all day, and he'd have been dead all day."

Katherine ignored her son-in-law. "We should have a Mass said."

Pete said morosely, "You maybe would have baptized him into Heaven, but you sure as shootin' would have baptized him clean outen this world."

Stella said sternly, "It was the power of God, Peter. The flower of birth arrived with its petals unopened, and God's Grace let him bloom. We will have a Mass said. To thank God for the first son."

Pete attended the Mass. He was filled with scorn. The seeds of doubt, sewn in ding-aling-aling Sweet Water shame, were by now weeds of apostasy, full-sprouted, sere and burred in his soul. He went through the motions at the Kyrie and the Gloria. He lost himself in dreams of heroism at Carnegie Tech and heard not a word of Father Hannigan's fatuous sermon on a miracle, or at least a near-miracle, that could reaffirm, for all to see, the closeness of the Blessed Savior to his believers, even in Sweet Water, West Virginia. If even Father Hannigan was amused and bemused with the superstitious claim, Pete Dankowski couldn't be expected to listen with gravity.

For one moment, when Father Hannigan knelt and raised high the Eucharist, there shot through the apostate a twinge of uncertainty that turned instantly to full dread, and in that one frantic moment he flailed wildly with the scythe of his childhood religion to cut down those foul weeds, to stamp them out with his miner's shoes, to cast them out before they choked his salvation. For one moment he uttered a prayer of thanksgiving for the deliverance of his son. But the more he fought at the vetch with the hoe of his indoctrination, the more it flourished in the fertility of his skepticism, and there came on his face a down-turning, one-sided smile of contempt, and there came in his heart a derision that he knew he would never tell in confessional, and in that great moment of celebrating the

137

birth of his first son, he was beset, then willingly over-whelmed, by a heresy that was more than agnosticism. It was the nihilism of atheism, and though he was drained by his dread thoughts, he was as soon filled with a strange, new passion of emancipation, a great surging of power in his arms and hands and mind, and it was as clear to him as the sun-bright sky, that he had in that moment been freed forever from that thralldom to which his stupid, cruel, debilitating religion had subjected him those igno-rant, supine years.

In the night the train whistle wailed down Murder Hol-low, and Ellen said to her husband beside her in the dark, "It blew so lonely when he was born, just the way it did when we committed the mortal sin. He's going to die."

Pete felt a cold wave come over him.

She said again, "He's going to die. I know it. We're going to be punished for what we did. God is going to punish us."

Then he was fully awake, and the relief ran through him. He laughed sharply, almost hysterically. "You scared the living bejeezus out of me, waking me up like that. I thought maybe there was something wrong with him. There's nothing wrong with him. That's ten pounds of Pete Dankowski in there."

"The way he was born, Pete, that was a sign. I know it as sure as we're lying here, God meant him to die, and he was saved that time, but there will be another time, and that will be our punishment."

He burst out, "Sweet Jesus, will you once stop talking like a superstitious Mick? Leprechauns, and fairies, and an almighty Christ! Haven't you got it figured out? You never saw a fairy, and you never saw any almighty Christ who gave a good goddam what goes on in Sweet Water, West Virginia. You tell me the last time God came down here and helped somebody spitting his lungs out with the TB's, no matter how hard anybody prayed. Or even bothered himself giving anybody the TB's. He just ain't that in-terested. There was no God had one damn thing to do with that cord around the baby's neck."

"Don't talk like that, Pete."

"You go on believing in God the way you want to, if you got to. But He's not the littlest bit interested whether I stick my thing inside you before or after a priest makes some mumbo jumbo and says now it's all right to do it.

And if he's not interested in the first place, He's sure not going to go round killing babies for it. It's stupid to talk like that. It's stupid. There's nothing wrong with him."

But she insisted in the days that followed that their son would die. It was a premonition, she insisted, not superstition. It was something she knew without knowing how she knew. As surely as her husband lay alongside her in the nights, their son would die, and this would be their dreadful, earned punishment for sinning against God and the Church, and Pete shouted at her, "If God killed all the kids that got born from adultery, there wouldn't be room in all the graveyards," but it didn't do any good, because she knew, and he hated the train whistles in the mountains that called so mournfully to her their wail of recrimination and doom.

As she grew steadily more depressed, he finally took it up with Dr. Black. "Ellen says the baby's going to die, she knows it. Every time that sweet-Jesus train whistle blows, she says it, and it's like shivers in your veins and bones. You got to tell her different, or she'll make a wreck outen all of us."

"She's got the postnatal blues. That happens. Women get depressed after the baby is born. Some women, it's worse than it is with other women."

"Is there something wrong with him?"

"Not a blessed thing. I looked him over yesterday. He's a big one. A healthy one."

"When the cord was around his neck, could that do something to him? You know, like make him die later on?"

"I just checked him, Pete. He's all right. Don't you start worrying, too. I'll have a talk with Ellen."

"You might as well know it when you talk to her, she says it's punishment, that's what she thinks."

"For having a six-month baby? Did you reassure her?"

"I said if God got hisself upset about quick babies, he'd be plumb wore out running back and forth without ever getting out of Parker County."

Black said drily, "That was delicate and gentle."

"I told her ever'body did it, and been doing it since people stopped swinging on their tails, and will still be doing it going up the golden stairs—some man's going to get restless awaiting of his turn at the judgment bar, and pass the time away with one last touch of the thing he liked best on earth. I get blue in the face telling her."

"I can see you've reassured her. I'll talk to her this afternoon. All right?"

Ellen Dankowski spoke no more of her premonitions. But they still existed, despite Black's earnest rationalization. Pete was aware of them in her silent brooding, the solemnity where once her Irish smile had flashed.

Then when Theodore Dankowski was seven months old, Black rode up the hill on his big black horse on a wonderful Indian summer evening. He informed the senior Dankowskis he had something private to discuss with the young couple, and he took Ellen by the hand and led her to the back porch, where Pete lounged in the washtub, watching the ducks as they waddled on the steep path and idly stirring the coal-dust black water around his hairy midsection.

Black's open-book face alarmed Pete. He asked, "What's wrong?"

Black offered Pete a cigarette, stuck it between Pete's lips when Pete held up his wet hands, and scratched a lucifer on the porch wall.

Pete mumbled as he drew in, "What's wrong?"

Ellen sat in the straight-backed chair on the porch, her arms folded over her swelling midsection, resigned to whatever Black could impart to her.

Pete smiled nervously and said, "If you're going to tell me she's pregnant, don't bother. I know."

Black searched for a way to begin. The young Dankowskis couldn't help him. They followed him with their eyes as he walked about the porch. Finally he stepped off onto the bare ground and looked up at them.

"Pete, Ellen, it's a hard thing to tell, and it will be a harder thing to take the telling."

Ellen asked, "How long will it be before he dies?"

Black wouldn't look at her. "He's not going to die. But there's something wrong with him. Pete, I called a doctor on the telephone, in Wheeling, and told him about it. A consultant. A specialist. He confirms my diagnosis."

"The TB's?" Pete asked fearfully.

"No, not tuberculosis. And not typhoid, or diphtheria, or anything like that. He's not going to die. Maybe it's worse than that, I don't know. Now I'm going to tell you straight out. He's not normal. There's something wrong with him. Something went wrong."

Pete asked sharply, loudly, "What do you mean, something wrong? What's wrong?"

Ellen said, "It couldn't be any other way. I tried to tell you."

Black said with asperity, "He's not going to die. Let's not have any more talk about your premonitions. That's got nothing to do with it."

Pete said, "For Christ sake, will you tell me what's wrong?"

Black drew a deep breath. "I told you. He's not normal. Your boy is not going to develop."

Pete stirred the water, watching it swirl as he digested the news. Then he said with sudden belligerence, "He looks all right to me. He looks just like any other kid. You better start looking him over again, before you come around here saying things like that. You and your specialist on the telephone. He never even laid eyes on him!"

"Your boy's not going to develop, Pete. That's it. He's not normal. The eyes, the responses, not developing."

"Sweet Jesus, he's seven months old! What do you want him to do, get up and run around?"

"You know I'd give a lot not to have to tell you young people this about your first-born. Listen to me carefully. Get this through your heads. Your boy will be three or four years old before he walks. He'll be seven before he begins to talk. He'll never get any better. There it is."

Pete stood up and began drying himself. He said as sternly as he could, "If there's something wrong with him, then you just fix him up, that's what you do."

"There are some things that can't be fixed. Here there's nothing to fix."

"Well, I've got you figured out. If somebody's going to get well, you say you did it. But if somebody's not going to get well, you say there's some things doctors can't do. The hell with that! You and that high and mighty guy from Wheeling, you say there's something wrong with my boy, then you just fix him up, you hear?"

Black snubbed out his own cigarette, took a pipe from his corduroy jacket pocket and lit it carefully. Finally he said, "Pete, you've got certain privileges at a time like this. But don't carry it too far. I'm your doctor. I'm a learned man, skilled in my profession, and I work hard for you. You think about that. You give me your respect. And when you've given me the respect I've got

141

coming, then start giving yourselves the respect you have coming. Both of you. You're adults. You were old enough to get married, old enough to have this baby. Now you find out something went wrong. Something beyond the understanding of the medical profession. Beyond the understanding of men. It won't do you any good to resist the facts. Or to have false hopes. The sooner you accept the fact of it, the sooner you will take the next steps. There's no blaming God for this. There's no blaming the doctor. There's no blaming yourselves. There's no blaming."

"No blaming?" Ellen asked.

"There's no blaming. If this was the first time it had ever happened, maybe you could blame. But it's happened to millions of people before it happened to you. We don't know what causes it. An injury while you were carrying him? Maybe. The cord around his neck, cutting off the oxygen to his brain? Possible, but not likely. German measles? Did you have them, Ellen? We don't know. Maybe just an unlucky accident. I mean in the way the genes got together. It could be a lot of things. And unless there is some miracle breakthrough in our medical science, we never will know. All we know is that it's happened to your boy, and that there aren't any miracles to help us. Or to help all the other millions of people it's happened to. And those people? Were they sinners? Many of them were, I have no doubt. And many of them were not sinners, I have no doubt. This thing has happened to the most intelligent parents, to the most virtuous, to the least virtuous and most stupid. There isn't any rule. It's an accident that happens. An accident that you don't think much about when it happens to someone else. You didn't think about it when it happened to Dwight Culpepper, up at Settle Creek. But it overwhelms you when it happens to you, and you start looking around for things to blame or for miracles to get you out of it. No blame, no miracles. Pete, we had one talk about guts. So now face this and decide what you're going to do about it."

Pete pulled on his fresh clothes. He buttoned his clean denim shirt without a word. When he finished tying his shoes, he asked with a calm voice, "What do you do about it?"

"That's better. You put him in the new state home,

142

where he belongs. The Frogsburg Home. They'll take care of him there. I'll put in the application for you."

Ellen said, "No, we did it, we'll take care of what we did."

"Ellen Foley, you're playing the martyr to the hilt." His face softened. "No, I take that back. It's the instinctive reaction of the mother. Now you listen to me. You've got another child on the way. You'll have plenty more children, you with your fine Irish pelvic structure, and this big Polack here, and so you should decide right now to do for the ones that can use it and forget the one you can't help. That's the best thing to do. Send him to the home, where he can live the best life possible, with the others with the same affliction."

There were no tears on Ellen's somber face. "Dr. Black, you don't stop loving him just because there's something wrong with him. You start loving him more. He needs it more."

Pete said, "He goes to the home where he belongs."

Ellen looked up at him. "For his sake? Or yours?"

"You heard Doc Black. For the boy's sake."

Black said, "For the boy's sake. That's it."

Ellen said, "I don't consider you the arbiter of something like this. It's not your province."

"Is it yours, Ellen?" Black asked gently. "Is it really your province to decide, when maybe your mother love won't let you see the forest for the trees."

"I'll let Father Hannigan decide whether we should pay our penance for what we did."

Black said quickly, "I will, too. I'll leave it up to Father Hannigan. I'm sure he'll agree with me that even if it would give you some morbid satisfaction or expiation of guilt, it wouldn't do one good thing for the boy, and that's what counts, the boy. I'll leave it up to the good father."

Father Hannigan disappointed Dr. Black. In the priest's way of seeing things, the unfortunate little boy clearly belonged at home where there was mother love. Privately, the connotations of penance appealed to his celibate heart. Ellen Dankowski took a grim satisfaction in the decision.

But Pete Dankowski had no intentions of abiding by the priest's arbitration. He agreed with Dr. Black. But his motivations were quite different. Once he had accepted, there on the back porch, the permanency of the frightful blight, he was through with that bad fruit of his loins. From the C & O station, he telephoned the state home at Frogsburg and made application for admission of his boy.

The official advised him, "We're not prepared, yet, to accept children that young. We'll put your application on file, and you contact us again when the boy is three."

Pete went home and stared down at his son. The vacancy in the face reproached him and galled him. He said softly, "You're not for me. I'll get you out of here, one way or other."

He bore the thorn in his side through the birth of his second child, Kathleen. He bore it another year until his resentment and frustration grew so great he could see the vacant face floating always before him in the Stygian darkness of the mine tunnels. When he came home to the gray house and the monstrous reality of the idiot, he grew ever more sullen.

A week before his third child was born he got drunk in Green Billy's blind pig in Shawnee and muttered hotly into his whiskey, "I'll kill you first, before I put up with you!"

Steve Dvorak asked curiously, "Whad you say?"

"I said none of your friggin' business."

Pete took off for Frogsburg and accosted the officials of the state home. "You said when he was three. Well, he's three. You got to take him."

The official informed him blandly that the home was much too small for the thousands of unfortunate children who needed it. There were too few nurses, too few doctors, and too few beds. Theodore Dankowski was on the waiting list, but it would be some time before expanded facilities would provide an opening.

Pete burst out, "I've been on the waiting list more'n two years. Who's getting ahead of me? Who do you have to know to get in here?"

The official just shrugged.

"Who's got the influence? How come people are getting ahead of me?"

The man didn't bother to smile. "I wouldn't know about influence. We have an admissions' board, and you're on the waiting list. That's all I can tell you, Dankowski. We'll let you know when we have room for your boy."

"You got any Polacks in here?"

"I don't know what you mean."

"You know damn well what I mean. You got any Catholics in here?"

"We'll let you know by mail when there's an opening."

Pete held his peace until Ellen had delivered herself of the second girl, and when Dr. Black's whiffs of chloroform had worn off, Pete asked her casually, "What girl's name goes good with Battle?"

She looked at him hazily, puzzled.

"You're looking at Peter Battle, Ellen Battle."

She didn't comprehend, but Dr. Black knew. "You did it, Pete?"

"I did it. At the courthouse in Frogsburg."

"That's a shame."

"Now just why is it a shame, Dr. Kowalski?"

"Because you'll regret it, like I have, I suppose. But mainly because now two of us have let our people down. The two of us who had such a good chance to do things as Poles. To make people around here think better of Poles. That's the shame. The best people of the benighted groups, they're too often the first to bust out."

"Dr. Kowalski, whatever you say just can't ring with me, now can it?"

"That's what I said. It's a shame for both of us. It keeps gnawing at me that sooner or later the Carstairs and the Parkers would have let Dr. Kowalski minister to them, and after that they'd just naturally realize that Pilsudskis, and Wrobleskis, and Dankowskis were just like other people, good ones and bad ones, and that might have made a bigger contribution to the world than anything Dr. Black has done or is likely to do."

Ellen asked drowsily, "Will somebody make sense?"

"Pete's changed his name."

"To Battle?" she asked incredulously.

Pete asked belligerently, "Anything wrong with Battle?"

Ellen said, "There wasn't anything wrong with Dankowski. I agree with Dr. Black. You didn't have to be ashamed of what you are."

"What I am? The way you put it shows you believe it yourself. I'll say one thing, I'd rather be a Polack than a Shanty Irishman, any day of the week."

The doctor said, "This ain't no time for anybody to be getting het up. You got a little baby here that ain't really seen the light of day yet."

145

Pete said, "I didn't change it for me, anyhow. I reckoned this one might be a boy. And I figured when he played ball, Battle would make a better name, so people could remember him. Make it easier for the reporters, and things like that."

Dr. Black said, "Good ole self-abnegating Pete Battle, always thinking of somebody else."

"I don't rightly recall asking your opinion, Dr. Kowalski."

"But you tell me, Pete Battle, just how do you think people are going to take to your new name in Sweet Water? Did that cross your mind? Do you think anybody's going to call you anything except Dankowski? The miners, let alone your folks? Don't you realize that even the ones that never did think much one way t'other about you being a Polack, are surer'n Billy Blue Blazes going to think of you that way now, since you came right out and admitted that you think there's something wrong with what you are? At least I had enough sense to put a hundred miles between me and my old name."

Pete relaxed and said, "Well, Dr. Black, if you want to know, that's exactly what I'm going to do one of these days. Get in my big washtub and wash the coal dust off me once and for all. Some other Polack can stick around and get the medals from his people."

Dr. Black shrugged. "Sure."

"You bet on it."

"Sure. Ellen, you take care, you hear? You pop children out like a mouse, but that doesn't mean you should get up and plow the back forty. I want you to stay in bed two or three days and take life easy. Give the grandmothers a chance."

She said, "They're so jealous, they'll break their backs seeing who can do the most."

"You'll be doing them a favor." Then he looked again at Pete. "I'm sure you'll be around Sweet Water a few days yet, Mr. Battle. I'm going to be mighty interested in the way people take it." He shut the bedroom door behind himself harder than he had intended.

Ellen asked, "Is it really done? Or are you just thinking about doing it?"

"It's done. We're Battles."

She smiled. "Maybe you should have picked Carstairs. Or Parker. That would fool 'em."

"I like Battle. It sounds like what it means."

"For a football player."

"You're damn right. For a football player."

"I hope you get one."

"Next time."

"Pete, are we really going off somewhere?"

"We're going. We're going far."

"Where?"

"So far they don't even know what coal is, except it's black stuff they put in the furnace. Maybe Akron. Reckon I could build tires. A man with my arms. They need strong guys to build tires."

"If you got your mind set on going, I'll go with you."

"Sort of counted on that."

"But promise me one thing. Promise we won't go without any money saved up. We ought to have enough to get by while you're getting started."

"How much you reckon we ought to have?"

"A thousand dollars."

"A thousand dollars! That ain't possible."

"I'll settle for five hundred."

"Including the two hundred you got from Mr. Carstairs?"

She hesitated a moment, and then said, "Including that." She was still safe. Pete Dankowski could never save three hundred dollars. Ellen Foley Dankowski would never have to leave Sweet Water. She smiled. She thought to herself: I'm probably the only person that ever lived in Sweet Water that didn't want to escape! Then the smile went wry. Ellen Dankowski? She was now Ellen Battle. Could they stay in Sweet Water as Battles? She said, "Pete, our new name's going to take a heap of getting used to. Not just by other people. By me, too."

9

PETE BATTLE withstood the gibes of his fellow mine workers and the outrage of his father with equal equanimity. He was a man with a purpose. The opinion of others was no longer important to him. He was no longer Pete Dankowski from Sweet Water. He was Pete Battle from Akron, Ohio. That is, he would be from Akron as soon as he saved three hundred dollars. Three hundred dollars.

When he had saved twelve dollars, he took the ferry across the Kanawha to celebrate in Green Billy's saloon, now operating as an open blind pig in West Virginia's new prohibition. After celebrating the saving of the first twelve dollars, he had only three dollars left, because he bought three rounds of drinks for a table of strangers who accepted him, without question, as a man named Pete Battle.

Three hundred dollars, a great deal of money to save out of one hundred dollars a month. He buckled down to it. By October, 1917, he had on deposit in Vincent Carstairs' safe one hundred and twelve dollars, and he was overcome with despair. On October 12 he stacked his pickaxe and said, "Reckon I'm in the mood for Green Billy's. You in, Wes?"

Wesley Culpepper said, "Reckon I better head home. She's about due."

"Mine, too."

"A man can't go to Shawnee when his wife's about due. Not that we do any good."

"You twist my arm, I'll twist yours. I need a drink."

"I got two bottles moonshine. Sell you one for fifty cents."

"Script?"

Culpepper shrugged. "Makes me no never mind. One's good as the other. I get real money, I spend it like a sailor."

As they entered the red house on the bank of the Kanawha, Ann Culpepper let out a yelp, then bore down, nearly ready to drive the baby out of herself into the hands of her waiting mother. Wesley bounded to the door of the downstairs bedroom. He asked anxiously, "Where's Doc Black?"

His mother-in-law said through clenched teeth, "Up in Murder Crick stalkin' flu. Dying like flies up there."

"Any of the kin?"

"Bound to be some of the kin."

"Can I help you, Ma?"

"By being still. Won't be but a minute now. Going to be the easiest she ever had."

Ann Culpepper smiled wanly and said, "Glad you told me, Mama."

Her mother said, "Dying like flies up the holler, and getting born like flies in Sweet Water."

"Who else?"

"The Foleys. Ellen Dankowski and Norah Foley."

Wesley turned and shouted, "Reckon you better light out runnin', Pete. Ellen's in labor."

"Where's the moonshine?"

"Kitchen cabinet. Help yourself. Listen, I got no time to talk to you. Mine's coming any minute."

Pete found the moonshine. He opened the bottle and drank deeply. He corked it and walked out of the house and slowly sauntered down the Charleston Road to Murder Creek and up the hill to the gray house. Casimar sat rocking on the front porch. He said, "Ellen's in labor, Peter."

Pete asked almost indifferently, "That so?"

"That some moonshine you got there, Peter?" When his

149

son didn't answer, Casimar held out his hand, and Pete reluctantly passed the bottle over, watched with alarm while the big man drank deep, and held his own hand out almost imploringly to get the bottle back. Casimar said, "Doc Black is up the holler."

"Seems to me he's always off somewhere when he should be here."

Stella Dankowski, come to the front door for a breath, said in her gentle voice, "It is easier to predict the time of dying than the time of birth. Dr. Black knows they are about to die in Murder and Settle."

"How's she doing?"

"It is difficult. I think it is another breech birth."

Pete asked with asperity, "Well, what are you doing down here then, Mama?"

"Just for a moment of air. Mrs. Foley is with her now."

"I'll bet. Making Signs of the Cross all over the room, long about now." Pete walked up the stairs and looked in on his wife. She smiled at him. He asked, "Feeling all right?"

"Just fine, Pete."

Her mother wiped beads of perspiration from her forehead.

Pete asked, "Can I do anything?"

Ellen said, "Not a thing, Pete. Just don't stay with me right now. I might have to holler, and I don't want you to hear me holler."

"I'll be here. Let me know what I can do. Where are the girls?"

Katherine Foley said, "At our house. Mike's with them."

"Hear Norah's in labor, too."

Ellen's mother stood up. She was distraught. "Who's with her, do you suppose?"

Pete said with some sarcasm, "There's two grandmothers, you know. I reckon her mother's with her, where she belongs." He said to Ellen, "Babies coming out all over the place. Ann Culpepper was just about to get her muffin out of the oven."

Stella Dankowski came in the room. "You go off, Peter, and we will have this baby."

Pete walked across the hall to the bedroom where his idiot son lay, the face blank in sleep as it was in waking. He raised his hand as though to strike away this monstrous blot. He drank long and deep from his bottle of moonshine. It made him feel a little queasy. Maybe it was a bad lot. He corked it and stood watching his son. His frustrations assailed him with a new fury. He raised his hand again, as though to strike the small boy. His self-pity flooded him. What had he done to deserve these things? How could it be, that so many lousy things could happen to a man who deserved more from Fate?

Carnegie Tech, lost. He'd studied hard, he'd played hard football, but Carnegie Tech, lost. He'd have been all-American, everybody said it. Everybody but that sonofa-bitch Joe Kowalski Black. What had he done to deserve the loss of that golden opportunity? Nothing. Nothing at all. They just took it away from him with no rhyme or reason. Carnegie Tech, lost. Instead, he had coal in his hair and in his eyebrows and under his fingernails, and if he scrubbed himself clean for a hundred years, he'd never get it out of his soul. Coal, sooty black coal, and the hands-and-knees chopping in the black-coal bowels of the earth, so that Vincent Carstairs' cold wife could go to Europe. There could be no possible justice in that. Two years, and only one hundred twelve dollars saved, and escape seemed as far away as ever it had been. A paying boarder in the gray house, but still treated like a Polish son, worse than a boarder. Two daughters where there should have been good sons to take the place of this blank-faced monster. This accusing fruit of his loins, silently yelling at him: "You were faulty when you made me, Peter Dankowski Battle!" And the state home would not take him away, because somebody else had influence, and somebody else wasn't a Catholic foreigner, and this monster would be forever with him, this monster embodying all the crushing weight of his frustrated life. Then, now. He'd thought about it, a thousand times he'd thought about it. Then, now, no more thinking about it.

He wasn't sure he could go through with it, but it was easy once his hands picked up the pillow. He turned the small boy on his side, looked once to make sure the door was closed, then with one decisive motion covered the small head with the pillow and shoved down. He closed his eyes so that he could not see the feeble struggle, the futilely clawing hands beneath him. He kept them closed long after the struggles ceased. He raised the pillow and looked closely. His first-born son was dead. He arranged the pillow so that it would look as though the boy had got-

151

ten himself tangled in it. Then he walked out of the room, down the hallway, and stood in the doorway of the delivery room so that the grandmothers could see him. He wondered how he could be so calm. He had just committed murder. He had murdered his own son, in cold blood. But he said to himself, "I'm calm because it wasn't really murder. It was something that needed done, for the boy," and he shut his mind to the knowledge that it was a mercy killing in which he gave himself the mercy.

The new baby came. It came breech, with the umbilical cord wrapped around the neck. Stella cut the cord before the baby was out of the mother, and tugged and pulled until she held the bluish thing in her hands, and as before, she thumped and whacked until it squawled and turned bright red.

Stella said almost to herself, "A fine boy, Peter. A fine, beautiful boy."

Pete was thunderstruck. This one, too, had been smitten by the hand of God to punish the sins of the father. He heard the train whistle, mournful, hoo-hooooahhhhh, and realized it had been blowing that way since the moment he had decided to kill. But there was no God. There was no punishment. No punishment that man himself did not measure out. If Ellen had done it to him again, if she had delivered to him again a blank-faced monster, he wouldn't wait as long. Once done, the second time would be even easier. If this child was choked into idiocy by the cord in the faulty structure of his wife, he would not live long enough to fill Pete Battle with shame. This child would die very soon.

When the grandmothers had gone for a while, Ellen pulled her husband down beside her. "You want to know something funny? I'm sort of sorry this one is a boy. Do you know why? Because up till now you've been my little boy." She stroked his hair with his face against her breast, and he was repulsed by the cloying excess of the mother love in her. If she only knew! She stroked his face. "Remember when I told you a long time ago how much there was in Sweet Water that people other places didn't have? I bet this is just about the happiest place in the world. But it's all right with me, if you still want to go to Akron. I'll still have something nobody else has got."

"Like what?"

"Like holding your head against me like this. Nobody

152

else in the whole world can do that. I'm happy with you." He didn't answer. She thought she could sense a reaction, and it worried her a little. "Can anyone else, Pete?"

"Can anyone else what?"

"Hold you close like this?"

He said, "Don't be stupid." He said it quickly. He thought of Ethel Parker, who always held him close in those weeks when his wife was no longer available to him. He thought with grim amusement that she would hold him close again before another night had passed. They would drink moonshine whiskey and make love like furtive animals back in the hills, and he would feel the great lust for her and the even greater glow of satisfaction that for him the daughter of the high and mighty Caleb Parker was a wanton, a tramp. How he loved the Eden-tree fruit of her. How much more he loved the pleading distress in her as he visited the degradation on her! High and mighty daughter of the high and mighty Caleb Parker! Pete smiled against his wife's bosom. He was a murderer and an adulterer. He wondered if she'd cast him, horrified, away, if she knew. Adulterer. Why did he do it? There was no enduring emotion in it, not even a lasting flow of relief, just moonshine liquor and that hot but fleeting satisfaction of debasing the Parkers. He didn't know the clear answer. He didn't know why he did it, but he knew he'd do it again and again in that time before his wife was again available to him and he could send the tearful Parker girl away with the cruel dismissal, "I'll get you again when I need you, Ethel." Ah, that was better. It gave him pleasure to think of that Parker misery. Pete Dankowski Battle, an atheist, an adulterer and a murderer. By God, he thought with grim pleasure, I'm a monster!

Stella Dankowski found the dead boy. Dr. Black pronounced accidental asphyxiation as the cause of death. "Poor little guy. He didn't have the co-ordination to get himself untangled." He looked at Pete until Pete's eyes averted. "Maybe you can say that God did finally act in mercy with this poor little boy."

Pete said, "It is better for him, isn't it?"

Black said, "It's better for a lot of people," and Pete thought the doctor knew his crime.

Ellen Foley Battle said, "Nobody believed me when I said he would die. The train whistle blew. I heard it, just

153

before the new boy came. So far off, I wasn't sure I heard it. And I worried about the new boy. But it was mourning for the other one."

Dr. Black said, "We lost ground today. Samuel Culpepper, Joseph Foley, and this new boy here, three boys born in one day, isn't that something? And two old men, an old woman, a strong husband gone with the flu, and that poor boy—five dead, we lost ground by two today." His face was gray and drawn with utter fatigue. He burst out, "God, why can't I make them live?" His discipline returned immediately. He said, abashed, "I'm very tired. It's been a very long day. Ellen, you're fine. The boy's fine."

Pete thought to himself, I heard that one before . . . and that one is dead, where he belongs.

He thought he would eventually feel pangs of remorse. They never came. For a long time he was concerned about Dr. Black, but he comforted himself with the thought that if the doctor knew, it was a secret shared by Dankowski and Kowalski who had turned Black and Battle, and there had to be a bond between them, a pact of some sort that would prevent the doctor from giving him away no matter what his detestation. But Dr. Black didn't know. He thought he knew, but he didn't know. Pete was off scotfree. He hadn't even religion to lose. The murder merely sealed his bargain with atheism. Now there could never be a turning back. Could he ever again go to Confession when he had this grim tale to relate? The thought amused him. He pictured Father Hannigan's futile horror, if only he could be apprised, within the confines of the confessional, of the foul deeds. Wouldn't that frustrate him, to know the ghastly truth and not be able to do one damn thing about it? Pete was tempted, but only in daydreams. He had not the slightest intention of ever again entering a church of any denomination, and most of all, nothing Catholic would ever again make him miserable. He was free! It amazed him that he could get off so easily. He had anticipated a long struggle and surely some torment. He wondered if other apostates took the finality of their severance with God as inconsequentially as he. He wondered if other murderers accommodated themselves as easily to that greatest sin save one. He was free! It was pleasant to contemplate that he could henceforth sin whenever the fancy or need struck him, and there need be no limits on the gravity of his sins, because he had committed

154

the two greatest, apostasy and murder, and there would not be even the penance of a discomfited conscience to pay. He was free of the blank-faced monster! He was free of all restrictions! He was free!

In Sweet Water, only Ellen Foley Dankowski Battle cried because Theodore Dankowski Battle was dead. The new boy, they named him David Battle.

BOOK
III

1

WORLD WAR I was a brave war.

George Hawkins, a notions drummer traveling out of Huntington, exhausted his supply of American flags two hours after he alighted on the Sweet Water platform, and he telephoned a rush order for more Old Glory so that he could proceed along the rail line to Coalburg, Cabin Creek and Chelyan.

This was unabashed patriotism.

There was the deep whistle call of the showboat. Sherman's Band, outfitted in khaki uniforms, played "Over There" four times during the performance, the black-face end men told Hun jokes, and the miners pushed forward to raise their arms to the pretty society girls from Charleston and commit themselves to Liberty Bonds beyond their means.

Parker County's draft board functioned more for dissuasion than compulsion. Volunteers from the red houses and the white houses of Sweet Water, and from the shacks of the fierce descendants of pioneers up the creeks, oversubscribed the county quota the first day, and Chairman Vincent Carstairs was forced to call a halt lest there be none left to dig coal. As his last official act, Vincent called himself to duty. By virtue of his ROTC duty at Morgantown, he was commissioned a captain in the

United States Army and went off to war at the head of the Sweet Water contingent exactly in the way English barons went off at the head of their foot soldiers in other holy crusades.

The Snakes of West by God Virginia fought their war with the same cheerful ferocity with which they fought the happy, violent life of their coal town, and they covered themselves with blood and renown. Four were killed. Three of them were slammed into oblivion by bullets or shrapnel without enough time to know for sure that they were dead. Wilbur Parker was hung up in the dark on barbed wire, holding his guts in his sundered stomach with his frightened, cold fingers, grunting with the hurt and the animal fear in a dreadful hour before Vincent crawled out all alone in the dark, found him, and all alone in the dark talked to him gently and encouragingly and slithered behind him so that Wilbur couldn't see, and all alone in the dark shot him in the back of the head and cried out once, "Oh, sweet Jesus!"

The four were killed. The four died violently for the glorying town. Four more were gassed, and at Armistice were sent back so that they could die at home with their tuberculosis.

Oh, it was a brave war! Sweet Water was fervent for the valor of its sons. Colonel Vincent Carstairs was the single greatest hero, which was fitting. His Government awarded him the Congressional Medal of Honor for his conspicuous, heedless gallantry. Marshal Joffre himself pinned on the Croix de Guerre. Vincent came home with his empty left sleeve pinned to his tunic, and there were no bounds to the pride of the town in its proprietor and for those honored dead who had fallen, alongside Vincent's arm, among the poppies. A new monument took its place next to the Old Sod plot, and this time the C & O, quite carried away, donated the property outright. It was over the dedication ceremony that the dying foursome cast their pall.

On a granite block, the town fastened a bronze tablet with the names of their fallen idols—George Dankowski, John Hall and Wilbur and Franklin Parker, two of Caleb Parker's three sons. On the great day of dedication the mines were closed, and even the feud up the creek was suspended so that all could attend Davis Parker, brother of Caleb and minister of the Church of Christ, as he indulged himself in two hours of William Jennings Bryan oratory. Every man, every woman, every child from twenty miles around came dressed fit to kill. That included Cassius Childress. He was dressed fit to kill. He was dressed appropriately. He chose that inopportune time to die, his gassed lungs bursting with his blood. This was unpleasant for the celebrants. It took the edge off the glorification of the great struggle to end all struggles. The war which they'd thought of as shouting doughboys leaping into Valhalla had suddenly been distorted into mud, blood, mustard gas and red-spewing agony. They wished Cassius had possessed the good sense and good taste to stay away from the ceremony when he knew his time was so near. Even when his body was carted away to the mine office, his blood stained the clay, and Pastor Parker delivered his oration with noticeable diminution of enthusiasm.

Now the knotty problem presented itself—whether those who would die of war-incurred disabilities deserved inclusion on that bronze roll call of honored dead who had had the propriety to die far away.

Caleb Parker said to Vincent, "We just plain forgot. Ain't room for any more names on the tablet."

So Vincent paid for a new, larger tablet. The substitution was made without fanfare a month later. Vincent came down, all alone in the dark, and said, "Well, Cassius, you got your name on here now just as though you'd died as decently as Wilbur Parker." Now the three young men waiting their turns to be dead could see three vacant places on the plaque waiting impatiently for them. Sweet Water was relieved when these grim reminders of the horror of war were admitted to the state sanatorium to die out of sight. And only the widows, the orphans, the three waiting families and Vincent Carstairs wept in their solitude.

2

VINCENT had no confidants. Caleb Parker, his superintendent and next-door neighbor, came close. James Lee Parker, the seven-year-old son of Caleb, came closest.

Caleb said to his wife, "He's run his daddy's mine since he was twenty-four, and everything he done in his life, he done thinking of the Red Flash. But the war and the killing and the dying, it's got the mine outen his head."

India Parker said, "He's a mighty lonely man. I feel sorry for Vincent."

Caleb sucked his black pipe. "Better save some feeling sorry for Sweet Water."

India pulled on her own small pipe. "Forty-four years old and not a son, just a mine. A mine and her. At least we got one son left."

Caleb didn't want to be reminded. When he let himself be reminded, the agony was unbearable. He repeated quickly, "Better save some feeling sorry for Sweet Water. I've got the idea Vincent's going to keep Charles running the mine."

"Did you tell him, Caleb?"

"I talked to him."

"They won't put up with Charles. Not any more. Not with Vincent back."

"I said I talked to him. I told him."

"Did you tell him how the miners feel?"

"I said I talked to him."

"No need to get huffy, Mr. Parker."

Caleb thought to chide his wife sternly for her lack of respect. He thought better of it. He said, "I'm irritable."

"Reckon we all are. He better get Charles out of Sweet Water before something happens."

"Vincent just don't seem interested. He can't get his mind on it."

They were silent awhile.

India Missouri Parker said, "He'll get over it. Give him a while, and he'll get over it."

Late at night, seven-year-old James Lee Parker came up behind Vincent at the Soldiers Monument.

He said matter-of-factly, "Hello, Vincent. How yew?"

Vincent turned and looked down. He didn't smile. He didn't have to, to show he liked Jim. "Your folks ought to tie you down."

Jim pointed to the left sleeve, all pinned up. He said, "Vincent, I been wanting a long time to ask you. Can I touch your sleeve?"

"Sure, Jim."

Jim patted the sleeve. He said, "It sure feels funny, patting nothing, where something is supposed to be."

"Feels funny to me, too."

"Is that what makes you sad, Vincent?"

"I didn't know I was all that sad, Jim. Does it show that much?"

"Papa says you are. You look sad, Vincent. Papa says you can't get your mind on the mine. Is that how come you walk around the monument at night?"

"Yes, maybe so. I come down here and think about the brave men that were killed, and I try to figure out just what all the things mean."

"Papa says I should be proud of my brothers. Boy, Vincent, I think if I go to war, I don't think I want to be one of the ones get shot. Does it hurt when you get shot?"

"A little bit, maybe. But it didn't hurt your brothers. They died real quick, and they didn't get hurt."

"Well, I think I'd rather get hurt, than I would die."

"I guess you got a point, Jim."

163

"I'm proud of my brothers, even if it seems kind of dumb—you know, war."

"You should be. You should be proud of all the things that go to make you up."

"Sweet Water?"

"Yes."

"And West by God Virginia?"

"Yes. And America. I think you're going to have a good life, Jim. Restless, inquisitive, confident. You're enthusiastic about life. I'm getting preoccupied with death."

"I don't know what that means, Vincent."

"I think you see things as they should be, not as they are. That's good."

"Do you know what, Vincent?"

"What?"

"I know how you can get over being sad."

"How's that, Jim?"

"Throw that cold woman out on her ear, that's how."

"Jim, that's personal. You shouldn't say things to people about their personal affairs."

"Well, you should."

"Because then I'd look at things as they should be?"

"Yes."

"Get on home, Jim, before Caleb and India miss you and have to get out of bed and go looking for you."

Vincent Carstairs searched himself through the long night in his library and in his separate bedroom in the big white house, and then he determined to make a change in his life before it was too late.

He paid off his cold wife handsomely, divorced her, and took off in search of a better woman. He was gone a year to the day before he returned with his new bride, a warm young blue-eyed girl from a good Pittsburgh family. She bore a marked resemblance to Ellen Foley. Vincent looked ten years younger. He was ready to take up once more the responsibility of his heritage. He was too late to undo the damage. A bloody war raged in Sweet Water. It was a war whose deadly hate made sweet by comparison the confrontation of Hun and West by God Virginian in Argonne and Flanders.

Pete Battle avoided both wars as best he could.

3

WHEN THE TRUMPETS BLEW in 1917, Pete Battle fled. He needn't have run. The draft would never have touched him, the father of three, in Parker County where volunteers elbowed and shoved to get to the head of the line. But he took no chances. He struggled only briefly with his conscience and courage, then, because he was a man without a cause beyond his own boundaries, he steered well clear of Vincent Carstairs and his draft board and, instead, announced boldly that now he, too, would uproot himself and go off to Akron to make his contribution to the war effort in the rubber plants. If the mountaineers would think him craven, a crime for which there was no forgiveness, then so be it. A man who could kill his own son without remorse could bear dishonor to save his skin.

Even in this he was secure. His luck held. It couldn't occur to Sweet Water that their football hero was a poltroon. "Atta boy, Pete! You get us all lined up, you hear? We'll come straight from *Ber*-lin to Akron long about six months from now!"

Nor did Ellen Foley Battle know the coward in her husband. She did see the opportunist. "Sure and it's a golden chance to get what you want." In a moment she asked, "Are you taking us, Pete?"

"I'll get settled."

"Will you send for us?"

"Soon's I get settled."

"Write. We'll miss you, the kids. Be sure to write."

He kissed her perfunctorily. "I will."

Dr. Black knew. He was the only one who knew. He apprehended Pete at the C & O station. "Miss Liberty needs coal as much as she needs rubber."

"You're the expert? Wilson consult with you now?"

"Miners will be exempted, just like rubber workers. You don't have to run out."

"You know everything, don't you."

"I know you're pusillanimous."

"What's that supposed to mean?"

"Look it up."

"Don't bother me."

"Well, go your way, Dankowski."

"I'll do that, Kowalski."

"I'm the worse off of the two of us. I've still got some conscience."

"But not enough."

"No, not quite enough to stand up in front of Sweet Water. You, you're better off. I think you're past the point of no return."

Pete contemplated the doctor. Unwanted emotions assailed him. With difficulty, he said, "Doc, you appointed yourself the thorn in my side. I invite you out. Heal thyself, physician, then maybe you got something to say to me."

With the Akron fund, grown to one hundred and seventy-nine dollars, he left on the morning train to Charleston, thence to Akron. In Ohio, his seatmate asked, "Where you headed for?"

Pete grunted, "Akron."

"Me, too."

Now with some interest, Pete asked, "You work there?"

"For Goodyear."

"Doing what?"

"Travel out of Akron. Servicing the West Virginia and Western Pennsylvania territory."

"For tires?"

"For tires."

Pete grunted again. "Reckon you're not selling a gang of tires in West Virginia."

"You'd be surprised. You been in Wheeling or Charleston lately?"

Pete didn't answer.

"Where you from?"

"Sweet Water."

"Got any cars in Sweet Water yet?"

"Vincent Carstairs. He's got a Steamer."

"Mine owner?"

"Mine owner. And the mine's got a couple of Mack trucks. Ain't no place to go with any of 'em."

"They got to pave the Charleston Road. One of these days, they'll do it. Then cars will make sense. How do you get to Charleston?"

"Train. Or streetcar out of Cabin Crick."

"You miss it?"

"Miss what?"

"I mean, living in a place like Sweet Water, do you miss a place like Charleston?"

Pete didn't answer. He suspected that derision, more than curiosity, was involved. He asked, "They need hands at Goodyear?"

"Like field hands?"

"Well, whatever you call workers."

"They need arms. Arms like yours, for tire builders."

"That the best job?"

"That pays best."

"That's for me."

"Try Goodyear. It's the company. Biggest and best. And they're hiring. Strong backs and weak minds, they need 'em."

"What's that supposed to mean?"

The man grinned. "You Snakes always take things so serious. I'm just saying they need strong guys like you."

Pete said evenly, "Mister, I reckon you better take that back, right now."

"Snake? What the hell, I've heard you call each other that."

"You don't call me that, mister."

The grin was gone. "So what the hell, I take it back. Why don't you mountaineers come out and join the United States? People don't mean you half the offense you're always taking."

Pete gripped the top of the seat ahead to pull himself

167

up and leave. But his self-interest overcame his pride. This man could maybe help. He sat irresolutely with both arms stretched out ahead.

The man grinned. "Relax, mountaineer. My name's Jack Kelly, and I can tell you how to go about getting in Goodyear."

Pete drew his arms slowly back to his sides. They rode on for five silent minutes. Pete took a bottle of moonshine from his poke. Without smiling, he said, "Reckon you could be some help at that." He handed the bottle to Kelly. Kelly pulled the cork and drank hard. He corked the bottle. Then he said, "Whoo-eee!"

Pete pulled the cork with his teeth and took a swig, washing his mouth before gulping. He wiped his mouth with the back of his hand.

A young man across the aisle asked with interest, "Moonshine?"

Pete turned his head briefly, then ignored him.

"Guarantee, I'm no revenooer. Guarantee, I'm a man dying for a drink."

Pete said sullenly, "Like to oblige. Not enough to go around."

"I'll bet you a drink you got some more in your poke."

Pete didn't answer.

"Give you fifty cents for a swig."

Pete turned his head. "For one swig? Fifty cents?"

"That reached you."

"Fifty cents, you got a drink."

"Warn you, I'll get my money's worth."

Pete passed the bottle across the aisle. The young man drank long and deep, his throat gurgling. Pete reached out his hand in alarm. But then he laughed and said, "Reckon you warned me."

The young man took out a wad of money in a clip. He peeled off a dollar bill and handed it across the aisle. "You must be fresh out of the hills. Here's the dollar you should have clipped me for."

"Just give me the bottle back and keep your remarks to yourself."

The man smiled disarmingly. "You sensitive about being from the hills?"

"Just keep your remarks to yourself, or you'll bite off more than you can chew."

The man appraised Pete. "I believe it. You look strong as a horse."

Kelly said, "I think our mountaineer is going to take on the whole town when he gets to Akron."

Suddenly the young fellow thrust his hand across the aisle. "My name's George Gipp."

Pete eyed him suspiciously. "From where?"

"Laurium, Michigan."

"You really George Gipp? From Notre Dame?"

"Sometimes. I'm not sure where I'm from right now."

"What you doing on the train? How come you're not in South Bend?"

Gipp shrugged slightly. "Got a chance to hustle a pool shark in Pittsburgh. It was too good to pass up. I took him for three hundred."

"Three hundred dollars!"

Gipp smiled. "If you weren't so goddam big, I'd say something about the hills."

"You really George Gipp?"

Jack Kelly said, "By God, it's him."

Gipp passed over a box of cigarettes. "Be nonchalant. Have a Murad."

Pete took the smoke. Gipp waited for him to pass the bottle back. Pete made no such move.

Finally Gipp said, "Dollar for another swig?"

Pete held out his hand and took the money. Then he passed the half-empty bottle.

Gipp drank. He said, with his slight smile, "Guess I thought I'd impress you enough to get a free drink. Guess I was wrong."

Pete asked, "What kind of team you going to have?"

"Couldn't say."

"How come? Don't you know?"

"Been playing some semi-pro baseball up in Kenosha. Simmons Baseball Club."

"Aren't you going back to South Bend?"

"I guess. Can't think of anything better to do. Besides, I like Rockne."

"We hear he's the new head coach."

"You hear it right."

"What happened to Harper?"

"Had his fill, I guess."

Pete shook his head. "Don't see how a man could get his fill of winning football teams."

Gipp said enigmatically, "Man can get his fill of winning, right enough."

"I reckon Rockne's the best coach anyhow."

"Everybody's glad Knute got it."

"Sure comes in at a lousy time. Reckon you'll be losing some ballplayers in the draft."

Gipp smiled just a little. "Knute's got a plan."

"What kind of plan?"

"He'll be athletic instructor over at Fort Sheridan, sort of volunteer. And just accidental, he'll have his ballplayers in the Student Army Training Corps."

Kelly said, "Good plan until they get commissioned and shipped off."

Gipp said, "That's what will happen. Then he'll have to think up a new plan. The draft board's got to get up early, to keep ahead of Knute."

"How about you? You going to get drafted?"

"I'll worry about it when it comes."

Pete asked, "Did Rockne really spot you kicking the ball with your street shoes?"

"Most stories are true. That one's true. I came to Notre Dame to play baseball."

"Who really said it, Rockne or Harper?"

" 'Knock 'em up in the nickel seats'? Both of 'em. That earth-shaking argument's never going to get answered."

Pete handed Gipp the bottle.

Gipp said, "Thought you'd never get around to it. Never talked so much in my life for a drink."

Pete said slowly, "Well, I guess there's another bottle where that one came from."

"Or two or three. What's your name, mountaineer?"

"Pete Battle."

"Too good to be true."

"What the hell do you mean by that?"

"You got a name too good to be true, that's all. Whether it's true or not, it's too good to be true."

Kelly said, "I told you, he's ready to fight all us furriners."

Gipp asked, "Ever play any ball, Battle?"

"I played a lot of ball."

"Who for?"

"Parker County High."

"Any good?"

"You're damn well told. We were the first team they

170

had, and we won every game. Didn't even have uniforms the first two games."

"I meant were you personal any good."

"I was good."

"Where you heading for?"

"Akron."

Kelly said, "He's going to build tires. That beats the trenches any day."

Pete said hotly, "Kelly, that's the last crack I'll listen to out of you."

Kelly said tiredly, "Relax, mountaineer. It takes a draft dodger to know another one."

Gipp said, "It was a compliment, Battle. Hell with Akron. Come on over to South Bend with me, and we'll get you in a Notre Dame uniform."

"One hitch. Didn't finish high school."

"So?"

"Could I play ball without finishing high school?"

Gipp nearly grinned. "At Notre Dame?" He drank and nearly killed the bottle. "Pete, let me tell you about Notre Dame. We got a mission. Anybody can help us with that mission, we don't ask stupid questions."

"What kind of mission?"

"A holy mission. A holy Irish mission. We're fighting for the poor benighted Irish. For every Mick that ever had a door slammed in his face. We're taking out the resentment of the Micks on this country. That means winning, and we don't care how we do it, or who plays, or high school diplomas, or pro ballplayers, or any other damn thing, just so we win. And that includes you don't even have to be Irish. Your name can be Battle or Pilsudski, if you play on that team, you're Irish on a holy mission."

Pete said sharply, "My name's Battle."

Gipp did grin. "Step on your pet corn?"

"Just lay off the cracks."

"Pete, if you're as mean and rough as you look, Knute can use you. You come along with me, and we just won't say nothin' about high school diplomas. They won't ask, we won't answer anything they don't ask."

"You serious?"

"You believe it."

"You finish high school?"

"Nope. I was driving a dump truck, and working as a

171

lineman for the telephone company, and promoting YMCA basketball games, and then they spotted me playing semi-pro baseball in Elkhart, and next thing you know I got the free ride to play for the Irish."

"How much you get in the free ride?"

"You mean cash money? None. That's the only catch. They tried to make me wait tables, but that ain't for me. Hell, I can make enough money hustling, I don't have to wait tables for anybody, anywhere."

"You just run around the country and do what you want?"

"Didn't say they liked it. But they got to put up with it. You remember that, Battle, when you got something they want, you got 'em over a barrel. Man, particularly now with the draft. Ten lettermen, gone. Little Dutch, Walt Miller, Joe Brandy, Slip Madigan, Dave Hayes, Chet Grant, and now they need the Gipper like they never needed him before. I don't even stay in the dorm any more. I'm out at the Oliver Hotel when I'm in South Bend. The pool sharks hang out there." He drank again and handed the bottle back with just the dregs left.

Pete looked at it ruefully. "Reckon you could hold your own in Shawnee."

"That where you're from?"

"Across the river. Sweet Water. Look, you think I could work out some money to play for Notre Dame?"

"You need money? I'll help you hustle some on the side."

"I need it steady. I got a wife and three kids."

Gipp whistled. "You got yourself four problems. How old are you?"

"Twenty-three. That too old?"

"Not too old to play for Rockne. Old enough to have a wife and three kids."

Kelly said, "I'll solve the problem. No need to go to Notre Dame and hustle for a living. You go to Goodyear and play on their semi-pro team. They give you a job building tires, but mainly they give you a job playing football." He grinned his own crooked grin. "It's the most draft-proof job they got, Battle." Before Pete could remonstrate, Kelly said, "Next to me. I got punctured eardrums."

"I'll bet."

"Like I said, it takes one to know one."

"You really got punctured eardrums?"

"I got a medical certificate that says so."

Gipp said, "Hell, Battle don't have to worry with three kids. Time they get to calling him up, Wilson'll be in Berlin, or the Kaiser in Washington, one."

"Goodyear's your bet, Battle."

Gipp said, "Hate to admit it, but your partner's right. You play for Goodyear, that beats anything we've got to offer."

"Except playing for the Western Champions."

"That and a nickel will get you a cup of coffee. You got to hustle your own, wherever you are. You figure I'm the biggest star in the game?"

"Everybody figures you are."

"I still got to hustle. Even hustle you out of a drink."

Pete said, "Maybe your nose ain't hard enough. You could put the screws on Rockne good and proper. He'd have to ante up. Why don't you come over to Goodyear? We'll both sign up."

Gipp was silent a few moments. Then he said, "Well, that's a good idea. On the other hand, there's the Rock, and he's dead if I don't come back."

Pete went that night with Jack Kelly to an Akron saloon. A hillbilly from Tennessee called him Snake. Pete broke his jaw, and before the police came, he and a handful of Snakes tore up the bar and withstood a dozen men, with Kelly cheering them on. At midnight Pete and Kelly went, drunk, to a cathouse, and Pete's whore washed his face solicitously. "Must have been some fight." She dabbed at caked blood above his eyebrow. "Where you from?"

"West by God Virginia."

"Me too."

"Whereabouts?"

"Wheeling."

"Big-city girl. I'm from Sweet Water."

"Red Flash Mines?"

Pete asked, "How you know?"

"You know Charles Carstairs?"

"I know him. You want to tell me you got something to do with him? He laid you? I don't believe it."

"I never set eyes on him. My sister worked in his home in Wheeling. You know, housework. And he never so much as laid a hand on her. And she tried."

"I believe it. He's a cold fish."

"Anyhow, I hear tell he's running the mine down in Sweet Water."

"Until his uncle comes back from the war."

"You all don't have to fret about your women with Charles Carstairs. They could climb in bed naked with him and be safe as in church. Old Pinch Nose."

"Old Pinch Nose, that's good."

"Miners cotton to him? Don't see how."

"They don't. That ain't my problem any more."

"You going to be in Akron awhile?"

"Awhile."

For a moment she paid attention to a bruise. Then she said offhandedly, "I got a place to stay. Three-room apartment. And just me there."

"And you're looking for somebody to pay the freight?"

"Well, a good-looking mountaineer like you, I could use a roommate." She patted gently. "Wouldn't ask you to pay all the bills. Not if I was to keep on working. And I would keep on working, lest a man was to decide I had plenty to do around the apartment. You wouldn't be sorry."

"Prove it."

She smiled and took off his clothes, then her kimono, and made love to him both heatedly and tenderly, and when he had subsided, she held his bruised face against her breasts and asked, "Do I satisfy you?"

"Reckon."

"That takes a heap of doing."

He grinned against her. "You're a sweet-talk drummer."

"I'll meet you outside."

The two of them walked in the early morning four blocks to her apartment building. She fed him six scrambled eggs and black coffee, and when she took him to bed, he asked, "What's your name?"

"Melanie."

He snorted.

"What's so funny about Melanie?"

"You don't strike me as a belle just off the plantation."

"My last name is Anton. I'm a Magyar from Wheeling."

"A Hunkie named Melanie. I'm a Polack from Sweet Water named Pete Battle."

"We go halves on the apartment, okay?"

"You got a deal."

174

"But if you use me as much as you're going to want to, you go three quarters. And all you got to do to keep me just for yourself, you pay all the bills, that's all you got to do, that and a little bit of saving money."

4

GOODYEAR FOOTBALL welcomed Pete Battle. He was two hundred pounds of hard muscle. In his big arms he had the strength of a bear, and he had the meanness to go with his strength. He lusted to hurt. The men across from him were his conscience. He reveled in the bone-crushing charges. Down in the melees of the line, he slugged with both fists, slammed with his elbows and knees, leg-whipped when he missed blocks or tackles, and despite his lack of skill, he was moved into the starting line-up after the first game and was the terror of the semi-pro league, the unchallenged bully, the master intimidator.

Goodyear taught Pete how to build tires. He was agreeable to the farce which put the frosting on his draft-free status, but then he was dismayed to learn that Goodyear intended that he actually work as a tire builder when the football season closed. He solved that by turning to basketball. He made the Wingfoot squad by virtue of his great strength and natural co-ordination. In the basketball of 1918, a wild man under the boards was more valuable than an accurate shot.

It wasn't until spring that they finally got him into the plant. He tried to stave it off with baseball, but no amount of wishing could make him a fielder or could help him hit the curves the good pitchers threw at him. Pete went glumly into Plant One and began his contribution to the war effort.

Through the war, he stayed at Goodyear, draft deferred. His pay was double his Red Flash hundred dollars. He lived high, a Wingfoot hero. He and Melanie Anton lived high.

Once a month he wrote home. "Everything's okay here. Hope the same is with you and the kids. Here's the money. Save most of it and don't tell Papa how much it is. Well, be seeing you soon." Having discharged his family obligations, he turned back to Melanie Anton. At least once a month he was unfaithful to her with Akron women who were infected, even more than the men, with war spirit and consequent abandonment. Blond, strong Pete Battle was an excellent repository for their patriotic fervor. When they took him in their beds, their lust was martial and holy. When they sent him away, hours later, they were aglow with his animal strength and the warming knowledge that they had contributed their utmost to a man who was contributing to the war effort. Akron fitted Pete well.

The first letters from Ellen Foley Battle said: "We're so lonely without you. The kids miss you. Can't we come soon?"

Then the letters became rote, they became habit, without feeling. Just one more time she broke down and said: "Your son David doesn't even know who you are, Pete. He doesn't even know who you are. And I'm beginning to wonder if I know who you are."

This time he telephoned her. She came to the C & O station, and they spoke as strangers over the hollow wires. He turned from the phone, took Melanie Anton by the arm and went off again into his Akron.

In 1919, emancipated from his draft-dodging by the Armistice, he quit Goodyear and went over to Massilon to try out for the pro football team. The Tiger coach received him with open arms, because his Goodyear reputation preceded him. The Massilon Tigers! Now the great football honors would at last be his. He dreamed a perpetual-motion daydream of the long-deferred recognition that was imminent. He said to the coach, "Tell Fats Henry to stand from under. There's a new number-one tackle in the United States."

He was appalled when he didn't make the starting line-up. "I can play better than those guys any day of the week."

The coach said, "You just think you can. You're rougher. But you're not as good." He softened the blow by adding, "You got the makings. You just haven't got the experience. These guys played college ball. And pro, not semi-pro. They're the best in the business. Give yourself some time. You'll get there."

"I'm there. I'm the best."

"Pete, you need a Dutch uncle. You got a real future ahead of you. There's a future in pro football. Thorpe is talking a league. He'll have George Halas and the Staleys for sure, and Curly Lambeau from Green Bay, maybe three, four more teams, and this game will be on its way. This sport is going to take America by storm. It's got to. This is a rough, tough country. With prohibition, people got to take their hots out on something. We think it will be pro ball. Two, three years from now, you'll be a good performer in a successful game. No sense your being too impatient. You're not quite ready, that's my lecture."

Pete said belligerently, "You just put me in where I belong. You put me in against the best, that's all I ask."

Then the coach said without smiling, "Well, maybe I'll just do that."

But it wasn't until 1920 that Pete got his crack at Jim Thorpe and the Canton Bulldogs in the new American Professional Football League.

The air was electric. Massilon against Canton! Sunday afternoon the stands filled early to capacity. Blood and sand! Massilon against Canton!

The Tiger coach said, "Your chance, Battle. Steve's leg can't make it. Show me you've learned something."

Pete said, "You just watch me."

On the kick-off, he sought out Jim Thorpe. The Indian came lazily down the field in the general direction of the Massilon ball carrier, determined to stay completely out of the play unless an emergency developed. Pete drove in from the blind side. He rammed his forearm under Thorpe's chin and sent him crashing to the grassless ground. He lay on top of Thorpe, grinning down. He said, "Going to be a little rough on Injuns out here today."

178

Thorpe said nothing. His Indian face was impassive. He lifted himself painfully and walked slowly into the defensive backfield.

Massilon scored. On the final plunge, Pete found Thorpe again and clipped him after the play was over. He lay heavily across Thorpe's ankles. He said tauntingly, "There's more where that came from, Injun."

The referee raised his whistle to call the penalty. Thorpe shook his head almost imperceptibly. The referee let the whistle drop against his chest. He whispered to his field judge, "Watch out for Battle."

The field judge said grimly, "Battle better watch out for himself."

In the Canton series, the plays ran against the opposite tackle. Pete was elated. He had met the best and put the fear of God in 'em. He wrestled and lashed out and piled on like a madman. On fourth down, Thorpe passed twenty yards to Gus Dorais for a touchdown. Pete bore in intending to crash Thorpe again to the ground, his forearms flailing menacingly. Thorpe skipped out of the way, avoiding the charge.

"Reckon I got your number, huh, Injun?"

There was still no expression. Thorpe said in his mild voice, sadly, "Sonny, you hadn't ought to have acted this way with old Jim."

"There's more coming," Pete said exultantly. He had him scared! He had the great Jim Thorpe scared and hopping to get out of the way! It would be in the papers. They had to put this in the papers. Would they read it in Sweet Water? The new terror of the pro league! Pete Battle, battling his way to overnight fame, a year on the bench and now suddenly the new sensation of the Massilon Tigers!

On the kick-off, Thorpe drifted downfield. Pete filled himself with new adrenalin and anticipation. He avoided one rusher he should have blocked and went for the Indian instead. Thorpe cut as though to evade the block. Pete swerved to get him . . .

He looked up at the swinging light in the dressing room. He moved to sit up and fell back with a sharp pain in his chest, and the light dimmed.

The trainer asked, "You coming out, Battle?"

"What happened?" He had to mumble. His jaws hurt. His lips were thick, his tongue cut.

"You with us now, Battle?"

"What happened?" Pete repeated.

"Well, sonny, couple things you didn't know about the big Injun. First place, he's still a savage, won't ever be anything else but. Second, he wears steel sheets instead of shoulder pads. Sonny, you asked for it, and you got it."

Pete mumbled. "What happened?"

The trainer said, "Doc, he ain't quite with us yet."

The light came back into focus, and Pete asked a fourth time, "What happened?"

The trainer and the doctor peered down on him. The trainer said with considerable pleasure, "Tough guy, you messed with that big Injun, that's what happened. You thought he was going to dance away from you like before, that's what you thought, and all of a sudden he turned and run right into you like a great, big, fast freight train, just aslammin', and abangin' with those steel shoulder pads, and stompin' for all he was worth, and then that big Wysocki, he come over and give you a stomp for good measure, and nobody lifted a finger for you, sonny, not even the referee, they just let old Jim and Wysocki teach you a lesson you won't ever forget, and that's that you can think you're mighty tough, but sometime you're going to run up against somebody just that much tougher. And when old Jim got done stompin' you, and I came out to pick up the pieces, he looked down and said: *Sonny, I told you you hadn't ought to have done that to old Jim.* So now you got some busted ribs, and two of your back teeth knocked out, and the rest of 'em loose and hangin' on, and you'll be lucky if you don't have to gum your food the rest of your life, sonny. That's what happened, sonny." He grinned wide, peering into the clearing eyes.

The doctor said, "You may have a concussion, Battle. We'll put you in the hospital overnight for observation."

The hospital kept him two days. Not one soul came to see him. He lay waiting for the coach to come tell him he'd played a hell of a game before the steel shoulder pads got him. The coach didn't show. None of his teammates showed. Melanie Anton did not come to see him. The hospital turned him loose, looking like the wrath of God.

When he came to the apartment seeking solace, Melanie was markedly indifferent to him.

180

"Guess I got it pretty good," he said. "I can use some taking care of."

She said calmly, "Reckon you're old enough to take care of yourself."

"What's that supposed to mean?"

"You expecting something out of me, Pete?"

He stared at her. He said heatedly, "You're damn right I expect something out of you."

"Hope you get what you're expecting. I wouldn't bet on it."

"Where you getting off, with this kind of talk?"

She turned her back on him. He grabbed her and turned her around.

She said, "Get your hands off me."

"You listen to me, Melanie."

"What for? So you can tell me what a big man you are? I listened to that long enough."

"I get it. Well, you listen to me, Thorpe hasn't got the last of me. He gets that next time."

"Next time. There won't be no next time."

"What kind of talk is that? I'll be back, five, six weeks. And this time with my own pads. That's what it was, you know that, don't you? It was his steel pads, it wasn't man against man."

"You won't be back."

"What kind of talk is that?"

"I know you. I've lived with you."

"You tell me what you know, you're so goddam smart."

"You've had it. You got no real guts. I knew that all along. A man like you, he's got no real guts. You won't ever go back and play against that Injun as long as you live. I know you. You're a no-good bastard, and you can get out of here as soon as you're ready."

He was incredulous. "Just because I got hurt in a football game?"

"I'm tired of you anyway," she said indifferently.

He was devastated. He said, "Melanie, we been here for too long a time, for you to do this."

"You're right, too long a time. I should of kicked you out when I got sick of your big mouth. That was after the first day."

He said bitterly, "You decided you don't need my loving any more? You got somebody else?"

181

She laughed aloud. "Need loving! You simple bastard, I hate screwing!"

He said very softly, "You whore. You dirty whore."

"Sure," she said calmly. "Didn't you know? Don't you remember where you found me? You, you had to quit Goodyear and play football for a lousy twenty-five dollars a week."

"If that's it, I'll go back to Goodyear. I can do both."

"You simple bastard, can't you figure it out that I'm sick of looking at you!"

He grabbed her by the back of her hair and wrenched her face up close. There was no expression of either pain or fear in her broad Hungarian face. He let her go.

She said, "Out, Mr. Battle."

He found a boarding house and holed up for six weeks until his battered ribs had healed. He ran himself into shape. Then he presented himself in the Massilon dressing room at Canton on the Sunday of the return-go with the Bulldogs. The coach looked up and said noncommittally, "Battle."

"I'm ready to play."

"Then get suited up."

"I figure I got seven weeks back pay coming. Isn't that right?"

"You'll get it."

Some of the players nodded in response to his greeting, but no one spoke. It got on his nerves. He stood sideways of the coach while he laced his pants and asked, almost rhetorically, "How come nobody pitched in to help me? Hell, I'd of helped one of the guys in trouble."

"They figured you were fighting your own fight, tough guy. You're on your own, Battle, until you prove you've learned something."

"Like what?"

"Like how to be a team player."

This time he turned and looked at the coach. "I play to win. Any objection?"

"You help the team, I'm all for you. You hurt the team, I've got no use for you. Battle, I've got my own problems. We've got a ball game today. If you're here to play ball, we can use you. If you still got the taste for the game, you show it on the field."

"You think my mind's changed about anything?"

The coach said, "It better have. If it hasn't, they'll kill you." He turned away.

His teammates watched with great interest as he pulled on sheet-steel shoulder pads. No one said a word. They just watched. He pulled on his jersey and clattered out of the dressing room with the team. In warm-up, he whacked shoulder pads with the right tackle. The tackle winced at the impact. He grunted and said, "Save it for the Injun. He's got his eye on you."

Pete looked downfield at the Bulldogs. Thorpe was sending long, lazy spiral punts down the field and not paying the least attention to the Tiger squad.

The tackle said, "Thought that would get you, Battle."

The coach came by and said, "You start, Battle."

Pete nodded grimly.

The coach smiled just a little. "I hear you got some new shoulder pads. I'm looking forward to the clash of steel on steel."

The Tigers won the toss. Pete lined up on his forty and flailed his arms nervously. He'd show them. He'd show them all. Most of all, he'd show Thorpe. This time it was even. This time it was steel against steel. The ball came end over end to the Tiger backs. Pete took aim on Thorpe, went all the way across the field to meet him. Thorpe accelerated. Pete girded himself for the impact. At the last moment he flinched. He was sent flying head over heels. The Canton crowd, eyes on the personal feud, roared for his blood. The impassive Indian knelt with his knee in Pete's stomach and said, "Next time you get what you got before. Next play."

Pete looked up into the cruel, handsome face. He pushed at Thorpe to get him off. He felt the steel shoulder pad beneath the jersey. He jerked his hand away and said, "They should throw you out of the league. You'll kill somebody."

Thorpe didn't change expression. "That's right, sonny. You."

Then Pete lay where he was, flat on his back. The trainer came out with the water bucket and sloshed the sponge in his face. "Hurt anywhere besides your guts?"

Pete said, "Ribs again."

"That so? Way I saw it, you were so busy running backwards he couldn't get you that hard. Better luck next time."

"Ribs," Pete said.

No one helped him off the field. The coach didn't even look at him when he walked on past the bench into the dressing room. He sat for a long time listening to the shouts from the field. He said to himself, "Nobody calls me a coward." But they did. Melanie Anton. Doc Black. The ballplayers. They all called him a coward. "Nobody calls me a coward." He walked to the dressing-room door where he could see the field. He watched the slam of bodies, elbows and knees in the pro league in which no quarter was given. He winced. He urged himself, Walk back to the bench and ask to be put in the game. He watched Thorpe, the magnificent athlete, dogging it two out of three plays, and then on the third, bursting out with violent energy to commit mayhem on opponents who'd crossed him. It was Thorpe's league. He started it. He was the single greatest star. He could wear steel plates on his shoulders, he could play football like his forebears played lacrosse or tortured settlers, and no one would help Pete raise a hand against him. It wasn't fair! Get out there, Pete, get out there and show them! His own shoulder pads were steel. It was man against man. But his feet were leaden. For long minutes he tried, and then he was devastated by the realization that they all knew him for what he was. He was a bully, and bullies were cowards when called. A bully? Was that all he was? He was a child murderer, he was an adulterer, he was a man that even whores despised. He said softly to himself, "Sweet Jesus!" and he thought he had better go home to his wife and children. He dressed quickly to get out before the team came in at half-time. He took the interurban to Akron and the next train to Sweet Water. There was a war in Sweet Water, waiting for him.

5

THEY KILLED Vincent Carstairs. They shot him dead. He brought home from Pittsburgh the pretty girl who looked like Ellen Foley, and she spent one day in the big white house with him, and three more days with his casket.

She asked that Caleb Parker accompany her on the train back to Pittsburgh, or at least as far as Charleston, and he was quick to acquiesce, because he had loved Vincent Carstairs, and also because Vincent had said that when he died, the Red Flash would belong to Sweet Water and that Caleb Parker would run the Red Flash for Sweet Water, and Caleb was eager to hear this news from the widow.

Before the train was beyond the Sweet Water limits, she said, "Mr. Parker, I'm going to sell the mine to my husband's nephew, Charles Carstairs."

Caleb Parker looked as though he'd been given the revelation that St. Mary's was the true Church.

The widow said, "Mr. Parker, I'm going to have a baby. I was going to tell Vincent after just a little bit longer, and all of a sudden it was too late. I know Vincent wanted the mine to go to the town, but the will leaves it to me. And I can't run it, so I have to sell it. And I'd sell it to the town, but the lawyer says I should sell it to Charles, because that will be safer—I mean, surer, you know, getting the money, because who knows how a mine will run with the miners themselves owning it?" Her blue eyes were earnest. "Mr. Parker, Vincent always talked about you. All the time. He thought so much of you. I don't suppose I've got any right to ask, but, you know, for Vincent's sake, for his baby's, will you help Charles keep the mine going at its best?"

Caleb stood up in the aisle. He said, "Madam, I've got no intention of helping Charles Carstairs. I'll do everything I can to get him out of Sweet Water."

He and young Jim got off the train at Chelyan and went back to Sweet Water, and in the time they were on the short round trip, the fat had gone into the fire. There was another killing. First a Pinkerton had got his skull cracked by a club, and then Anton Dvorak got shot dead. There was a meeting at the tipple. The yelling swelled up the track to the station house.

Caleb ran to the tipple. Rourke was up on a mine wagon, waving his arms and yelling, and miners who would have spit on him the day before, yelled back like maniacs. Rourke pointed up the hill and screamed at them, "He's up there! Vincent Carstairs not yet cold in his grave, and Charles is up there in that white house! Do we let him get away with it!"

And the crowd screamed, "No!!!"

Mother Jones climbed on the wagon, and she talked. She talked. She talked over the miners' heads, but she talked, how she talked, and she was a spellbinder, and the miners shouted and cheered and whistled as though they knew what she was talking about, and when she was all done orating, she finished up, "Hurrah for John L. Lewis!"

Then Rourke jumped up again on the wagon and yelled, "Three cheers for John L. Lewis."

And the miners yelled like it was the first day of the world.

Rourke shouted, "The strike is on! You are slaves no longer! This town is yours! If the owner sends Pinkertons, kill them! If the bookkeeper crosses you, kill him! If the superintendent crooks his finger, shoot him! Men, get your guns!"

Then Walter Dankowski jumped onto the wagon alongside Rourke and yelled, "Just a minute! Men, just a minute!" And when they quieted enough, he demanded, "Since when do we listen to radical scum like this?"

The miners tried to hoot him down, but Walter lit into Rourke, and Mother Jones, and John L. Lewis, and the United Mine Workers, and shouted louder and louder, and the crowd began to pay attention to him.

But Rourke yelled, "What do we do with this company suck?"

A miner shouted, "Shoot him!"

Leo Dankowski said, "Walter, you better get home while the getting's good."

But Walter stood his ground.

They'd have shot him, they'd surely have shot him.

Caleb Parker stepped forward. He climbed up on the wagon, and the miners hooted him, even though they knew he'd been fired as superintendent. Caleb raised his arms. The men of Sweet Water could not resist their acknowledged leader. They quieted. He said, "Men, Charles Carstairs started this fight. We'll finish it!"

Then the miners yelled their heads off, because they were on the right side if Caleb Parker was on their side.

Rourke smiled broadly.

6

TWENTY-FOUR MEN rode the railcar with Pete from Charleston to Sweet Water. Twice Pete tried to engage the man across the aisle in conversation. The man ignored him the first time, and the second time said, "You don't get the message. I got no interest in talking to you."

When the train squealed, huffing, into the C & O station, Pete rose and loomed over the man. "Mister, you got a right not to talk when you don't feel like it. But sometime somebody's going to teach you some manners."

The man's expression didn't change. He put his right hand inside his coat and came out with a .38 revolver. He looked Pete in the eyes and pointed the gun where he was looking. He asked, "Colby, you reckon this is one?"

A man behind Pete asked, "Who are you, mister?"

Pete turned and looked into a double-barreled shotgun. He looked up and down the car. All the men opened cases and assembled shotguns as though it were an everyday occurrence.

Pete asked, almost under his breath, "What's going on?"

The man named Colby said, "I asked you who you are. What's your name?"

"Battle."

"Where you from?"

"I'm from here."

"Which side you on?"

"Which side of what?"

Colby called, "Hart, you got any Battles on your list?"

The man named Hart said, "This must be the Dankowski that's been in Akron playing football."

Colby said, "Okay, Snake, get back in your seat and stay there. Until we're off the platform."

A man said, "Colby, they're waiting for us out there."

Pete said, "Nobody calls me Snake."

"I call you Snake, and I'd just as soon blow your guts out as look at you. You listen good, ballplayer, we got no grudge against you. You got no part in this, keep it that way. Now sit your ass in that seat and keep it there, or get it shot off."

The train humped to its dead stop. Pete lurched into Colby. He saw other shotguns level down on him. He said quickly, "I'm sitting down."

The men filed out onto the platform. A hundred men surrounded the platform, waiting for the twenty-four. The noon sun glinted on rifles, shotguns and revolvers. The men from the train formed a hollow square, their shotguns at waist level.

Caleb Parker stepped forward. He said evenly, "Now then, we got the drop on you. I reckon you just better break those shotguns and get right back on that train. Or be dead."

Colby said coldly, "We're reporting to Mr. Carstairs. You men get out of the way and nobody will get hurt."

Caleb said with equal calm, "Don't reckon you're calling the tune, Pinkerton. You want to get shot, you step one foot off that platform."

Colby asked Hart beside him, "That Caleb Parker?"

"That's him. Rourke's the one next him, without a gun."

Colby said, "Parker, I'm to tell you, you show any resistance, the militia will be here."

"That what Carstairs has to say?"

"That's what the Governor has to say. If you resist, the militia will come and wipe you out to a man."

Caleb smiled a little. "Well now, Pinkerton, where you from?" Colby didn't answer. Caleb said, "Reckon I better make you a little speech. You got something to learn about West Virginia and Parker County. Yesterday they was going to try a Hatfield for shooting a McCoy, over

189

at the Frogsburg Court House. Only the Hatfield never got to the top of the steps, when Harley McCoy blew him to Kingdom Come. That give you a message?" Colby still didn't answer. "We don't rely on strangers to get our jobs done, and we don't count on interference from strangers when we're getting a job done. Put it in your pipe, if Carstairs sends Pinkertons, or the Governor sends militia, we're going right ahead and get our job done, and any strangers that come in here won't be going back. And if you send any more of your spies, you'll find him floating down the river like the last one. That clear, Pinkerton?"

Colby said, "Last chance, Parker. You can't fight the Army."

Nine-year-old Jim Parker yelled shrilly from among the Sweet Water men, "Pinkerton, it'll take two armies."

Caleb didn't turn his head. "Jim, told you to stay away from here. Git."

Colby said, "Be women and kids killed when the shooting starts."

Caleb said, "Be Pinkertons killed. Now you break those shotguns and get back on that train, stepping real easy. You got one minute, then we shoot."

"There will be a lot of dead Sweet Water men, Parker."

"There will be every last Pinkerton dead. You got less than one minute."

Colby said calmly to his men, "Break the guns. We'll board the train."

When the guns were broken, Pete Battle stepped out onto the platform. Leo Dankowski yelled, "Hey, Pete!"

Pete smiled broadly and waved the wave of the returning, conquering hero. He said in a loud voice, "One of these scutters shoved a shotgun in my belly and called me Snake. Let's see how big he talks now." Suddenly he turned and rushed Colby, throwing a mighty blow. Colby warded it off with the broken gun, then smashed the butt in Pete's face, breaking his nose. The blood spurted over both of them. Pete sank, stunned, to his knees, but he grabbed Colby's legs and pulled him down, and as his head cleared he got his strong hands at the man's throat and began to choke the life out of him. Another of the invaders sprang to help. Some of the Baldwin-Felts detectives assembled their shotguns frantically.

190

A shot rang out, and one of the agents pitched face-down on the platform, a squirrel-rifle bullet between his eyes. Men yelled, and a barrage of shots followed. All of the invaders went face-down on the platform, the dead and wounded sprawled out or curled up, and those still uninjured in positions of surrender. At the first shot, Pete Battle released his death grip, rolled off the platform and huddled against its protection.

Caleb Parker yelled five times, "Cease fire!" before his command was heeded. He surveyed the carnage. He thought to himself: Oh, Christ, why did it have to be! But he said steadily, "Now you Pinkertons pick up your men, and you get on the train. And you take back the message, you or the militia, we don't care which, you come to Sweet Water again, you don't get another chance to go back."

There were five dead men and three wounded in the car that was backed all the way to Charleston. The invaders had been repelled. Sweet Water had shown they would not be intimidated. The men nearest Caleb Parker hit him on the back and congratulated themselves, the brave, independent Americans of West by God Virginia.

Nine-year-old Jim Parker said, "We showed 'em, Papa."

Caleb said, "You get home, Jim."

Leo and Will Dankowski helped their brother to his feet. They took him into the station and wiped the blood off his face. Dr. Black said, "You're going to have a mighty sore and ugly proboscis, Pete. I'll fix it up best I can."

Pete watched the doctor's face. Black-Kowalski seemed pleased enough to see him. Pete looked around at the other friendly faces. He grinned and said, "This ain't much compared to the kicking around against Thorpe."

Jim Parker asked, "Pete, who's the best ballplayer, you or Jim Thorpe?"

"What's your name?"

"Jim Parker."

"You're getting mighty growed up."

"Man gets growed up in a hurry these days. Who's the best?"

"Some as say Thorpe, some as say me."

Dr. Black asked, "How come you're home in the season, Pete?"

191

"Got hurt."

"Bad?"

"Besides, thought I'd come home and fight Pinkertons."
Black narrowed his eyes.

Pete said, "Comes a time to come home and help."

The good-looking young man in the seersucker suit
stepped forward. "I'm Rourke. We can use you."

Pete put his hand out cautiously. "What you doing
here, Rourke?"

"Don't you know? Caleb and I are heading up the
union."

"Caleb?"

"Why not Caleb?"

"Where's Vincent Carstairs?"

Dr. Black said, "Dead."

"When?"

"Nobody write you?"

"Guess they didn't think it was important."

Rourke said, "Pete, soon's you get reacquainted with
your bride, you come talk to me."

Pete said, "I'll do that."

His brothers walked with him to the gray house. Leo
hollered up the hill, "Hey, Ellen, come see who we got
here!"

Ellen Foley Battle came out on the front porch. Light
sprang into her pretty face. She ran down the steps and
would have thrown her arms around Pete's neck, but then
she stopped and both of them rubbed their hands self-
consciously.

Pete said, "How you, Ellen?"

"Just fine, Pete."

"I'm home."

"For good?"

"Depends. Yeh, for good."

The two little girls came hopping and dancing, calling,
"Daddy! Daddy!" and he hugged them embarrassedly, and
his father came out and said noncommittally, "Pete," and
his mother came to him with tears in her eyes and hugged
him fervently while he stood with his hands at his side.

Ellen asked, "Where's David? Get David."

One of her daughters went skipping up the hill to the
back yard and came back leading her brother by the
hand. Ellen said, "He doesn't know who you are, I guess,

192

Pete." The boy looked up solemnly, his bright blue eyes searching. Ellen said, "This is your daddy, David."

Pete asked, "How old's he now?"

Ellen smiled. "Three, you big lunk."

Pete said, "Not very big for three, is he?"

7

THE MILITIA CAME. A battalion of the West Virginia National Guard occupied Sweet Water, and the town that had known no law except the distant sheriff at Frogsburg now knew martial law. The troops came on flatcars and set up their tents in two encampments, one between the tracks and the Kanawha, upstream, and the other on up Murder Hollow, beyond Casimar Dankowski's gray house, toward Red Flash Number Two. Soldiers patrolled the Charleston Road, marched in squads among the company-red houses, occupied the C & O station in platoon strength, and guarded the mines themselves with complete combat units. There was no resistance. The ferocity of the miners evaporated when confronted with that much steel. The men who had sworn death before dishonor now chose life. Sweet Water filled up with sullen resentment, more bitter, even, in its fear than in its frustration.

The militia colonel convoked the principals. Caleb Parker, Rourke and Pete Battle marched past the troops into the mine office. The colonel sat to the right of Charles Carstairs, who sat erect behind the president's desk, where Roger and Vincent Carstairs had sat before him. Charles looked older than his thirty-five years. He was drawn and haggard, but determination glinted in his eyes behind his rimless glasses, and showed in his thin lips beneath his pinched nose. Caleb, Rourke and Pete seated themselves before the desk.

Charles said abruptly, "Colonel, Caleb Parker was superintendent of the mines. Now he's the leader of the union. Give your orders to him."

The colonel asked, "Which one's the Wobbly?"

Charles picked up a letter opener and pointed it at Rourke. "That one."

Rourke said, "Wrong. I'm United Mine Workers of America."

Carstairs said, "Chameleon. The miners wouldn't take the IWW, but they swallowed the Mine Workers. He's still a Wobbly, for my money."

The colonel looked at Pete. "What's your name?"

"Pete Battle. What's yours?"

The colonel asked Charles, "What's his part in it?"

Rourke said, "He's president of the local."

Carstairs asked sharply, "Since when?"

"Since yesterday."

"Thought you were president, Caleb."

"My name is Parker, Carstairs."

"It's still first name with me, if you want it."

"I got no wish to be president. They put Pete in."

Carstairs said to the colonel, "Battle's the town football hero. He's been playing with the Massilon Tigers."

The colonel said, "I don't know the names of all the pro players. Can't say I've heard of you, Battle. What position did you play?"

Pete said, "We're even. I sure never heard of you."

The colonel said mildly, "I'm sure more people know you than know me." He smiled just a little. "From now on they'll know both of us, here in Sweet Water."

Charles said, "He's a Dankowski."

"That's the family you consider sound."

"Not so sure about Leo and Will. Walter and the others, okay." He looked at Pete. "Don't like to see you choose the wrong side."

Pete said evenly, "I know which side I chose."

Charles said, "Colonel, no matter who's president, the miners listen to Parker."

The colonel said, "Then let's get on with it." He raised his voice to a bluff, friendly level. "Parker, things have gone wrong around here. I'm here to straighten things out."

Caleb said, "That will take some doing."

"It will. It's late in the day to let bygones be bygones. But we've got to get together. It can't go on th s way. We all know that. Or there will be more men killed. That's why the Govenor sent me down here. To keep peace while things get worked out."

Rourke said, "You were sent down here to court-martial the miners that shot the Pinkertons."

The colonel puffed on his cigar. "You'd like that, would you?"

"What's that supposed to mean?"

"Just what I said. Wouldn't you like the miners tried? That would be a bonanza of publicity for you Wobblies."

"Are they going to be tried?"

"That's not in my jurisdiction. But the answer is, no, they aren't. The prosecution feels they wouldn't have much chance of conviction. We went through that at Logan."

"If the newspapers continue their allegations against the miners, we'll demand a trial."

The colonel said, "You don't make demands on me, Rourke." He bit into his cigar. He relaxed and said, "Parker, I'm here to work out a compromise. My job is to keep the peace and get the mines open. I'm going to work out an honorable give-and-take solution."

Rourke snorted. He said, "We give, Carstairs takes. You made your reputation at Logan."

The colonel said, "Rourke, this town is under martial law. I'm in command here. I have called this meeting, and I am conducting this meeting. If you have any doubt, my soldiers will prove it to you. The next time I consider that you are speaking out of turn, I will have you forcibly ejected from this meeting. Is that clear?"

Rourke smiled sardonically and said, "I have no doubt at all that you will use force on the miners. You're the mine owners' soldiers."

The colonel chewed his cigar vigorously. Then he said with renewed amiability, "Parker, you are the superintendent of these mines, and also the leader in this strike. You know the problems of both sides . . ."

Caleb interrupted. "I am not the superintendent. I'm a miner. Charles Carstairs saw to that."

Charles said, "You've never mined an ounce of coal in your life. You're a Parker." Then he said, "If you want me

196

to admit it, I will. I was wrong. I made a mistake. I'll rectify it. You're still the superintendent."

Rourke said, "Close the barn door after the horse is stolen."

Caleb said, "Sounds just a little like a bribe."

"Call it what you want. We'll get along without you if we have to, but we'll get along better with you. I want you to talk sense to the miners."

Caleb lighted his pipe, puffing while the others watched him. Finally he asked, "What's your idea of sense?"

"Cold, hard sense. Facts. If the miners don't know it now, they better damn well get it through their heads, this strike can go on forever, but it won't win one damn thing. Not one damn thing. They've already lost. They won't ever get back the lost pay. Never. Every day they're out, it's more lost pay. Unless this strike ends, and the men come back on my terms, this mine will never open again, and this town is dead."

Rourke said, "This mine will open again. And it will be with the United Mine Workers of America."

Carstairs said, "There will never be a union in this mine."

"You'll never dig a car of coal without the union."

"We'll never dig a car of coal with the union."

The colonel said, "That's enough. Parker, one thing is clear, this town is on its way to becoming a ghost town. Do you want that to happen?"

Caleb lit his pipe again, though it still burned. He said, "Before there was a Red Flash, this town was here."

"For you. But not for the miners. Do you want part of the responsibility for turning their coal town into a ghost town?"

Caleb said, "The responsibility is there." He pointed to Carstairs.

Carstairs said, "I'm ready to reopen the mine tomorrow. On exactly the same terms on which it closed. The same terms that have been good for years. It's your move."

Pete Battle said, "Carstairs, get out of the Middle Ages. The miners have got a union. You deal with it. We've got demands. We demand increased safety, less hours, more money. Slave labor in Sweet Water is over."

Charles tilted his head back and gazed down his pinched nose. "Just how did you get qualified to speak for the miners, Battle?"

Pete leaned forward and said, "I've dug coal, that's how."

"Then talk like a Red Flash miner and Walter's brother, not like a Wobbly."

Pete said, floundering a little, "I'm president of the union, and you better talk to me like it."

"Mr. President of the Union, let me tell you something about what's going on in Sweet Water, since you obviously haven't got the faintest idea."

The colonel said, "I believe I'll take over. Parker, Battle, we've studied it. There's no excuse for this strike. There are no conditions in this mine that the union can improve. They've told you you're going to get more money and better working conditions. Wrong. This mine has the reputation of being maybe the safest and best in West Virginia. That's a credit to the Carstairs'. The Red Flash doubles and triples the safety regulations. There is not one thing the union or anybody else can do to make this mine any safer than it is. There's danger in there, and we all know it. The union isn't going to make it any less dangerous.

"As for money, the Red Flash has the top rates. They pay more than the union mines. If your miners go somewhere else to dig, they're going to get a mighty unpleasant surprise. They'll find out they already had the best where they were."

Carstairs said, "That's right. The best. Caleb, you go ask the miners if they want me to pay the rates the union mines are paying."

Rourke said, "I want to know about your profits."

Carstairs said heatedly, "That's no business of the miners. None of their damn business." Then he forced himself to temperance.. "Caleb, you should know, if anybody does. If we give the miners more, it doesn't come out of my hide. It comes out of the customer's hide. And that's bad. We've got plenty of competition, you better believe it. We're just about too high-priced right now. We raise our prices, we lose business. If we lose business, we dig less coal. If we dig less coal, the miners get less pay. Now you tell me how the Wobblies think they're going to get more pay for the miners. They're not. You want to know how the miners can get more pay? You already know, Caleb. By digging more coal, not less. And the Wobblies can talk themselves blue in the face, but that's the facts of life."

The colonel said, "The facts of life, Parker. There is no such thing as a wage increase without corresponding increase in productivity. Otherwise, all prices go up, and if the miners would look beyond their noses, they'd know they couldn't buy one more bag of flour than they did before they got more money. They're right exactly where they started out, only worse off, because some other mine is selling coal, and this one isn't."

Pete Battle said, "Colonel, you haven't dug coal. I have. I know how much coal a man can dig. I know how hard they work in the Red Flash."

Carstairs said quickly, "Right. Before this I Won't Work bastard came down here, I had the best miners in West Virginia. And they got the most money. We got some new machines coming. We put those in, the miners dig more coal and get more money. That's facts."

Rourke said, "Now I've heard everything. You put in machines, miners get laid off. That's what you want. Less people. More property and machines, and the hell with people. The men are supposed to sit and starve while the machines do the work. Well, you don't get away with it, Carstairs. Not any more."

The colonel said, "Come back to the point. The clear fact is, this strike must end. And now."

Caleb said, "Just a minute. I want the answer. What happens to people that get shoved out of the way by the machines?"

Carstairs said, "If some get laid off, they go do something else for the ones that are now making more money digging coal than they used to."

"Just like that?"

The colonel said, "Just like that. That's what America is all about. That's why we live as well as we do. It's not just theory. That's the way the industrial revolution works."

Caleb Parker gestured with his pipe. "Carstairs, I don't say I buy it, I don't say I don't. Suppose what you say is so. If it is, the union is smart enough to know it. If they understand it, then what kind of game do you say they're playing?"

Rourke said, "You know what he'll say."

"No, I don't. I want to hear it."

Carstairs leaned forward, picked up the letter opener and pointed it at Rourke. "The radicals know what they're doing. They know they don't gain anything for the miners.

The miner doesn't mean a damn thing to John L. Lewis."

The colonel said, "He's arrogant, and insulting, and overbearing with everybody, miners and owners."

Rourke said, "And doesn't kowtow to you, Colonel."

Carstairs said, "Lewis is not on the side of the miners. He uses them. To put money in his own pocket. He'll sell the miners down the river any time it means money to him. He makes business deals with owners. He loans owners money out of the union treasury. He's going to end up one rich man, one rich man, and he doesn't give a damn for the workers. They're cannon fodder for him."

Caleb asked, "And the Wobblies?"

"They want something more than John L. Lewis wants money. They want power. Power for themselves. Mother Jones, Rourke, they get our miners stirred up for the revolution, but they know they're not going to gain anything for the miners, so they've just got one game, one idea. They want the union in. That's it. That's the whole of it. Not for the miners. For themselves, they want the union in at Red Flash. The miners aren't striking for themselves. They're striking for John L. Lewis' pocketbook and the anti-American ideas of the radicals."

Rourke watched Caleb Parker, distressed with the turn. He said, "I want to point out one significant thing. Carstairs talked about his miners. *His* miners. Just like he owned them, lock-stock. Livestock. That's the way he thinks of them. And I'll tell you one thing this union is going to give its members, and that's dignity. No more bowing down to the mighty emperor. No more ass-kissing. From now on this union is giving its members dignity and simple human respect."

The colonel used his cigar the way Carstairs used the letter opener. "Rourke, the Governor of this state knows about dignity in Sweet Water." He started to point the cigar at Caleb, but lowered it in an indication of deference. "Parker, the men and women of Parker County are known for their independence and dignity. Is this union going to add to that dignity? Or are they going to detract from it? They'll take pioneers and put them in a herd, like cattle."

Rourke said, "The colonel proves again that he has brought the owner's militia here to enforce the owner's will." He studied Pete Battle, but only briefly. Pete would not waver. He was completely taken with himself in his

200

grand new eminence. Rourke looked again at Caleb Parker. Caleb sucked his pipe, cogitating. Was Caleb defecting? Rourke said, "Colonel, you're sent here to do Carstairs' dirty work. Do you know what kind of man he is? The Governor sent you down here to bayonet his miners. There's nothing he'd like better. This man, Colonel, is a man who spent the war behind his uncle's desk, making a mess out of everything that was built up here, and when his uncle came back, he had him killed. This is the man that's talking the big talk about the greedy unions."

Charles went white. He contained himself with extreme effort. Finally he said, "You Wobbly bastard, if you were important, I'd get you for libel."

The colonel said, "I warn you, Rourke, it's libel. The official inquest states that Vincent Carstairs was killed by persons unknown."

Rourke said, "Around here, the persons aren't unknown. I challenge you, Carstairs, sue me for libel. I'll say it real plain for you. Vincent was killed by the Baldwin-Felts guard Charles Carstairs brought in here to shoot miners and anybody else he wanted shot. Have I said it loud enough for everybody to hear?"

Caleb Parker said, "You surely sound mighty anxious to get sued, Rourke. Or get tried. Or get something."

"You saying now Charles Carstairs didn't kill Vincent, Caleb?"

The colonel asked sharply, "Parker, did you ever say that he did?"

Caleb sucked at his pipe. He said, "I don't recall ever saying that he did."

"What did you say?"

Caleb studied Charles Carstairs. "I told it at the inquest. Vincent came home with his bride. He sent for me the day after he got home, and I came and told him how bad things had got under Charles, and how all hell was due to bust loose one of these days. So we set out for the mine, but we never got there. We were walking along, and there was a rifle shot from behind us, and I flopped, and I got up after a while, but Vincent was shot dead, through the back."

Rourke said triumphantly, "By Charles Carstairs. And it doesn't take much figuring. He didn't want to get out from behind that high and mighty desk."

201

Charles Carstairs said, "Colonel, I want this man removed from this office."

The colonel said, "Rourke, walk out or get thrown out, your choice."

Caleb Parker said, "Now just one minute, Colonel. Going to be everybody gets his say here."

The colonel locked wills with Caleb. Finally he said, "Rourke, you've got five minutes to talk."

Rourke said, "Good for you, Caleb. If it wasn't clear before, it's got to be clear now. The Army and this colonel are down here to break the strike, pure and simple."

The colonel said, "The militia is here to preserve law and order."

Rourke asked, "And prevent unionization of the Red Flash?"

"If necessary to preserve law and order."

"You got your law and order. For the time being. As long as you're here, Colonel, you've got law and order. Now what do you suppose is going to happen when you take your troops out of here? This union will not be thwarted."

The colonel said, "I call on this room as witness to this threat of riot and violence."

Caleb Parker smiled just a little. "Colonel, I reckon he's finally getting you provoked like he wants."

Rourke said, "We're five hundred strong in Sweet Water. Five hundred good shots."

The colonel said, "Without guns. My men are rounding up all weapons."

"You don't really expect to find them. You never do."

"It doesn't matter. Rourke, we met armed insurrection in Logan. We sent Coxey's army home with their tails between their legs. For all the big talk here, your miners got out of my way when I marched in here. Have no doubts, I will give the order to shoot. I will also give the order to throw you in prison for a much longer time than you are contemplating for your martyr role." He turned to Caleb. "Parker, I don't want to be provoked in this fashion. I'm not here to preserve peace at gun-point. That's no solution for the long run. I'm here to effect some kind of solution. We started out on a good note. Mr. Carstairs has agreed to reinstate you as superintendent. That surely is a step in the right direction."

Caleb said, "Well now, I was superintendent for Charles

Carstairs for quite a spell, and the trouble started while I was there, so I don't see how it changes just because I come back."

"Can you think of a better way to start, than starting all over again at the beginning?"

"I can think of a better way, yes." Again he lighted his pipe, while they waited for him. "I think I am going to have some say of my own, now." He puffed. "When Vincent was here, Colonel, we threw the Wobblies out. In all this town, wasn't a man had any use for the union. As fast as they came, we sent 'em back faster. Rourke can tell you. Then we got Charles. Things changed. And they can't change back. Not with Charles, because he won't ever change."

Charles asked, "Are you saying I should get out?" He was incredulous.

"I am. Somebody else behind that desk, maybe the miners will see it they don't need the union after all."

"You have somebody in mind, Caleb? Yourself?" When Caleb didn't answer, he said to the colonel, "When Vincent was killed, Caleb thought he'd be running the mine. My uncle's wife didn't see it that way."

The colonel asked, "Parker, is your own ambition anywhere at the bottom of this thing?"

Rourke said, "We're getting off the track. Charles Carstairs isn't all the reason for the trouble. The union is bigger than just one man. It's not that personal."

The colonel said, "Maybe it is. Maybe that's the stupidity of all this. Parker, is it a personality clash at the bottom of all this?"

Caleb Parker squared himself away to the mine owner. "Carstairs, you just aren't a man that men take to. Particular not men like you have in Sweet Water. You don't understand us. It's not what you do, it's the way you do it. It's not what you say, it's the way you say it."

Peter Battle said, "In other words, Carstairs, you're a horse's ass." He was proud of himself. Then he subsided uncomfortably before Caleb Parker's annoyed expression. He repeated, almost under his breath, "A horse's ass."

Charles Carstairs sat rigid. He spread his fingers on the desk top. He said in clipped tones, "I tell you now, Parker, you or nobody else sits behind this desk. The Red Flash is mine. I own it. I run it. Nobody else. No Polack tells me what to do. Especially one that hasn't got the guts to keep his own name. No Bolshevik comes in this town and tells me what to do. No John L. Lewis tells me what to do. And no Parker. No high and mighty Parker. I tell you now, this strike is going to end if it takes the militia from now till doomsday. The men are going back to work. Or starve. I have seen fit to let them live in the homes I own, even while they're striking against me. I may reconsider that. My patience is at an end." He clenched his fists on the desk. He struggled with himself. He said, "Caleb, all right, you hit me between the eyes with my shortcomings." He unclenched his fists. "All right, I accept it. By God, I'll tell you, and you should take it in account, it's not easy to follow Roger and Vincent Carstairs. By God, if I don't come off to you sometimes the way I mean to, it isn't for lack of trying. All right, I make you the offer. You come back with a new job. We'll call you general manager. I'll listen to your ideas. You can share the running of the mine with me." He managed a slight smile. "And you can make up for what I lack in personality."

The colonel said, "Gentlemen, I think we're seeing daylight. It's been a personality clash all along, and the radicals have come in like jackals to take advantage of it. I'll speak my piece now. This union, it's an un-American thing. It's not for a town like Sweet Water. These are men down here, not sheep. Right now they're all swept up in the union, probably because somebody's telling them they can't have it, and they're stubborn. Caleb, I think if you were to talk to those men the way we've been talking here, and tell them what we've had to say, they'd see the union for what it is. If you tell them the facts, Caleb, that's the end of the Rourkes down here. I'd say we've reached the solution."

Rourke said, "You'll play hell."

Caleb said, "The leopard can't change his spots. I say maybe Rourke goes. Maybe the union goes. But for sure, Charles Carstairs goes. Sell the mine, Carstairs. You've had your chance to make a go of it. Now it's too late for another chance."

Charles clenched his fists.

Rourke said, "You're wrong, Caleb. It's not Charles Carstairs. It's the conditions in the mine. Getting rid of him solves nothing."

Caleb asked, "You want him to stay? That's interesting."

The colonel asked, "Mr. Carstairs, is this a possible solution? Could you contemplate selling the mine? There are others."

Charles Carstairs said one word. He said, "Never."

The colonel said, "Mr. Carstairs, you know where the Governor stands. He'll enforce the law. Now then, let's conclude this meeting with the idea that some progress is made. Caleb, we'll meet again in three days."

There was no meeting on that third day, because on that day Caleb Parker was laid to rest in the Church of Christ burying ground, three days after the night he was bludgeoned to death by persons unknown.

8

THE NIGHT HE WAS KILLED, Caleb Parker sat at his dinner table asking questions and answering his own questions.

"Will–the union do the miners any good?" He held his finger up at India Parker and at his son James Lee. "Man takes his life in his hands when he goes down in that mine. But ain't one blessed thing Rourke or the rest of the radicals can do about it. For all their big talk, not one blessed thing. And that includes that fancy cathouse madam Mother Jones and that bushy-eyebrowed scutter that talks Shakespeare and still's got the manners of a pig. I'll tell you, it's God and John L. Lewis on one side, and everybody else down below somewhere. How come we kowtow to that scutter?" Caleb shook his white-haired head. "Anybody could see the nose on his face, could see that."

Jim Parker asked, "See what, Papa?"

"The union will do good only for the union leaders. India, you see any reason why Sweet Water men should be fighting on the side of socialists?"

India Parker said, "No reason at all, Mr. Parker."

Caleb Parker glared at her to tell her to mind her own business and not be answering his rhetorical questions. He lit up his pipe to get his thoughts going again.

"So what in Billy Blue Blazes are we doing? Killing

206

good Americans just to get that foreign union in. How come we got so mixed up in this thing we're bashing in heads and shooting each other dead? For Rourke? We're doing just what he wants us to do. How come? Was a time when we knew him. An anarchist. A no-good radical that we run out of town. Then how come this? What happened to everybody. How come the best town in West Virginia to go sour?"

Young James Lee Parker, nine years old, couldn't stand not putting in his two cents. "The men got no use for Charles, Papa."

Caleb Parker made out that he didn't hear his son, but the corners of his mouth moved as though he were going to smile, and he said, "So it comes down to the simple fact the miners got no use for Charles Carstairs, that's it, that's the whole of it. The miners and me got no use for him. So that's it. Charles goes, and the union goes, too, I've made my decision."

At ten minutes to eight Caleb set out up the hollow to meet Rourke and Pete Battle at Red Flash Two. James Lee Parker went out his bedroom window and down over the back porch and after his father.

Caleb emerged from the dark to where Red Flash Two was lighted up. A man came out of the dark behind him, struck him over the head with an axe handle, and ran back into the dark. Jim Parker came running. His father lay in the coal dust, blood trickling out of his mouth and spurting out of his ear.

Mine guards and militiamen came running. Four of the militiamen cut out into the darkness after the assailant. One of the mine guards shouted, "It's Caleb!"

Jim Parker stood looking down at his father, lying all sprawled out, with the blood gushing out of his ear and trickling out of his mouth, his face turning green in the light from Red Flash Two. Jim picked up a hunk of coal, threw it hard and hit the nearest guard in the chest. The guard didn't duck or flinch. One of the other guards said, "That's Caleb's boy."

Jim Parker picked up another hunk of coal. Then he didn't feel like throwing it, because he couldn't figure out what good it was going to do Caleb, and it was as though nobody had smashed in his papa's skull so that he could be mad at them, but that just *things* had done it, not people.

Pete Battle came running, and Rourke.

The mine guard said, "Take the boy home, Battle. We'll take care of Caleb."

On the night of the funeral, the miners and the pioneers from Sweet Water and Murder Creek came for revenge, five hundred strong. They advanced, in their hot rage, on the Red Flash, red bandanas of the union movement on their necks, armed with every weapon they could lay their hands on.

The militiamen came lickety-split from the tents, the bugle blowing its head off. The miners and militia ran side by side to the mine office. Then they formed up, not forty feet apart, five hundred red necks, and the battalion of militia.

The colonel yelled out, "Fix bayonets!"

The militiamen took the bayonets from their scabbards and fixed them on their Springfield rifles. The militiamen looked at the miners, and then down at their own bayonets, and they licked their lips nervously. The militiamen hoped that no one would start the battle, and the miners just waited for something to start it. One spark, one final step, and half a battalion of West Virginia National Guard would be dead, and the male population of Sweet Water, West Virginia, wiped off the earth. It was time for one small Armageddon.

Pete Battle stepped into the no man's land and yelled out, "Where are you, Carstairs? Hiding behind your desk?"

Charles Carstairs stepped immediately out into the light. In his right hand he held a short .38 revolver. He said, "I'm right here, Dankowski."

The veins in Pete Battle's forehead popped out. "My name is Battle, Carstairs."

Carstairs said, "You ought to be proud to be a Dankowski. Casimar Dankowski set every record for digging coal. Casimar Dankowski bought himself the gray house." He wasn't talking to Pete Battle. He was making a speech to the miners.

Pete yelled, "We come to get you, Carstairs. For killing Caleb."

Carstairs didn't turn a hair. His pinched nose was up in the air. He said, loud enough for everyone to hear in the strange quiet there was, "You haven't got the guts. Not one of you. You lost your guts. You lost your pioneer guts the minute you joined this radical union. I'll tell you one more time. This is my mine, and no anarchist bastards are going to tell me how to run it. Now get off my property."

The colonel stepped out front and said loudly, "All you miners, disperse. Break it up. Go home before more men are killed."

Wes Culpepper raised his rifle and pointed it square at Carstairs. Young Dvorak sighted down on the colonel. Neither Carstairs nor the colonel flinched.

The colonel shouted, "Battalion! Two paces forward! March!"

The militia took two steps toward the miners, the bayonets thrust out front. All of the miners raised their guns.

The colonel shouted, calmly, with just a little edge in his voice, "You miners, look right and left of you. On each flank, there behind the sandbags, those are Browning machine guns, manned by experts. They're sighted on you now. The squads with them are armed with hand grenades, and you're within their range. If one shot is fired, there will be no live miners left in Sweet Water. You can't fight machine guns and grenades. I order you, in the name of the Governor of West Virginia and of the President of the United States, to disperse forthwith and return to your homes."

Rourke came boldly out front. "These soldiers will never fire on fellow West Virginians. Let's get Carstairs!"

The colonel raised his arm to give the order to commence fire. It was time for the death of Sweet Water.

James Lee Parker ran from the dark out into no man's land. Every man froze.

The colonel shouted, "Get this boy out of here!"

Jim Parker called out, "Mr. Carstairs, did you kill Caleb? Did you have him killed?"

Charles was quiet a long time. He walked forward and said, so softly that only those nearest could hear, "Jim, I swear to God, not me, not anybody under my orders killed Caleb. Nobody from Sweet Water would want Caleb dead. Or Vincent, either one."

Rourke said, "You're not from Sweet Water, Carstairs."

Carstairs said, "I'm trying to be. You're not from Sweet Water, Rourke. Are you trying to be? Or would you rather tell this boy who killed his father?"

The colonel said, "Get the boy out of there."

Charles Carstairs took the hand of James Lee Parker.

He said, "I'll take you home, Jim." And then he said to the colonel, loud enough that everyone could hear, "Colonel, it's ended. We accept the union. There will be no wage increases, there will be no changes in standards. But we accept the union."

A sort of great sigh went out into the night.

But Pete Battle stepped closer and said, "No matter what, Carstairs, it's got to be you and me. You're going to fight me now, or admit you're a coward and a bushwhacker."

Carstairs said, "Dankowski, we didn't want Caleb dead. We didn't do it. Why don't you ask Rourke who did it?"

Pete said, "You're not talking to a nine-year-old boy now. You're talking to me. You fight."

Then Carstairs said, "I'll fight you. We'll even it up. We'll each have a gun and start from opposite ends of town. Does that suit you?" Pete Battle paled in the light from the Red Flash poles. Quickly he turned and went to his miners, and he grinned, and he shouted, "I knew the bastard would back down!"

Sweet Water lived.

The Sweet Water of Vincent Carstairs and Casimar Dankowski and Caleb Parker died. But the Sweet Water of Pete Battle and Rourke lived. Charles Carstairs acceded. In the moment that was the last moment, the man who could not accede, did accede. He acceded to a nine-year-old boy, Caleb Parker's boy, who was the brave embodiment of Sweet Water, who was the hope, if hope there was, of Sweet Water. Carstairs acceded to unionization of his mine, and though he laid down terms of his own, and though he kept his Baldwin-Felts guards to preserve law and order, the United Mine Workers came officially into the Red Flash Mines, and Vincent Carstairs' Sweet Water died.

Peter Battle headed that union, dancing on the puppet strings in Rourke's hands, but loud and proud in his own union militancy. He was a brave tiger, this union president, this father of David Battle, except at night when he was awakened by the whistles of the trains off beyond the mountains and lay frightened beside his wife in the dark, listening for assassins.

This was Peter Dankowski Battle.

This was the genesis of David Battle.

210

BOOK

IV

1

ROURKE GOT STABBED to death by Green Billy in Shawnee. It was just a joke when Rourke bought an hour of the Gypsy's time on her wedding morning, but Green Billy didn't see the humor of it, and slammed eight inches of hunting knife fifteen times in Rourke's back.

Green Billy was in love. He had met the dark Hunky girl in Steubenville on the very day that she embarked on her professional career. He was her first customer. He brought her home to Shawnee, dressed her, including golden earrings, like a Gypsy dancer, set a charge of ten dollars, and made her the star of his brothel. The Gypsy and her business both flourished, and Green Billy ate his heart out. In a burst of passion and jealousy he proposed marriage. The Hunky from Steubenville was pleased to accept with the provision that she be inaugurated madam as well as wife.

Rourke's sense of humor was struck. He offered the Gypsy twenty-five dollars. For twenty-five dollars the Gypsy would stand on her head. Therefore, while she was in her stall ostensibly dressing for the ceremony of holy matrimony, she was in fact laboring with all pride to perform a twenty-five-dollar trick. Of course, Rourke's friends were in on the joke, or it wouldn't have been much of a joke. In Clark's Department Store, Jim Parker overheard Pete Battle tell Wes Culpepper the hilarious goings-on. Jim consulted with India and then went to tell Green Billy about it. Green Billy listened without change of expression, continued to pull on his fancy pants as though he had all day, took himself quietly to the Gypsy's compartment above the saloon, and without so much as a howdy-do rammed his knife into Rourke's back, then plunged it home again and again, and the Gypsy couldn't get out from under the dead weight that collapsed on her; and while the blood gushed over her, she screamed bloody murder, and nineteen-year-old Jim Parker, from the doorway, said almost sonorously, "The wages of sin is death." He made his way down the hallway, down the rickety stairs to the street, the revenge at long last accomplished.

Green Billy ordered his bride to wash the worst of the gore from herself and to hurry into her wedding gown while there was still time. Then he took her below to the saloon and married her, and that was when the sheriff arrested him and took him off. They electrocuted Green Billy three months later, partly because a fight over a prostitute did not constitute sufficient crime-of-passion grounds, partly because he had been high-handed in his bribery dealings with the law-enforcement officers, but principally because West Virginia was so delighted with its electric chair that the juries and judges seized every reasonable opportunity to verify again and again that electricity did kill people.

This was the third time that Jim Parker had been in on a dramatic event that changed the course of Sweet Water. As a boy, he had played a remarkably pertinent role in the unfolding dramas that changed Sweet Water from a Carstairs principality into a United Mine Workers thralldom. Vincent Carstairs had listened to him and found in a child's candor the courage to do what he wanted to do, and because Vincent went off to find a warm girl, his brave Sweet Water disappeared from the face of the earth. Charles Carstairs had called off a war because Jim Parker was the embodiment of the futility of it all. To close the ring, Jim was the messenger who brought death to Rourke, the man who had brought the union to Sweet Water. It was revenge on the revenger.

Sweet Water always did treat Jim Parker as something extra special, even for a Parker. Jim always did have unusual quantities of forthrightness, or confidence, or maturity, or self-importance, or whatever the qualities were that set a future leader apart. When he went off to the University of West Virginia at Morgantown, he became an authentic hero. The coal miners took the deepest personal pride in the scholastic accomplishments of this first college man in the history of the town. Not even Vincent, born and raised in the white house, escaped the mines long enough for this much education. Not even Davis Parker, brother of Caleb, uncle of James Lee, mighty orator, Church of Christ spellbinder, had formal education. The miners of Sweet Water, and their wives and children, themselves well read and well informed on their own time, gave an unstinting admiration and deference to a genuine scholar. Morgantown! They were more than deferential, they were almost reverential. Jim Parker was a college man and could say no wrong. Not that any miner went so far as to change his way of thinking because of what Jim had to say, but he could say no wrong.

By the time he was twenty-one he was accustomed to the role of savant. In all the town, only the cousins, impious Joe Foley and pious David Battle, resisted Jim's all-encompassing wisdom, and even they deferred to him enough so that he never did learn that with all the kowtowing that came to him, with all the rapt attention to his pontifications, with all the genuine admiration for his accomplishments, he persuaded no one. There was now a higher authority than pure reason in Sweet Water. There was the union.

In June, 1932, Jim was graduated from Morgantown. He was not yet quite ready for the automotive industry. First would come Massachusetts Institute of Technology. Jim Parker knew exactly where he was going. He had a timetable. He knew that he was going to be president of National Motors. He knew this. While other young men in Sweet Water wondered if they could rise to be foreman in the dying Red Flash, Jim Parker knew that he would get to Detroit and one day be president of one of the ten largest corporations in the world.

2

JIM PARKER sat himself in the wooden-slatted swing hanging on rusting chains on the porch that ran the entire width and around one corner of the Parker house. The fifteen-year-old cousins, Joe Foley and David Battle, perched on the porch rail with their muscular rumps pointing down the hillside to the deep-green Kanawha. Jim liked the cousins, big Joe Foley and small David Battle. He was pleased that they had come to see him on his first day home from Morgantown. He didn't suspect the malice-aforethought of their call. They had come, as a matter of fact, hoping to cadge a ride in the green Franklin parked precariously in the steep driveway, but Jim Parker, full of himself, blissfully assumed they had come to sit at his feet and drink up his wisdom.

Pro-American, anti-union James Lee Parker was particularly pleased to get in his grasp the son of the devil. David Battle had been born with the original sin of unionism, and James Parker was the man to exorcise and proselytize. He settled down in the swing, undoubting, bold, just a little condescending, ready to make the most of the golden opportunity to confound Pete Battle's son.

It took Jim only three minutes to work the conversation round to where he wanted it. It took him the ensuing ten minutes to divest himself, in monologue, of a full spate of opening remarks filled with righteousness, vituperation and abiding conviction. Having worked himself into a proper fervor, he rose from the swing, walked to the rail, and waved his arm dramatically at the company homes moldering beneath them on the barren flat land beside the river. His voice was the Voice that thundered down on Eden. "There, Davey, is the desolation they brought to Sweet Water. Not social justice. Desolation. Not dignity to the miner. Desolation. Look at it. Take a good look. Those houses used to be painted spanking-red every three years. Do you know how long it's been since they've been painted? Twelve years. Do you know how long the union's been in Sweet Water? Twelve years. Take a good look, Davey."

Jim reared back and pointed his avenging finger down to the silent tipple—huge, dusty, black against the river and the sky. "The tipple was *never* quiet on a weekday. That, Davey, is what the union brought here."

He waved his arm next door to the Carstairs house, where Harold Scott now lived, the new owner come down from Wheeling. "You should have known Vincent, Davey. You should have known Sweet Water when Vincent was here, and Caleb, and when Uncle Davis first got his pulpit. And I'll tell you the difference. This town was hard, but it wasn't *mean,* like it is now. And all the miners talked like Akron had pearly gates, but that was just blowing off steam, and the Snakes left in droves out of Coalburg and Chelyan and Logan, but for all the talk, nobody left Sweet Water, because they liked this town, that was the difference. And I'll tell you why. Because Vincent didn't *own* the Red Flash, he *was* the Red Flash, and so was everybody else the Red Flash—the Parkers, the Dankowskis, the Dvoraks, the Foleys, the Culpeppers—everybody part of it, and the difference now is the Red Flash is the enemy of the miners, and that's what the union did to this town, and this town is gone."

David Battle looked as though he might smile. "Well, Jim, as for not painting the houses, some might say Charles Carstairs was a cheapskate, and so is Mr. Scott. And as for being mean, the company isn't exactly any more friendly to the union than the union is to the company. And as for not digging as much coal, there's the depression and the Wall Street guys, and mainly, you can't blame the union for being down to strip mining. Good luck's just moved up the hollers to new coal."

Jim Parker raised his arm like Jehovah. "Does the hand of God make itself manifest? I do know this town did what was not right, and it has suffered ever since. Do you want to say it's just coincidence? I think it's more."

Joe Foley burst out, "Oh, I like your style, Jim! You should talk to Father Hannigan about that. You'd give that champeen penance-giver a happy month of Sundays thinking about this town paying for its sins."

Jim frowned. His deadly earnest, gratuitous, well-meant offering of truth wasn't going well at all. He was preaching. He wasn't asking for comment, let alone opposition. He wasn't sure which should affront him more, the patient, respectful resistance of David Battle, or the impious levity of the irrepressible Joe Foley.

Jim said, "If I were you two, I'd be paying some serious mind to what I'm saying. You've got a long time ahead of you in this town, and you've got to make up your mind whether you're going to live it like Americans or Bolsheviks."

Without warning, Joe tumbled backward off the rail. Jim shouted, "Look out!" But Joe flipped and landed on his feet. He climbed back up, grinning, saying, "You like to scared me outen my pants, Jim, with that Bolshevik talk."

David hadn't moved. He'd seen Joe in action before. He asked with perfect equanimity and no apparent resentment in his voice, "Jim, you saying Papa is a Bolshevik?"

"I say it. Bolshevik. That's what the union is, and anybody connected with it."

"Papa? John L. Lewis?"

"Bolsheviks. They think like Bolsheviks, they talk like Bolsheviks, they're Bolsheviks, Q.E.D."

"Well, Jim, some would say they talked union talk."

Jim Parker's voice raised as he came in for the kill. "Union talk? Now I want you to tell me the difference between union talk and Bolshevik talk. You can't, because there isn't any difference. It's word for word. And it doesn't make any difference if it's Karl Marx, or Mother Jones, or Rourke saying it, or Pete Battle. Davey, you're going to get your eyes opened. I want you to read Karl Marx and pretend it's Rourke or Pete saying it. You're going to get the shock of your life, because it's word for word, and the unions of this country share the revenge philosophy of the Bolsheviks."

There was silence. Jim was sure he'd scored.

He had. David was impressed. He didn't know for sure who Karl Marx was, but he was impressed. He said earnestly, "Jim, could be it makes sense. I been hearing things one way, that's for sure. Could even be that the truth's been going its own path with everybody off one side or the other. That could be, and I'll stack what you got to say up against what Papa has got to say."

Jim asked himself, "Who is this fifteen-year-old kid to offer me tolerance?" Then he forced patience and a smile. It was good that David Battle was a worthy adversary, because it would be a worthy conquest. Besides, there was that earnest, guileless look on the bright face. It was no wonder that everybody in Sweet Water was inordinately fond of David Battle. Jim would accept this charge. He would do for David Battle the things that needed doing. Yes, he would be David Battle's best friend.

Joe Foley stood up on the porch rail. He said, "Try this, Davey." He dove off the rail headfirst, flipped, and landed gracefully on his feet, his arms wide, his knees bent. David followed him. He hit hard and went skidding. He was hurt, but he jumped up quickly. He joined his big cousin, and the two of them stared longingly at the car Jim Parker had built for himself in Morgantown out of scrap parts.

Jim followed the look. He smiled more broadly. The example of his own success, that would be his best argument. He said, "Only capitalists get to ride in the Parker Special Franklin Air-Cooled. Come on, I'll run you down to Chelyan and back."

The cousins shouted. They boiled into the car.

It was on the ride to Chelyan that Jim learned that Walter Dankowski, first son of Casimar, had, within the week, replaced Wilbur Parker as superintendent of the Red Flash mines. He was thunderstruck. It took all his budding discipline to keep a stoic face. A Dankowski the superintendent of the Red Flash? A Dankowski, where Parkers had always reigned! Unthinkable! A hundred questions were on the tip of his tongue. He bit them off. They'd humiliate him before these fifteen-year-old non-Parkers.

Joe Foley said with high-spirited malice, "Reckon

219

you'll be moving outen the white house any day now, and Walter moving his statue of St. Joseph in."

Jim's voice was icy. "The white house belongs to Mama as long as she's alive. That's the terms of the pension."

Joe said, "Then Walter better forget it. He'll never outlive India, if he lives to two hundred."

The youngest Parker of Sweet Water didn't hear. He was lost in his appalled thoughts. The great aplomb that sustained him was shaken, and he was uncomprehending. How could it be? What could the Lord God Jehovah be thinking of, to permit this sacrilege in the Sweet Water of Caleb Parker, and Davis Parker, and Wilbur Parker, and James Lee Parker, and all the Parkers before them who had brought God, and rectitude, and stability, and leadership, and Americanism to the wilderness! But James Lee Parker was a fighter. When he'd arrived at Morgantown, the young men from Wheeling had asked him if he lived in a Shawnee teepee in Parker County, but at the end of the four years, the number-one student was a Parker, and the men from Wheeling knew Parker County. Was Sweet Water gone? Had it given up its coal-dust soul, irrevocably, to Hunkies and union tyranny? So be it. Jim Parker's future was not here. His future was in Detroit. In Detroit they would ask him if the girls wore shoes in Parker County. But in his time in Detroit, Detroit would become Parker County. He would take David Battle along with him, this bright, earnest young man, and show him the truth, and let him partake of a new Sweet Water of the Parkers.

3

JOE FOLEY? Jim Parker wrote off Joe Foley as a buffoon. That was a mistake. Joe Foley was an uncomplicated young man of great complications.

Late in the afternoon, the cousins pushed the Franklin off the Charleston Road back into the mouth of the driveway. Jim Parker said from the driver's seat, "Leave it here. I'll get some gas from the Red Flash in the morning."

Joe Foley said, "Thought for a minute you was going to have us push you to Huntington."

The cousins raced up the hill. Jim followed, doing his best not to breathe heavily. Joe Foley picked up an egg-sized rock and in a burst of enthusiasm shied it all the way down the hill, across the Charleston Road, across the railroad tracks, almost to the Kanawha.

Jim Parker said, "I wouldn't believe that unless I'd seen it."

David Battle said, "He can throw a football that far."

Joe Foley said, "I can throw a cow turd that far." He swooped his hand and picked a chickweed. He stuck the stalk between his teeth and chewed, the tassel flicking. "I wonder if you throw a cow pie like a discus." He lounged on the concrete steps to the porch.

221

David said, "He'll be first-string halfback right off, and for four years."

Jim said, "And when he gets to college, he'll be better than Red Grange and Jim Thorpe put together."

David said, "You bet."

Joe said airily, "I do believe that's true."

Jim asked, "And your Red Flash team is going to be the best ever?"

"I do believe it will."

"You got to go some, Joe. That first one, that was great. They haven't had anything like it since."

David said, "There's going to be a coach. I mean a regular coach."

"I wasn't talking about the coach. I was talking about that first team, those guys had muscles on their muscles. They didn't even have uniforms the first three games, just extra sweaters, and they wiped up everybody. I got to admit, Davey, your daddy was the best. The best ballplayer this town ever had."

David said solemnly, "He's the best."

Joe Foley snorted. He said, "Mr. Big Hero."

Jim jerked his head at the tone. "What's that supposed to mean? I thought you had the sun rising and setting on your uncle."

"Maybe that was some other year."

David said, "Joe and Papa are on the outs. Don't pay him too much mind."

Jim said, "I mean, I had the impression you were on the same side of things as Davey and Pete. Isn't that how it is?"

"You mean does the union and all that crap make me no never mind? It don't. But when it gets to Mr. Big Crap and his big talk, he's got another think coming, he thinks I swaller it." Coming off Joe Foley's Irish tongue, the words were not entirely harsh. Now he grinned before he said, "Only swallering I do, I been vomiting so much listening to Mr. Big Hero, I got to swaller quick when that little ole round, hard knot gets in my mouth, on account that's my A-hole on the way up." Then he said with sudden, real vehemence, "Ain't Mr. Big gets me so goddam het up. It's Davey gobbling up that crap like he was a big-mouth fish. He's so goddam gullible, it makes you vomit. And he's just so plain stupid he don't know when his old man ain't got no use for him and ain't never going to get no use for him. Mr. Big Hero craps all over him, and

222

he comes back just begging to get crapped on again. Oh, boy, is he stupid."

David wanted to protest. But he didn't know quite what to say, so he said nothing. He looked off to the Kanawha, his bright face as troubled as ever it could get.

Jim Parker said severely, "Joc, I suggest you watch your language." But his curiosity overcame his sensibilities. He was a true son of India Missouri, the champion gossip. "What docs Pete brag about? Maybe I can set the record straight. Of course I got no wish to tear a man down in front of his own son." The young man who had already proved he had no such compunctions smiled in appreciation of his own sanctimonious lie.

Joe Foley said, "Okay, the night your daddy got his skull bashed in, what did Mr. Big do that night?"

Jim drew in a long, slow breath. "What does he say he did?"

"Did he fight?"

"There wasn't any fight. There wasn't anything to fight. The guy that did it came out of the dark and hit Papa over the head, and he ran back in the dark, and that's the last anybody saw of him."

"He said he fought the guy that did it, and the guy hit him with the axe handle and got away."

"Well, I'm afraid his memory is a little bit faulty there."

Joc said, "Har-de-har-har-har. You listening, Davey? And he dared Charles Carstairs to a fist fight, and he got dared back to a gun fight, and he chickened out, right?"

"That's it."

"I can take him."

"Take Pete? In a fight, Joe? I'm not sure I'd go that far. Man that would say Pete isn't the best in town, I don't think I'd want to be on that man's side. You better wait a few years before you try it."

"I can take him."

David said, "Okay, that's enough."

Jim said, "Of course, Joe's sticking up for you, Davey, same as me and your other friends who don't like to see you getting the short end of the stick. Tell me something, is it because you're too little for football, is that why your dad has it in for you?" David didn't answer. "I hear that. India says he scarce talks to you. That really true?"

Joe said, "There's one thing you missed on, Jim. Davey's

going to be a ballplayer, you better believe it, and I mean a ballplayer."

Jim ran his skeptical eye up and down David Battle's small frame.

Reading his mind, Joe said, "That's only Mr. Big's idea. Just because Davey ain't size enough to be a horse in the line. But him and me, we been banging around, and that little knocker would run hisself right through a brick wall and make it, Ellen or me ast him. And he's going to be just one helluva ballplayer, we have to kill him."

"Who, Ellen and you?"

"Sure, me and Ellen."

"Well, that makes sense, Ellen and her spunk, wanting Davey to be a football player. Hope you got her fight, Davey. You sure are the spit of her."

Joe said, "Ain't he jist? If he was a girl, I'd of had him up in the hills by now, and I ain't sure I won't anyhow, one of these days."

Jim said, "Knock off that kind of talk around me, Joe."

Joe said, "Oh, for Pete's sake." Then he said, "Anyhow, Mr. Big Crap says you can't make a silk purse outen a sow's ear. Then Ellen says Davey ain't any bigger than a sow's ear but he's got the guts of the whole pig, and he'll be a ballplayer."

"I trust she said it more elegantly."

Joe's smile looked sober. "Well, I reckon she couldn't be anything but elegant if she tried." The smile left completely. "If he says one more time that Davey ain't his, he's Vincent's, that's it."

David said sharply, "You shut up, Joe, you hear?"

Jim was alive with anticipation. "Well, Davey, Sweet Water isn't exactly Charleston. When a man talks like Pete talks, ain't nobody in this coal town doesn't know about it. Is that his latest? Davey is Vincent's?" Then he realized the thing had gone too far, and he said, "You're right, of course, Davey. Joe and me owe you an apology. But you should know one thing. Nobody in this town would ever think anything wrong about Ellen, that's for sure. As for you, Joe, a man that's going to be star of the football team, he should be an example to the rest. It's tough deeds, not dirty talk, that makes leaders of men."

David said, "Limited vocabulary. Father Hannigan says."

Jim said, "Here's some more sound advice for both

224

of you, from somebody who knows. Don't either of you get so filled up with football you forget the books. Just remember that."

Joe said, "Now, Jim, didn't you know I get all A's in school? I got eyes like a hawk, and I get the same grades as Davey, exact."

"I trust you don't really copy another man's work. Outside the moral wrong involved, there's the practical consideration that you don't really learn anything when you copy another man's work."

Joe said, smiling pleasantly, "Lor-dee, Jim, you so full of righteousness, just got to overflow all over me. I thank you kindly, Jim, I surely do, for those little sermons."

James Lee Parker said, "You show me proper respect, young fellow."

Joe Foley refused to be abashed. His temper was rising. "Reckon preaching comes natural to you, Jim. I think you oughter join St. Mary's, then sin wouldn't upset you so much. You Church of Christers, you can't lie, and steal, and commit adultery, and all those good things, like us. That's why we got Confession. You Protestants get stuck with your sins. You join up with us, Jim, Father Hannigan will scrape your bottom once a week and get it all fresh and ready for new barnacles. Salvation every Saturday in Hannigan's little black cubbyhole, and you don't have to take sin so serious."

Jim opened his mouth but Joe refused to be interrupted. He said, "How do sins stack up with you, Jim? How high *is* dirty talk? High as cards? High as making the Sign of the Cross? Now you take Davey, it's sex curls his toes. Look at his feet. You can see his toes curling right now inside his shoes, just mention sex. With me, I think being stupid is the worstest sin. And I think people are being stupidest when they think they're being smartest about what sin is and what sin ain't."

Jim Parker said, "I consider you impertinent, and I resent it. I won't have any more of it."

"Now you been giving me add-monishing, Pastor Parker, and maybe I got my own sermon to say. Both you holy guys, you all the time ready to jump on me, I just say something everyday like anybody else in this coal town says. You two guys get so you act like you had some God-give right to tell me I'm something worsen you are. Now, I just don't happen to think God opened hisself up outen

225

the sky to either one of you and had any such conversation about who knows what, and who doesn't. So as of right now, I want you to know I got the feeling my ideas on things might be just about as good as yours, or Pastor Davis, or Hannigan, or anybody else. Anyhow, save your breath. You're farting against the wind, you think you can preach your kind of talk into a coal town. You ever stop to think maybe the rest is right, and you wrong? Anyhow, talk out loud never hurt anybody that wasn't looking to get hurt. Frigging. Look at your pissy-ant faces when I say frigging. Like saying it was going to bite you. Now I say maybe it's when you hidey-hole think about sex and don't do it and are scared shootless even to talk about it, it gets dirty. Me, I'm for Swaney Wood."

He held up his middle finger obscenely.

"Why don't you holy bastards relax? Once in awhile relax? And that goes for that Gerry, too. Why don't you all three get yourselves set up for beatification? Do you know what that is, Jim? That's when the Church makes you official saints. Boy, you're the three sure is qualified, and all they have to do is ask you, you'll tell them."

Jim Parker said, "I won't have it. I don't care if I'm the only one in Sweet Water that doesn't like dirty talk, I won't have it. Maybe you just better go home, Joe. I've heard enough out of you."

Joe Foley rose and stretched elaborately. He waited for reassurance from David. None came. Joe was suddenly crushed. How could he leave without his cousin? He'd be lost.

Jim said, pointedly ignoring Joe, "Davey, how old's Gerry now? Seventeen?"

David said, "Eighteen, Jim." His eyes were on his cousin's back.

Jim said, "Maybe I'll come over and see her while I'm home."

Joe said meanly, "You got to go to Confession first. And you don't so much as touch her tippy toe with yourn. I guarntee, Davey's one hillbilly ain't banged his sister."

David said, "Joe, I let lots go by. I don't let that go by."

Joe said cheerfully, "Okay, I take it back. You do bang her." He walked a few steps down the hill. He turned and said, "Reckon I'll go down and write piss a few hundred times on the tipple."

David watched his friend down the hill.

Jim said, "Well, now what will we talk about?"

David stood up. He said, "Well, Joe is Joe, Jim, and you got to take it in account. Reckon I'll go along with him," and he left.

Jim's mother appeared in the doorway. Her sixty-year-old face, with a thousand lines, bore grim glee. "Jim, that boy sure talks awful."

"Didn't know you were listening, Mama."

"You were talking right outside the window, Jim." The dark eyes sparkled. "What do you make of it between Joe and Ellen?"

Jim was startled. "Joe and Ellen?"

"You saw him. You heard him."

"About what, Mama?"

"Joe and Ellen," she whispered, hissing. "Joe and Ellen, and him wanting to fight Pete. Why don't you invite those boys over here for supper tomorrow, and you keep your eyes and ears open."

"I'll do that, Mama. You, too." He meant it to be sarcastic. It didn't come off that way.

4

Some of the Dankowski clan gathered in the evening on the porch of Casimar's gray house.

David said, "Uncle Walter, who killed Caleb?"

Walter Dankowski, the superintendent of the mines, said, "Davey, nobody knows."

"But who do you think?"

Pete Battle said, "What kind of stupid question is that? Why ask him? He's not going to tell you."

"Well, I just wanted to know what he'd say, Papa."

"Well, don't be stupid."

David fell silent, burning to know.

Stella Dankowski said, "A boy has a need to question things, Peter. You were the same way."

Pete Battle said, "I wasn't stupid."

Walter Dankowski asked his brother, "Who did kill Caleb, Pete?"

"The same one that killed Vincent, and you know it, even if you are the high muckety-muck now and can't say it."

Walter asked, "Davey, Joe, who do you think?"

Joe Foley said, "You didn't tell me different, I'd got to say old Pinch Nose."

"Which goes to show people's looks count for what people think about them."

Joe said, "Hannigan told me people's sins showed on their faces. I told him I hoped I'd be plumb ugly by the time I was sixteen."

Walter said, "I'll tell you about Charles Carstairs. You could say a lot against him, but he sure had guts. When they carted him out of the white house, I bet he didn't weigh eighty pound, but he was still fighting."

Joe asked, "What's cancer, Walter?"

"Something that eats your insides up."

"I mean, what is it?"

"Guess people don't rightly know."

"Well, is it like, you know, the kind of thing you get when you're up to no good? Excuse me, Mrs. Dankowski. But is that how come people hush up about it?"

"Not that kind of disease, I don't think."

Pete Battle said, "I thought the mine superintendent knew everything."

Walter said, "Only union leaders know everything."

David said, "Jim Parker says it was Rourke had Caleb killed, and before him Vincent."

Pete said, "I'll tell it once, and you listen. Carstairs had his uncle bushwhacked so he could keep the mine and the white house. And he killed Caleb on account he told the Pinkertons to kill off all the union leaders."

"Jim says his papa had quit the union before he got killed."

"Well, that just shows how stupid he is. Everybody knows Caleb was the first president of the union, right before I got elected. Just don't you be stupid."

Walter puffed on his pipe. He swung around in the rocking chair and put his feet up on the porch rail. He said with mild-toned malice, "In the first place, Davey, if your daddy got elected, it wasn't so anybody could notice. He got picked by Rourke, and that was that. And Jim's right, he should know. Caleb quit the union and was going to run both the union and Charles out of town, and Rourke couldn't see neither one happening."

David said, "Well, that just doesn't make sense, does it, Uncle Walter? The miners wanted to get rid of Charles."

"The miners got no use for Charles, but Rourke did. Charles was the excuse for the union. No Charles, no union. Okay?"

David shook his head slowly. "I don't know. Hard to think of a union man doing the killing. But I guess if you

229

can think of a company man doing it, you can think of a union man doing it."

Walter said placidly, "Well, nobody will ever know for sure. They had the *in*-quest, and everybody said what they knew, and nobody knew nothing, and that's the way it always was. It was a war. I'll tell you, Davey, don't you ever get the idea it wasn't a war. More people got killed than this country will ever know about. But nobody ever knew who shot who, or bashed whose head in, and wasn't ever a killer got caught. And between the cancer and Green Billy, Carstairs and Rourke are dead, and the dead, I reckon, will just have to bury the dead."

Pete Battle said, "That's what I'd expect out of you."

Joe asked, "How come they called him Green Billy?"

Ellen Foley said, "Because he was green."

Joe said, "Hoo ha! Did they call Grandpa Foley Red Mike?"

Ellen said, "Be respectful, Joe."

Joe grinned. "You got to add-mit, there's plenty Injuns ain't as red as Mike. His nose looks like a map, those purple things in it."

Stella said, "For shame, Joseph!"

Kathleen, the older Battle girl, said, "Mama, right in the middle of a family fight seems a good time to tell it. I'm going to get married."

Pete Battle pointed his big finger at Kathleen. He said, "You tell that no good sonofabitch he sets one foot around here, I'll show him who's going to get married."

Casimar Dankowski said, "Girl, you tell that no-good bum he don't move in here with you."

Kathleen said, "Papa, Bernie's going to get a job. We're going to Akron and work at Goodyear or Firestone, one."

Ellen Foley said, "We'll get the banns published if you're set, honey. But you better think about it."

"Mama, I'm eighteen, same as you."

Pete Battle asked sharply, "You got to get married, Kathleen?"

Gerry, the beautiful younger sister, rose from the porch steps and walked swiftly into the house.

Pete asked, "What's eating her?"

Stella said, "Peter, that was not a good thing to ask Kathleen."

Pete said, "I'm going to want to talk to you, Kathleen. If you got yourself in trouble, I'll fix you good."

Kathleen rose and smoothed her dress. "I'll tell you one thing, I don't *have* to get married. And I'll tell you another thing, I'm eighteen, and you or Mama don't tell me what to do. I'm going to marry Bernie, and you can like it or lump it." She walked down the front steps, swishing. She turned and smiled at Joe Foley. "Right, Joe?"

Joe grinned and said, "I get the pick of my kin to marry, I pick you, Kathy." He watched approvingly as the girl swung on down the hill and disappeared toward town.

Ellen Foley watched her daughter go. Kathleen was the bad seed, Pete's, she had to be. David and Gerry, they were her children.

Joe Foley said to the silent group, "Now what'll we fight about?"

Pete Battle said, "You mind your own business."

David said, "Uncle Walter, I've got to know, you and some other people that got no use for the union, you can make some arguments for the way you look at it . . ."

Pete Battle said, "They got no use for the union because John L. Lewis and me makes them give the miners what they got coming, period."

"But what I want to know is, the miners joined up, Uncle Walter, and they aren't all that dumb, so they got to have a good reason, and what is it?"

Walter said, "Reason? Men don't have to have reasons for things."

David said, "Well, that's not much of an answer. Excuse me, Uncle Walter, but it's not."

"No, it's not. I don't know why they did it. I sure have thought about it lots. Maybe the war, Davey. The ones that stayed home and didn't do any of the fighting, seemed like they had to get their turn. And Rourke, he showed up like coming outen under a rock, and it was like the miners couldn't get poisoned fast enough to suit them, and there weren't a Hunky in the crowd knew what Mother Jones was saying, but there they were, listening to that female, and she was a spellbinder up on that wagon, and they were the IRA, and the Polacks fighting the Czar, and they just had to do some fighting."

"Did they need the union, Uncle Walter?"

"No."

"Did the union do them any good?"

"It did not."

Casimar said, "Stupid. Union is stupid."

Pete Battle said, "The company sucks can talk themselves blue in the face, but you just take a vote in this
town, you'd find out the truth."

David Battle said, "How can you vote on the truth,
Papa?"

"What's that supposed to mean?"

"The truth's the truth, isn't it, Papa? You can't vote on
it."

Walter Dankowski said, "Good thinking, Davey. Union
says the ones get the most votes, they're the ones right.
That's like saying might makes right, and everybody
knows that isn't so. No, sir, Davey, you got it, true is
true, and right is right, for rich people and poor people,
and Church of Christ and St. Mary's, and company and
miners, and wrong is wrong. What do you think, Ellen?"

Ellen Foley Battle said, "I'm not sure."

Pete Battle said, "Then keep out of it."

Ellen said, "Shaw said there was a different right for
each person."

Pete demanded, "Where did he say that?" He wasn't
objecting to the principle, he was questioning his wife's
knowledge and authority.

She said, *Major Barbara*. And that could be the case,
each man has his own particular kind of right. The union
does say that the way most people vote is right. Alexander
Hamilton said the aristocracy should decide what's right.
Is that what you say, Walter?"

Pete Battle snorted. He resented it, as always, that his
wife was well-read. It was a common cross he bore with his
father.

Walter said, "A person knows what's right and what's
wrong, and sometimes they do things they know are
wrong, but they work on themselves, and before they're
done, they make believe they're right."

Pete said, "Well, hallelujah, the superintendent admits
the Red Flash could sometimes be wrong."

Stella Dankowski said, "The Bible, David, that is where
it comes from. Right is God's right, and not man's right.
And the Declaration of Independence, it would say that,
too."

Casimar Dankowski said, "Water. Pump it cold."

Stella said, "Yes, Papa," and she sprang to do her
husband's bidding, chastened.

Pete Battle said, "Stupid. You don't even know what

232

you're talking about. It's not *right* the union talks about. It's *rights*. It's miners' *rights*, that's what counts."

Walter said with some heat, "What rights? The rights are in America for everybody to take. You don't have to holler for them, unless what you're hollering for is really something that belongs to somebody else, and you're going to take it away from him. That bird Childress, all about him being for the common man, and going to soak the Red Flash enough taxes to make all the miners rich, well, that's not rights talk, that's chains talk, that's what that is, and you put that bird in Congress, you'll find out how much rights you got left before him and that kind get done with you. This country's going to vote for that Roosevelt sure as shooting."

"You're damn right we are. And it's the majority that's going to talk. It's time we told the minority and Wall Street where to get off. And that's what right and rights are all about, and if you don't understand that, you don't understand what social justice is all about."

Joe Foley let out a loud groan. They turned to him. Ellen asked, "What's wrong, Joe?"

"It hurts my head."

Walter said, "Mine, too, Joe. I'm not as smart as the union men. I haven't got all the answers to the questions that can't be answered."

Joe said, "You guys don't understand about politics, anyhow. Now, the Foleys, we'd be Republicans if we was richer. I think some of my kin'll vote for Hoover just to show off. Whoo-eee, I been hearing all day about what a mess Sweet Water is, and perdition just around the corner, and I'm going to go build me a ark before God takes the Kanawha and drowns us all, and if he do, I got dibs on Swaney Wood for my ark, on account what I got to say with her don't hurt my head."

Ellen Foley said, "Joe, I'm ashamed of you."

Pete Battle said, "He's a smart ass." He looked at his son, but he wouldn't call him by name. "Stupid. You keep away from that Jim Parker."

Walter Dankowski asked, "And me, Pete?"

Pete said, "Why don't you keep your company-suck ideas in your house and out of my house?"

Casimar Dankowski roared, "What is this! What is this? The gray house is my house."

5

AT INDIA PARKER'S reconciliation and gossip-hunt supper, Joe Foley spooned out a pound of beans, selected three huge hunks of salt pork, cut a five-inch square of hot corn bread and spread a great gob of butter between the halves.

Jim said with wonder, "That's how you throw rocks so far and run so fast."

Joe gulped the food whole. He said, "You sure are one good cook, Mrs. Parker. Any truth to you being part Shawnee? You sure cook beans good, and you got kinda high cheekbones."

Jim said, "Papa always claimed Mama was the nearest kin to Logan alive."

India said, "Land's sake, Jim, stop telling these boys such a thing."

Her son said, "You just let somebody find Logan's treasure, she'll own up fast enough." He smiled complacently. It was good to have again as his friends these other two of the three most intelligent young men in Sweet Water.

But if he thought Joe Foley would be reconstructed, he had quick disappointment coming. Joe could only be himself. Without any warning, he asked, "Jim, when your daddy was lying there with his skull bashed in, did you know he was dead? I mean for sure?" At Jim's distressed expression, Joe said, "Just wondered, that's all."

"You ever see anybody dead, Joe?"

"Sure. Saw Billy Culpepper get run over by the train last year."

"Did you know for sure he was dead?"

"If he weren't, he were in trouble, since it cut off his head."

"I knew, too. Papa was dead. What other pleasant thing do you want to talk about?"

"How come you going on to school some more? You going to get so smart you'll make yourself sick, not to mention everybody else."

It was said so pleasantly that Jim didn't know where to take hold of it and be offended. "I got my bachelor's at Morgantown, now I go get my master's at MIT."

David asked, "Does it cost much to go to MIT?"

"I wouldn't be going, if it did." David looked surprised. Jim said, "Did you think we were rich?"

"Well, we sort of got the idea you weren't poor. Papa says you got the, you know, the money, the pension."

Joe said, "The blood money for Charles killing Caleb, that's what Davey is trying to say."

"The pension and Uncle Davis keep the white house running. I'm partly working my way through MIT and partly on scholarship."

Joe demanded, "What for?"

"Believe it or not, Joe, they sometimes give scholarships for something besides football. Sometimes they give them to scholars."

Joe said, "Well, bust my bee-hind. Excuse me, Mrs. Parker."

Jim said, "You keep that in mind, Davey. You have to be mighty good and mighty big to get a football scholarship. Keep in mind the other way to skin the cat."

David said, "I'll get a football scholarship."

"To prove something to Pete? I can understand that, but don't kill yourself in the process of trying to do the impossible."

Joe said, "Oh, boy, is he stupid."

David said, "You just wait. He will."

Jim Parker asked, "Will what, Davey?"

"Come around. When I'm playing ball."

India Parker said, "Talking about Pete, somebody was

telling me they saw him over in Shawnee with you two boys. What would fifteen-year-old boys find to do with a grown man in Shawnee at night?" When nobody answered, she said, "Not much doing in Sweet Water for young men. What do you men do these days?"

James Parker said, "Something is going right over my head. What's so important about Pete and Davey and Joe going to Shawnee?"

India asked, "Important? I wasn't making anything important out of it. Was there something important, David?" When no one answered, she asked, "What's the name of that saloon over there, that blind pig?"

Joe Foley said, "You must mean Green Billy's, ma'am. The Gypsy, that's his widder, she runs it. They sell hard likker, and there's some dancing girls, but I reckon you wouldn't know about that. I saw Pastor Parker going in there the night we were in Shawnee. I reckon he was calling to help some of the sinners in there."

The light dawned for Jim Parker. Pete had taken his son and his nephew to Green Billy's, and India, in her mysterious ways, knew about it.

Joe asked innocently, "Where is Pastor Parker tonight? Shawnee again?"

Jim said, "Joe, you know darn well Uncle Davis hasn't ever been in Green Billy's. As a matter of fact, he's got a woman up the holler needed his services."

Joe Foley's grin spread across his face.

Jim said, "Don't, Joe, I warn you."

"I won't. If he's up Murder Crick, he's got competition tonight. There's a traveling snake-handler preacher up the holler going to have a barbecue, handle some rattlers, sing bass, kiss a copperhead, and fetch a woman's baby that's two weeks late. Like to see Pastor Parker top that one. No wonder the snake-handlers are taking away the paying customers."

India said, "Joe Foley, you ought to be ashamed of yourself, talking that way about a man of God."

"Yes, ma'am. Which one, Pastor Parker or the snake-handler?"

"It's not right for a young man to be irreverent."

David said, "Impertinent, ma'am, more than irreverent."

Joe said, "Davey, I surely do add-mire the way you talk."

Jim Parker said, "If you spent less time memorizing

236

the dictionary, Davey, and more time trying to understand this town and the union, you'd be further ahead."

Joe said, "That Jim Parker, he oughter be a halfback. He spots a opening, he's in there *right now* with all four feet flying, and I reckon it runs in the family."

India asked, "Did you and Pete and Davey see a movie in Shawnee, Joe?"

Jim said, "Oh, for Pete's sake, Mama." He didn't disapprove of her curiosity. He disapproved of her handling and timing.

David said, "I'd like to build a car like yours, Jim."

"It can be done. Mine's one-third Franklin and two-thirds junk. I'll help you guys build one this summer."

Joe asked, "You got any eye-dee where we're going to get junk in Sweet Water?"

"You got a point. How many cars are there here now?"

"Mr. Scott's Packard, Doc Black's black Ford, Grandpa Foley's Graham, and Walter Dankowski's Model A."

"That's all?"

"Well, I guess you know your Uncle Davis took his down to Charleston and come back on the train."

"No, I didn't know it. I haven't seen him since I've been home. How come, Mama?"

India said, "He didn't have the use for it."

Joe Foley said, "Way I hear it, with collections going to the snake-handlers, he went up to talk the car people into cutting down the payments, only they were Jews or something like that, and not religious people, and they kept the car."

India said, "There's talk Father Hannigan wants a car."

Jim asked, "What do the parish think of that, Davey?"

Joe said, "The parish don't like to see Hannigan sulk, on account he takes it out on you in his cubbyhole. The parish will cough up. And if I know Hannigan, he won't settle for less'n a Buick or Packard to go with his big see-gars." He said to Davey, "Forget it. We're two hillbillies wouldn't know their hinders from a axle. Reckon we'll make it out of Sweet Water running with a football, not in any car we build."

Jim said, "This hillbilly built his own car."

Joe Foley said inadvertently, "A Parker?"

When the implication came through, Jim Parker laughed out loud. "We *are* the hillbillies, not *you!* That tickles my risibilities. Since when did it get twisted around that

237

you think of yourselves as the hillbillies, you fish-eating Johnny-come-latelies? We're the real McCoys!"

Joe Foley looked a little sheepish. "Hillbillies is at the bottom of things, and that sure ain't Parkers."

"I'd never thought it of you, Joe. That you'd ever drink from the humble cup."

Joe Foley smiled with a hard jaw. His blue eyes slitted. He said without trace of accent, "I don't drink out of anybody's cup but my own."

But Jim Parker savored the small triumph, the momentary accession over the self-assured Irish boy. "That's latter-day Sweet Water for you. Everybody wants to be something besides what they are. Everybody's a little bit ashamed of what they are."

David asked, "Like what?"

"Fish eaters want to be hillbillies. Hunkies want to be Anglo-Saxon. Hillbillies want to be Southern gentry. Everybody in this town spends half the day and night wanting to be something else."

David said, "That's the way it's supposed to be, Jim. Aren't you supposed to want to be something more than you are, and that's what gets you there?"

"Not quite right. Me, I want out of here so bad I can taste it. But there's a difference. I want out to *do* something, not to *be* somebody else. Just leaving here, that isn't getting out. If you go to Akron and work in the rubber plants and never get off the calendar, or Dee-troit and never get off the line, then you never did get out of Sweet Water after all, because you took the coal dust right along with you, no matter how fast you run. Davey, this is some of the best advice you've ever gotten. You've got four years ahead. Boy, play it to the hilt. You're bright guys, both of you. Give the best you've got all the time, and not just football. And you'll get out of here, both of you, walking out to something, like me, not running away from something. And then you come up to Dee-troit, after you go to college, and I'll give you a good job at National Motors."

Joe Foley said, "Jim, that's right kindly of you. When you get to Dee-troit, I wouldn't give a nickel for anybody's chances that was up against you."

"You believe it, Joe."

"I do, I do. You going to be so important, the Pope and the King of Siam going to have you to tea and get

238

your add-vice on the union, I can see it. On the other hand, you got yourself one problem, Jim, and that is you all the time see things for other people like they was you, and they ain't. You see this town like it was sour, on account that's how it is for you, but that don't mean it's sour for ever'*buddy*."

Jim interrupted, challenging. "You heard anybody laughing their heads off in this town lately?"

"Sure. Swaney Wood. She laughs her head off at all the old men come running after her, their big ole tongues dragging in the coal dust. There's some don't want outen town. Mr. Big Hero, he's too busy being Kingfish. Doc Black and his black car, he's got his black roots in the coal dust, and I figure if he ever gets hisself a little ole black housekeeper and paints his house black, he'll never dee-part. Walter, he's a Polack done the most a Polack can do, and he ain't just ay-bout to leave this town. Your Uncle Davis, I don't reckon you could prize him outen the pulpit with a crowbar, less'n he could be a Presbyterian or something proper like a Episcopalian. There's lots get along just fine in Sweet Water."

Jim said scornfully, "Big frogs in a small pond."

"Jim, what you think the Parkers been all along? Well, you going to do something about it, but you ain't the onliest one. Davey and me, we ain't going to walk outen Sweet Water, no, sir, we going to run on a red carpet all the way to South Bend, Indiana, and right on up to the moon. Do you know what I'm going to be? All American halfback, that's what. And do you know what Davey's going to be? Captain of the Notre Dame football team, that's what. And the fanciest people in the country going to come cozying up to us, and some that ain't even Irish."

David Battle said, "Maybe we'll all end up in Dee-troit, Jim. Joe, and Mama and everybody."

Joe Foley said, "Ellen doesn't have to leave."

Jim asked, "She's happy here?"

"Sure."

"What makes you think so?"

"There ain't no coal dust where Ellen is."

There was silence.

Jim Parker said, "That's a good thing to say about somebody."

Joe said gruffly, "Pass the corn bread, please, ma'am."

India Parker smiled unctuously. "You ever write her a

239

poem, or anything like that, Joe?" Joe looked at her but didn't answer. The old squaw pursued him. "How do you get on with your Aunt Ellen?"

"I get on fine, Mrs. Parker," Joe said. "Anybody that wouldn't get on fine with Ellen, there's got to be something wrong with that somebody."

"Don't your mother get after you, you spending so much time over at Ellen's instead of your own house?"

"Why should she mind? One less for Papa to get supper for, while she reads. Casimar ain't exactly enthused, I got to admit."

David said, "Joe's on the outs with Grandpa. Grandpa is provoked because Joe eats there."

Jim said, "I can't understand that. Joe doesn't eat much."

India Parker said, "Ellen sure is a good-looking woman. She sure don't look like a woman in her thirties. Prettiest girl that ever was in Sweet Water, and still looks young enough for a young fellow to be courting."

6

ROBERT EMMETT QUINN dreamed a day-long, night-long heavy dream that he would one day go into the Hall of Fame the greatest coach of them all, greater even than Knute Rockne. He plotted his course precisely. Three years with the pros, then a backfield or end slot with a major college power, then the top, the top.

Coming out of Washington and Jefferson in 1930, he was forced to seek out the pros when the pros did not seek him out. He offered himself to the Giants, the Bears, and Portsmouth. There were no takers. Unannounced he made his way into the Green Bay Packers training camp and lasted long enough to be convinced that he was at best a good end who couldn't carry Johnny Blood's helmet. With this string played out, he revised his schedule and hastened back to W & J. He said to his head coach, "Guess I'll have to coach without pro experience. I'll take the backfield job."

"We filled it. We wanted you, but we couldn't wait."

"When will you have another opening?"

"Who knows?"

"Well, guess I should have taken it when I had the chance."

"Spilt milk."

"Yes. Any suggestions?"

"There's an opening at West Virginia. I'll write a letter for you."

Quinn was interviewed at Morgantown. The head coach said, "Wish I could be sure you know as much football as this letter says," and Quinn lost out to a graduate. He sent a dozen letters of application following up a dozen rumors. Those coaches who bothered to reply suggested that he arm himself with experience. He came back to his coach and said, "There's got to be a place for somebody who knows as much football as I know. I've wasted a whole damn year."

"I've found a spot for you."

"I'll take it. Sight unseen."

"Man named Harold Scott owns the Red Flash Mines at Sweet Water. He's got a morale problem in his town, and he figures a winning football team will do the job for his miners. You teach algebra, and you get paid on the side by the mine."

"High school?"

"Parker District High."

"Wasn't quite what I had in mind. How much do I get?"

"I get the impression that depends how good you do. You might as well know it, Scott wasn't too enthused about taking a beginner. I did some fast talking for you."

Quinn smiled. "High school? With the Snakes? The hillbillies? The coal miners?"

"You'll have a whole squad of hard-muscled kids who want out of Sweet Water. Way the coal business is, they're hungrier than ever. Go make yourself a reputation."

Quinn grinned wider, and it was a grin of anticipation, not humor. "Yeh," he said. "Yeh, that will do it. Those Hunkies are going to shove me ahead of them right up the ladder," and he came to Sweet Water to teach algebra and coach football.

Algebra bored him nearly as much as it bored the coal miners' sons who were his pupils. After the frantic year away from the game, football excited him even more than it excited the ball-rabid fathers in the bleacher stands yelling the coal dust out of their lungs for the glittering product he created. He was a world beater. He was a master.

In Quinn's first year, the Parker Red Flash team went through their eight-game schedule undefeated and demanded the state Class C championship. The Charleston sports reporter, enraptured with the class and precision of Quinn's product, wrote: "Coach Bob Quinn's Parkers run the Notre Dame box with a split-second timing that must bring a smile to the face of Knute Rockne, wherever it is the Master now watches football games . . ." Bob Quinn drank that wine deeply.

The Parkers were the idols of Sweet Water. Harold Scott paid Quinn $120 a month on the side and got his money's worth. For the first time since the death of Vincent Carstairs and the accession of the United Mine Workers, there was community identification at the junction of the Kanawha River and Murder Creek. Attendance at home games went over a thousand. Every miner and every mountaineer up the crick knew every player on the squad, and they knew football. Suddenly, in surly, depression-ridden, union-ridden Sweet Water, they knew football. They lived from Saturday to Saturday. Bob Quinn was the man of the hour, and he was only twenty-three years old and in his first year of coaching. A fifteen-year-old phenom named Joe Foley was his principal instrument of success.

At the end of the season, David Battle approached Quinn and said earnestly, "Coach, I want to play next year. What should I do between now and then?"

"Get bigger."

"What should I do in case I don't get bigger?"

Coach Quinn brought out Speech Number Three. "Davey, we can use everybody. We're not like the big schools, where we can pick and choose. You sat on the bench because you're not big enough, and we've got some fellows who are big enough. But you run pretty good. Pretty good. And you're only a freshman. Joe Foley's the only freshman could make this team. But you've got a future. So you spend the next nine months running. Winter, spring and summer, you run, Davey, run. And punt, because we can always use a kicker. And don't get discouraged. You've got three years ahead of you, and you'll play a part in our plans. You believe that and keep believing that, because a ballplayer with desire will make it. Desire, that comes first, Davey. Drive, drive, drive, Davey, and make a place for yourself on this ball club."

Bob Quinn didn't believe his own pep talk. David Battle believed it, and Ellen Foley Battle believed it, and though Joe Foley didn't believe Bob Quinn, he believed in David Battle, and the two of them ran, winter, spring and summer. Mainly they ran down the railroad tracks, because that made a game of it. For an hour they kicked the ball down the tracks and ran after it at full speed, sometimes stepping only on the ties, sometimes only between the ties, and sometimes full-tilt down the rail until David could run forty yards before losing his balance, while his good-natured cousin yelled, "Go it, Davey!" When the afternoon train came by, they hopped it and rode back into Sweet Water, dropping off at Carstairs Field, where Ellen waited to retrieve the ball for them.

Joe said, "Follow through higher with your leg, Davey." He took the ball from his small cousin and sent it fifty yards, spiraling. "Did you see how I did that?"

"Can you tell me, Joe?"

"No. I just do it. Watch me again. I think it's mainly the follow-through."

David punted twenty-five, thirty, times, for thirty-five and forty yards, sometimes spiraling, sometimes end over end, while his mother, in a skirt and shirt and tennis shoes, ran them down.

Joe said, "Better. Let's go, dropkicks."

Ellen wiped her forehead with her dusty hand. "No more dropkicks, Joe. That's out. From now on, it's only place-kicks." She took the ball from her nephew. "Latest issue of *Football* says dropkicking is out for good with the new shape ball. So we place-kick."

Joe said admiringly, "You're the coach, Ellen."

With one arm Ellen hugged her strong, sweaty nephew and kissed his cheek spontaneously. She said warmly, "Joe, in case I haven't told you lately, David and I are mainly appreciative."

The blood coursed through Joe Foley.

With her palm she felt the hard muscles of his back, and she doubled her fist and hit him gently. "Goodness, Joe, you're not made out of muscle, more like iron."

Joe didn't move.

She faced him and wiped some of the water off his face with her forearm. "Sure hope I'm not as sweaty as you. I feel like a mess."

"You look fine." His voice was strained.

"I'm a thing of beauty. A joy forever."

"That you are, Ellen."

She looked up at him, with some puzzlement at his tone.

244

He said, "I'm sure glad you don't marcel your hair."

"I haven't got the nerve."

"Marcels look so frizzy. How long is your hair?"

"Shorter than it used to be. Maybe two feet. You don't think I should bob it, Joe?"

" 'Twould be a mortal sin. Somebody's got prettier hair than you, I never saw that somebody. Reckon that goes for the rest of you, too."

She wiped his forehead again with her sleeve. She said, pleased, "You're my best beau, Joe."

"That Injun squaw sure is a sharp one."

"Who's that? India?"

"Yes."

"What's she sharp about this time?"

"She figured something out even before I knew it myself."

"What's that?"

"Something."

"What on earth are you talking about, Joe?"

"Nothing."

"Well, it's something. What are you being so mysterious about?"

"How come you think a lazy Mick like me runs his feet off to the knee bones on a hot day like this?"

She studied him. She hit his biceps and smiled. "You shouldn't be embarrassed for being such a good guy. For David, Joe, because you think the world of him and both of us think the world of you."

He said abruptly, "David's you, Ellen."

She looked in Joe's blue eyes. Suddenly she comprehended, but she didn't want to comprehend. Suddenly she was flustered. She was unsure. She wiped her hands nervously on her skirt, and she scuffed her dusty tennis shoe on the turf like a schoolgirl. She said, "Don't say things like that, Joe. Even in fun."

David Battle, from twenty yards, said with unusual asperity, "Talk, or practice?"

Joe said, "Him, too."

"What, Joe?" she asked severely.

"Him, too. He's sharp like India. He knew it before me. And that's not the half of it. We're rivals."

Ellen said sharply, "Stop that kind of talk, Joe."

He didn't look at her. "When I say one more thing. Sometimes a guy knows he got a need for something, but

245

he don't know what it is. When he figures out what it is, and he finds out the one he's got the need for's got the same need, then you stay awake thinking about it. You got to think there's something wrong with you, thinking like that. But after a time you decide it doesn't make any difference if it's wrong or right, the need's so great. And then you decide if the need's all that great, and it's for somebody who's so good, then it can't be wrong, no matter what anybody would say . . ."

Ellen said, "Stop it, Joe. You're not making any sense. Stop it." She wondered why she felt odd, deep in her stomach.

Joe said, "No, no sense. No sense at all." He trotted up the field. "Let's place-kick, Davey."

David said, "Maybe tomorrow."

Joe tossed the ball in the air twice, then hollered, "Yar I come, Davey! Bring me down!" He tucked the ball under his arm, trotted, then turned on his blinding speed. David stood with his arms at his side.

Ellen yelled, "Get him, David!"

Joe cut, his right arm out in the classic showboat pose of the halfback. David launched himself and smacked his shoulder into the thigh, and they went down in a heap, the ball flying away. Joe tried to get up. David held him, pinned. Joe disengaged his cousin's arms and got to his feet. He walked in a circle, limping a little. David rose and walked away, down the tracks toward Murder Creek and the Dankowski house. Ellen walked up to Joe, and the two watched David disappear.

Joe said, "He hit me good. It hurt."

Ellen said, "Serves you right."

"I guess so."

Impulsively she put her arm around his shoulder again to walk off the field with him. She felt the rippling muscles in his shoulder. She pulled her hand away as though it were burned. She said severely, "I don't want to hear that talk out of you ever again." She walked away from him, after her son, not looking back. She wondered why she continued to feel odd, down deep in her stomach.

In the Parker house, India Parker let the curtain fall back in place, and her Injun-black eyes glowed.

7

Bob Quinn laced his ballplayers with sarcasm and soothed them with lavish praise. He said to Joe Foley, "You go into the line on plunges like Nagurski, great. But when you get through, don't stop to applaud. Get your head up quicker and look around."

Full of good spirits, Joe asked, "How's that, Knute?"

Quinn was stunned. After a moment he said sharply, "You show me respect, young man. I'm your coach."

Joe said, straight-faced, "I call my coach Knute, and he doesn't know it's a compliment."

"Then wipe that smile off your face." He was further chagrined when he realized there was no smile on Joe's face.

Joe said, "Yes, sir!" Then he said, "Relax, Coach. Nobody else can hear us. You think you got some ideas how I should run with a football, I'll listen. What was it you played at W & J? End, wasn't it?"

"Foley, I knew you'd get too big for your britches. Well, no man's too big for the team. Discipline comes first. No man's too big to ride the bench."

Joe shook his head. He smiled his engaging smile. "No, sir, discipline doesn't come first. Winning ball games comes first. If these other Bohunks don't know it, you and me

247

know it. So when it's just us, let's relax and win ball games."

"The team comes first. You just better remember that, Foley."

Joe Foley wasn't at all distressed. "Sure glad I can run like a deer. Sort of evens things up, doesn't it?"

Quinn said, "We'll see about that." He blew the whistle, ending practice ten minutes early. He left the field struggling with himself. It was his own fault. He'd brought it on himself. Why did he have to play the big shot and give advice to a ballplayer who was beyond his advice? His bluff was called, and he was agonized, because he knew damn well he'd never keep Joe Foley on the bench, no matter what the provocation, since an undefeated football team was his passion, and integrity and honor as a man would have to take second place behind the fulfillment of that passion. He went to his room in Aunt Polly's boarding house and sat glumly on into the dusk. A brash, self-confident young man had nailed him and would do it again and again for the next three years, and there wasn't a damn thing Quinn could do about it, because that young man contained in his solid 185 pounds the ingredients of the brew of Coach Quinn's success.

On the Dankowski front steps, Ellen kneaded a lump in David Battle's leg. David asked, "Joe, you think it was a good thing to talk to Coach like that?"

"Didn't think anybody heard. That was between Quinn and me. Just joshing him some."

"Doesn't seem right, to josh the coach."

Joe said airily, "He's just the driver, we're the horses. We win the race for him."

"Player's got to respect his coach."

"Davey, smarten up. We got it made, you and me. They need us. Leastwise they need me now, and when Gary goes, they'll need you. The coaches need us from now on out, long as we can move that football."

"Coach is teaching me a lot."

"So he knows football. So let him teach, but you don't have to take him so all-fired serious."

Ellen said, "Don't listen to that IRA rascal, David. You show respect for the coach. Joe's wrong about that."

Joe said, "Ellen, Quinn didn't show respect for himself.

Now you try to tell me he did. I joshed him and he took it. If you saw it, Davey, you saw him back down."

Ellen said, "You certainly didn't gain respect for yourself by making another man lose his self-respect."

Joe shrugged his shoulders. "He had his chance. I gave him the test. Maybe I was hoping he'd measure up. But that's the way it is. With all coaches. Wait until those college coaches come after us, their tongues all hanging out. They'll come down here to Sweet Water holding out their free rides, and when I tell 'em sweeten it up, maybe that'll wipe the shoot-eating grins off their faces. They know it, they know they need us more than we need them."

Ellen said, "Sure hate to see you getting ideas like that." She slapped David's calf. "That ought to do it." Then she said, "You listen to me, you two, I don't want to see either one of you getting too big for his britches."

David looked as though he were smiling, though his expression didn't really change. "I can't even get *my* britches out on the field."

Ellen said, "You remind me of Pete, Joe." She didn't see the involuntary clench of his fist. "When he first started playing, it was a game. And all of a sudden it was business."

Pete emerged from the doorway onto the porch. He said, "It's a business. And the sooner you figure that out, the better off you are."

Joe said, "He comes out that door like India."

Pete asked, "What's that supposed to mean?" When Joe didn't answer, he said, "When football's a game, I'll eat it. Notre Dame wanted me with two years high school. They wanted me again right from Goodyear, when the war ended. Don't give me any high and mighty Notre Dame and football being a game. They had players on that team could scarce sign their own names."

Ellen said mildly, "That was a long time ago."

"Joe Savoldi was a long time ago?"

"Well, Pete, do you know much about Joe Savoldi?"

"Know they had to tell him the plays in Eye-talian, on account he didn't speak English."

"Well, that makes him even with a few around here." She rose and smoothed her skirt. Joe followed her motions. She looked at him and clasped her hands uncertainly. "You two listen, maybe some schools will take you

249

even if you're just smart-alecky blockheads. But not the good schools."

Pete asked, "You think Marchy Schwartz and Marty Brill and Frank Carideo and those guys had to get down on their knees to get into Notre Dame? You think they didn't get just what they asked for?"

"You don't know anything about what they got, Pete."

"Oh, I don't?"

"No, you don't. You haven't talked to anyone from Notre Dame since 1922."

"Don't give me that. I know Hunk Anderson."

"You *knew* Hunk Anderson."

"I know him. Hunk knows the score, and with him down there, a horse can get what he wants."

"You *knew* Hunk Anderson. When he was a ballplayer. Not when he's coach. You might be in for a surprise. My bet is no ballplayer gets into Notre Dame unless he hits the books."

Pete was containing himself with great difficulty. "Since when you know everything there is to know about what goes on in football? When's the last time you played?"

"This afternoon. After regular practice."

"Stupid."

Joe said, "We don't figure it's so stupid."

"Nobody asked you. Stupid waste of time. A woman spent more time around the house, that's a better use than messing around with a punk kid that's got no chance." He walked across the porch and down the hill, turning toward the Kanawha and the ferry landing. Silently they watched his retreating back.

Joe said sullenly, "Must be a union meeting in Shawnee."

Ellen Foley Battle's white skin turned whiter still.

David said in an unaccustomedly loud voice, "You interested in report cards, Mama?"

Ellen still looked off toward the Kanawha. "Any B's, David?"

"Nope. Joe got all A's again, too."

Joe said, "Can't help it. Just get 'em no matter how hard I try not to." He tossed his football against the porch ceiling, caught it, held it up. "That's my ticket of admission, not A's."

Ellen turned to him. "Pete got all A's. For the two years he was in high school."

Joe lapsed into the unwonted sullenness. He didn't like

the comparison. He said, "Nuts," which didn't mean anything except discomfiture.

Ellen said, "You do remind me a lot of Pete when he was sixteen."

"Well, I don't know how that could be."

"Not in looks. You don't look like he looked. But you're strong, like he was. And smart, like he was." Then she said with a surprising ferocity, "Joe, don't let them take it away from you."

"Who's going to take what away from me? Nobody."

"They took it away from Pete."

"Well, maybe he let 'em."

"Maybe he did. Don't you let 'em."

"I'm not like Pete. Not like he was, and not like now. By Jesus, I'll tell you one thing, if I was him, I'd know when I had something good, and not be heading for Shawnee."

Ellen couldn't reply. She felt drained.

David said with an exasperation as rare as his cousin's sullenness, "Okay, okay, nobody's anybody else. Forget it."

Ellen walked behind her son, and to do something with her hands, began kneading the muscles of his sturdy neck. Joe watched her. He wanted her to do it for him. She read his thought as clearly as if he'd spoken it. She should do it. She should make that friendly, harmless, warm gesture of her loving regard for the big, strong nephew who gave himself so unstintingly to her small son. She was afraid to touch him. Her fear provoked her. Why couldn't she caress her nephew fondly, as she did her son? She walked with her gliding, feminine, athletic movements behind Joe, and dug her fingers into the muscles at the base of his neck. Instead of relaxing, the muscles bunched. She wanted to jerk her hands away. She thought to herself: Don't be stupid. This is Joe, who has grown up with David. She jammed her thumbs as hard as she could, and the hard muscles gave not a bit. She thought: Pete was hard-muscled and tense when I touched him when he was sixteen. She nearly said it aloud.

She asked as casually as she could, "David said anything yet about the big plan?"

"Like what?" Joe's voice was as tense as his shoulder muscles. "Don't hear two words out of him a month."

Ellen felt her son's eyes. She looked at him. He was watching her hands working in his cousin's shoulders. She pulled her hands away almost guiltily. She said, "Like Navy. Like Annapolis."

Joe whirled his head around. "Annapolis? Like Army-Navy Annapolis?" He turned back and grinned at David. "You thinking about Annapolis, Davey?"

"Just mentioned it, that's all."

"Better keep him in out of the sun. And out of Shawnee. He sees a stupid movie, and the next thing you know he's seeing himself in those brass buttons with about a million girls falling all over him." He grinned his broadest. "How about that? Can't you just see us coming home in those spanking-white uniforms and parading around in the coal dust?" He threw the ball as hard as he could into David's midsection. "You got yourself pictured singing lollygag songs to all those million women?"

David couldn't answer. The wind was knocked out of him. When he got it back he lunged at his cousin, and they went rolling off the steps and down the hill, flailing wildly. At the track, Joe was on top, his knees on David's biceps. He let him up and they walked slowly back up the hill. There was a trickle of blood in the corner of Joe's mouth. He said, "Whoo-ee, he's a tough little knocker!"

Ellen said, "You and David would make handsome midshipmen."

"You see that movie, too?"

"Just thinking I'd be proud of both of you."

David said, "Got to get a drink." He went in the house.

Ellen asked, "Think he's hurt? Sounds like he might be."

Joe said, "Maybe shook up a bit. We hit the bottom hard."

"Joe, you don't think we're doing wrong with David?"

"Football? Size for size, he's tougher'n I'll ever be."

"You're a good guy, Joe."

He sat down close to her, his arms wrapped around his legs. "If you want Davey to go to Navy, he'll go where you want him to go, and I'll go where Davey wants to go."

"Well, you've got a lot of time to think about it. But you better not forget the books while you're being too big for your britches on that football field, in case that's where you decide to go."

He said airily, "Just can't hep being smart."

"I'm proud of you and David, Joe. I couldn't be prouder if you were my own, too."

His smile belied his tense intent. "I'm your own."

She felt the nervousness returning.

"If I went up there, Ellen, and I had on that uniform, would you come up and be my girl at a dance? Like in the movie, with all that moonlight, and all?"

She said warningly, "Joe . . ."

He looked up at her. "I said it like I was kidding."

"I told you that other time, Joe, don't kid about something like that."

"Ellen, I wish . . ." He stopped. He said again, "I wish . . ."

She waited. He didn't finish his wish. She wanted him to go away. She wanted to hear his wish. Every orthodox instinct demanded that she feel revulsion. She watched the movement of his bunching muscles beneath the denim shirt. She thought of her husband, now, in Shawnee. She thought of her husband, then, young and full of the world, with the hard muscles of his shoulders bunching at her touch. She remembered. She remembered the wonderful, terrifying constriction deep in her stomach when she touched the hard muscles of Pete Dankowski, before he married her and became Pete Battle. Loneliness assailed her. Bitter tears fell inside her. One tear, another tear, another tear. Far off, the evening train called. The lonely wail put its shiver in her. She wished Joe Foley would go away, and she wanted him to stay.

8

DAVID BATTLE played not one minute of football in his sophomore year. For the first seven games of his junior year, he played not one minute. On the eve of the last game, Joe Foley stopped Bob Quinn in front of Aunt Polly's boarding house.

Quinn nodded curtly.

Joe said, "I got a favor to ask you, Coach."

"Coach? What happened to Knute?"

"Give you some idea how bad I want the favor."

"What kind of favor do you want out of me, Joe?"

"Sort of a tit-for-tat favor."

"I'm playing you. No matter how hard I have to swallow, I'm playing you. What do you want me to do now, kiss your rump in Old Sod Square?"

"I want you to play Davey at right half tomorrow. I want you to start him, and I want him to play the whole game."

Quinn turned away to go into the house. Then he turned back. "The answer is no. I play the men I think will win. You know that better than anybody else, I play the winners, no matter what."

"You're wrong. Next to me, Davey's the best halfback you got."

"I'm the judge of that."

"He's up to a hundred and fifty pounds, Coach. And pound for pound, he's a better ballplayer than me. I know."

"You play. Battle doesn't. I start the line-up that's won seven games. That's final."

Joe shook his head. "You got a real problem."

"What's that supposed to mean?"

"I was counting on playing myself tomorrow. Sort of looked forward to beating Shawnee."

"Don't say it, Foley."

"I've been bothered with a cramp in my leg. Might be a regular charley horse by morning."

Quinn said in a rage, "I'll throw you off the team."

"Well, I wouldn't blame you. Wonder what would happen if you did? You ever count up how many touchdowns I've scored for you the last three years?"

Quinn's nose was whitened alongside the nostrils.

Joe continued conversationally. "Eight the first year, and you got an undefeated team. Fourteen last year, and we won 'em all again. And nineteen TD's this year and still one game to go. I don't have to play tomorrow to make all-State. Charleston and Wheeling papers already got my picture and told me I made their teams. But you, you still got to win tomorrow to get your season."

Quinn barely managed control. "The answer is no. I'm the coach of this team, and I'm the one that picks the best ballplayers. If you don't play, or if you don't put out, I'll yank you off the team, and I'll let everybody in Sweet Water know why."

"Well," said Joe, "I reckon that would go over like a turd in the punch bowl in this town. Reckon we both know who the miners would blame if the coach couldn't get along with his star halfback. And Mr. Scott, he's mighty anxious to win. I reckon we both know that."

Robert Emmett Quinn walked away from his star halfback without another word. On Saturday afternoon he faced his men in the pre-game huddle, and he said, "There's one change in the starting line-up." His courage was up. He had the strength of his night of determination. Now all he had to do was to say it. Just say it. Corby starts in place of Foley. All he had to do was say it. He looked at Joe Foley. He couldn't say it. As in a dream, he heard himself saying, "Battle starts at right half."

The squad let out a sharp yelp. Quinn looked around

at them in surprise. They were pleased. Why were they pleased? Even Deke Webber, captain of the team, right halfback for seven victories, clapped David on the back and said through his disappointment, "Go get 'em, Davey!" Why were they pleased? Quinn looked around the huddle and said to himself, "I don't know these guys. I coach them, I teach them, I teach them better than anybody in the country could teach them, I'm a great coach, and I don't know what makes them tick." He said aloud, "Men, one more game. Just one more, and Parker County has its third undefeated season. They tell you Shawnee is a pushover. Well, those Snakes didn't come across the river to get plastered by Sweet Water. They came to win." He paused just right for dramatic effect. "But *we* came to plaster them. *We* came to send them back across the Kanawha with their tails between their legs. Go get 'em, Parkers!"

The team yelled loud, and the starters rushed on the field. Robert Emmett Quinn stood on the sidelines with his captain beside him. He had to ask it. "The guys are sure for Davey. How come?"

Deke Webber had a tight throat. He wanted desperately to play. He said, "He's Davey."

"He's Davey?"

"Sure. You know."

No, Quinn didn't know. He felt very lonely. He didn't know.

David Battle played thirty minutes in that final game of his junior year. He didn't cover himself with glory. He played solidly and dependably, and he blocked for Joe Foley, and he was the first man bounding back into the huddle after each play, and the Parkers played with new enthusiasm. Robert Quinn wondered at it. The lonely perplexity consumed him.

David Battle kicked four extra points from placement. It was David who scored the final touchdown. Four times they gave him the ball from the five-yard line on in, while Quinn screamed vainly from the bench, "Give it to Foley!" When David made it across the line on the last try, the Parker team sprang at him, thumping him wildly, and Joe Foley bear-hugged him and lifted him high in the air, so that David flushed and hurried with his head down to kick the final extra point.

When the referee raised his gun and fired, the Sweet

Water miners erupted onto the field. They caught up Joe Foley and Whitey Culpepper. They caught up Coach Quinn and ran, shouting, around the field. The biggest throng of all, they carried David Battle, passing him along, heaving him high in the air. On the shoulders of the miners, Coach Quinn smiled his professional smile and waved his hero's wave. His eyes followed David Battle. What did he have? What did that guy have that brought out such warmth? He couldn't understand it.

In the new dressing room in the high school, Quinn silenced his shouting, dripping players, and called the slow ones out of the shower. He assumed his Rockne pose. "Men, we've completed another undefeated season. The third undefeated Red Flash team in succession. Well done, men. Parker County is proud of you. Enjoy yourselves at the victory dance. You've earned it." He paused. "This season is over. Now we think about next year's undefeated team." His men let out their dutiful yell. Quinn said, "Webber, as captain you have been a credit to this team and to Sweet Water. You have been an inspirational leader. As your final act of duty, as soon as everybody's dressed, you will conduct the vote for next year's captain. He will be introduced at the dance tonight. You will do it by secret ballot, men. Let me know when you're ready. Everybody returning next year gets a vote."

Webber said, "Coach, they already got their captain."

Quinn nodded. Well, Joe Foley deserved it, every bit of it.

But Joe Foley put his hands on David's back and propelled him into the center of the dressing room. David looked perplexed.

Webber said, "Davey, the team has elected you captain of the Big Red Flash for 1934."

His teammates cheered him.

David struggled for words. Finally he said, "I voted for Joe Foley."

Joe said, "I did, too. I only got two votes."

Webber said, "Don't let him kid you, Davey. He got only one vote."

Quinn asked, "Battle, as new captain do you have anything to say to the team?"

David looked at him, he looked at Joe Foley, he looked at the team. He tried desperately to think of something to say. He hadn't a word to say.

Whitey Culpepper said, "We finally got a captain with enough sense to keep his mouth shut!"

The young men got into their dungarees and their shirts and went off to Sweet Water's celebration. Joe Foley was the last to leave. He started to speak to Quinn.

Quinn said, "What now, Foley?"

Joe changed his mind. He said, "That was a good idea you had, playing Davey."

Quinn burst inside with his anger and frustration. He went to the victory dance and played his role mechanically. He accepted numbly the hundred-dollar bonus check from elated Harold Scott. He left as soon as he could. In his bachelor room he sat far into the night, reading and re-reading his Charleston clippings, and still he suffered. What kind of man was he? Why couldn't he understand a David Battle? Why couldn't he face up to a Joe Foley? What profited it a man to gain undefeated football seasons and suffer the loss of . . . suffer the loss of something he couldn't even define. He said aloud to himself, "The coppery taste of golden victory!"

Then Pete Battle came by. Pete was drunk enough to say what he had to say. Quinn opened the door of his room and asked with quick hostility, "What can I do for you?"

Pete closed the door and sat himself in the rocking chair the coach had just vacated. "Bob, next year you should let Davey run more with the ball. Davey and Joe will open up the defense for each other."

Quinn smiled sardonically. "I might have known. I might have known you'd come hopping on the bandwagon. Now let me get you straight in my mind. Aren't you the guy called Davey useless as tits on a boar?"

"Got to talk tough to get a kid to drive." Pete slurred his words. "Who you think's been teaching him how to make up for his size?"

"You?"

"That's right."

"You're a liar."

Pete turned white. "Nobody calls me a liar."

"You're a liar. A goddam liar. You taught him nothing. Joe and Ellen and me, we taught him. You never had any use for him and you know it, and I know it, and everybody knows it. Now you see the town making a hero

258

out of him, you come sucking around wanting some of the glory."

Pete clenched and unclenched his fists. The anger went slowly out of his face and was replaced with a drunk's mollification. "I didn't come to get in a fight."

"What did you come for?"

"Bob, I thought I'd coach the line for you."

"Thanks, no, thanks. I'm doing just fine."

"You'd do better if you had a line coach. And there's nobody around Sweet Water knows more about line play than me."

Quinn contemplated the big man impassively.

Pete said, "You're losing most of the line next year. You got a hard row ahead. What are you figuring, one more season here, then a big college?"

"Could be."

"Reckon you'd like to go out never losing. The backs are set. You need a line. Extra coach would help."

Quinn said, "Yes, I guess that would help."

"I don't have to get paid."

"That's for sure. There's no money for a line coach."

"Well, I'll do it. I'll teach that new line you got coming up. And I've got some good ideas for using Davey."

Quinn sat on his bed. There was no longer any amazement in him for his own cupidity. He smiled the non-smile again and said, "Maybe I'll take you up on it. But if I do, you can forget about any good ideas you got. If you're line coach, you're going to remember every minute, I'm head coach. I'll decide who runs with the ball and when, and when I want advice from you, I'll ask for it."

Pete swallowed. He said maliciously, "Too bad you can't talk that tough to your left halfback."

Quinn said softly, "I need Joe Foley a lot more than I need a line coach. I'm going to make it very plain to you. I've been sitting here tonight wondering what kind of man I am. I know what kind. I'm the kind that wants to win football games more than I want to stand up to Joe Foley. If I had the guts, I'd make him ride the bench until he treated me with respect, but I haven't got that kind of guts, I'm not that kind of man. As for you, I've never liked you. I've got no respect for you. I don't like your motives now. You never came down here volunteering all those years before I came, when the Parkers were losing. You want in on the glory, because Sweet

259

Water is forgetting about Pete Battle, the great hero. You had nothing to do with your son except to say the worst things a man could say about his son, until you find out tonight that the whole town thinks he's the greatest little guy in the world. Now you figure you'll get on the bandwagon and strut around your union office, because every Hunky and hillbilly in Parker County worships anything to do with this football team. If I had any guts, I'd tell you to go bag it, with your Johnny-come-lately offer. But I'm not that kind of man. I want to win football games more than I want to have guts. You can help me, so I'll take you on. And you can strut around and puff yourself up all you want because the town thinks your son is great, and you can pretend you had something to do with it, but you're talking to the wrong man, if you try to convince me you're anything but what you are, a low-class sonofabitch, just like me. So you come on in and teach the new line how to elbow and slug and hold without getting caught, and we'll win ball games, and the Notre Dame thing will open up for me, and some of your elbowers and sluggers will get gobbled up by the colleges, and you can brag up and down the Kanawha about how you did it, but when it gets down to just you and me, you understand me once and for all right now, this team is winning because I'm running a Notre Dame offense like it isn't seen outside South Bend, and because I've got Joe Foley. I've got one job, and that's to win football games. If you help me do that, I'll take you on no matter what I think of you personally, because that's the kind of guy I am. Win football games. All of them. Wherever I go, win all of them. As long as you help me win, you can stay. But I don't want any advice from you, and I don't want any lip from you. If I get either, I'll kick you out so fast it will make your head swim."

Pete Battle sat thunderstruck. Finally he said, "Men don't talk like that to me around Sweet Water."

"This man does."

"Quinn, you're talking plain stupid."

"I've heard you're the roughest man in Sweet Water."

"This time I'm letting it pass. From now on, you remember that."

"I'll tell you your problem, Battle, I don't believe it."

"If I'm not, I'm waiting for somebody to prove it. You got a candidate in mind?"

Quinn smiled slightly. "I'll tell you one could take you right now. Joe Foley could take you."

Pete snorted. "He's seventeen years old and I outweigh him twenty pounds."

"Then you shouldn't be afraid to take him on. Maybe I can arrange it."

"He's seventeen years old, for Christ sake!"

"Then you want to try a grown man?"

"I'll try any grown man."

"Then try me."

"Maybe I will."

"Don't give me maybe. Give me yes or no. I'll help you make up your mind. I know how good you are. Maybe you ought to know about me. I was a second-rate end, but I was heavyweight boxing champion at W & J, and somehow you don't scare me one little bit. So any time you say."

"I just might try you."

"Any time. Any way. Right now?"

"I'll try you, one of these times."

"That's what I thought. So we understand each other. You're a blowhard living in your great might-have-been, and me, I'm a gutless wonder that will do anything to win football games, including having you around. So you run the line, and I'll run you and the ball team, and one of these days, Joe Foley is going to call you down, too, and I hope he'll do it in front of the whole town. Enjoy yourself while you can."

Bob Quinn sat on by himself into the night, glorying because he had confronted the bully, glorying because his name was across the state for his undefeated football teams, and yet tasting the copper because he had played Joe Foley every minute of every game, and because he had played David Battle when Joe Foley gave him no choice. Joe Foley, who called him Knute. He wished he were Joe Foley. No, he wished he were David Battle and that other men loved him.

Pete Battle went home thinking of ways to show his son that the roughest man in Sweet Water was Pete Battle.

9

ELLEN FOLEY watched from the porch. She shuddered each time her son was hit. When she couldn't bear it any longer, she came off the porch and called down the hill. "Pete, David, get cleaned up for supper."

The father came quickly up the hill. The son came more slowly. Pete said exultantly, "I'll make a ballplayer out of him yet."

"Or kill him, one."

Pete snorted.

"Next time maybe he should wear the pads."

"Why? I wasn't wearing any."

"You all right, David?"

Her son nodded. He went into the house walking gingerly, no unusual expression on his bright, eager face.

Pete snorted again. "Kill him! You think those big goddam tackles are going to say pardon me when they hit him?"

"Pete, he played a hard game yesterday. Maybe you should take it easy."

"Not like he'll play next season. After I get done with him. You notice the ball pop out when I hit him? Way he was going, he'd be the champeen fumbler. Not when I get done with him."

"You hurt him, Pete."

262

"Did you hear him holler? I didn't hurt him."

"David doesn't holler. Pete, he tries hard to impress you. Don't take advantage of it."

"Listen, you been giving me about all the advice I want to hear, you understand? And get that snot look off your face."

"If there's a look on my face, it's telling you not to hurt him again."

"You get that look off your face, or I'll wipe it off." He walked away, seething. He came on his son washing up at the basin on the back porch, bare to the waist. Pete looked uneasily at the bruises and abrasions. There was a purple swelling on David's left side. The son looked up but said nothing. For one suffocating moment the father was suffused with regret. This was his son. His own blood flowed in this boy. This boy tried silently, desperately to measure up to the hard requirements of the father. Pete thought of that long-ago day when his own father had been cruel. He thought of saying something kind to the boy, sought for kind words.

Ellen said, "I told you he was hurt. Can I do something, David?"

Her son said, "I'm okay, Mama. I'm okay."

Pete said, "A few lousy goddam coal scrapes. What's the big deal?" He thought of his own mother, that warm Polish Jewess filled with softness and romanticism. This was the same thing over again. A hard man and a soft woman. What practicality had there been in Stella's sentimentality? Casimar Dankowski had condemned his son to the coal mines, and that woman who was his sentimental mother had wept tears for him, but to the coal mines he had gone. This Foley woman would weep tears, and her son would stay forever in Sweet Water. No, it wasn't tears that would get David Battle out of Sweet Water to do the things denied the father. A thousand gallons of sentimentality would not get David out of Sweet Water. But Pete Battle would get him out. Pete Battle would toughen up this boy who was too much like Ellen Foley to get out of Sweet Water.

Ellen touched David's swelling side with her finger tips. She said, almost to herself, "He made the team, without this much beating. He got elected captain, without this much beating."

263

"On the Tigers, a man didn't even notice a few bruises like that."

David looked again and said, "I didn't say anything." He looked in his father's eyes a moment, then walked into the house, drying his face on a towel to hide his expression.

Ellen said, "So you proved you could take him. I hope you're proud. You only outweigh him seventy pounds."

"You knock it off, I'm warning you."

"Or you'll give me some of that? No, I won't knock it off. Did you see what you did to that boy? I sure hope you're proud of yourself."

"You wouldn't understand. Stupid women. He's got to learn what it's like to get hit hard and still come back for more. That's what separates the men from the boys. Before I'm done with him the colleges will be down here with their tongues hanging out, and we'll write our own ticket."

"You listen to me. Mr. Hero, we were getting along just fine without you. Where have you been the last ten years? Crying about he wasn't big enough, that's where you've been. Crying about he must not be your son, that's where you've been. Oh, I've heard about you. Now you see him making it without you, so Mr. Big has to go down and make himself coach, and he has to come home and beat up his son. Well, you get this straight, we can get along just fine without you. We did it when you were in Akron. We've done it since you came back. We get along just fine without you. Now you sit in your union office, or you stay over in Shawnee with your women, or you do whatever you damn please, but I'm telling you right now, Mr. Big, don't you ever hurt that boy again."

Pete took one step and raised his big hand. "I'll slap some respect in you."

She grabbed up the washbasin and slammed it in his face, the porcelain stunning him, the soapy water drenching his shoulders. He knocked the basin out of her hands, and it shattered on the porch floor. She went after his face with her nails, raking the skin, drawing blood. He got a wrist in his powerful hand and forced her quickly to the floor at his feet. She breathed hard. He twisted the wrist. The pain contorted her face.

He said coldly, "I'll teach you respect."

264

She said, "If you hurt him again, you better kill me, or I'll kill you, Pete, I swear it."

He let her go. She slumped to the floor. He was shaking with rage and consternation. Why didn't people understand? He was only thinking of his son. Where did Bob Quinn and Ellen Foley get off with their accusations? They just didn't understand. A man had to fight lonely battles. He had to do what was right, no matter what they thought.

Stella Dankowski said, "The boy is hurt, Peter."

Pete said, "He got banged up in the game yesterday. He's all right. Just banged up."

Casimar Dankowski said, "Stupid game. Stupid."

Pete said, "Go put your shirt on, boy."

David left for the front of the house and the stairway to the bedrooms. They heard him say, "Hi, Joe."

Joe Foley came in the kitchen, his hands in his pockets. "Thought I might stay for dinner, Mrs. Dankowski."

Casimar asked, "You can't get any food in your own house?"

Stella said, "Always for Joe, plenty."

Joe asked, "What happened to Davey?"

Casimar said, "Stupid football."

Joe said, "He didn't get hurt in the game."

Pete asked, "Now just how would you know, Mr. Know-it-all?"

"Well, maybe I just seen him in the dressing room after the game, and maybe he just didn't have any bangin' up."

Ellen stood in the doorway from the back porch. "Maybe there was some more football today."

Stella said to her son, "Your shirt is all wet, Peter. What happened to you?"

Joe asked, "A little scrimmage down below, just the two of you, Uncle Pete?"

Pete said, "I spilled the washbasin on myself, Mama."

Joe asked, "A little scrimmage, Uncle Pete?"

"You mind your own business."

Joe was smiling just a little. "Reckon Davey's my business."

"Since when?"

"Since a long time ago, Uncle Pete. Maybe he's been my affair when he should have been somebody else's."

"I'm sick of your face around this house. Now why don't you git while the gitting's good."

Joe asked in the same matter-of-fact voice, "You think maybe you could bang me up like that? Think you could do it without getting banged back?"

"You thinking of trying me on for size?"

"Might be this is the time."

Stella Dankowski said, "Stop! You should be ashamed, a boy and his uncle. What is this?"

Old Casimar said, "Women, keep out of this. That boy needs some respect knocked in his head."

Ellen took Joe's arm. "Walk with me down the hill, Joe. I think Dr. Black should take a look at David."

Pete said, "Don't bother coming back. Stay home where you belong."

Joe Foley tensed.

But Ellen propelled him firmly through the house and down the hill to the Murder Trail. They walked in silence. Dr. Black's new young housekeeper agreed to send the doctor over when he returned from delivering the Whitestone baby.

Joe said, "I'll walk you back, Ellen."

"Let well enough alone. Come tomorrow, Joe."

"Kinda like to know what's with Davey."

"If there's anything wrong, we'll let you know. He'll be all right, Joe. We'll see to that."

"You and me?"

She felt the odd feeling springing in her.

He said, "That was peculiar, that talk about me being the man that was bringing Davey up. Wouldn't that be peculiar if a guy like me got to thinking a guy his same age was like his kid that he had to take care of?"

She smiled gently. She said, "Guess you would say it was peculiar. But I guess somebody else would say the man that felt that way, he has something to him he didn't want other people ever to know about him. You're a nice guy, Joe."

Then his words came in a sudden torrent. "And if he felt that way about the kid, like he was the kid's old man, then he'd be bound to think about the mother like he was her husband. I guess that's peculiar. I'd guess it was particularly peculiar if he's been in love with her since he was maybe ten years old, and maybe even before that. And he talks big about what he does to other girls, but that's just big talk, because he can't get the one out of his head. Reckon that's peculiar enough. Reckon I've tried

266

enough times to bang it out of my head against a rock. Or dive in the crick and get the water to wash it out of my brain. But I get out of the crick and I stand there naked, and I look at my arms and my hands, and it seems like they're so strong I could break a tree on my knee, and it seems like they're so weak I couldn't even reach out and touch you if I had the chance." When she didn't answer, and when she looked distressed, he said, "About eight million times I decided I was going to tell you. And you always stopped me, because you knew what I was going to say. And when I finally did tell it, it didn't come out right. I wish I could have said it right." In a moment he asked, "You much provoked, Ellen?"

"No."

"What are you? How come you look like that?"

"Just thinking. I'm glad it's finally said. It seemed like such a terrible thing when it was in the shadows."

He said, with great hope springing in him, "Ellen, if you let me, I want to do it with you. Lord, I do."

But Ellen Foley now felt smug! She smiled almost patronizingly. "Well, Joe, I'm almost forty years old. I guess I should be flattered. But you, don't be silly. You'll get over it when you meet the right girl, and we'll both be glad we had it in the open this once and got over it."

Then there was no trace at all of his carefully cultivated accent. He said evenly, "The last thing in the world you can do is treat me like a boy. I may be peculiar to be in love with my aunt. I may be somebody they should lock up in jail. But I'm not a boy, that you can pat me on the head. If you can't feel the same way I do, because it's too terrible to even think about, or whatever it is, you can still have respect for me."

Her supercilious composure was shattered completely. Her mouth was dry. She swallowed vainly. "Joe, I'm married."

"No, you're not married. I don't call what you have, being married."

Her voice was now strangled. "I'm your aunt."

"I can tell that to my head."

She said, terrified, "Oh, Joe, I wasn't patting you on the head. You're scaring me. You are." She wished she could cry.

"Ellen, let's go where there isn't anybody around except us."

She said more sharply, "Don't, Joe. Just don't say any more than you've already said."

"You want to come. I can tell."

"Don't say another word!"

She left him by the silent black tipple. He walked to the river bank and took the ferry to Shawnee. In the room of a chalky-white prostitute at Green Billy's, he changed his mind, and first she tried to tease him into going through with it, and then she laughed at him when he left without his dollar's worth.

10

LATE AT NIGHT, the train whistle blew. The mourning cry came down through the valley, and Pete sat up in bed. Ellen was not beside him. She sat in the rocker. She said, "The whistle never changes."

Pete was shaking and drenched with sweat. He said with a voice he sought to make calm, "I had a nightmare."

"About breaking a boy's ribs?"

"They're not broke. They're cracked."

She didn't answer.

"Okay, I hit him too hard. I'll go easier next time."

"What was the nightmare?"

"Papa was sitting there in the rocker, staring at me. Not saying anything. Just staring."

She came over to the bed and put her hand on her husband's forehead. "You're wringing wet. Go back to sleep. It was me sitting there, not Papa."

"What are you doing up?"

"Thinking."

"What about?"

"Pete, I was sitting there thinking we knew each other once."

"What kind of dumb talk is that? We been living together twenty years. We got two grown girls and a grown boy. I'd say you can't know somebody much more than that."

"Just once we knew each other, Pete, just once. When we were on the hill, that first time, and you talked about the creek and the snow and seeing me all naked. You made me feel so peculiar. So aching and longing and feeling wonderful. I'd do it again. I know I would. I'd commit mortal sin all over again. You were so strong, so handsome, so young and afraid of everything, just like me. Just once, that's all we knew each other."

He didn't answer. He didn't know what to say. Her dramatic tone made him most uncomfortable.

"When people get married, it seems like that's the end of knowing each other. From then on it's just doing without knowing. And all of a sudden you get to wondering if maybe Sweet Water was just coal dust all along, and not the wild flowers and the sweet hunger and love that made you sin. The time's going, Pete, it's going."

"Are you drunk?"

"Is that all you've got to say?"

"You sound like some stupid story. Will you just talk like you're a hillbilly from Sweet Water?"

"You just don't understand, Pete. The time's going."

"Are you getting old? I'm not. You thinking we don't get enough sex? Reckon most women around here would change places with you."

"Reckon they would. Particularly if they've decided they don't really know their own husbands and get hungry to be known at least once more."

"You threatening me?"

"I'm not old. Men look at me."

"What men?"

"I'm relieved to know you're jealous."

"Well, for Christ sake, you look good, I never said you didn't, if that's what you want to know. You get your share of sex from me, and that must mean you look good."

"There's more to making love than just getting in bed and going at it."

"Oh, is that right? Do you want me to read poems when I do it?"

"Pete, I've got so much love to give, and nobody to take it. Sometimes I think if just once you'd look at me again like you did on the hill, I'd give you so much love you wouldn't know what to do with it."

He snorted.

"Give it a chance, Pete. Maybe you'd be surprised."

"I'd be surprised, all right. You sure didn't act like you felt that way this afternoon."

She didn't answer.

"Okay, I didn't mean to hit him so hard."

"Don't take out your frustrations on him."

"What frustrations?"

"Whatever they are."

"What makes you think I've got frustrations?"

"Pete, I'm begging you to love me. To be in love, like we were. Twenty years, Pete. Twenty years, just existing. Fooling myself. Always convincing myself things aren't that bad. Always telling myself I'd be ungrateful if I said anything, because it looks like we have as good a life as the next people. But maybe sooner or later, you've got to say something, before it's too late. I don't think you understand it, Pete, or even know it, how much in love with you I've been. Always have been. Oh, Pete, you're killing it. I think maybe I really have been play-acting all this time. Acting at being in love. To save myself. Because, where could I go? I've shut my eyes to your faults, and pretended I was satisfied, that it really hadn't changed all that much. I can't do it any more, Pete."

"Will you, for Christ sake, come to bed and stop letting that train whistle get you all upset?"

"Pete, how could you hurt that boy? A million times you've hurt him, in every way you can think of, and all he wants is for you to love him and be proud of him. Good God in heaven, look at yourself, Pete, does it give you pleasure to destroy love?"

"If you and him don't like the way I do things, then why don't you just get out? I'm inviting you."

"Pete, I might. I just might. I got a shock, sitting in the dark, thinking. The happiest I've ever been is when you were in Akron. Then instead of having you with me, I could daydream about it. I used to think about all the great things we'd do together. Go somewhere and do things, or stay here and do things.. And then when the reality returns, you know you're not really going to go off to some big adventure, and you know all of your life is right here in Sweet Water covered with the coal dust your husband puts on things, and your life is in your husband just the way he is in Sweet Water, and you

271

know you better not even put too much love in your children, because they'll grow up and go away, while you and your husband stay on, and you know you better find whatever of living there is right here with him, because that's all there's going to be. I'll tell you what the train whistle is, it's the dying while we're still alive, and that's the greatest loneliness there ever can be, dying while you're still alive, and you feel like you're bursting and crying inside you, and you want to put out your hands and pick up something that would make the loneliness stop, but it doesn't stop, it just goes on. And if a hundred men look at you and tell you they want you, you don't want to pay any attention, you just want the man you fell in love with the first time. Pete, it bloomed so sweetly just for a minute, and all of a sudden it was gone, and the loneliness came and stayed, and you keep looking for the flower from then on, and sometimes you think you see it starting to bloom again, but then something happens so that it's like coal dust stifling morning, and you just keep holding out your hands to the flower that never comes back, and wondering what you can do to make it come back like that, even if it was just for once more."

He said gruffly, "I don't even know what you're talking about. I don't think you do either."

"You better know, Pete. You've got to know. Before something terrible happens. Pete, I'm so lonely!"

"I don't know what you're talking about."

"You do. You're lonely, too. That's the nightmare. Papa just staring at you, and you want to be close to him, but he won't let you, and he makes you feel like you've done something wrong, but you can't even imagine what it was, because you never meant to do anything wrong to him, and you don't know what to do about it. You just don't know what to do about it."

He ran his hand through her thick black hair. He said harshly, "Mama used to want me to sit on her lap even when I was twelve or thirteen, because I was the youngest one. That can make you think nothing in the world can get you, when you're sitting in your mama's lap. But it didn't stand up against Papa. Mama cried when he did it, but she could have saved it, because she could have drowned Sweet Water, and Papa wasn't going to change his mind. So that's the world. That's the way it is. And the sooner you know it in this world, that's the sooner they

272

can't get you, and that's when you get over being lonely."

"Pete, why are you so ashamed of sentiment? Please, please, tell me just once that you love me! I think maybe I'd be that flower myself, blooming out all beautiful for you, just once, if you told me just once you loved me."

He wanted to tell her. But the words wouldn't come. He couldn't let them come, for if he did, there would come the bitter devastation of knowing himself. Ellen couldn't know the nightmare for all it was, only Pete could know it. His father was sitting in the chair staring at a child killer, an adulterer, at a bullying coward, at a man who had broken his own son's ribs to relieve his frustrations. How could he confess this sorrow? He wanted to tell her before the moment was gone.

He said, "Listen just a minute. I'm not going to talk like some women's magazine. I'm going to say something straight out you don't want to hear. You heap it on my head. All of it. Maybe I've got it coming. Maybe I haven't played kid's games with you like sweethearts up Beulah Crick. Heap it on me. But do you know where it comes from? Do you know where it starts?"

She didn't answer.

"You don't know. Your mind doesn't work that way. Sweet Ellen, everybody says, sweet Ellen, poor Ellen, that dirty black bastard she's married to. I wish just once they could look inside you and see you, and hear you say it—mortal sin, mortal sin, mortal sin. I was up there on the hill and full of life, and you said mortal sin, mortal sin, mortal sin, and you can't see that, what you did, and you can't take it, but you did it, boy, you did it, and made all this what it is."

He rolled from the bed, pulled on his trousers and went from the room, down the stairs, out into the open, staring off into the dark at Sweet Water.

She couldn't see it, she couldn't take it. She thought to herself: Please, Joe, don't hold out that terrible flower again, in your strong hands, in your youth all hungry, like he was. Oh, Lord, where do the thoughts come from that make terrible sins!

11

IN MAY the backs and ends met with David Battle on Carstairs Field. They clustered around him.

Joe Foley took charge. "Okay, we got two pass plays with Quinn. We got the screen to the fullback, and we got the ends running like hell no place in particular. What we need is pass patterns, like we got running patterns. That's what the pros are doing. That's what they're doing in the Southwest. We're going to throw that ball come fall."

Whitey Culpepper asked, "You talk to Coach about this?"

"What's to talk? Quinn wants to win ball games, he's got no squawk long as we win. Us, we got to get ready for the big time."

Whitey said, "I see the fine Irish hand of Ellen Foley in this, right?"

Joe turned his face to where his aunt watched from the porch of her father's house on the hill. "She says the Notre Dame box will go out, if they don't open up the offense. Too much grind 'em out. Here's Ellen's and my idea of it. The spinning fullback. It gets more out of the fullback and the right half."

Horvath, the fullback, said, "That's sweet talk."

"You run it from the single wing. Fullback gets the

274

ball from the center, spins, and then he can give it to the tailback for one of our regular off-tackle or end runs, or he can fake it to me and give it to Davey on a cutback or a wide reverse, or he can fake to Davey, too, keep it hisself and spin back into the line. Or he can even jump pass as he hits the line."

Horvath said again, "Sweet talk."

"Now the pass patterns. First off we'll try the slant. That means just what it sounds. The end slants across, quick. Ball comes direct to me. The end gets just beyond the line of scrimmage. I straighten up and hit you quick. That's it, it's got to be quick. It's not a TD play, Whitey, unless you get a head of steam and keep going. But it breaks their back for five or ten before the defensive backs can react. It's a sure cure for their throwing a seven-man line on you. What we do is run it a couple times, then throw to Davey down deep off the fake."

Whitey said, "Only one coach knows more than Quinn. Reckon that would be Ellen."

David Battle said, "Whoa up, Joe."

"Isn't that the idea, Davey?"

David said evenly, "That's Ellen's idea. It's the right general idea. We're after deception. The spinner gives some deception. My notion is Pop Warner."

"Pop Warner!"

"Jazzed up. Warner quarterback under the center, with the fullback three yards back of him. Both halfbacks line up in a T with the fullback, or one back goes out on the wing."

Joe asked, "What's wrong with the spinner? I think I'm with Ellen on the spinner."

"Not quick enough, Joe. This way the quarterback straightens up and hits the slant end right now."

Joe said dubiously, "I don't know. I think I'm with Ellen."

David said calmly, "She's not the coach of the team, or the captain, either one."

Joe Foley stared at David Battle.

David said, "Joe, in the Warner, you'll be the quarterback. That's where you put your best man, your passer. Let's give it a try. Billy, you center."

Billy Stone said, "I don't get it. I'm supposed to throw the ball to a sumbitch standing right on top of me?"

Whitey said, "No, stupid, you hand it to Joe, back between your legs."

"Is it legal?"

Whitey said, "If Davey says it's legal, then it's legal."

David said, "It's legal. Whitey, you and Wayne at ends. Vince and me at half. Carl, fullback. Joe, quarterback. Count of two, snap the ball, end slants in, Joe hits him. Whitey, you slant. Wayne, you flare to draw the defense. Let's go."

Joe Foley said wonderingly, "Hup, let's go."

Quinn, coming from Aunt Polly's, saw the practice and hurried down. Pete Battle came from the union office. The two coaches watched in silence while Joe Foley took the ball from center, straightened up, hit the slanting end, and, next time, the flare end. Quinn called David over. The players came with him. Quinn asked, "What's all this?"

David said, "The Warner system, Coach."

Quinn looked at Joe. "I know it's Warner. I get the impression somebody is figuring they should be the coach."

Joe said, "Just in case we bog down with the box, Knute."

David said sharply, "I'll answer him, Joe." His cousin cocked his head, startled. David said, "It's my idea, Coach. This is captain's practice."

Quinn said, "Just what the hell is that supposed to mean?"

Pete Battle said, "There's your answer." He jerked his thumb toward Ellen on the porch, a hundred yards away. "They're horsing around with a woman's idea of football."

David said, "No, sir. The Warner formation is my idea."

His father said, "Same difference. Knock it off. You got better things to do than horse around with that sissy stuff. You're supposed to win ball games, not tippy-toe, Fancy Dan around the field."

Joe Foley said, "Everybody line up for the flying wedge!"

Pete said, "You wouldn't have the guts. You wouldn't last five minutes in one of our games. When we locked arms, and Wilbur Parker come running behind us without a helmet, wasn't nobody going to stop us. You wouldn't have the guts for that kind of football."

Joe smiled just a little. "Why don't you get your cleats and we'll have a little guts practice right now?"

Pete ignored the challenge. "Listen, you gutless wonders,

knock off this woman football. Your job is to win ball games. It's four-yard football that wins." He grunted. "You want a fancy play, we had one on the goal line where Wilbur and Franklin took a hold each side of Wes and flung him right over the line. Like to broke his neck a few times, but it never missed. That was football, not this basketball. You try that one with Davey."

Whitey Culpepper, taking courage from Joe, asked, "Break his neck?"

Pete said doggedly, "Guts football."

Joe said, "Hail the Parkers, champeens of the Neanderthal League."

Pete said harshly, "You be careful, smart aleck."

"Get your cleats and show me some guts football, Uncle Pete."

David said, "There's no sense in the argument. Those rules are gone. The new rules, they're opening up for passing."

Pete said scornfully, "Fairy football. You play guts football, and you'll have what the colleges are looking for. Now get back out there and do it right."

Bob Quinn said, "Just one damn minute." There was silence. He said, "Well, I'm hearing everything. Now I'm going to tell you, there's only one coach of this football team. Only one man going to say how we play it. Anybody got any doubts about that?"

Before Joe Foley could reply, David said, "No, sir. You're the coach. I'm the captain."

Bob Quinn surveyed the young man. He looked at the other players gathered around. Was Davey Battle calling his bluff? It sounded like it. Was he pulling a Joe Foley? No, there was no biting sarcasm, no good humor. This was a statement of fact. This young man took himself seriously as captain of a football team. What ridiculous kind of notion was that? A captain of a Bob Quinn team who was more than a figurehead? That's what this young man was telling him, this young man who excited such loyalty and admiration in his peers. Was it rebellion? Was it mutiny? If it was, how would Bob Quinn go about quelling it? He didn't understand this young man. He didn't know how to grab hold of him.

David said, "Coach, this is the way I figure it. We've got a good backfield and good ends. We lost a lot in the line. Maybe we can't move on power this year. Maybe

277

there comes a time to adjust to the material. You're the coach, Mr. Quinn, but I figured we'd horse around with some deception."

Quinn didn't know what to do. Finally he said, "Davey, won't hurt a thing to horse around. Football is winning, but it should be fun, too. You run it in summer like you want to. When I take over again, I'll run it my way." He walked off the field, doing his best to look unconcerned.

The backs and ends waited for command. David said, "Okay, let's get with it."

Pete asked, "Joe going to do all the passing?"

David turned to his father and said, "He's the natural-born passer."

"Well, if you got to horse around, you take a crack at it, Dave."

"Hands aren't big enough."

"Well, for Christ sake, you can try. Stop making excuses and try."

Joe hollered, "Heave it, Davey!" He flashed down the field and David threw to him. The ball wobbled through the air, came down on target but unlovely. Joe came hipper-dipping back up the field. He motioned to David, and the captain of the team flashed away. Joe waited, waited, then threw fifty yards, floating spiraling on the mark. Joe said without looking at his uncle, "First you want him to play break-his-neck football, then you flip-flop and want him to pass. You don't know what you want. If I was you, I'd leave Davey to me. He'll leave Sweet Water on his strong points, not his weak ones. Why don't you just march yourself up to your union office and sit there looking at your belly button, you'd be more use than out here." Joe waited. His stomach felt empty, like before a ball game. This time it had to be. This time the fight had to come. He waited and wondered if he'd lose. He waited.

Pete Battle pretended not to hear. He left the field white-faced, his insides churning. Could Joe take him? How could he? How could that snot take Pete Battle? Turn around, Pete. Go back and teach that punk snot a lesson he won't ever forget. He wouldn't even know how to fight. They didn't fight in Sweet Water any more, not like they did in the hard days. That punk wouldn't know how to use his heavy shoes. He wouldn't know how to use his knee, or use his elbow in close. Go back and teach him a lesson he won't get over ever. Go back. He thought of the sloping shoulders, the long, strong arms, the muscle-bursting neck, the muscle-rippling back of Joe Foley. Go back, Pete. Go back. But he couldn't go back. Joe Foley relaxed and was limp, because he didn't know if he would have won.

Pete ordered a hand exerciser from Sears, Roebuck, and he said, "Dave, you got the alibi your grip ain't good enough to pass, then squeeze this until it's good enough." Twenty times an evening for two months, he shouted, "Squeeze, boy, squeeze. Get your nose up out of that book and pay attention to squeezing."

Ellen said, "And maybe squeeze himself right out of a college education."

Pete snorted. "You just don't get it, do you? You throw that ball good enough, you run good enough, you play hard-nosed enough, won't be a college in the country won't be glad to guarantee you a degree. On their hands and knees, they'll guarantee you a degree, on a silver platter, you get the whole damn college. And when they come—Pitt, Carnegie, Penn, Southern Cal—we just listen to what they have to offer, and then we'll tell Notre Dame, here's what we'll come for, Hunk."

"*We'll* come for?"

"What's that mean?"

"Just wondered if you were going with David."

"You know what I mean."

"Yes, I do."

Pete said irritably, "Squeeze that thing, Dave."

The grandfather said, "Stupid."

Pete said, "Keep out of it."

Casimar Dankowski roared, "What is this? What is this?"

Pete said loudly, "Oh, shut up, Papa!"

Stella Dankowski cried out, "Peter! Shame, Peter, shame!"

Pete said, "Okay, Mama, okay. Dave, you just do what I tell you. Squeeze that thing."

Ellen said, "He's squeezing it in his sleep. You tried his grip lately?"

Pete's eyes glinted. He put out his big hand. "Shake, boy!"

They clenched hands. They gripped. They gripped hard. There was no unusual expression on the face of David

Battle, but the veins of determination stood out on his forehead. He fought the big hand. It was a closer thing than Pete expected. For a moment he felt a surge of panic. Then David couldn't keep it up, and his father's big hand crushed inexorably while the smile of triumph spread, and David went to his knees, fighting to keep his face immobile.

Ellen said tensely, "It's enough, Pete. Can't you see?"

Pete let him go. He said triumphantly, "Can't beat the old man yet."

Casimar Dankowski, past seventy years of age, rose from his chair and put out his strong hand. "Now I teach you a lesson."

Pete said, "Oh, sweet Jesus, sit down, Papa."

Joe Foley, watching from the doorway, said, "Try me."

"Sweet Jesus, haven't you got a house of your own?"

Stella said, "Peter, we will not have that kind of talk."

Joe asked, "You got a house of your own, Uncle Pete?"

Ellen said sharply, "That's enough, Joe."

Casimar said, "All of you, out. Out of my house."

Stella said, "Papa, Peter didn't mean it."

Pete said, "I meant it. I ought to leave him here to starve to death. Sitting on his fanny for twenty years, it would serve him right."

Stella rocked her lined face with her hands. "Peter, Peter, Papa."

Joe Foley said, "Want to try me in a grip fight, Pete? Indian-rassle? Arm-rassle?"

"You're really asking for it."

Ellen said, "That's enough. Everybody, that's enough."

Joe said, "You say you will, but you don't. Let's set a time. A time so there's no backing out. The day I leave Sweet Water for college, we'll arm-rassle. Right out there on the C & O platform, in front of everybody, one shows up the other one. Is it a deal?"

Pete said gruffly, "Any time."

"Not any time. That time. The day Davey and me leave."

"You got a deal. Now get out of my house."

"My house," Casimar Dankowski roared.

Pete said to Ellen, "Let's go to bed."

Ellen rose and followed her husband out of the room without a word. Joe listened to the stairs to the bedrooms creak under them. His chest ached.

280

David asked, "Want to do anything, Joe?"

"Reckon I'll go on home."

"Joe, would you do me a favor? In the long run, I can take care of myself with him."

"Sure you can. He'll beat your brains out, that's what he'll do, if I don't make sure he don't."

"Passive resistance, that will wear him down. He was so dead set against throwing the ball, and we got him around to where that's all he can think. Passive resistance. And besides, I got to admit, my grip's getting good using that thing. It will work out, Joe."

"I'll by God make sure it does."

Stella said, "For shame, boys talking like that. David, for shame."

David Battle said to his grandmother, "I will take care of this." His square jaw was set, his Foley-blue eyes glowing. "Joe, I want you and everybody else to know, if I want help, I'll ask for it."

David took his big cousin by the arm and led him to the front of the house and down the front steps. Joe was perturbed. What was Davey talking about? Davey needed him. Davey needed taking care of. Davey needed the big-brother strong-father he didn't have in Pete. Davey needed him.

But David said, "Joe, listen just a minute. You go on all those years, not measuring up, you're too puny and you never do anything right and wishing you could do just one thing, just one lousy thing to make him proud of you, because he's the greatest in all the world, and then all of a sudden you realize it's not you that's got the problems, it's him. And then you feel sorry for him, and wish you could figure out what you could do to help him."

"Davey, you've gone soft in the head. He's a no-good bastard and always was. He'd crucify you if there was a nickel in it for him. Not a thing he could think of, he didn't do to make you miserable. Now you trying to tell me you feel sorry for a miserable bastard like that?"

"He's a sinner, Joe."

"Sure, he's a sinner. What's that got to do with it."

"You feel sorry for sinners. You try to forgive them."

"And you sound like some Holy Joe. Look, Davey, I think you're coming along just fine. This captain thing, that's great. But you get me worried when you start talking like a Holy Joe. You ask me, you're getting worse."

"Getting worse because I'm more aware of sin? That doesn't make sense." David turned and walked toward the house. He stopped and looked briefly at the lighted window of his parents' bedroom. Without turning, he said, "Maybe you could look in yourself, and get rid of some sin, do you think?" He resumed his way to the house.

Joe watched his back. Was it coincidence, that upward glance to Ellen Foley's bedroom? He wondered how much David did know. This young fellow that needed him, had to need him, how much did he know? Did he know for sure that Joe was in love with Ellen? Did he know that? Did he know that Joe had asked Ellen to give herself to him and let him make love to her the way she needed to be loved? Did David know that? He must. Maybe out of intuition born out of jealousy. Was this coming between them? Was this the barrier erecting itself? Would it shut out the father-son relationship that David needed so much, that Joe needed so much?

Joe sighed inside himself. He sauntered down the hill to Murder Road along the rail track and Murder Creek. There he turned and looked back up at the gray house. For a while he watched the light in Ellen's bedroom. The light went out. Joe pounded his fist in his palm and cursed out loud. The gall filled him up, burning. He walked fast up the tracks toward Murder, turned off along Black Beulah Creek, which ran deeper than the Murder. He took off his shirt and loosened his belt. He heard the male voice and the soft answer, Whitey Culpepper and Swaney Wood. Joe put his shirt on again, saying softly, "Why? Why? Why? Why did it happen to me?" Swaney giggled. Whitey said she always giggled just before he did it to her. The sound of her, the knowing what was to happen, excited him. The want of woman was a fire. He listened again for Swaney. He couldn't hear her now. He thought of Swaney, Swaney giggling with him. Swaney. Swaney. And then Swaney Wood disappeared in the night, and the firm, ever-young body of his father's sister walked naked toward him, there in the wilderness, every way he turned, and he wondered if Pete was doing it to her, the way Whitey was doing it to Swaney, and he said softly to the night, "Oh, sweet Jesus!"

12

BETWEEN Cambridge, Massachusetts and Dee-troit, Michigan, Jim Parker averaged nearly seventy miles an hour in his Parker Special boat-tail Packard. He drove directly to the Embassy plant and put himself in line at the Salaried Employment office, all hot-shot engineer and MIT, and he said to himself, "Here I am, Mr. National Motors! Are you ready for me?"

An hour later he spent four minutes with the Salaried Supervisor, who said to him, "Are you kidding, kid? There's a depression on, remember?" Jim departed that office somewhat subdued.

After some contemplation, he took himself with renewed resolution to the Engineering Department of the Embassy Division, and told the male receptionist that he wanted to see Mr. Carl Pearson. The receptionist gave him a snide look and let him talk to Pearson's secretary on the phone. The secretary sounded as though he smelled bad, right up the wires, and she demanded to know just what it was he thought important enough to present to Mr. Pearson himself. James Lee Parker of Parker County, West Virginia, resented her attitude. But he had an axe to grind. He yes-ma'amed the secretary and told her that he was a student from MIT and wanted Mr. Pearson to see the hot car he'd built. The secretary said that she would

283

inform Mr. Pearson, but that he was quite busy and would undoubtedly turn Mr. Parker over to an assistant. Carl Pearson surprised his secretary and the male receptionist, but not Jim Parker, and came below to see the car.

Pearson walked around the yellow beauty and looked inside it and at the engine, and he said, "Not bad. How fast will it go?"

"One hundred plus."

"This I've got to see."

Pearson was up to eighty on the street alongside the Embassy plant when the police officer's siren set up a plaintive yell. The motorcycle was not about to catch Jim Parker's Packard, but Pearson pulled over dutifully. He said to the officer, "Just testing, Dick."

The cop said, "I might have known it was you, Carl. One of these days you're going to beat my ass for not arresting you, if you don't knock your own off first."

Pearson then drove at closer-to-legal speed through the streets of Detroit, enjoying the feel of the well-built automobile. Jim Parker waited. Finally Pearson asked, "What did you want to see me about, Jim?"

"Sir, I'll have my master's in automotive engineering from MIT this June. I stand third in my class. I built this car to show you what I can do and I want a job working for you."

Pearson studied young Jim. He said, "MIT and a nickel will buy you an apple on Woodward Avenue. But this car is just great, Jim. Just great. And I wish there was something I could do for you, but I can't. We're not hiring."

"Well, who do you think I can ask for a job around National Motors that can give me one?"

"Good Lord himself couldn't. There's a depression, remember? We're laying off, not hiring."

"How about the mother of God? Your secretary. Could she give me a job?"

"Is she that bad?"

"Yes."

Carl Pearson narrowed his eyes. "When you're important enough to have a secretary, you'll be entitled to opinions how secretaries should act. I'm more impressed with your car, I'll assure you, than with your judgment. Don't you think you might be just a little brash?"

284

Jim Parker said, "Mr. Pearson, I've got a lot to learn. But I know quite a bit, too. It's for sure I know who you are. I know I want to go to work for you. That's because I can learn some things working for you that will help me get ahead fast. My selling point is that I'd do a good job for you. I think I'd earn my money."

After a moment Carl Pearson said, "Now that sounds better. That's not smart-alecky, brash talk, that's confidence. Where are you from, Jim?"

"Sweet Water, West Virginia. That's up the Kanawha Valley south of Charleston."

"You don't have any discernible accent."

"Just some colloquialisms left over. You can get any kind of accent you're looking for in West Virginia. All the way from Deep South mushmouth to maybe the most accent-free speech you'll find in America. I've got some hillbilly in me under Morgantown and MIT."

"Your father a coal miner?"

"My father was superintendent of the Red Flash mines. My family has been there a long time. The county is Parker County. I think the main family occupation is the ministry."

"Oh? What denomination?"

"Church of Christ."

"Fundamental?"

"Quite."

"That's good. That's very good. I'm Fundamental myself. I've done some lay preaching. Jim, tell me your ambitions at National Motors. Do you have any big dreams and schemes all laid out?"

"Yes, sir. They're quite specific."

"The intention of my question was to bring you down to earth. To face the present, not the future."

"Yes, sir. But my answer is that I intend to do a good enough job that I'll go a long way in the Corporation, and while I'm getting there I'll be doing my best to push my boss on ahead. Loyalty is something we know in the mountains."

Carl Pearson, the future president of National Motors, said, "Jim, we haven't hired an engineer for three years. But National Motors has to be here after the depression, if it ever does end. I won't promise you it will be any more than sweeping out my office, and I do promise you, you darn well better get along with my secretary, but you've got yourself a job. Report July first."

Jim went home to Sweet Water and proposed marriage to Coby Warren, a quite plain girl.

13

Jɪᴍ ꜱᴛᴇᴇʀᴇᴅ the Parker Special boat-tail Packard at high speed off the macadam of the Charleston Road. He ricocheted up Murder Trail, along the rail spur and the creek, to the foot of Casimar's hill. David bounded off the front steps, then put his hands nonchalantly in his pockets and sauntered down. When he couldn't contain himself, he shouted, "Man!"

"Get in."

Jim drove back to the pike and headed upstream along the Kanawha, past the tipple, past the Red Flash office and company Store, past Carstairs Field and Parker District High School, past St. Mary's Catholic Church and Old Sod Square, past the dingy C & O station, past the Church of Christ.

At the side of the road, Swaney Wood turned from Whitey Culpepper and waved. David nodded almost imperceptibly and sank lower in the bucket seat. Swaney watched the yellow car disappear, and Jim Parker watched Swaney in his rear-view mirror.

Jim said, "She sure gave you a look."

David shrugged like a turtle.

"She really the kind of girl she's got the reputation of being?"

David shrugged again.

"She probably is. India always thinks the worst of people and she's generally right." When David still didn't answer, Jim said, "I think maybe you're more taciturn than ever. When you grow up, they ought to make you ambassador to the Orient. You'd get the Chinese talking about the inscrutable Americans."

David straightened up in the seat. He said, "I get all A's, and somehow people get the notion I don't get all A's. I talk, and people somehow get the notion I don't talk. I run with the football and I don't ask anybody for anything, and somehow people get the idea I want a hand up after I been knocked down. Well, I'm captain of the football team, and I do my job." He slumped back down in the seat.

Jim said, "I'll have to think about that." He depressed the accelerator until the speed was very dangerous. David leaned his head back with the wind in his face, and through slitted eyes watched the beautiful Kanawha Valley mountain sides flow by. He vowed that he would one day own a car like Jim Parker's.

Jim asked, "How's Joe?"

"Feisty."

"I bet he is. Uncle Davis says he's the best high school football player in America. He says you're not far behind."

"I'm behind."

"How much do you weigh now?"

"One sixty."

"That's good."

"Joe's one eighty-five. They timed him in the hundred in ten flat in tennis shoes."

"Uncle Davis says you're shiftier, and if Joe wasn't on the team, you'd come on the greatest. Has that occurred to you?"

"That kind of speculation doesn't have much point."

"Colleges after you?"

"Some. But they know I'm a made ballplayer, and Joe's the natural. They're mainly after me because they figure Joe and me will go to the same place."

"Which one? Notre Dame?"

"Joe's driving 'em batty. He won't say."

"You guys going to win tomorrow?"

"I think."

"Any doubt?"

"Shawnee's undefeated, too. They're gunning for us. We've been lucky to get by some games."

"I'm not asking questions just to hear myself talk. I'm listening to the way you answer, to see how you've changed."

"Have you changed, Jim?"

"I'm sure I have. I think my self-confidence has a little sounder base than it did. I suspect I'm mellowing just a little bit. I'm bound to be maturing. I better be mature. I just got a job in Dee-troit. Did you know up there they call it Detroit?"

David asked enthusiastically, "Engineering cars?"

"With Carl Pearson himself."

"I don't know who that is."

"Chief engineer at Embassy. The hottest hot shot. His picture was on the cover of *Motor Magazine* this month. You bet on him for president of National Motors, right before me. I'm on his team. And he's a fundamentalist, that won't hurt."

"Do things like that count?"

"Don't things like that count everywhere?"

"How old is a guy like Pearson?"

"I'd guess maybe thirty-five."

"How much money do you reckon he gets?"

"I haven't the faintest idea. Maybe ten thousand a year."

"I bet it's more than that. Papa says the bosses get maybe fifty times as much as the workers in those factories."

"For all I know, he makes a hundred thousand. I didn't stop to think how much you got. Just how big and famous you get. How many magazines they put you in. All the cops in Detroit know Carl Pearson for his speeding. That'll be the day, when they know me, too." He jammed the accelerator to the floor. The Packard jumped. Jim shouted over the roar, "I'll be so famous you can just write me Jim Parker, Detroit, and I'll get it." He slowed down reluctantly for a series of S-curves.

David said, "Joe Foley, World."

"Reckon you got me there. More people know Red Grange than know the president of National Motors. Or the President of the United States, for that matter."

"Does that make you mad, Jim?"

"Some. But it's the natural selectivity of the capitalistic

system, and I can't really object just because some sexy, stupid movie star gets more money than the President."

"Do you talk much about politics and things at MIT?"

"Sure. Bull sessions all the time."

"Do those smart guys think like you?"

"I'd have to say most college guys are for the New Deal. The depression mixes people up, and besides, college guys are natural rebels."

"Everybody is wrong except you?"

"Most everybody, yes. Do you expect that to bother me? It doesn't. Most people thought the world was flat. Just consider that all dumb people are for Roosevelt, and that means most smart people are the ones who voted against him. Are you still on the side of the dumb ones?"

"I think maybe you've changed some, all right, Jim. You don't seem so het up as you used to be. Or least-wise, even if you haven't changed your notions, you're spending time thinking about your job and things, and not about unions and things. Papa says that's one reason the union always wins. The union thinks about their things all the time, and the bosses, the fat cats, they think about their money most of the time and the union only part of the time."

"When I'm president of National Motors, I'll show the union I haven't changed."

David didn't say anything, but he disagreed. It seemed to him that Jim Parker was already in the grasp of power and success, and his brave ideas would be lost.

Jim thought about it, too. Was he losing his zealous-ness? Was he abandoning his crusade? Were his convic-tions altering? He said, "When I said the money wasn't important, I didn't mean it to come out that way. I just meant I didn't know what I was going to get, but I want lots, because I'm no Hindu sticking skewers through my jaws. The American idea is to reward good performance. Money is like people applauding you. I want a lot."

"I thought maybe you were deciding we should all be like preachers and teachers and such, and working for the common good, like Papa says, and for the honor."

"Is that what you think people should do, Davey?"

"It sort of sounds like a Bible way of doing things."

"If it does, that's where me and the Bible part company. That's what communism is all about, Davey. Work for the common good and the glory of the State. And I'll admit,

290

if you could repeal human nature, it would probably work. In theory it's perfect. It breaks down because people aren't perfect. The union and the communists assume that the workers are more altruistic and moral than the bosses, but they aren't, of course, and the noble idea ends up with bums wanting to ride the coat tails of the producers, particularly where you've got diverse populations, like America, where there are great blocs of nationalities that want other people to take care of them."

"You sure are cynical, Jim."

"Of course I am. More so all the time. About everything except me and where I'm going, and National Motors."

David pondered. He wondered whether or not to say it. He said, "I'm cynical, too, maybe. Do you know what I asked Uncle Walter? I asked him since Roosevelt and Hitler and Stalin and Mussolini all wanted a big government that was the boss of the people, what was the difference between them?"

"What did Walter say?"

"He said it didn't sound like much of a thing to do, to lump them all together, with Roosevelt being an American. But I can't see the difference between them."

"By golly, you're right. And by golly, I'm glad to see the day."

"Well, I didn't say I went whole hog. I mean, maybe there's a middle of things. Only I got to say, it seems like the middle is sometimes on the opposite from Papa and the union and all. I mean, when I want to do something with myself, and it's the union supposed to be for the common man, how come they all the time try to keep the common man where he is? That kind of thing. I don't say the bosses are right on things, but they're the ones want to give the guy like me a chance to be somebody."

"Want to be my best man, Davey?"

"Your what? In politics, or National Motors, or something? I don't get it."

"Like getting married best man. I asked her."

David stared at him.

Jim U-turned and headed back toward Sweet Water. "Didn't you ever hear of anybody getting married? Man gets to be twenty-three and's got himself a job in Detroit, and he thinks about it."

"Does Mama know?"

Jim Parker's face clouded. "Davey, it's not Gerry. It's Coby Warren."

"Coby Warren!"

"Davey, it couldn't be Gerry, you know that."

A red Auburn Speedster with the top down sped past them, Harold Scott, muffled against the briskness, waving haughtily.

Jim asked excitedly, "When'd he get it?".

David said woodenly, "Two months. He sold the Marmon to Uncle Walter."

"Has he still got the Dusy?"

"He gave it to Artie, and Artie ran it into Murder Crick."

"Going up there with Swaney, I'll bet."

David didn't answer.

"When I get to Detroit, I'm going to drive me nothing but experimental cars. The ones three or four years ahead, like Carl Pearson drives. Davey, you know I couldn't marry Gerry."

"Sure."

"I guess you know I would if I could. Gerry's got to be the prettiest girl in Sweet Water, next to Ellen. And Coby is a plain girl, you'd get me to admit that. But that's all right. She's the right one for me. She's got the household virtues I want. Davey, she's Church of Christ."

"You don't have to explain, Jim."

"I sure gave it a lot of thought. I figured for a while I'd look around up in Detroit, where there's millions to pick from. But then I got to thinking if I did that, I'd be lolly-gagging around when I should have my mind on the job of being president. And why should I go to all that trouble just to find the same thing I already found in Sweet Water?"

"Would you pick Coby if she was a Catholic?"

"No."

"Well, I guess that's fair enough. I think it's fine, Jim." David wished Jim Parker well. But he had a gnawing doubt. He wondered if Jim had picked Coby because she was a Warren, and Gerry was only a Dankowski-Foley.

They drove in silence.

Jim said abruptly, "How's Joe's Oedipus complex?"

"I don't know what that is."

"You know darn well what I'm talking about."

David said, "Oedipus is when it's your own mother." He wished he hadn't said it, because it committed him.

Jim said, "We both know what we're talking about. Did you think I didn't know about it? If you want me to, I can even tell you why he's got himself so mixed up."

"Well, Jim, did you ever stop to think maybe there's some things you just got no business asking about? How come you and India figure everybody else's business is yours, too?"

Jim said, "This time you're doing me an injustice. I think that's one of the things I've improved on. I'm so busy with myself, I'm just not as nosy as I used to be. Maybe you ought to stop and think that I consider myself your friend. I want to help where I can."

"Help who?"

"Help you, Davey, wherever I can."

"Well, maybe I just don't happen to need that kind of friend."

"I'm going to do it. I'm going to say what I've got to say. If you decide you don't want to be my best man, or want to call everything quits when I get done, that's up to you. But I've been involved in what I've got to tell you, so maybe I just do have the right to talk. I'm going to start with Joe and lead up to you. I'll start like this. With Joe, it's simple. There isn't enough outlet in a town like this, even for the football star. Not enough normal release for a terrific guy like him, with all that drive. But don't worry about Joe. He'll get over it. Going away is going to be the best thing that ever happened to him. Not just him. You, too. Davey, do you ever go out with Swaney?"

David was tense. After a long moment, he said, "No."

"Does Joe?"

Again there was a wait. "How should I know? He says he does, but he's big talk."

At the sign that read Sweet Water Unincorporated, Jim pulled the Packard off the road and up against the bank of the hillside below the company home of Dvorak.

"Davey, you ought to go out with Swaney."

David said sharply, "She's a slut."

"You mean she does it for money?"

"She would."

"Davey, who said so. Ellen?"

"You sound like Papa." David braced himself. He didn't want to talk about the dreadful things. He wanted

293

desperately to talk about them. "Jim, I'll ask it, do you think there's something wrong with me? Do you know what I mean? I mean, Joe and me go to the dances some, but we don't take a girl, just sometimes dance with the ones the other guys bring." Again he took a hitch on himself. "Jim, Papa says we're queer, because he took us four times to Green Billy's and we wouldn't do it." He heard his own voice saying these things as though in a nightmare. How could he thus expose his innermost fears to Jim Parker, who might be a true son to India Parker and tell the world, and in any event was a young man whose admiration David very much wanted? How could he be doing this to himself?

But Jim said calmly, "Good, we're coming out in the open. There's nothing wrong with you. Probably you dissipate some of your sexual drive in working so hard at football. I do that studying hard at MIT."

"Jim, do they teach you about things like this at MIT?"

"These are elementary things. Classic cases from the psych course. In this case, I have my own experiences I'll be getting to."

"Jim, when he gets me outside that place, and you know what's going on in there, I get sick like I'm going to throw up."

"Well, in the first place, I'm sure not going to try to talk you into that. Or taking Swaney anywhere except dances. For sure, I don't want you to take her up Beulah Crick."

"Sometimes I think maybe I'll tell Mama what he's trying to get me to do."

"Very likely she knows. In any event, I think you're old enough to handle it yourself."

"Mama says there's lots of things in the world they tell you a man has to do or he isn't a man, but she says the sinners just want company."

"I'd say I agree with her."

"She says no matter what anybody says, it's mortal sin, and you can't get rid of it just going to Confession and then doing it again."

"Well, I don't have to worry about mortal sins in my church, but I don't think men should commit adultery any more than women. That's what I get from reading the Bible. And maybe I wouldn't admit it around MIT, but when I get married, it's going to be the first time I do it, same as for Coby."

"Jim, I reckon I want to hear what you're going to say about Joe."

"We're talking about Joe and Ellen."

David nodded fearful assent.

"Don't take it too seriously. There are a lot more serious things you should be concerned about. Joe, that's just thinking, that's not doing."

"Thinking is the same as doing it, you know that."

"Is that what they teach you in the Catholic Church?"

"God said so."

Jim smiled. "I repeat my question."

"Well, I don't think I want to joke about it."

"Good heavenly days, if you have to worry about what you think, everybody's in trouble. Davey, we're getting down to what I've got to say to you."

"Do you think things, Jim?"

"Sure. All the time. Every time I see that Swaney walk like that, I think things. I been thinking things all my life. I can remember when I was six years old, I used to think about being a naked slave for Charlene Culpepper when we had the same desk in school, and maybe I didn't know what I was doing, but on the other hand, I knew darn well what I was doing. I can remember a spell when I kept thinking about doing it to nigger girls, and maybe I'm not over that one yet. That's just the way people are. Everybody thinks things that would be terrible in the light of day. Everybody looks at dirty pictures, just so long as he figures he won't get caught at it. And everybody can have the same kind of dirty thoughts, but let somebody else's get out in the open, people are all the quicker to say he's perverted, or something. I'd like to be a mind reader on Uncle Davis or Father Hannigan some day."

"Jim, are you really saying there's nothing wrong with Joe thinking that way about Mama? Are you really saying that?"

"I just said Joe's got plenty of company, that's all. When a guy realizes he's not a unique ogre, the obsessions go away quicker. Dirty books, playing with yourself, all those kind of things that everybody does or is a liar if he says he doesn't."

David was nearly frozen with humiliation. He said, almost strangled, "It's a sin."

"Playing with yourself? I don't know. I know it's not polite. That's why you lock the door. It's just an im-

295

propriety. Are you sure it's a sin? Davey, you sure think a lot of things are sins."

"Jim, I went this far, I guess I'll ask it. Jim, when I do get to thinking, you know, what kind of woman, and all that, I think she should be like Ellen. I mean look like her. You got to say that's kind of funny."

"I'd say for sure you've got good taste. I never had that problem. India's not exactly my idea of a dream girl."

"How can you talk that way about your mama?"

"You mean without due respect? It's not hard. I'm cut loose, Davey. Maybe too much, but that's better than still being tied. At this point, I'm going to be president of National Motors and marry Coby Warren, and Mama is just another woman in the world to me. You'd be amazed how good you feel when you cut loose. Maybe you ought to cut loose like Kathleen. Do you hear from her?"

"No. We don't. She's in Akron, but we don't know where."

"Good for her. She got out from under. Davey, I'll tell you about Ellen. That's the blackest hair on any white woman on the Kanawha, and the bluest eyes and fairest skin this side of Ireland, and I think she's found the Fountain of Youth right here in Sweet Water. And I think maybe she's got some frustrations that are mixing her up some, and I'm not going into them, because if you want to, you can figure them out for yourself. Now let's talk about you, because that's what I've been aiming at. You don't like it when people always try to give you a hand up, when all the time you can stand on your own feet. Well, in the first place, you got to admit you do look like a natural-born mascot. And in the second place, you've got some maturing to do. You're doing some great things physically. And they tell me you're the brightest student in Parker High. People don't really underestimate you, not the people that know you, anyhow. But strangers would. You are maturing some ways. You resist Pete. You're thinking for yourself about things and disagreeing with him some. You're coming on like a tiger. And all the time, you're regressing emotionally. I see that in you. Other people see it, too, even if they don't know the background so they can define it. But I know exactly what it is. Ellen is mother and father to you. And she's putting all her ideas in you. And not all of her ideas are necessarily good ideas."

"Jim, don't you say anything against her."

Jim started the car and slewed out into the Charleston Road, the wheels spinning in the coal dust. He drove to the gray house. He said, "Go ask Ellen if it's all right for you to be my best man in the Church of Christ. When you come back, I've got something to say that's been burning a hole in me."

David hesitated. He wanted to tell Jim Parker to go to hell. He was dreadfully unhappy. He was agonizedly dissatisfied with himself. He had committed the most extreme impropriety. He had exposed himself to Jim's prying, exposed his deepest concerns and emotions, and worst of all, gotten no real comfort, no real explanation of the devils that beset him. He tortured himself with self-recrimination. He wished that Jim would out with it, the coup de grâce.

He went to the house and asked the question. When he came back down the hill to the car, he said, "Mama says I should tell you I'd be honored, and nothing's going to bite me in the Church of Christ."

Jim showed surprise. "And what did Pete say?"

"He said he didn't reckon anything was going to bite me in either church."

"There I reckon he's right."

"I don't think he means it like you. It got Grandma started on him again. About going to church."

"Casimar?"

"He got up and went out back."

"Davey, was your mama sore about it not being Gerry?"

"Didn't seem like it, Jim."

Jim's face brightened. "Of course! That's it. She's relieved that Gerry won't be getting married. Davey, here it comes, first the slug between the eyes, then a surprise. Davey, Joe said it. Do you remember when we talked the day I came home from Morgantown? Joe said it, about you and Gerry and Confession and beatification. Davey, it wasn't Gerry being Catholic that I didn't ask her to marry me. Here it comes. It was because it was all the time like I felt I was mortal sin just walking around on the face of the earth when I was around her. I couldn't even accidentally touch her bare arm without her jumping like I was the snake trying to give her the apple. She sees sin everywhere. Do you know what she told me? She told me Pete made a pass at her. Can you imagine? I don't know what happened, but I'll sure bet it was in her mind, that's all, because I know first-hand how she is. Davey, you've got to do something with her, before it's too late. And for yourself, too. That's what I had to tell you."

David Battle said, "Jim, you better know it, I've got my idea of what sin is, and if you think different, that's too bad. I thought you were different, and you're just going to have to not tell me you think different, if you still want to be friends, and that's it."

"I'm sure not sorry I told you. It was burning a hole in me. All I ask is that you think about it. And Suzanne Carstairs is coming to Sweet Water. Suzanne is Vincent's daughter."

David's blue eyes opened wide.

"Mrs. Brady wrote India and said Suzanne wanted to see where her father lived, and would it be all right if she stayed with us for a spell. That's her new name, Mrs. Brady, Vincent's wife that was a dead ringer for Ellen. What's your bet that Suzanne looks like Ellen?" Jim smiled warmly. "She's fifteen years old, if that's not too young for you. I'll bring her to the dance for you and Joe." His smile broadened. "Maybe she's just the one to lead you and Joe out of Sodom and Gomorrah." He turned the car around to drive off, stopped briefly, and called back, "I'm counting on you to help out with Suzanne."

David watched the yellow boat-tail car carom down the trail, and despite his best efforts, felt an excitement.

14

Bob Quinn called his squad to the huddle on the sideline. He wore his usual uniform—the sweat shirt, baseball cap, baseball pants, low-cut football shoes and sweat socks. A whistle hung on a cord around his neck. Joe Foley came first and stood next to him. He said out of the corner of his mouth, "It's the last game, so I'll tell you you've had it wrong for four years."

Quinn stared straight ahead, but Joe knew he was listening.

"Rockne just wore the whistle at practice."

Quinn's hand shot to the whistle, then he lowered it slowly.

"As a matter of fact, the whole get-up is wrong, Knute. Where'd you get your information? Rockne wore a business suit on game days. You've copied the wrong picture for four years."

Quinn turned in suffocating mortification and took Joe's jersey front and pulled him close. He said softly, "You try to run like Red Grange, me, I try to coach like Knute Rockne."

Joe grinned. "I hope I come as close as you."

Quinn let go the jersey. He was nonplused. Was it another of Joe's sarcasms? He sounded sincere. It must be some sarcasm, and Quinn would get the point before long.

The crowd roar increased noticeably. Sweet Water boiled with unbearable anticipation. The invading Warrior adherents, come over the Kanawha from Shawnee, raised their own answering sea roar.

Quinn got a hold of himself. He was a professional. He could not be turned from the job at hand. He said in his Rockne voice, "Men, you've come to the final day. Seven Saturdays in a row you've got out on the football field and carried the Parkers to glory. Your task is not yet finished. Your mothers and fathers are in those stands. They've got faith in you and the great Parker football teams. They count on victory. They count on you. Are you going to let them down? Are you going to put the Parkers in the losing column? Shawnee stands between you and your goal. Are you going to let defeat come to Sweet Water? Men, around here we don't know what defeat is. Now get out there and drive, drive, drive. Get out there and win, win, win!"

He waited for the shout from his squad. They swatted their sweaty palms together, but they stayed in the huddle on the sideline, while the referees waited in midfield.

Quinn said in anticlimax, "Let's go get 'em, Parkers!"

Joe Foley said, "Davey, I reckon you know we made you captain because you kept your mouth shut. Now you got to say something."

The entire squad, bending over in the huddle, watched David Battle. He was prepared. He wanted desperately to say something grandly inspirational. He was the captain. All year he'd lived up to being captain. But to say something inspirational? His throat and lips were dry, and he had no words at all.

Joe Foley grinned and put his arm around his cousin's shoulder. "Davey, you say more'n most people when you don't say nothing." Then his voice turned raspy. He sounded more like Rockne than Quinn sounded like Rockne. He said solemnly, "Men, let's win this one for the Gipper!"

They grinned, they roared.

Before they stopped roaring, David knelt down in the huddle and made the Sign of the Cross. He said, "Jesus, Mary and Joseph, protect us during this hour of our ʳecreation." There was dead silence, there in the huddle,

300

while the crowd noise swelled. David made the Sign of the Cross again, and the Dankowskis and Harry Gallagher, Dvorak and Joe Foley moved their arms with him. But still the squad waited. David straightened up. He said, "I got three cousins on this team, they don't come through, they got to answer to me. Nobody on this team has played a losing ball game. Shawnee's lost before. That's the difference. Let's go."

Then the young men, the sons of coal miners, railroaders and mountaineers in depression-ridden, ruined, shabby, hungry Sweet Water, West by God Virginia, burst onto the field with one great yell of fervor. At the last minute Joe Foley stopped and turned back to the coach of undefeated football teams, growling like a lion and making the face ballplayers make for photographers. He said between his teeth, "We're winning this one for the Gipper, Knute."

Quinn didn't smile. He said within his head, "Go, you Irish bastard. Win this one for me. Win this last one for me. Win it for me and go to hell!"

This was a day of Shawnee inspiration. From the moment David won the flip of the coin and the Parkers received, they had their backs against the wall. The kick was short. Whitey Culpepper, the left end, picked it up on the first bounce, was hit before he had it tucked away, and the Shawnee Warriors took it on the thirty. They weren't stopped until a fourth down pass went off the fullback's finger tips at the four. Quinn released his breath. The play should have scored. The Parkers hadn't defensed against a throw to the fullback, and it should have scored. Well, it didn't, and it was the Parkers' turn.

But the big Red Flash team couldn't get out of its own tracks. The determined Shawnee line poured in before the plays got under way. Sweet Water made one first down on main strength, then was forced to punt in the next series.

Pete Battle raged on the sideline. "Get in there and charge, you chicken-livered Snakes!" He was drowned out by the Shawnee din.

It went that way. For the entire first half, Shawnee flung themselves at the Parker goal. They were stopped on the twelve, on the two, and on the eight-yard lines. Coach Quinn faced his squad at half-time in the locker room. They waited for a tongue-lashing or inspiration, prepared to ignore either one as much as possible. He said nothing, and the players looked wearily at their cleated shoes.

Pete Battle couldn't take the silence. He said, "Listen, you bastards, who said you could play football?"

Joe Foley straightened up and hit his palm with his fist. David put a restraining hand on his arm. Joe relaxed just a little. He said, "I assume the brain trust has figured out what's happening?"

Pete said, "I'll tell you what's wrong, you're not charging. You're playing gutless ball. They're outfighting you, that's what's wrong."

Joe addressed himself to Coach Quinn. "They're on to us. They've got us scouted right down to the last move. We've beat them and a gang of other teams for four years with the same moves, but now they're wise."

Quinn turned away. He couldn't spoil his planned dramatics by speaking now.

Pete said, "Those plays work, if you put some charge behind them."

Joe said with remarkable patience, "Mr. Quinn, we're a great coached team, if fundamentals and precision are all there is to coaching. But sometimes you come to the end of that line. This is it. Shawnee's throwing a new play at us every series, special for us. Our stuff, they're in on us before fundamentals and precision can count. It's time to pull something out of the hat."

Still Quinn said nothing.

The team waited.

Quinn looked at his watch. He stood up and said, "All right, girls, let's go."

He waited expectantly for the growls of protest. It was the master stroke. If it had worked for Rockne against Princeton, it surely would devastate these high school mountaineers with their fierce pride.

His squad sat silent.

Then Joe Foley said, "Oh, sweet Jesus!"

David Battle got to his feet, and his cleats clattered loudly on the concrete as he walked out in front of his team. He looked at Quinn, looked him right in the eye. He said, "Coach, this is a four-year team. The first years we got whipped up to winning. Now we don't need that. We'll win this ball game. Shawnee will never score on us. We're asking for permission to throw some surprises at them."

302

Quinn said coldly, "Get out there and play the football I've taught you. There aren't any alibis. You execute those plays properly, they'll move like they've moved for four years."

David said, "Let's go, men. We'll score."

The Shawnee team was lined up when the Parkers returned to the field. The Shawnee fans booed lustily at the delaying tactics, and the referee took courage from this and walked off a fifteen-yard penalty. When the Parkers lined up to kick off, the Warrior fullback yelled out, "Reckoned you'd give up. Come and get it."

The Shawnee left half nearly broke away. David Battle caught him at the ankle on the twenty-five, and Joe Foley came piling in to make the tackle secure. The Warriors went for a first down on the thirteen, and there they were repulsed once more by the men determined to win. But the Parkers of Bob Quinn could not move the ball. Joe Foley broke loose for one twenty-five-yard run before two men brought him down. It was their only threat. They ran for no gain on their thirty as the quarter ended. It was a long walk to the other thirty. David Battle wrestled with himself. How could David Battle flout authority? He was a young man who honored even his father. But he was also a young man who would not lose. In the huddle, before John Hall could call the signal, David said quietly, "We do it." They waited expectantly for his orders. "Pop Warner. Let's go."

Whitey Culpepper and Anton Dvorak, on each side of David, pounded his back enthusiastically, and a yell came from the huddle. They burst out into a T formation. Bob Quinn sprang to the chalkline, a protest on his lips. The Shawnee backs straightened up in obvious consternation, and their line relaxed just a little and looked up. Joe yelled, "Hup!" and took the ball with no count. He threw instantly, catching Whitey Culpepper on the slant. Whitey cut past the startled fullback, ran straight down the field, then veered to the sidelines with the safety man angling him out. David Battle came flashing by, poured his shoulder into the Shawnee safety and took him out of the play. Whitey ran down the sideline with the other halfback in futile pursuit.

The stands were stunned. Then a hysterical shriek burst from Sweet Water. They shouted. They yelled at one another. "Did you see it? Did you see it?" Shawnee

303

stood in silence, in shock, in dismay in the stands. The Shawnee coach called to the referee. The referee cupped his hands and said, "It's legal, Coach." Joe Foley held the ball and David Battle kicked the extra point. Bob Quinn stood on the sideline, the protest caught in his teeth.

The hopped-up Parkers took a fumble on the third play. They came out of the huddle with a loud "Hup!" and snapped into the line. In the T, Joe shouted, "Hup-one," and the Shawnee line lunged off-side. Joe continued, "Hup-two," and took the ball; he stood up to fake the same slant pass, kept and swung around end behind his backs, past the sprawling Warriors, and went untouched for thirty yards into the end zone. The Sweet Water stands were in pandemonium, and the Shawnee stands in deathly silence in the mutual disbelief. When they lined up for the extra point, leather-lunged Mike Foley yelled out, "Quinn, you beauty, where you been hiding it!" The kick was good. Pete Battle raced up and down the sideline, yelling, "Way to go! Way to go!" Bob Quinn turned and walked to his players' bench. He sat down and watched his team win for him.

With five minutes to go, the Parkers took over. Sweet Water howled expectantly. In the huddle, Joe Foley said, "Davy scores this one, right?" The huddle yelled back, "Right!"

On the first play from the Shawnee forty, Joe handed to David on a swing around left end. The Warrior fullback broke through the blockers and knocked him off stride. He picked up his balance, but the timing was lost and the pursuing end brought him down, no gain.

On the second play, Joe faked the slant. Whitey Culpepper kept right on running for the deep sector, drawing the two right defending backs with him. The other end went after him overloading the sector, and when David came flashing by there was no one to pick him up. He raced into the end zone for the pass. It was overthrown. He left his feet and dove headlong, clutching with his finger tips. His head struck the goal post simultaneously with the ball contact, the ball went flying out of the end zone before there was retention, the referee waved his arms violently, no completion, and David lay unconscious on West Virginia's brown November turf. The crowd was throttled into silence, then murmured like surf.

The players on each team gathered around the fallen hero.

Dr. Black hastened out. He thought to himself: Not even the enemy is David Battle's enemy. God, don't let that young man be hurt. He rolled David over. The legs began to twitch. At the end of another long twenty seconds, he began to jerk his head vexatiously at the smelling salts. He tried to get to his feet, but Dr. Black held him down. When his head finally cleared, he hopped up, walked a few steps, while the crowds on both sides of the field shouted for him, trotted and pranced, knees high, then scampered to his team as they huddled.

Quinn turned to Bernard Dankowski and started to wave him in. He hesitated. Why take Battle out? This game wasn't over. Anything could happen in five minutes. If this young man was the mysterious inspiration, why take him out?

Pete Battle asked incredulously, "You're not going to take him out?"

Quinn's eyes shut. If he knew how to have compassion, surely he would have it for this David Battle. If he knew how to love a football player, surely he would love David Battle, who would run through a brick wall or a goal post. If he knew how to respect a ballplayer as a human being, surely he would respect David Battle, the Sphinx, the enigma, whose enemies were not enemies, who roused in his friends the hot mixture of admiration and protection, David Battle, David Battle, the young man who won unknowingly all that Coach Quinn had lost to get his winning football teams.. Did he have compassion for his wingback? Well, this wingback had defied his orders and used plays the coach had never heard of. Have compassion for him? The hell with him, the coach had greater compassion for his own coaching aspirations. Keep the best eleven men in there. He opened his eyes, smiled sardonically and said to Pete, "What made you think I was going to take him out?"

The Parkers lined up for the next play. Suddenly Joe Foley called time. He took David's arm and led him toward the sideline. Quinn met them. He asked matter-of-factly, "Out on his feet?"

Pete said angrily, "He's not hurt. What are you trying to pull?"

Joe said quietly, "He doesn't feel it when he's hurt,

305

remember?" He said to Quinn, "He's all right, Knute. Just wonder if it occurred to you, if he gets hurt now, you get yourself one lousy reputation."

Quinn said sarcastically, "Thanks for your concern, Foley."

Joe said evenly, "You got more of my concern than you maybe think. You're a good coach. Maybe the best in the business. You just got some things to learn, that's all."

Quinn felt suddenly tired. "Sit it out, Davey." He turned and waved Bernie Dankowski into the game.

In the huddle Joe said, "Well, everybody gets a chance. For the Gipper." On the first play, he handed off to Carl Horvath, and the fullback slammed fourteen yards up the middle. Then he tried John Hall, the quarterback, playing left half in the T. Hall went off left tackle for six more. Dankowski for three, Hall for eight, Hall for six more. Then Joe said, "If you guys don't mind, I've got some people in those stands to impress, so I guess I'll take it myself this time." He dropped back and faked the long pass. The strong Shawnee fullback came in fast. Joe cut to the end. The fullback grabbed him by one leg. Joe lunged and the fullback's grip slipped down to his ankle, but he held on while Joe dragged him. The tall defensive halfback came full tilt. Joe twisted and looked for help. He shouted, "Bernie!" and lateraled off in an unrehearsed, unknown quarterback option play, just as the halfback climbed all over him. They clung desperately to him, trying to bring him to earth, and he threw them off with his strong hands, yelling, "Let go of me, you dumb bastards, I haven't got the ball," and Bernie Dankowski, the son of Walter, went down the sideline unmolested for the third touchdown in the twelve-minute quarter.

In the wild shouting, the exultant leaping in the Sweet Water stands, Bob Quinn said, "Well, I did it. I did it. Four years, and not one defeat."

Pete Battle said, "What do you mean, you did it? It's my line held Shawnee out all day."

Quinn glared at him. "You're a crummy, no-good bastard, Dankowski. And I'm no better. Wasn't either of us won this last game. Was David Battle, that's who. And Joe Foley, that's who. But if they don't tell, I'm going to take the credit, you can just bet. And it wasn't me took Davey out of there. And it sure wasn't you. I'm sick of it."

306

But then David Battle ran on the field to kick the extra point, slapping his substitute on the back, shouting, "Way to go, Bernie!" Quinn clenched his fists and sweated out the last minutes, and the lust for his victories grew back in his heart. Victory. Who cared how it came? Victory! Where will the records say it was other than *my* victory? What Sweet Water miner will ask me what a miserable sonofabitch I really am? They wanted victory, I wanted victory, we've all got victory, and I'm their hero.

At the final gun, when the Sweet Water fans erupted on the field, and the Shawnee men and women melted silently away, Quinn waited expectantly for his young men to rush to him and carry him triumphantly aloft. He had brought this benighted town four undefeated seasons in a row. God, what more could a man do for a couple thousand Hunkies and hillbillies? He'd pulled them out of their coal dust. Pulled them out of their sour lives. He had brought them pride where there had been no pride since the death of Vincent Carstairs. Well, he was leaving them. How could Notre Dame fail to give him the backfield opening? How could they fail to see in him, inevitably, their next head coach? How could this Sweet Water fail to know him, now, as their great emancipator and supreme hero?

The squad came running, but it was David Battle they hoisted high in the air, and they ran with him through the shouting throng, yelling, "Hubba, hubba, hubba!" David protested. Joe Foley whacked the thigh riding on his shoulder and shouted, "Look out, Army, here comes Battle and Foley!"

One group of Shawnee spectators stood sullenly on the field. When the elated Parker team came shouting their way, they couldn't stand it any longer and one of them tripped Whitey Culpepper, and David was thrown to the ground in the melee. David hopped up, unperturbed. He turned toward the dressing room.

The Shawnee man said, "Yellow, Snake?"

David turned and looked at him.

Joe Foley took off his helmet and swung it in his big hand. "You looking for trouble, mister?"

The young man said, "You're a yellow copperhead, Battle."

Joe said, "Now, mister, you got yourself more than you bargained for."

David said, "He's drunk, Joe. Let's go."

Another of the Shawnee men said, "Forget it, Coop." They had nothing against David Battle. How could even Shawnee men have anything against David Battle?

But the man lunged for David. He didn't make it. Joe Foley intercepted him and crashed him to the turf. In one quick move he pinned the man on his back, knees on his arms, and pumped his big right fist five, six, seven times in the face until the struggle ceased. David Battle's teammates ringed him. Any Shawnee wanting to get at David Battle would have to go through Whitey Culpepper, or Bernie Dankowski, or John Hall, or Anton Dvorak, and the entire Parker squad. And the Sweet Water crowd ringed the scene menacingly. Joe Foley asked, "Anyone else want to take a chance?"

Without a word the invaders lifted their fallen companion and walked him, groggy, off the field.

Joe asked, "You okay, Davey?"

David nodded imperceptibly. He was okay. But he wasn't okay. Why did Joe do that? Why didn't Joe let him fight his own fight? David Battle was frustrated, but it didn't show on his bright face, and his teammates resumed the shouting walk to the locker room.

Jim Parker called to him. David lifted his arm. There was the girl with Jim. David felt a clutching in his stomach. She had black hair, and blue eyes, and Dresden-china skin. She could have been the daughter of Ellen Foley. She could have been Ellen Foley. He couldn't look at her any longer. He looked at Joe. There was no smile on Joe's face. Joe said quietly, "That's got to be her, Davey."

David said, "Yes."

Joe said soberly, "Man!"

The team went into the locker room. Pete Battle stayed on the field to revel with the hero worshipers. Coach Robert Emmett Quinn trailed behind his squad. He said in his lonely chest, "It'll be different at South Bend. Different when I'm a big name. They'll all come sucking around me then," and in his wonderment about David Battle, in his envy of David Battle, he scarcely noticed that the riotous fans of Sweet Water reached wildly out to touch the coach and clap his back as one of the greatest of the conquering heroes.

15

On this cold November West Virginia day, under leaden clouds at Sweet Water, the Four Horsemen rode again. This time they were a blockbusting fullback named Carl Horvath, a rough-and-tumble quarterback named John Hall, an inspirational leader and all-round halfback named David Battle, and most of all at superb tailback named Joe Foley, who must be the best high school football player in America. These successors to Miller, Layden, Stuldreher and Crowley, thwarted and stymied at every turn by an aroused opponent for three full quarters, broke out a dazzling new series of new plays in the eleventh hour, ran by Shawnee 21-0, and led the amazing Big Red Flash of Sweet Water to their fourth successive undefeated season.

If there could have been doubt before, there can be none now. There is no one in high school coaching, and perhaps not even anyone in the college ranks, who has brought the Notre Dame offense to the peak of perfection attained by Parker District High under Robert Emmett Quinn, the coach who has never known defeat. Today he proved his coaching genius and versatility. With a scoreless tie, and even defeat, staring Sweet Water down the throat, he rose to the occasion, dug deep in his bag of tricks and came up with an exciting and devastating formation that swept the Warriors right back across the Kanawha to Shawnee, unable to believe what they had seen. It is rumored that Quinn now leaves the Parkers to accept the backfield coach position with one of the greatest national football powers. No coach could leave under better auspices.

As for Joe Foley, the college coaches, the alumni, the bird dogs from coast to coast are already descending en masse on the Kanawha Valley mine town to lure this phenom into their camps. One backfield coach of a major Midwestern university, who watched the game from the stands, said frankly, "He's the greatest college prospect in the history of the game. He's big, he's strong, he has savvy, he can throw, he can run like a bullet, and best of all, he loves the game, he's got desire. . . ."

This was the day Gerry Battle packed the barest necessities, left a note behind and took the train to Charleston, then on to St. Theresa to become a novice in a cloister. Ellen Battle was dry-eyed. "It had to come. I knew it when she talked about it."

Pete Battle raged. "If that isn't the stupidest goddam thing I ever heard of, I don't know what is. Well, we'll see about it. You get her back."

"Just how?"

"Well, she's got to get her people's permission."

"If she does, she's got mine."

Pete spread his hands. He was apoplectic. "Stupid! Stupid! What does a good-looking girl like that want to do throwing her life away in a cloister? Throwing her life away! Do you know she won't even get to talk to anybody? And that includes you?"

Ellen said, "It's what she wants."

Pete stormed onto the porch of Casimar Dankowski's gray house. David Battle sat on the steps. Pete said, "Stupid! Stupid goddam girl!"

David looked up. "Why do you think a girl does that, Papa?"

"I just told you. Stupid, that's why."

"Maybe it's the call."

"The call! Call for what? What good is she going to do anybody in a goddam cloister? What good's it going to do to shave her hair off and say penance the rest of her life? You think she's going to do God any good, doing such a stupid thing? I'll tell you what it is, it's escaping. Any woman that would do such a stupid goddam thing, she hasn't got the guts to face up to the world. Self-abnegation, is that what you're going to say? Screw that. It's selfish, that's what it is. It's self-serving. She can't face up to the world, so she goes in a goddam cloister and makes herself ugly, and takes it out on herself with flagellation, and lets other people donate the money to take care of her, and never does a goddam thing back for the world but say prayers. You tell me the last time some nun in a cloister got some good for anybody saying prayers for them. I can't believe she'd do such a stupid goddam thing."

David said, "Maybe you're right. Maybe she is escaping."

"From what? That's what makes me so goddam mad. What's she got to escape from? A pretty girl like that. Just because Jim Parker picks that ugly woman over her? You think that's it? Christ, there are a million Jim Parkers in the world for a girl that pretty."

"Maybe she was escaping from you."

"What's that supposed to mean?"

"If she is, you don't have to ask."

"What are you talking about? You got something to say, say it."

"What did you do to her?"

"What did *I* do to her?"

"Gerry told Jim what you did. You made a pass at her."

Pete raised his arms to the heavens, "Oh, sweet Jesus, I've heard everything."

"Did you?"

"Oh, sweet Jesus!" Then instantly Pete Battle was calmed. "Boy, I got something to say to you. And you listen good. There's a lot of things I'd do in this world. There ain't a lot I wouldn't do, if I was of a mind. That's the difference between you and me. You're a puking punk. You haven't got the guts to take on a whore and be a man when I stick it right in your face. Maybe you think that makes you holy and me stink to high heaven. I got news for you. I *know* when I stink. You don't *know* when you stink. You're so goddam pious, and you still got stinking ideas festering like pus in your pious head. Well, you're goddam right I made a pass at her. And you listen real good. I'm forty-three years old. I'm in the stabbin' prime of my life. When I see a good-looking woman, I can feel the want of her all through me, and that's something you couldn't even understand, you're so goddam scared of pussy. And I include any girl, any girl, you understand? You think that makes me any different than any man? It doesn't. You show me a forty-year-old man with a grown daughter built like Gerry, and when he looks at her and sees her undressed, or running around in her slip, or she puts her arms around him, and if he says that idea doesn't cross his mind how she'd be in bed, I say he's a goddam liar, or a goddam eunuch, one. And I'll tell you what kind of pass I made at her. I patted her on the ass and told her she was looking great, and that any man that got that was getting something great, and it was too bad I was her old man, that's what kind of pass I made at her. And if she's so goddam sick in her mind she thinks that stinks, maybe she's best off to go rot in a cloister and save it for the worms. And that goes for you. You think you're pious and holy? You stink!"

Pete Battle walked swiftly down the hill, toward the ferry and the prostitutes of Shawnee.

Joe Foley stood up and stretched his arms luxuriously. "I can kick the bucket right now. Man couldn't *find* a better obituary than that."

Suzanne Carstairs, in the Parker porch swing, said, "There's more. Should I read it?"

Joe said, "I couldn't stand it." He jumped up, caught the overhang and chinned himself. He dropped to the porch and dusted his hands. "I got to marry that reporter. Unless Bob Quinn beats me to it. Does he say anything in there about money and convertibles?"

"I don't get it."

Jim Parker said, "He's pulling your leg. He's talking about what the coaches will offer him to get him to their schools."

She said, "I don't think Joe pulls other people's legs. He pulls his own leg."

Joe asked, "How come you to say that?"

"I know you, Joe Foley. You make it seem like you're laughing at other people, and all the time you're laughing at yourself."

Jim Parker studied the fifteen-year-old girl apprecia-tively. "Is that right, Joe? Has she got you pegged? I think so."

Joe said offhandedly, "Maybe better than some. If people are all one, a joke on one of us is a joke on all of us."

Jim asked, "What is that, some Irish mysticism?"

Suzanne Carstairs said, "I understand. It's what I was saying about him."

Jim said, "Well, that was Vincent's greatest gift, a sen-sitivity to others."

The beautiful, lively girl asked, smiling broadly, "Was my father really all that wonderful as people say?"

"You must know by now. Haven't they all said it?"

"I'm greedy. I want to hear it again."

"I'm sure it makes you feel good."

"It does. It's wonderful. Mama told me. But it means more when you hear it and see it right here in his town. Is it all right to call it his town?"

Jim said, "It was his town."

"Being here, it's just like he was still alive."

Jim said, "He's still alive."

"Like your daddy, too, Jim. He must still be alive here." Her white teeth flashed. "Sweet Water's got new heroes, now, Joe and Davey."

Joe said, "Pass over that paper, Sue. I got to read me that part again where he calls me a phenom."

She tossed the paper to him, and he did read it, thor-oughly and unself-consciously pleased with himself.

She asked, "How about you, David? I liked what he said about you being the inspiration."

He couldn't bring himself to look at her.

"Cat got your tongue?"

He nodded. Then he said, "He said some good things about us."

She said to Jim, "Do you know he danced with me three times last night, and I don't remember that he said one word. Oh, excuse me, David. Twice when I asked him about the game, he said Parker was lucky to win. And

313

you might as well know it, he did ask me to dance the first time, but I had to ask him the other two times."

Jim said, "Our town Sphinx, that's Davey. Don't let him fool you. He's got Webster memorized, and I've seen him downright voluble."

She asked, "David, do you think I look all that much like your mother?"

He said, "You sure do, Suzanne."

"That's nice. I think she's beautiful. I wish I looked exactly like her. You know something, I think I look more like her than I look like my mom. It made me feel funny, like looking in a mirror. I'm not sure she liked me."

David said, "Well, that's a strange thing to think. She'd be bound to like you. What makes you say a thing like that?"

"Just sort of had a feeling." She moved her head back and forth, deliberately tossing her glowing black hair. "Wish my mom had come down. She wanted to, but then she was afraid to. I mean, like old memories. But it was Scott's idea. My stepfather, Scott Brady. He thought I should go, and he thought Mama should go with me. He's a great stepfather. He says he wishes he'd known Vincent. Do you know what he said when he put me on the train? He said Vincent had made him richer, knowing him through the two of us, and to find out more about Vincent, so I could tell him. Isn't that a nice thing to say? I'm sure glad I came."

Jim Parker said, "You and Davey will make a perfect match. He'll listen."

She asked, pleasantly bright, "Do I talk all that much? I do, don't I?"

Joe Foley tossed the paper aside. He stood on his hands on the porch. Upside down, he asked as carelessly as possible, "When you going back to Pittsburgh, Suzanne?"

She said just as carelessly, "Oh, I don't know. A few days."

Jim said, "She was supposed to go back today. Wonder what changed her mind."

Suzanne said, "That's a terrible thing to give away, Jim Parker. Up until now I thought you were a nice boy."

Jim smiled. A nice boy. He was eight years older than this beautiful girl, but she treated him as an equal, and the amazing part of it was his anxiety for that acceptance.

314

A remarkable girl. A remarkably mature fifteen-year-old girl. Not like Swaney Wood. Swaney had been mature when she was fifteen, but not this kind of mature. Swaney was always sex-mature, from the time she was twelve. Maybe from the time she was nine. Sex-mature. Jim smiled broader. Didn't this one have sex appeal, too? Even more than Swaney? Swaney was breasts and thighs and hips and melting, and the love of sex fairly oozed out of her. This one, this fifteen-year-old girl, she burst with womanhood that had nothing to do with breasts and hips, but had to do with the wonderful force of her feminine manner, with the quick knowledge she implanted in every male that she was a *woman*, a woman who probably never ever had been touched, but who was entirely aware of what it was in her that brought out such obvious ardor in every male she confronted. It was pleasant, it was good, it was unsettling, it was devastating. Devastating. Jim stopped smiling. She was looking at him. He felt as though she could read his thoughts, and he wasn't sure he wanted her to do that.

Joe Foley came crashing to the porch floor. He asked, "How come you get out of school, just like that?"

"I go to Miss Campbell's. If you do well, you get a reward. I've got two weeks off."

"Two weeks? That's good." Joe did rapid push-ups.

Suzanne said, "Joe, if they could hook up all that energy, you could run the electricity or something for the whole country."

Joe stopped and, lying prone, said, "You should see Davey. He can do most as many one-arm push-ups as I can do two-arm, and he can stand on one hand and chin hisself eight thousand times and probably play the Spanish guitar while he was doing it."

Suzanne said, "David, will you do a one-hand handstand?"

He said, "Maybe later."

Joe asked, "Suzanne, would you like to see the night life of Sweet Water tonight?"

"Now you're just funning me. My mom told me before I came down here they took the sidewalks in at dark. Only you don't even have any sidewalks."

"Well, we had the dance last night. We got two churches, the district high school, the station, a pop stand, and the big ole black tipple. But you got to include Shawnee.

315

That's the big city. Clark's Department Store. Green Billy's blind pig. They even got a restaurant over there. And a gas station. People in Sweet Water that's got cars, got to bring gas back on the ferry from Shawnee in cans. Let's go see the metropolis tonight."

Jim said, "He's exaggerating only about the gas. We're not that benighted. We can always steal gas from the Red Flash pump."

Suzanne said, leaving herself an out, "India is counting on dinner here. What would we do if we could get away?"

Joe said, "This guy from Wheeling, he's a Notre Dame alum, and he's coming all the way down here to take me to dinner in Shawnee, and I just thought maybe you'd be interested in what he's got to say."

"You going to Notre Dame, Joe?"

"Me and Davey are going to Navy. The Naval Academy. But I figure I might just as well get a dinner from this Notre Dame guy. And I'm going to go around and see some of the other colleges, you know, just to see some places."

"Are you really going to Annapolis, David? Gee, that's exciting."

David said, "We have to pass some entrance exams."

Jim said, "That won't be any problem for these two. They're better students than they are football players."

David said, "In a mine town we're good students."

Jim said, "When did this Navy thing happen? You've sure kept that a secret."

Suzanne said, "I think it's wonderful. I'll bet you'll look wonderful in those uniforms."

Joe said, "You'll have to come see us. Do you think your mother would let you?"

"I think she just might. And you can't tell, I've been try-ing to decide on finishing school, and I just might pick one near Annapolis." She smiled with wonderful coquet-tishness. "Then by the time you two have taught me the ropes, I'll be ready for the new midshipmen that take over when you leave."

Joe asked, "When will you get there?"

"I'm most sixteen, you know. Two years. Unless I decide finishing high school up there is just what I need. David, when you're a high and mighty college man, would you think a high school girl was too young to date?"

David said, "I sure wouldn't."

Suzanne said, "Let's all go sightseeing in Shawnee and talk about it."

Joe said, "That alum will have a green hemorrhage if this many show up, but it will serve him right."

Jim said, distinctly regretful, "Count me out."

David asked, "Why don't you take Coby and make it four?"

"To Shawnee? The city of sin?" He said to Suzanne, "Coby doesn't approve of Shawnee."

"Is it really all that bad?"

Joe said, "You better believe it. Sin doesn't skulk around in Shawnee. It walks down Main Street proud as you please."

She said, "Come on, David, Joe, we'll do it."

David said, "Can't. Got to be home."

She said quickly, "Well, then we can do something else. Like play cards, or something."

David said, "You and Joe go, I won't horn in." He rose and said, "See you guys."

Jim said, "I'll drop you off on my way to Coby's."

The two of them climbed into the yellow boat-tail Packard. Jim backed down the steep, winding driveway to the Charleston Road and drove in silence to the Dankowski-Battle gray house. David opened the car door.

Jim asked, "How come?"

"How come what, Jim?"

"You know darn well how come what. That pretty girl's got all kinds of interest in you. How come you walk off and leave her like that?"

"I've got something to do."

"You're the world's worst liar. Without Joe, you got nothing to do. Let me guess. You figure it's more important for Joe to get it out of his system than for you to get it out of your system, right? And Sue Carstairs is heaven-sent for him, right? Is that it, Damon?"

"Jim, Gerry's gone. She went off to be a cloistered nun."

After a moment Jim said, "You got to be kidding."

"Would I kid about something like that?"

"No."

"She's gone."

"That's a terrible thing."

"Is it? She's out of this sick town."

"I don't understand you, David."

"Yes, you do. She's out of this sex-sick town."

317

"David, come on, it's not that bad."

David didn't answer.

Jim said, "Davey, you're letting things get all out of perspective. This isn't good. It's getting out of hand. It isn't all that bad."

"I don't know how it could be any worse."

David Battle walked up the hill to the house. Jim Parker sat for a while in his yellow Packard and worried. Then he drove off to pay his respects to his plain girl.

16

Suzanne Carstairs twisted the butterfly doorbell of Casimar Dankowski's house. There was no sound. The mechanism had long since succumbed. She stood uncertainly. She screwed up her courage and rapped on the glass of the front door. From behind her, at the foot of the front-porch steps, David said, "You got to make enough noise to raise the dead, to get in this house. Or just walk in, one."

She whirled and looked flustered. "Hi, David."

He set down a hod of coal.

She asked, "What are you doing?"

"Carrying coals to Newcastle."

"That little bitty bunch of coal?"

"It's not for the furnace. We've got a coal stove."

"You mean in the kitchen? For cooking?"

"Sure. That's the best kind of stove."

"We've got an electric stove. And before that we had a gas stove. I never heard of a coal stove."

"Most people in Sweet Water got a coal stove."

"It's fascinating. There are fascinating things in Sweet Water. Like your old-timey doorbell. It doesn't make any noise."

He nodded his head.

She said, "I was just taking a walk."

He nodded again.

She said with exaggerated diffidence, "Just thought I'd walk up Murder Creek. How far would you have to go before you ran into a moonshiner?"

"About half a mile."

"Would they do anything to me if I came poking around?"

"Don't think you'd find one. Revenooers don't. They can be right under your nose, and you wouldn't see it."

"I think you're pulling my leg. I bet there aren't any moonshiners. Jim says you pull people's legs, and they never know."

"This time I'm not. Most of the miners drink white lightning. They don't have to go too far to get it."

"Will you show me a moonshiner?"

"You want to get shot?"

"Now you are kidding. They wouldn't shoot us."

"Can't tell about a moonshiner. They're peculiar. You could mess around his wife, before his still."

"I want to see. I'm inviting you to escort me on a Cook's tour of the wilderness."

He studied her. He said, "I better get a lumberjack. It will get cold."

They walked down the hill to the trail. Ellen Battle watched them from the living-room window. Stella Dankowski said, "Such a pretty girl. Such a handsome boy."

When Ellen didn't answer, the grandmother said, "Joe, we haven't seen him for a week. That's good, for those boys to get an interest in such a pretty girl."

Ellen said, "She had to come get David. She's chasing him. A girl should have more pride than that."

Suzanne Carstairs said to David, "I'm ashamed of myself, I guess you know." He turned his head and looked at her quizzically. "I chased you. I gave up waiting for you to ask me, and came over to chase you."

He said, "You wouldn't really do that."

"You're exasperating. And you do it on purpose. Mr. Hard-to-get. That's supposed to be me."

"I wouldn't do that," he said earnestly.

They walked in silence until they came to Black Beulah Creek, the deeper branch of Murder Creek. He led her upstream. It was chillier in the shade of the trees along the bank. She clutched her coat.

He said, "You wouldn't think it now, but this is our swimming hole."

She smiled a little, not looking at him. "Tell me the truth, do you skinny-dip?"

He didn't answer. They walked further. He turned and watched her. He said, "You sure do have pretty clothes." He stumbled on a root and went hopping to keep his balance. He said, "Guess I better keep my eyes in the boat."

She stopped and stood at the bank. She turned to him and asked, "Do you think I'm pretty, David, or just the clothes?"

"Sure."

"You don't act like it."

"Guess I just wouldn't know how to say it."

"Yes, you would. If you wanted to. Sometimes when you're not watching, you say things like out of a book."

"I think things better than I say things."

"I'm glad there's just the two of us. Jim said you talk when there's just two people. Do you get shy in crowds? Is that what it is?"

"Maybe other people have more important things to say."

"I don't think you're really all that modest. Either you're just pretending you're modest, or Pete really did beat you down. Is that what happened?"

"I guess you know a lot about this town, for only being here a week."

"I'm staying with India. She's the all-time champeen gossip. And I did ask her about you, if that's what you want to know."

He turned and walked further upstream, and she trailed slightly behind him.

She said, "Stop a minute, David. This sure is pretty."

He said, "We don't have much in the way of scenery in Sweet Water. Unless you like beechnut trees and buckthorns and dandelions growing out of hard scrabble and coal chips. That's why this is such a good walk, up the crick. If you really want to see something, we should go to the top of the hill. You can look back down on the Kanawha, and you can't see much of Sweet Water and Shawnee for the trees. And when you turn around and look the other way, it looks like nobody ever saw it before

321

right now, when you're seeing it, and you could be the only person in the world."

"That would scare me, to think I was the only person in the world."

"It doesn't scare me. It's a good feeling. It feels clean and good, just the way God made it."

"I know why you feel that way. I don't blame you."

"Well, I wouldn't bet you knew."

"Sure, I know. It's Sweet Water. I've got a confession, David. I've been very polite and told everybody it was exciting to see Sweet Water, but I'm so disappointed I could cry. I guess it was so long ago that my mom forgot how it looked, and she built it up as being a spanking-bright clean place. I guess that was because she was in love with my daddy, and any place would have looked good."

"It *was* like that. I don't remember it, because by the time I remember, the paint was already off the houses."

"David, it's an awful place. It's just an awful shabby place. What happened to it?"

"Times change, I guess. When your daddy was here, there was prosperity. And he had more of a personal interest in seeing everything bright than Charles or Mr. Scott ever had. It's been fifteen years since the company houses were painted, and I bet ten since any of the white houses."

"It's not just the houses, David. It's the people."

David Battle was taken aback. After a moment he said, "Yes, that's so. You should see the pictures of Mama and her girl friends, they wore clothes every day nicer than Sunday clothes now. You know, those middy blouses with the big neckerchiefs, and their hair piled up, and their clothes didn't just hang on them like gunny sacks, and they looked ironed and new, and the young guys, they even had ice cream suits and straw hats for dress up, and you sure wouldn't see something like that now. You're right. The people have changed, along with the town." Then he said with renewed resolution, "Blame the depression, and the mines playing out. Prosperity went up the cricks after the coal."

"Up the cricks, is it like Sweet Water was when my daddy was here?"

He hesitated. "No, it's not. It's maybe not shabby, up

322

Cabin Crick and places like that, but it's not bright and shiny, either."

"Then it wasn't just the prosperity. It must have been pride."

"Jim Parker been talking to you?"

"No. I've been too polite to say anything about how disappointed I am. That Jim Parker, he's got to be one of the smartest people in the world. What does he say?"

"He says the pride went out of the town when the union came in."

"Could that be, David?"

"I don't know. I don't see how."

"Maybe it's true."

"Well, maybe it's true for Sweet Water, I'll go that far, it's maybe a special case. But I bet other places the miners got more pride. Now they've got the union. I don't know. I'll have to think about it."

"This sure is pretty. I didn't think there was going to be anything pretty in West Virginia. I never saw anything as pretty as this. Except maybe the Pennsylvania hills when the trees turn." She smiled again. "Joe says this is lovers' lane, up this way. Is that true?"

He said with sudden asperity, "Why ask me, if you already know?"

"I didn't come up here with Joe. I came up here with you. This is the first time. Is it lovers' lane?"

"Well, not in November." When he realized the implication, he stared helplessly at her.

She smiled again. "I guess you're as much a saint as Joe says you are. How come you to be so good? I feel downright wicked next to you."

"Well, Suzanne, are you wicked?"

She stopped smiling. She sat down on the bank. She reached for his hand and pulled him down beside her. He let go her hand quickly. He picked up a stone and threw it in the creek. He threw a twig in and watched it drift downstream a few yards before an eddy caught it and jammed it against a turn.

He said, "Suzanne, what kind of girl are you?"

She cocked her head. "Like good or bad?"

"Just what kind of girl."

"I'm a fifteen-year-old girl, almost sixteen. I guess that's what kind." When he looked at her, she asked, "What are fifteen-year-old girls like in Sweet Water?"

323

"Depends."

"In Mount Lebanon, we got the idea fifteen-year-old girls in the wilderness are, you know, pretty much grown up. Maybe the girls down here think that about us in the big city." She smiled mischievously. "I met your girl friend Swaney. I bet she's sassier than I'll ever be. I just think about things. Do you think about things, David?"

He turned his eyes away and threw another twig in the water. "Sometimes it's hard not to. The devil can put an attraction in sin."

She smiled a little uncertainly. "Now you're just kidding me. You don't really think the devil has anything to do with girls and boys. You make me feel funny, David. I bet it's good for me, to have the tables turned. But when it's happening, I'm not sure I like it. I feel like a hussy, or something, chasing you." She watched his profile. "It makes me mad at myself. And mad at you. I feel like I want to get even. Like get you so stirred up you'd make a fool out of yourself, and then I'd slam the door in your face. Only I'm not even sure I'd like to slam the door. You've got me all mixed up, David. I'm spoiled. When the boy is all after me, you know, a girl's so busy enjoying her power and so busy keeping his hands away, she doesn't get a chance to feel anything herself. But when she's after him, then it makes her feel funny. I feel funny all over."

He looked up at her and said, "I do, too."

"Why don't you kiss me, David?"

"Do they kiss you?"

"When I let them. Why don't you?"

"Well, I got the idea Joe's staked his claim."

Her composure burst. She cried out, "Oh, you're so dumb, you're so dumb, you're so dumb!"

Her sudden anger put consternation in him. He sought frantically for something to say to mollify her.

She said, in the same hot tone, "You're eighteen years old, and that's the oldest boy I've ever been with, and I bet you're the dumbest. What are you going to do, step aside for your best chum? Well, didn't you ever stop to think maybe I don't want you to step aside for him?"

His mouth was dry. His pride strove to assert itself. He tried twice before he could speak, then he said, "Well, Suzanne, did it ever occur to you I'm not interested in you?"

"It couldn't be. It just couldn't be. You do want to be

324

with me, and I know it. You want to hold my hand, or kiss me, or something, and I can tell it, the way you look at me. The way you look right now, you do want to do something to me."

Then almost in a whisper he said, "Maybe I want to, and maybe I can't."

"David, what's wrong?" When he didn't answer, just looked at her miserably, she said, "It is it. Joe said it was. It's because I look like her, like Ellen. And it would make you feel like incest, like you were kissing your family. Well, what's she got to do with you and me? Nothing, that's what. No more than Joe Foley's got to do with you and me. Haven't you got better control of your mind than that?"

His jaw set. "Well, Miss Freud, why don't you look inside yourself before you go off with your psychiatry lesson?"

"Well, I don't know who your Miss Freud is, and I don't know anything about psychiatry, but I think you're dumb, and you can take me back to Sweet Water."

"Who do I look like, just tell me. I look like my mother, and that means I look like you. Do you kiss yourself in the mirror, Miss Narcissus? You and your tossing your hair, admiring yourself for how pretty you are, don't come around talking to me about peculiar. I don't want any part of your messed-up thinking."

"I don't know what you're talking about. I just know you're dumb."

"Then stop it, stop it. I don't want to hear any more about it."

Her lips parted, her teeth were clenched. "Incest! Incest!"

He grabbed her by the hair, and with his face close up to hers, said hotly and softly, "Shut up, shut up, shut up!"

She threw her arms around his neck and pressed her open mouth on his lips. He pulled violently away, but she clung, and when he fell over backward, she was on top, and her mouth stayed hotly against his. He burned with the revulsion. He burned with his anger. He put his arms around her to throw her off. He rolled and was on top of her, and when he wanted to pull away, he no longer could, and the strange, wonderful glow of wanting shot through him, and he looked at her closed eyes and closed his own and kissed her fiercely, and with the weight of him on her, she moved her knees apart in a movement for ease that was even more a movement of abandonment, and when he felt her thighs against his hips, he

325

pressed himself against her, and through the layers of cloth that separated them, she moved under him, and she made a sound that was almost a moan and bit his lip, and he covered her face, her eyes, her throat, her lips with his lips and moved with her movements, and the courage and heedlessness built in him, and he began to think of how he must now tear aside the red skirt that kept them apart, and he wondered what he would find underneath that would still bar him and how he would go about the penetration of that barrier, and her hips thrust and were fluid, and he thought of Swaney Wood, and he thought of Swaney Wood giggling with Whitey Culpepper just before Whitey did it to her, and he thought of Joe Foley saying he did it to Swaney, but he must be lying, and he thought of Joe Foley wanting his mother, and he thought of his own bitter emotions and not being sure whether it was anger or jealous resentment he felt against Joe, and he thought of Green Billy and the Gypsy and the whore his father had stuck in front of his face, the horror of that chalky-white, slatternly slut, and he thought of his father disgusted with him because he was a saint, nothing but a saint, and he thought of his father patting his own daughter and saying sex things to her, and he thought of his own father accusing Ellen of adultery, it was Vincent who did it, David was Vincent's, Pete Battle said so, and this girl, this black-haired, blue-eyed girl who was a mirror reflection of himself, she was the daughter of Vincent, maybe it was true they had the same father, maybe it was true, oh, God—and the ugly horror of the sex of Sweet Water, the utter debasement of Sodom and Gomorrah, the dreadful, ugly, ugly, foul sins came smothering him like stinking excrement, and he looked into the face of the girl whose body moved underneath him, and he saw his half sister, and he saw his mother, and his mother screamed at him, like the terrible wail of the train whistle through the valley, screamed, "Mortal sin! Mortal sin! Mortal sin!" and he sprang off and away from this foulness who was his sister and his mother underneath him, and he pounded the earth on the bank of Black Beulah Creek and pounded it again, and called out in himself, "Oh, God, please don't let me die with this foul sin on my soul!"

Suzanne Carstairs sat up. She said in a flat voice of awful hurt and mockery, "Well, who's going to cry, you or me?"

He stood up. There was now no expression on his face. "Come on, Suzanne, we'd better walk back."

"Sure, David. I hope you're proud of yourself."

"No, I'm not proud."

She rose and brushed the leaves and humus from her coat. "We'll hurry. I imagine you have to get to Confession."

The misery utterly overwhelmed him. He walked beside her in silence all the way to the Parker house. She held out her hand in a mocking, polite gesture. "Thank you for a lovely lesson on how a girl can make a fool of herself."

The unhappiness clouding his face again, he said, barely audible, "It's not you, Suzanne. I think a great deal of you, and not very much of myself."

She fought against the tremble that wanted to come in her lips. "I don't know who's the dumbest. For a minute I wanted to be eighteen, but I'm only fifteen. It was a good lesson. You, you could have had me. Next time it happens with a girl, you'll know." She tossed her hair and said with difficult lightness, "I'll be going home tomorrow."

"Do you have to, Suzanne?"

"No, I don't have to. I could stay here and keep on being more unhappy than I've ever been in my life. Is that what you want?"

"It isn't you, Suzanne, it isn't you, I swear. It's me. I don't know even know what's the matter with me. What's the matter with me, Suzanne?"

She searched his grave, handsome face.

He asked urgently, "What's the matter with me?"

"David, David, I'm only fifteen, I don't know!"

"Will you come back sometime?"

"Will you hurt me, David?"

"Will you come back, when I know what's the matter with me?"

"Will you write a letter to me, David, and two or three or four letters and tell me you want to see me? So I can feel like I'm pursued, like a woman should be, and not throwing myself at you."

He said softly, "I'll pursue you. I'll find out what's the matter with me, and I'll pursue you."

Then there were tears in her bright blue eyes, and she said, trembling, "David, I'm as much in love with you as a girl could be with somebody she doesn't even know." Impulsively she kissed him, gently lingering, and the

327

dread evil sprang up in him, and he pulled away, but this time she didn't know, and she smiled happily and walked into the house without a backward glance, and David stood rigid, watching her, hating her, and it was foul excrement coursing in his veins, not blood, and he cried in himself, "Oh, God, what's the matter with me!"

Behind the living-room curtains India Parker watched, and her black eyes glowed as she contemplated the pleasure of divulging in detail to Ellen Foley Battle the fact and fancy of the triumphant invasion of Sweet Water by Suzanne Carstairs, and the abject state of love to which she had reduced David Battle and Joe Foley. India was curious to know which loss would hurt Ellen most.

17

If there could have been any doubt before, there can be none now. There is no one in high school coaching, and perhaps not even anyone in the college ranks, who has brought the Notre Dame offense to the peak of perfection attained by Parker District High under Robert Emmett Quinn, the coach who has never known defeat. Today he proved his coaching genius and versatility. . . .

QUINN SENT THE ARTICLE to South Bend to add to the file on his application for the backfield vacancy. While he waited, full of confidence, a dozen other offers came his way as word of his prowess and accomplishment spread through the professional fraternity. Bob Quinn rode with vast pleasure down the daydream of coming national public recognition.

Pete Battle said, "You got two chances, Quinn, slim and none. Only alums coach at South Bend."

Quinn replied complacently, "They'll take me. Why did they get rid of Hunk Anderson? They want those Rockne days back, that's why. They're smartening up. They're looking for winners, men with the winning complex, that's me." He raised one eyebrow. "Besides, I've made a solemn vow

329

to go to Mass every Sunday if I get it. The Lord can't afford to pass up a chance like that."

The letter from the new Irish head coach was succinct:

We have studied your record and credentials with great interest and much admiration. We feel that you are eminently qualified to coach at Notre Dame. However, we are continuing our long-standing practice of selecting our coaches from the alumni. Should this policy change in the future, we will be quick to contact you. All good luck in your future coaching career.

Quinn rocked slowly in his rocking chair in his room in Aunt Polly's boarding house. Ten minutes later he burst out cursing and sat at the table to write a letter of acceptance to the offer from Fordham. Three days later Fordham wired their regrets; the position was filled. Quinn churned with frantic desperation. This was the same as five years before, when he turned down offers only to find them evaporated when he sank to accepting. He hurried to the C & O station and phoned the president of the University of Detroit. He said, with his chest constricting, "Father Koenig, this is Bob Quinn in Sweet Water. If you still want me, I want the job."

Koenig said briskly, "We understand that you placed the backfield vacancy at Notre Dame ahead of the head coach position at Detroit."

"Yes, Father, I did."

"Well, so would I, Mr. Quinn. You haven't written us since your interview. Tell me briefly just what are your feelings toward us now."

"Father, my feeling is that my teams win football games. I expect to win with Detroit."

Then Koenig said, "You know Jesuits. We're practical and worldly. This school has decided to win enough games so that Notre Dame and Michigan can't continue to ignore us. We wanted you because you are a winner. We still want you on that basis. I will send you confirmation of our appointment as head coach at the terms discussed. Just one more thing. We hope that you will bring Joe Foley with you."

Quinn drew a deep breath. "Is the offer contingent on my bringing Foley?"

"If I knew how to make it contingent and still do justice to our respect for you, I'd do it. No. It's our hope, not our requirement."

"I'll do my best, Father Koenig. And thank you. I'll see you in a few weeks."

He went first to work on his secondary stars. When he came a cropper, he was utterly confounded. He hadn't counted on Joe Foley. But the rest of them, surely they would be eager to follow to new glory behind the coach who had taught them glory in the first place. It was now that he learned the bitter lesson that Horvath, the Dankowskis, John Hall and Whitey Culpepper had fought their hearts out for the Big Red Flash solely that they might blow away the coal dust that lay on them, behind them and ahead of them if they did not excel. They were selfish beyond belief; they had fought for themselves, not for him.

Leo Dankowski's son Casimar asked incredulously, "Dee-troit? I'm going to Pitt." His cousin Bernard, son of Walter, chose to play against him and accepted the bid from Carnegie Tech. Southern Cal came that long distance with stars in their eyes to get Joe Foley. Failing, they left with John Hall signed and sealed. Whitey Culpepper listened to talk of a dozen Swaney Woods in the South and accepted Duke. One by one, the men who'd made Quinn great, the men Quinn had made great, peeled off from him. Pete Battle was pleased to tell him the truth. "Your ball-players just don't like you, Quinn. How does it feel?"

Quinn said with honest resentment, "It's stupid. Popular coaches don't go undefeated. I made undefeated football players out of those hillbillies, and they're too stupid to know that's what counts."

"So go to Dee-troit and make some more undefeated football players that don't give a rat's ass for you."

"I will. I'll do just that, and you know it." He swallowed his pride. "I'd like to take Davey with me."

Pete snorted. "I thought you been cottoning up to me. Well, when you're ready, we'll listen to your offer. But if I was you, I wouldn't count on it."

Bob Quinn went to Joe Foley. He said, in man-to-man fashion, "Joe, we've had our differences. Or maybe you could say we've really had our mutual understanding. You know I'm going to Detroit. I want you and Davey to come with me. In the first place, we'll win football games. In the second place, I give you my personal guarantee we'll match any offer you get from anybody. You give us the opportunity, we'll match any offer."

Joe Foley smiled. "Knute, we never had a mutual understanding. I understood you, but it was one-sided."

Quinn asked as mildly as he could, "Well?"

"You never understood I figured you got to be just about the best football coach in the U.S. of A. Next to Ellen Battle."

Quinn smiled tentatively. "Then we go on to new heights?"

Joe shook his head. "No. I wouldn't go to Dee-troit for a million dollars. And you don't even know why. It's not the money. That's just talk. Colleges don't give money anyway. It's just all talk. I'm going where I'll be all-American, it's as simple as that."

"You could make it at Detroit. You could make it anywhere."

"Not in a million years. They'd never hear about me far away as Cleveland."

"We'd make sure. Believe it, we would. Those Jebbies are bound and determined to come up in the world, and they'll go all out for you."

"Our minds are already made up."

Quinn's heart sank. "You and Davey both? Where are you going?"

"Better ask him. In the meantime, I'm going to take a few trips."

"To campuses?"

"East, west, north and south. This hillbilly is going to see some of the world. Free."

They continued to come for Joe from across the country, from nearly every state. Six head coaches and twelve assistant coaches made the pilgrimage. Twenty schools sent near-by alumni as emissaries. Twenty more wrote personal letters signed by the head coach himself. Michigan came. Pittsburgh came. Southern Cal came. Penn came. Illinois came. Alabama came. Notre Dame came often.

Each weekend Joe climbed on the train and set off for new adventure. Three weekends he spent in Pittsburgh, and the Panthers grew optimistic. The backfield coach said to the head coach, "We got it made. He's got a black-haired dolly in Mt. Lebanon."

The head coach said, "See if she wants a scholarship."

The backfield coach said, "She's a sophomore in high school."

"What's the matter with Foley? He go for jail bait?"

The backfield coach smiled. "Not her. Believe me, not her. She might be fifteen, but . . ."

"Well, see if we can hold his hat, or hold her down for him, or do something. Don't let him get away."

Coach Quinn sat down with Pete and David Battle to make his last-ditch presentation. "Davey, I understand you and Joe will go to the same school. That's a good idea. You make a great pair in the backfield. I want you to go to Detroit with me."

Pete said, "Well, now, Quinn, you can save your breath. We've decided."

David turned his head to his father and looked surprised, but he didn't say anything.

Quinn asked, "That right, Davey? Have you signed a tender?"

"No, I haven't signed anything. Joe either."

"Then you should consider Detroit. You won't get a better deal or a better education anywhere. They want a football team. And it's Jebbie, as good a Catholic school as there is."

Pete said, "And he'll ride the bench for you for the first three years."

Quinn said defensively, "That was before he weighed one seventy." Then he said, "David, I can't put it any better than this. Come to Detroit. You'll play great football, and you'll get a great education. The best."

David looked as though he might smile. "I'll get a better education at MIT."

The two men shouted at the same time, "MIT!"

David asked, "Why not?"

Quinn said, "You got to be kidding. There's no football at MIT."

David said, "I know."

Quinn said, "He's pulling our leg."

Pete looked at his son. Then he said, "If you're not, then get that stupid idea out of your head right now. The only way you get to go to college is on scholarship, and you're sure not going to be so stupid and work your way through MIT when football will get it for you on a silver platter."

Quinn asked, "You do like football, don't you, Davey?"

"Sure. I think it's great. Maybe it's not the most important thing in the world."

Pete snorted. "Sweet Jesus, I never heard anything so stupid. The world on a platter, and he talks stupid."

"MIT stupid?"

Pete said, "Oh, sweet Jesus, I think he means it."

Quinn turned devious. "Well, Pete, football's the most important thing in the world to you and me. We can't force our ideas on somebody else . . ."

Pete interrupted. "I know what's best for him, so forget it."

Quinn said, "Don't misunderstand me, Davey. I think football's the best bet for you, too. You should combine it with a good education. That's playing it smart. But Pete and me, we got no right to try to force our ideas on you. But you're overlooking two important things."

"What's that, Coach?"

"Two things. First, what does your mother want you to do?"

David just watched him.

"Wouldn't you say, all the time she's spent with you down on Carstairs' field, all this time, she wants you to play football. Isn't football what Ellen wants most of all for you?"

Still David watched him.

"The second thing, this talk of MIT, it's not fair to Joe. Joe's going to go where you say, you know that. And you just got to admit, Joe's not cut out to be a student with horn-rimmed glasses. He's cut out to be the greatest ballplayer in the country. Maybe the greatest ever. Maybe better than Red Grange and Jim Thorpe put together. You wouldn't be fair if you took that away from him."

Pete snorted again. "At Dee-troit?"

Quinn said quietly, "I'll be at Detroit. Don't forget that. I put Sweet Water, West Virginia, on the map. I'll put Detroit on the map, and Davey and Joe along with it."

Pete said, "I don't know what all the argument is about. I've got them both committed. Won't nobody beat the deal I got for them."

"Detroit will. Or at least match it."

"Not the deal I got."

"Just what kind of deal did you get?"

"One you can't match."

"Davey and Joe are good Catholic ballplayers. We've got

334

good Catholic alumni who want a football team. Let's stop fencing and come out with it."

David said, "I could tell you both something."

Quinn asked, "What's that, Davey?"

"The offers aren't as big as people make out. Not even Joe's. Mr. Quinn, this is your first time at recruiting. I mean, excuse me, sir, but . . ."

"Go ahead, Davey. You're absolutely right. I'm green as corn."

"People have talked to Joe and me you don't even know about. I know what they offer. It's not like people talk about. No convertibles. No big money. Just a free ride and a little bit of help on the side, and you got to work for that. The biggest offer Joe got is a lot smaller than people talk about."

Pete said, "That's because they're talking to kids not dry behind the ears. While you been listening to the snow jobs, I got down to business and got something that makes sense."

David said, "Papa, I guess I better tell it. Joe and me really are going to go to MIT. But that's for graduate school, and it'll be Navy sending us, after we finish up at Annapolis and serve some sea time."

Again the men exploded in unison. "Annapolis!"

David said, "They play football at Navy."

Pete said, "Some football! They haven't beat Notre Dame since the year one!"

"They were the national champs in 1926."

Pete said, "Sweet Jesus, what next! Listen, boy, did it ever sink in your thick skull you go to Navy, you've had it? No pro ball?"

David shrugged. "Joe and me are going."

Pete said, "You're not going to any pissy-ant, whistle-pants school, and that's that."

"The man's coming to talk to us tonight. He's coming over with Joe."

"What man?"

"Assistant director of athletics. And their bird dog from Charleston. He's been talking to us, the bird dog."

Pete asked scornfully, "Just how do you figure you're going to get there, in the first place?"

"The bird dog says they want ballplayers there, same as any place else. He'll get the appointment for us. He says it's no problem."

"I didn't mean the appointment. You got to pass an exam, right?"

"Right."

"And you think you can pass an exam like that?"

"The guy says you don't have to be a genius to get in Navy. People just think that."

"Well, maybe you don't have to be a genius, but you can't be a Sweet Water dumbbell, either. And you're talking like a Sweet Water dumbbell right now."

Joe Foley came in with the Navy bird dog and Leo Carter, Navy's assistant director of athletics. Carter was a ruggedly handsome ex-tackle out of Cornell. He had a bluff, professional heartiness. He shook hands with a respectful Bob Quinn and a reluctant Pete Battle. He sat himself next to David. He grabbed David's thigh with his big fingers. "Not bad," he said. He looked at Quinn. "You meet a little guy like that, you got to feel his leg to see what's there. I wouldn't have guessed he was one seventy. Have I got it right, Davey?"

David said admiringly, "Yes, sir, exactly."

"How tall?"

"Five nine."

"Where did I get the idea you were a squirt? Legs and neck like yours, we can use you just fine."

Pete said, "Carter, you might as well know right off the bat, you made a long trip for nothing. Davey's committed."

Carter asked, "That right, Davey?"

David looked at his father. "I haven't signed anything, no, sir."

"You want to hear more about Navy?"

"No, sir. I mean, me and Joe, we've decided. But maybe you could tell us what it's like, you know, the things you do and things like that, when you're a midshipman."

Pete grew livid. He said loudly, "You listen to me, you're going where I tell you."

Carter asked, "Where's your mother, Davey?"

David said, "I'll get her."

Ellen Battle stepped into the room, and it was apparent she'd been listening all along. David said, "This is my mother, Mr. Carter."

Carter said, "How do you do, Mrs. Battle. You've got a fine boy here. This is Mr. Gregg from Charleston."

Pete said, "Now just what's she got to do with it."

336

Carter said affably, "Mama makes the real decisions. Particularly with football players. The old man, he thinks he's the one that makes a ballplayer. Never. It's Mama. She's the one. A ballplayer, he cuts loose from his old man mighty quick, but he still listens to Mama." He looked at Quinn. "That's how ballplayers are, right, Bob?"

Quinn nodded. He hadn't the faintest idea how ballplayers were. He said, "That's right."

Carter said, "I hear you're going to Detroit."

"That's right."

"Remind me to get some bets down on the Titans. Wish we had you at Navy. People that don't know how to lose, they're the ones win. Sounds obvious, but it isn't. That's why we want Joe and Davey."

Quinn's avaricious football heart leaped. He said casually, "When you make a change down there, put me in line."

"We're back to officer coaches again. If I had my way, we'd have you down there right now. The admirals decide those things."

Pete said, "Some helluva football school. The admirals decide. Do they decide who carries the ball?"

"No, they don't. I better set the record straight. I gripe about the admirals, but the system works pretty good. I wish we had a civilian coach, but that's a small thing compared to the things a midshipman gets out of Navy."

Ellen said, "Can we ask some questions, Mr. Carter?"

"I came down here by mule back just to answer questions, Mrs. Battle."

"All right, the most important. Is David, are David and Joe, are they smart enough to get in?"

"Transcripts say they are. The proof will come when they take the exam. They take it next week. Where did you say they could get it, Forrest?"

Gregg said, "In Frogsburg. At the post office. I'll drive them over."

Ellen asked, "Is it as tough as they say?"

"It's tough. But these are all-A students, Mrs. Battle. They'll breeze through."

Pete said, "In a hillbilly high school they're all-A."

Quinn asked, "Are you guaranteeing they'll pass?"

Carter appraised the coach. "No, I can't do that. Our entrance exams aren't even graded by us. An Ivy League bunch does that, and they'd like nothing better than to cut a couple horses out from under us."

"Just what kind of offer does Navy make?"

"Bob, no offer. And the best offer. We can't give them a thing. But they earn more than they can get any place else. Midshipmen are in the United States Navy. They get paid. Paid for getting the best education in the country. Paid for living a life young fellows would give their right arms for. Room and board. The best chow in the world. Cruises to foreign ports and sixty dollars a month, and when they graduate, they step right into an officer's commission."

"Do you guarantee the commission?"

"No guarantee. They're their own guarantee."

Pete Battle said, "Now I'll tell you about Navy football. You slog it out four yards at a time. That's what they call football up there. Carter, you know damn well you got no use for Davey. You want him just to get Joe. You want those big backs. Slog away, and everybody in the stands knows what play's coming next, because it's always the same, and you run up and down the field between the twenty-yard lines and then bog down and don't score, and then you talk about what a moral victory you got, because you beat 'em on statistics. Well, that's not Davey's game. He's a break-away runner. You got to spring him loose. I'm telling you right now, Davey, they got officers as coaches, and they may know how to steer a battleship, but they don't know enough football to fill up their fancy omelet hats."

Joe Foley said, "Hunnh!"

Pete asked belligerently, "What's that supposed to mean?"

"The marvelous contortionist from the circus, the India-rubber man, he twists the same story to fit any idea he happens to be pushing at the time. Last time I remember you were preaching the holy gospel of slog-em-out football."

Leo Carter looked at Joe with curiosity at the clear spite and venom. He turned and appraised Pete, his professional smile masking his distaste. "You know your football, Mr. Battle."

"I should. I played with the best."

"Who was that?"

"Massilon Tigers."

338

"When was that?"

Pete said uneasily, "Nineteen twenty-one." He breathed an inward sigh of relief when Carter said, "Before my time. I played some with Portsmouth in '24 and '25 before I got smart and started telling other people to get out there and take their lumps. Now let me give you a thought. A coach tailors his game to his matcrial. You'll agree with that, Bob."

Quinn said, "No, I don't agree. I had the system and taught it to my horses."

Carter raised his eyebrows. "Mr. Gregg was telling me about the Warner T you broke out to beat Shawnee."

Joe Foley said, "Our coach is modest. He's got every bit as much imagination as Knute Rockne."

Quinn said, "They sprung the formation on me. I didn't think it was sound football. But it worked."

"Who sprung it?"

"Davey Battle." Quinn felt good. He had admitted the truth. The taste was good. He said, "Don't try to fool them, Carter. We're all alike. We promise the break-away back we'll play his game, but when the time comes, we'll still play it close to the vest. The winning coaches, we'll still leave the hipper-do to the losing coaches, and we'll play Rockne football."

Joe Foley said, "You can all knock off the talk. Davey and me made up our minds already."

Ellen Foley asked abruptly, "How long would they have to stay in the Navy?"

Carter said, "Three years after graduation. Then they can resign if they want to. They might not want to. It's a good life." He sized her up and said boldly, "It's a long way from the mines."

Pete said, "It's a long way from pro football, that's what it's a long way from."

Ellen asked, "How long would they be away from home at a stretch?"

"Mrs. Battle, they're away from home the moment they leave Sweet Water to go anywhere. But you'll see him, don't worry. They get leaves. And you'll come down to Annapolis and see him in that uniform. Mama always asks that question."

Ellen said, "Well, I don't know about all this. I thought it was a good idea at first, but now I'm not so sure."

For the first time Carter was concerned. He put on his

339

most affable, sanctimonious expression. "Davey, Joe, as you know, this is a decision you have to make for yourselves. Joe, if you're set on playing pro ball, don't go to Navy. If you're set on being a lawyer, or a doctor, don't go to Navy. If you haven't made up your mind what you want to do, then go to Annapolis, because Navy fits you for everything else. You know, pro ball is a lever to get you into a good job when you quit playing. Hell, the Navy does that automatically, so why get your brains knocked out like your dad and I did? Now listen to this. You're going to school to get an education. Not basket weaving, or home ec, or phys ed. That should be your answer right there."

Carter said, "Yes, we are recruiting. We want football players. They make good officers. And they're good for the morale of the Academy."

Pete Battle said, "You're wasting your time, Carter. This isn't up to eighteen-year-old kids to decide."

The Navy recruiter looked his adversary in the eye. "The best thing about going to Navy is you're on your own. You take the load off Papa's back and cut loose from Mama's apron strings. You're self-supporting from the moment you enter those gates. Isn't that what you want, Joe, Davey?"

Ellen Battle said, "I've been thinking, if there was a war . . ."

Leo Carter was disappointed in the mother. He said patiently, "Mrs. Battle, if a war comes, young men are going to war. This way they go as officers." David searched his mother's face. She had been so set on the Academy for Joe and him. Why now the misgivings? He said, "Mama, you can't plan anything, when you plan on the worst happening. Nobody would ever do anything worthwhile."

Forrest Gregg, the Navy bird dog, said, "Leo, I told you Davey had a head on his shoulders."

But Ellen Battle said, "These boys are Catholics. I think they should think about that."

Carter said quickly, "More than half of last year's squad was hard-nosed Polack and Irish Catholics." He smiled broadly. "Catholics get the best deal at Navy. They go on a church party out to St. Mary's in town, before breakfast, and get church over with. The Protestants go to ten o'clock chapel, and their whole morning's shot." He searched his mind for the clincher. "Here's maybe the most important thing of all. Think about this. At Navy nobody ever asks you if you're Protestant or Catholic. Or if you're rich or poor, or what your family is, or anything else except what *you* are. You put on that uniform, Joe, Davey, you're all alike. The only thing that counts is what you can produce."

Pete demanded, "You saying they should be ashamed of their families?"

Carter thumped his palms on his legs. He didn't know how to answer. He'd come to Sweet Water to close a deal, and hillbilly parents were baffling him, thwarting him. He said with bluff heartiness, "Joe, Davey, are you in?"

Joe Foley looked at his uncle. He looked at Ellen Foley Battle. He said, "Davey's got his brains in his feet, and his feet always come out pointing in the right direction."

David looked only at his mother. He said firmly, "We want Navy. That's what we've wanted all along."

Pete Battle stood up. He clenched his fists in towering rage at the complete insubordination. He remembered. He could still feel the sting of his father's hand when he'd ventured his own tentative insubordination. Now was the moment. Knock respect back into his son's head. Roar "What is this!" and knock respect into his son's head. He didn't know how. How could he instill respect where none had ever been? He didn't know the truth. He didn't know David Battle's desperate longing all those years for approval and acceptance. He didn't know his son. He only knew himself. He knew only that he was the furthest thing from an object of respect. Casimar Dankowski? Strong-willed, staunch, father-image Casimar Dankowski? No, he was Pete Battle, not Casimar. If he tried it now, what would he do if he met full resistance from David? And maybe he'd have to fight Joe Foley. Yes, he'd have to fight Joe Foley. He knew it, as sure as he was in that room, he'd have to fight Joe, and the empty fear was in his stomach, and the sour fear was in his mouth. He walked out of the room and up the stairs.

The following day Bob Quinn came to UMW district office. "Pete, this time we're on the same team. Navy's no good for those boys."

"Well, they're not there yet."

"You going to use brute force, or a new argument?"

341

"Quinn, I got too good a deal. You know Davey. In the long run, he won't queer it for me."

"For you?"

"What did you think?"

"I guess I thought something stupid, like you were negotiating a deal for Joe and Davey. I should have known better. What did you get?"

"A deal you can't match."

"I talked to the Detroit boosters. They haven't got much experience in this kind of thing, but they said they'd back me up if I got Joe. So?"

"Let's get down to hard facts. The only way you'll get Joe is to get Davey. The only way you'll get Davey, is if I put the heat on him about paying his obligation to me."

"How do you get your money? It is money, isn't it?"

"Man can have two jobs. Job as a consultant, that doesn't take too much time away from the union."

"How much?"

"Why don't you test it out?"

"Fifty dollars a month?"

"You're warm."

"We'll go seventy-five, if you deliver."

"How will you guarantee it?"

"I'll have to talk to the boosters. We got some doctors and dentists doing okay. Maybe through some plant, if we got somebody that owns one. I think we better stay away from Father Koenig on it. I'm not sure whether he'd approve. All I know is, I want Joe. You think you can deliver? They're sure set on Navy."

"They're wet behind the ears. I'll dry 'em out between now and the time."

Quinn said, "I've got my own ace in the hole. They got to pass the exam."

"Thought they were a lead-pipe cinch."

"Just because they got A's in math? I was the teacher, remember?"

18

THE MAY FLOWERS BURST OUT. Ellen Foley Battle followed them up the mountainside, stopping often to drink in the wonderful, warm air. Halfway up, she sat on a rock outcropping and looked out to the Kanawha at the mouth of the Murder. She felt glorious. The air was magnificent. The setting sun glinted off her black hair. She was strong. She was vital. She was youth.

Joe Foley made his way up the hill after her. She watched his approach. He surmounted obstacles effortlessly. He moved like a big cat. She thought to herself: The two of us, we're young and strong.

From fifteen feet, he smiled broadly and said, "Seen you from the crick. Can I join you?"

He sat on the rock with her.

She said, "It's beautiful. Just a beautiful day. It will be a beautiful evening."

He breathed deeply. He said, "It seems like you can't get enough spring air inside you. It's like all the parts of you were shoutin' hallelujah!"

Ellen Foley said, "Yes."

He said, "Ellen, you sure look good, the way that light is hitting you."

She leaned back so that her black hair hung down and nearly touched the rock. She said, "I feel good. I just

343

feel wonderful." She straightened up and clasped her knee in her hands. "How do you count age? Not by years, I'm sure."

"Not in your case, Ellen."

"No, I'm as young as you, I think, Joe."

With a brogue he said, "Sure and you're comely, Ellen Foley."

She watched his face.

He said calmly, "Ellen, hold still. There's a copperhead about four feet to your left. Hold still, I'll get him."

He turned his head slowly and looked for a stick, but he saw none. He rose in slow motion, bent over and picked up a rock, straightened up and lashed out with his right arm. The rock crushed the snake's head. The body writhed furiously.

He said, still calm, "Got him."

She said, smiling tensely, "Snakes scare me. You'd think somebody born in West Virginia would get used to them."

He walked around behind her on the outcropping. He knelt and put his hands on her shoulders, his thumbs at the base of her neck, and he kneaded gently.

She said, "You have such strong hands."

"The better to strangle you with, my dear."

She closed her eyes. The strong, young hands sent warmth through her. Because he was strong, he was a match for her. Only he in all the world was a match for the raging passion which her strong, young body could release. It was spring, and she had the gift of long-lasting youth, and her husband would not accept her youth, would not take it up and taste the fierce joy of it. She opened her eyes and turned them to the Parker house with its four chimneys visible through the trees. India Parker was a fool, a meddlesome fool, and dead wrong. No fifteen-year-old girl could hold a candle to a beautiful forty-year-old woman. No little girl could divert David Battle and Joe Foley. Joe's strong fingers touched the bare skin of her neck. He put his hands inside her collar, so that he could work them into the bare skin of her shoulders. She closed her eyes again. In just a few moments the sun would go over the hill, and the warm evening would come down on them like the walls of a bedroom, and he would ask her as he had asked her before, and she would be very gentle and understanding as she turned him down. She would turn him down. There was no possibility that she would turn and give herself to him, to know once again the wild, sweet, abandoned ecstasy. Oh, she had so much to give. If she would turn and give herself to him, he would receive so much. He would give back to her so much. She felt as though she were trembling.

She said, "It's been a long time." Her voice was not quite steady.

"What's been a long time, Ellen?"

She didn't answer. She leaned back against his leg, and he continued to massage her neck and shoulders. Suddenly he took his hands away. Still kneeling behind her, he said, "Ellen, it won't be long now, we'll be going off, Davey and me. I wonder if we'll get back."

"Your roots are here."

"You're here, that's what. I want you to know something, Ellen. I think you've been good for me. There's been times I wouldn't have believed that. I don't think I should go into it, but I think in the long run you'll prove good for me."

Without looking at him she asked, "Are you practicing a farewell address of some kind?"

After a moment he said, "I'm not practicing. You'll be glad to know it."

"Don't play games with me, Joe."

"I'll tell you something, when I'm all-American, I'm going to have sixteen girl friends and not get a crush on any of them. I'm going to be like Davey, hard to get. You know me, when I get a crush, I just throw myself down like a big ole hound dog just begging to get my belly scratched, so Suzanne ends up head over heels for Davey. You only have to hit me over the head twicet with a sledge hammer, then I catch on."

Ellen asked sharply, "What's between David and that girl?"

"I'll tell you the truth, I don't know."

"Well, David can take care of himself against her."

"Against her?" He grinned. "I reckon that is the right way of putting it."

"India says David took her up to Black Beulah. Joe, David wouldn't do that."

"Are you asking me, or telling me? I don't think he would take her up there. I think she might take him."

"How about you, Joe? Did you take her up there?"

"I'll tell you the truth about that. I tried. And that's

what I'm telling you. Next time I'm going to play hard to get. Or maybe stick to the Swaney Woods." His eyes lighted up. "Swaney Wood, that's the best thought I've had this week."

"Joe, I don't appreciate this kind of talk. You know better."

"Yes, I do. And I guess you know what I've been trying to tell you."

"I don't know what you're talking about."

He said, "Well, I don't know how to say it any clearer without coming out and saying it. I'm going away, and times and things change, and . . ."

"I don't know what you're talking about, and I don't care to know."

He hopped off the rock. "Coming down?"

"I'll stay here awhile. You go ahead."

"I'll stay with you."

She said quite loudly, "Get out!"

He cocked his head and studied her.

At the top of her voice she said, "Get out!" Just a little softer she said, "Leave me alone." And then in normal tones she said, "I just want to be alone, Joe. I just want to be alone."

Without a word or a backward glance, he made his way down the mountain side. When he had disappeared from view, she stood and held her clenched hands stiffly at her sides and looked down on Sweet Water. In a fervent voice, she said aloud, "Lord, have mercy on us, God, have mercy on us. Oh, God, drive the sin out of this iniquitous place. God, help me drive it out of my son. Oh, God, don't let him be a vile sinner like his father, like his vile cousin. Lord, don't let David succumb to that whore. Oh, God, help me keep my son pure!"

19

ELLEN FOLEY BATTLE SAID, "David, come sit on the steps. I want to talk to you about it."

When he would have sat apart from her, she tugged him close enough so that she could stroke his hair while she talked.

"David, it would be for the glory of God. Doesn't that give you a good feeling? Do you remember how we talked about it when you were little?"

He didn't answer.

"David, we've got to discuss this before it's too late."

"Mama, I want to go to Navy. I already told Mr. Carter that I'd go."

"He wouldn't expect you to ruin your whole life, just because you thought you promised."

"I don't think I promised, I know I did. Mama, I'll tell you what. We won't talk about it now. There will still be plenty of time if I went to Navy. I could still be a priest after I went through Navy. Maybe I could be a chaplain."

"No, David. You'd be changed. You'd live the wrong kind of life, and then you could never be a priest. This is the time. David, we're alike, you and me. We've seen the terrible things that sin can do to a person. It's too late for me to do much about it, but now I've got one daughter

347

who will do something, and I could have a son who would."

He turned his head and studied his mother. He asked, "Mama, was it Gerry's idea to be a nun? Or was it yours?"

"Of course it was her idea."

"Did you talk to her about it before she decided?"

"Of course I talked to her. What is it you're trying to say?"

"I don't know. Mama, I knew you were maybe changing your mind some about Navy, when you were talking to Mr. Carter. I thought maybe it was just, you know, worry about me going away."

"Isn't that the most natural thing in the world?"

"Yes'm, that's what I said, like you wanted to hold on to me a little bit, that's what I thought it was."

"David, I'm not trying to hold on to you. I'm just thinking of what's right for you. Annapolis sounded glamorous, but it was a wild-goose chase, when all the time you've been cut out to be a priest. That's all I'm saying, David."

"Tell me again, did you tell Gerry to be a nun?"

"David, if you knew what happened to her, you'd know why she had to do something quickly. The worst of all sins was right in front of her. I wish I could tell you about it. I can't."

"I know."

"Do you?"

"Yes, I know. It's a terrible thing. I wonder if he meant it all as bad as it sounds."

"He meant it."

"Do you know for sure, Mama?"

"He meant it. This time don't try to forgive him. David, it's the thing we've had to face. He's capable of any sin. She had to get away. Now she's doing something worthwhile with her life, where sin can't reach her."

He stood up. He sat down again. "Mama, I'm sorry. I want to be a naval officer. I've got my mind set on it."

She stroked his hair again. "If you've decided once and for all, there's nothing I can do about it. David, I wish you'd consider me enough to think about it. Just think about it, that's all I'm asking. This is the most important thing in the world to me."

"Mama, I can't just up and be a priest, you know that. I haven't even been thinking about it."

"You've been living it, haven't you?"

David didn't answer.

She said closely, "David, you have been living the right kind of life to be a priest, haven't you? That girl. India is up to her tricks. She says you took that girl up to Black Beulah."

"Mama, we've talked about me playing ball, right? That's what we've been planning, right? You can't just up and get a fever and think I'll catch it like that. I don't feel the call."

"You do. You know you do. You were meant to be a priest. You've got to know that. David, are you meant to be a sinner, like the other men in Sweet Water?"

His neck stiffened.

"You're not, David. You're not meant to be a sinner. You're not meant to succumb to temptations like that girl would put in front of you. You know how terrible sin is. You've had a better chance than most people to see mortal sin and what it does to people. David, answer me, I've got to know, have you been living the celibate life of a priest?"

He didn't answer.

"Swear to me that you have, David."

"Yes," he said loudly.

She said triumphantly, "Of course! I told India. I know you don't think about sex all the time, like the other ones do. David, you're strong, but you should be careful about the company you keep. It could expose you to temptation. If you only knew the terrible things some men would do, so awful you can't even talk about it. You're not like them. You're not a sinner. The Grace of God is in you."

He said nothing. He was miserable.

She said confidently, "David, we'll compromise. If you don't want to go to a seminary right away, go to Notre Dame. Play football. But prepare to be a priest. That way you'll get to do all the things you want to."

He stood up.

She said, "I know you, David. I know you better than you know yourself. Being a priest is the thing for you. You can do God's work. That's for you, David. God's work."

He said, "Mama, I don't want to be a priest. I want to be a naval officer."

She was now confident. "David, fight mortal sin."

"Please, Mama."

"We'll talk about it later," she said soothingly.

The letter came.

DAVEY:

Congratulations! The secretary of the Academic Board advises that you have passed the entrance exam and you're all set. You'll take the physical exam when you report here in July. You can plan on passing it. You will receive notice of your alternate appointment from Congressman John Pennell of Mississippi, a good friend of Navy. Be sure to write and thank him for his courtesy and interest.

Sorry about Joe Foley. You just did make it on algebra, and he just missed it. I've written him suggesting that he attend prep school for a year and enter the Academy next year. This will give him an excellent background for the work here. If you think you might like to go with him, let me know immediately and we'll arrange scholarships for both of you, based on financial need, of course. Then you could both enter the Academy the summer of 1936.

Sincerely,
LEO CARTER

Aunt Polly, the postmistress, asked hopefully, "Was it what you boys have been looking for?"

David asked his strong cousin, "What do you want to do, Joe?"

"Your letter tell about me?"

"Yes. I don't get it. How come both of us, all that trouble with algebra?"

Joe shrugged. "Every man on the squad got an A from Quinn. And that's just how much it was worth."

"What do we do?"

"I suppose you go to Navy."

"Want to go to prep school for a year? Might be a good deal. Sounds like both of us can use some cramming."

Joe shook his head. "You go ahead, Davey. You made it, you go ahead."

They walked out of the C & O station and stood on the platform. David said, "Joe, you sure lost your enthusiasm about Navy, somewhere along the line."

Joe said firmly, "If I'd of passed the exam, I was going to Navy. And I tried my level best to pass it."

"From obligation? Obligation to our deal? Joe, have you lost your enthusiasm for going where I'm going?"

Joe hit him so hard on the arm muscle that David had all he could do to keep from rubbing. "Let's take a swim. Crick oughter be cold enough to clear our skulls for planning."

The train in the station pulled out. They hopped the last car before the conductor could pull up the platform. The conductor said, "You'll kill yourself some day. Now get off."

They dropped off at Murder Creek, with the train moving at ten miles an hour. They watched the train disappear toward Charleston. Joe stooped and picked up a round rock. He threw it from the tracks halfway across the Kanawha. David tried it. He barely made the water.

Joe said, "Maybe I'll take up baseball, when we get some place you don't have to be a mountain goat to run the bases."

"Where's that going to be?"

"Davey, I want to play pro football so bad I can taste it."

"Well, for Pete's sake, why didn't you just say so?"

They left the tracks and walked slowly up the trail past the Dankowski house. Ellen Foley stopped in the yard when her son and her nephew waved at her. She half-waved back, her arm going only to her shoulder. David would have turned in to speak to her. Joe kept walking. David followed his big cousin up the trail until the gray house was out of sight.

Joe said conversationally. "She's a mite provoked with me."

"That's no secret. What for?"

Joe picked up a long, bare branch and threw it, like a javelin, to the far bank of Murder Creek. "Maybe I can be a decathlon champeen, like Jim Thorpe."

"How come she's provoked?"

Joe Foley said in a pleasant tone of voice, "I think some day I'll heave India in the Kanawha."

"What for?"

"On account she's half Injun, half Snake, and all big mouth. She makes me feel like a bug she stuck a pin into to look at under a magnifying glass."

"She been giving you the third degree? Me, too."

351

"She fixes those beady black eyes on me, and the wrinkles in her face kinda grab hold of you, so you can't get away, and she says: *"You kinda taken a shine to Suzanne, Joe?"* He talked in a leering falsetto. *"You kinda get to thinking Ellen and Suzanne are one and the same?"* He stopped and looked at his cousin. "Not sure I meant to let the cat outen the bag, Davey."

"Oh, I'm sure you did."

"Well, maybe I did. I just didn't know if you knew."

"I know."

"Do you know?"

"I know."

"I wasn't quite sure you did. Don't know if I'm glad you know or not. I think I'm going to explain some things. Can I talk to you a minute, Davey?"

David Battle said, "Suit yourself." He felt the sickness in his stomach; the revulsion against sex was coming over him. He wanted to close his ears and eyes and run frantically for Black Beulah and the cold water, or the warm bath his mother would pour for him in the galvanized washtub on the back porch of the gray house that was the womb. He couldn't move. Sin transfixed him.

"That old Injun bat wants to know who it is I'm thinking on when I spark Suzanne."

David waited.

Joe smiled. He picked up a hunk of coal from the track bed and threw it deep into the trees on the slope. "It was a good question, only some late."

"What does that mean?"

"Davey, do you really know? That I had sort of the" —he threw another baseball-sized hunk of coal—"the hots for her?"

"Yes. Joe, did Ellen know it?"

"Yes."

"Joe . . ." David couldn't ask it. He picked up his own lump of coal and threw it, and the two of them went on up the track like grade-school boys, acting diffident.

"Davey, I'm over it."

"Are you?"

"I sure am, Davey, I sure am."

"Suzanne?"

"Could be. Guess I was bound to get over it anyhow."

"Does Ellen know you're over it, Joe?"

"I reckon she can tell some difference. She knows. I do reckon that's why she's some provoked at me."

They were silent awhile.

David said offhandedly, "I do think she's got her nose out of joint."

Joe stopped and sat on a stump against the hillside. "There's a perverseness in people that they're natural born with. The things you can't have, you'd give the most to have. I think maybe perverseness is at the bottom of most sin. The more lowdown the sin is, the more you got to fight off the perverseness in you that makes that lowdown sin look so good."

"I guess I've had enough speculation about sin thrown at me, between you and Jim Parker."

"My speculation's got its point. But I'm more mixed up now than I was when I was mixed up. I'm wondering if there was ever anything to get over, or if it was just something I made up and then went along with. When you get over something, you wonder how you got yourself so het up about it in the first place."

Joe began skipping shale in the lengthwise direction of the narrow Murder Creek.

"Davey, I'm sure glad I popped off and explained some things. Like a big load lifting off me."

"That's not why you did it. You've got something to say you haven't said yet, and you're just leading up to it."

"You're perspicacious." He grinned. "Do you know what that means?"

"Sagacious. Astute."

"Well, then you can go to hell, because I've been saving that one up to throw at you. Suppose I do some more supposing out loud. Davey, you got to know it was all on one side, you got to know that."

David said loudly, "I know that," and an explosion of relief went off inside him to know at last that nothing physical had transpired between his mother and his cousin. He wanted to smile, and it was hard to keep his lips firm.

"Davey, she's got a problem. And it's going to get worse before it gets better. I got to say this, because it's important to you. She was provoked when I was thinking things I shouldn't think, but it was like she was hanging on to a chance, like it was a compliment she needed, like it was reassurance, and she wouldn't maybe ever do anything about it, but if she wanted to, she could get even with him for Green Billy's and the rest of it, so when it's gone, she's more provoked than ever, and she's going to take it out some other way. Davey, I can see that, in the way she's talking."

"What's your point, Joe?"

"She doesn't want you to go to Navy, right? She wants you to be a priest, right?"

"How did you know that?"

"She told me herself. Like flinging it at me. Do you know why she wants you to be a priest?"

"Because she's a good Catholic, and that's reason enough."

"I think because she wants to hang on to you."

"Well, that's just stupid. A mother doesn't hang on to a priest, for Pete's sake."

"Doesn't she? She knows a priest ain't laying up with some tomato, she knows that. Except I'm not so sure about Hannigan. I trust a priest that smokes and drinks, he's got something to take his nature out on."

"Joe, why don't you just forget the cleverness for a while?"

"Davey, it's true, and you know it's true, she just plain don't want you having anything to do with girls, and doesn't want me having anything to do with girls, and you know that, or you're blind. And she's tying you tighter to her apron strings all the time, you got to know that, particular now that her and me are on the outs you're the last of the Mohicans for her to hang on to. That's what I'm leading up to, Davey. You got to cut loose."

"It's not true, Joe."

"It's true. She's got you hooked."

"If you want to know the truth, it's Papa's got the hold on me. I bet I tried a million times to hate his guts. And all I end up with is wanting just one time, just one lousy time, for him to say okay, I did one thing okay, and I feel that way so much I even think sometimes I want to sin like he does, and it's her keeps me from it. Wasn't for her, Joe, I'd probably be like the rest of Sweet Water, so I'd say she's done only good for me, and not tied me up."

"Do you good, Davey! Putting that stupid mortal-sin-thinking in you! Oh, sweet Jesus, Davey!"

354

"You think your way, Joe. I'll feel sorry for you, and I wish I could help you, but I can't."

"Listen, it's not my way. It's human-being way, that's what it is. Sweet Jesus, don't you think I know? There's spells when Hannigan scares the living shout outen me in that black cubbyhole, and I swear I ain't going to think no bad thoughts again, not ever. And that's when them bad thoughts come just a-leaping over the trenches like Huns, and I'm just stabbing everywhere with my bayonet, and can't get 'em all, they're coming from all directions. So the only thing you can do then, you just lie there and let them thoughts have their fill of you, and then they go away and don't come back as soon. Davey, you got to get free of her."

"You just don't make sense, Joe."

"All right, you go to Navy. That's where you want to go, right? That makes it perfect. You get to go where you want to go, and at the same time you cut loose from the apron strings."

David Battle said, "Yes." It was true. He wanted Navy as much as Joe Foley wanted pro ball. He wanted Navy. He wanted Navy. All he had to do was accept his appointment and go. But Ellen Foley Battle didn't want him to go to Navy. She wanted him to be a priest. She would let him go to Notre Dame and then be a priest, but that was as far as she would go. He said, "But I made you a deal. We go the same place. I'm not all that keen on Navy. Where do we go?"

"All right, just so we go somewhere they don't want us to go. Pete, he says he's got a deal. I think he's full of crap. At least we know for sure it isn't with Notre Dame. And I don't think it's Pitt. Now maybe we ought to go to Pitt. Mount Lebanon's mighty handy. Davey, I'd do that if I was you. That Suzanne. In case you got any doubt, I'm slag in the coal vein far as she's concerned, but she'd do handsprings, you asked her."

David Battle thought of Suzanne Carstairs, who had filled his loins with such hunger and who was his mother and sister under him, and was such foulness, and he said, "Pitt's out. Okay, you say they don't want us to go to Notre Dame, that's where we'll go." The lie of it was ashes in his mouth.

Joe Foley grinned. "That's just great. Just great. And

355

sure as pot's to piss in, Suzanne will end up at St. Mary's, and you'll get to bang her all the time we're there."

David said sharply, "Joe, I've got this to say. I've had my fill of that kind of talk out of you. Any more of it, I'm going some different direction from you."

"Davey, I accept that, if you let me say this just once. Just once. You got to do something. She's getting you so filled up with mortal sin, you're going to get to the place you can't touch a woman without thinking you're getting some horrible dirt all over your hands. Boy, I've had my problems, but thinking women are dirty ain't one of them."

"Have you said your piece?"

"Yes."

"Once and for all?"

"Yes. I swear. And we're going where nobody but us wants us to go, that's great."

"Joe, do you think Notre Dame will give me the ride? They haven't said anything to me."

"David, I just got a feeling they will. A package deal. I guess you know it's not the best deal. We get the free ride. We get some tickets to scalp. They'll get us a job if we want it. That's about it."

"You want to put a gun in anybody's ribs, Joe?"

"No."

"I don't either, even if we could."

"I did once. I'm growing up. Now I just want a square deal. We'll beat our brains out for 'em on Saturday, we make the coach a hero, we make a few million shanty Irishmen happy enough to get drunk, and we got a free education and a first-class ticket into pro ball. That's not bad."

"Tell you what, Joe. When we get out of Notre Dame, we'll make sure we get drafted by the same pro club. We'll tell them they got to take both, right?"

"Sure, Davey."

They walked back into Sweet Water. From the C & O station, Joe called collect to South Bend. He said, "It's Joe Foley calling," and the backfield coach was so anxious to accept the call that he stuttered to the operator. Joe said, "We're coming. David Battle and me. If you still want us."

"We thought you lost interest."

"We've got the interest."

"That's the one thing we've got to be sure of. We don't take ballplayers at Notre Dame unless they really want to come here." He held his breath, having made his required speech. Then he asked, "What can we do?"

"Can somebody get us a summer job in South Bend? So we can get a little money ahead? And maybe kick the ball around a little?"

"I think we can do that. Joe, at Notre Dame you have to earn the money." Again he held his breath.

Joe said, "We'll dig ditches."

"We'll get you a job."

"Will you send us bus fare?"

"Train fare. Your friend from Charleston will get it to you tomorrow. When will you come?"

"Inside a week."

"Call me when you get here."

"Coach, we'll win some ball games for the Irish."

"Joe, we're counting on that. And tell Battle we're glad he's coming."

Joe hung up and said to his cousin, "That was easy." He grinned. "Oh, by God, I can't wait to see Pete's face. Sweet Jesus, I hope he really did have a deal lined up. You going to tell your folks tonight?"

"Sure. Why not?"

"Just wanted to make sure. I'll tell mine, too."

David Battle thought to himself: It's perfect. I'm going where I want to go. Navy wasn't really for me, not really. And it's not as though I'm going to be a priest. That's four years off, and a lot can happen in four years. Thus he rationalized away his submission to his mother, but he was not so successful that he wiped completely away the uneasiness that Joe Foley had put into him.

Joe said, "Come on, let's get that swim."

They met Swaney Wood swinging along the Charleston Road toward the station. Joe took her arm and turned her in the opposite direction. She asked easily, "Where we going, Joe?"

"Black Beulah. Skinny-dipping."

"All three of us?"

"Sure. Anything wrong with that?"

She put her arms through the arms of both of them and smiled prettily. "It took a long time, but now I've got both the handsomest beaux in Sweet Water," and David felt the protruding, wonderful softness of her breast against his arm, and for the minutes they walked together, he thought giddily that he might go skinny-dip-

357

ping with Swaney Wood, and the thought of this filled him with the utmost anticipation.

But when they reached the Dankowski house, he turned off. He said, "I've got to write Mr. Carter and tell him I won't be going to Navy."

They didn't urge him to reconsider. David walked slowly up the path to the house. He turned and watched strong Joe Foley and pretty, sexy Swaney Wood up the trail. He watched her hips. He watched her hips. Would Joe do it to her? Would Joe do such a terrible thing? Would she giggle and then let him do it to her? Would she spread her legs apart and pull him down on top of her and drive him into herself! The thought filled him with panic and revulsion. He said half aloud, "Oh, please, God, give him strength! Don't let him commit mortal sin with that girl!"

And all he could see was her hips.

20

DAVID DIDN'T TELL HIS PARENTS. They learned it from India Parker, who learned it from Joe Foley's mother the day before the departure and sent the news hurrying through Sweet Water.

Pete Battle came boiling from his union office and apprehended his son on the Charleston Road. He shouted in a towering rage, "I've got you signed up. Don't you understand? You're signed up."

"Where?"

"Just you never mind where."

"Papa, we're going to South Bend right enough. On the morning train."

Pete raised his big fist. "I'll knock some sense and respect in you!" Then the father looked quickly up to the Foley house to be sure the mother wasn't visiting and watching from the porch.

David said soberly, "It's ironic. In the long run, no matter how strong you are, the woman is stronger."

Pete opened his hand and lashed out with his big palm. David caught the wrist and held off the blow. Pete shook him loose, like a terrier shaking a rat. He stared at his son, baffled. Then he looked guiltily around him once more to be sure that no one was watching. This time he saw Bob Quinn, taking in the tableau from the door of the company store.

Quinn walked to the father and son. He said evenly, "Save your strength, Battle. You'll need it for the arm-rassle with Joe, on the platform. In front of the whole town. Remember?"

Pete Battle asked, "Just what the hell business is that of yours? And who's been talking to you about that, anyway?"

Quinn said, "Your humiliation will be my business and my pleasure. As to who told me, that's up to you to find out. I'm just guaranteeing, if you come to the station, that match is going to be held." The football coach walked on.

Pete Battle watched the broad back. He turned to his son and said, "Dave, the reason I fly off at you is I don't want you to be stupid. Now don't be stupid. I'll get you the right deal."

"Papa, does that mean you really haven't got a deal yet?"

"I practically have it. It's all set."

"Do you mean with Coach Quinn, Papa?"

"I've got others. Practically set."

"Papa, I was going to tell you tonight. I'll see you at supper."

Pete Battle said, "Dave, don't be stupid. Just wait a few days, I'll have it set."

He watched his son's retreating back.

Ellen Foley Battle took her son's hand as he came up the porch steps. "You should have told me yourself. But that's all right. David, I'm glad you decided to do the right thing."

David said, "Mama, I'm going to Notre Dame to play football. After that my plans are to play pro ball."

She sat him in Casimar Dankowski's rocker. She said confidently, "When the time comes, I know you won't disappoint me. David, do you have to go so soon?"

"They've got jobs for Joe and me. We'll need some money when school year comes."

"Then you don't have to go. I've got some saved up. Why don't you just wait until September, and I'll send you off with a good start."

He looked at the walls of the gray house. He looked down the hill to Murder Trail, and then along the creek to the Kanawha. He heard the familiar grumbling complaint of Casimar Dankowski, taking out his miseries and frustrations on his half-Jewish wife. He looked at his beautiful mother, who loved him. He was tempted. Notre Dame could wait until September.

But he said, "Save it for an emergency. Save it to come see me sometime, and I'll show you around the campus."

She sat beside him in the swing and pulled his head down against her shoulder. She said, "I'm going to be so proud of you, David."

He studied his emotions. It felt good to have his head against her. He was secure. There was nothing wrong with that. He sat up straight, but he let her hold his hand in hers.

She asked carelessly, "Is that Carstairs girl going to St. Mary's?" As soon as the careless question was out, she turned her head sharply for his answer.

"I haven't the faintest idea."

"India said it."

"I told you, I haven't got the faintest idea. I hope not."

The fond smile came back on the beautiful face of Ellen Battle. "That's what I thought." The smile left. "David, when you get there, don't you think it would be a good idea if you met some new people? That's one of the things college is for. You don't have to room with Joe, just because he's from Sweet Water."

"I'll think about it. I don't think it will make much difference either way."

She said earnestly, "David, you should have a proper roommate. One that won't lead you into doing wrong things."

"Joe couldn't do that."

"No, of course he couldn't. But be on your guard, David. He'll try, if you give him an opening."

"Mama, Joe and Papa are going to have the arm-rassle tomorrow. Joe must have told Mr. Quinn, and Coach is going to make sure they do it. I was thinking, maybe between us we could talk them out of it. There doesn't seem much point in it."

His mother said, "That's between them. We'll keep out of that one. They can go their way, and you and me, we'll go our way."

In the night, Ellen said to her husband, "In the arm-rassle, you win tomorrow, Pete. You show him."

In the dark, Pete tried to see his wife's face. His own showed the surprise. He said gruffly, "I somehow got the idea you might want him to win."

She said, "I want him to lose."

Her husband wondered at the intensity of her emotion.

21

THE WORD SPREAD that the three heroes, Quinn, Foley and Battle, were leaving for Charleston on the same train, and the miners of Sweet Water gathered in the early morning at the C & O station.

Old Davis Parker made, in his pulpit voice, the first oration. He went on and on, until Mr. Scott, the owner of the Red Flash, moved in front of him and looked significantly at his pocket watch. The pastor concluded in resentful tones. "May the Good Lord, in his infinite wisdom, watch over these fine lads and see their works favorably. In God's name, we ask it."

Father Riley, the young man who would in one month complete his take-over of the parish from the retiring Father Hannigan, got the second crack. He smiled cheerfully to the crowd, disposed himself into a one-of-the-fellows attitude, and said with patent boisterousness, "Sure and it's a foin day for the Oirish." The listeners forced their appreciative chuckles. "Robert Emmett Quinn to lead the Jesuits out of the wilderness. Joe Foley to bring new glory to the Green of our Lady at South Bend. And David Battle. Davey, if you're half Irish, sure and you're all Irish. God be with you all."

Mr. Scott appropriated the center stage of the platform. He knew he didn't own this town as absolutely as the Carstairs' had owned it, and maybe he didn't control it like a baron, the way they controlled it, and maybe he didn't hold the town's affection as Vincent and his daddy had held it, but he was the man who had brought pride back into the town, and he was the man who dominated this town, and he knew that all the way.

"Sweet Water is proud of your exploits. We are proud to have played a part in your victories. When I brought in a coach, I hoped he would be good, but Bob Quinn exceeded my fondest expectations. He wasn't good. He was perfect."

He waited indulgently for the cheers to subside.

"Joe Foley and David Battle, if they aren't the two best halfbacks in America, somebody will have to show Sweet Water a better pair."

Again he waved his arms to let the cheers subside.

"The football teams of Parker District High have meant a great deal to this town. No one has contributed more than these three young men. I propose a proper send-off cheer. Hip-hip . . ."

Now the miners responded a little self-consciously, "Hooray!"

Bob Quinn made the first reply. "I won't forget Sweet Water. I came here unknown, and the men of Sweet Water brought me a reputation that's taking me to Detroit. I won't forget the men and the town that gave me this opportunity."

In the cheering, Joe Foley muttered, "Way to go, Knute."

Quinn said out of the corner of his mouth, "I'll still take you, Joe. Either one of you, or both of you. You wouldn't regret it."

Joe said pleasantly, "I'll put in a word for you at Notre Dame."

Quinn pushed him forward.

Joe said to the crowd, his Irish grin broad, "You all get one promise. When Davey and me get on that field against Army, all they'll see will be a cloud of Sweet Water coal dust. Amen!"

The cheers were long and lusty, and in them the yells, "Now, Davey! Let's hear it, Davey!"

David was pushed forward, his bright face and bright blue eyes earnest. They expected him to strive for speech and fail. They were prepared to give a warm, fond cheer for the silent one.

He said, "We aren't leaving Sweet Water. We aren't even taking Sweet Water with us where we go. We *are* Sweet Water, and wherever we go, we'll do our best to be a credit to what we are."

The crowd was strangely quiet.

Quinn said behind David, "I wish I knew what it is he has. I wish I knew." Then he stepped forward and said loudly, "One last thing. The big match we've all been waiting for."

Joe watched Pete Battle. Would Pete back out, somehow, the way he had always backed out? Joe hoped he would. He'd lost his desire for the fight. There didn't seem to be much point in it. He said to himself, "Back out, Pete. I'll let you out gracefully, if I can."

But Pete strode forward and said in a loud voice, "Let's give it a go, Joe. Leg-rassle, you know the rules."

Joe asked, surprised, "Leg-rassle?"

David whispered urgently, "There's a trick in leg-rassling, Joe. He knows it."

Joe brushed his cousin aside. "I'll leg-rassle you, Pete. But first we arm-rassle, like we agreed."

Bob Quinn raced to the baggage room and brought back a wooden box. Joe knelt quickly before it and put his elbow down with his hand raised and ready. Pete licked his lips. Without a word he knelt down on the other side of the box, and the middle-aged man and the young man gripped fists.

Quinn asked, "Ready."

The hands clenched hard.

Quinn yelled, "Go!"

The muscles bunched. The tendons stood out in the forearms. Joe Foley grinned. Pete Battle was grim. They struggled. They fought. There was tension in the watchers. The full story unfolded itself to the miners. This was a grudge. This was a deadly feud. This was no game. This was no half-serious banter.

Joe forced his uncle's arm an inch to the left. Pete forced it back vertical. The grin left Joe's face. The veins stood out on each forehead. The sweat formed and rolled down into their eyes. The teeth were bared.

Ellen Foley Battle said softly in the silence, "Get him. Get him." She didn't say who.

David said tensely, "The train's coming. It's a draw. Call it a draw."

Joe Foley asked heavily, "Draw, Uncle Pete?"

The light of triumph flushed over Pete Battle's face. "No draw," he grunted, and he gave out a mighty paroxysmal effort. Joe's eyes narrowed into agonized slits. He grunted twice. Slowly, inexorably he forced his uncle's hand to the left, an inch, three inches, suddenly all the way, the back of Pete's hand striking the box with a dull thud. There was dead silence. The grips relaxed. Pete knelt there with his arm bent double, breathing heavily, his eyes closed. Joe stood up and backed off, grunting and rubbing his right shoulder with his left hand. He said, "You're a helluva man, Uncle Pete." The grin came to his face. "No matter what, you're one helluva man."

Pete rose to his feet. His right arm hung limply at his side. His eyes burned. He said, "Leg-rassle."

Joe said, "The train's at the bend."

Pete said in a strained voice, in the agony of defeat, "Leg-rassle." He lay on his back on the platform.

Joe looked at the train coming up the track a quarter mile away. He rubbed his hands on his best clothes. He looked at the crowd and at his cousin. He shrugged and lay down beside his uncle.

They gripped right arms. Pete winced, but he tightened his own grip.

Quinn asked, "Ready?"

The two raised their right legs, passing the leg of the opponent. Joe's mind raced to figure the trick. He brought his own leg as far back as it would go, so that the thigh muscles were coiled like a spring. The engineer of the train hit his brakes again, and the locomotive huffed and squalcd.

In the noise, Quinn yelled, "Go!"

Joe smashed his leg forward to lock his uncle's leg. He was too late. Pete's great leg lashed home, catching at the precise moment when the forces combined to Joe's disadvantage, and the 190-pound young man was flipped backward head over heels, and when he struggled to right himself, he went on over the edge of the platform and onto the track, and though he twisted like a cat to get off, it was too late. The trucks of the engine caught him spread-eagled, smashed into his groin and on up the middle of that proud, strong body, smashing it and pulverizing it into bloody, flat pulp, and the two halves of the body fell each on one side of the track, and the severed

366

head was knocked fifteen feet away by the undercarriage.

No one screamed. Joe Foley's mother said softly, "Oh, God in heaven, merciful God." She sank sitting on the platform.

David looked down on his friend, and though there was no change at all in his expression, his heart broke.

Pete Battle jumped up and ran to the edge of the platform. There was in him a wild moment of exultation. Then he began saying, "I didn't do it. I didn't do it."

The train men came rushing out of the cab. They stared at the mangled, obliterated human being. The fireman retched violently, spewing against the great black wheels of the locomotive.

Dr. Black, who had been so silent throughout the proceedings, stepped forward and said, "I will do it. The rest of you go. I will pick him up." Then he flung himself on his knees on the platform and made the Sign of the Cross, the first he had made in thirty-five years. He said in a loud voice, "Oh, God, for the small good that is in any of the rest of us, accept unto Thy bosom a young man in whom you planted the seeds of greatness." He jumped off the platform and kneeled in the cinders. "Oh, Joe, I'm so sorry!"

Father Riley came out of his shock and knelt beside the doctor, the pitch of his voice belying his regained composure. He gave the Sacrament of the Last Rites.

David stood wooden.

Ellen Foley took him by the arm. "Get on the train, David."

He looked at her with utter disbelief.

"Get on that train and go to Notre Dame. Do I have to say it? Do I have to tell you to go on for Joe?"

He thought to himself: She doesn't want me to go to Joe's funeral. Why wouldn't she want that? She looked at Bob Quinn.

Quinn said, "This is a violent town, David. The hand of man strikes in anger, and we understand that. The hand of God strikes so cruelly, so carelessly, so coldly, so heedlessly, that we don't understand." And in his mind, he said: *Why Joe? It should have been me. Oh, God, it should have been me!* Bob Quinn closed his eyes and changed his thoughts, because the tears burned, and he was devastated.

They sat and waited for an hour, side by side, silent, staring straight ahead. When the debris of the human being had been swept up and laid gently away, when the reports had been made out, when the engineer had taken two deep swallows from a bottle of moonshine whiskey, the train chuffed slowly away from Sweet Water, and ten minutes later it came to Black Betty Creek, and the whistle called our mournfully *Whoo-hoo-ahoo-oo-oo-oooooo*, and David Battle could not cry. Bob Quinn cried for him, silently, unseen, unheard.

And Pete Battle cried. When it was dark he took the ferry across the Kanawha to Shawnee and the place that had been Green Billy's, and he told the Gypsy that he didn't want the young Irish girl from Charleston, he wanted the madam herself, and he drank a great deal and made such violent love, that the Gypsy rose on her crepey legs, pinched his creek and said, "You're a wild man, Pete. Like ten years ago."

They brought him a new quart of moonshine. He drank half of it.

The Gypsy said, "I've got something new. Maybe you can give it a try." She bent over him on the bed in a stall, and though no one else could hear, she whispered, "I got a nigger girl."

He sat up. He said, fumbling for his clothes, "I don't do it with niggers. I'm going to tell everybody you got one here."

"You should take a look, Pete. Just one look. She's sixteen, and her boobies aren't all the way out yet, and she's got the sweetest, little old round ass you ever seen, and she's the color of chocolate, like milk chocolate, and just as smooth, without a bump on her anywhere that don't belong there, and she's got the whitest teeth you ever seen in that sweet, little ole girl mouth, and the blackest eyes that'll just look you up and down while she figures what she's going to do to you next, and that little ole red tongue, and I got to tell you, Pete, you just got to be the first one to try this—I wouldn't give her to anybody else until you had the first crack."

He sat on the edge of the bed, one leg in his pants, his head whirling. He asked as though from a great distance, "How much?"

"Whatever you say, Pete."

"I say free," he said thickly.

"Then she's free, Pete."

"Where is she?"

"Be here in just a while. She's out to see Leadbelly."

"The nigger?"

"The singer."

"What's he doing here?"

"Singing, what do you think he's doing? Somebody came in and said he's down by the ferry, singing. That little nigger girl snuck off to see him."

"How come you let him in Shawnee?"

"We got nothing against niggers in Shawnee."

"That's the trouble with you."

"No, that's the trouble with you in Sweet Water."

"He just better not come across the river."

"Let's go see him. You pull your clothes on, we'll go down and see him, and then we'll come back, and you take that little ole girl and see what kind a bag of tricks she got herself."

He grunted. "Yeh. We'll just do that. We'll just do that."

But when they emerged into the night, they found that Leadbelly had crossed over into Sweet Water. They hurried to the ferry, and in Sweet Water hurried up the tracks to the C & O station where the crowd was gathered. The man they called Leadbelly stood on the platform from where the blood of Pinkertons had run onto the tracks to stain the coal ships, where the blood of Joe Foley, in its turn, had gushed and spewed. The platform light was turned off. One torch burned and sent its smoke up into the warm night. The full moon and stars lighted Leadbelly's gray hair. The crowd of white men and three Shawnee whores watched him in silence. He strummed his guitar once.

Dvorak called out, "What are you trying to prove, nigger?"

Leadbelly strummed once more.

"I asked you what are you trying to prove?"

Leadbelly said, "To prove I can sing."

Pete Battle lurched to the front of the crowd, stood below the platform. He yelled, "Since when do we let niggers in Sweet Water?"

Wes Culpepper yelled, "You just get on outen town, nigger, while you still can."

Leadbelly strummed his guitar. His Negro-Indian-Egyptian face looked impassively and nobly out over them. He said, "When I was in Washington, there was a meeting. About folk singing, this meeting was. And it was an interracial thing, so they booted us out of the hotel. Then we went to a rooming house, but they booted us out of there, too. And Paxton, he said to me, *Don't let it bother you, Leadbelly. Washington's a bourgeois town.* That was my country's capital, and I got the bourgeois blues . . ."

He sang it, "Bourgeois Blues," while the moon and the stars and the torch lighted his strange face.

When he had finished, there was silence. It was uneasy silence.

The Gypsy whispered to Pete, "There's that little ole nigger girl now." She motioned with her arm, and the young colored girl came hesitatingly from the dark and stood beside her madam, and the Gypsy whispered to Pete, "This little nigger girl going to kill you, Pete. You climb on top her, you ain't never going to get off."

And Pete Battle looked her up and down, and his eyes stayed at the young thrust of her breasts for a long time and then on her thighs and her pelvis in the tight skirt.

On the C & O platform, the Negro they called Leadbelly said, "I was in Huntington. They liked me to sing in Huntington. Somebody said Sweet Water. I remembered about Sweet Water. A long time ago a man came through here. He walked down the railroad tracks, and they flung rocks and hunks of coal at him. And he walked on through the town. I came to sing the song to you. No charge. *Washington's a bourgeois town.* That's all I came to sing."

He took his guitar from around his neck. He turned to leave the platform. Pete Battle climbed unsteadily onto the platform. "Nigger?"

Leadbelly turned to him. "You want to call me nigger?"

"I want to tell you something."

"Then tell it."

"When you talk, you don't sound like a nigger. But you don't sound like a white man, either. I don't know what you sound like."

"Is that what you had to say to me?"

"No. What I got to say, just because a man digs coal and keeps his thinking behind his face, that doesn't mean he doesn't have feelings."

Leadbelly nodded slightly, his strange, handsome face impassive.

Pete said, "I was there."

"You flung rocks and coal?"

"I flung a hunk of coal and hit him right between the shoulder blades—clunk—and he just raised his head and kept right on walking out of town."

"That man was my friend."

"It wasn't you?"

"No, it was my friend."

"Is he dead?"

"They lynched him. For rape."

"Did he do it?"

"Maybe he did, maybe he didn't. I think he did. But he did no rape in Sweet Water."

"I hit him—clunk. Boy, I hit him a good one."

The Gypsy called hoarsely, "Let's go, Pete."

The Parker County sheriff took her by the arm and said, "You know the rules, Gypsy. Get back across the river."

Pete said to Leadbelly, "You got no call to hate me. When I get hit, I don't put my head up. You got no call to hate me."

The Gypsy said with growing concern, "Let's go, Pete."

The sheriff looked the colored girl up and down. "You got nigger girls now?"

The Gypsy said, "Just one. This one. You come over, Sheriff. This one kill you. I swear, this one will absolutely kill you."

Leadbelly said into the night, "I sang my song."

He walked off the platform and disappeared up the track into the dark. Sweet Water let him go. Pete Battle yelled wildly after him, "You show your head in Sweet Water, we'll show you how to treat niggers!" He turned and stared up and down the young colored girl with the Gypsy.

Dr. Black took him by the arm. "Go home and sleep it off, Pete."

Pete said pleadingly, "My papa was just sitting there staring at me."

"You're making a fool out of yourself. A bigger fool. Sleep it off. You'll be all right in the morning."

"That poor bastard. That poor bastard."

"Who, Leadbelly? Seems to me he told you all off."

"Not him."

"Who?"

"Joe."

Dr. Black shuddered. "Oh, God, yes!"

"No, not him, either."

"Who? You?"

"Yes. Me. Pete Dankowski."

BOOK
V

1

The conductor shook David's shoulder twice and said, "South Bend, son."

The wind catapulted rain in bursting, blinding green-yellow torrents against the windows. David put his face against the glass. He could see nothing.

The conductor whispered hoarsely, "It's there, son. South Bend is out there somewhere."

David retrieved his father's black simulated-leather suitcase from among cardboard boxes, hats and other cheap valises on the overhead rack. He made his way, half awake, through the littered aisle of the day coach, past the sprawled or curled-up dozers on their way to Chicago. One woman, the side of her face against the seat back, looked at him unblinkingly and unseeingly. One man winked at him solemnly and closed his eyes again.

The conductor said, "Good luck, son."

Not another soul got off the train at South Bend. David hesitated on the steel step and held his hand into the waterfall from the platform canopy. He turned up his collar and leaped for cover. That quickly, he was wet. He didn't know which way to head. He stood uncertainly, sopping.

At the baggage car, handlers in green slickers and sou'-westers unloaded mail bags and rail-express shipments.

The bare-bulb lights did not quite penetrate the mist and vapor that swirled under the canopy. The wind pressed in gusts against the slickers of the handlers and flopped the brims of their sou'westers. David slanted toward them, against the wind. They did not look up from their work. They pulled their iron-wheeled baggage carts into the baggage room and paid no attention to him.

He went back to his rail car to ask the friendly conductor for advice. The steps of the car were withdrawn, the door closed. Then he saw the shaft leading down into the earth from the platform, and he hurried through the double doors. His wet feet went flying out from under him, and he banged and skidded wildly down the ramp, his suitcase flying open and his belongings spilling on the damp concrete. Grateful that no one saw his humiliation, he stuffed the clothes back into the suitcase. He went carefully around the U-turn of the shaft and at the bottom of the second ramp emerged into the high yellow-tiled tunnel between the tracks and the passenger station. He went into the deserted lobby, wondering that his wet heels could clack loudly and hollowly. He looked up at the high ceiling of the miniature Grand Central station. He turned back toward the tunnel and saw, high on the wall, the marble clock with brass hands. He said half aloud, "Whoo, boy."

Then he saw a ticket agent behind brass bars of the one cage that was open. His heart leaped up. The agent looked for all the world like Mike Foley at his C & O station in Sweet Water. He wore the same green eyeshade and the same garters to hold up his long sleeves. David walked hopefully to him. He struck an ashtray stand with his suitcase, and the metal clattered loudly on the marble floor. Clumsily he tried twice before he could make the stand stay erect. The agent watched him. When David moved again toward the cage, the agent reached up and pulled a dark green shade between himself and the brass bars.

David stood helplessly looking at the shade. Finally, in desperation, he said loudly, "Excuse me, sir."

After a long time the shade rose. The agent had the look of a man accosted. He waited.

David said, "I missed my train and got here late."

The agent waited. Finally he asked, "And?"

"I'm supposed to call somebody, but it's mighty late."

The agent turned back to his work, filling in penciled

notations in spaces on manila cards. He prompted again, "And?"

"Where would you spend the night and call him in the morning?"

The agent wouldn't look at him. He said, "We got hotels."

"Yes, sir."

The agent looked up briefly. "Call a cab. He'll take you to the Oliver." He looked down again.

"I was thinking of walking, if it's not too far. Can you tell me if there's a YMCA?"

The agent put his pencil down and leaned on his folded arms. He said gruffly, "Boy, you'll drown out there."

"Yes, sir. I been wet before."

"You got a mile walk. If you haven't got any money, sleep on a bench. You got the place to yourself."

"Yes, sir. Maybe I'll do that, if you think it's all right."

"Where'd you come from, boy? You ever been in a city before?"

"Yes, sir. I been in Charleston."

"You from Sweet Water, West Virginia?"

"Yes, sir."

"You Joe Foley?"

"No, sir. I'm David Battle."

"Isn't Joe Foley from Sweet Water? They were looking for him a few hours ago."

"The train got hung up."

The agent asked, "You a ballplayer?"

"Yes, sir."

The agent said, still gruffly, "Why didn't you say you were a ballplayer? I'm no mind reader. You're in South Bend. You should say when you're a ballplayer."

"Yes, sir."

"Call Coach Reagan. He left the message if you fellows from Sweet Water showed up." He handed David a note and also a nickel from his own pocket.

"Should I call Mr. Reagan this time of night?"

"You call him. Then come back here while you wait for him. I got some hot coffee."

"Yes, sir."

He dialed in a booth. After four rings, a woman said with deep weariness, "Hello?"

"Excuse me, ma'am, is Coach Reagan there?"

"What time is it?"

"Four o'clock, ma'am. I'm sorry."

"Mr. Reagan's sick. He has the flu. He needs his rest."

"Yes, ma'am. I'm sorry."

"Who's calling."

"David Battle."

"From Sweet Water?"

"Yes, ma'am."

"Just a minute. I'll tell him."

David said, "Don't bother him, ma'am. I'll call tomorrow." But there was no answer.

Then the coach asked in a hoarse voice, "Where are you?"

"Train station, Mr. Reagan. I'm sorry to bother you this late, but the man said call you."

"Stay where you are. I'll be right down."

David said, "Mr. Reagan, Joe's not with me." He said it into a dead phone.

The agent said, "You don't look much like a football player. You should have said you were. I was closing up."

"Yes, sir."

"You must be good. We been hearing about the Sweet Water Flash."

"That's Joe Foley, sir."

"Four Horsemen weren't so big, either. They went maybe one sixty. You weigh that much?"

"Yes, sir. Some more than that."

"They looked meaner than you. They were the best. Won't be another team like that come along. You want some coffee?"

"Yes, sir. I sure do."

"Make yourself at home. Coach Reagan will put you up at his house tonight. He does that when the hot shots come in."

Coach Reagan burst in out of the rain, his topcoat over his pajamas, his hatbrim dripping. He came to David holding out his hand. He croaked, "You're Battle?"

"Yes, sir."

"Where's Foley? In the can?"

"I tried to tell you, sir, before you hung up. Joe's not with me. He won't be coming."

Reagan stared at him. He shrieked hoarsely through laryngitis, "Why not!"

"He's dead, sir. He was killed in an accident."

378

Reagan felt a wave of nausea and dizziness. He sat down on one of the high-backed benches. "I think I got pneumonia."

"Yes, sir."

"If you think that's a stupid thing to say, it's because I can't think of anything else to say. My mind is racing. There's always a way. When something goes wrong, you just got to buckle down and figure out the way to make it right. That's what my mind is doing. Figuring out how to get around this, and make Joe Foley show up." He coughed a great, racking bark, and then was seized with a spasm of agonizing coughing. He put his big hand on his chest, and his voice was like a train whistle. "I'd as soon wire-brush my bronchial tubes as cough again." He stared at David through puffed, veined, watering eyes. "You know who almost got this backfield job instead of me?"

"Yes, sir. Coach Quinn."

"That's right. Me, I got pneumonia, and I get out of bed to come get Joe Foley at four o'clock in the morning in a hurricane, and you tell me he's dead."

David couldn't think of anything to say.

"So what do we do now?"

"Sir?"

Reagan croaked louder, "So what do we do now?"

"Mr. Reagan, I came down to go to Notre Dame. And play football for you, if I can make the team."

Reagan wiped his miserable nose with the back of his hand. "Maybe it's the light in here, but you don't look like much of a football player."

"Mr. Reagan, I came to play. If the deal's off because Joe isn't coming, just tell me."

Reagan stood up. He clutched his coat to his chest. He said grimly, "A deal's a deal, Battle."

David followed him to the Studebaker parked at the station entrance. They were drenched before they could close the doors. The engine was a long time starting. When they drove off, the wind in gusts rocked the car. The windshield wipers were inadequate against the onslaught of solid water. The road nearly disappeared in the sheets of flood that blew in every direction. Reagan used his handkerchief to wipe the steam from the inside of the windshield. He said hoarsely, "I got pneumonia in June!" Then he was silent. He made his way into the Notre Dame campus. He drove to the stadium. He stopped but didn't turn off the ignition. He handed David a key. Finally he spoke once more. "Through that door, you'll find some bunks and lockers in there. Take your choice, won't be anyone in there besides you. Be somebody around in the morning tell you where to get breakfast. I'll talk to you when I get over my pneumonia."

Reagan waited until David got the door to the locker room open. Then he drove off, disappearing in the first twenty feet into the rain, the taillights evaporating suddenly. David closed the door behind himself. One light burned. He searched, sloshing, until he found the bunks. He took off his clothes and hung them in a locker. He found the shower room and stood for ten minutes in a hot deluge. He opened his suitcase and put on dry drawers. Then he lay on his back on the bunk, put his hands under his head and looked at the ceiling. The ticket agent had said, "Coach Reagan puts the hot shots up at his house the first night."

Should he feel resentment? How could he? He wasn't a hot shot. Joe Foley was the hot shot. David Battle didn't look like much of a football player, and that was his problem, not theirs. Well, he'd played football over Robert Emmett Quinn's dead body. He would play over the dead body of Joe Reagan. He would play for Notre Dame. Right here in this locker room, right here, he'd pull on the bright-green jersey. This was the place. Right here, he'd fall into the group and go, cleats clattering, up the ramp. Right here. Right out there in the wild rain was the turf that would be bright green on a sharp, clear October Saturday, when the stands would scream blindly, full-throated, wildly, like Romans in the Colosseum, for victory . . . victory . . . victory! They would roar for David Battle. They would shout his name, roaring from the students in the corner, swelling from the men in the center, bursting in the sky above the field: "David Battle! He's the man! He's the man!" He filled with hot determination. They would shout his name into the blue sky over the bright-green field. They would do this. He dedicated himself. He would do for Notre Dame those things Joe Foley would have done, and they would know him, these maniacal shouters, they would know him, they would know him . . .

On this first night of being away from home, he was utterly lonely.

But they'd know him! He was the elected captain of the Big Red Flash team. He would be the captain of an undefeated Big Green team! The green, green turf, the bright uniforms, the thud of shoulders, the thwack of arms and helmets, the flash of his legs, his cut, his fake, his burst of speed, the sprawled tacklers, the crowd noise swelling into a great, sustained, pagan paean for him, the jack-in-the-box cheer leaders, the terrier with his shamrock-green blanket, the shrieking, open-mouthed girls from St. Mary's, the open-mouthed alumni, the open-mouthed priests, the fists all raised in the madness of touchdown on Saturday afternoon on the green, green turf, victory, hot victory, the "Victory March" and the band like drunken peacocks, gyrating in exultation for him, and his name bursting out of the green, green turf, bursting into the blue sky, bursting against the golden dome, bursting in the savage, adoring hearts: "David Battle! David Battle!" They would know him. They would know him in Chicago. They would know him in New York. They would know him in Boston, and Philadelphia, and Detroit, and Baltimore, where Catholics gloried in victory, and the priests in South Bend would be proud of him at the victory cocktail parties, and the trustees would glow because of him, and Pete Battle would be proud, oh, God, yes, then would Pete Battle at long last be proud of his son, proud of his son, proud of his son . . .

He stared at the ceiling. He missed his mother. She came filling his throat and eyes. He missed her. On the train it was good to be away from her. It was good to be away from Joe Foley. It was such sweet relief from the slow suffocation. He could breathe. They were no longer with him, around him, on him, in him, he was free of them, and he could breathe.

He missed them.

Was Joe Foley dead? Did it happen? Was Joe Foley smashed and pulverized before his eyes? Was he really? Was he really gone forever? How could that be? It wasn't really true. It wasn't real when it happened. It wasn't real now. Instead it was good, just once, to be away from Joe Foley. Just once, it was good to be away. In the locker room of the Notre Dame football stadium, without another living being within a hundred thousand miles, David Battle missed Joe Foley, and he missed his mother and wanted the love and protection they would lavish on him,

381

if only they could. God, don't let me be ungrateful for their love! He couldn't bear those thoughts.

He thought of Suzanne Carstairs. Suzanne would come to St. Mary's to be near him, he was sure she would do that. Don't do that, Suzanne! What would happen? What might happen if sometime they were on the bank of the St. Joseph as they were on the bank of Beulah Creek and sin came swirling up in both of them again? He thought of the way her legs gave under his weight, her knees going apart . . . what if they did that sometime and didn't stop and took off their clothes and didn't stop! It's sin, it's sin, don't think of it!

He thought of Swaney Wood. Did Joe do it to her? Did he? David thought of Swaney Wood. He thought of the way she walked, happy with living, the way her eyes looked him over so unself-consciously, the way her hips talked to him when they moved so fluidly. Her hips talked to him. They hummed to him, called to him, folded him in fluid hotness in the wonderful, terrible mystery between her legs, talked to him, hummed to him, called him to be with her as he was with Suzanne and not stop, not stop, not stop. He thought about Swaney Wood. He thought about her. He thought about her. In the locker room beneath the great stadium of Notre Dame, with the rain and loneliness drowning the world, with the wind blowing Sweet Water away, away, with no one within a hundred thousand miles of him, he thought of Swaney Wood and succumbed to mortal sin.

Then he took the pillow and pulled it down on his face and said aloud into it, "Notre Dame!" Then he said frantically, "Oh, my God, I am heartily sorry for having offended Thee . . ."

2

JOHN COBB drove his big-wheeled monster 368 m.p.h. on the Bonneville Salt flats. That was big news in the Detroit sports pages. Bobby Riggs, Ted Schroeder and Joe Hunt in the Nationals, that was big news. Gehringer, Greenberg and Ruby York and the Detroit Tigers, they were the lead stories on the sports pages, and especially the upcoming fight between Bob Pastor and the Brown Bomber, that was big, important sports news in Detroit. The Detroit Lions, training at Cranbrook, were relegated to the second and third sports pages, because professional football was a minor sport in 1939.

But David Battle, reporting to Cranbrook direct from the All-Star game in Chicago, he hit the front page of the *Detroit Ledger;* the paragraphs were dwarfed by the big black headlines and double columns of Roosevelt's appeal to Hitler and Poland and Europe poised on the brink of war, but they were front-page nonetheless. David Battle was just as big sports news as Joe Louis and young Joe Di Maggio.

Wellman, the head coach, escorted him to the chow hall. The assistant coaches trailed behind with the two new linemen, Turner and Karcher, stiff the day after the pounding the Giants gave them in Soldiers Field. The forty strong men, dressed in T-shirts, turned from their food. Bight, the four-year veteran tackle from Purdue, rose from his table and came bowing elaborately, strewing imaginary petals. In a booming voice he cried out, "All hail! All hail! King Heisman is here!"

The veterans rose, raised their hands over their heads and salaamed in obeisance, calling, "All hail, all hail!" The rookies who had been in camp three weeks grinned self-consciously, relieved that new targets had arrived.

Winkworth, the sophomore end out of Georgia, pulled an empty chair from his chow table. "Your throne, your Majesty, you all."

David blushed furiously.

Coach Wellman pointed to the chair. "That's your spot, Battle." The coaches left the hot-shot rookies and sat at the council table with Dipper Coogan.

Turner and Karcher hastened to empty chairs. David stood uncertainly.

Winkworth said, "Your throne, Heisman."

David slipped hurriedly into the seat.

Bight stood on a chair and commanded attention. "Gentlemen, this is a moment you will never forget. You will tell your grandchildren about the day you sat down to lunch with the mightiest of them all. I give you David Battle!"

Winkworth shouted, "Who's he?"

"I give you Mr. Notre Dame!"

The squad shouted hurray.

"I give you Mr. All-All-All-American!"

Winkworth shouted, "Who's he?"

"I give you Mr. MVP of the All-Star game, the star of stars!"

The squad shouted.

"I give you Mr. Not-once-but-*twice* HEISMAN!"

They shouted loudly, and half the squad jumped to their feet and salaamed again.

Winkworth shouted, "A speech!"

Bight raised his arms. He said sonorously, "A pontifical blessing. Your Holiness, will you give us your blessing?"

David colored even deeper and was frozen.

Belcrank, the tackle from Southern Cal, hollered, "His clippings. Who's got his clippings?"

Bight asked, "Mr. Heisman, you did bring your clippings with you? Of course, you did."

David sat rigid, miserable.

Bight said, "I think our hero's modest. Well, it just so happens I've got a clipping for him." He tossed the front page of the *Ledger* on the table. "Now you just get over your modesty and tell us all about it, Heisman. You're among friends."

David looked down at the headline of the story: LIONS WELCOME DAVID BATTLE.

"Read it, Heisman."

David stared straight ahead in utter agony.

Dipper Coogan, the quarterback, said calmly from the council table, "Get on your feet and read it, rookie."

David turned his eyes to the great man. Coach Wellman, beside the quarterback, jerked his head upward ever so slightly. It was a clear command, a friendly command to co-operate.

David stood. He picked up the paper. He began softly. "'David Battle, everybody's all-American . . .'"

Bight shouted, "Louder, Heisman. They'll want to hear this in Birmingham."

David raised his voice. "'. . . two-time winner of the coveted Heisman Trophy as the outstanding college football player, most valuable player in the All-Stars' losing cause against the Giants, captain of the Notre Dame football team, winner of more awards than any player in the history of the game, reports today to the Detroit Lions training camp at Cranbrook. Reportedly he becomes the highest paid rookie since Red Grange joined the Chicago Bears . . .'"

David's voice trailed off in total embarrassment.

Bight said, "Oh, there's much more!"

David put the paper down.

Belcrank said, "I want to hear that part about our title hopes riding on you. Is that right, Mr. Heisman, do our title hopes ride on you?"

David sat and began to eat quickly, not knowing what he was eating.

Bight said, "I'm disappointed in you, Heisman. Were you that modest at the trophy dinners? I'll bet you were. I'll bet you gave credit to the team, and your mother, and your high school coach, and the jock-strap factory, and Divine Providence, I'll just bet. I'd like to hear that speech."

David swallowed the food without chewing.

Bight waved to the squad. "I don't think you all really

appreciate this man. Do you know what this football player did? I mean, do you really know?"

Winkworth asked, "What did he do?"

"He really did, he won the Heisman twice, can you believe it?"

"That little bitty feller right there? He won the Heisman twice?"

"Yes, sir, that little bitty feller right there. It's on his shoulders, our whole season, that little bitty feller right there."

David set his fork down. His jaw was tight.

Bight commanded, "Silence! King Heisman is about to speak!"

Head Coach Wellman tried in vain to catch David's eye again. David started to push back his chair. Suddenly Billy Turner, the tackle from the All-Star game, went over backward in his chair. He got to his feet, grinning sheepishly. He said, "Morning, you all!"

The heads turned from him, back to David Battle. Once more David started to speak.

Turner didn't give him the chance. He said, "Long's I'm on my feet, might just introduce myself proper. I'm Billy Turner, from Arkan-zuss. I want to tell you, I been looking around, and you all are a right likely-looking bunch of fellers."

Suddenly there was real hostility in the chow hall, where there'd been rough good humor.

Bight asked, "Now just who pulled your chain?"

"Pulled my chain? Took me a minute there to catch on. We don't have them new-fangled toilets in Arkansas that you pull with chains. We got the old-fashioned kind that you flush with a handle. Boy, that's a laig slapper. I got to remember that one."

Burlingame, the six-year running back, said in a cold, flat voice, "Sit down, rookie!"

Billy Turner smiled broader. "Cain't the rest of us rookies get in on this? Don't seem hardly fair, letting Davey get all the fun."

"Sit down, rookie."

Turner's smile stayed, but his voice changed. "When I finished my say, I'll sit down."

Bight came close and pointed his finger at Turner's chest. "Butt out, rookie. I reckon you said too much already. What kind of wise guy you supposed to be?"

Turner looked straight into the face of the strong tackle whose job he'd come to take. "I'm a little ole country boy what likes funnin'. I was hoping maybe you city slickers would pay some attention to me, and not let any little bitty ole halfback get all the runnin'."

Bight jabbed again with his forefinger.

Billy Turner said, "One of my nicknames with the Hogs was Lip. When I get talking, they have a helluva time shutting me off. One of my other nicknames was Straight Nose. Take a look. It's straight. I was the only man in the Southwest Conference never got a deviated septum. How 'bout that? That's on account I don't take lumps, I give lumps. Now, sir, I like good clean fun and good sport . . ."

Dipper Coogan, the great man, said, "That's enough, Turner."

Turner shook his head. "Not quite, Mr. Coogan. Just thought you all might like a ree-port from Chicago. Davey Battle, after he was in camp a few days, we made him team captain. He's one helluva ballplayer. That summabitch is one helluva man. Just thought I'd tell you that."

Coach Wellman wrestled with himself. Should he interfere? He decided against it. He wouldn't know what to say. Turner looked around the room. He sat down lazily, elaborately unconcerned. David Battle said silently, "Why? Why? Why did you have to do it, Billy? For God's sake, just let me alone to fight my own fights!"

The hall was thick with ill will. Dipper Coogan rose without haste. He unwrapped a blunt cigar. He lit it and blew smoke at the high ceiling. He looked at David, he looked at Turner. He said in the voice that was peculiarly gravelly and high-pitched all at once, "I got no use for loud-mouth rookies." He walked from the chow hall, blowing smoke at the ceiling.

Dick Keene, the backfield coach, whispered to the head coach, "Christ, that's all we need, dissension."

Wellman whispered to Holmquist, the line coach, "Make sure they beat that loud-mouth Turner's brains out this afternoon." He stood and said to the room, "Skull sessions. Linemen with Holmquist in Room 101. Backs and ends with Keene, 102. Scrimmage at three. Full pads."

3

Characteristically, David sat in the rear seat in the Cranbrook classroom. Coach Keene said, "Why don't you take this one, Battle." David walked to the front of the room and took the seat waiting for him next to Dipper Coogan. Coogan looked him over insolently but said nothing.

Keene handed David a black loose-leaf notebook. "Your bible, Battle. From now on, this one's more use to you than the one you use in chapel. How many plays did you have at South Bend?"

David said, "Forty. Maybe fifteen basic."

"This bible's got one hundred fifty. You got some homework ahead. You count on the next three nights, your nose in the play book. You guard that book. You lose it, you're fined three hundred dollars. Any questions?"

David shook his head. He had no questions. One hundred and fifty plays? How did you learn one hundred and fifty plays in three nights?

Keene asked again, "You got no questions?" This time he waited for an answer.

David said, "I'll have some questions when I know a little more."

"Do you know our general offense?"

David nodded yes.

"What do you know about it?"

"Wellman's offense from the Coast. Unbalanced line. Most running and pass option plays go to the strong side. But spread formations. A wide-open game, compared to anything the pro league has seen for a few years."

"Keep going. A dissertation."

David didn't know whether they were running the rookie again, or seriously testing his knowledge. He would co-operate either way. The earnest, bright expression was on his face. He spoke for five minutes on Coach Wellman's short punt with a spread. He concluded, "Wellman's system is supposed to combine the surprise and open game of the T, with the strength of the single wing or short punt."

Keene regarded him speculatively. "Will it work?"

"It should. It's suited to the personnel."

"Wellman tell you your spot?"

"When he talked to me in South Bend he said I'd be trying out for wingback."

Burlingame, the veteran right half, snorted. David knew exactly what was in his mind. He was thinking: Try out, hell, you've already got my job. They're not going to let the hot shot sit on the bench, even if I'm a better man.

Dipper Coogan said, "If we've had enough kindergarten, let's get down to business."

Keene, the backfield coach, hopped to the command of the backfield star. He turned to his blackboard and began drawing his circles and x's and curved arrows. He talked traps. David listened with straining attention. Traps, he knew traps. They had traps at Notre Dame. It was a draw play, it was a trap, it was simple. But it wasn't simple. This was different. There was something a little different about it. There were subtle variations. There were some new words. There was a refinement. This wasn't Notre Dame. This was pro ball. This was a business. These were the *best* players. These were the strongest, fastest, *best* backs. These were the *smartest* backs. It was a simple trap or fullback delay, but there were endless possibilities, endless, subtle variations. The curving lines, and the bars for blocks, flew on the blackboard. David's head whirled. He listened with all his strength, but he couldn't hear. A simple trap? One hundred and fifty plays? How could you learn one hundred and fifty plays as subtle as this in just three days!

Keene said, "That's it. Tonight's session, half on pass

389

patterns, half on pass defense. Get suited up. Full pads. Full contact. Three o'clock."

The twelve veterans rose and walked out in twos and threes, talking animatedly, relaxed. Nine rookies trailed behind them, with nothing to say to one another. David Battle came last, alone.

Dipper Coogan waited for him in the hallway. He jerked his thumb at David. David came to him and stood respectfully waiting. Coogan said in his high rasp, "Heisman, right now, you get one thing clear. There's only one boss on this football team, and that's me. There's only one star on this team, and that's me. You got that clear?"

David just looked at him and waited.

"You got that clear, Heisman?"

Still David just looked at him.

The great man was a little bit disconcerted by the bright blue eyes and the earnest, handsome face. He said, "Don't forget it, Heisman, not for one minute." He jerked his thumb down the corridor. David walked away from him, his head still whirling. Coogan waited for Coach Keene to emerge from the classroom. He said, "Dick, got something I want to know."

"What's that, Dipper?"

"This story about Heisman and his ten thousand dollars. That true?"

Keene didn't know how to reply.

"You know how much I get, Dick?"

"I got some idea. Not exactly."

"You know it's a lot less than ten grand?"

Keene said uneasily, "I guess it would be. Don't know anybody in the league getting anywhere near that much."

"Except Heisman?"

"I wouldn't know, Dipper. You better ask Wellman. He's the one signed him up."

"What did Battle get?"

Keene said, greatly unhappy, "I wouldn't know, Dipper. I do know Battle didn't come easy. He might give the idea he wouldn't be a tough guy to deal with, but I hear he was. I hear he said maybe he wasn't so all-fired anxious to play pro ball and that some Notre Dame alum had a big job for him. I hear he played it pretty good."

"He got a bonus? You think he's getting ten thousand?"

Keene edged away. "I couldn't say, Dipper. You better ask Wellman. Or the GM."

Dipper Coogan walked down the corridor after the back-field coach, considerably displeased with himself. He had displayed venality and envy unworthy of the greatest name in the game.

4

COACH WELLMAN blew his whistle. "Let's go, Dipper. Take 'em down the field from your thirty. Yesterday's second string on defense."

David Battle and Burlingame looked at the head coach.

Wellman said with a mixture of malice and curiosity, "The varsity is on offense."

Both halfbacks hesitated momentarily. Then both of them trotted out on the field.

Keene said to Wellman, "Well, Heisman's got confidence, I'll hand him that."

Wellman said, "Dipper will take some of it out of him in about one minute."

Twelve men went into the offensive huddle. Coogan gave no sign that he noticed. He called numbers and colors that meant nothing at all to David Battle. Just before the huddle broke, Coogan rasped, "Burlingame, check-block the end before you run your pattern."

Eleven men burst from the huddle. David stood where he was, looking forlorn. He watched as Coogan took the pass from center, faked a run to the strong side, and threw for eight yards to Burlingame cutting back to the middle. Coach Holmquist, the referee, blew the whistle. The offense picked themselves up and came hustling back to the huddle. They ignored David completely. He trotted off to the sidelines, doing his best to look unconcerned. On the second play, Coogan again faked to the strong side, this time handed off to Burlingame on a reverse, and the blockers went all out with Mr. Heisman in camp and sent one of their favorite veterans on his way for thirty yards before a rookie back pulled him down with the extreme effort of a man making the squad.

Looking at the field, Wellman said in David's ear, "He's a good runner. He's a ballplayer." He turned and watched David's face. David watched the field intently. Wellman said, "I told you when I signed you, you're our wingback. When you see how good a man Burlingame is, you know how much you got to live up to." In another moment he said, "I'm not much for interfering. This is a man's game. Men take care of themselves. They'll blow off some steam with you, you just take what they dish out, they'll come around."

David looked at the head coach and said sharply, "I can fight my own battles."

Keene pulled the head coach away. "We better get Mr. Loud Mouth in there. If they don't get a crack at him, we're going to have a problem on our hands."

Wellman shouted, "Turner, right tackle on defense." The Razorback grabbed his helmet and raced on the field. Wellman said, "Battle, right half on defense." David trotted quickly after his friend from the All-Star team.

Keene said, "They'll kill him."

"Who, Battle or Turner?"

"Both, but mainly Turner. How stupid can a rookie get, shooting off his mouth like that?"

Wellman said, "Just don't be too sure. I saw him in the All-Star game. He gave as good as he got."

Billy Turner charged into the defense line like a full-back, shouting to the man he was relieving. Dipper Coogan raised his head in the huddle. He rasped softly, "Here's Big Mouth."

The offensive line snapped into position. Bight said, "Hello, Big Mouth."

Turner said, "Not Big Mouth. Lip, remember? And Straight Nose."

The ball came to Coogan. He trotted lazily toward his right end, watching the battle on the left side. Bight's forearm came up at Turner's face. Billy warded the blow with his own arm. Then the varsity line climbed all over him, while the defense watched with curiosity. The second man to get to Billy hit him from the side, buckling his legs. Winkworth, the end, came in straight up, elbows high, and smashed him over backward, and as they hit the turf, Bight rammed his elbow into the midsection, and Billy let out an involuntary grunt. They untangled. Not a word was said. The offense headed for the huddle. Dipper Coogan was on the ground where he'd been laid low by David Battle.

Coogan picked himself up and went cursing into the huddle. He said, "Same thing."

They lined up. They repeated. This time, when they untangled, Billy Turner swung his elbow and caught Winkworth on the point of the jaw, dazing him. Winkworth dropped slowly to his hands and knees, shaking his head. Billy bent over him and patted him on the shoulder. He said amiably, "Sorry, fella, didn't see you there." Winkworth walked slowly to the sideline, gingerly raising and lowering his head.

At the other end of the line, David Battle stood with blood pouring down his face, and Dipper Coogan lay on the ground, gasping for breath that wouldn't come.

Coach Holmquist ran to the great man and bent over him. In a moment he called with great relief, "Just got the wind knocked out."

Wellman asked Keene, "Did you see what happened? I was watching Turner."

"Battle come in on Coogan again, and the Dipper rared back and gave him the ball right in the face and knocked him right off his feet. The little sonofabitch got up and came at Coogan right through the air, feet first, and got him right in the chest."

Wellman said, "Good Christ!"

Billy Turner came, all solicitude, to his friend. David turned away impatiently, soaking the blood into the arm of his jersey. Only then did Holmquist go to David and, over his protests, examine the blood-smeared face. He sent David trotting to the sidelines. Wellman held his hands on David's face, examining. "Broke?"

David didn't answer.

"It's broke. You got a nose twice as big as you used to have." He motioned to the trainer. "Take him in and fix him up." He said to Keene, "Get Turner out of there. Put in Karcher. And send in Hunk for Coogan."

Coogan came and stood by his head coach, breathing a little heavily. Wellman made sure none of the squad could hear. He said, "Dipper, you're through for the day. This is football, not a street-corner fight."

Coogan flushed with rage. When he could control himself, he said, "Wellman, I been running this team long before you came around. I'll be running it when you're gone. All right, you coach it. You get us ready. But I'll run it on the field and run the squad, and that's the way it is."

Wellman said coldly, "There's only one man running this team, that's me." But his voice betrayed his uncertainty.

Coogan heaved two more breaths to calm himself further. He said in a more friendly tone, "Don't get your ass in a uproar. Turner's the best thing's happened to this team. It's the first guts they've showed since camp opened."

Coach Wellman didn't want to fight with his quarterback. He said, "He's going to be one helluva tackle."

"You want to win football games, you leave the squad to me." Coogan turned away, then turned back. "And you leave Battle to me." He walked away toward the showers.

David Battle and Dipper Coogan toweled down together. David's nose was pressed back into shape and taped, but it was greatly swollen and there was caked blood in his nostrils.

Coogan said to the shower room, "Learn something, Heisman?"

David stopped toweling.

Coogan said, "There's more where that came from."

David said, "Take a look at your chest." He pointed at the angry cleat marks. "Next time you get it in the face." He took another step. "There's just you and me in here. I came here to play football. You want it some other way, you just say so."

Coogan stared at him incredulously. "You want to fight me?"

"Any time you say. Right here and now, or any time you say. But I came here to play football."

"Then you listen to me, Heisman. Cold-cocking me, when everybody is taking care of Turner, you call that football, or you call that playing big hero? You got plenty to learn, Heisman. And if you don't learn fast, I'll make

395

sure your ass gets booted off this team, Heisman or not. You got that straight?"

"You afraid, Coogan?"

Dipper Coogan turned deep-red. "Of you?"

"You said there was only one star on this team. You afraid to find out which one it is?"

Coogan clenched and unclenched his fists. The violence of this unstable man was now all on the surface. David braced himself for the attack.

The color left Coogan's face. He said, "That's the way it'll be. You'll get your chance, Battle."

He turned and walked lazily to his locker and began pulling on his clothes.

On the field, Keene asked, "What are you going to do?"

Wellman asked testily, "What do you want me to do, kick them off the squad? Turner's too good. He'll be first string by opening day. Kick Battle off the squad? Mr. Heisman? The owners would have our balls first."

"We're going to have trouble. Real trouble. I think we've already got it."

"Coogan will work it out."

"Well, I'll tell you something, you don't know what's going on in Coogan."

"Who knows what he thinks? Not me."

"I do this time. He's got a hard-on, for Mr. Heisman. For the money. If he finds out for sure Battle's making more than him, the fit is going to hit the shan."

Wellman said, "Well, if no one tells him, he won't find out."

5

WHEN THE EVENING skull session ended, Dipper Coogan climbed into his Cadillac convertible and drove off to Birmingham to spend the night with the grass widow who was the latest substitute for the rich wife he kept stashed away in her big home in Santa Barbara. Most of the veterans and some of the rookies piled into Fords and Chevies for the nightly beer ritual behind Haley's beer store on Maple. David Battle hurried to his room to immerse himself in the black loose-leaf notebook.

A half hour later Billy Turner filled the doorway. He grinned with difficulty, his upper lip cut and puffed. There was a purple abrasion alongside his mouth. He said, "Davey."

"Hey, Billy."

"Them's tough guys. Is my nose still straight?"

"For now."

"Yours, too. Big, but straight. Hurt?"

"No."

"Sure looks like it hurts."

"I got a high pain threshold. It doesn't hurt."

"Wonder how the Dipper would like a busted proboscis."

"Billy, I'll fight my own fights."

"Sure, Davey."

"You got enough to worry about."

"Me? I made the team today, man. They give the best they had, and it weren't good enough. 'F I wasn't sure when I got here, I'm sure now, this little ole country boy is all-pro. You get some money down on it, Davey."

"Billy, just let me worry about Coogan and me."

"Sure, Davey. You got a phone call. Some pussy."

David closed his notebook. He stood up. "My mother."

"Oh." Then Billy said, "Thought maybe it was that Suzanne."

They walked down the corridor into the lounge. Four men playing bridge looked up but said nothing. Burlingame, writing a letter, looked up but said nothing. Charlie Dean, the sophomore halfback from Florida, looked up from the radio he was tuning. He said, "Yankee stations wouldn't know good music if they heard it."

David said into the phone, "Hello?"

"David?"

"Mama, I'm not sure I'm supposed to get calls here."

"I'm sorry, David. I won't call any more."

"I didn't mean it that way."

"I didn't either. I've got us a place. In Birmingham."

"Whatever you pick, Mama."

"Upstairs, downstairs apartment, two bedrooms up. Forty-five dollars a month, is that all right?"

"That's fine, Mama."

"What's the matter with you? You're stopped up."

"Got a bloody nose."

"Broken, David?" she asked anxiously.

"Just bloody."

Charlie Dean had found hillbilly music on the radio, and he turned the volume high. Belcrank sprang from the bridge table and pulled the plug, and they wrestled over it.

Ellen asked, "David?"

"Just watching a fight."

"A real fight?"

"No. Just horsing around."

"How did it go today?"

"Just fine. Billy Turner was great. Mama, I've got one hundred and fifty plays to memorize in the next three days. Evening's the only chance you get. We have breakfast at seven-thirty and the day's full from then on."

"I'll let you go, David."

"What's our phone number?"

398

"We haven't got one yet. I'm calling from the drug store. I'll give you our number when I come out to practice."

David was silent.

Ellen asked, "They do allow spectators, don't they?"

"I didn't ask yet. I guess so."

"If you don't want me to, I won't come out."

"Maybe not until things get settled on the squad."

"You'll be able to come into Birmingham, won't you?"

"When I get the plays memorized. Sure."

"I called home to tell them we were settled. Mama says to say hello. Grandpa Dankowski wants to come up for a visit."

"Is he coming?"

"He's lonely, David."

David didn't say anything.

"When you get left alone in the world, it can get pretty lonely."

"Sure. He can bunk in my room."

"I'll get our number to you as soon as they put in the phone."

"Or I can get it through information."

"Well, good night, David. Take care of yourself."

"Good night, Mama."

When he had hung up, Charlie Dean, lying on the floor where Winkworth and Belcrank had left him, said, "What's it like, being Heisman with big ole blue eyes? Pussy just throw itself at you?"

David's jaw tightened, but he said nothing.

Belcrank, who had tried to eavesdrop, said, "I think it was his mother. That's nice."

Winkworth asked, "Them stories about you true, Battle?"

David asked tensely, "What stories?"

"You being all-American nice boy off the field?"

Billy Turner said, "Don't believe everything you hear. Davey had the prettiest little ole black-haired, blue-eyed Suzanne gal you ever seen, come up to the All-Star training camp to call on him. Man and boy, wasn't a ballplayer in camp wouldn't give a pair his fifty-yard-line seats to sink his teeth in that woman. You oughta seen Davey handle her. You could practical see her begging for it, he give her such a hard time. Tomcats around here could take some lessons from Davey, you better believe it."

Through raging mortification, David said, "Okay, Billy."

399

"Just thought they oughta know. She be coming up here, Davey? These tomcats oughta get a look at some *real* coo."

"Knock it off, Billy."

Dean said, "I leave it to you, Battle. Man from Sweet Water, he oughta know good music. You ever heard prettier music than I had on that radio?"

"It was fine."

Dean said to Winkworth, "Battle says so, that's good enough for me, and it sure oughta be good enough for a lineman. Let's plug it in, Battle."

David held up the notebook. "Got some homework." He walked through the lounge and back to his room.

Dean said, "Serious little son of a gun, isn't he."

Winkworth said, "You be serious, too, Coogan laying for you."

"You see Battle light into the big man? All four feet was just aflyin'. Not sure I mightn't bet on Heisman. He's got more guts than's good for any one man."

Winkworth said grimly, "I didn't see it. I was right busy at the time."

"Coogan got himself another think, messin' around with Heisman, that's my bet."

"Coogan'll kill him. He'll kill him. Dipper gets down on him like that, Heisman don't gain a yard, and he'll be hollered out of the league."

Belcrank said, "The Dipper wouldn't do that. He wants to win ball games too bad, not to use a ballplayer like Heisman."

"Balls. Foster was here, Coogan wouldn't throw to him, just because Foster was Catholic. Where's Foster? Saying his rosary on the Chrysler assembly line, that's where."

"I say that was because Coogan figured Foster for no guts."

"I say it was account Foster was Catholic, and Coogan's got no use for Catholics. And if the Heisman ain't enough to do Battle in, Notre Dame is. And one more thing, the Dipper takes care of his'n. The ones get drunk and chase pussy with him. You think the all-American boy ever going to get in Coogan's gang? Battle's dead."

Charlie Dean rolled over and crawled on his hands and knees toward the unplugged radio cord.

Winkworth said, "You plug that noise in, I think I'm going to have to kill you."

Dean asked Turner, "Razorback, you like my kind of music?"

"Is there some other kind?"

"Think you can hold those Yankees off while I plug it in?"

Winkworth set down his cards.

Billy said with no grin, "Reckon I better save my energy for the field."

Winkworth said, "You'll need it. Mighty rough out there today?"

"How's your jaw?"

"Fine. How's your mouth?"

"Hurts. But just as big. I got one ree-quest, Winkworth."

"What's that?"

"I got a ambition to be the only lineman in the National Football League with a straight nose. You can kick me in the nuts, or anything you want, or kill me, just don't deviate my septum."

The corner of Winkworth's mouth twitched, but he didn't say anything. He picked up his cards.

Dean said, "By golly, that's a reasonable ree-quest. I think this big ole razorback is the fustest and onliest good-looking lineman I ever seen. Be a shame to spoil it."

Looking straight ahead, Winkworth asked, "You going to make this team, Turner?"

Wrobleski, across the table, said, "I got a feeling he made it."

Winkworth said, "I'll give you some free add-vice, Turner. Bight's the morale of this ball club. Maybe you think he was laying it on Heisman kind of thick, and maybe he was, but you dug yourself a hole for butting in, you're going to be digging out of a long time. I think you better talk to some of the rookies that was here while you were starring it up in Chicago, and maybe you'll get some smart. You beat Bight out of his job, you be playing alongside me. I can make you look good, or bad, and you better know it. You just get some smart and start digging yourself out of that hole." Then he added, "And leave Battle to Coogan."

Billy Turner didn't smile. There was little trace of Arkansas accent when he spoke. "Winkworth, you started that out just fine. You sure got off the track again when you start threatening me. I'm going to be left tackle, and if I ever figure you're not putting out, we're going to find out who's who and what's what. But I'm easy to get along with. Man doesn't play in the line this long without being easy to get along with. I got one weak spot. That's Davey Battle. Every man on that All-Star team, he got the same weak spot for Davey. You'll get it, too, sure as shootin', and then you'll figure out why I dug myself that hole, to keep him from digging one for himself." Then he said, "Winkworth, you and me, we got to be friends, wouldn't you say that?"

Winkworth didn't say yes or no.

6

THE FOOTBALL FANS, 15,107, came to the University of Detroit stadium to see the new, wide-open football of the new head coach of the Detroit Lions. They came to see Billy Turner, the wild rookie tackle from Arkansas. They came to see the old master, Dipper Coogan, the perennial all-pro, the perennial hero. Most of all, 15,107 fans, an all-time record for the intrasquad game that closed the training season, came to see Mr. Helsman himself, America's number-one football hero.

The squad was divided, ostensibly, into old-timer and newcomer teams. In actuality they were divided into varsity and scrub, since David Battle and Billy Turner were assigned to the old-timers.

Battle and Coogan stood on the goal line for the kick-off. It came dead center, between them. They both moved for the ball. The Dipper expected to take it, because that was the way they did things on the Detroit Lions. David Battle took it out of his arms, because that was the way they did it at Notre Dame. He ran straight up the field, cut to the sideline, avoided a slow lineman, gave a limp leg to an end and went to the forty before he was hemmed in and crashed out of bounds. He bounced up like a rubber ball and trotted to the huddle as the ball was marked.

Dipper Coogan was livid. He stepped out to meet the wingback. He rasped quietly, "That was my ball, Heisman."

Three of the linemen heard him. Belcrank said to the right tackle, "Well, I guess that means we got a job to do."

They expected it when Coogan called for a wingback reverse into the center of the line. The Dipper took the snap from center, ran at the strong side, and then handed off to David cutting back. The veterans opened the gates. The defensive line charged through without opposition and threw five hundred pounds of beef on Mr. Heisman. David folded himself and went limp. The referee unpiled them. From the bottom, David squirted out and bounded into the huddle.

Wellman let out his breath.

Keene said, "He's tough, by God, he's tough. He's got the savvy."

Then Wellman made known his concern. He said grimly, "He better be tough. It's a long season. A long season. Man that size, he better be tough."

In the huddle, Dipper Coogan put his face against Belcrank's. "You summabitch, who told you you could play football?"

Belcrank looked up in surprise. Hadn't Coogan wanted the gates opened on Heisman? Didn't he want the hot shot taught a lesson?

Coogan said, "Same play. You mothers, if you can't hold out the scrubs, what in Christ are you going to do when the season starts?"

They blocked. David took the hand-off, cut in, broke loose and went to the twelve-yard line before Burlingame cut him down.

Dick Keene said almost to himself, "He's good. He's good."

This time the Detroit Lions moved to the front sports pages of the *Detroit Ledger*.

Before 15,107 fans at the University of Detroit football stadium, the Detroit Lions unveiled the razzle-dazzle offense they will throw this year at the National Football League, as the old-timers defeated the newcomers 21-6. David Battle, the two-time Heisman Trophy winner, lived up to every bit of his advance billing. This year the Lions will have a double threat in their backfield, all-pro quarterback Dipper Coogan, and Battle, who looks like an all-pro wingback every minute he's on the field. Coogan and Battle, the Big Dipper and the Little Dipper. . . .

Dipper threw the newspaper down and snorted, "Oh, Christ!"

His grass widow asked, "What's the matter?"

"Big Dipper, Little Dipper, for Christ sake!"

"Sounds sort of cute."

"Grow up, will you?"

"He's cute. He sure is. What kind of fellow is he?"

"What do you care?"

"I don't care. I mean, he just seems like a nice person."

"You want a nice person? Is that what you want?" She said, "You don't have to be on your ear."

"Well, I'm asking you." His voice was even higher and more rasping than usual. "You want a nice boy? Or do you want me?"

"He's sure got you on your ear, Dipper. You got no reason."

"No reason, except you talking about him being cute. I'll let you in on something. He's queer as a three-dollar bill. Now how cute you think he is?"

"I don't believe that."

"Well, I'm telling you."

"Who ever heard of a queer football player?"

"You're hearing about one now. You know where he lives? With his mama, that's where. And no women. This tomato comes sucking around after him, and he acts like she's going to get him down and give him a dose of the Old Joe. I don't think he'd know what to do with some pussy if it was staring him right in the face."

"Don't talk like that, Dipper."

"You don't like the way I talk, you just say the word, I'll be out of here so fast it'll make your head swim."

"Dipper, I don't want you to go. Take it easy. He's not doing anything to you. I don't want him. You've got no reason to be jealous. With me *or* football. I mean, everybody is saying it, with him in there, you'll look all the better. I mean, the both of you, you'll have that much more chance to look all the better."

"Now you're a football expert?"

She smiled pleadingly. "Dipper, don't be so grumpy."

"Get me a drink."

"Before breakfast?"

"Just get me a drink. And let me worry about Heisman, I can take care of him."

Winkworth said to Karcher, "I don't get it. Dipper hates his guts, but he wouldn't let us open the gates on him."

Turner said, "Nobody hates Davey Battle's guts."

"You don't know the Dipper like I know him."

"Man doesn't live could help liking that hard-nosed little summabitch."

"You saying Dipper's a man? I mean, like a human man? He ain't. Takes more than a human man to chase coo all night, and get out on that field still drunk, and play all-pro ball. You can't count on what Dipper thinks about things, by figuring out what human beings would think about the same things."

"I say he likes Davey. He made him look good out there. He bent over backwards."

"I say he hates his guts, because he can't stand the idea of anybody cutting in on his headlines. On him being the only big hero to the team itself. That's what makes the Dipper tick, being Mr. Big."

"Then, why'd he make Davey look good last night?"

"Maybe because he's a competitor. Maybe because he's got to win in a fair fight. If that's it, we oughter have one helluva season while they try to get ahead t'other."

"He ast me I'd go out with him Monday night."

"You going?"

"Couldn't wild horses keep me from it. I got this team made, I'm going to do me some relaxing."

"You go with the Dipper, fill you with booze and coo, or kill you, one. I know. I tried to keep up with him more'n twicet."

"That why you look so old?"

"That's why."

"That man's a sure nuff puzzle. When I figure him out, I'll let you in on it."

Winkworth shook his head. "More time you spend with him, less you know about him. One thing, the more time you spend with him, the drunker you get, until you don't know nothin' about nothin'. But I'll tell you, he's got to hate Davey's guts. He's got to. Davey's Catholic, and the Dipper hates Catholics almost worse than he hates losing football games. I hear he played his best games against Notre Dame."

"All-pro quarterback, he couldn't think that way. You take me, they had a nigger next to me in the All-Star game, you think that black boy and me didn't fight our black and white hearts out in that football game? Man's life at stake, or his football game, he don't think about niggers, and Catholics, and Jews, and stupid things like that."

"You're a dreamer. You a nigger lover, Straight Nose?"

Billy said mildly, "Not so's you could notice. We had a little nigger halfback on the All-Star team, just as cute and fancy as you please, and he got moves made even Davey sit up and take notice, and he turn on that speed, he just burn the worms as he go by. But he got no guts, and I got no use for him, not because he's a nigger, but because he got no guts, but that big black buck played guard next to me, he got a couple pounds of guts in his black soul, and he says to me, 'Billy, them Giants pushing us around pretty good. I think you and me got to turn a crank and show 'em what's *mean*, and I say, *mean*.' I'll tell you a thing, Wink, them Giants stopped running at me and that black buck, we showed 'em what *mean* was. That was a nigger you didn't ast was he a nigger, because he was a man, I'm telling you, a man."

"Would you be his buddy in Little Rock?"

"Nope."

"Why not, you got these ideas?"

"Because I'm not stupid, that's what. I might could like that nigger up here, but I'm not stupid."

"Wait'll you live around Dee-troit a time. You going to have niggers shoved down your craw, you like it or not. And you got no pick and choose, like between your no-guts halfback and your guts buck. You don't get to choose, like you get to choose 'tween white folks. Up here, they want you to think all niggers is the same, and that means all good. You going to see some race riots in this town."

"Got no time for that. I only got time for booze and coo and football."

Winkworth grinned. "What you going to do, you go

chasin' pussy with Dipper and it turns up blacker than the ace of spades?"

"Dipper do that?"

"Dipper does that. When he's in the mood. What you going to do?"

"Maybe say he's got more sense'n I give him credit for. You ever had it?"

"I'm from outside Tallahassee, boy."

"You had it."

"Good, ain't it?"

"Spoils a man."

"What you make of Davey? I mean, him and women."

"Clean mind, clean heart, clean mouth. Got to admire a man like that."

"You think there's something wrong with him? I mean, don't stick up for him for a minute. You think there's something wrong, him living with his mama?"

Billy said slowly, "I think there's something wrong with his mama living with *him*. It's not Davey, it's the other way around. He got to get rid of her, that's what he's got to do. He'll get around to it. Nothing wrong with that little man. I'm telling you, Wink, won't be a man on this team wouldn't cut off his arm for that little bastard, another week goes by."

"But not Dipper."

"He'll come around."

"Not in a million years. I'd give a nickel to know what he's figuring on. He's got to get him. Heisman? The new star? And a Catholic to boot?" Winkworth shook his head. " 'F I was Davey, I wouldn't turn my back on that killer."

Billy Turner said grimly, "Dipper come at Davey's blind side, he just might find me there."

Winkworth grinned. "Okay, Straight Nose." He grinned wider. "I sure got to admit that little knocker gets to you. You find yourself reaching out to pull him up, and you ask yourself how come you're doing it, but you just cain't hep it."

Billy said, "And all the time he hates it."

"How come?"

" 'F I knew, I'd tell you. You think Dipper's a enigma? You try to figure out Davey Battle. Maybe he's too proud to have people thinking he needs taking care all the time, maybe that's it."

"He's not all that little, you know. He must go a good one seventy-five. He just looks little. Man, he met Olzewski head on, and you could hear Ole's teeth rattle." Winkworth grinned again. "You got me doing it. I got to admit, I'm joining Heisman's fan club."

Billy said, "Shake, brother Vizier."

7

FOR DAVID BATTLE, World War II was football. He didn't intend it that way. For the first weeks after Pearl Harbor he heeded his mother's admonitions, adhered to the promises she extracted, and waited for the military to come get him. Straight Nose Billy Turner rekindled in him the fire of heedless, Sweet Water, Little Rock patriotism. He did it in a roundabout way.

"Davey, I got me this cave about fifty mile from Little Rock and least ten mile from where people leave off. I got it stocked pretty good. Victuals, dirty pichers and white lightning."

"No women, Billy?"

"Well, I give some thought to that. Then I give some more thought. You have a woman in your cave, only two things could happen. One, she's bound, sooner or later, to get woman-type patriotic, you know, send the menfolk off to get slaughtered, and she'd turn you in, surer'n hell. Or if that don't happen, you spend enough time with a woman, you're bound sooner-later not to change something about yourself she wants you to change about yourself, and she'll march herself down and turn you in just for spite. No, sir, no women in my cave, Davey. Except this black bear. She got a glossy coat, Davey, soft and silky, and she's warm and nice, and almost half-tame,

and her claws don't hurt too much when you get tough-
ened up to it. And she don't talk. Just woofs once in a
while when you're doing things just right. Now, I been
thinking, somebody might get stubborn, and this war go
on a long time. Man in a cave, he oughter have a buddy
to say something to, every week or so, and since you
don't talk much more that that sweet ole girl bear, I been
thinking inviting you in, when the draft board starts blowing on our neck."

David shook his head back and forth, smiling despite
himself.

"I'll sweeten it up. I don't want you messin' round *my*
bear, but I'll see if she got a sister. Your bear have to
be Catholic, Davey?"

"Billy, what say we volunteer? They're going to get us
sooner-later, anyhow."

"I been thinking about that. I asked myself, Billy, why
don't you volunteer? And the answer came back, just as
clear. Billy, when the Lord went to all that trouble to put
any brains at all in a back-country Arkansas boy, seems
like the least you could do is use 'em. They got to come
get me, Davey. Take half the men they got to find my
cave. And the other half to drag me out. Did I ever tell
you about my daddy?"

"I didn't know you had one."

"Only reason you don't know about him, Sergeant York
got credit for all the Huns my daddy shot. That's a fact."
Billy Turner stopped smiling. "My daddy joined the Marines. He was at Château-Thierry. And got killed. So
you're right, Davey, I don't have a daddy. And never did.
He was just a dumb country boy that stuck me in my
mama's belly before he went off to get killed, and instead of a daddy I got me some medals, and I got me a
old-timey picture of him the day he got married, and I
got me a cigarette case he bought in France and had on
him when he got killed, and I got me a letter. You'd
think a man that was 'most illiterate, he wouldn't waste
time writing a letter, now wouldn't you think that?" He
rose from the chair in the living room of his bachelor
apartment. He went to the desk and took out the letter. He
held it, uncertain.

David Battle waited, very still, hoping that the spell
would not be broken.

Turner turned and sat again the chair. He held the

letter up. "Davey, nobody besides me ever saw this. Ever heard it. You understand?"

"Yes."

"Maybe it's got something to say, maybe it doesn't."

"Read it."

Turner smiled just a little. He put on his thickest accent and read:

"Son, I thought I would tell you what it's like over here, and that is what I am going to do, because it just might could help you sometime.

"Son, a man like me does a lot of puzzling and still don't know much about man's ways or the Lord's ways. The ways of man and the Lord put a test on you, sometimes, you don't know if you can meet.

"Man like me, when he is home, don't think much about the Lord. Man like me sure don't live like the Lord wants him to live, or least like people say the Lord wants him to live. But I got this much figured out, even if it isn't very much. The Lord let me be in the world, and feel the sun, and the rain, and the wind. Man's got to appreciate that. And the woman, and the son, and the gun, and the dog, they're good things. The Lord is good things. Now it seems to me like you would be turning your back on the Lord, you ever turn your back on the good things He put in the world and don't enjoy them. You remember that, son, since I took the trouble to figure it out for both of us.

"But maybe you got to face up, sometime, and do what scares the pants off you. And young Billy Hobart from Louisiana, and old Wesley from Oklahoma, they got shot and laid there looking right through you, just asking questions you can't answer them, and you get scared some more, and get a longing, and it's a terrible deep longing, to run out of here and get home and see your son. You got to watch that. Reckon that is when the worst side of a man comes out.

"If you watch that, you can get the best side showing again. So I figured it out for Billy and Wesley and maybe me. And it might could help you some day, boy. When you try to figure the sense of something and just get a bigger puzzle than your head can handle, that is when you stop trying to *know* things, and start in to *feel* things, because truth has a way of coming to *feeling* when it won't come to all the *knowing* in the world. That puts you back on the track. Like you say to Billy and Wesley, no use fretting it makes sense, or don't make sense. Or the Lord wants it this way, or don't want it this way. The answer is, a man's got no right to enjoy the good things he found in the world, if he don't get up when the time comes and do what he feels he's got to do. That's advice to you, boy. You depend on your feeling, not your head, when you got the biggest things to decide. Then it's like the sun coming out, and morning busting out, and you don't need anybody's words to tell you you're doing the right thing. It was good enough for them to get killed over. It's good enough for me if I have to get killed. I don't want to. Lord, I don't want to! But if I do, you understand, son, a man's got to do what he feels he's got to do. Son, if I don't see you, you *be* somebody, you hear?"

Billy Turner sat curling and uncurling his big hands, the letter in his lap.

David said, "Well, I guess we know what we've got to do."

"I reckon we do."

"Let's go."

"It would be stupid. You know that, don't you? Let's think it over."

"Is that why you read the letter? To think it over?"

They went to the Federal Building in downtown Detroit and joined the queue at Navy Recruiting. They were recognized by one of the other volunteers. The word spread. They were taken by a CPO directly to the officer in charge. The commander was elated with his prize catch and showed it. He made them comfortable and went off gleefully to phone BuPers.

In half an hour he said, "Mr. Battle, Mr. Turner, we've got the best billet for you."

Billy asked, "What kind of billet?"

"Great Lakes. They'll have an appropriate spot for you.

And you don't have to report for two or three more months."

David said, "Commander, you could presume we didn't come busting down here just to get a delay. What's wrong with now?"

Billy said, "Now hear the man out, Davey."

"You having second thoughts, Billy?"

"Just wondering how my wife is going to take it."

"You're kidding."

"Didn't I ever tell you about my wife? I got me two kids, Davey, would of starved to death, wasn't for the football fund at Arkansas."

"Where are they?" David asked skeptically.

"Back in Little Rock with her mama, where they belong when a man's out in the world playing football."

The commander asked, "You're married, Mr. Turner?"

"You want to see a picture of my bride, Captain?"

"I'm a commander. No, that won't be necessary. If you gentlemen will fill out the forms, we'll get things moving."

David asked, "Sir, what's this billet at Great Lakes? Just so there's no mistake, we came down here to find out about officer's training, or direct commissions. We've got our degrees, both of us. Don't we qualify?"

The commander said soothingly, "Everything will be taken care of. You'll be notified when to report. The chief will get the necessary details from you."

Billy Turner asked, "Davey, you got the same railroad feeling I got?"

The commander said, "You gentlemen just leave everything in my hands. I'm personally guaranteeing you'll get a better deal from us than the Army or Marines could ever dream up."

David went home, puzzled and frustrated. Ellen asked him, "Where were you, David?"

"Over at Billy's."

"I called over there. Two hours ago."

"Just taking care of some business."

She said with accusation, "You wouldn't volunteer, David. You wouldn't do that, after I asked you not to."

"Mama, it's a matter of sooner or later."

"Not if you have an essential job, they won't draft you."

"If."

"Just talk to Jim. I know he'd get you an essential job. Why don't you just talk to him?"

"Did you know Billy Turner was married?"

"How would I know that? Is he?"

"He sure is. He's got two kids and one more on the way."

"That's terrible, going off and leaving them like that. That's terrible. I knew there was something wrong with Billy."

"Because he went off to play football and left his family home? It's been done before."

She said sharply, "David, don't you dare ever again say something like that to me."

He said, just as sharply, "Don't use that tone of voice with me, Mama. I'm grown up."

"Are you? Since when? A grown man doesn't talk about volunteering to go off to war and get killed. A boy does something like that. I'm sick and tired of your disrespect. You straighten up, young man. You listen to me. I know what war is like, and you don't. You haven't seen it, I have. It's spitting up blood and waiting to die, that's what it is. And that's not going to happen to you while I'm alive, do you hear me?"

David didn't answer. He couldn't trust himself.

She yelled at him, "You answer me, young man, when I speak to you."

He began to shake visibly, like a small boy. It took him a long time to regain some composure. He said, as gently as he could, "Mama, everybody could tell us what it's like, but we wouldn't believe it. Each generation has to find out for itself. And a man's got to do what he knows he's got to do."

Her moods shifting quick as the wind, she was then patronizing. "David, you've been such a good boy. Don't turn selfish now, that's all I ask."

"Selfish!"

"I know what it means to you. But think about me, just this one more time. Wait until I'm used to being without Grandpa during the days, then maybe the nights with nobody here won't be so bad."

He paced the room restlessly.

Now, quickly, she was softly maternal. She pulled him to the couch beside her, put his head down in her lap, and gently rubbed his forehead and eyes. She said consolingly, "David, you're just one man, and they can get

415

along without one man. It's not as though you'll be making any difference."

Her words were more prophetic than she knew. David Battle and Billy Turner contribute to victory? Came their orders to Great Lakes. Ellen Battle railed at her son for his duplicity, his stupidity, his selfishness. In an hour-long tirade, she pleaded and demanded that he get his orders changed before it was too late. He couldn't stand up under her onslaught. He phoned the commander at Navy Recruiting and said, "I don't want the Great Lakes billet, whatever it is."

The commander said sternly, like a movie commander, "Battle, you've got your orders. Carry them out."

The orders directed them to report for boot training. If they received boot training, they didn't notice. They were assigned to the athletic department. They were made comfortable. Officers of all ranks accorded them deference. They were bewildered. Nobody could tell them exactly what they were supposed to do. After frustrating weeks of time-filling, came Dubois from the Cardinals, came Henkle from the Giants, came some other pros, came some strong linemen and shifty backs from colleges and sandlots—came the dawn. David Battle was finally embarked on the naval career they had selected for him. He reported to Paul Brown. He became left halfback on the Great Lakes football team.

The following season he and Billy were sent, as chief petty officers, athletic specialists, to St. Mary's Preflight in California, where the starting eleven were mainly all-pro, and wiped up the Army, the El Toro Marines, and every other team they could get their hands on. Ostensibly he and Billy and the other footballers came west to drill aviation cadets. Ostensibly David Battle was a calisthenics and obstacle-course expert. During the football season the only cadets he saw were those in the stands. Even in the off-season the St. Mary's executive department was hard put to find tasks for twenty-five athletic instructors. Straight Nose Billy Turner loved this duty. He was enthusiastic about San Francisco and the war-struck girls. He enjoyed this World War II without reservation. He couldn't understand David Battle. He said, "Davey, not as though we didn't try to fight. Relax."

David chafed. He was miserable. He pleaded with his superiors. He begged to be enrolled in the preflight school as a cadet. He wrote formal requests for an opportunity as a ninety-day wonder. He even volunteered to go overseas with his CPO rating or as a seaman, on aircraft carrier or honey barge.

His commanding officer said, "Battle, look at it from our point of view. You're making your best contribution to the effort. Nothing could be more important to Navy morale than this football team."

"You've got ballplayers to burn."

"We can't spare you. This is the greatest football team in the history of the game, but it's still David Battle that's the magic name."

David said with a most unusual bitterness, "Ted Williams gets to fly airplanes for the Marines."

The captain shrugged. "There's no all-star baseball team."

"They say when he's supposed to show up and play ball for the station team, he shows up if he feels like it, and doesn't show up if he doesn't feel like it."

"Is that some kind of threat, Battle?"

"I'm not sure. I agree with Ted Williams. If he's going to be in the Marines, he should be a marine not a baseball player. I want to be a naval officer. Before I went to Notre Dame, I was all set for the Academy. I wanted it. This is my chance come up again to be a naval officer. I think I'd make a good officer. I want to make a normal contribution to the war effort, not football."

The captain studied the agitated David Battle. He leaned back and put on his kindly look. "I commiserate with you, Battle. I know what you're going through. I'm Academy Class of 1920. A lot of my classmates are making admiral. Most of them are out where it counts. Me, I was recalled to active duty after being passed over and retired. Do you think I wouldn't like to be out there? Well, I've got to count myself lucky just to be playing this part. To each his own."

Chief Petty Officer Battle said stubbornly and audaciously, "Captain, I'm not interested in your problems, or anybody else's problems besides my own. I'm entitled to a commission. If I have to, I'll take it all the way to the top. I won't be put off."

The captain sighed. He said, "I'll see what I can do."

So the Navy commissioned David Battle a lieutenant, just like that, skipping ensign and j.g. He was no longer

417

an enlisted man playing left halfback for the mighty St. Mary's Preflight football machine. He was now an officer playing left halfback. They did make him assistant coach. His teammates did salute him elaborately, and Billy Turner demanded and received his own commission as a j.g., and his own mock, friendly salutes. But their regimen changed in no appreciable degree. David had achieved his ambition. He was, at long last, a naval officer in the service of his country. For all that counted, strive as hard as he could to be a correct and proper officer, he remained David Battle, the all-pro halfback, the Little Dipper, the man for whom both teams gathered when he was slow getting to his feet—still a football player, not quite an officer in the United States Navy. Now that he was an officer and could live in town, he moved out on Billy and became the roommate of Ellen Foley Battle.

In August of 1945 the Alnav made him lieutenant commander. Before he could get the new braid on his uniform, V-J Day destroyed the war and his last hope of glory was crushed. He celebrated dispiritedly. In the Persian Room he met Kelly Brand.

He sat at the bar with Billy, his protector. He played with his horse's neck and wondered if this was the time he should try booze. He listened to very little of what his friend rattled at him.

Then Billy asked, "You got permission to spend the night in town?"

David said sharply, "Knock it off, Billy. I'm in no mood."

"Why don't you kick over the traces and go tomcatting with me, Davey? Never be a better chance than this. Girls in this town gone plumb outen their skulls. 'Fore this night's over, be a hundred thousand of 'em just beggin' to get jabbed by their nation's heroes. Davey?"

"Knock it off."

"Davey, I never bugged you. You know that. Not when ever'body else give you a hard time, I never bugged you. Well, hang on to your hat, I'm going to bug you some now. Davey, you got to let loose them apron strings right now, or maybe you ain't never *going* to let loose."

David flushed. "If it's a problem, it's my problem."

"No, it ain't. Damn it, it ain't. I'm the one's plumb wore out sticking up for you."

"Sticking up for me? Do you think you have to apologize for me, just because I don't run around like a crazy Indian? If that's what you think, you're no different from the rest of them."

"You listen to me, little buddy. Don't get on no high horse with Uncle Billy. You ain't no pope to sit in judgment on me or anybody."

David's jaw tightened, but after a moment he said, "All right, I accept that. I didn't mean to give that impression."

"Well, you do. You're getting more a goddam saint every day. And I mean the kind tries to make other people feel dirty. I can remember the day when the ballplayers figured you was just a clean-living boy, and you got some admiring for it. Not any more. Now you get the kind of admiring a pissy-ant preacher gets, a holier-than-thou gets. Davey, ain't a man on any team you ever played on wouldn't break his ass for you. That's real admiring. But soon's you get off that field, la dee dah!

"You're so scared to death sin's going to bite you in the ass, you're scared to take a deep breath. It ain't no human being thinks like that. You know who you're like? Dipper Coogan. How does that grab you? You think Dipper's a human being? He ain't. He's a *thing*. He's a thing he made up hisself. He's a fire, that's what he is, burning away and burning up everything that gets in his way. He's a football thing. He gets on that field and you got to love the guy most just when you hate his guts most, because he's a burnin' fire out there. That's the only time he's alive. You think he's alive when he's boozing? When he gets blind drunk and jabs anything that moves? That ain't no human being, that's a guy his own fire is burning him up, and he's got to do something wild until he can get back on that football field again, or die. It's you, too, Davey. I'm telling you, it's you. I bet that's something never occurred to you, you and Dipper two of a kind. The only time you're a man, the only time you're alive is when you're out on that football field, doing things nobody would think a little summabitch like you could do. You get off that field, you die. Just as sure as Dipper, you die. He takes his out sinning, and the worst sin the better. You ain't no different. You take yours out in no-sin, and the worst no-sin the better. And I don't know which is the worset of the two, the sin of screwing the low-downest women you can find, or pissy-ant, self-righteous no-sin. Davey, you got to do something. You're

419

a mighty long way down that road of no return. You got to stop turning your back on the Lord and pick up in your hands the beautiful things He put here for you in this world."

Billy Turner stopped. He gulped his drink.

David asked, "Are you through?" His voice was unsteady.

"If I could think of something else to say, I'd say it. If I knew how to make myself clearer, I would. It's some more complicated than a dumb razorback like me can figure out. But I had to have my say, even if you got so pissed off you never had anything to do with me again, and that's how serious I am."

Billy ordered another drink for himself. He drank half of it down.

David asked, "What do you want me to do? You want me to get drunk? You want me to shout some dirty words? You want me to pick up a girl?"

"I don't know. I don't know where living leaves off and sinning begins. I don't want you to sin."

David snorted.

Billy Turner said, "I don't feel too good. I got the feeling things won't ever be right between you and me again. Man can't take a beating like this from another man and ever think quite the same of him. Ain't that right?"

"That's right, Billy."

"So I did it knowing what I was doing. So you done lost yourself a watchdog. From now on we're just plain, ordinary friends, not buddies, if you want to go even that far."

"Want to go your own way tonight?"

"When I'm ready. Not until then. I spend most of my life with plain, ordinary friends. Fair enough?"

After a moment David said, "Fair enough." He was miserable.

"Why don't you blow your stack?"

"I don't blow my stack. I'm not human, remember?"

"Pity. That's a pity. Davey, here she comes."

They watched the girl approach.

David asked, "Here who comes?"

"The girl I'm going to fall in love with. Oh, sweet Jesus, look at that proud, pretty walk. I'm in love, Davey, I'm in love."

Billy moved over one stool. Kelly Brand slipped herself into the opening between them. She took out a cigarette and made fumbling motions in her purse for a match, ignoring the Persian Room matches under her nose.

Billy struck a match. He was too late. David already had a light to her cigarette. Billy said, "Glory be, them halfbacks is fast."

Kelly Brand turned and smiled at David. In a moment she said, "Thank you, Mr. David Battle."

He was accustomed to recognition. He said, "You're welcome, miss."

Billy asked, "Will you have a drink, ma'am?"

She smiled again, a wonderful smile. "Admire it."

Billy asked, "Texas?"

"Houston. Leastways a farm near Houston. No ranch. No oil wells. Just a farm. My name is Kelly Brand, and that's my life story."

"I'm Straight Nose Billy Turner. I've got the only undeviated septum in pro ball, and you got to add-mit, I'm some handsomer than any lineman's got a right to be. You already know my silent partner here."

"You're a great tackle, Mr. Turner. Some say the best."

"You a football fan, Kelly? I like girl football fans."

"I'm a fanatic, Mr. Turner. Is that redundant? Fanatic, is that where fan comes from?"

"Ask Davey. He's the brain. You name it, any subject, we just ask Davey."

David twisted his glass in his hands. "That's where fan comes from. I think Miss Brand knew that."

Billy smiled. "That's our Davey. Brainy and blunt. Now what would you like to know about me?"

Kelly sipped at the drink that was set in front of her. Her eyes sparkled. "How are the kids, Straight Nose?"

"Oh, sweet Jesus!"

"Told you, I read all the football magazines, like some girls read *Photoplay*."

"Then you know I been married long enough to be a good date."

"I know you're the *best* tackle. And the *best*-looking. And I know you're giving me exactly what I deserve, Mr. Turner."

He was discomfited. He said lamely, "V-J Day."

She patted his hand on the bar. "Buy me lots of drinks, Mr. Turner."

He said with renewed confidence, "Forever. I'm in love with you, Kelly. I been in love with you from the time you walked across this room."

She smiled at him and lighted up his heart. "I beat you to it. I stood there looking over the bar, and I asked the man at the door, Isn't that David Battle, the football player? And then I asked, Who's that handsome man with him? But the man didn't know you, Mr. Turner, so I came over to find out for sure that it was you."

Billy said, "Oh, Lordy, I'm in love." He let his head drop sideways onto his shoulder, his eyes closed.

Kelly Brand said soberly, "Yes, men love me."

David Battle asked, "Miss Brand, do you live in San Francisco?"

"No. If I told you the truth, you wouldn't believe it. I came up here to see St. Mary's Preflight play football."

Billy asked, "All the way from Houston?"

"Can you think of anything better to do, when you haven't got anything in particular to do?"

Billy squeezed her hand. "Well, no more football, but you sure nuff come to the right city and found the right guys to celebrate with." He said to the bartender, "Another round."

Kelly Brand said to David Battle, "The fan magazines, they tell whacks. They say you don't drink."

Billy said, "Horse's necks."

She said, "Oh." Then she leaned forward and inspected David's face. "Do you have a straight nose, too? Do you have any disfigurements, Mr. Battle?"

He did his best to keep his expression steady under her close scrutiny.

Billy said, "He's one up on me. He's still got his own front teeth, and mine are store-boughten. But when it comes to noses, he ain't in the same league."

She leaned even closer and stared at David's nose. "Texas, we'd call that straight."

"See that there little crook on the side? He got that when Dipper Coogan let him have the ball, wham, in the schnoz. And that bump on the bridge, can you see it? He got stopped at the goal line by the safety man's knee. I bet his nose was two inches across when he got up. He was the ugliest halfback you ever saw."

Kelly said, "I bet he stayed in the game, right?"

"Right. Until he got sick swallering blood."

"And you got the safety man, right? I read how the Lions get back at the ones that get David."

"That time Winkworth got the safety."

David said, "And caught fifteen yards, just when it hurt most."

Billy said, "You see, Kelly, he can talk. Usual he needs an interpreter. Not the translate kind, a mind-reader kind."

Kelly Brand said, "I've got a confession, David Battle. You're my hero. When Notre Dame played Southern Methodist, I rooted for Notre Dame. My daddy like to skinned me."

"Kelly? Not Irish?"

She smiled, and he almost smiled back at her. She said, "My daddy named me after a man that got shot dead helping him against a drifter. Wasn't until that Notre Dame game, came home to him what he did to himself. Catholics aren't quite as popular in Texas as Baptists this year."

David said impulsively, "You sure are a pretty girl."

She cocked her head at him. "When you finally do say something, you come on like Texas."

"If everybody from Texas looked like you, I don't think I'd think about Texas the way I think about Texas."

"I'll tell you the truth, I've always felt I was a little bit too much of a tomboy, you know, the farm and all, to get men stirred up."

David did smile. "You're a girl. Some girls that look a little more like girls than you do, they fall short of you."

Billy said, "By golly, the Little Dipper's got unsuspected depths. I think you've plumbed them, Kelly."

She smiled again, most warm, most attractive. "I like you two. I surely do. I just couldn't believe it when I saw you, Mr. Battle. Will you let me celebrate the great victory with you?"

Billy asked, "Do you have a friend, Kelly?"

"I know two people in San Francisco. David Battle and Straight Nose Billy Turner. And I maybe came to San Francisco to see the best football team in the country, and I maybe came to get to some place where I didn't know one soul."

Billy Turner said, "And it could just as easily be somebody besides us. Okay, I haven't assumed anything else."

423

She looked at Billy steadily. "Just say I've got the feeling this is going to be the best day in a lot of days."

Billy stood up. He said, smiling just a little, "It's a far, far better thing I do. Davey, you take Kelly and get us a table. I'll scout around for somebody in a mood to celebrate victory."

David said warningly, "Don't play cruise director, Billy."

Billy said with sudden heat, "Don't you think I know when I been kissed off by a girl? I'm not doing you any favors, she is." He turned his face away from them, drained his drink, then walked off, slowly searching the room.

Kelly Brand took David's arm and led him to a table. He didn't resist. She said, "I'm glad I got up the nerve to come sit next to you."

"Did it take nerve?"

She sat down. He lit her cigarette before he sat. She was quiet a moment. Then she said, "No, it didn't take any nerve. I've done it before. We'll assume that I do everything but lie, cheat and steal, and I came to San Francisco to grab hold of a minute and enjoy it for all it's worth. Now I've told you all you need to know about me."

They sat, silent, a long time.

She asked with a new, a false, smile. "Want to send my kind of woman packing, David? I wouldn't blame you."

He said, "I like your tan. I like your hair. I like the way you move, the way you walked coming in here, sort of wiggle and glide like a jig halfback that's got all the moves and knows it. I like your looks. And the way you talk. That most of all. I think I like you very much."

She returned his earnest look. As though she were taking a deep breath, she said, "I think I better tell you a little bit more about me. Those nice things, I thought I was all those things once. My husband thought so when he married me." She shook her head no to his unasked question. Her chestnut hair swirled. She smiled the crooked, rueful half-smile again. "Long gone. The son of a gun went over the hill three months after he quoth ever more. The Lord and him know where he is now." She smiled wider and tossed her hair again. As though with mockery of herself, not him, she asked, "Will you be consolation, David Battle?"

"If I could. If I knew how."

424

She raised one eyebrow and cocked her head at him again. "You really are all that modest, David. I thought that must be just publicity talk." When he didn't answer, she asked, "Are you as nice as you sound, David Battle?"

"What does nice mean? Inexperienced?"

"No, I mean nice. You have such a guileless look. How old are you, David?"

"Twenty-eight."

"I'm twenty-three. How tall are you?"

"I'm five ten. I weigh one seventy. I'm only small next to other ballplayers. Kelly, tell me about your husband."

"He ran off with a Mexican girl that looked like Linda Darnell. For all I know, maybe it was Linda Darnell. He's a lieutenant in the Air Force. Or was. They're looking for him. He's been over the hill for a year."

"Are you?"

"Looking for him? Or over the hill? I'm not looking for him any more. The tie that didn't bind is officially severed. Just Leavenworth's looking for my shining knight. His rich daddy, he quit a long time ago. He quit when my hero married me instead of that girl whose daddy's company my daddy-in-law wanted to merge with. Not a cent. Not a cent. Do you know what the irony is, David? I didn't marry him for his money." After a moment she said, "I think maybe my daddy is looking for me. Maybe I'll call him tonight and tell him I'm out with you. That would drive him outen his cotton-pickin' Texas Baptist mind. I told you about my daddy. I got no reason to be proud of him. The day my daddy buys hisself a new denim shirt, that's the day he thinks he's rich. We're the poorest white folks in the county, including drunks and ne'er-do-wells. The church mice come around my daddy just to feel better. I think you'd like him. He wouldn't give himself a chance to like you, but you'd like him, I think, David. I like him. I like him just fine. Do you like your daddy?"

"He's dead."

"I'm sorry. For a long time?"

"Seems like a long time. Sometimes it seems I only saw him two or three times in my whole life."

"What did he die from?"

"He died."

"I didn't mean to pry, David. I didn't mean to rattle on so, either. You make a good listener. Except you bring out some things that shouldn't be thought about. I'm sorry. I'm much better company when I'm flip. I'll do better, honest. I'm really very good company."

"How are you getting along?"

"Living? By cadging drinks from strangers. And an occasional meal. You going to feed me tonight?"

"Sure."

"Will you put me up? I haven't got a place to stay."

After a moment he said, "I might do that."

"Will you want something in return?"

His mouth was dry. "No, no demands."

She smiled the slightly crooked smile. "I think you missed the boat. I couldn't have argued, in my starving condition."

"I don't think I believe you when you're flip. I think you're saying the smart-alecky things you think are expected."

She took his hand between her hands, held it up, kissed his fingers quickly. "I suppose we'll be better off if we believe it from the beginning, everything but lie, cheat and steal."

"Maybe I don't want you to be pensive, but maybe not too flip, either."

"I'm not a nice girl. I smoked a marijuana cigarette once, that's one thing."

"Did you like it?"

"Yes. Sort of. I guess because it was exciting. I was seventeen."

"Just be bright, and intelligent, and very pretty. Those are my demands."

"Then can I brag?"

"Be my guest."

"I will, if you take a turn after me. I was homecoming queen. I was a cheer leader, and then I was homecoming queen. That made me feel pretty."

"Where?"

"University of Texas."

"Did you finish?"

"Three years, before that dude turned my head. You should have seen me, David, when I was cheer leader. Just aprancin' my fool head off at the Cotton Bowl. Can I brag some more? I was at Texas on scholarship." The smile went. She said half sarcastically and half wistfully, "That's how smart I am." The smile came back. "I like

426

what you said, about the way I walk, like a skittery half-back. I like to walk. I like to move. I feel good. I mean, I feel physically good almost all the time. And when I'm moving, I like it because I feel like all the parts of me were put together good, and it feels good to move them. You don't think I walk sexy, do you? I mean, it's not that kind of walk is it?"

"Sexy, yes. But not that kind. You've got class. That's not a good word, but I can't think of one that takes its place. You walk as though you know you've got class. Proud. That's good. And that *is* sexy. It isn't the movie sex symbols that are sexy-looking. It's women like you."

She put her elbows on the table and her head in her hands, looking in his face dreamily. "I'd love to sit here and let you say things like that forever."

"What happened to your Texas accent?"

"Same thing happened to your hillbilly accent. It comes and goes. David, are you married?"

"Would it make a difference?"

"No, of course not."

"You mean you're not a prude?"

"Of course I'm not a prude. Would I ask you to put me up?" She smiled again. "It would be best if you are. I'm a black widow, and if we mated, I'd devour you. Your friend Billy Turner just went out the door with a redhead in a black dress. Do you suppose he's taking her some place to tell her about his wife and children? I want a steak. Cow size. But not rare. If you Yankees knew how to cook steak as well as we know how to grow steak. That's what we know how to do in Texas, grow steaks and girls."

"That you do."

"I hope to kiss a pig, we know how to grow girls. You won't be disappointed in me."

"We fatten up Texas cows in Kansas City, and Texas girls, we sleek them up in San Francisco. Why did you marry him? I mean, what were your feelings?"

"David, I was in love with him. Or infatuation, or whatever you call it. He was a dashing boy, David, and turned my head. Okay? What did Billy mean?"

"About what?"

"About not watchdogging any more. I had the feeling you two were having an argument. And he was doing the explaining, and you the one mad."

427

"Yes."

"Want to tell me? Or eat your steak?"

"Eat my steak. And listen to you be bright and chipper. And fall in love with you."

"Well, don't say that. I don't like that."

"What's that supposed to mean?"

"Serious or kidding, just don't say that. Do I have to explain?" She tried to smile. "I guess you didn't see me wince when Billy Turner said it. I'm sorry, David. I'm being difficult."

"I don't understand you. How many kinds of girl can you be?"

"Do you want me to go away now?"

"Go ahead, if you want to."

"David?"

"What?"

"It would break my heart to leave. I just want to be near you tonight. And not think about tomorrow. Will you dance with me?"

He said gruffly, "I don't know how. Sure, come on."

They danced, they ate, she drank, they went out into the milling, wild celebration, and then David Battle drank, too. It was early morning when they took her suitcase from the Greyhound terminal and registered at the Mark Hopkins. He went to the room with her, tipped the bellboy, and then fitted the night chain.

8

She slipped off her shoes and sprawled in a chair. "Gee-oopiter, shoes and me don't get along."

He grinned.

She said, "That's the first time I've seen an honest-to-goodness, bust-your-face smile on you. It looks good."

"You break me up. I'm feeling the poundings of romance, and you flop out like a rag doll."

"Do I excite you, David? That's nice. Have you known a million pretty girls?"

"I've met a hundred pretty girls."

"How many have you known?" When he didn't answer, she said, "You puzzle me, David, you surely do. I think Billy was right. It would take a mind reader to interpret you. Such a guileless, open, handsome face, and sometimes I think your mind is just as guileless, and then, when you're not careful, I get a look at some real, earthy guile showing through. The unhappiness, I know that's there, even if you do keep that well hidden. I wish I could penetrate you. You scare me, a little bit, when I don't have the least idea what you're thinking. Are you tight at all, David?"

"No, I don't think so. I feel very good."

"I'm not, either. But I don't see how I can feel so exhilarated and sleepy all at the same time. I guess it's the long trip, and then the fun of meeting you. I'm so sleepy, David."

She rose from the chair and slowly took off her clothes. She hung her dress in the closet, and she folded her slip and put it in a drawer and unhooked her brassiere and put it in the same drawer. When she turned around, wearing only white, tight panties, he bit at the inside of his lip.

He said, "I didn't notice you weren't wearing stockings."

"I hate girdles. Don't you?"

"I thought your hips were flat. They're not. They're round and stick out like a girl's hips should. I think you've got the best legs and hips I've ever seen."

She turned and looked at herself in the mirror. She watched his eyes directed at her firm, high breasts.

She said, "David, I think I'm embarrassing you."

She pulled the covers back on the double bed. She sat on the edge and slipped off the panties with one motion and twisted under the sheet. He took off his jacket and hung it in the closet. He took off his tie and put it on the bureau.

She said, "You're staying, then."

He sat uncertainly in the upholstered chair. She watched him studiously.

She said, "You don't really know what to say or do, do you?"

He rose resolutely and quickly took off the rest of his clothes and came into bed with her. He lay there not touching her.

"David, before you do anything to me, talk to me a little bit."

He turned and looked at her. He could see the push of her breasts against the sheet. He could see the lines of her legs, spread apart, so that the sheet formed a hollow. A wild surge of wanting came over him. He reached out his hand and found hers and squeezed her fingers, and the touch of her excited him beyond endurance, and he knew that he had only to roll over and be on her, and be enveloped by her, and he knew he was ready to do this, and then the wild, mourning train whistle in his mother's soul came wailing at him, screaming) at him, "Mortal sin! Mortal sin!" and he let go her hand as though it had burned him, and he lay rigid.

After a long time she asked gently, "What is it, David?" When he didn't answer, she said just as gently, "Don't you want me? Is that it? If that's it, will you just go as quickly as you can? I couldn't take that, making such a fool out of myself."

With his mouth dry, he asked, "How old am I, Kelly?"

"Twenty-eight, David?"

"It would be the first time."

After a very long time of wondering what to say, she said, "Well, that isn't possible. You're pulling my leg again with that straight face."

"It's possible. It's true. I can't give you at least one very plausible explanation. There was the sort of planning that I would be a priest. I guess it just got out of hand, even when I didn't go to seminary."

"Yes, that's plausible. David, I'll seduce you gently?"

He said with sudden ferocity. "No, you would never seduce me. If the time comes, I will make love to you."

She said contritely, "I just want to help. That's what I'm here for. I need to be wanted, I need to be needed by somebody I admire. I can tell you about my needs, David, and you can help me. But I need more to be able to help you. Let me do that. Just tell me what I can do."

He said, "You were a long time getting here, Kelly Brand." Then he repeated, "A long time." Then he said, "The cloying possession. The cloying, enveloping, smothering possession. The guilt, the sin, the unbearable agony."

"Me. David? Is that me?"

"Her."

"A girl?"

"Her, too. She came to St. Mary's. I knew she would. She's so beautiful, it would make your heart break. But it's her. Her all over again."

"Your mother?"

"Yes."

Kelly smiled tentatively. "Tell me what dark things go on in Sweet Water."

"Don't be too flip for just a minute."

"Have you ever laughed at yourself, David? You could stand it. I'm laughing at us right now. It helps."

"What does it help?"

"If I knew, I'd tell you. Tell me about your father."

"I told you, he's dead."

"How long?"

"Long enough. He's dead."

"How did he die?"

"He's dead, Kelly, that's all."

431

"Did you love your daddy a great deal?"

"Love him!" He raised both clenched fists toward the ceiling. He said more softly, "Sure, I guess I did. I guess maybe the only one I felt that way for. You want to know why? Because he didn't smother me, that's why."

"And everybody else did?"

"He was a sinner. I bet the Lord Himself couldn't keep track of his sins. Boy, I remember when I was three and he came home from Akron and hadn't ever really seen me, and he looked at me like I was some bug he'd like to squash. He was the only one that hated me, and didn't smother me, and made me do things on my own. And I busted my heart to make him proud of me. Do you want to know something? I think I got to be all-American at Notre Dame just to make him proud."

"Was he proud?"

"He was dead. Before it got selected. He was such an unhappy man. So much good in him that never got out. How do you feel sorry for the worst of all men? So he's dead. Boy, is he dead! And me, I'm just the opposite, I've got so much bad in me that never got out, and I'm just as dead. Boy, am I dead! But some of the ones that smother you, the smug do-gooders, they're dead, but they get resurrected after three days and come back in somebody else and start in smothering you all over again. Kelly, I'll tell you somebody that you don't even realize you know. You know a guy named Joe Foley."

"I don't remember."

"Now he's Straight Nose Billy Turner. Or he's Winkworth. Or a hundred other guys, all of them trying to fight your fights for you, when you just want them to let you alone and let you fight your own fights. You know who I like? I like Dipper Coogan. He'd kill me, if he could. He'd like nothing better than to see me break a leg on that field. Break it right off. He'd pick it up and throw it so far they'd never find it, so he could keep me off that field where he wants to be the only star. He never gave me a thing. Not the sweat off his balls. And he gave me everything I wanted out of him. My daddy and Dipper, the evil ones, they're the only ones been good to me."

"And your mother?"

"She's good. Oh, boy, is she good!"

"And the girl?"

"I don't know what she is. She looks like my mother,

almost exactly like her. She could be my twin sister. Lord, I feel sorry for that girl. She doesn't want me all that much. She just wants what she can't get. Or did. She finally quit. She got married."

"Are you sorry?"

"Sorry!"

"I guess you're not."

"No. I'm not sorry."

"Would you like your mother to get married and go away?"

"I don't know. I don't know what I want. Yes, I do know exactly what I want."

He rolled over and put his arms around her and pulled her against him, and felt her breasts on his chest, and put his open mouth against her face, her lips, her eyes, and kissed her a hundred wild times until she breathed deeply and pressed herself against him, and he said in her hair, "And do you know what you are? You're sin. You're mortal sin, that's what you are. You're warm and beautiful and something God made, but never mind that, you're mortal sin . . ."

She stopped breathing. Holding her breath, she pushed him away, and her eyes were big and searched his.

"You're sin, you're sin, you're sin."

She said ever so softly, "Oh, poor David, poor David."

He asked bitterly, "Poor David? You, too, Kelly?"

"David?" He didn't answer. "David, you can have me, you know that. I owe it. Something to eat and drink and a place to sleep, you can have me." He turned his head away. "You can have me if you want to prove something. If you want to sin to prove something to your father and yourself against your mother, you can have me that way, if you want me. Or because I am sin, and if it would make you feel good to sin, just once, sin, you can do it for me. I'd sin for you."

"You'd sin!"

"Don't be too cruel. Don't be as cruel as I deserve. Wait until some time when you know all that there is to know about this, before you pass your judgments on me. I came here to sin to help myself, and now I'll sin if it helps you. Don't treat me too cruelly."

"I have a sister who doesn't sin. She's in a cloistered convent. She's probably shriveled up like a prune between

433

her legs by now. I know the difference between sinners and the sanctified ones. Come over."

He turned and pulled her up against him, her head on his chest. When she knew that this was all he wanted of her, she pushed her face hard against him, and when after a long time of lying there, after the tears had come flowing from her eyes and run down her cheeks and wet the hair of his chest, they slept peacefully like grown children, and in the last dark of the night he awoke and felt the warmth of her body against him, her firm breasts, her strong, lithe back under his hand, her firm, long leg doubled over his legs, so that her pelvis was thrust against his hip, and he rolled over on her, and she put her arms sleepily around his neck, and he said, "I've got to tell you, it tickles my risibilities, all this time so saintly, but this time the worst of all, a beautiful girl like you next to me for the whole night, and if I let you get away, I should be shot."

She squeezed his neck tighter, refusing to wake up.

He said, "I think I'm in love with you."

She disengaged her arms from around his neck, slipped them under his arms and wrapped them around his waist. She said sleepily, "Just stop talking and do something about it."

He smiled against her cheek. He said, "Yes'm."

9

IN DAVID BATTLE'S NAVY, it didn't make any difference to anybody that he didn't show up for three days. When he finally checked in, he was told that he could head for Detroit whenever he was ready. He was further informed that the San Francisco police were looking for him. He figured that one out. He girded his loins and went to see his mother. Kelly Brand insisted on driving over with him. He insisted that she wait in the car for him while he bearded the lioness.

Ellen Battle took it hard. She railed at David for his callous disregard of her feelings. Each time she seemed about to run down, a fresh calumny occurred to her, and she heaped it on his head without respect. She said, "David, she's a tramp. She's nothing but a tramp," and only then could he get another word in.

He said mildly, "She's a girl of surpassing excellence."

"A girl you can pick up in a bar, she can't be anything but a tramp."

"I'm sorry I told you the truth. That's a bad habit I'll have to break."

"You were throwing it in my face. David, you picked her up in a bar!"

"What percentage of people do you suppose met in a place you'd approve?"

"David, please! Don't marry a girl like that!"

"You misunderstood. I just said we were going to get an apartment. You can keep this apartment, or go back to Detroit, suit yourself."

Ellen Foley Battle said with vast relief, "Well, I did misunderstand. All right, you move in with her. You sin. You just do that for a while. Then you'll come to your senses, and you'll see a priest, and you'll come home."

"You'd rather have me sin for a while than get married forever? That's a refinement of your morality philosophy I hadn't anticipated."

When David had packed, Ellen insisted that she accompany him to the car and meet the woman. Kelly took a cigarette from her purse as they approached. David lighted it for her. There was a slight trembling in her fingers.

Ellen spoke her first words to the woman who was stealing her son. "Emancipation. In Sweet Water I'd have been flogged and branded for smoking. Especially in public."

Kelly said, "Yes, ma'am, my daddy would take the hide right off me, he caught me smoking."

"You're a polite girl."

"Yes, ma'am. I hope so."

"You look like an intelligent girl."

David said, "She won a scholarship to Texas."

"You don't look like a girl who would do something stupid."

David walked around and climbed in the driver's seat. "Time to go."

Ellen said sharply, "Not quite yet." Then she modulated her voice. "I want to talk to you for just a minute, miss. I think you should listen. What kind of feeling do you have for him?"

Kelly said softly and a little nervously, "I think it's evident."

"No, I think it's far from evident. In the first place, people just don't fall in love in three days. Particularly in the kind of three days you spent."

David flushed violently. Kelly put her restraining finger tips lightly on his leg. She said, "I'll show you our diary, Mrs. Battle, if it will help."

"I'll have respect from you, young lady."

"Yes, ma'am. I'll have the same respect from you, ma'am."

Ellen Foley managed a faint smile. "I apologize. And

436

what you did, that could happen in a celebration, when people get caught up in a mob. The important thing is from here on. Miss, if you think you have his interest at heart, would you let him ruin himself?"

"With me? Ruin himself?"

"It would, you know. If you two move in together, it would be all over San Francisco inside a week. David is too well known to do something like this. I assume you know David has no intention of marrying you."

"Did he tell you that?"

"He doesn't have to. David still has intentions of being a priest, when he's through with football."

Kelly Brand turned and cocked her head at David, a tickled smile on her face.

David said, "After I finish the thing I'm going to do after football, that's when I'm going to be a priest."

Ellen said, "Now I have a sensible suggestion. David, you take me home to Detroit. You wait a few days, or a few weeks, and then you see her again and see if you still feel the same way. Don't you think that would be an intelligent thing to do?"

There was silence.

Ellen gained confidence. "You just don't destroy the good habits of a lifetime. You just don't flaunt something like this at society." She grew overconfident. "And you don't flaunt something like this in your mother's face. That's just plain cruel."

Kelly Brand said, "Of course it is, Mrs. Battle."

David started the engine. He said, "Mama, you'll just have to accommodate yourself to the fact. You're going to have to start living your own life."

"Just a minute, David. When am I going to talk to you? You can't just leave me all alone like this."

"Cash a check, Mama, if you need anything. Mama, if it will make you feel any better, there's really been nothing happened between us so far. And we do intend to get married."

Ellen Foley watched the car disappear down the street. Her eyes were not wet with tears. They glowed with anger. She had nursed an ingrate, a traitor. He was Pete Battle. He was the despicable Joe Foley.

10

DAVID SAID, "I've finally figured out how it is you walk. As though you were throwing flowers to the world."

"I'd rather walk like a jig halfback. David, let's talk."

"Where should we look? Nob Hill? We've got to get something overlooking the Bay."

"David, take me to the bus station."

"What kind of joke is that?"

"No joke. I've decided to go see Daddy for a while." He didn't say anything. "Did you think I was going to move in with you?"

"I thought you were."

"Well, I'm not."

"You've got to be kidding. Don't. I don't think it's funny." He pulled the car to the curb. He turned and studied her. "What is it you're saying, Kelly? That you've been playing games? You've been playing watchdog for me? Making me do something you thought would be good for me?"

"Well, hasn't it worked?"

"What do you want now, a letter of commendation? Are you proud of yourself because you got me to give my mother a hard time?"

"David, you did that for yourself."

"Just a minute. This is stupid. I did it for you." With a

touch of desperation, he said, "This conversation can't proceed like this. I'm not a stranger to you any more, remember? I'm in love with you, remember?"

"I know you think you are. But your mother's right, people couldn't say they fell in love in three days. And I asked you not to say that to me."

He tried to sort his whirling thoughts. "I don't care how short a time. I saw you, I wanted you, I've had you, and I'm in love with you, and I'd do anything for you."

"David, don't."

"Don't give me don't! You're going to have to tell me what's going on. I'm not very bright."

She leaned back against the seat cushion. "Would it help to know I love you? Would that help? David, it wouldn't work. People aren't supposed to fall in love on the spur of the moment."

"Well, the hell with that, we did, and that's that."

"Lonely in San Francisco on V-J Day?"

"When I held you, you said you could stay there for-ever. What happened to that?"

She didn't answer.

He demanded, "What happened to that?"

"There has to be morning."

"What's that supposed to mean?"

"When it was night, I didn't have any other life. But in the morning, you remember."

"Kelly, I haven't asked you any questions."

"But you just gave yourself away. You knew right away what I was talking about. No, no questions. But they'd come. There'd be recriminations, sometime when the first bloom was gone, sometime when we had a fight. I'd get the worst end of that fight. That would hurt too much." She opened her eyes and smiled just a little. "So you see I'm not being unselfish sending you away. I'm thinking of myself. I'm sure I knew from the beginning, there couldn't be anything that would last."

He said with the bitterness obvious, "Are you trying to tell me you just picked me up and helped me like you'd help a stray dog? Just abstract kindness, is that all?"

"Two strays, David? Both of us looking for a substitute when we're lonely and bewildered? David, I don't even know what I'm doing. I can't think straight. Don't make me talk. I just knew you had to get away from her, and I had to help. I'm so sorry if I did anything wrong."

439

"Well, I am away from her. I left to go with you."

"You can't. I can't."

"She won't give up that easy. I won't break my own habits that easy. I'm twenty-eight years old. In a week I'd need some clean shirts, and I'd be back over there. So you see you can't go, Kelly."

She smiled. "I was afraid for a minute she had you again, and your great love for me was going to collapse like a summer romance."

"Well, I'll tell you what I think. I think you're being stupid. Just plain stupid, Kelly. Playing psychiatrist. Playing games, when it looks like there's something real that's here for us. Whether it makes sense or not, for three nights there's been nobody in the world except us, and for three days we've walked through San Francisco owning every brick and cobblestone and cable car and hill. You can't go, Kelly. You're the entirety, and I'm not going to let you be stupid."

Her lips trembled. She fought against tears. She said with difficulty, "I don't want to do anything stupid. I just want to get so far away from you that you can't ever hurt me. David, I'm a girl you picked up in a bar. I'm a girl you made love to the first night you knew me . . ."

"You're the first girl . . ."

"And you think you love me? Warm girl. Attractive girl. Bright girl. Loving girl. With such frightful loneliness under the smile. You think you love me? You don't even know what love really is." She stopped. "David, just take me to the station. I've done something good for you. Now let me go away."

He said angrily, "It's obviously meant a great deal more to me than it has to you, is that the problem?"

"David, I just don't believe you! I don't!"

"What is it you don't believe?"

"I'm not the first for you."

"I told you you were."

"You've made love to me for two days and three nights."

"And you're experienced enough to pass judgment on my skills?"

"I didn't mean that. Yes, I did. I've been married, David. David, I don't want to come to San Francisco and be wanton, after all. I just want to go home to my daddy, before I get hurt so bad I never get over it. I don't even know what I'm talking about. I can't make sense. I just know I've got to get away. Please, David, please."

He sought in vain for words and understanding.

"Please, David. Oh, God, let's not talk any more. Just take me to the station. Or put me in a cab. I've got to get away."

He tried to put his arm around her. She resisted.

"Listen, David. You can't stay in San Francisco. You've got to play football. They'll be waiting for you."

"Does that matter all that much?"

"Be sensible."

"All right, I'll be sensible. I have to support you. We'll head for Detroit right now."

"We can't do that!"

He grabbed her hair in his fist and twisted her face up to him. "Now you shut up and listen to me. Do you think I understand what's going on? I don't. I don't know why we met, or why we're like we are, in love without rhyme or reason. But if you think I'm going to let you get away from me now, you've got another think coming. I think maybe I'll marry you. But that can wait. To-night we'll drive as far as Jackson Hole. Except I think we'll stop and spend an hour in a motel at least twice before dark. Now you just shut up, you hear?"

He drove out of San Francisco and headed east. They were a considerable distance on the highway, and she hadn't said anything. She put her hand in his lap, and he took it. She moved closer and put her head on his shoulder.

She said, "I'll be the motel spotter, all right, David?"

11

THE NEW GENERAL MANAGER of the Lions asked with agitation, "Where you been, Davey? We pull strings to get you out of the Army before anybody else, and you take two weeks between San Francisco and here."

"I was in the Navy."

"Army, Navy, where you been?"

David smiled. "Seeing some of the country."

"Well, the team's over at Assumption College. I guess you know Bob Quinn is the new head coach."

"Yes. He's a good coach."

"Should be like old home week for you. He'll build us a winner. We're counting on it. He's a winning coach."

"He lost a few at Detroit."

"He won more than he had any right to."

"He's a good coach. He's conservative."

"You've got some reservations? Don't. Mr. Wakeman told him to play the T. Wide open. It's your game."

"That's good. I wouldn't want to play somewhere where I couldn't do my best."

Martelli raised his eyebrows. What did that mean? He said, "I've got your contract, Davey. Let's get it signed, and you get over to Canada and start catching up with the squad."

"I've got some ideas about my contract, Mr. Martelli."

442

Martelli asked warily, "Like what?"

"I want twenty-five thousand a year. I want a two-year, no-cut contract."

"Out of the question."

"Suit yourself."

"What's that supposed to mean?"

"I've played football a long time, Mr. Martelli. I don't need it any more just for the fun of it. The war cut me out of five good pro years. Now football's got to pay."

Martelli smiled with false friendliness. "Davey, in the first place, we haven't got no-cut contracts with anybody. Not with any of the players. Not with the coaches. Not with me. That's out of the question."

"Suit yourself. That's what I want."

"As for the twenty-five, that's five more than Connor will be getting."

"I read about Connor. What happened to Coogan? I didn't think he was ready to hang 'em up?"

"Several things. He thought we'd make him the new head coach. When we didn't, he quit. Just as well. He's not a T quarterback."

"Connor's good. I played against him when I was at Great Lakes and he was at Notre Dame. If you want him to get the same money as me, then give him twenty-five, too."

"The quarterback has to get the most, you know that. We were thinking eighteen for you. You report in this afternoon. I'll bring the contract out. Maybe we can up it a couple thousand, but that's the limit. And we can't break the one-year deal, or everybody would want in on the act."

David stood up. "That's your problem. My phone number is Midwest 4-9876. Call me when you're ready. But don't wait too long."

"Davey, you miss too much more of training camp, you won't be as valuable as you are now."

"That so? That a threat? Maybe I'll have a threat of my own. There are other football teams."

Martellie said stiffly, "Our option is still in force. You can't play anywhere else."

David asked innocently, "Does that include a new league?"

Martelli narrowed his eyes.

David said, "I won't beat around the bush. There's not

only talk of the new American League, I've got feelers from three Canadian teams. The way I see it, with the Dipper gone, you need me just about as bad as the Canadian clubs do. If you don't need me, just tell me, and I'll make other plans."

Martelli picked up the phone and dialed. When he got through, he said, "Carter, David Battle is in my office."

On the other end, Carter Wakeman said, "Good."

"He doesn't like the offer."

"What does he want?"

"Twenty-five thousand, two-year no-cut. He's indicating the Canadians are talking those figures."

Wakeman whistled. After a moment he said, "Put him on."

David said, "How are you, Mr. Wakeman?"

"I'm looking forward to meeting you. Are you free for dinner tonight?"

"I'll make sure I am. May I bring a guest?"

"Who, your lawyer?"

David smiled. "No, the girl I have a date with."

"Fine. Would you mind discussing a little business on a social occasion?"

"No. Not if it's football business. I heard Martelli tell you what I have to have."

"We'll discuss it. Don't be too difficult, David. I paid a lot of money for this lousy franchise. I stand to lose a lot in the operation. It's a hobby with me, not a business. It can only be my hobby long as I can afford it."

"Yes, sir. It's my business, not a hobby."

"We'll discuss it. Maybe I can come up with something."

"We'll be there."

"Seven o'clock. Martelli can tell you where."

Carter Wakeman lighted a cigar, beginning to talk through the opening puffs. "All right, you like this house. I'll tell you about it. I grew up on the near West Side of Detroit. Compared to us, Corktown was high society. I want to tell you, I got hungry. I don't mean for food." He waved his arm at the forty-foot living room. "I had the idea I'd end up in Grosse Pointe, in one of the big mansions on Lake Shore. So I take Bloomfield Hills. I mean, I don't know whether or not I settled for second best. But I didn't have any choice. There won't ever be any more Lake Shore Drives. The socialists made sure of
444

that. So I settle for a twenty-room house. It's pretty good. It gives me a pretty good feeling. I thought maybe I'd feel new-rich, but I don't. Or at least I don't feel any different than the other nigger-rich that live out here. And I belong to the best clubs. And go where Marge wants for the winters. And spit out a few jillion stampings a year in my plant. And I'm accepted. And I own the Detroit Lions, and all this goes a long way to getting rid of that hungriness I got on the West Side." Wakeman crossed his legs and pointed his cigar at David Battle. "There's a moral to this story, Davey. You got to plan for something like this a long way ahead. It doesn't just happen. Luck doesn't work that way. You got to be lucky, but you have to plan a long time ahead for when the luck comes. Now tell me about your plans, Davey."

David was caught off guard. It took him a moment to say, "I get the feeling I've been a grasshopper, not an ant."

"That's the trouble with you ballplayers. You've got the greatest opportunity in the world to use your ballplaying as a stepping stone into business. The pro ballplayer of the future is going to be half businessman. How long are you going to play ball?"

"Should I tell you?"

"I think you should."

"Probably just the two years of the no-cut contract I want."

"Well, I'm disappointed. You could play at least five or six more if you wanted."

"As an all-pro? I'm not so sure. Running backs don't last that long."

"Have you been hurt in the past, Davey? I mean, do you have a tendency?"

"No. I missed two games my sophomore year. I got clipped and it pulled a ligament in my ankle. I've never been hurt running with the ball, just on defense."

"You won't be playing both ways. This league's going into specialization."

"That would be good for the game. I like playing defense, but it takes a lot out of you, being in there all the time. A man could do better if he came off the bench, fresh. That's good."

"So you could play several more years."

"I've pretty much made up my mind, I want to quit
445

while I'm on top. And also get started somewhere when I'm not too old."

Marge Wakeman asked, "More coffee, Kelly?"

"Yes, ma'am, please."

"David?"

David put his hand over his cup. "No, ma'am, thank you."

Wakeman asked, "Cigar, Davey? I didn't think to ask you."

"No, sir, thank you."

"That's good. Can't destroy the image."

David's mouth tightened. "No, sir."

Wakeman didn't notice. He said, "I'll lure you, Davey. I'll bribe you."

"How's that, Mr. Wakeman?"

"That's what I've been leading up to. You've got to start your future right now, not wait until you're through with ball. How did you get along with Dipper Coogan?"

"I'd say good enough. Why?"

"I'm putting you on the spot. I know Coogan had his nose out of joint with you. But it's important to know just how it stood between you two."

"He never liked sharing the limelight. That never stopped him on the football field. He's a winner. Maybe the greatest winner. Connor will be good, but I'm sorry Coogan's gone."

"Did you hear it he quit when we wouldn't make him coach?"

"I heard that."

"I thought he was a great field leader, but too impatient to run things from the bench. Dipper's still a college kid, and you need that on the field, but not on the bench."

David smiled. "Hard to think of Dipper as a college Joe. You always think of him as the old pro from the year one."

Marge Wakeman said, "I like Dipper Coogan. Next to David Battle, he's my favorite ballplayer."

Kelly Brand said, "Mine, too. Next to David Battle."

Wakeman said, "He wasn't ready to quit, but it was the end of the line for him. I don't think he could have made the transition to the T, and I think there'd have been murder if we put him at halfback and somebody else at quarter."

David said, "You're right. Murder."

446

"Dipper's going to do all right in business. That's my guess. It won't be easy for him to change his ways, but that's my guess."

"Do you know what he's going to do?"

"I should. He'll be working for me. I didn't want him as a coach, but I sure can use him for the stamping plant."

David said, "I never figured he'd hang around Detroit. I thought he'd go back to Santa Barbara. Or maybe start out around the world and never stop."

"He can't afford it."

"His wife can."

Wakeman shook his head. "No wife. Divorced."

"I didn't know that. That surprises me. Why would she wait all this time, then divorce him?"

"She didn't. He divorced her. For infidelity. Ain't that something?"

The honest-to-God grin came on David's face. "*He* divorced *her* for infidelity!"

"How he got away with it, nobody will ever know. Or why he would throw all that away. That's sex for you. He's got a tomato he's living with in Birmingham, maybe she put the squeeze on him."

"A divorcée?"

"I don't think so. That must have been another one. This is a young one, maybe only nineteen."

"Money?"

"No. That's what I would have thought. Dipper had to go to work serious. Do you know King Smith?"

"I met him. He's a friend of Dipper's. A salesman."

"A manufacturers' representative."

Kelly asked, "What's that?"

Wakeman said, "He sells for more than one company. He provides the sales force for companies that for one reason or another don't have their own sales force."

Kelly asked guilelessly, "Is it a good business?"

"It can be. The top agents make just about as much as some of the biggest men in the auto companies. It can be a darn good business, if you get the right accounts."

Kelly said, "That might be a good field for you, David."

Marge Wakeman said, "Carter, you're keeping David in suspense."

Wakeman said, "You're right. On purpose. I told you, Davey, I want to bribe you. Did you know Dipper was King Smith's partner?"

"No. I knew he did some public relations work for him, just before the war. You know, he went to dinner with King and some of his customers and talked football, that kind of thing."

"Well, they're full partners now. That's because I gave Coogan and Smith the representation of Wakeman Metal Products with the condition they'd be partners. Would you like to know how good a deal that is?"

"Yes, sir."

"You probably don't know, most of our business has been in the appliance field. We sell to washing machine and refrigerator people, places like that. We do about seven million a year in the appliance field. I didn't think I wanted my auto business. But I got some, and it's pretty good business. That's the part I turned over to Dipper. Last year we did one million in car parts. I turned it over at a straight five per cent. That's fifty thousand dollars in cold cash."

David said, "That's a lot."

"I wanted to do the right thing by Coogan. But I was betting it would be a helluva deal for me, too. It's working out. This next year they're getting almost two million business. They get three per cent on everything over one million. That's eighty thousand for them, and I'm making a good profit on it. And I'm betting it's just the beginning. I bet in a few years they'll get eight, ten million dollars' business a year. They're good. That King Smith is good. Davey, they'll need more help. Can you guess what I've got in mind?"

David waited, not knowing whether or not to speak.

"I'd like you in with them. What do you say in Texas Kelly? You're my kind of folks. Do you think you'd get along with the Dipper?"

David said grimly, "With that much involved, the Little Dipper just might make sure he got along with the Big Dipper."

Wakeman smiled. "I'm not saying you'd be a partner. Just that you'd get in on the ground floor. Partner, that would come later, between you and Dipper and King. But you could start right away. Even during the season, you could do the dinner things you were talking about. That would be an asset to the business. And work full time when the season ends. Sound good?"

"Yes, sir. How much do you think they would pay?"

Wakeman smiled. "Ten thousand?"

"That sounds good."

"Davey, I need you to play ball. This franchise is going to cost me a bundle before I'm through. I need every customer we can get through those gates for the next few years. And you're my drawing card. Will you give me your word that you'll play at least four more years?"

David said quickly and clearly, "No, sir, I will not. I intend to quit on top. I'll promise to play two years, no longer."

There was a very long silence.

Carter Wakeman asked, "How about the contract?"

"I think what I asked is fair."

A cloud came over Wakeman's face. He said angrily, "Well, when I stand to lose more than a hundred thousand, why should I worry about a lousy seven thousand to get David Battle?"

"And the no-cut?"

"All right. All right. Just don't let anybody on the team find out about it, or we're all dead."

"Does the job offer still hold?"

Carter Wakeman stared at David Battle. Then he grinned. Finally he heaved a deep sigh. "You be as tough for me as you are for yourself, we'll all be rich."

"I'll be in camp tomorrow."

In September of 1945 David Battle began his final two years as all-pro halfback for the Detroit Lions. In the same month he went to work for King Smith and Dipper Coogan.

12

King Smith was a formidable, implacable man. He had traveled a hard, flashy route to respectability and business eminence. He was the hardest soft man in Detroit.

He cut his teeth selling used cars on Livernois, the used-car capital of the world. He wore herringbone suits. His shoes were pointed and polished. On his right hand he wore a two-carat diamond ring. He lied glibly. He had no conscience, no pity for the suckers. He was the archetype successful young car hustler. The razzle-dazzle, near-nefarious business suited him perfectly. In the Trenton streets and fields, down river, where he grew up, there were few holds barred. Livernois, with its stretchable rules, was but a sideward step, and he operated there with cocksureness and abandon. They knew him on Livernois. They admired him on Livernois. If there was any love on Livernois, they loved him on Livernois.

By the time he was thirty he was earning fifteen thousand dollars a year. He was independent and sought-after. He switched back and forth among the big lots on Used Car Row as the fancy suited him. With his huge income, he kept up with the flashy people, the fight buffs, the friends of baseball players, the men who looked for action. He liked show girls all the time, and sometimes, when the mood was on him, he liked honky-tonk girls and frequented

450

the kind of places frequented by Dipper Coogan. King Smith was a Detroit hot shot.

The day after his thirtieth birthday his landlady found him delirious in his bachelor apartment, and he was packed off to Receiving Hospital with a 106-degree temperature. The doctors never did diagnose his mysterious ailment. They ordered him sponged with alcohol and wrapped in ice, and the temperature left as suddenly as it had come. The fever left a remarkable legacy. Overnight, King's black hair turned snow-white. In the morning, looking at himself in the mirror, he was astounded by the drastic change in his appearance. He was not at all dismayed. He was pleased. Suddenly he was distinguished! His car-salesman's mind leaped to the possibilities here unfolded. A distinguished used-car salesman! It was a natural. King Smith grinned at himself. The grin looked, somehow, now honest and reassuring beneath the white hair. Now there'd be no more skeptics, no more wary shoppers looking at him out of the corners of their eyes to betray their distrust of a black-haired, fast-talking kid with a diamond ring. Suddenly the world was King Smith's oyster. Who wouldn't repose complete trust and faith in this distinguished-looking gentleman grinning back at him from the mirror! He blew on his diamond ring, polished it on his hospital nightshirt, and said aloud, "Livernois, you ain't seen nothing yet!"

But there was a further unexpected repercussion. In those first few weeks with his new white hair, he cut a hell of a swath through the gullible shoppers. His income soared. Singing Sam, his current employer, fearing to lose him, offered him a chance to buy into the lot. But he looked at Singing Sam with a sudden distaste. Sam was a man with brown baggy trousers and a toothpick in his mouth. In those few weeks King Smith had been treated with a respect he'd never known. The wand had been waved to transform him overnight from a car peddler to sales executive, and he savored the new regard. Now, suddenly, Singing Sam and used cars were beneath him.

In his new respectability, he married Kitty Corbin. In his new respectability, he took the only possible business step that could occur to him, and he became a new-car salesman. His white hair and his record of success started him high. Hugh Holiday made him sales manager of his Chevrolet agency. King put a hustle into his salesmen. He established quotas and rewards. He assigned demerits when prospective customers escaped the showroom. Hugh Holiday said, "The guy's a pistol." In little more than two years the agency advertised itself as the largest Chevy dealer in Michigan. King Smith was properly rewarded. But now his ambition leap-frogged to a decision to acquire his own General Motors agency. He lacked one essential ingredient. He lacked money, because money he spent as fast as he could make it.

He tried to interest people with money to back him. They were willing to associate with the distinguished young hot shot. They were also understandably adamant in requiring the lion's share for themselves, and they offered, instead of the senior partnership King demanded, opportunity for future participation based on success. King Smith was impatient. He wanted his own agency sooner than others would give it to him.

To supplement his income he answered a blind newspaper ad for a commission tool-and-die salesman with contacts. Contacts, schmontaks, King Smith could sell. Meyer Tool & Die gave him a trial and never regretted it.

King had no clear idea how to proceed. His direct mind leaped to one conclusion. If he was going to wear more than one business hat, he must be, above all, efficient. This meant making a sale on almost every call. That would require, in turn, instantaneous acceptance and friendliness from each new prospective customer. How get that?

He went to a Detroit Lions' practice session and waited until Dipper Coogan came off the field.

"Remember me, Dipper?"

Coogan looked him over. "You King Smith? What the hell happened to your hair?"

"Turned white."

"I can see that, you dumb bastard." He grinned. "Some pussy's old man scare it white?"

"I got a proposition for you, Dipper."

"Where you been, King? Haven't seen you around any of the places. Christ, it's been two years. Come around."

"I will."

"Stick around until I get dressed."

"I will. I've got a business proposition for you."

Dipper Coogan's expression changed. "I don't do business with guys I screw with."

"I'm starting a manufacturers' agency. To sell products to the automotive industry. I'm offering you a cut."

"And you want me to put up the money, right?"

"Wrong. I want you to put up your name. We don't need much money to start. Just some entertaining, and I'll put that up."

Dipper surveyed the distinguished-looking young man who had been his occasional boozing and raiding partner. He started to walk off. He turned back and said, "I'll see you after I get a shower. I'll listen."

That evening they formed Coogan & Smith. Dipper Coogan did it in a look-see, what-the-hell frame of mind. He made a few calls with King, talked to some customers through a few dinners. It was a revelation to Dipper. Particularly after ball games, the customers were enthusiastic at the opportunity to discuss the plays with the great man himself. They bought. Coogan & Smith filled Meyer Tool & Die to the bursting point. In the first six months their commissions were $12,000 and the Dipper took his one third and blew it in a wild week in Miami Beach. When he came back, thoroughly debilitated and thoroughly unchastened, he rasped in his high voice, "King, I got me this coo needs high life. You and me got some money-getting to do."

This was the pattern of the first year. In 1940 King took the second step and went after new, bigger principals. Frazer Products was pleased to be associated with Dipper Coogan, who in a fit of sobriety half promised his full effort. Frazer manufactured rotary shock absorbers for the gyp market. For three years they had battered against the entrenched automotive sources to no avail. The first year with Coogan & Smith, they were awarded ten per cent of the National Motors business, whereupon King Smith resigned as sales manager for Hugh Holiday. His die was cast. Though he did not completely abandon his ambition to acquire his own agency, he knew that he would be, first and foremost, a manufacturers' agent for the remainder of his business life.

Dipper Coogan and King Smith were as close as men could be. They were alike. They were both tough as nails. They were both shrewd, instinctive businessmen. When Dipper stopped carousing long enough to work, he accomplished wonders, and King Smith worked ceaselessly and most effectively and kept the business on the track.

453

Above all, they were both inherently honest men. Each trusted the other implicitly. The customers trusted both of them completely.

This was the ultimate business maturity of King Smith. He looked into the mirror and thought to himself: When I peddled cars, I lied about mileage and piston rings. They were normal lies, lies we called white lies. They were lies. There will be no more lies.

King was a hard man. He gave no quarter, he asked none. He took every legitimate advantage of his competitors, and when they realized what a threat he was, and tried to cut him up before he could get off the ground, he responded with deadly ferocity. When all went his way, he was gracious and charming. When he was crossed, he was vindictive, unrelenting and painstakingly patient in working his revenge. He became, quickly, controversial. There was no middle ground among the men who dealt with him. All of them admired him. Half of them liked him, and half of them hated his guts. He let none of this disturb him. Like him, hate him, he had his own objectives, and he achieved them. He achieved them without lies. The white-haired King Smith was an honorable man.

In 1940 Waycross Mills nearly went under in the last throes of the depression. In 1941 they came to Coogan & Smith. "Break us into the automotive fabrics business. We haven't needed it before, but we need it now."

King said, "With your name, I think we can do it. When people think home fabrics, they think Waycross. It still won't be easy. But if we're successful, you'll have a multi-million-dollar burden carrier, and you might even make some profit. We work on straight commission. We gamble. Our terms are a straight three per cent."

The president of Waycross said, "That's fair enough."

King warned him, "It sounds fair now, when you haven't got the business. When you're paying us a quarter million dollars a year, will you change your mind?"

Charles Cook said, "Mr. Smith, we've been in business seventy years. Waycross is an honorable company."

King said, "You've got that reputation."

Cook said, "You do, too, Mr. Smith."

In 1940 they bought, with loss prices, a small chunk of the Plymouth fabric business. Waycross performed well. King Smith, at the peak of his vigor, performed well. The war stopped their auto business cold.

King Smith sold tools and dies and machined-parts from 1942 until 1945. He made a considerable amount of money, a great deal of money, an astounding amount of money. After the war he built a 30,000-square-foot office building on James Couzens Highway and moved in, determined to fill it up with salesmen and purchase orders. He came back that year with a smashing eight-million-dollar fabric business for Waycross at Chrysler, GM and National Motors. The total billings of Coogan & Smith would reach a whopping fifteen million dollars. With twelve salesmen and engineers, with eight girls, they had suddenly become the largest manufacturers' agency.

Dipper Coogan said, "I've quit the Lions, King."

King Smith said levelly, "Good."

"Carter Wakeman's the new owner."

"I know."

"He won't make me coach. I quit."

"Then you're ready for full time here, right?"

"Wakeman says he'll give us his stamping account. Fifty thousand commissions go along with it."

"I think we'll take it."

"Wakeman's got a condition. He says I'm to be full partner."

"What did you say to him?"

"I didn't say anything. You got to tell me how to let him know it isn't in the cards."

"It's in the cards, Dipper."

Dipper Coogan rasped a great oath. Then he said, "I got to go to work. I need money."

"We're partners. I never intended anything else. Don't worry about deserving it. If nobody else knows it, I do. I wouldn't of got off the ground without your name."

Dipper Coogan stared at him. After a long while he said, "I'll take it. Do I have to come to work every day?"

King Smith said, "You call your own shots like always. When the time comes we have to worry how the other guy goes about getting his own job done, that's the time we have to worry about the partnership."

Dipper Coogan held out his hand. "If you ever figure I don't rate my share, that's good enough for me, you give me what I got coming. We don't need no paper, right?"

King Smith took the hand. "Right."

They hired Bill Robinson for the Wakeman account. They swiped him from Joe Blackwell's agency. Bill was thirty years old. He was a handsome, bright-faced young man with the David Battle air of complete honesty. He was intelligent, industrious and ambitious. He was an unsuccessful young man. In eight years he had held six jobs. For Joe Blackwell, he manned a desk in the office as a follow-up man on Joe's soft trim accounts. With Joe, he had no responsibility, no opportunity.

He said, "Mr. Smith, that's the best thing you're offering me. A chance for responsibility on an account. I can handle it."

"That's why we want you. You haven't mentioned salary."

"I know you'll be fair. You've got that reputation, Mr. Smith."

"Bill, you've got yourself a real chance here. The sky's the limit. You'll have every latitude. It's to our interest that you succeed. But it won't all be in the future, either. We start you at ten thousand and what you can steal from the expense account. You're on the Wakeman account one hundred per cent. Get into everything. Learn it all. It's going to prosper, and when it does, you will, too."

Bill Robinson said, "King, I just want you to know how much I appreciate it. You've got a lifelong friend."

David Battle came to work that same month.

Dipper said, "Heisman, we didn't have any choice."

King Smith said, "Don't let him put you on, Davey. We got all the choice in the world. We just let Wakeman think he's getting his own way."

David Battle said, "I'll do my best, I guess you know that."

King Smith said, "We know that. You always do."

But after two weeks Dipper Coogan said, "King, I been thinking, maybe we oughta have some kind of contract with our salesmen. I'm thinking about Robinson and Battle."

King asked, surprised, "What for? They know what they're getting and where they're supposed to work. What else is there?"

"I got a feeling."

"With Davey and Bill?"

"Well, I just got a feeling. We should get some agreement they can't work on any of our accounts for two years after they leave here."

456

"Come on, Dipper. You know Davey better than that. And I'll bet you couldn't find a loyaler, harder-working guy than Bill Robinson. Bill's so glad to get a chance like this, he'd never turn on us."

King Smith enfolded Bill Robinson to his bosom and nurtured a viper.

13

It unfolded like a detective story. It began in the well-deserved misfortunes of Trent Jones.

Trent Jones, Senior, ended his distinguished automotive career as Vice-President Engineering at National Motors. There was no more respected man in Detroit and Bloomfield Hills. He worked with the best, belonged to the best clubs with the best, and bore up with the rottenest son of all of them.

The son learned about soft trim in the body engineering department of National Motors, where his father had installed him, complete with new title, "Fabric and Color Coordinator." He learned about venality second-hand and inaccurately in the rumor mills of the automotive giant.

Trent considered himself a natural-born big frog. He had no patience for normal progress through the Corporation. He gorged himself on the scuttlebutt speculations on the grand incomes of the big soft-trim agents like King Smith and James G. Blaine, and he took particular note of the deep suspicions in the Engineering Department that these unscrupulous men were selling their goods to buyers who could be bought. That appealed to young Trent. He wanted in, at the top. He could be as crooked as anybody, if he just got the chance. When he resigned

458

from National Motors and went to Blaine with his father's name on his lips, it was with every intention of carving a chunk out of the golden hide of this second biggest, second roughest, toughest agent in Detroit.

The carpet company was Belmont Mills in Belmont Heights, Pennsylvania. It was a rich, tempting target. It grossed for Blaine more than one hundred thousand dollars a year. Blaine assigned young Trent to the account as leg man and general factotum. Blaine had only himself to blame. It had required the highest order of rationalization to take on the young man who had a reputation for general undesirability. Blaine had, of course, hired the son to get the father.

Trent jumped in with all four feet. He was zealous, he was enthusiastic, he was capable, he was ingratiating. He brought himself favorably to the attention of the Belmont personnel on his frequent trips East to the mill. His master plan might have succeeded, if the impatience hadn't gotten to him again.

After a bare six months, Charles Belmont, the president of Belmont Mills, phoned Jim Blaine and said, "Your boy Jones just marched into my office, announced that you're sitting on your fanny while he's doing all the work, guarantees me that his father will give us more business than ever, and he's offered to take the account for half commission."

When Trent Jones presented himself, unabashed, to his boss, Blaine said coldly, "You're fired. You got ten minutes to get your stuff and get out."

Then, with thoroughly aroused malice, Blaine told the industry what the sonofabitch had tried to pull. He could have spared himself that effort. No one in Detroit was more than mildly curious about such larceny. So there were crooks in business? So what?

Quite unrepentant, Trent Jones betook himself to his father's practical solace. The Trent Jones Company, Sales & Consulting Engineers came into being. The father found accounts for his son to represent. While Trent Senior was active, his friends and associates forgave him for steering business to his son. Trent Junior, through his father's efforts, became a well-to-do slob. When the father retired, the son's manufacturers' agency fell swiftly into deep trouble. The wolves tore at him. He lost his big engineering design source. He lost his big prototype shop.

He was beleaguered, nearly desperate. He was left with only Buckeye Stamping, and Blaine still pursued him relentlessly.

Blaine said to the Chrysler purchasing agent, "Buckeye is shipping junk to Long Beach and Newark. Jones told them they could get away with it at the remote assembly plants."

Quince asked mildly, "How do you know all that?"

"First-hand. I just know. We let Buckeye know that Jones is getting them in trouble."

"That was friendly of you. Where do I get the impression you're still after his hide?"

"You know damn well I am. If I can, I'll run his ass right out of this business."

"Jones says you're shipping rejects. I got to admit, it's the first time I ever heard competitors knocking the other guy."

Blaine snorted. He said, "Jones is a liar. He's a goddam liar." He teed his ball on the fourth hole at Orchard Lake Country Club, the second of his three golf clubs. While he waggled his driver, he said, "Did you ever try to get Jones to look you in the eye? He even walks sideways. Every time he gets near me, I get the feeling he's going to try to sell me a hot diamond. You can't trust him any further than you can throw a grand piano." He lashed into his fast backswing, grunted and lunged and smashed the ball two hundred and thirty yards down the right side of the fairway. Before he finished his follow-through, he was saying, "He's a no-good, sneaking pipsqueak. Nobody ever could trust the crawling sonofabitch."

As they walked down the fairway, the purchasing agent said, "Then he'll survive in this business. He seems to have all the necessary ingredients."

"You better take it serious, Arn."

Quince asked with some frost, "Why? As far as I'm concerned, I'm buying from good sources. Nothing cools me off faster than a man knocking a competitor."

"I'll tell you why. Jones is the one spread the rumor I was buying my business from you. If you want proof, I've got the witnesses."

They played out the fourth hole. They walked slowly, past the seventh tee and the sixth green, the long hundred yards to the fifth tee, with no one ahead or behind on Tuesday afternoon.

At the tee, Quince said, "I'm on vacation."

"Okay, I've had my say."

"I was just thinking I might go off vacation long enough to make one phone call. To Quality Control and get them checking Long Beach and Newark."

"Good! And I don't want the business, I just want Jones. Give the business to King Smith or Joe Blackwell."

Quince said sharply, "I'll decide who gets business, and when, and where, and why."

But Jim Blaine was satisfied. He'd driven Trent Jones from another pillar to another post. The Buckeye account couldn't survive this blow.

14

TRENT JONES suspected that he was held in low regard. He didn't know for sure. After all, he did have all those years of acceptance as the son of a mighty man of National Motors. After all, he had been a junior member, then a senior member at Bloomfield Hills Country Club for years before James G. Blaine and King Smith even dared make application. He had grown up with other junior members, who inevitably accepted him as a fixture. After all, his wife was the daughter of a senior vice-president of the National Bank of Detroit. She was a Junior Leaguer. Everyone who was anyone liked her. She belonged. And he belonged. He *did* belong. No one could deny that. He belonged by inheritance, he belonged by tenure, he belonged by his wife, and he belonged by virtue of the inability of the young men and women in the group to discern either faults or virtues in those they had known all their lives. His belonging was his source of ultimate comfort when new people saw him for what he was.

And he was tough. Nobody could deny that. He could make his way in the jungle. All right, his father had helped him and now could no longer help. The son had made one abortive effort to claw his own way. From now on, it was no-holds-barred. He needed accounts. He would get accounts. From now on he was smart. The cold-turkey approach to Belmont Mills had failed. Obviously you had to work from the inside. If you wanted to steal the Waycross Mills from King Smith, you got next to somebody and gave them a stake in your success.

Waycross it would be. Did you approach the division manager or sales manager and offer to cut him in? For a few thousand dollars, somebody might just see things your way. But if you picked the wrong guy, you'd be on your ass again, and you might even be in law trouble for bribery. How do you know when you have a man you can approach? Who do I know at Waycross or King Smith's, that's the question. He knew Bill Robinson, that's who he knew.

The second link in the detective story was forged.

Bill Robinson said, "I've only been with King less than two years, if that's what you have in mind."

"Would you leave for the right figure?"

At the Fox and Hounds bar, Bill said, worldly-wise, "Everybody's got his price. It would have to be a good one. I'm doing good with Dipper and King."

For an hour Trent Jones fed Bill Robinson martinis and listened to him brag about his employers, about the job he was doing on the Wakeman account, and about his bright future.

Trent said, "Everybody knows that. And everybody in town knows you're the one doing all the work."

Bill couldn't hide his pleasure. He said brightly, "I've taken over everything except Purchasing. I haven't negotiated any purchase orders yet."

"You could. That's the easiest part."

"I guess I could. I've met all the buyers."

"Too bad you're not getting the loot to go along with the work."

"Are you making me an offer? Don't fence. If you've got a good price, I'll at least listen. I don't want to get the reputation as a jumper."

"This is your sixth job in seven years, and now you're worried? I'm just kidding. I'm going places, Bill. I'm young, like you. I'm going to need a partner. Give me a couple weeks. I might have something to talk to you about."

Robinson went home and told his wife about the partnership offer. He portrayed it as a firm proposal.

She asked, "How much money?"

"I'd guess it would be splitting maybe fifty thousand or more, when we got going."

"I thought you said Trent Jones was no good."

"Well, King doesn't like him. That's because King and Jim Blaine stick together. I've got nothing against Trent."

"I'd sure listen, Bill, to what he has to offer."

Robinson took Thursday afternoon off to play golf with Jones at Bloomfield Hills.

"King going to buy you a country club membership?"

"He says we'll talk about it at the end of the second year."

"You're too good a golfer not to get to play. The way I figure it, a guy's got to have his own membership to do the job right in this business."

"Let's get down to it. What's with this partnership?"

"I've got room for you."

"On what basis?"

"If you're worth it, a full partnership. You'd have to contribute."

"Well, I'd figure to contribute. You're not just about to give away the store."

"You'd have to contribute something special, Bill. Like an account."

The light dawned slowly, and then Bill Robinson realized he'd known all along it would be this. "I bring in the Wakeman account, right?"

"No, the Waycross account. I'm best at soft-trim. You do that, you're a partner."

"Now just how the hell do you think I could do that? I haven't got a damn thing to do with Waycross. Besides, Dipper and King would make mincemeat out of me if I tried it. Besides, I owe King."

"Like hell you do. He's screwing you every day, and you know it."

"Supposing I could find a way to do it, why wouldn't I just take it myself? Who is it that has to worry about making a contribution?"

"Both of us. My plan calls for both of us to work on it."

"Well, I don't think I want to talk about it right now."

"You don't have to commit yourself. We've got plenty

464

of thinking to do before we move. Have you ever been to Bloomfield on Saturday night?"

"I've never been here any night. This is the first time I've been on this golf course."

"There's a formal dance this Saturday. Let's take it in. I'd like you and Cora to meet some of the young members."

The pattern of bribery was so obvious that Bill found it difficult to shut his eyes to it. But the Robinsons broke a date with ordinary friends to accept the invitation to Bloomfield Hills Country Club, and Cora Robinson asked her husband, "If you join up with Trent, do you get a membership here?"

"No, they couldn't get me in here. But he'll get me in Oakland Hills, or Plum Hollow, or Birmingham."

"Birmingham, that's the one. I can duck over with the kids during the day."

"Cora, this thing isn't all that simple."

"It sounds simple to me."

"I'm not just thinking about how hard it will be to do. I don't know if it's the right thing."

"You're in business, aren't you? That's how business is, dog eat dog. It's not like it was illegal, that would be something else. But to fight to get somebody's account, that goes on every day."

"I guess so."

"You've got your family to think about, before you think about King Smith. Do you think he'd think about you for one minute if you got in his way? You bet your sweet life he wouldn't. They got one thing in mind, Dipper to drink it up, and King to live it up, while you do the work for them, and you know it."

At this moment Bill Robinson felt the knot of degradation tying itself irrevocably inside him. From this moment on, there would be only rationalization of his actions as he joined Trent Jones to cuckold King Smith. He was grateful to his wife for giving him the strength, and he hated her for helping him succumb to his greed.

Bill Robinson said to Trent, "Supposing we agree to do it, it can't be Waycross. King's too solid. He's taken them from zero to ten million dollars. I haven't got any contact at Waycross. I asked if I could get some soft-trim experience and do some work on the account, and Dipper said I had my hands full with Wakeman. So it's got to be Wakeman. That's the one we have a chance at."

Trent Jones said, "I'll take your judgment." He looked over Bill's left shoulder, then over the right shoulder, never in the eyes. "Is Wakeman big enough? Tell me the story."

"We'd have all the money we need, even at a cut-rate commission. As for the facilities, they're outstanding. The main plant is up at Green Arbor, non-union. The die shop and Carter Wakeman's offices are here in Detroit. What do you want to know?"

"The people. Are you in good with them?"

"Yes. So is King."

"All right, the first job, you start spreading the word with the Wakeman people that things aren't right."

Bill said, "Things *are* right on the account. That's the problem. They've never been better."

"Are they? Seems to me King and Dipper aren't paying much attention to it. That's the way it looks to me, with you doing all the work. Dipper whoring it up all the time. King spending all his time on the Waycross account, the one that's important to him. And the other thing, word of dissension might get back to Wakeman. Oh, and there might be some sabotage on the account, only nobody would ever find out about that. But not so much it would hurt the account permanently."

"Dipper's working. Not all the time, but he's working pretty good. And King's in there pitching all the time."

Trent said sharply, "You don't get the message, do you?"

"Sure, I get the message. I'm just telling you it won't be easy. And if we get by Coogan and Smith, we still have to get by Davey Battle."

Trent asked surprised, "How's that?"

"He's working on the account. I've got Chrysler and General Motors, he's got Ford and National Motors."

"He's actually working on it?"

"Damn hard. And he stands in good with Carter Wakeman. Boy, I'll tell you, just how the hell we figure we can get the owner of the Detroit Lions to take an account away from Coogan and Battle and give it to us . . ."

Trent puffed his cigar, rolled it in his mouth. "I always figured when you got over being nervous, you were well on your way to stealing. That's just the easy part. The hard part is when the thing you want to steal don't just get up and walk to you." He said with decision, "You're

466

right. We can't get Wakeman. Back to Waycross. Let's figure out something on that one."

They explored the possibilities. They could come to no sound conclusions. Bill Robinson went back to work for King Smith with renewed determination to do a good job for his employer. Trent Jones went to his office and read a letter from Buckeye announcing the effectiveness of their termination of contract. They were at a dead end.

Then two things happened. Wakeman hired Stub Cook, a dissatisfied assistant chief body engineer of National Motors, to be their new automotive manager. Trent Jones had worked with Stub Cook and exchanged rumors and gripes. That was the third link in the chain.

The following day Carter Wakeman was rushed to St. Joseph's hospital with a drastic stroke. Within a week it was made known that he would not return to work for at least six months, if then. The major obstacle was removed. The fourth link in the chain made possible the climax of the detective story.

15

A SYNDICATE of Detroit businessmen bought the Detroit Lions from Carter Wakeman. The new general manager said, "Davey, we'll do anything reasonable to keep you playing. What do you want?"

"I've committed myself. I'm hanging them up."

"Thirty thousand?" David didn't answer. "You're used to the money, Davey. You've got a rude awakening coming when you try living on your business income."

"Dipper's paying me fifteen and bonus. I'll get by fine."

"You aren't making sense. You could have that and our thirty."

"And I made all-pro this year because the writers have got in the habit. So I'm from now on a full-time businessman."

David went directly to the apartment in which he kept Kelly Brand. He said, "Honey, you're looking at an ex-football player. I wasn't sure I could do it, but it's done."

She said gravely, "Nobody but me left to tackle."

He stretched out on the living-room couch, his head on the arm. "Kelly Brand?"

"Want to eat here, or go out?"

"I want to talk to you. I'm now one hundred per cent respectable."

"Bully."

"Do you think I'm respectable enough that I should now make an honest woman out of you?"

"No."

He sat up. "Kelly?"

"What, David?"

"I'm in a marrying mood."

"I wish I could accommodate you."

"I'll get somebody else."

"Will you?"

"No."

"That's good." She came and sat on the couch with him. He pushed her down and lay alongside her. She asked in his ear, "Don't you like it this way, David?"

"No, I don't. I can't afford three apartments any more. I've got to move in with Mama, if you won't let me in here."

"Then you'll just have to get a raise. I don't want to get married. I like my love affair. I don't want it to change, ever."

"It's dumb."

"Be nice, David." She kissed his cheek.

He said gruffly, "I'll be nice. But I'm warning you, if I ever meet a girl as sexy as you that will marry me, you've had it."

"There is no such girl."

"No, there is no such girl."

David said to King Smith, "Now that I'm full time, should we discuss salary?"

King Smith said, "Which would you rather get paid, what we're paying you, or what you're worth?"

David said, "What you're paying me, thanks just the same."

Bill Robinson said to Trent Jones, "We've got the opening. Stub Cook's already on the outs with King. He's pissed off because King won't roll out the red carpet for him like he always did for Culligan, when Culligan had the division." He grinned. "I don't blame King. Stub's a bore. And he's incompetent. No wonder he wasn't going any further at the Corporation. If we get that account, that's the next thing to work on, getting Cook out of there before he ruins the company."

"He'd like to do King in?"

"And it burns him up to see Dipper and King getting all that money, when he's just on salary. He's coming down from Green Arbor tomorrow. He's going to close Wakeman's Detroit office to save money."

Trent said, "We got to be careful. We get him to thinking along the lines we want, he might go all the way and go direct on sales, and nobody will have the account."

"That's where Davey comes in."

"Why Davey?"

"Stub thinks he's the greatest thing on wheels. We got to get Davey in on this."

"That's too bad. That means a three-way split. If it has to be, it has to be. At least until we get rolling."

Bill Robinson said, "Trent, I want a contract between you and me about this account. Iron-clad. No small print."

"It would be incriminating."

"That's too bad. I want it."

Trent said, "Sure, Bill, whatever you say."

Bill Robinson went to King Smith and said, "Can I talk to you about something?"

"What's on your mind, Bill?"

"Well, I'm thinking about money."

King said slowly, "Well, it seems like you're getting quite a bit. You don't think it's enough, Bill?"

"I don't want to say it isn't fair, but I'm sure having a helluva time getting by from month to month."

"What did you do before you came here, when you were making half what you're getting now?"

"We were using some of the money Cora's mother left her. It's gone."

"Bill, you've had a raise every six months. You've got a helluva future here. And you're doing a helluva job. When you've contributed as much as Dipper and me, we can talk about arrangements. You ought to be a little patient."

"Those are mighty big checks coming in from Wakeman every month."

King lit a cigarette to calm his rising anger. "Bill, I've got nothing to hide from you. I don't recall inviting you to see the checks, but that's not important. If you'd like, you're welcome to look at the books from the beginning and see just how well we've made out on the Wakeman account. It would surprise you. There's more expense than you think. Why don't you total it up for yourself? You'll have a better perspective."

"King, I guess I better tell you what's on my mind. I wouldn't do it, except my first loyalty is to myself and then to you. Davey isn't pulling his weight."

"What makes you say that?"

"The customers say things to me they wouldn't say to you. Most of them don't go for that ballplayer jazz, that big-hero jazz. You could save yourself a lot of money there. That way there'd be more for the rest of us."

This bothered King. Was it true? It could be. David Battle could be glamorous dead weight. But then he shook his head resolutely. "His accounts are in good shape. And anyway, I made him a two-year deal, and a deal's a deal. I think you're underestimating his contribution. And maybe overestimating your own."

Bill Robinson's face was blank. He could take such a remark with equanimity. He was no longer the naïve desk clerk from Joe Blackwell's agency. He was a wheeler-dealer, spreader of discontent, accomplished subversive. He was covering himself from every angle, playing every end toward the middle. No matter how this turned out, Bill Robinson was going to prosper.

King wanted to satisfy the crackerjack young salesman. "I'll tell you what, Bill. I'll talk to Dipper and see if he'll go along with a car for you. Will that help? That's a hundred a month tax-free."

"Sure," Bill Robinson said, "that will help a lot. I appreciate it, King. I don't want you to get the idea I don't still appreciate the opportunity here. I've learned a heckuva lot."

He went to his own office, walking on air. His campaign was proceeding nicely.

King was delighted when Robinson offered to take Stub Cook off his hands. "Take him out to dinner. Blow him to a good time, if that's possible. Don't skimp."

But Robinson took Stub home to dinner and made him feel part of the family. His wife and children made a fuss over Uncle Stub. In the kitchen, Cora Robinson said to her husband, "God, he's a bore!"

471

Bill said urgently, "Don't you forget for a moment, he's going to bore us right into that account."

She said impatiently, "Don't worry, I'll do the job. Thank God, at least he's not a fanny-patter."

Bill slapped his wife's bottom. "Get the kids to bed and I'll get old Stub drunker, and you can come back and take over laughing at his jokes."

When the time was appropriate, Bill said, "Stub, Wakeman is sure a great account. It's been a great chance for me to handle the business from start to finish."

"How do you mean, Bill?"

Bill displayed surprise. "I thought you knew. I didn't mean to say anything out of school."

"Knew what?"

"Wakeman is my account. Dipper and King assigned it to me. They turned everything over to me."

"Don't they work on it?"

Bill said with clear loyalty, "They do the important entertaining. You know, the vice-presidents and that kind of thing. The purchase orders and the day-to-day stuff, the business, that's my end of it. They do the golf and football entertaining at the highest level, that kind of thing."

Stub Cook said morosely, "So some bastard from the Glass Tower can pick up the phone and tell Engineering what's what. Well, we always fixed the bastards that had that done."

Bill said, "I'm with you. I like straightforward business. Sometimes I think King goes overboard with the big shots. I guess that's just a difference in sales philosophy." He smiled. "They've sure got it made. I sure wish I could get in as much golf as they do."

"How often do they play?"

Bill said diffidently, "Well, I sure don't keep track of what my bosses do. Both of them belong to both Bloomfield Hills and Orchard Lake. I guess maybe they get in four rounds a week. I know it's sometimes not easy to get a hold of them when there's a fire to put out."

"Do they play with the guys on the firing line, or with the big shots?"

"I'd have to say with big shots. They both like to play Bloomfield, and you can't take a buyer there. I mean, with the bosses playing, a guy down the line can't relax. Far as I know, guests are discouraged at Bloomfield, anyhow. You're not supposed to do any business out there. A salesman, he's wasting his time playing there. I think maybe I ought to belong to Oakland Hills, then I could entertain the guys that count. But that's just my opinion. King told me he was sorry he couldn't get together with you tonight, I forgot to tell you. He had an important date."

"Who with?"

"I think Vanderhoven. He's Vice-President Forward Planning at Ford."

"What's that got to do with Wakeman business?"

"Well, nothing. But you can't ever tell, he might come in handy some day, that's the way King figures it with the big shots. Face it, he hasn't got much time for the working guys like you and me."

"Will I see him on this trip? Do you think he'll be able to spare some time?"

"I don't know, Stub. He told me to take care of you. It's not like when Culligan was running the division. I mean, King usually had time then. I guess he's busier now."

Stub Cook said, "I guess."

"King knows he's a fixture at Wakeman. Even with Carter Wakeman out of the picture. When's he coming back to work?"

"Maybe he won't. Until he does, I'm running the show."

"I must admit, King figures he's boss with Wakeman sick."

King Smith, at home, had no date with Vanderhoven. He sat puzzling over the morning's conversation with his employee. He asked his wife, "Do you know anything I've done to Bill Robinson?"

"What could you have done to him?"

"I don't know. But he's acting sort of peculiar. Like maybe I did something to him."

"As much as you've done for him? I wouldn't worry about it. He's probably got something on his mind. Bill's a good guy, and he sure likes you."

"I've seen other guys brown-nose the boss. I wonder if you know it when it's you being brown-nosed."

"Bill's not that type. I can tell when a guy's a phony. And why wouldn't he like you, and no apple-polishing connected?"

In the morning Bill called King at home and said, "I'll take Stub off your hands today. I'll get him over to Ford

473

and see the production line. That'll keep him occupied for a while."

"Would the two of you like to meet me for lunch?"

"If you want to. But I don't think it makes much difference to Stub. You know him. So why don't you just get some things done and let me worry about him."

King said, "I talked to Dipper about the car. He says for you to go ahead and pick out what you want. Within reason."

"Boy, King, I sure appreciate that."

"Stay with it, Bill. Dipper and me both know what a good job you're doing. It will be worth your while."

Bill Robinson said to Stub Cook, "I suggested to King we have lunch today, but he had to beg off. Would you like to get together with him this evening? I'm sure he will, if it's important."

"I wouldn't put him to the trouble."

"Well, okay. Stub, next time you come to town, stay with us. You sure made a hit with the kids. All they talked about this morning was Uncle Stub."

Stub Cook glowed.

Bill Robinson smiled warmly at him and said silently, "Oh, you jerk, you farmer, you'd swallow anything!"

Robinson requested permission to make a plant trip to follow up on production problems. King Smith made an offer that was most welcome. "Take Cora. She'll enjoy a couple days in the country."

"She sure will. You mean take her on the expense account?"

"Sure. Good business relations. You're getting on pretty well with Stub, from the looks of things."

"Well, I talk his language."

"I get the feeling his nose is maybe a little out of joint. Maybe I'd better spend some time with him next time he comes in."

"Hell, King, he couldn't care less. He knows you've got nothing in common. He said he prefers it out at the house, you know, with the kids. I'll take care of him. King, I think I better tell you this. Stub and some of the other people at the plant don't think too much of Davey. They wonder if you're getting your money's worth out of him."

King's temper edged. "I think I'll be the judge of that. I've thought about what you said before. You did under-

474

estimate him. I think I better have a talk with Cook."

"As a matter of fact, you won't have to, I set him straight." Bill smiled. "King, the negotiations coming up, do you think I could get in on some of them?"

"I don't know why not." He leaned back in his chair. "As far as I'm concerned, the more you know about the account, the better."

Bill smiled. "Not worried about me doing a good job?"

"It's to our credit if you do a good job. We picked you out, didn't we?"

Bill said soberly, "Yes. I make sure you get the credit."

"That's not necessary. It will come automatically."

"Well, I just want you to know I appreciate how much you've done for me."

King said to Dipper, "Maybe we should get Bill into some of the contract negotiations."

Dipper Coogan shook his head. "He ain't ready. He's got blind spots. He don't understand the whole picture. He's got some cronies in Engineering and Styling and Production Control, and I get the impression he figures that's the whole show. Some of the buyers, I get the feeling they don't want to do any business with him. He's still wet behind the ears."

"What about Davey?"

"What about him?"

"Are you satisfied with the job he's doing?"

"I'm satisfied. But I don't feel right about those guys. King, I used to know when we were getting a weak spot, even before it got there."

"Well, what do you want me to do? Make a big issue of a contract after all this time?"

"No, I guess we can't do that."

King called Bill Robinson in. "We want to give you more responsibility on the account. But do some more preparation for it. Spend some more time with Purchasing. And with some of the engineers you don't know, not just with your buddies."

Bill said earnestly, "I think I get along with the people that count. I think maybe you and Dipper concentrate too much on the big shots."

King said, surprised, "That's twisting off the subject. I'm talking about you spending more time with more

475

working guys. In the second place, as far as I'm concerned, everybody at every level is a big shot."

"Seems to me you spend a lot of time with the vice-presidents."

"Are you being critical, or asking for advice?"

"Advice."

"It doesn't hurt to know vice-presidents." King grinned. "They class up your set of friends." The grin left. "Bill, the big shots are like a fleet in being. Sometimes you'll really need help. Sometimes you'll be right, but some jerk will say you're wrong, and you'll have to appeal it to the high court. I admit, I like being with the top men. Outside of the business implications, usually you like a big shot for the very qualities that made him a big shot in the first place. You like a man like Jim Parker or Cleary, even when they're still just on the way up. I enjoy being with them. As for advice, this is it, you have to treat everybody the same, because the next gang of big shots is coming right out of the working level. I don't think either Dipper or me is remiss in that."

Bill Robinson said, "As usual, you're right." He was satisfied. Now he knew King's answers, if King should be confronted by Stub Cook. Bill would make sure he primed Stub with answers to the answers. He took his wife to Green Arbor to work further on the doing-in of his employer.

16

Deke Harbert, a body engineer from National Motors, was well qualified to play a role in the conspiracy. First, he knew Trent Jones well and still did not dislike him. Second, he was venal.

Trent said, "Deke, I'm going to tell you something. If you ever let the cat out of the bag, I'll kill you."

"You know me better than that, Trent."

"I may get the Wakeman account away from Coogan & Smith."

Harbert whistled.

"It's not set yet. I'm still working on it."

"Does King know about it?"

"Hell, no."

"How about Davey Battle?"

"No, he doesn't know, either. What's your feeling about Battle?"

"Good guy. He works hard."

"Well, when the switch is made, we'll probably want Battle to come with us."

"That's smart. He sits pretty good with some of our brass. Jim Parker practically sponsors him. Who else is with you in it?"

"Bill Robinson, Davey makes three, and we'll need a fourth. Somebody who knows automotive stampings."

"You asking?"

"Interested?"

"Yes."

"It would be a good deal."

"I'm interested."

"Good. We'll keep you posted. There's one thing we might call on you for. You know Stub Cook, he's got the Automotive Division of Wakeman."

"I know. I know Stub. We get on pretty good."

"He'll be down to do some checking. He may want to prove something to somebody else from Wakeman to back himself up. Like prove that Smith and Coogan don't get along very well in National Motors Body Engineering."

Deke Harbert said blandly, "Then I'll just tell the truth. That should help us a lot."

Bill Robinson sat down with Stub Cook and Herman Worth, the treasurer of Wakeman Metal Products. "I might as well tell you, I'm going to quit Coogan & Smith."

Stub said, "I'm not surprised."

"I can't go their route any more. I guess you know how I feel, Stub. I'm doing all the work, and they're making the money. And I guess you know, we disagree on sales policy, too."

Stub Cook, the ex-engineer, said to Worth, "King concentrates on the big shots and on Purchasing. There's nothing that used to burn me up more than that."

Bill said, "It's catching up with him. The engineers are ready to do him in."

Stub said, "They can do it, too. They'll fix his clock for him."

"So I'm quitting, while the quitting's good."

Herman Worth asked, "Where are you going, Bill? I'm sorry to hear this."

"I've got a couple of good offers."

"I think we ought to tell him, Stub. Don't jump too quick, Bill. We've got something in mind. Do you think we should level with him, Stub?"

Stub said, "Frankly, Bill, we've been thinking about taking the account away from King."

Bill's heart leaped. He said earnestly, "Well, I hate to see it happen to King, but I guess he deserves it. Where will you put it?"

"I'm thinking of going direct."

Bill's heart sank.

Stub continued, "If I go direct, I was thinking of you and Davey staying on."

Bill was now again most hopeful. "Run the Detroit office for you?" That could be better than his deal with Trent Jones.

"Frankly, Bill, I think we would put Davey in charge, because of his name. But there would be a substantial raise in it for you."

The loyalty to Trent Jones returned in a hurry. "I think that would be a mistake. I don't think you should go direct at this time. The competition is getting tougher all the time, and you need the best sales you can get. That usually means a manufacturers' agent."

"Well, that could be."

The treasurer said, "On the other hand, we can save a considerable amount of money."

Bill said, "I think you could anyway. A new agent, taking the account intact, he could afford to cut his commission. I mean, he wouldn't have the start-up expense. It doesn't make any difference to me, I'm leaving anyway, but if you don't have anybody in mind, I'll suggest Trent Jones."

Worth asked, "Why him?"

"Because he's an eager young guy with all the contacts in the world. I know him and I'd recommend him, that's all. He is hungry, I'll vouch for that."

Stub asked, "Are you involved in this with Trent, Bill?"

Bill Robinson said forthrightly, "No, I am not. Not under any circumstances. Wakeman's been good to me, and I'm just offering my best recommendation. I'm sure you can scout up another agent just as good as Trent."

Stub said, "I always liked Jones. I'm not sure he stands as well with some other people as he does with me."

Bill said carelessly, "Then if I were you, I'd do some checking, put it to some people at the auto companies, who stands best, King Smith or Trent Jones. In any event, I'd talk to the customers before I made any move."

Herman Worth said, "Bill, will you do one more thing for us? Set up an appointment for Stub and me with Jones, and also, on the same trip, set us up to see some people in Engineering and Purchasing so we can be sure of our ground here."

Herman Worth and Stub Cook closeted themselves with Deke Harbert, the engineer who looked forward to associating with Jones and Robinson, and they were given an earful. By the time the unbiased report was concluded, there was no doubt in Worth's mind that Coogan & Smith had the worst possible relations and reputation with National Motors Engineering.

Bill Robinson then drove them to Chrysler Purchasing to see Quince, the man selected after exhaustive study of the possibilities. Quince had one characteristic that suited the purpose. He was noncommittal.

Herman Worth, speaking for Wakeman, said, "I have just one question, Mr. Quince. If we were to change our representation, how would that affect us here at Chrysler?"

Quince lit a cigarette. "Not satisfied with Coogan & Smith?"

"We're contemplating a change."

"Care to tell me to whom? Direct sales?"

"We're not at liberty to say quite yet, Mr. Quince. You'll be the first to be notified."

"What are you asking me? Does King Smith have an in with me? Will I crucify you if you let him go?"

Herman Worth shifted uncomfortably. This was exactly the question he had asked.

Quince said, "Don't come to me with your problems, Mr. Worth. As far as I'm concerned, your representatives have done a good job for you. You have a lot of business, and they handle it well. It's not my prerogative to go further than that. We do business with the principal, not the representatives. You've been judged on your merits in the past, and I'm sure you will be in the future, no matter who's selling for you. Does that answer your question?"

"Yes, sir, it does. I hope this wasn't an improper call."

"Not at all, Mr. Worth. I'm sure Stub knows all the proprieties of this business."

Stub said, "I just wanted to reassure myself. And I wanted Herman to form his own opinion. Thanks, Arn."

Quince said in his flat voice, "You're welcome."

In the lobby, Bill Robinson betrayed some anxiety as he asked, "How did it go?"

Herman Worth said, "If you ask me, Quince didn't like it."

Stub said, "Well, nobody can say we didn't play fair

480

with King. We chose a Purchasing man who was in his corner, and you notice he didn't go down the line for him at all. My reaction to it is that one of King's good friends just said it didn't make any difference to him which way we went. That satisfies me."

Herman Worth said, "On that basis, I'm satisfied, too, Stub. I'll vote with you."

Bill Robinson said, "Well, I'll stay on until you make the change. But I've already accepted the other offer."

King Smith seated himself in front of Stub Cook in the Green Arbor office. Stub said abruptly, "King, I'm going to come right out and say it. We're taking the account away from you. We'll live up to the cancellation clause in the contract."

King Smith was utterly devastated. His mind went flying off in a dozen directions, searching for reason and possibility. With a calm face hiding his turmoil, he said, "I expect there's going to be some explanation."

Cook wouldn't look him in the eye. He said, "King, first of all, we want to assure you that this is a straightforward business decision. It is nothing personal against you, or Dipper either, of course. We have always had the greatest respect for you, and we still have it. But some reports have come to our attention, and we've investigated and have decided to make this move."

"Just what kind of reports?"

"That you have been neglecting the account."

"Neglecting the account!"

"That you have been spending too much time on the golf course and other activities, and not enough time for us."

"Just where did you get these reports?"

"They came from your own man. They came from Bill."

A whirlpool sucked at King. "Bill Robinson said this to you? Why would he do that? It isn't true."

"Believe me, we took into account that he might be bucking for the account. Personally, I don't have much respect for a man who would do this to his boss. But that's neither here nor there, the point is, he told us what was going on, and we checked his story, and your customers have confirmed it for us."

"What customers confirmed the story?"

Cook said uneasily, "We got corroboration." How could he tell King Smith that the corroboration had come from one minor engineer? "They confirmed that you were spending too much time with the big shots, that you relied too much on Purchasing, and that you had most of the working guys down on you. We can't afford that."

King lit a cigarette. His hand was not entirely steady. "Now that is interesting. The testimony you have has come from a young man who works for me and from some unknown informants at the auto companies." He drew a deep breath. He shouldn't lose his temper. This thing might still be salvaged, and he might still have to work with this man. "Stub, before I say anything else, let me remind you that we've done a good job for you. I think that deserves some consideration you're not giving us. This move could have a devastating effect on my professional career. I don't deserve that. I request that you reserve your decision until you make a more complete investigation."

"King, you've known this was coming. You've had severals weeks to combat it, if you had some facts on your side."

"Just how was I supposed to have known it?"

"Your own man? You're sharper than that, King. You must have known."

"Well, I'm telling you right now, this is a complete surprise to me, and it will be to Dipper. No, not quite. He had the instinct. He smelled a rat. Stub, I think we've got just one helluva misunderstanding here, that's what's happened. First, I want to know exactly what Bill said to you and what your other informants said."

Stub Cook wouldn't look at King. "That wouldn't serve any purpose. The decision is made."

Now King said with heat, "I won't accept that decision. Instead of talking to people with an axe to grind, you better come to Detroit and talk to people I'll suggest, who really know the score. You owe that to me."

There was silence. Finally Stub said, "The decision is made."

King stood up. "Just who the hell do you think you are? In the first place, you've got no right to question how I spend my time. I'm not your employee. My firm is retained to do a specific job. We have accomplished that job. We've done more than you could have reasonably expected. It's none of your business how much time I spend, or Coogan spends, or Battle, or Robinson, or anybody else spends, just so long as we do the job we contracted to do. In the second place, you didn't hire us, and you can't fire us. Carter Wakeman will make this decision."

"He's in no condition to make decisions, King. The responsibility for running this Automotive Division is mine. I have the authority from the Board of Directors. I'd advise you, don't try to carry it further."

"Well, you can just bet your sweet ass I'll carry it further. I'll tell you one more thing, if you try to turn this account over to Bill Robinson, I'll spend every hour every day until you're out of business."

"That's one thing you won't have to worry about. He's quitting you to go somewhere else."

"And David Battle? Where does he fit in this?"

"The assumption is that he'll go with the account."

"Where did that assumption come from?"

"The new representative. That was one of the conditions."

"Who are you trying to turn my account over to?"

"Trent Jones. We've signed the contract."

King Smith was stricken absolutely speechless.

17

BILL ROBINSON couldn't stand it any longer. He came into King's office. "Good morning, King."

"Good morning, Bill. What's up?"

"Nothing much."

"I'll be with you in about half an hour. I've got to get this finished."

Bill blurted out, "What about Stub Cook?"

"What about Cook?"

Bill didn't answer.

King repeated, "What about Cook?"

Bill had turned pale. He said, "Well, I guess I should tell you, Stub called and told me what he did."

"Is that so? I'm glad he keeps you posted."

Bill stood nervously waiting. He said, "King, I just answered their questions, that's all."

"Have a seat, Bill, I'll be with you."

"King, they'd already decided to take the account away from you. They did that on their own. What I answered had nothing to do with that."

"Is that right?"

"That's true, King. It was Stub's idea. Frankly, the whole thing was they wanted to save some money. What are you going to do now?"

"About the account?"

Bill smiled tentatively. "About me."

"Nothing." •

"I mean, aren't you going to fire me?"

"Why should I? You're young. You made a mistake. Why should I put a black mark on your record? You're entitled to a mistake, even one this serious. No, you're not fired. When Dipper and I decide, we'll tell you what account you go on."

Robinson left in near nervous prostration. King went to Dipper. "Bill asked me if I was going to fire him. I guess that means he wants an excuse to go with Jones. It's hard to believe."

Dipper Coogan rasped, "I'll get that bastard in here and fire him, if you won't. And kick his ass right out of here."

"Dipper, he's a good young guy. He made a mistake."

"Mistake, my ass. Before this is done, we're going to find out it's been figured out to the last inch. And that includes Heisman."

"Have you seen him?"

"No. He's probably divvying up with Jones right now."

"That's the last one I'll believe, Dipper."

"King, you've been away from Livernois too long. You've gone soft in the head."

David Battle came in. "Good morning."

King asked abruptly, "Davey, what do you know about the Wakeman account, and what part did you play in it?"

David just looked at him.

King said, "Well?"

"I don't know what you're talking about."

"Do you know they took the account away from us?"

"Are you serious?"

"Nobody discussed it with you? Stub Cook? Herman Worth? Bill Robinson? Trent Jones? Anybody?"

"Nobody. I had lunch with Bill yesterday. He didn't say anything. Did he know? Have we lost it?"

"We've lost it. And Bill knew."

"Why would they do that? It doesn't make sense."

Dipper said, "When the niggers start coming out of the woodpile, it will make sense."

David Battle said, "Maybe one thing makes sense. Maybe that's why Bill has been spending a lot of time with Jones."

"You saw him?"

"Sure."

"Why didn't you say something to us?"

"I didn't think it was any of my business, and I didn't make anything of it. King, I didn't think Mr. Wakeman would ever do a thing like this to you and Dipper."

"He doesn't even know. I tried to talk to him, but he's *non compos mentis*. We've had it."

David asked, "What do we do now?"

King said, "Well, I imagine you talk to Jones and Robinson. I understand your staying on is a condition of their contract with Wakeman."

"Don't you still have a job for me?"

King said wearily, "You're still on the pay roll, Davey."

Robinson was waiting for King in his office. "I guess I better tell you. I thought maybe you'd fire me. You're a good guy for not doing it, but I've got to quit anyway."

"That's up to you. We're ready to keep you on."

"Well, there's something come up. I was going to quit and take another job. But Trent Jones just called and offered to make me a partner."

"Out of a clear blue sky?"

"Jones said Stub insisted they make me a good offer, so they can get some continuance of the representation. I'm going to take it. It's too good to turn down."

"I'm sure it is."

"I'm really doing you a favor. I appreciate your offer to keep me on, but you don't need me any more, and I'll be getting out of your hair. I guess I better go right away. Stub decided we should take the account over immediately. I mean, you'll be getting your commission, but there wouldn't be much sense in a lame-duck thing, you know."

King said, "Give me your car keys, the registration, get your stuff cleared out." His voice was mild.

"I have some money coming, King. The salary through today, some expense money. Do I get two weeks' or a month's severance?"

"I'll figure out what you have coming. I'll mail it."

"You're sure taking it like a gentleman, King. I guess you know by now, this is the breaks of the game."

"Sure," King Smith said.

Dipper Coogan was devoid of compunction. He bribed the janitor of the Wayland Building and spent only fifteen minutes going through the files in Trent Jones' offices

486

until he found what he wanted. This was a copy of the agreement between Bill Robinson and Trent Jones, dated weeks before, providing that Robinson and Jones would be equal partners in the representation of the Wakeman account, and that they would share the net return, which was defined as the gross commission less prorated expenses and less a share for David Battle to be agreed upon.

Dipper Coogan sat in Trent Jones' chair and spent eight cents of Jones' money for the double-unit call to King Smith. "King, I'm looking at it. Right in front of my face. It's a put-up deal. Robinson and Battle both were in on it. I'm taking their contract back to our office to get it photostated."

Bill Robinson was bright, feverish, elated, triumphant. He served drinks to Trent Jones and his wife, and to Cora Robinson, Kelly Brand and David Battle. He raised his own glass to them. "I guess this calls for a toast. Here's to a good association."

The glasses raised, except for Kelly Brand's. David Battle put his glass to his lips, but he didn't sip the drink. He put the glass on the cocktail table and said, "I don't know if this is the place to talk, but we better."

Trent Jones said, "Sure, Davey, there's no better place, all three of us here."

"You mean the two of you. I don't know anything about this. You may think I do, but I don't. That's what I'm here to find out."

Trent said, "You're a full partner with us, Davey. It's as simple as that."

"I've still got a job."

Bill asked, "Didn't King tell you?"

"Tell me what?"

"He's going to dump you so fast it will make your head swim."

"Why would he do that?"

"He thinks you had something to do with getting the account away."

"He's got no reason to think that. He knows better."

"I guarantee, you're dead at Coogan & Smith. Even if you talk them into letting you stay, you'll never make it now. Your bet is with us."

David asked, "May I use the phone?"

Bill said, "Sure, David,"

487

David dialed the home of King Smith. He said, "David, King. I've got one question. Do I still have a job with you?"

King Smith said, "You're fired."

David asked with iron discipline, "Will you explain?"

King Smith hung up.

David returned to the living room. He said, "I'm fired."

Bill Robinson released a sigh.

Kelly Brand said, "David, I think we should drive over right now and talk to King."

"What for? He hung up."

"Don't get peeved, David. Make allowances."

Bill Robinson said, "I told you. Your bet is with us."

David said, "There's more to it than you're telling. The account could be handled by two men. Why don't you come out with the whole story?"

Trent Jones said, "I'll tell him, Bill. Davey, you're right. We did something maybe we didn't have any right to do. When Stub gave us the account, he told us he wanted you in on it, and we promised we'd get you. I guess you'd say you got us over a barrel." He smiled with a comradely expression. "That's why we're offering you a full partnership."

"Does Stub think I've already agreed?"

"Yes, he does."

"And what if I don't go with you?"

"Then we'll just have to face it. We've already got the contract. It's a corporation contract with no mention of names. The names are on a separate, personal agreement. We've got at least one year."

"How much money is involved?"

"Well, the first year we get half of King's commission, and of course we take over handling of the existing purchase orders. If we hold expenses down, I'd say we'll get maybe twenty thousand each the first year. The second year we get the whole commission. It's two thirds of what King got. I'm sure we can count on better than thirty thousand apiece starting the second year, with full expenses."

David said, "That's not bad."

Trent said, "And that's just the Wakeman account. We'll be getting other accounts now. We're on our way. Davey, with you, that will be a big help getting good accounts."

David said, "I'll think about it."

Bill Robinson asked brightly, "What's to think? We've got a great team here. We'll set this town on fire."

Kelly Brand said, "I want to know something, Bill."

"What's that, Kelly?"

"Bill, did you help put this deal over on King?"

Bill Robinson's mouth turned dry. He said, "I had nothing to do with it. It was Stub Cook's decision."

"Are you saying you had nothing at all to do with it?"

"The only thing I did was answer some questions. I answered them truthfully, that was all."

"What kind of questions, Bill?"

"Just about the account. Kelly, I had nothing to do with it. King killed himself with Stub Cook. King and Dipper lost the account on their own. Now that it's lost, we'd be nuts if we didn't pick it up. If Davey and me don't, Trent will have to get somebody else."

Kelly pursued, "Did you know it was going to happen?"

"I had an idea, that's all. I didn't know."

"Did you tell King that you had an idea it was going to happen?"

Bill Robinson was silent.

Kelly repeated, "Did you tell King you thought he was going to lose the account?"

Bill asked, "What's all this third degree, Kelly?"

"I think there are some things that David ought to consider. You say you had nothing to do with King losing the account—I want to get that very clear. You say you didn't know you were going to end up a partner with Trent Jones."

Bill interrupted heatedly, "I was getting the short end from King, and everybody knows it."

Trent Jones said, "That's right. Bill and Davey were doing all the work, and Coogan and Smith were riding the gravy train."

Bill had caught himself. "I had nothing to do with them losing the account, period. That was between them and Stub Cook, and that's that."

"And you were loyal to King?"

Bill didn't answer.

Kelly said, "I mean, you and David, you were getting paid to do exactly what you were doing. You couldn't say you were getting any short end of the stick, now could you? King Smith was paying good salaries to get

489

the job done. You two were taking the money he paid you, and were expected to do exactly that job. Didn't King pay you fairly? Now didn't he? Didn't he treat you awfully well?"

Bill said, "Sure, I've got nothing against King. He's a darn good guy. You won't ever find me saying anything against him. And I don't think he holds anything against me, either. He's got no reason to."

"Because you were loyal to him, right?"

"You're darn right I was. I worked hard for him and stuck up for him whenever anybody said anything against him."

David Battle said, "Kelly, I have a feeling you better let this drop right here."

Kelly Brand said, "I'm not quite finished. I will be in one minute. Bill, you stick to your story that you didn't plan this thing from beginning to end. I'm sure you'll be able to convince a lot of people it's the truth. You won't convince me." She stood up. Her Texas accent came on strongly. "Sir, I don't think you've got a drop of loyal blood in your body. All right, even if you've convinced yourself you didn't do it, just answer me one question. Could you have prevented it?"

Bill Robinson was appalled.

"If you're as almighty loyal as you're making out, couldn't you have gone to bat for the guy that did so much for you? When you were talking to Stub Cook, if you had fought for Dipper and King, don't you think they'd still have the account? Could you have prevented this?"

There was silence. Bill Robinson was sick. It was out. No matter how much he rationalized, no matter how much he could explain it as Wakeman's actions and none of his own, this question he had not prepared for, and it brought the moment of truth. He could not explain to her, nor explain to himself, that he had not lifted one finger to help the man who had helped him. Knowing this, he would have to accept forever the dreadful truth that he had been driving away from his mind, desperately hiding behind the rationalization of self-preservation. He was a liar. He had lied to everyone else, and then, to preserve his self-esteem, lied to himself. There could be no more rationalization, no more self-delusion. It had indeed been a deliberate plot from start to finish. He had conspired

490

with an unsavory man to steal from the man who had be-
friended him, and though for the rest of his life he could
lie to friends and strangers, he would not be able to lie
to himself, and he would know himself for what he was,
and looking into the accusing, scornful eyes of Kelly
Brand, he thought to himself, as the blood drained from
his face: Don't feel sorry for King Smith. He lost an account. Feel sorry for me. I lost my self-respect. A million
times, no matter how often I put it out of my mind, it's
going to come back at night to haunt me. I lost my honor
when I did this terrible thing.

Kelly Brand said, "Sir, you are despicable."

She rose and walked from the living room out the front
door.

David Battle stood up. "I guess I better apologize for
her. I don't know what set her off like that."

Trent Jones was unperturbed. "That's okay, Davey.
You'll be able to talk her out of it. And of course we're
still expecting you to be a full partner."

David said, "I'll let you know no later than noon tomorrow."

David said, "That was unforgivable."

Kelly Brand was silent. She smoked nervously.

David backed the car out of the driveway and headed
down the street. He said, "I apologized. You were rude."

"David, don't you see what kind of people they are?"

"Kelly, you haven't got the faintest idea what went on.
Bill told you straight out, he had nothing to do with it."

"David, you just can't believe that. You just can't."

"I do. I've got no reason to believe it any other way."

"Does that mean you're going with them?"

"Have you forgotten I'm out of a job?"

"King's just upset. You can't blame him. He probably
thinks you were in on it. Why don't we drive over and
see him right now?"

"He made his move. Now I'll make mine. Not the way
Jones and Robinson think. That's one thing that came out
tonight, they put themselves over the barrel promising I
was part of the deal."

"So now you're going to put a gun in their ribs?"

"Somebody has to be the boss."

"David, you couldn't!"

"Just calm down and listen to me. Aren't you the one

always telling me I should stick up for myself? Wasn't it you told me to ask the Lions for the moon? I'm doing now exactly what you've always said. I'm fighting for what I've got coming. What do you want me to do, tell King thanks for firing me, and thanks for thinking I stole his account?"

"David, what's happened to you?"

David said, "That will be enough. You were unforgivably rude to Bill Robinson. Tomorrow I think you better call and apologize to him and Cora. And hope they'll understand you were upset, or something."

He pulled up in front of her apartment. He started to get out to hold the door for her. She said, "Just a minute, David."

"We can talk inside."

"No, you're not coming inside."

"Oh, is that so?"

"David, don't do this thing. You'll never forgive yourself. All right, you got your feelings hurt, but that's no reason to shut your eyes to the truth of people like Trent Jones and Bill Robinson. If you do, you're no better than they are. If you do, the truth's going to come back some day and make you so sick of yourself you'll never get over it. David, this is the time. Take me right now and marry me, and we'll just keep going somewhere else and start up again."

He was outraged. He said, "I wouldn't marry you on a bet. Where do you get this high and mighty stuff all of a sudden? Now *you* want to give *me* morality lectures?"

She didn't say a word, just reached for the car door handle.

He said, "Get out. I'll call you in the morning when you've had a chance to think what an ass you're making out of yourself. I just don't want to hear any more lectures from you. They've got a hollow ring."

Looking straight ahead, she asked, "Because I'm a girl you picked up in a bar? Because I went to bed with you without knowing you? Because I'm a mistress? Is that why I have no right to tell you when you're losing your honor?"

"You're saying it, Kelly, not me."

"David, if what I did changed you like this, I'm sorry."

"You're giving yourself too much credit. I'll call you in the morning."

"Good-bye, David."

"Don't be stupid."

She went from the car to her apartment door without looking back.

At Bloomfield Hills Country Club, a friend said to King Smith, "I hear Battle's with them, too."

"He is."

"Well, that's a crock."

"It is."

The friend said, "Well . . ." Then he said again, "Well . . ." And finally he said, "Well, that's business."

It was at this moment that Trent Jones came through the locker room, smiled cheerily and said, "Good morning, Ben, King."

King's friend said, "Good morning, Trent."

They watched Trent out the swinging doors toward the starter.

King's friend smiled tentatively at King's expression. "What do you want me to do? He's a fellow club member."

"Yes, he is. A fellow club member did this to me."

"King, it's business."

"That's the twentieth time I've been told that."

"Sure, it's a lousy deal, but it happens every day. Somebody is always stealing an account. You just weren't very smart to let them pull it on you. Next time, you'll put the guy under contract."

King Smith said, "I've been taught a lesson. More than you know. You'll never know the full story of this, because I don't intend to tell it. But the pieces have been falling into place. From the start it's been such a dirty deal you wouldn't believe men could do such a thing. And you sit there and say it's just business." His dam of self-control was finally bursting. "That makes me sick. Just business! What kind of business are we supposed to have in America? That kind of business? I ask you, would you do what they did? You know damn well you wouldn't do it. Then why do you let them off? That's what encourages them to do things like this, you let them off. Why? Because you're too lazy to do anything about it, too lazy to trouble yourself? Because you're too busy with your own affairs to really worry about somebody

493

else's affairs? Well, I'm telling you, this kind of thing is your affair. I'm not sure you've got any right to call yourself an honorable businessman if you shrug it off when people do something like this.

"I'll tell you exactly what's going to happen. Some of the customers are going to be sore as hell about it. They'll think about getting even with guys who would stoop that low. That's exactly what they'll do, they'll think about it. And then they'll forget about it. Just like people can get upset by the Syndicate or juvenile delinquency, but really can't be bothered to do something about it. The first few times they'll look at these three crooks and wonder how anybody could stoop so low, and in just a little while they'll forget all about how they got the account, and they'll just ride with the winner, because that's more comfortable. They'll have lunch with those crooks, and they'll play golf with them, and after enough time they'll begin to believe the lies themselves, because that's more comfortable, too. But a lie is a lie, even if it's believed. And thieves are still thieves, even if people forget it. Ben, don't you ever say to me again this was just business. It is not business. It is chicanery. It is crookedness. It is thievery. It's lying, cheating and stealing. It's dishonorable. It's all the things that business isn't. When you condone something like this, you're contributing to the decline of morals in America. It's not just passive acceptance, it's active approval of thievery. These guys who stole my account should be thrown out on their asses wherever they go. They should be avoided like lepers. They should be held up as object lessons of what America doesn't want to be.

"Well, I know it's not going to happen that way. Ten thousand people are going to say, just like you, that's business. And when they do, the lying, and the cheating, and the stealing are going to rub off on them a little bit, too. I feel sorry for them.

"I feel sorry for Jones. I don't think he has the sensitivity ever to be ashamed for what he did. Isn't that a terrible thing, to be such an animal? The only one I don't feel sorry for is me, because at least I'm angry. I'll tell you right now, David Battle and Bill Robinson are going to die ten thousand times for what they did, because no matter how many people forget what happened and how it happened, no matter what passes for truth from now on,

494

Battle and Robinson and Coogan and Smith know the truth, Battle, Robinson and Jones are dishonorable. Feel sorry for them, Ben, and for yourself. And for business."

King Smith stood up.

He said, "I'm not sure I want you as a friend any more."

Both men were white-faced.

David Battle began his rounds for Battle, Jones and Robinson. On the third day he took Deke Harbert to lunch. Harbert said, "Well, I'm ready."

"For what, Deke?"

"Maybe they didn't tell you. They promised to talk about a spot for me with you guys."

"I didn't know that."

"Well, they did."

David told Trent Jones of the conversation. Jones phoned Harbert in David's presence and said, "Deke, just as soon as things settle down and some things break." Deke Harbert now began to realize that he had been used, but rather than face it, he resigned himself to wait for the promised land. He had committed himself to the crooks. There was no turning back.

David asked his partner, "Just what did you promise him?"

Jones said casily, "That we might have an opening for him some day, that's all. He apparently misunderstood."

"And what did he do in return."

"Do in return? Nothing."

"He told me Stub Cook and Herman Worth talked to him about King's job performance. What kind of report did he give?"

"I wouldn't know, Davey. You'd have to ask Stub. Simmer down, Davey. This thing is working just fine."

Straight Nose Billy Turner waited for David at his apartment. David asked, "How'd you get in?"

"You should try locking your door, little buddy."

"Maybe I should. How's the team?"

"Fine. Could use you, you change your mind."

"I won't. I'm in business."

"So I hear. How's it feel, being birds of a feather?"

"What's that supposed to mean?"

"I reckon you know, little buddy."

495

"Billy, we decided a long time ago we were going to be just ordinary friends, isn't that right?"

"Right. Hard to hold to a decision like that, you think as highly of a body as I think of you."

"Just keep your nose out of this."

"Kin I have three minutes your valuable time?"

"What do you want?"

"As I understand it, you been able to swaller those crooks stealing that account, and maybe even got yourself convinced they didn't do it. I got a thought to add to the thoughts you been already give. I reckon I'd hold some blame for that company, that Wakeman. Any company that would crucify a man just to save a few lousy bucks, they're crummy. I think they smell. Davey, do you want to sell for a company that smells?"

David smiled just a little. "Aren't you the Billy Turner that lays down bets on ball games? I'm getting plenty of advice from people maybe not qualified to give it."

"Sure, and I'm Billy Turner, and you're David Battle. Or at least you used to be David Battle. Maybe now what's good enough for Billy Turner is good enough for David Battle, and wouldn't that be a crying shame. That would make me mighty unhappy, Davey. If I had anything to do with changing you, I reckon I'm as sorry as I can be."

"That's a reprise, too. I assume you talked to her."

"Yes."

"Did she call you? Did she have to blab it to somebody?"

"She called me. Do you know what I did, Davey? I asked her if she would marry me. I truly did. I told her I truly loved my wife, but I loved her more. And if she was done with you, I wanted her."

David couldn't answer. He knew what Billy Turner was going to tell him.

"She's gone, Davey. You lost that little Texas girl."

David turned without a word and ran to his car. He drove to the apartment of his mistress and let himself in with his key. He walked swiftly into their bedroom. The closets and drawers were quite empty. He lay on their king-size bed and stared at the ceiling. He took up the football lying on the bed, a game ball, a trophy of one of his excellent performances for the Detroit Lions. He tossed the ball in the air, playing catch. He thought of

496

Kelly Brand. He thought of the way she walked, like a jig halfback, like a little girl throwing flowers to the world. He thought of her wonderful smile, of the chestnut hair that swirled when she tossed her head. He thought of her glowing eyes, and of the glowing intelligence that stimulated him. He thought of her sweetness when he pulled her close, and of her want of him when she pulled him closer. He thought of her. He thought of her. He stared at the ceiling of the Notre Dame locker room, with the rain and loneliness drowning out the world, with the wind blowing Sweet Water away, away, with no one within a hundred thousand miles of him. He thought of Kelly Brand, and the wailing, mourning cry of the train whistle of Sweet Water set him to shaking violently, and he missed her, he loved her, he missed her.

He sat up on the bed. He said aloud to her, "Go to hell. Go to hell."

The phone rang in the apartment he shared again with his mother. Billy Turner said "Davey, I been over talking to Dipper Coogan."

"I got nothing to say to you, Billy."

"I'm drunk, Davey. Just drunk enough, you don't listen to me, I'll come over there and beat the living hell out of you, and you're going to listen one way the other. I talked to Dipper. And I said, Dipper, I'm just a country boy, but I got that pre-law and some toward the dee-gree, and the way it seems to me, you can throw this Robinson in jail for conspiracy, that's the way it seems to me."

"What conspiracy?"

"Well, now, David, when you're of a mind to know, you'll know it right enough. You know it right now, soon's you'll accept it."

"Give me a fact."

"Cora Robinson, she told a friend her husband's been working for Trent Jones for months."

"That's a pretty good fact. Also could be fancy."

"They got lots of facts like that one. They also got the contract."

"I don't know about any contract."

"Don't you, Davey? It's got your name in it."

"If it does, it still has nothing to do with me. Is it signed by me?"

"Davey, you better see Dipper or King and get it straightened out."

"What's Dipper going to do?"

"He's in favor to sue Robinson's Judas ass and take him for everything he gets for the next twenty years. They already got an attorney who says they got Robinson dead to rights. While he was on their payroll he was in an active conspiracy and was working for his competitors. They can nail him to the wall. Dipper's got to talk King into it. King says what good would it do, it would just make a martyr out of Robinson."

"Well, I don't believe they could win all that easy. But I'll talk to King. Billy, thanks."

"Don't thank me too soon, little buddy. The way it looks now, you done something, too, you could get throwed in jail for. I'm just giving you a chance to square away. As of right now, little buddy, I want you to know, I think you smell, and Kelly Brand thinks you smell. You stink."

David slammed the phone down. He was white and shaking.

A half hour later, he phoned Trent Jones. He said, "Trent, I've moved. My new phone number is Midwest 4-7631."

"Good, Davey."

"Trent, that's not really what I called you for. I've been doing some thinking. Wouldn't you think Stub Cook and Worth would just about take my way of thinking, whichever way I turned right now?"

Trent was alarmed, but he said calmly, "We made you a good deal, Davey. What's on your mind?"

"Do you think we need more than just the two of us to handle this account?"

Trent Jones said eagerly, "You won't believe this, but I was thinking of talking to you about that. I mean, how do you trust a guy that knifed his boss once? He'd do it again, right?"

"Right. I'll talk to you about it in the morning."

"Good deal, Davey. First thing tomorrow."

Ellen Battle asked, "David, can I get you something?"

"No, thanks, Mama. I've got some more calls to make."

"Well, don't work too late. And if you want anything, just let me know."

He called Bill Robinson. "Bill, I've been doing some thinking, and I want to ask you a blunt question. Could you and me handle the Wakeman account? I mean, just the two of us?"

Bill Robinson said, "We handled it before, just the two of us."

"Do you want me to say it, or do you want to?"

"I'll say it. The two of us can get the account from Stub, I'm sure of it. We don't need Jones."

"I thought you'd say that. Do you know something, Bill?"

"What's that, Davey?"

"We stink. All of us, we stink."

He sat staring at the phone. His mother called from upstairs, "Are you sure I can't get you something, David?"

He picked up the phone and dialed the unlisted number of Dipper Coogan, and the maid asked, "May I tell Mr. Coogan who's calling?"

"Mr. Battle."

The maid came back and said, "Mr. Coogan's not home, Mr. Battle."

David dialed the listed number of King Smith. He said to the maid, "Mr. Battle calling Mr. Smith."

The maid said, "They're over at Mr. Coogan's house, Mr. Battle."

David said, "Thank you."

He found a Coke in the refrigerator and drank from the bottle. He set it by the phone and called the home of Jim Parker. He said, "Jim, it's the full circle. I want the job you promised me back in Sweet Water."

BOOK
VI

1

WHEN JIM PARKER went to work for Carl Pearson at Embassy in 1934, he hitched his wagon to a star. Pearson, the chief engineer of one division of the Corporation, was already running fast for the top. Jim Parker bet all his chips on him. Jim came to Embassy filled with zealous loyalty to the man who had given him his opportunity. He came determined to justify Pearson's high regard for him. He came filled with the precise intention of riding Pearson's rocket.

Pearson started him in the Balance Laboratory as a technician. Jim refused to see the assignment as menial. Instead, he quickly assumed so many prerogatives that the manager of the lab was torn between resentment of the upstart and satisfaction that the tasks were shifted from his own shoulders. Jim came to work early and left late. He was the despair of other young engineers who would have preferred a healthier balance between hard work and normal male extracurricular activities. Jim was a trial and a delight, depending on the point of view.

He was not a brilliant engineer. He did not have a blue-sky inventive mind. But he was a solid, thorough innovator. Very shortly his name was on a National Motors patent. In his third month he devised a new torsiograph for measurement of torsional vibration in engine crankshafts. It was not an invention born out of inspiration. In that sense, it was not an invention at all, but a product of his orderly mind, a step forward in engineering, a logical progression of the art and practice of the laboratory. Carl Pearson personally commended him. Pearson saw himself all over again in Jim Parker, the solid, dependable, hard-working, religious, ambitious engineer starting the long climb from the very bottom to the very top.

In that third month Jim felt himself well enough established to send for Coby Warren Parker. She came from Sweet Water on the Greyhound bus, and he met her in the terminal after midnight and took her to a three-room apartment on West Grand Boulevard across from the Henry Ford Hospital. If Coby had expected a resumption of the three-day honeymoon he'd allowed himself before he'd hied off to Detroit, if she expected hearts and flowers, she had to think another think when he reported to Embassy, as usual, at seven the following morning.

The apartment location was convenient. The three-day honeymoon in Charleston had been fruitful, and now she swelled, and in March of 1935 Jim Parker was late for work for the first time in his career, because at six in the morning she walked with him across the street to the hospital and delivered a son at seven, and he didn't make it to the lab until nearly nine.

Jim Parker was an ebulliently thorough young man. In matters of engineering, this was an ideal combination. In matters of money, his ebullience remained but his thorough good sense deserted him. He was inclined to buy what struck his fancy. He was as childlike with money as any Sweet Water coal miner. On the other hand, Coby Warren was a natural-born miser. With the added responsibility of the son, she requested permission to manage their fiscal affairs, and he acceded willingly. For the forty dollars they'd paid as rent, she acquired a five-room starter home in a new development in the northeast, still within the city limits. She negotiated the satisfactory price and the minimum down payment, and transacted the entire arrangement. She furnished the home for six hundred dollars, half of what it would have cost her husband.

They were pleased with their life. Coby was a meticulous housekeeper and an excellent cook. For his part,

Jim supplied two hundred dollars a month, more than adequate income in 1935. Coby's management was spectacular. She arranged a fifty-thousand-dollar, thirty-pay insurance policy on her husband, and she put fifty dollars a month into a savings and loan association. They were substantial members of their young community.

They didn't waste time on frivolities. They stayed home. They listened to the radio, read library books, and played at intercourse for endless hours. Only the first nights were they hesitant in their love-making. They went to bed their wedding night completely inexperienced, and the consummation was less than satisfying. This was as much due to the Sweet Water Church of Christ as it was due to their virginity. To these two favorite disciples of Pastor Parker, the order of vice ascended, as Joe Foley had insisted, from blasphemy to sex, and finally, at the top, to card playing. But during the three-day honeymoon Coby Parker decided sex didn't hurt quite as much as she had expected, that her husband was not quite the ogre that her mother expected, and that the full, tingling feeling of him inside her was even more pleasurable than her religion had warned her it would be, and by the time she had him again in Detroit, a deck of cards would still have set her teeth in indignation, but sex was a face of the devil she leaped to greet. The sober, stable front they presented to the neighborhood vanished in the sequester of their bedroom, and their sex life sprang into abandon that outdid the big talkers in the Embassy plant. It was typical of frugal Coby Parker that she wrested additional pleasures from their hours of sexual divertissement in the knowledge that it was free.

In four years they had three more children, another boy and two girls. At this point they adopted preventive measures. Since this severely dampened their spontaneity and ardor, Jim suggested they experiment with the rhythm system. Coby turned this down cold, since it smacked of Catholicism. Thereupon they threw caution back to the winds, surrendered anew to abandonment, and loved unhampered through the evenings and nights, and, congratulating themselves warmly that she was never again pregnant, Jim and Coby Parker once again took their secret place among Detroit's leading practitioners of the art and joy of sex.

Inevitably Jim began to grow beyond his wife. His daily

association with pagans blunted the edge of his Sweet Water fundamentalism. Now it came to him as a revelation that decent men occasionally laughed at off-color jokes, occasionally cussed. There was a young buyer named Fairfax who cussed as happily, as luridly, as colorfully as Joe Foley himself, and caused Jim to think of Joe with great fondness and regret, and he began to warm to men who had the cheerful impiety that the big, strong young ballplayer had shed, like fresh rain and fresh air, on Sweet Water for the few years of his life. Jim's ultimate liberalization came on the night he accepted a Scotch and water at Belden's retirement party and was not struck dead.

Surely he remained among the most moral of men. Though he had at last acquired the tolerance that Joe Foley had asked of him, his religious approach was still amply stern to satisfy Pearson the Calvinist. The problem was just that Jim's new accommodation could never be understood or accepted by the unswervable, hardshell Coby Warren. This was a fork in the road for them. Furthermore, Jim began to acquire, if not a social grace, at least a social polish. With his obvious success in those early days in the Corporation, he was accorded genuine respect from the men who admired him professionally in the laboratories and inevitably carried the deference into their social relationships. Jim was pleased. In Sweet Water he'd been the big frog in the small pond. He was now growing big in Detroit. He was keenly aware of the advantage this gave him in the jockeying for position that took place among the yearlings.

David Battle was a useful instrument to Jim Parker. When David came to Detroit and the Lions, he and Jim picked up their friendship almost as though it had never been interrupted. If Jim Parker was big in his own bailiwick, this was as nothing to the importance of the right halfback in Detroit's scheme of things. Three hundred people knew and admired Jim Parker. More than half a million were in love with the Little Dipper. Jim Parker didn't mind David's ascendancy. He had his own great confidence and pride, and most of all, at this stage, he was quite happy using the respect reflected from David Battle as a further wedge for acceptance.

Having gained all this respect and acceptance, it didn't occur to Jim to be in any way concerned that his wife was falling behind. Why should it? She was no part of

506

his professional life. She was his wife. He loved her, he loved his home and his children, he loved her management and frugality, and in particular he loved the haven she provided him, so that in the hours he spent with her she replenished him and sent him back in the morning with undiminished vigor and unquestioning optimism for his eventual success.

In 1940 Pearson moved him into the Engineering Department proper as assistant chief chassis engineer, a promotion of considerable significance. Pearson knew what he was doing. He wanted to keep Jim Parker satisfied. He devoted considerable thought to the development of loyal, capable associates who would surround him when he reached the top. There were other men besides Pearson, in National Motors, who had the same confidence in their own destinies and were planning their own organizations. Carl Pearson made sure his men were satisfied to be on his team, lest Albright or Williams come to them and woo them away with blandishments and encouragements. Jim Parker didn't know these details. He was not aware of Carl Pearson's meticulous planning. Jim knew only that ho was irrevocably on Carl Pearson's team and had been since the morning Pearson drove the Parker Special Packard at breakneck speed down the street in front of the Embassy plant. Jim was Carl Pearson's man. He congratulated both Pearson and himself, in June, 1940, when Pearson moved from chief engineer to vice-president and general manager of the Embassy Division. The tandem stars were rising swiftly from the horizon.

In 1942 Pearson insured that Jim would not be wasted by the war. He sent Jim off to the Embassy tank plant as chief engineer. This suited Jim. He was honorable enough and brave enough to march off to war for his country if it came to that desperation, but he also remembered the blood spewed by Cassius Childress, and contemplating that futility, he found ample practicality of philosophy to abide the sacrifice of staying at home to further his career. Let less valuable men go off. Jim Parker would consent to stay home and make what was, in truth, his greatest possible contribution to American industry's victory over Germany and Japan.

With the end of the war, National Motors was ready for deferred reorganization. Embassy's chief engineer was sent to the corporate staff, and Pearson rushed Jim into that stepping-stone position. For four years Jim served with great distinction in that post. In 1949 Pearson made another great leap, all the way to Group Vice-President Automotive, and thus stood on the threshold, with Albright and Williams, as likely successor to Warren Court in the presidency. Jim was now thirty-eight years old, the bright young man of Detroit automotive engineering. He was given immense credit for the excellence of Embassy, National Motors' premier car. Pearson attempted to install Jim as his successor as general manager. Court forestalled him. "Too young." Instead, Court himself selected Jim to succeed in the vacancy as chief engineer at the Cutlass Division. Cutlass was the volume car. This was the highest divisional engineering post.

In this crucial post he served for two action-filled years. The Cutlass enjoyed unprecedented popularity, and once more Parker was accorded a major portion of the credit. He was now on the big bonus roll. His income shot overnight to an astronomical one hundred and fifty thousand dollars a year, and Jim Parker, born in Sweet Water, West Virginia, was among the important men in Detroit, Michigan.

Coby said to him, "That's a lot of money."

"Yes, it is."

"That's just an awful lot of money. You're making just about as much as the president of at least two of the companies."

Jim replied seriously, "NM appeals to your loyalty where it counts, right in the pocketbook. Chief engineer of Cutlass is a lot harder job to get than president of some companies."

"It's just an awful lot of money. We'll change the investment program."

"Coby, we can't get away with living here any more. We're going to Bloomfield Hills."

"Jim, don't be too quick. If you think it's necessary, maybe Birmingham, but not Bloomfield Hills."

"Mrs. Parker, I don't think you know how important your husband is. As of yesterday I'm a member of Bloomfield Hills Country Club. That's it. That tells you right there you made it in the auto industry. We've got to live up to it."

"We have to be careful, Jim. Until the stock options come through, we really don't have anything permanent

508

to count on. Just taxable income, and that won't leave too much."

"You can have forty thousand dollars to furnish the house."

She stared at him incredulously. "We could build the house for that, let alone furnish it."

"The house will cost three times that much. It will be ready in six months. Start shopping."

She looked at him reproachfully. "You did it yourself?"

"Yes. Carl bought a lot on the golf course, and he talked me into the one next to him."

"Jim, we should have talked it over."

"You might have talked me out of it. How would I explain to Carl that the hot shot's wife wouldn't let him buy a lot?"

"I wish you'd have consulted me."

"You'd have gotten a better price. This is Jim Parker's folly. That's what we'll name it. Do you know who I'm going to have for the housewarming? Carl, of course. And I think it would be smart to ask Mr. Court and see if he'll come. And I guess Bud Volk and Tony Campbell. And maybe the Fords and Dodges?" He smiled at her distress. "Seriously, I'll have Davey Battle. And I think I'll ask Gene Sarazen, and Bobby Layne, and Al Kaline. And Bob Quinn. And then I'm going to ask some people from Sweet Water. That's for sure. Who do you think we ought to ask from Sweet Water? Are you listening?"

"I was thinking about the money we'll have to invest. The Lord has been good to us, Jim."

He said patiently, "Yes, the Lord and National Motors."

"Of course we'll take all the stock options. And the stock bonuses. That's the important thing for the long pull. We'll have about sixty thousand a year out of the straight income."

"Not quite that much, but go ahead."

"Oh, it will be that much. Just leave that part to me. With the deductions we can manage, we'll have that much. But the important thing to do is use the tax money itself."

"Just how do you propose doing that, Mrs. Baruch?"

"We should think about oil. We'll get that twenty-seven-per-cent depletion allowance. But that's very dangerous, so we won't extend ourselves there. The important thing will be pseudo corporations."

He said, "I haven't the faintest idea, what's a pseudo corporation?"

"Group investment, with not more than ten men. Invest in a new company, with a new product, with risk involved. Then any losses incurred in start-up can be written off as direct deductions against your income. It becomes a regular corporation only after it begins to return a profit. I think you'll find that's what Mr. Pearson and the others are doing to keep some of their money."

"It must be one Walter Reuther hasn't found out about yet. Carl wants to talk to me about investments. I'm pretty sure they're going to include me in from now on."

"And of course there's real estate. That's the safest and best return of all. I think we should buy some frontage along James Couzens. There are some new office buildings going up along there, small buildings. It's selling now for one hundred fifty dollars a front foot, and in five years it will be more than three hundred. And of course that's capital gains."

Jim Parker contemplated his Sweet Water wife with candid admiration. "When I'm president of National Motors, I'm going to install you the next day as Vice-President Finance."

"Jim, this is too fast. We shouldn't be in Bloomfield yet."

"You mean we can't quite afford it? How many people out there do you think can afford it? Besides, Carl says I'll get the division. And soon. Then we can come closer to affording it." He smiled. "Besides, when I make president, I won't have to move. I'll already be there. Why such an expression?"

"Jim, I'm not up to it."

"What are you talking about? Up to what?"

"Bloomfield Hills. The Country Club. The people. Carl Pearson. The Campbells. People like that. I'm not up to it. Jim, we both know it, I don't keep up with you. You know what I mean. I can't even have people in the house five minutes, without dying a thousand deaths. You've gone so far already. You have so much. You're going to go so much further. Jim, I wouldn't blame you if you looked at somebody else."

"Another woman?"

"I couldn't blame you."

"You forget, I'm no Apollo."

"It's different with a man. You're intelligent. That's the

510

first thing a woman looks for in a man. And so full of energy. I know how attractive you are to other women. I've seen them."

"Who? This interests me considerable."

"Just women."

"Name one."

"David's wife."

"Sarajean? You're out of your mind. I like the idea, but you're out of your mind."

"She does. She's the kind of woman that can't help looking, and she looks at you. She admires you."

"Do you know where our new lot is? Four doors down from Davey's house. Remind me to check out your notion about Sarajean."

"Don't tease me too much, Jim. Women admire you. But other men don't look at me twice. How could they? I wouldn't blame you if sometime you looked at another woman. A younger woman."

"But you hope I don't?"

"Yes, I hope you won't."

"I wouldn't worry. We're like Carl and Evie. They're used to each other, like a pair of old shoes or something, and so are we. Matched bookends. I'm holding things from one side, and you're holding them from the other side. Besides, mistresses cost too much. You keep me so broke with the investments that I couldn't possibly afford a mistress. And the nicest thing you ever said is that Sarajean Battle makes eyes at me. I can't wait to tell Davey."

"Jim, don't you dare!"

"I will. Or better yet, I think I'll just drop by in the middle of the day and tell her I'm hers, take me."

"Don't mind me, Jim. Once in a while I feel inadequate. It's hard to keep up with a man that's going as far as you."

He smiled. "You know what you're overlooking, don't you? We've got a good life, you and me. We've got great kids. At least we will, if we get your daughter's mind off boys."

"I wouldn't trade our life for anybody's."

"I'm sure you wouldn't trade with Sarajean."

"No, I wouldn't."

"Coby, I've got too much sense to lose you. I'd go broke without you. Remind me to ask you sometime how much you've made me worth." He pulled her against his

511

chest and stroked her graying hair. His voice wasn't at all that of a passionate lover; it was his normal, eager but almost expressionless voice, but the truth and ardor were clear to her. "I love you, Coby Warren. Let's hit the rack."

"The kids are all gone."

"That's what I said, let's hit the rack."

Her arms tightened around him and she said, with the boldness that came out at these times and pleased him mightily, "There I can keep up with you, Jim Parker."

In 1951 the dice came up seven for Carl Pearson. Albright and Williams, his formidable rivals, had to settle for executive vice-presidencies. Warren Court backed Pearson all the way and swung over a minority of the board who were holding out for Williams, the financial man. Carl Pearson was President of National Motors. The Detroit headlines shouted his name. The men in his coterie shouted silently, just as loudly.

Now Jim Parker took over the Cutlass Division. The timing was perfect. Cutlass sales soared to ever greater heights. Both by his prowess, and by his luck of the draw, Jim Parker was the undoubted man of the hour and the future. When *Time* put his eager face on its cover in a run-down of the automotive business, his rivals in National Motors shuddered and buckled down the harder and knew that they weren't going to make it. They were bucking a man with a sudden national reputation. They were bucking an engineer who understood dealer relations and understood assembly lines. They were bucking a hardworking leader who inspired utter loyalty in his subordinates. They were bucking Carl Pearson's protégé. Everyone in Detroit and Wall Street said it: "Jim Parker is a cinch when Pearson retires."

When he was called to New York for his first Board of Directors meeting, he waited outside the Board Room with pounding pride, and he looked about himself and said to himself, "Boy, this is a long way from West by God Virginia . . . and you told Davey you were going to the top, and you meant it, and you were full of confidence, and the closer you get, the more you know you weren't quite as confident as you said . . . and boy, it's just great!" and he was smiling when he was sent for. When they brought him into the room to introduce him, the senior member of the board rose to his feet, his legs shaking ever so slightly under him, a warm smile on his surprisingly young face, and clapped his old man's brown-freckled hands, and the rest of the board rose with him and applauded, and Jim Parker took his waiting chair with a bright, expectant look on his face and the sense of the awful importance of his responsibility to the United States of America for his part in running this giant. When the meeting had concluded, Old Dankworth said, "Jim, I've been a member of this board for thirty-two years. Avery Winston did something that's never been done before. This is the first time this board has ever stood and applauded a new member. I hope it makes you feel good. It does show the measure of Mr. Winston's hope, and our hope, for the job you will do for us in the future."

Jim Parker took the hand offered him. He knew he should be humble before that great revelation. He tried. He could not be humble. He could only feel elation, a small boy's elation for a paternal expression of ultimate fondness and approbation. Jim Parker's cup ran over.

In 1956 came his succession to Group Vice-President Automotive, and if there had been any unbelievers, they were now silenced, because he was on Pearson's own exact route to the presidency. One of the Big Four, in trouble, took highest cognizance of his stature. In 1961 the Board of Directors of that automobile company, having received permission of the National Motors Board, sent a representative to Jim Parker.

"Jim, we need a new president. I guess you know. We've got men in our own organization who could do a decent job of it. But you've got the key things our men lack. You know how to run the Cutlass dealer organization. We want you to come with us and set up our dealers. We'd want you to bring some of your own top sales people with you. We'd count on that. Second, with your name and reputation, you'd pull us up by our bootstraps. You'd put confidence in the public, you'd put confidence in our own people."

"You've talked to Carl?"

"Yes. And it's up to you."

"Why should I consider it? I've got some hopes here."

"For the same reason Carl gave permission to talk to you. National Motors is interested in our prosperity. That's the biggest responsibility. To the industry itself, and the country. Carl knows that, and so do you."

"Carl might. I'm too provincial. I've had my nose in National Motors, and I've been thinking about nothing but beating your head off."

"You don't have that privilege any more. At this level, you're institutional. You know that. You're spending half your time making speeches and running campaigns. Where did you speak this week?"

"National War College. I enjoyed that. The top-ranking men of all the services."

"United Fund? Red Cross? Boy Scouts? Detroit Symphony Orchestra? The President's Commission on Industry? Your press conference on NBC? Does that sound like National Motors? Or does it sound like you're representing all of us?"

"I'm afraid I'm still provincial. I think of most of those things I do as part of the job."

"Well, we can make it worth your while to come."

Jim smiled. "I'm doing well here."

"We can match your salary. You might think we couldn't match your stock, but we can. If you become president of National Motors, what will you come out with, three million dollars would you say? We can give you stock options that you can run into ten million dollars and a lot more after taxes."

"Providing the stock appreciates that fast?"

"With the *knowledge* that it *will* appreciate that fast, with you as president."

"Would I have a free hand."

"Subject to the board, I'd say freer than you'll ever have here."

Jim Parker said, "Give me a week to think it over."

When he came back, he said, "The money doesn't tempt me quite enough. I've already got all the money I can possibly spend. The challenge does tempt me. I'd like to do the job that needs to be done with you. That would give me the greatest possible satisfaction, probably more than I'll get if I get the chance of running our well-oiled machine." And then, at the moment when the representative's hopes had sprung up, Jim said, "But I can't take it. There's more than just me involved. There are other people to think about. All the men who have been with me since 1934. Whatever it is, it gets into your blood. You don't

514

leave those men. They're *counting* on you. Their own ambitions are tied up in you. I don't mean my superiors. They can get along without me. National Motors can get along without me. But the men I've got on my team, where would it leave them? I couldn't bring them all over to you with me. I'm sure Carl would draw the line there. Besides, you can offer me, just one man, enough money, but you couldn't offer the others, all of them, enough to make the switch with me. No, if I went with you, it would mean leaving them when they've been counting on me and based their plans on me." He smiled again. "And I surely am provincial. I live and breathe my own corporation. Live it and breathe it. I'm glad you asked me, and mighty proud, and I wish I could, but I can't."

In the plane, en route to the next board meeting, Pearson asked, "Going, or staying?"

"Staying."

"Was there ever any doubt in your mind?"

"Yes. Considerable doubt."

"I'm surprised. I don't know whether I'm disturbed."

"It would be a good challenge. There's a lot to be done over there."

"And not much to be done here?"

"Carl, you know the difference. You know exactly what's to be done here."

"Yes, run it. That will be more of a challenge than you realize, looking at it from where you are now. The day I took over, I got a little bit of the feeling the President of the United States must feel when the awesome responsibility settles suddenly right square on him. All of a sudden it's not quite so simple as it looks, running the great, well-oiled machine. You'll find out, Jim."

"Will I?"

"Yes, when it's your turn."

"That's the first time you've said that."

"God willing, you'll run it."

"I'll tell you one more thing, Carl. When I was listening to them, and then went back and thought it over, all of a sudden I wasn't so sure I wanted to be president of any automotive company. For the first time in my life, it occurred to me that I'd already done quite a bit with my life, and maybe I didn't have to prove anything any more."

Carl turned and watched Jim's face.

Jim smiled. "But the doubt didn't last long. I want it. You've got to want it, after you've wanted it this long."

Carl said, "Yes, you've got to." In another moment he said, "I think I had some doubts one night, too. But they left and never came back. It's the fulfillment, Jim, for people like you and me, and you'll have it, you'll have the fulfillment."

In 1963 they headed for New York in the company plane to announce the culmination of Jim Parker's destiny at National Motors. Jim Parker died in agony and dread. Coby Parker mourned desperately. Her heart and soul mourned in utter grief and fathomless devastation. Coby Warren had before her the lives of the children she had borne her husband, but her own life died with the man who knew he had been loved but never had known the exalted heights of her adoration, because she had had no way of telling him. Coby's life ended, her existence continued.

And the scramble began to see who would succeed Jim Parker at National Motors. Who would it be? Tony Campbell? David Battle? Bud Volk?

2

IT WAS IN 1947, when Jim Parker was still just chief engineer at Embassy, that David Battle came to him to exact the promise that had been made at India Parker's kitchen table.

David said, "I'm singularly unqualified, but I have a specific job I want."

Jim Parker said, "As a matter of fact, you're eminently qualified. Not as an engineer, though, I wouldn't think."

"My degree was a ticket to a dog fight. That's not what I have in mind."

"Davey, before you get too wound up about joining the Corporation, there's something else that makes a lot more sense for you. You ought to look at a dealership. With your name, it's a natural. Could you raise a hundred thousand dollars?"

"If I sold my mother, I could raise about forty."

"That might do it. The Corporation would arrange most of the financing. I mean, they'd back you. Davey, you could get rich with the right Cutlass or Embassy agency. I'll talk to Carl Pearson, and I'm sure he'll help us with Sales."

David shook his head. "There's one job I want. I want to be in Purchasing."

Jim Parker smiled. "That's like a virgin saying she wants a job in a brothel. Sales, even in the Corporation, that I

517

can see. Why on earth would you ever, in your right mind, want to be in Purchasing?"

"I've got a reason. I want it. I want you to help me get the job."

"If I'm going to help you, at least you should take my advice about some things. I know what I'm doing. If I came out for your football team and didn't know the first thing about it, you could tell me where I had the best chance, right? National Motors is my football team. If you're bound and determined to go this Corporation route, you're best fitted for Sales. You've got the name, you've got the personality. That's where they've put Tony Campbell. It makes sense for people like you." Jim Parker suddenly drew back and looked at David Battle with an expression of surprise on his face.

David asked, "Why the look?"

"You've got the personality. When you know a man through the years, you don't notice the subtle changes. It just hit me in the face." He smiled again. "Where did the Silent Knight go? You took my advice and started talking."

"Jim, I want a job in Purchasing."

"You surely have changed, Davey."

"We've all changed, Jim. You've changed more than you know."

"In what way?"

"I'll tell you sometime when it's appropriate."

"I'd like your view."

"You've narrowed. You've lost a great deal of the wide idealism you had in Sweet Water."

"Wide-eyed?"

"I said wide."

"I know what I'm doing."

"I'm sure you do, Jim."

"I'm going to be president of this Corporation."

"We always knew that."

"If that narrows my view, it will just have to narrow."

"Some of us knew that, too, back in Sweet Water. Remember?"

"Just biding my time, Davey. What's your excuse for changing?"

"Do you disapprove?"

"Not really. I think you make me a little bit uneasy. You're certainly not the self-effacing, quiet, modest man

518

the sports writers still want to make of you. I'd have to say that's a change for the better. Can I guess? I'd say Kelly. She's good for you. She's a wonderful girl. Why don't you marry her so Coby can stop clucking?"

"Kelly's done her job. She's gone back to Texas."

"You let her go!"

"I let her go."

"Well, if you did, you've changed to being stupid, that's what you've changed to."

David Battle said, "I hope that's all you have to say on that subject, Jim, because I have no intention of discussing it with you or anybody else."

"Just how much do you want to change our relationship? I do read that as unfriendliness."

"Read it the way you want. She's none of your business."

"Well, now, David, you're the one coming here asking something. I'm used to meeting tough-talking men every day, and I'm used to coming out on top. Tell me again what kind of relationship you want between us."

"I want a job in Purchasing. I've got my reasons. I want you to help me get it. If not through friendship, that's your choice, then I'll hold you to the promise you made in Sweet Water. I want the job with no questions asked. And from there, I'll make it on my own. Fair enough?"

Jim Parker said icily, "Fair enough, David. I'm sure our personnel office will do it for me. I'll call you when you're to report." Then suddenly his face softened. "Sometimes I'm not as bright as everybody in National Motors thinks I am. Davey, take this piece of advice or lump it, it's meant to be friendly. If you've had a fight with her, why don't you just this one time unbend and make the move. And marry that girl, David. I doubt you could ever find another like her as long as you live."

David said, "Jim, thanks for the job. I appreciate it."

Embassy started him in Production Control. He was disappointed. He wanted Purchasing. But Jim Parker had said to the Director of Salaried Personnel, "It will be a personal favor to me if you get him a job, but I want him to start at the bottom and work up."

David plunged in with grim determination. For a time he was the object of respectful curiosity from his co-workers and of a certain resentment from his supervisor, who thought he could see the handwriting on the wall, and that he'd be working for the football star before this was over. In six months the bloom had worn off, familiarity had bred its nonchalance, and David reported in each day pretty much just another guy. He was assigned to the scheduling books for rubber goods, primarily tires, and he bent his thoroughness to each day's task, so that at the end of six months he felt that he was finally earning his weekly eighty-five dollars.

At that point he knew his way around sufficiently to make at least a preliminary move in his campaign of expiation. He went to the man who handled the major stamping books and said, "Chris, I want a favor from you."

"Sure, Davey, name it."

"A favor between you and me, nobody else to know about it."

"Name it, Davey. I'll do it if I can."

"On the seat back, when you need some extra production, if everything's equal, give it to Buckeye instead of Wakeman."

The production control man slowly shut his book. After a long time he said, "Davey, Buckeye is represented by Coogan & Smith. You used to work for Coogan & Smith."

"Do you think I still do?"

"I'm asking."

"I do not. If you don't know me well enough to know I wouldn't do anything dishonest, I've misjudged our relationship."

"Take it easy. You got to admit, I've got to know what's in your mind."

"Okay, you've got to ask. Chris, I want to see Jones and Robinson get hurt. I want to see Coogan and Smith get Wakeman's business away from them. It's a personal matter, and something very important to me. If it's no skin off your nose, will you give them every break you can, everything being equal?"

"Davey, is it a good personal reason?"

"The best."

"Davey, I'm no great, loyal NM fan, but I want to know, is this in the interest of the Corporation?"

"It's important to the Corporation. You have my word on that."

Chris Martin opened his book. "That's good enough for

me. I'll do it. Dipper and King will get what breaks I can give them."

It was Friday. David raced home. He was stopped and ticketed for speeding.. As the officer wrote the ticket, he came to the name and said, "Gee, Davey, I should have recognized you. I've got the ticket started. I'll erase it, if you say so."

David Battle smiled. "I deserve it. And you don't deserve getting in trouble." He took the ticket and drove off again, almost as fast. He packed a bag. He phoned American for a reservation to Chicago, Dallas, and on to Houston. He spent six restless hours in the Houston airport motel, and in the morning, very early, he rented a car and drove fifty miles to the farm of Wes Brand.

Kelly Brand's father said, "Good morning, sir."

David held out his hand and the two men gripped firmly.

Wes Brand asked, "Looking for me, sir?"

"Yes, sir. Mr. Brand, I'm David Battle."

Brand's eyes narrowed suddenly to slits in his brown face.

David asked, "You know who I am, sir?"

"Yes, sir, I know who you are. You looking for Kelly?"

"Yes, sir, I am."

A slow smile came on the brown face, but the eyes stayed slitted. He drawled, "I'll tell you where you can find her, Mr. Battle. You should have stayed right where you were in Houston. She's at Forty-three Redmond Drive, you got that?"

"Yes, sir."

"I suggest you stop at a gas station just before you get to the city limits and get your directions."

"Yes, sir. Thank you, Mr. Brand." He started to hold out his hand. Wes Brand made no answering move. David said again, "Thank you, Mr. Brand. If you think I've got some things to make up, I think so, too."

Wes Brand said, "Mr. Battle, I wish you and my girl all the luck in the world." The smile was still there, the eyes still slitted. "I surely do." He turned and walked into his house.

David drove into the rich suburb with growing premonition. He stopped at the address. He looked at the estate. He forced himself to look at the mailbox. "Bowie Lee Hankins." His heart constricted. With a violent motion

521

he turned the ignition and started the car. He moved only ten feet. With another violent motion he stopped the car and leaped out, went through the gate and up the long walk nearly at a run. His mouth was dry. He could hear his heart pounding in his ears. He rang the doorbell, immediately rang it again, then again and again.

He heard her say, "I've got it."

She opened the door. The vexed expression left her face. She turned dead-white.

David said, "I'm sorry, Kelly. I'm so sorry."

Her hands dropped to her sides. She looked very tired.

He said, "I'm so sorry, Kelly."

The color came slowly back to her face. She smiled a little. "Hello, David. Come in."

He followed her through the door. She said, "Come on out on the patio. It's cool there. I'll get you a drink. What would you like?"

"I want to talk to you."

She sat on a green, wrought-iron chair with a pink cushion. "Sit down, David. How nice to see you."

He said softly, "Kelly, I'm here to see you. Whatever you do or say, I won't have this sophistication from you. You will treat me with respect."

The color began to drain again. She said tensely, "I think you better not stay, David."

"I've got no choice. I've come to get you. You can have your revenge on me, your father already got his revenge on me, but I came to take you back with me."

"David, sit down. Please, sit down. Don't say things that you haven't any right to say."

"First, I want to know how long you've been married. We can fix that."

Now Kelly Brand flushed with anger and resentment. "Well, now, sir, I'll tell you. I've been married since the minute I decided you were gone, that's how long. You didn't come. You didn't call. You didn't write. Now you show up six months later and want to pick up where you left off. Well, things just don't work that way, David. Not even for you. What do you think I am, some baggage you can check until you're ready to use me again? I'm Kelly Brand, David, and not even the high and mighty David Battle treats me like that. I think I better tell you some things you don't know about me."

David interrupted. "I know all I need to know about you."

"Sir, you don't know the first thing about me. I told you, and even when I was telling you, I knew you didn't know. Well, I'm going to tell you one last time, and maybe this time you'll get it through your high and mighty head. I'm Kelly Brand. I'm a girl that loved a man and married him, and he broke my heart, and I cried for a long time. And then I got up and stopped crying and went to San Francisco and decided I was going to do something just as terrible as I could, so my heart wouldn't be broken any more. And I did it, just as terrible as I could. I did it with you. I let you use me any way you wanted to, for as long as you wanted. And I thought maybe it wasn't so terrible, because I was in love with you. Do you want to know what you could have done? You could have married me, that's what you could have done. Oh, no, not you. I told you I couldn't do that to you. Do what to you? What do you think you were doing to me? Do you know what you did, sir? You believed it, that's what you did. I told you I wasn't good enough for you, and I wasn't sure that I was, but you believed it, down deep you believed I wasn't good enough for you, and you never got me down and made me marry you, that's what you didn't do. The great, pious David Battle, playing at sin for the first time in his life, and, boy, weren't you clever to pick a whore to do it with, so if you ever got tired of sinning and decided to go back to being pious again, you could just go to Confession and Hail Mary me right back out of your life, just like I wasn't ever there a thousand times in the night, loving you until my heart was breaking. Do you know that's you, David? Just like the other one? Just like the other one. The second man in my life to lose his honor. David, you'll never know, even now, how much I loved you, and then how much I hated you and pitied you for what you did to them. The great, pious David Battle, living with his whore, and joining the jackals to pick the bones of the man who was good to him. Do you want to know who Bowie Lee Hankins is? He's the other one. He's the first one that broke my heart, that's who. He's the man that ran off with a Mexican girl, and they caught him, and they gave him a dishonorable discharge, that's who he is. And he's the man came to me and said, 'Kelly, there's no forgiving what I've done. I'll never ask

523

forgiveness of you or my country.' And do you know what I said to him? I said, 'Bowie Lee, we'll get married again just as soon as you can get the license.' And he's a fine husband, and he's doing fine things, and people are forgetting that he was despicable. That's who he is. And he's a man getting it fixed all over again in his mind, just like his daddy, that I'm a whore who came back just to get his money, and that's who I am. Now tell me who you are, coming down here to tell me what you're going to do and what I'm going to do."

He couldn't talk.

She said, "Tell me, David. I want to hear it."

He said very softly, totally crushed, "Kelly, I love you. That's all I can think of to say. I think I could kill your husband. If I thought that would help you, I would do it."

She stood up. She said, "You love me too late, David Battle. Good-bye."

He took her wrist, and his strong hand turned it white. "Kelly, I'd be abject, because I love you. But not for long. And not truly abject. Don't come weeping and wailing to me with your great problems. You're supposed to be so all-seeing and all-knowing. You play psychiatrist. Fix up poor little Davey Battle. Get him off his mother's apron strings. Fix him up in bed. Make a man out of him. You play games and cry when I don't know the name of the game. Kelly, I couldn't possibly tell you who I am. I'm not sure there ever has been anybody in me. If there was, it got lost a long time ago. In Sweet Water, and Joe Foley, and Ellen Foley, and little Davey that they pick up off the ground and dust him off, and the whole goddam mess of it. But I know one thing—before I'm done I'm going to be David Battle. You sit here and cry your eyes out if you want, I'll give you something to cry about. Not once, not ever once did I think anything but the best of you. There wasn't once I didn't know you for the good things you are. Cry about it, Kelly. And when you think about me becoming David Battle, you think about if you're ever going to become Kelly Brand for me to love again."

He walked through the house, out the front door, down the walk to his car. He drove away.

The phone rang. She picked it up and said woodenly, "Hello?"

The big male voice drawled, "Honey, this is your little old Straight Nose buddy. How you?"

"Where are you, Billy?"

"Dee-troit, where you think? Honey, we're going to play an exhibition in Dallas in September. You think you could come up and hold hands with me for a evening? You kin bring Bowie Lee, you got to."

"Billy, David was just here."

There was silence.

"Billy, did you ever tell him about me and Bowie Lee?"

"Of course not, honey. I didn't figure there was any point to it."

"Have you seen him much, Billy?"

"Off and on. We're not the greatest buddies like we was oncet. Honey, I never figured him to go down there. I figured he was over and done with. I swear to God, he never once mentioned you. He had, I'd of tole him."

"What's he doing, Billy?"

"Honey, you just better forget it. If he's gone again, this time it will be for good."

"What's he doing, Billy?"

"When you left, he quit those crooks. He just up and quit 'em. He's working his heart out in a little bitty old job at National Motors."

She said, "For me, do you think?"

He said gruffly, "I don't think anything, Kelly. When I try to think, I just get me in trouble. I lost my friend when I tried to think. Honey, I love that little ole Davey, and I thought myself right outen his life. Did I do the same with you, now, for not being smart enough to know what to say to the both of you?"

She said, "No, Billy, neither of us could blame you when we're the ones stupid. Billy, you let me know when you'll be in Dallas, we'll be up to see you."

"Honey, you don't get too blue, you hear?"

She smiled a little and said into the phone, "Sure, Straight Nose."

"Say hello to Bowie Lee, and you take it easy, you hear?"

"Billy, will you tell me once in a while what David's doing?"

There was another silence. Then he said, "I surely will, honey."

She hung up the phone. She sat again in the iron chair and lit a cigarette. She crushed it out and said, "Oh, damn, damn, damn, damn, DAMN!"

3

THERE WERE TWO CATEGORIES of women who went un-escorted to Detroit's bars. There were the hookers. A trend-setter would say, "RonJo's, that's the place," and the professionals would arrange themselves on the bar stools that night waiting for the rush of men, who came overcrowding the new spot like excursionists all rushing to one rail of the boat. For the next few weeks RonJo's, Merri-weather's and the Red Fox would be the spots, and then someone would say, "Town Talk, that's the place," and the excursionists would go rushing off to the other rail.

The bored housewives and young secretaries, dedicated boozers, sexless, followed the hookers. Some of the married women came as early as lunch, more came in the cocktail hour, and most came at dinnertime or after bowling. They disposed themselves at the bar rails among the prostitutes and smiled to get free drinks, and they all had bottomless pits into which vast quantities of V.O. could be poured without apparent effect. The secretaries came after work. Their method of operation and their motivation were exactly those of the housewives. They came to do men out of drinks, to lead them on like B girls, hinting at sexual relationship, only to go home at the witching hour, two girls to a car, no men. The gallants deluded themselves, saying, "Another ten minutes and I'd of got that one in the sack," when the truth of the matter was, they never had a chance. The hookers were delighted with this kind of amateur competition. They plied their best business very late at night, when the men with egg on their faces, learning the hard way that they were lonely in Detroit, had drunk enough whiskey that they could bring themselves to buy surcease. David Battle met Sarajean Court in such a bar. He would have drunk alone. Two girls sat down on the stools to his immediate right. He paid no attention to them, nor, ostensibly, they to him. After one drink the bartender looked significantly at David, then half nodded at the two girls. David turned his head, was less than overwhelmed, and went back to his drink.

The bartender said to the girl next to David, "Sarajean, do you know David Battle? You know who he is. The Little Dipper."

The girl said to her friend, "He's a football player. Isn't that right, Joe?"

The bartender said, "The best." He said to David, "You were the greatest, Davey."

David Battle said, "Buy them a drink."

At midnight the two girls went off alone in the one car, to drop Sarajean Court at her own car, but David followed.

Sarajean said to David, "Please, I've had too much to drink."

He said, "Your keeper's gone. Now you can do what you want."

"I want to go home by myself. Please, I'll see you again some other night."

"And play easy to get until going-home time? Maybe I'll just make you pay the piper."

"David, please don't be that way. I don't do this much. Just when Jo wants to go out and not get involved."

"Which accounts for the bartender knowing you? Does he know you're Warren Court's daughter?"

"How did you know?"

"I know."

"Please, David, I shouldn't have been in there. Won't you let me go home?"

"Why do you do it?"

"Just for the fun. For the excitement. Oh, please, please, please!"

"Do you know you're the lowest of the low? The whores in there, they come right out and say what they are. You lie. You pretend. And then you throw cold water in a man's face."

"They deserve it. It serves them right."

"Is that what your friend Jo says? Men deserve anything women can do to them? What do you deserve? Do you think you're so almighty special that men should be glad to buy you drinks all night just for the pleasure of some kind words and some teasing that you might be interested? I'll tell you what you deserve. You deserve to get caught like you are right now."

"David, you've had too much, too. Go back to your car. I'll see you some other time. Honest, I will."

"Do you realize that there isn't a soul on this street? Your buddy's gone, and there's just the two of us. When I rape you, there's going to be nobody to stop me. You didn't think it would end up this way, did you?"

She said, terrified, "Oh, please, David! I'll tell! I swear I will!"

"What will the daughter of the president of National Motors tell the police? That she was out cadging drinks from strangers?"

"I don't have the money. Daddy doesn't give me any. I have to earn my own. You don't understand."

"Do you really hate men? Are you like the housewives in there, getting even with all men? Are you like Jo, hating men because her mother taught her to, or because somebody did something to her? Are you a dreadful woman like them?"

"They're not dreadful. Not all of them. What are they supposed to do? They just want a little bit of excitement, something different, and nobody to get hurt, that's all. David, I'm getting sober. I swear I am, and you'll be in trouble if you don't get out and go away."

But he took her face in his hands and kissed her while she struggled futilely, and then he kissed her long and tenderly until she finally put her arms around his neck and clung tightly. When he put his right hand beneath her skirt, she clamped her legs tightly together and once again fought to get free, but she was no match for his strength, and while she said, "No, no, no," against his lips, she gradually surrendered. He took her from there to a motel and made love to her as though she were Kelly Brand, and he didn't take her to her car again until it was nearly three o'clock.

She said tensely, "Good night, David."

He said soberly, "Good night, Sarajean."

"Will I see you again?"

"Of course."

"I'm sorry, David. I wish it hadn't happened."

"But it's not the first time it's happened."

After a long time she said, "No, but it's the first time it happened like this. Good-bye, David."

Without smiling, he said, "Oh, I'll see you again, don't worry. We have National Motors in common. We can't let this drop here."

"Would you make love to a sort of plain girl, just because her father was president of the company you worked for?"

He squeezed her hand. "Good night. I'll see you tomorrow. We'll have dinner, all right?"

She said, "All right, David. Come in and meet my folks tomorrow when you pick me up. Do you know where I live?"

"I know."

"I thought you would. How will I explain you, that I picked you up in a bar?"

"Why not? It's done all the time. No, we met through friends. Good night, Sarajean."

He made love to Sarajean Court for four years. Then he asked her to marry him, because it seemed like a reasonable thing to do. He thought that Ellen Foley Battle would not object to this girl. She did. She said, "She's a drinker."

"Yes, she's that."

"So are you. David, you've got to stop."

"I have stopped. For several months now."

"But not her. She's a drinker and a sinner."

"I am going to marry her. Then she won't drink any more, and the sinning automatically stops, and that should please you."

But Ellen Battle went back to Sweet Water and didn't return until David asked her to come live with them.

4

In the big paneled office, Trent Jones sat in a chair facing the desk of the new purchasing agent of the Cutlass Division of National Motors. Trent was in considerable turmoil, but no agitation showed on his face. He said, "I thought I should make a courtesy call, Davey."

David said, "I hear Bill Robinson's gone to California."

"That's right."

"Squeezed out?"

Trent smiled. "I wouldn't say that. He just didn't fit the picture any more. You knew him at Coogan & Smith. He just never was a big-time guy. He was always just the order-desk clerk."

"Things are going well for Wakeman, right?"

"We have our share of the business. So does King. I guess you know he took on Buckeye."

"I've been checking. The pricing Stub Cook gives you is better than he ever gave King. Is he trying to prove he didn't make a mistake in switching?"

Trent said evenly, "I've shown them how they could cut costs, that's where the good pricing has come from."

"Has Wakeman's profit been as high with you as it was with Dipper and King?"

"I couldn't say."

"I would have thought that was the first concern of a representative."

"We're doing fine, Davey. Wakeman's a good, sound company. That's the most important thing, right?"

David didn't answer.

Trent asked, "Have you seen much of the Dipper or King?"

David said in a level voice, "I haven't said one word to either of them in the four years since you stole their account and I got as greedy as you."

Trent Jones took out a cigar. He lighted it with a steady hand. He said, "Davey, we did get the Wakeman account, and we have held the Wakeman account. We've got more dollar volume now than when we took over. We've done a good job representing them. I work hard at it. Maybe by this time it doesn't matter how we got it in the first place. This is today, not yesterday. I'd say we're in strong now. We've got good friends in all the Big Four, now, that don't see one thing wrong with the way we do business, because we do it right. I came over here to be friends with you. Do you want it that way?"

"You were not my friend then, you will never be my friend. I can't make it any plainer than that."

"Then I'll tell you, we've got friends up the line here now, just in case. I've got my own football player now. Did you know Jimmy White is with us? And you know Jim Parker, how he goes for football players, the ones still playing. I want to get along with you, Davey, I want you to judge us solely based on our performance, but if you don't, we won't take it lying down. Is that the way you want it?"

"I have a feeling you're going to need your friends up the line."

Trent softened his tone. He said, "Davey, you got no reason to make it hard on us. We offered you a good deal with us. Anything else was between King Smith and me, not with you. We were going to take care of you."

"I know all about that. I know you were going to cut me out, until you found out Stub Cook wanted me as part of the deal. But that's not the point. The point is that King Smith got screwed. The point is that you did something so wrong it's hard to find words for it. Now a lot of people are saying that one man isn't important, that the important thing is that Wakeman is a good supplier, and they're entitled to all the privileges and prerogatives of a good supplier. But the way I remember it, King Smith did just as good a job for National Motors as Wakeman Sheet Metal ever did, and maybe that just entitles him to consideration, too. I'll tell you just how it's going to be between you and me. I've got no use for you. You deliberately stole the account. You lied and cheated to get it. Both of you, you're men of no honor, and I know that better than anybody else, because I ended up part of it. You're no good. In this office, or out of it, I'm no friend of yours. I'll make it plainer, I'm your enemy. The rest of the people in this Corporation and the rest of the automotive industry may have short memories and may be able to accommodate themselves to you, rather than stand up and go to all the trouble of being counted on the side of doing the right thing in this world, but I'm standing up, I've just been waiting for this chance to stand up. If you hope I'll even go so far as to treat you scrupulously, forget about it. I'll treat you as unscrupulously as I can. You've got no right to be in this automotive business. You're the kind of people who make other people think that all business is crummy. Well, business isn't crummy. You're crummy. I'm going to do my best to take away every bit of business you've got at Cutlass. Now you're free to take this information to your friends higher up."

Jones stood up. He said easily, "Davey, you cross me once, I'll just do that. I'll hang you higher than a Christmas goose, I guarantee. By the time we're done telling the deal you offered to make us if you gave us some more business, you'll be out on your ass. It's your move."

David made his move.

The director of purchases called David in. "I don't go along with your split. What's your justification for taking the heater shroud from Wakeman and giving it to Buckeye?"

David said, "I made this split in what I considered the best interests of National Motors. Is that sufficient reason?"

"I don't see the justification for it. The pricing is identical. You don't kick out an old source, if they meet the pricing."

"I just did."

532

Fairfax asked curiously, "What is your relationship with King Smith and Dipper Coogan?"

David's jaw tightened. "We haven't spoken since the day I quit. Does that answer your question?"

"Yes, it does. Davey, I'm going to reverse your decision."

"I want my decision to stand."

"I see no justification for it."

"I want you to take my recommendation."

"I'm sorry, Davey, I just don't happen to agree with you, unless you can come up with better reasons than you've given me."

David Battle went to his office and phoned the division manager.

Jim Parker said, "Davey? How are things down in kickback land?"

"I've got a problem. I want you to hear it."

"Come on over."

"No, on the phone. King Smith's Buckeye Stamping has the same price as Wakeman's. I took the part away from Wakeman and gave it to Buckeye. Fairfax is reversing the decision. I don't blame him, but now I'm going to put the bite on you for the second time in four years. I want that decision to stand. I want Buckeye to end up with all of Wakeman's business."

Jim Parker didn't say anything for a while. Then he said, "I guess you know King Smith is one of my closest friends. I might want to do something for him, but I don't dare stick my nose in it. I can't interfere with Purchasing. I've got to let them run their own show. Besides, if I ever put pressure on for King or anybody else, they'd crucify him down the line. You should know by now the million ways they can do it. I just wouldn't be doing King any favors if I got into this one."

"And I think you're begging the question."

"Just what is the question, David?"

"Justice. Does our corporate responsibility require that we stand by and watch a guy get it in the neck from a bunch of crooks? We're taking the easy way out if we just ignore the whole ugly mess and let them fight it out among themselves."

There was another silence. Jim Parker said, "A light dawns. Now I know why you were so set on getting into Purchasing."

"Now you know."

"Well, Davey, I think this time I'll just leave the decision up to the director of purchases. As far as I'm concerned, his decision will be final."

"Jim, I think I'm disappointed."

"By the way, I just hung up from calling Fairfax. I gave him the news that he's moving to Corporate Staff for his last year. He'll be calling the new director of purchases right about now. If you'll hang up, his girl can probably get you."

King Smith's Buckeye took all of the Cutlass business of Trent Jones' Wakeman. King called the president of Buckeye. He said gleefully, "Well, this is one time we got good enough prices to undercut those bastards at Wakeman. We cleaned 'em out." Then he said, "But there's bad news, too. That other bastard is the new director of purchases."

"Battle?"

"Battle."

"What do we do now?"

"I'll tell you one thing we don't do, we don't ever call on the director of purchases. And if that bastard ever crosses me just once, we'll see who's who and what's what."

5

In 1958 David Battle went to the corporate level as Vice-President Purchasing. In 1960 he was given broader responsibilities with the new, ambiguous title, Vice-President Administration.

There were those who said, "Work hard and long, then marry the daughter of the president, and you're in."

There were others who added, "And when your father-in-law retires, make sure you've got a home-town buddy heading the Automotive Group."

There were very few who knew the extent to which David Battle was active and effective in the operation of the Corporation. Among those who knew were Jim Parker himself; Bud Volk, who reported to Jim Parker and hence worked constantly with David Battle; and Dana Albright, the Executive Vice-President Operations, to whom Jim Parker nominally reported. Among those who did not know the job done by David Battle were Carl Pearson, the president of the Corporation, and Tony Campbell, the Vice-President Sales.

On the Wednesday before the Friday of President Kennedy's assassination, Tony Campbell and David Battle boarded an American Airlines jet for Los Angeles. Tony was pleased with himself. In six hours he would plumb the pleasant depths of Sue Cross. Four hours from Detroit to Los Angeles, an hour and a half to freshen up at the Beverly Hills Hotel, and ten minutes to get to her apartment. That left twenty minutes to get her in bed. He'd make it, with time to spare. The first time, which was in another year, took all night. That first time she finally succumbed just as he was about to say the hell with it and chalk up another failure. Each trip it was quicker. Now she'd be very glad to see him. She'd hesitate a moment and turn her cheek for his kiss, but he would take her face in his hands and kiss her lips, and her resolve would melt quickly, because, once broken, her resolve was not strong.

Sue Cross was in love with Tony Campbell. He was not aware of this. He liked Sue Cross. She was a bright, witty girl. He liked her model's good looks. He liked the way she trembled when he rubbed her breasts with the palm of his hand, the way the sex sprang up so quickly in her, the way she cried out urgently and threw herself up against him. Sue Cross was a great pleasure to him. The time he spent with her would be idyllic if she could forget about her son. She talked about him constantly. She wanted, even, to bring him up from her parents' home so that Anthony could look him over. He had no taste at all for that. He'd as soon meet the divorced husband himself. What did a four-year-old son have to do with an affair? He had his own four-year-old son, and a six-year-old son, and a two-year-old daughter. What did they have to do with affairs?

Sue Cross. He would make love to her for an hour, then he'd take her out on the town until she had drunk her fill of sorrow-drowning martinis. Returning to her apartment, she would devour him and still not fill the void of her loneliness. She would sleep with her arms around him to make sure he was still there. In the morning, when she left for the studio to play at secretary for the producer who kept her, Anthony would sleep three more hours, and awakening fresh and strong, would hold his meetings with the Los Angeles zone manager and the West Coast staff.

He would enjoy their deference. These men depended for advancement on the good opinion of the National Motors Vice-President Sales. They would point out to him three or four times how much they had gone beyond their quota for the quarter, and they would get his warm smile

536

and friendly, almost benign encouragement. He wondered what the obsequious zone manager would think if he knew that he was not thought suited for further promotion. Would the brown-nosing stop abruptly? Probably not. The habit was too deeply ingrained.

Through the afternoon they would believe that they had his rapt attention, while his mind would wander and he would scarcely hear them. Why listen? He knew it backward and forward. Why listen? How could things possibly be going better than they were for National Motors? Sales were up, the stock was up, and the Government pondered possible moves against both NM and GM because they were successful. He would pass the afternoon with a bright, warm smile over his boredom.

In the evening he would call Connie and say, "I got free after all," and she would be relieved that he had not forgotten her even after four years of love-making, and probably she would insist on dinner at home. That would be pleasant. He'd be in the mood for her tender ministrations. Of all of them, only Connie would he let rub his back and put him to sleep. Connie was the old one. She was thirty-eight; she reminded him of Wendy. She was not as beautiful, and she didn't have quite the charm and intelligence, but she had the same volatile personality that could fly between calm surveillance and wild wanting. Connie would rub his back and put him to sleep, then she'd lie beside him as long as she could stand it, and then she would wake him up and demand more of him, and while he loved her, he would think of Wendy. This would be a good two days, and he was pleased with himself. But what the hell was he going to do with David Battle?

The stewardess smiled down on him and asked, "Seat belt fastened, sir?"

Tony appraised her swiftly. She moved on. When she came back up the aisle of the first-class passenger compartment, he watched the motion of her hips.

David said, "Not bad, huh?"

Tony's first instinct was annoyance. Then he smiled his handsome, mechanical smile and asked, "When did you take up mind reading?"

The jet taxied to Metropolitan's Runway 19. The girl on the speaker said, ". . . the possibility that it will ever be necessary to use the emergency oxygen system is extremely remote, but we are required by Government regulations . . ." His mind said idly with her, ". . . just cover your nose and mouth when the mask drops down and breathe normally . . ."

Over the plane's loudspeakers came a labored gasping for breath. The stewardesses dissolved. The girl with the good hips, coming down the aisle, stopped and said to Tony, "He's a nut. An absolute nut."

"The pilot?"

"You know what he did yesterday? We were at thirty thousand feet, and he announced that there would be a lot of Air Force jets flying around, so he would advise the ladies to pull the curtain over the lavatory porthole. He's cracking up. Excuse me, I'll see you after take-off."

Tony Campbell decided that Connie would not see him this trip. He turned to David and was annoyed by the awareness obvious in David's amused expression. He asked almost gruffly, "How's Sarajean?"

"Just fine. Wendy?"

"Couldn't be better." Tony thought to himself: Just fine. Sarajean's just fine. That's why she drinks herself blind at every party. She's feeling just fine. That's why she's always telling her troubles to Wendy and anybody else who will listen. She's just fine. In a pig's eye she's just fine. He said aloud, "Understand we're coming to a party at your house Saturday."

"For Jim. Celebrate the big day."

"You can include me in the celebration. I'm going on the board at the same meeting."

David said, "Yes, I know."

Tony looked straight ahead. How did Battle know? Did the Group Vice-President keep the Vice-President Administration advised on board matters? Probably. Then he did turn his head to take one long look at David's profile. Just what the hell was the Vice-President Administration doing on this trip? Was he checking up on him for Jim Parker? Just where did Battle fit into this picture?

David said, "I'll be going on the board at the same time." He added politely, "I assume you know that."

Tony Campbell nearly jerked with surprise. He lied, "Yes, I know that. Congratulations to both of us."

The jet roared down the runway, bounced, clunking its wheels, and ran steeply up into the air.

538

Tony came out of his thoughts and said, "I suppose you got to know Jim Parker pretty well in a town the size of Sweet Water."

David turned and observed the handsome Tony Campbell. He knew exactly what the question implied. He said, "We got on fine, considering that he was six years older."

"Do you get much chance to see him now?"

"Socially? Not too much. You know Jim."

"Yes." But Tony Campbell didn't know Jim Parker. Not once had they been together socially. He decided that there was no reason to pussy-foot. He was curious, and if the largest block of stock couldn't ask questions, who could? He asked, smiling pleasantly, "David, what are Jim's plans for you? Would you say that you're Jim's protégé?"

David smiled a little, but he didn't answer.

"I'm glad you came on the trip. I'll get to know you a little better."

"Yes. That's good."

"What is it you expect to learn?"

David smiled again. "You make it sound cloak-and-dagger."

Tony was chagrined. He'd betrayed his thoughts.

David said, "I guess my girl didn't convey the entire message to yours. I just want to get some exposure to Sales. I'm deficient there, among other places."

Tony said, "Yes." He wasn't sure he believed the explanation. In committee it seemed that David knew a great deal about Sales. "You mean this is your own idea?"

"Did you think it was somebody else's?"

Tony said, "I didn't think much about it one way or the other. Glad to have the company." There was a long silence between them. Then Tony said, "David, I assume you know the line-up of the new committees?"

David said, "Yes."

Tony waited. He couldn't bring himself to ask the point-blank question of the man he considered his junior.

David said, "I'm not sure of the propriety, Tony. I mean of jumping Jim's gun. But I've got no reason not to tell you, as long as you're surprised when Jim tells you in the board meeting. Jim will be on all the committees except the Bonus committee, that will still be Mr. Winston, Mr. Dankworth, and the three outsiders. I assume you know you'll be chairman of the Marketing committee."

"How about the Operating committee, am I on that?"

"No, you're not."

"Administrative? Policy?"

"No, as a start you're only on the Marketing committee. I would assume Jim will have more plans shortly."

"And you?"

"I'm on all the committees except Bonus and Finance."

"Engineering?"

"Yes."

"You mean you're on Policy and Operating?"

"Yes.

"Well, how about that?"

David didn't say anything.

Tony Campbell asked, "Does your Administrative committee get the say of who's on the other committees?" He was smiling.

David smiled, too. "It would sound that way. No, the assignments will be made by Jim at the meeting Friday. Subject to the approval of the board, of course. The selections are his."

"Just what job does Jim have in mind for you? He wouldn't by any chance be giving you the Automotive Group, would he?"

"I couldn't say."

"Davey, I sure got to hand it to you. You're an empire builder. Most guys that get stuck in Administrative, that's the end of them. You've made something out of it."

"Yes, I think so. When I got it, it was a paperwork job. I think it's more than that now."

"I hear you're taking on Engineering Services."

David nodded. "Purchasing, Security, Engineering Services, Technical Data, we get all the cats and dogs. That's one way to get more people working for you than anybody else in the Glass Tower. Carl Pearson's got two secretaries reporting to him. Me, I've got staffs on top of staffs."

The plane leveled off for the flight to Chicago, the first leg of the journey. Tony Campbell turned and looked at David again. Where had this guy come from? Just who the hell was this guy turning out to be?

He said aloud, "Davey, I sure remember you on the ball field. You and the Dipper were the best. I sure never would have guessed we'd end up on the same plane for NM."

540

David nodded.

"You deserve your old Silent Knight reputation. I have to extort answers from you."

"I think it was a little bit exaggerated."

"What was your route to here?"

"You mean through the Corporation? I started in Production Control and Purchasing at Embassy, then director of purchases at Cutlass. I was there for six years, then I got to be VP in 1958, on my forty-first birthday."

"I beat you by one year. I made it just after my fortieth. I'm the youngest in history. That proves that my stock beats your football. How old are you, forty-six?"

"Forty-six."

"Doesn't seem possible. How can the Little Dipper get to be forty-six years old?"

"One day at a time."

"David, let me ask you. I do get the impression you're going to succeed Jim with the Automotive Group. I'll ask the question rhetorically. Do you think you'll succeed Jim the rest of the way when the time comes?"

After a moment David said, "You did say the question was rhetorical?"

"Do you have that ambition?"

David said, "I have ambitions."

"That's funny."

"What is?"

"I don't mean that you have ambitions. I mean my reaction to them. I keep thinking of you as a ballplayer. It's hard to realize you've been away from football so long. So long that you have the big ambitions at NM."

"Whizzer White? Do you think of him as a ballplayer, or as a Supreme Court justice?"

"As a ballplayer. I'm not knocking you, David. I'm just curious. We haven't known each other. It's about time that we did."

"What are your ambitions, then?"

Tony grinned. "Mixed. You combine Spanish fly and phenobarb. It makes you want a piece of tail, but if you don't get it, you don't give a damn. That's me. I combine my ambitions with my stock, then I want to go high, but if I don't make it, I'll still have the sweet consolation of my stock."

"I assume you want to be president."

"The thought's crossed my mind. I'm sure I've never said it aloud."

"Well, we all have a long time ahead to think about it. Twelve years. Assuming Jim doesn't drop dead somewhere along the way. In twelve years there will be some people you already know about, plus probably some guys that crawl out of the woodwork between now and then and make a name for themselves." He smiled. "I guess you'd be the Winter Book favorite."

Tony smiled more warmly. Now he felt more disposed toward the man beside him. Obviously David was an ambitious man, and a capable man, but he did have the sense of perspective to know that Tony Campbell and his stock were the logical succession to Jim Parker, when that far-off day would come. Tony suddenly decided that when his time came, he would do well by David Battle. The Little Dipper could be a great asset to his administration.

He was startled when David appeared to have read his mind again. David said, "I think we could do some worthwhile things together for the Corporation. We may be needed."

"You sound as though you have something specific in mind."

"I do. The administration of Jim Parker is going to be the greatest in the history of NM. He's like Herbert Hoover, the best qualified for president there ever was. Like Hoover, he's going to come a cropper."

"Do I detect some disloyalty to your Sweet Water comrade?"

"I hope quite the contrary. Jim's going to take this Corporation to new heights. I sure intend to make a contribution. I have the feeling we're going to do so well that the Government will break us up."

"Then you're predicting a Pyrrhic presidency for me?"

"Unless we prevent it."

"Spit against the wind?" Tony shook his head. "The rape is inevitable." He grinned. "Maybe we'll *all* be president of National Motors. You, and me, and Bud Volk, and Cleary. We may all get to be a president of the pieces. How will you prevent it, David?"

"By spending some time leading the country, not just leading our corporations."

"Have you heard of Romney?"

"Have you? He's a breaker-upper. I meant the people that think as we think. I think the presidents and vice-presidents of the world's most powerful industry should spend as much time in politics as the presidents and vice-presidents of the world's largest unions, or else we'll gradually be taken over by default. We've got to be something more than hired managers slicing up the big melons that were planted by the geniuses that started the automotive industry."

"Now there's a sentiment that will win you no prizes in Detroit."

"I think we could make our crusade palatable. Appeal to the better instincts. I think it's necessary. I think we can do something about it, Tony. Save NM and the country at the same time. What's good for GM is good for NM."

"I don't understand a word you're saying. I'm not sure I want to. And where do you get this Lindbergh stuff?"

"I suspect we'll be in this thing together for a long time. Cohorts, if that's the right word."

"Well, when the time comes, you tell me what you want me to do. As long as it doesn't mess with my stock, all right."

"With your stock, we've got a good start. If we had old Dankworth's with us, and the insurance stock, I think we could make our weight felt."

Tony turned and faced David full. "I think you're proposing that we get together and take over the Corporation."

"The other day my father-in-law came into the Administrative committee meeting, and he looked around and asked where the old gang had gone to. I told him he was looking at the old gang. Our time does come, Tony."

"Is this what you had in mind, coming on this trip?"

David Battle decided he'd gone far enough for the time being. He said, "Tony, I will be succeeding Jim as Vice-President Automotive."

After a long time Tony asked, "Do Volk and Cleary know it?"

"No. Outside of Jim himself, you're the only one. Pearson doesn't know it, either."

"Pearson will have a green hemorrhage."

"Why do you say that?"

"Never been a Catholic get this high before."

"You have to be kidding."

"I couldn't be more serious. There's never been a Catholic got that high before in National Motors."

"I just won't let him know I've got a hot line to the Pope."

"Well, David, congratulations. Does this mean I'll be reporting to you? I guess it does."

"Will you view it that way?"

"No, I won't. I'll co-operate, David, you can count on that."

"I do know that. I trust you know that I know you're the most eligible man in the Corporation." He smiled. "And that you have thirty-two million dollars' worth of stock."

Tony Campbell's smile was twisted. "No, don't forget my stock." Then he sat in silent turmoil. What did it all mean? Was David Battle to be the next president after Jim Parker? No, by God, it didn't mean that. It meant that David was to be, technically, his superior for a space of time. And then there would come another day, and in that other day Tony Campbell would assume his rightful heritage, and David Battle knew that and would play his cards accordingly. David Battle was all right. They would get along just fine.

Tony unfastened his seat belt. He said, "I think I'll go talk to someone prettier."

David watched him make his way up the passageway to the kitchen and the very pretty stewardess with the good hips. He smiled grimly to himself. He'd pulled it off. He'd given Tony the bitter lump and still kept his good will. If he stayed careful, he'd have Tony in his hip pocket. He'd be very careful.

6

WHEN ANTHONY CAMPBELL saw Jeanie Templeton for the first time, he decided that he had looked for her forever. His senses told him that she was a beautiful seventeen-year-old girl who would bring pleasure to him. His superstition told him that Fate had brought him the full circle to confrontation of himself, the reflection of a reflection. His premonition told him that having found her, he had found the disaster, devastation and desolation to which his urge for self-destruction had driven him through the hunting years.

He looked long and deep. He wanted to reach out and touch her tawny, cascading, hair, parted in the middle, one half flowing forward across her left eyebrow. He wanted to trace with his finger tips the outline of her high, broad, oriental cheekbones which gave her smoke-blue eyes an exotic cast, set them deep. Her nose was broad, like an oriental nose. He wanted to lean forward and touch her full fresh lips with his.

He said spontaneously, "You're beautiful, Jeanie, like morning," and she was pleased.

He carried the single overnight case to his gleaming, black, air-conditioned Embassy convertible. The sisters were dressed identically, except for color, in stretch pants, sandals and cowl-neck sweaters. He said, "You look like movie starlets. You're perfect for Palm Springs." He moved to open the door for them, but Jeanie Templeton vaulted over the side and took the middle of the front seat, preempting her sister's privilege. Tony pulled from the curb. He said, "Look out, Palm Springs."

Jeanie Templeton said, "Look out, Tony Campbell." She said it offhandedly, but he knew she did not say it idly. He knew this girl. He had never seen her before, but he knew her.

She tuned the car radio until she found the shouting music she wanted. She turned it so loud that the speaker vibrated. He said, "Good grief!" He turned it down. Momentarily she was angry, like a spoiled child. She was too young for him. Her motions and impulses were those of an impatient little girl. A commercial interrupted her music, and she jumped to dial a new station. When she found what she wanted again, she moved her hands and head in time, with a twist and a shimmy, and the while, she talked incessantly and brightly. She talked about the car. About the weather. About the music. About the trip to Acapulco on her sister's stewardess passes. About the road and the desert. Now her chatter pleased him. Her youth beguiled him. He grew progressively more enchanted with her, and he grew progressively more preoccupied with his presentiment of cataclysm. By the time they were well into the desert, he knew that he didn't want to go on to Palm Springs with these two girls. He knew that he wanted to go home. He wanted to see Wendy Barrett Campbell. That realization astounded him. He could not remember ever before wanting to see his wife. He didn't want to go to Palm Springs with a twenty-two-year-old stewardess and her seventeen-year-old sister. He wanted to get back to Detroit and get to work for National Motors. There was work to be done. He had to get back to Detroit and get cracking. He berated himself for not returning with his new friend, David Battle. David Battle did not know that Tony Campbell was headed for Palm Springs with two beautiful young girls. Tony Campbell did not know that David Battle was headed for Palm Springs to meet Kelly Brand.

Tony stopped to put the top up, because the sun burned too hot. He hit the dashboard gently with his fist while the top came to position and screwed itself home.

Jeanie Templeton asked, "What's the matter?"

He said, "Nothing." He switched the air-conditioning on, and the cold air filled the car.

Leslie Templeton said, "I love this car. Why don't you give it to me when you go back to Detroit?"

"Sure. Only it belongs to the Embassy dealer in Beverly Hills."

The sister of the stewardess said, "She already knows that."

Tony asked, "She knows what?"

"About the car and you being rich."

"Is that so? How does Leslie know?"

"She called up somebody and found out about you."

"Oh? Just who did she call?"

"Nobody that counts, don't worry. Leslie knows better than to do something like that."

"Who did Leslie call?"

"Somebody that sells Embassies."

Leslie said, "She's let that cat out of the bag."

Jeanie asked, "Aren't we supposed to know he's rich?"

Tony asked, "Who you been talking to, Leslie?"

Leslie said, "You were the second Vice-President Sales we had in one week. The first one said they had some kind of advertising deal where they loaned Cadillacs for a month to people. My dumb roommate, she gave him her real address. Can you imagine anybody so dumb? So when this guy showed up, he was driving a Hertz Chevy, and it turned out he owned a bar in Detroit. I think he was a white-slaver."

"Answer my question."

"I just thought I'd check up on you. I called that dealer and talked to the salesman, and I told him I was a secretary and my boss wanted to write a letter to the Vice-President Sales of National Motors, and I wanted the name."

"Did he know?"

"He sure did. He said you were in town, and they were sending a convertible over to the Beverly Hills for you."

Tony relaxed. "You're satisfied?"

"That salesman knows a lot about you. He says everybody knows about you. He says you have about umpteen million dollars."

"That would be a lot of money."

"That's exactly what he said, umpteen million dollars.

547

Mainly the conversation got around to what I looked like, so I told him, so he said he made more than fifteen thousand dollars a year, and he was twenty-eight and single, and he'd like to come over and give me a demonstration ride in an Embassy convertible."

"I can guess which one. Are you going to take the ride?"

"This is my second in this convertible. I beat you to it. Tony, do you really have umpteen million dollars?"

"Yes."

"How much? Twenty?"

"Anywhere from ten to a hundred million dollars, I'd say was umpteen."

Jeanie Templeton asked, "Are you one of the richest men in the world?"

"I'm not sure where I rank. I know I'm above average."

She twisted and knelt on the seat facing him, smiling pleasedly, searching his face. "What's it like, Tony? It must be nice having all that money."

"It is."

"Where did you get it?"

"I inherited it."

"That's good. You won't be so stingy with it."

Tony said sharply, "I don't like this turn of the conversation."

The younger girl was oblivious of his resentment. She said brightly, "Tony, I want to marry you."

He had to smile. He said, "I'm already married. I've got a full-fledged wife and three children. Okay?"

"I wouldn't mind that. We wouldn't have to tell anybody about us."

"You sound serious."

"I am."

"That's against the law."

"If you're that rich, they wouldn't do anything to you. Tony, I want a ranch. I really do want one. The whole thing—horses, cowboys and all. And you can keep me there, and then whenever you come West, I'll be there."

Tony asked, "Leslie, is she pulling my leg?"

Leslie Templeton said, "Yes. She does that. She's not quite as dumb as she pretends."

Jeanie Templeton turned on her sister with fury gleaming in her smoke-blue eyes. She said, "All right, Leslie. I'll fix you. I'll tell him you thought maybe you could get this car out of him. And I'll tell him a few more things."

Tony Campbell said sharply, "Knock it off. I you." Then he smiled. "Or we'll turn around and go back to Pasadena." He continued to smile. "Joke or not, I'll tell you this. I have a manager. He's seventy-three years old, and he managed the estate for my father for over twenty years, and he's a fine old gentleman and a tightwad, and he requires that we live off my current income so that we can contribute properly to organized charity. That doesn't include convertibles for beautiful girls. Okay?"

Leslie Templeton said, "Do you know what that sick captain did on the flight? He called me up there and said he was having trouble steering, and he wanted me to go look out the back window and see if the tail was still on. I think he's flipped his wig? Okay? The subject's changed? We'll all go and have a good time?"

They registered at the Ocatillo. The seventeen-year-old girl came to the pool in a tight black one-piece bathing suit, and the twenty-two-year-old girl came in a flowered, tight, soft, silky two-piece suit that was almost a bikini. The younger girl ran and dove headlong. She came up, smiling, at the other end of the pool.

Leslie said, "She's a beautiful girl. She has a wonderful figure, don't you think, Tony?"

"Yes, I do think so."

"I'm twenty-two."

"Yes, I know."

"I'm fully developed."

His teeth flashed white in his bronzed face. "I'm aware of that."

"Jeanie is seventeen."

The smile left. "I know that, too."

"Everybody says she's going to be the most beautiful girl in Pasadena. I was one of the runner-ups for Rose Bowl Queen. I bet Jeanie wins it two years from now when she's at Pasadena Junior College. I'm proud of her."

"And provoked with her."

Leslie Templeton didn't answer.

Tony smiled again. "I'm sure it's no secret, I'm fascinated with her. I'm enchanted by her. She's different. Unusual. Her cheekbones and the shape of her face and the shape of her eyes, they're almost oriental. But her coloring is Scandinavian, or Teutonic, like yours. Did some Chinaman sneak in? She *is* beautiful. Haunting. I don't know how somebody that's so young and fresh and lively can be haunting, but she's haunting."

Leslie Templeton said, "I'm glad you're haunted. And she's seventeen." She sat on the edge of the pool and let her ankles down into the water. Tony sat beside her.

Jeanie Templeton called from the other end of the pool, "Come on in, you guys."

Leslie said, "I was offered a job in Las Vegas. A nude show girl. I sure wanted to do it. It was a lot of money. And, you know, like doing something you shouldn't do. Daddy would have died. Do you know why I went with American?"

"Glamour? Travel? To meet a rich bachelor?"

"Travel. To see places. I like it. It's hard work, but it's glamorous, too, sometimes. I guess you know that. You probably know more about being a stewardess than I do. So I've been to New York, and San Francisco and Dallas, and some towns that don't count, and I've been once to Bermuda and Acapulco, and I've got the travel bug, and maybe I'll go with Pan American, because I want to go to Hawaii and Europe."

"And you're twenty-two. And you can do whatever you choose."

"Yes, I'm twenty-two."

"And you're beautiful. Why did you bring her? It's the most ridiculous thing I've ever been involved in. How could you do it?"

Leslie Templeton put her hands on her hips on top of the thin, brief, printed silk of her swim pants, then ran her hands down her legs to her knees, smearing the drops of water that had splashed on her thighs. The fine blond hairs glistened wetly on her legs.

She smiled almost ruefully. "I think I outsmarted myself. Should I tell you?"

"Yes."

"When you asked me, it made me mad. I've never dated a married man. It's not right. And it made me mad that you'd just up and ask me to go to Palm Springs with you. And I'll tell you the truth, I wanted to go, and that made me all the madder. So I decided to bring her. That would fix you. All your plans, and nothing." She brushed her legs again. "So I brought her."

"Did you change your mind when you found out about all the money?"

"I didn't say I changed. I'm still angry with you."

"I like you. I surely do, Leslie."

"I'm angry with you. You're too old for me, and too married."

"I'm sorry you brought her."

"I am, too."

"What are we going to do about it?"

"I don't know. Tony, I don't know if it's the money, or just because you're so damn handsome, or because you'll be like a sexy father to me, or what it is. Does it matter what my reasons are?"

"Yes, it matters."

"Will you believe what I tell you?"

"Yes."

"It's all those things, but mainly it's because from the first time I saw you, I felt the same way I felt when I was thinking about being a nude show girl in Las Vegas. Does that make sense to you?"

"Yes."

"Tony, we can come to Palm Springs again, just the two of us, or go to Hawaii or Europe."

Seventeen-year-old Jeanie Templeton came up behind Tony Campbell, threw her arms around his neck and flung herself into the water, taking him with her. They came sputtering to the surface. She clung tightly to him, her breasts pressing against his chest, her fingers clinging tightly to his strong back.

He said fiercely in her ear, "I'm in love with you."

She said, "Yes, I know."

7

STRAIGHT NOSE BILLY TURNER had written a letter to David Battle.

DEAR DAVEY:

I'm getting so fancy, I got me a secretary now. Only she's got some fool idea she's going to type my letters, but this is one letter going to get done one finger at a time, by me.

I hear you're very large in the Corporation now. That's good. Did you know I'm president of this little ole bank in Little Rock? I usta think them fellers that ran banks was all millionaires. I wore my frock coat, my stripey pants, and my stove-pipe hat to work the day they made me president, and one of the tellers pushed the burglar alarm. Davey, you won't believe this, but a bank president in Little Rock gets about the same as I got for beating my brains out in the National Football League. And to boot, some irate customer is bound to walk in here some day and deviate my septum.

I just couldn't defend myself, either. I wouldn't like to say I was running to fat, but I've seen houses smaller than me. I understand you look just about the same as you did. I understand you could probably step out and play yourself a ball game this afternoon. I guess you know where I hear about you.

Davey, a man that writes one letter in seven years, he ought to have something important to say. I got it. Davey, I haven't made such a good widower as I thought I would. When I was married, I usta think that was the wrong condition for me to be in. Man's a widower for three years, he gets a different opinion on his natural state.

David, I'm going to marry Kelly. I asked her, and she said yes. She said she would tell you herself, but I reckoned it was maybe my place, under the circumstances.

David, will you wish us well?

BILLY

This letter came to David on November 13, 1963. He phoned Kelly Brand at Houston. He said, "I heard from Billy."

She waited.

"Don't do it, Kelly."

"David, I've been divorced for four years, Billy's wife has been dead for three years, and it's as simple as that."

"It's not simple at all. I don't want you to marry him."

"David, I'll say it again, I've been divorced for four years. Should I remind you that you're still married?"

"I want you to meet me in Palm Springs. November twenty-first. I've scheduled a trip to the West Coast. I'm sure we can use Jim Parker's house again."

"No more, David. No more."

"You must come, Kelly. We'll talk. We'll resolve things."

He sat with her at the enclosed U-bar of the Racquet Club. Their conversation had been stiff and difficult, as though between wary strangers. They sipped their drinks in a long period of silence.

David said, "A rose by any other name isn't really as sweet. In most places you'd call this a crummy bar. Because it's the Racquet Club, it's chic."

"I don't really like Palm Springs."

"I thought you did. All this time."

"I don't."

"I don't blame you in the honky-tonk daytime. But not even at nighttime?"

Kelly Brand turned her head to him, and her hair swirled as it always swirled when she moved.

He said, "I've liked the nights here with you. And the days, too. Kelly, I don't want you to marry Billy."

"I'm sure you don't, David. I'm sure you like it just the way it is. You'll have your cake and eat it, too."

"That's not true, Kelly. You know better than that."

"Do I?"

"You know better."

"Then divorce her, David. Divorce her."

"You know I can't do that."

She sipped her drink, watching his face as he looked straight ahead. She said, "You can sleep with me, that's moral, but you can't divorce her. David, you know I just can't accept it any more."

"I don't want you to marry Billy. You wouldn't be happy. It wouldn't work out."

"Don't be too sure, David. I have the greatest respect for him. The greatest fondness." She smiled wryly and sipped her drink again. "You have to admit it would be the first time I've showed any sense. I sure never have showed it with you. David, I had no intention of ever coming out here again. But I did. I think to see if I was right. I was right."

"About what?"

"About you."

"Tell me about me."

"I'm sure you know about you."

"No, tell me. Then maybe I'll know what goes on in your mind."

"You've changed. Changed so much since I first knew you."

He smiled faintly. He held up his glass. "I drink and I sleep with girls."

"Do you, David? More than just me?"

"What do you want me to do, sign an affidavit of my feelings for you? You know how I feel about you. You know how I've always felt about you. There are no others and never have been."

"I'm glad, David. I'm glad of that. But I don't think you think of me the way you did. I just don't think that. You've gotten remote and detached. I don't have the feeling of knowing you any more. You've gone off somewhere and left me behind. Where did you go?"

554

"I think you're imagining things."

"No, I'm not imagining. Oh, I know you carry a torch for me. I know you love to make love to me. And I also know you want me to love you desperately so that you can keep me dangling. I think you've turned selfish. God help your poor wife."

"What kind of remark is that?"

"God help her. I feel sorry for her. Sometimes I feel ashamed of myself."

"I don't care to discuss this."

"David, what's your wife's name?"

He looked at her, puzzled. He said, "Sarajean."

"That's the first time in all these years either one of us has ever spoken her name. David, does she know about us?"

"I'm sure not. She may suspect, but she has no way of knowing. Besides, I don't think she's been sober long enough to know." A shadow crossed his face. "I apologize, Kelly. I've never said such a thing about her before. I apologize to you."

"David, you should probably try to get closer to her again. You owe her that. David, I'm going to marry Billy. I know I am. Give your wife a chance, there may be more for you with her than there ever could be with me."

He said in a low tone, "You can walk out of my life whenever you're of a mind to, but when you go, don't try to direct what I'm going to do after you're gone."

She said contritely, almost stricken, "I'm sorry, David. I didn't mean it that way."

He drank and ordered another. He said to her, "Kelly, the way you've been acting, some of the things you've said, I could get over you."

"Do it, David. And send me away. That would be the best thing you ever did for me."

"Listen, Kelly. I just want to time it right, that's all. I can't afford a divorce just when the big move comes along. I've got to let it sit for a few months. Maybe a year."

"David, I don't think you have the least intention of marrying me. Even if you think you do, I'm sure you don't. You'd have married me when we both had the best chance. Instead you married for advantage. You did do that, you know. You've got to know you did. I amaze myself. I thought I was so sophisticated. Instead, I'm the one that's just the little ole country girl. And you've been having sport with me all these years."

"You're doing yourself a disservice, Kelly. That's a habit with you."

"Do you love me, David?"

"Yes, I do."

"Will you divorce her and marry me?"

"Yes, just as soon as it's feasible."

"Then you love me when it's feasible. And there will always be a reason why you can't. Even if you have to fall back on your ace in the hole, your religion. David, I'm not angry with you. If anything, I admire you all the more, at least in some senses. I remember when I was so concerned about you and your mother. You've come a long way. I felt sorry for you when your mother moved in again. Now I just feel sorry for your wife. David, I just hope you haven't lost some of the good, moral things that you had when I first knew you."

"Do you think I have?"

"I'm sure you expect me to say I don't think you have. But I can't say that. I'm not sure. I'm just not sure about you any more."

"Honey, that fellow that just came in with the two young girls, do you know who it is?"

"No."

"Tony Campbell."

Tony Campbell and Jeanie Templeton and Leslie Templeton went directly into the dining, dancing area. Jeanie Templeton's arm was through Tony's. He was smiling down on her.

David said, "Well, he didn't see me. I think we should go."

"Why? Are you ashamed of me?"

"You know better than that. I just think I'd be doing him a favor if I didn't see him with the two girls."

Kelly Brand regarded David Battle with prime curiosity. "I don't think I believe that. I think you prefer to have the advantage over him—you've seen him but he hasn't seen you. Did you know he'd be in Palm Springs?"

"No. Or I wouldn't have come here. Kelly, give me some credit, will you?"

"I will, David, I will. The more you suddenly unfold to me, the more credit you get from me. David, I'm going to make a speech to you. Listen carefully. I'm not young,

556

like Tony Campbell's two girls. I'm forty years old. When I look in the mirror, I can still see the bright girl from Texas, the cheer leader, the queen, and other people still see it, too. But when I get closer to the mirror, I can see, after all, that all that time really has gone by. I'll probably be going through my change of life one of these days, David, one of these years soon. I'll go through it and then have gone through my whole life barren. That's a lonely thought. I look back and don't have too much to show for all those years that I was very attractive. Married twice to a thorough scoundrel, that's not much to show for it. A running affair with a man who doesn't even have the time to do the job properly, and I think maybe not even the full inclination to do the job properly. Is that much to show for it? Just two years, David, the ones we had in Detroit, when you were the hero, and everybody loved you, and I loved you, and I think for that time you did love me, and so we've been spending all these last years trying to get those two years back, and I guess I've just got to face up to it. I've been the stupid one, I've just been the autograph hunter, sort of hanging around outside the stadium, so you can come out and smile at me every once in a while and sign your name, and then go on home to your real life. I've got to feel that way. If you could get outside yourself and look at it from my standpoint, you'd see that. If people knew the role I've played for you all these years, they'd tell me I was out of my mind. And they'd sure be right. David, take me back to the house. I have no intention of letting you make love to me, but I know that when you touch me, I will, because I'll be stupid all over again and think we're going to get Detroit back. But when I leave here, I'm going back to Houston and tell Billy Turner I'm for sure going to marry him in six months. And that's just how long you'll have, David. Six months. And if I hear in six months you've got your divorce started, then I'll be cruel to Billy and I'll wait for you. But if I don't hear that, I'm going to go ahead and marry him and start falling in love with him. David, you'd better make love to me skillfully tonight. It will be your last chance for a long, long time. Come on, before Tony Campbell sees you."

8

DAVID CONSIDERED all the angles, then went ahead with the party for the corporation people even though Jim Parker was only a month dead.

Sixty-nine-year-old Ellen Foley Battle sewed a fourth and last patch onto a disreputable black dress. She pulled the dress on, walked across the shell-pink carpet of her beautiful bedroom, and examined herself in the full-length mirror on her closet door. She wasn't quite satisfied. She hoisted the skirt and ripped loose the hem. Now the dress hung three inches longer in the back than in the front. Ellen smiled with approval and with anticipation.

She left her big bedroom in the big home which was owned by the father of her daughter-in-law. She marched, determined and purposeful, down the corridor past the four other bedroom suites, and then with her head held high, like a queen, made her way down the wide white-carpeted staircase toward the noise of the gathering. She paraded herself into the formal living room and swept up to Carl Pearson. She held out her hand, regally, and said, "I'm David's mother."

Carl took his cigar out of his mouth. His eyes ran quickly up and down the black dress with the four crazy-quilt patches. Carl Pearson was president of one of the world's largest corporations. He was a man of considerable aplomb, but it was insufficient for this marvelous performance. He said numbly, "I'm Carl Pearson, Mrs. Battle. This is Marion Williams."

Ellen Battle said, "Yes. Of course I know your names very well. I should have met you before this, but David's wife prefers that I not meet their friends."

Not knowing what else to say, Carl Pearson said, "This is my first time in your son's home. This is a lovely place."

Ellen said, "Yes. My son is very well off."

A white-coated Negro waiter came by with a tray of drinks.

Ellen said to him, "I wonder if you would mind getting me a drink?"

"Of course, ma'am. What would you like?"

"I'd like some of that champagne, but I'm sure my son's wife wouldn't approve."

"Ma'am?"

"Just find some wine in the kitchen. Some cooking wine. I'm sure she wouldn't begrudge me that, aren't you, Mr. Pearson?"

Carl Pearson said, "I'm quite sure, Mrs. Battle."

"I must apologize for my appearance, Mr. Pearson, Mr. Williams. I asked David if I could have a new dress, but he said this one would do just fine." She smiled a martyr's happy smile. "I guess beggars can't be choosers. I don't have any money of my own, only what my son gives me, and of course his wife's mink coat comes before a new dress for me."

Sarajean Battle came in from the adjoining library. She turned white. She went back to the library and said to her husband, "David, will you excuse yourself for a minute?"

David took one look. He said, "Oh, good God!"

Sarajean Battle was on the verge of tears. "I can't stand it, David. I've never been so humiliated in my life."

"All right, I'll take care of it." He took a step toward the widening group around his mother. She had the rapt attention of half the key executives of National Motors Corporation. David stopped. He asked his wife, "You got any bright ideas? Maybe we should make a joke of it. Maybe you should rip your dress, too. Or maybe we should just ignore it, and she'll go away."

Sarajean Court Battle said, "David, I can't stand it any more. This time, either she goes or I go."

"Relax, Sarajean. It's not the end of the world. Relax."

She whispered hoarsely, "David, I've had it. I warned you. I told you a thousand times, Don't bring that woman in this house. But you wouldn't listen. David, you call a cab and get her out of this house in ten minutes, or I'll go myself."

"Hold your voice down."

"Why? What could be worse than what's happened already?"

"Just hold your voice down. And be reasonable. I can't send her out driving around in a cab for the rest of the night. Where's she supposed to go?"

Sarajean whispered urgently, "I don't give a damn where she goes. I don't give a damn if she freezes to death and drops dead. I hope she does. She's made my life miserable, David, and I hope she drops dead. And don't tell me to hold my voice down, or I'll say it loud enough for everybody in this house to hear."

David took her arm. "You've got to admit it's funny. This is the funniest thing she's done yet."

"I'm sure Carl Pearson is just dying laughing."

"It is funny. It would take a wild sense of humor to think up something as diabolical as this."

"David."

"I'm stalling. I don't know what to say to her. Okay, I give up. She's got to go. But of course not tonight. Tomorrow I'll rent her a furnished apartment and move her in."

"Tonight, David."

He set his jaw. "I said tomorrow. You listen to me. This is an important night. Okay, I'm no happier with her than you are. I said she'd go. That's tomorrow. As for tonight, you're the hostess. You're my wife, and I have some people here who are important to me, and you are one of my assets, and you will measure up."

She added defiantly, "Or what?"

"There is no or what. There's just do. You will do what is expected of you. If you please, Sarajean, would you get me a refill? I'll be talking to Carl Pearson."

He went to the closet in the foyer and took out Ellen Foley's full-length black-diamond mink coat. He walked to the group gathered around his mother and said, "Mama, if you don't like your dress, why don't you wear your coat over it?"

His mother said, "That's Sarajean's coat."

"Is that so? It has your initials in it. Hers is blue, remember." He handed his mother the coat. "If you don't feel like wearing it at the party, just hang it back up, okay?"

Ellen Foley Battle turned from her son and looked triumphantly at her approaching daughter-in-law. She took her coat and walked away, regally, the hem of her dress hanging down to the calf.

Sarajean Battle handed her husband his drink. She said nothing. The silence was heavy and uncomfortable.

David raised his glass. "To Sarajean." The other glasses raised. David said, "Just a minute. The only people that may drink this toast are those who have had at one time or another in their lives, like Sarajean, their own cross to bear." He smiled broadly.

Carl Pearson said, relieved, "By golly, it's funny! By golly, I didn't know whether to laugh or cry. I can't help it, Sarajean, you should see the look on your face. David, can I ask you? Is she eccentric?"

"She's still twenty years away from being eccentric."

Dana Albright said, "You mean she did it out of just plain meanness? There's a woman after my own heart."

But the silence grew heavy and embarrassed again.

Carl Pearson said, "Well, David, if you've got a minute, I have something to discuss with you. Just take a minute."

David took the president of National Motors into a corner of the huge living room. "Can I get your drink freshened?"

"I'm fine. Nice to be in your home. You should have asked us before. David, the question of the new addition to the Embassy plant comes up for final disposition in the next board meeting. This was one of Jim's pet projects."

David said, "I know."

Pearson narrowed his eyes. "That's what I've been given to understand, you know about it. I get the impression that it might be your plan."

"It was Jim's. He presented it."

"Whose was it originally?"

"Mine."

"Then don't beat around the bush with me."

"I have no intention of doing that. At the time, it was my superior's plan."

"Some of us are against it. Williams and I don't think it's justified."

"The fiscal evidence is incontrovertible."

"Oh, is that so?" There was testiness in Carl Pearson's voice.

"In terms of return on capital investment, building the new wing beats rebuilding the old section. We didn't go into this on the spur of the moment. The economic factors are well documented."

"And Marion and I are just not with it, right? Well, we'll continue this discussion at work." With that abrupt closing, he walked back to the large group.

Dana Albright said, "You're championing an unpopular cause. Excuse me for overhearing."

David said, "Dana, it's not all that earth-shaking. It's sure not worth any big fight on the board. I had no intention of trying to shove this down somebody's throat. It just happens to be, in the opinion of some of us who have examined every angle, a sound, logical move to make."

"Probably Carl thinks you'll include a sacristy in the new building."

David chose to ignore the implication. "If the presentation has been inadequate so far, I'll be glad to make the presentation myself."

"Didn't he invite you to the board meeting?"

"No."

"Winston himself asked for you. It must have slipped Carl's mind. Consider yourself invited."

"Fine. Is there anything else I should be prepared for?"

"Where do we put the Ohio stamping plant?"

"Bryan."

"I see."

"Yes. I've been over that one thoroughly."

"Ten o'clock, my office, tomorrow. Are you free?"

"I'll make sure that I am, Dana."

"I'm supposed to be picking up the slack left by Jim. They aren't aware that the Vice-President Administration has concerned himself with so many details of the job of the Group Vice-President Automotive."

David didn't answer.

562

"Wouldn't you say that you are handling Jim's job as of this moment?"

"I'm handling my job."

"What is your job?"

"Until I'm otherwise directed, my job is the job assigned to me by Jim Parker."

"Ten o'clock. I need briefing. David, have you ever been up to the Blue River Lodge?"

"No. I know about it."

"It's about time you were. The weekend after the board meeting, some of us have been asked up for a wild-game dinner and some poker and what not. Why don't you plan on joining us? I'll ask King Smith to send you an invitation."

David said, his face expressionless, "Fine. I'd like to see it."

David said to his wife, "The party was a success. I think everybody was glad to get out of mourning."

Sarajean Court said, "David, I finished the evening for you. Now that's the end."

"Don't talk foolishness."

"And don't you talk down to me, like I'm irresponsible. David, I've had it. I just can't stand it any more. It's not just her. It's the whole thing. It's the whole damn, lousy thing. It's the way you treat me. You have no respect for me. You don't love me. I guess you never did. So I'm not blaming you, but I've had it, and I'm leaving while I'm still young enough that somebody else will want me."

"I'll talk to you in the morning."

"If you're going to talk, it better be right now."

He said levelly, "Sarajean, I'm going to say something to you I've never said. I have no desire to discuss anything with you when you've had too much to drink."

She laughed bitterly. "Then when can you? Everybody knows I always have too much to drink. Poor David Battle. His wife drinks too much at parties."

"Yes, you do. I'm sure it's time I said something about it."

"Did you ever stop to think just why I drink? It's because I'm lonely, that's why. It's because I'm married to a man that doesn't love me, that's why."

He turned his back and began to undress.

She said hotly, "You see, you won't talk to me. You

563

won't discuss anything. Do you know you scarcely said one word to me at the party?"

He faced her. "I was talking to other men. And while they were talking to me, they couldn't have been talking to their wives, either. Don't try to convince me you're uniquely ill treated. You're a married woman, and you have the same problems with husbands at parties that almost every other married woman has. Go sleep it off."

Her lip trembled. She said, "David, I want a divorce."

Then he said sharply, "I'll tell you why you drink. It's because you don't have any guts, that's why. You feel so sorry for yourself, poor Sarajean Court, people don't treat her like the Queen of the May, the way she wants to be treated. Sarajean, I haven't got time to take care of you. I've got enough problems taking care of myself. I expect you to take care of yourself. I've got some important things I want to do. I expect you to do your share. I don't expect you to hang around my neck crying about what a raw deal you're getting, and how unhappy you are, and how you just have to drink because everybody, and particularly me, is doing such terrible things to you.

"I can't work up that much sympathy for you. Maybe it is my fault. You're the second girl who decided I wasn't in love enough to suit them. I'm not sure just what my shortcomings are in this area. Probably I'm not demonstrative enough. But my fault or not, there isn't going to be any change. You've got to make do with what you've got, you've got to make do with me as I am.

"And for that matter, what on earth more do you want? I've enjoyed living with you. I've enjoyed your company. I've been proud of you as a wife. I've enjoyed making love to you. I wish we had some children. We don't, so we don't. Maybe I could wish a lot of things were different and better. But it's good enough that I don't have to go around complaining about it. And it's good enough that you don't have to go around crying about it and drinking about it.

"Where did you ever get the idea you're the only woman that doesn't get her husband's undivided attention? Do you think you're the first wife who has a husband married to his corporation? I'll guarantee you're not. I'm sure you can get all kinds of sympathy from some other wives who drink too much. Poor wives, neglected while their husband does his best at his job. National Motors gets all

564

the best that's in him, gets all the best of his time, and you just get the leftovers. Well. I've got no way of justifying my life to you. If I have to justify it, then I couldn't possibly.

"But as far as I'm concerned, you and the rest of them that drink too much, and some that flirt too much, and some that climb into the sack with the wrong men, you're begging the question. No matter what you say about it, when you drink too much, that's your own problem that got born within yourself, not outside yourself. There may be shortcomings in the husbands, I'm sure there are. But you drink because of the shortcomings in yourself, and I'm not buying your rationalization."

She said, "Get rid of that woman."

"Sarajean, I'm going back on my promise to you. I can't help it. She stays here. I wish it could be different. But it can't. Some parents, you can put them out on their own where they belong. Mama would get worse and worse. You don't know the half of it. Do you think she's made your life miserable? I could tell you a few things. My sister won't let her in the house. Honey, I told her if she ever pulls anything like that again, I'll ship her back to Sweet Water and she can sit by herself in the white house until it falls down around her. I've scared the pants off her, and she'll toe the mark for a while. But you know damn well she's going to get off the track again. Honey, don't be so polite to her. The next time she crosses you, you let her have both barrels. You'd be doing her a favor. She wants attention. Give her some attention that she'll really feel, and you'll blow some of your own steam off at the same time."

"David, for God's sake, get rid of her!"

He went back to his undressing.

She said, "David, I want a divorce."

"There won't be any divorce. There is no such thing."

"You want to bet? You just want to bet, mister?"

"Listen to me. If I'm not satisfied being married and living here with you, it's up to me to find within myself the things that will make me satisfied, not make some demands on *you* to satisfy me. If you find your life wanting, then look within yourself and make your life full. I'll still be here. You'll likely find a great deal more of me than you've been seeing for some time."

"You're making me ill. You're talking like a goddam

565

priest. You just get down off your high horse, mister. I know why you married me in the first place, to get my money, that's why. And you've been running around ever since with hot pants for Kelly Brand, don't try to kid me. And don't pull that holy act with me. You'd divorce me in a minute, if you thought you could have your dolly and still make president of National Motors."

"Sarajean, if you really believe that, then you go right ahead and divorce me and be damned. But you sure ought to know by now, I'm still concerned about you, and I still feel the same way about you I did when we looked at the geese on Upper Straits Lake, and we didn't say much, but we sure wished each other well. It hasn't changed. Except you want me to be different and say things. Honey, I didn't even say things then!"

"I scared you good, didn't I?"

"Like how?"

"When you know I want a divorce, butter won't melt in your mouth. You can see National Motors going right down the drain. Well, let me tell you something, you never had a chance in the first place. Marrying me didn't really get you any further than you probably would have gotten anyway. And now you've had it. Jim Parker's dead and buried, and you right along with him. Just who do you think's going to pay any attention to you now, without him to back you up? Tell me, just who?"

"Sarajean, I can't have anything else to say to you. I wish I could. But I'm no hero. I can't forgive you. Now I hate you, I finally hate you."

Her voice broke. "Get rid of her, David! For God's sake, get rid of her!"

He turned his back.

"David, I don't just drink too much, I'm an alcoholic! Don't you know that? Don't you even pay that much attention to me? While you've been busy, I'm an alcoholic!"

He walked from the bedroom.

9

THIRTEEN MEN at the long Board Room table turned to David Battle and his battery of charts. Of the thirteen, six were Corporation men, six were outside men, and old Avery Winston, chairman emeritus and the mighty power behind six thrones since vacating his own, was the balance wheel.

From the Corporation came Carl Pearson, president and chairman of the board, his term having been extended for the three weeks since the death of James Lee Parker. Carl Pearson presided.

On his right sat Winston. On Winston's right came Ruggles, an outsider, president of Columbia Steamship Lines. Next came Marion Williams, Executive Vice-President Finance. Next Holmquist, an outsider, senior partner of the brokerage house of Smith, Winchell, Hartman and Holmquist.

On Pearson's left came Dana Albright, Executive Vice-President Automotive, the man who had been nominally the immediate superior of Jim Parker, but had been in practicality his assistant in the final year of Jim's drive to the top. Next to Albright sat Carideo, president of the Bank of the United States. Then Wolgast, another outsider, president of the big chemical house that owned twelve per cent of National Motors.

Then came Werner Bud Volk, vice-president and general manager of the Cutlass Division, formerly heir-apparent to Jim Parker as Group Vice-President Automotive and now one of the two leading candidates to succeed Pearson as president.

Then came Hankins, who represented the insurance firm which had loaned National Motors three hundred million dollars in a mutually advantageous arrangement. Across from him sat old Dankworth, the wagon manufacturer, the largest individual stockholder in the Corporation. Between them, at the foot of the table opposite Carl Pearson, sat the newest member of the board, Anthony Campbell, Vice-President Sales, so that the largest individual stockholder and the second largest individual stockholder sat side by side. David let his eyes come to rest on Anthony Campbell.

Carl Pearson said, "We're at your disposal, David."

David said, "Gentlemen, I have ten charts here that are intended to prove that an expenditure of thirty-two million dollars for an addition to the Embassy plant is preferable to spending eighteen million for modernization of the existing structure. For the next ten minutes the charts will do my talking for me. Then for five minutes we will have a slide presentation of the project, including architects' drawings, to show what you will be getting for your money."

Carl Pearson said, "Provided we buy the program."

"Yes, sir. I believe that you will. Our presentation takes fifteen minutes. Several weeks' study by some competent men has gone into this fifteen minutes."

Anthony Campbell thought to himself: Don't be smart-alecky, Davey. That sounded just a little bit smart-alecky.

For twenty minutes David spoke calmly and firmly. He knew his subject thoroughly.

Carl Pearson said, "Good presentation, David."

Dankworth said, "Hear, hear."

Avery Winston said, "Mr. Dankworth prefers the chart and slide type presentations, Mr. Battle. For that matter, so does this entire board. I assure you, your presentation will play a part in our deliberations on this appropriation."

David said, "I must conclude my remarks in this way. If our concern here is for the next two or three years, the decision would be a close thing in my opinion. I would

568

still lean toward the new building, even on such a short-term comparison as that. In terms of our long-term building program, that is, if you wish to bracket this improvement with the over-all program, I think the issue is one-sided."

Marion Williams said, "So we gather." He said it drily, but without malice.

Carl Pearson said, "Thank you, David."

Dana Albright said, "I'd like to bring up another matter while we have Mr. Battle here. David, I would like you to tell the board your reaction to our loss of the armored-vehicle program. Gentlemen, Mr. Battle has suggested to me that we shouldn't take this loss lying down. He feels that we should fight back. If you approve, we'll do something about it. David?"

David said, "We're talking about the repercussions of our loss of the T-231 armored-vehicle program on this year's bid. Some of you may not be familiar with this program. I'll review it. We have been operating a Government-owned plant in Romulus, Michigan. We have had both the engineering and the production on the T-231. We won it originally on open bid. We have had a successful program for seven years now. Each year the production requirements have been put out again for open bid. Each year we have been the successful bidder. This year we lost. U.S. Machine & Foundry came in with a bid six million under ours on a sixty-four-million-dollar contract. We do not think their bid is realistic. We think it's possible that they intentionally bid below cost and hope to recoup through engineering changes. But that is not our concern at the moment.

"Our concern is the upheaval at Romulus. We will continue to handle the engineering and some administration. U.S. Machine will take over the production. It is our understanding that they will be moving in their own work force from their Wayne plant. You may know, they lost their railcar contract at the Wayne plant.

"We are suddenly faced with the prospect of laying off seven to eight thousand men. These are high-seniority men. The age level is considerably higher than average. As a result, there is not much chance that they will be picked up by U.S. Machine or anybody else, because of the retirement penalty this would impose on the new employer. This is one of those instances where the retirement benefits won by the Union work out to the great disadvantage of the union member. These men are out of a job, maybe permanently.

"It is my opinion that we should make the strongest representations to the Secretary of Defense, not only on behalf of these dislocated men, but on behalf of the country and of National Motors. We should remind him of the considerable inefficiencies which will likely develop out of this shift. The dislocation may well result in delayed production and an inferior product.

"From our corporation standpoint, he should be reminded that we have a considerable investment in this program. Our pricing has been sound. We should not be penalized by an apparently irresponsible bid. He should be reminded of the drastic effect this will have on our commercial operations. By laying off this many men, we have increased our unemployment compensation payments by several million dollars. Even though we have managed well, we have now been hit with a major assessment through no fault of our own. I have suggested, then, that we should make the strongest representation we can to the Secretary to see if we can convince him he should void the last bid and negotiate a satisfactory price with us. I feel sure that we can demonstrate to him that this is in the interest of national defense."

Dankworth said, "What you mean is, you can lead that horse to water. But if I know him, you might not be able to get him to drink. He might not drink just out of sheer cussedness, even if he was dying for a drink."

David said, "Yes, sir."

"My question is this, Mr. Battle. I have heard it suggested that we should withdraw from further competition in this area. If all of the large, responsible companies did this, it would bring the Defense Department to see reason. At the very least, it would limit the field of bidders and provide at least that much more likelihood of continuity in these important programs. What would your reaction be, Mr. Battle, if you could not persuade the Secretary to your point of view?"

"Sir, we don't have the option of withdrawing from future competition."

"Why don't we, Mr. Battle?"

"At some point we must reconcile ourselves, right or wrong, it is our defense we're talking about. National

570

Motors and the other automotive companies do have an obligation to do defense work, even when it's unpleasant. Furthermore, I think we should be reminding ourselves that the open-bid procedure is basically sound. It is the moral procedure. It is consistent with the notions we express when our own hides are not so directly involved. Mr. Dankworth, I think we should fight hard for solution of this thorny problem we've got, but even if we're not successful, we should go back after this program next year. I need scarcely remind you that some of our defense work has been not only patriotic but highly profitable. The bitter with the sweet. Mr. Dankworth, a portion of our chagrin is due to our complacence. Sometimes we're tempted to feel that we're so big and do everything so well, that we just naturally will, every time, do the job better than the next guy. That's not necessarily true. Sometimes an inventor in a garage will solve a problem we've had twenty of our best engineers working on for months. I think we should hit the Secretary hard, but I think we should also be prepared to come away with egg on our face. He may just be able to throw some figures at us proving that while we've grown complacent with this job after seven years, somebody at U.S. Machine has come up with some corner-cutting that beats the daylights out of us, fair and square. This meeting with the Secretary will have to be played by ear."

Dankworth asked, "Will you be the man calling on him, Mr. Battle?"

Dana Albright said, "He will accompany me. We have a meeting set up late this afternoon at the Pentagon."

Avery Winston said, "It strikes me that this meeting has the highest importance and significance. It will set a pattern. Carl, it might be a good idea for you to go along with Dana and Mr. Battle and lend the weight of your title."

Carl Pearson said, "I agree with you."

Albright said, "Fine, Carl. We have a helicopter standing by at the downtown port to take us to La Guardia. If it's all right with you, we'll go to Washington in my plane, as scheduled. We're returning to Detroit tonight."

Avery Winston said, "Do your travel-agency work on your own time, gentlemen." He was only half serious.

Dankworth asked, "Shall we pick any more of young Mr. Battle's brains while we have him up here?"

Avery Winston said, "As a matter of fact, I have a question. I was given to understand earlier today that Mr. Battle is the man in charge of our racing-team effort. If this is correct, Mr. Battle, how does this happen to come under the Vice-President Administration?"

David said, "We cover a multitude of sins, Mr. Winston. In this case, we recruited and trained a crew from our dealers, not from our Engineering Department. I felt it was appropriate to divorce it from Engineering or Sales."

"You decided, Mr. Battle?"

"Yes, sir."

"My grandson advised me this morning that we weren't on the stick in stock-car racing. On checking, I found that our Engineering Department was not involved at all. This concerns me. I'd like to know the basis of your decision. I might also like to know on what authority you made this unilateral decision."

"It was my decision that using dealer teams had two distinct advantages. First, we get better mechanics than we have in our Engineering Department. Regardless of our engineering abilities, racing is a specialized field. So we've recruited some specialists. Second, we hedged our bet somewhat. If our racing program isn't successful, it will be outside mechanics who weren't good enough, not our Engineering Department. The job of our Engineering has been to provide us a racing package. This they have done. The new 565-horsepower engine will do the trick. While we're on this subject, we have felt that with the new sports-car package, and this engine in its cut-down version, we should make a run for the big international road races in 1964. We're optimistic."

Avery Winston asked, "Who decided? Who is we?"

David Battle said, "I decided, sir."

"Is this within your authority?"

"Until someone delineates my authority differently from the way I now see it, it is within my authority."

Dankworth said, "Mr. Battle, our advertising people want to come out with a big contest to name the new sports car. We've just been asked to approve it. Will you save us the expense and give us a name?" He appreciated his own humor.

David didn't say anything.

Dankworth said, "I suspect you have one. Do you?"

David smiled. "Driving to work, I've substituted car-naming for driver-cussing. I've submitted a couple of names to our people."

Dankworth asked, "Well?"

David said, "For the sports car, Commando."

Dankworth said, "Not bad."

"For the new compact, one occurred to me that we've somehow missed all these years. The National."

Avery Winston looked down the table at Tony Campbell. "Mr. Campbell, have we ever used National? Has it ever been submitted?"

Tony wished he knew all the thousands of names that had been proposed for National Motors cars. He was forced to say, "I'll check it out, Mr. Winston."

Then Avery Winston waited for David to say, "I've already checked it out." David didn't say it. Winston was sure that it had been checked out completely, but David didn't use the opportunity to rub it in on the new member of the Board of Directors. Avery Winston thought to himself: Young Mr. Battle, you don't know how close you came. If you'd said it, you were done with me. This way, I don't like it that you know so much of what's going on, but I'll listen, I'll listen.

Aloud Avery Winston said, "I'm sure Mr. Battle and the board have more important things to do than name automobiles. Mr. Battle, we'll have one more report from you, now that we have you before us. How are things in your Purchasing Department?"

"I'm satisfied."

"No report?"

"We let one purchasing agent go last week for alcoholism. We transferred a senior buyer because he was too close to the vendors."

"On the take?" Pearson asked sharply.

"No, sir. Just so close to old friends that his judgment was getting cloudy. It wasn't exactly a disciplinary move. More in the nature of a warning. These are inconsequential things to discuss before the board. I have intended to send one report to Mr. Pearson, and I'll bring it up now. We do have something of a continuing morale problem in Purchasing. It's the problem of the balance of power between Engineering and Purchasing. As you know, one of the Big Four gives too much strength to Purchasing, and this takes the initiative too much away from their engineers. An engineer can design and specify something, but he can't get it on the car unless Purchasing approves the budget. At another of our competitors, Engineering has traditionally been too powerful. They send drawings over to Purchasing with specified vendors. They have unwarranted control over sourcing. Obviously this cuts the heart out of Purchasing and costs the Corporation a great deal of money. I would say we don't have either of those problems. I would say that in the past year we've struck a remarkable balance between Purchasing and Engineering. Will you concur, Bill?"

Bill Cleary, the Vice-President Engineering, said, "I concur. Our departments get on remarkably well."

David said, "But I still feel very strongly that the top Purchasing posts should be upgraded, both in title and compensation, to give them stature in their dealings within the company. I feel that the director of purchases should be a vice-president. I suggest that the board take this under advisement. The suggestion will be detailed in the next report to the Administrative committee."

Carl Pearson said, "We'll consider it, David. A good point."

Old Dankworth said, "Mr. Battle, with your wide range of interests back at the store, it might be simpler to ask you, With what areas do you *not* concern yourself?"

David wasn't sure he wasn't being put on. He decided to answer soberly. "Finance, sir. By that I mean pure finance. Of course all of us are concerned with Finance as it directly relates to our own projects. And Engineering is essentially out of my bailiwick. In both these cases I rely on the experts."

Tony Campbell winced for David. David had misspoken. He had said, just as though he were president of the Corporation, "I rely on the experts." Surely it wouldn't go unnoticed.

It didn't. Cleary said, "I appreciate your vote of confidence, David."

David smiled just a little. "I rely on Engineering, Bill, as I do the rising and setting of the sun."

Tony Campbell thought to himself: Not a bad recovery, David.

Cleary said, "Then may I assume you will withdraw your objections to our request for soft-trim research money?"

David didn't smile. "I am against that expenditure. There is no justification for it."

Cleary smiled, but it was a dangerous smile. "Please disabuse me of my misconceptions."

"An automotive company cannot profitably enter the soft-trim business. This is an area which Purchasing has had under constant scrutiny. I feel that your soft-trim engineers have gone just a little bit romantic on this one. The automotive portion of the fabric and carpet business is quite small compared to the domestic usage. The big textile mills use automotive business as a filler and as a burden carrier. The capital equipment and the research are carried principally by the domestic usage. A new company confining itself to automotives sales could not likely compete with the current domestic suppliers. I am convinced this would be the case, just as surely, if National Motors went into the fabric business. My opinion is that no money should be invested in this area. We have a detailed report on its way to you, Bill. You should have it early next week.

"On the same subject, I think I should say that we should let the Du Ponts worry about the new synthetic materials. There's no sense turning National Motors Research into a poor man's Du Pont. We can keep our hands full finding automotive uses for the things the chemical people dream up for us."

Avery Winston said, "You've done your homework, Mr. Battle."

David risked no answer.

"We could keep you here for some time and profit from your views, but it will be more efficient for our operating people to seek them out when you return to Detroit. If your reports in detail are as comprehensive as your generalities are incisive, I'm sure you can make a contribution in several areas. Will that be all from Mr. Battle, gentlemen?"

Old Dankworth said, "I would like to be indulged. I would like to ask our young Mr. Battle one more question. I ask it with malice aforethought. Or rather with knowledge aforehand. I have in my possession a memorandum sent under Mr. Battle's signature to his Purchasing Department. It came into my possession from a member of this board. I would like to read it to you, gentlemen, in case you have not seen it."

Old Dankworth adjusted his spectacles and held the paper at arm's length, straight out ahead of his face.

Dana Albright said, "If I may, Mr. Dankworth, I think I should say that this is an excerpt from a talk Mr. Battle gave to his department. A man can say things in person he hesitates to commit to writing, lest he sound pompous. The director of purchases made the transcript and distributed the memorandum."

David said, "Thank you, Dana. I had girded my loins to be considered pompous."

Dankworth said, "Then, Mr. Battle, please speak your lines, addressing them to all departments."

"Yes, sir. I spoke of our mission. Rather of our job, that's less pretentious and more accurate. Our job is sales. No matter what our department, our job is sales. Our mission as a corporation is to sell automobiles at a profit to the stockholders.

"There is a natural enough tendency for all of us to view our own areas as the be-all and end-all of the business. We have engineers, for example, who believe that the engineering job they do is an end in itself. From their own personal standpoint, this is valid. But from a corporation standpoint, I think it would be a healthy thing to remind those engineers occasionally that only that portion of their effort is pertinent which results in profitable sales for the Corporation. The same is true of Manufacturing, Quality Control, Purchasing, and even Sales itself. I think it would have a purgative and salutary effect to remind all of us that we justify ourselves within this Corporation only by what we contribute to selling automobiles at a profit. That is a condensation of my remarks to my Purchasing Group."

Dankworth said, "Sometimes the most obvious truths are overlooked, neglected. I think you have presented a good yardstick by which to measure the performance of all the employees of National Motors, including those on the executive bonus roll, wouldn't you agree, Carl?"

Carl Pearson said without noticeable enthusiasm, "I agree. We'll use that suggestion."

David asked, "Will that be all?"

Dankworth said, "Just a minute. I still haven't asked my question. Please humor me, gentlemen. Mr. Battle, you seem like a bright, alert young man with your feet on the ground. You have made this quite practical suggestion for the philosophical approach of all our men to their daily job. I would like to hear from you what you think should be the philosophical approach of our top executives? Of our president? Of this Board of Directors?"

David said nothing.

Dankworth said, "Well, Mr. Battle?"

"Mr. Dankworth, I have some definite thoughts. I feel perhaps they are not appropriate at this time."

"Just what would make them appropriate, Mr. Battle? Need I remind you that I have been on this Board of Directors since the Corporation was formed in 1908? Need I remind you that I am the largest single stockholder in this Corporation? I would think a question from me was automatically appropriate."

David looked as though he would smile, but he didn't.

Dankworth said, "I think I can read your mind, young man. You're thinking that between me and young Mr. Campbell here, we've got more stock than any other two people in the world, and for all that stock we've got just two out of the thirteen votes on this board. Is that what you're thinking?"

David wished he could knock them out of their chairs. He wished he could tell them that with the Campbell stock, the Dankworth stock and the insurance company power, he was sure he could indeed seize control. He smiled and said, "Yes, sir, that's a good approximation. Mr. Dankworth, I'm not bashful about my political ideas. In the appropriate forum, I would like very much to present them."

Old Dankworth said with strength in his voice, "I want to hear from you now, young man, and I'm sure this board will humor me."

Carl Pearson said drily, "We'd all be very much interested, David."

Avery Winston said, "It would appear you are still in demand at our board meeting, Mr. Battle. Do you care to answer the question, or to reserve your answer for another time?"

This was the opportunity to duck the challenge gracefully. David said, "I will answer."

Tony Campbell thought: Go ahead, David, kill yourself.

David said, "I should identify myself politically. I'm a moderate." He smiled his good smile. "I have yet to meet a man who didn't believe that he was the moderate and that those who disagreed with him were extremists. Most people call me a conservative. Or even a reactionary. That's because I have some unfashionable beliefs. I have a freedom obsession. I'm against organizations. I'm against government, the United Auto Workers and the CIO. I'm against the NAACP and the Anti-Defamation League. I'm against communism, socialism, Nazism and liberalism, and I'm not sure I'm crazy about motherhood, the United States Chamber of Commerce and the Boy Scouts. It is my consuming concern that individual men are gradually disappearing into one huge, homogeneous mass organization, rushing like lemmings to oblivion.

"But I'm not a true alarmist, I don't think. Only a fool beats his breast and shrieks from the housetops that the socialists are destroying mankind utterly. Socialists couldn't do this. Nobody could. We're pompous, socialists or reactionaries, if we think that what we do at this moment will determine for all time the course of history in the cosmos. Man will never destroy himself utterly. He can't. From his noble, foolish experiments, man always returns to the instincts the Creator put in him.

"I want to suspect that I have a sense of humor and perspective. It is the Birchers and the liberals who have an inability to see anything good in those with whom they disagree. All men do have good motivation. All men see themselves as the saviors of mankind. There is conflicting understanding of man's affairs and man's emotions and man's destiny, and this separates us, but we are always united in our wish to do *good* for mankind. Because of this I am optimistic.

"Man *has* an instinct for freedom, all men—white men, black men, yellow men, red men, all men. Men surrender their freedom in exchange for security. But it's always born again, that pride of man in his worth as an individual. Because there's that strong thread of dignity that runs through our philosophical evolvement from Eden to future Nirvana, the eternal philosophy intended by Creation when we were lifted from the ooze and pointed toward godliness."

Tony Campbell thought to himself: You're fancy, boy, mighty fancy. What kind of hole are you digging yourself?

David said, "The thread doesn't break. Mankind is resilient. Mankind rebounds from feudalism, from Stalins and Hitlers, from inquisitions, from puritanism, and will rebound from the American liberalism that now spreads its government over us like a blanket.

"We can sit here and wait for the pendulum to swing. We can sit here and wait a few hundred years until America falls of its bureaucratic weight and a new, vital civilization ascends somewhere else. In Einstein's continuum, mankind would be just as well served. Wait. That's the comfortable thing to do. It's probably the smart thing to do. I have a great many friends who have accommodated themselves to the inevitability. I understand them, I accept them, and I have scorn for them."

Tony Campbell said to himself: Way to go, David. Get very specific. Stick your neck out.

"The socialists fight for their beliefs and deserve the victory that now is theirs. The men who believe as we believe have surrendered abjectly. Mr. Dankworth, I indict the leaders of the automotive industry."

Tony was startled and greatly pleased.

"I indict the businessmen of Detroit and America. I refuse to accept their plaintive cry that they can't stop the Juggernaut. I refuse to allow them the comfort of expedient surrender. They tell me that they are too busy being managers. They even excuse themselves on the grounds that they are not permitted to be controversial. I'm not quite clear whether they believe it is the Government, or the Union, or the Corporation which will throw them in jail if they are controversial.

"We are rapidly approaching the day when the President of the United States and his Supreme Court can do exactly what they wish. Then their orders may be neither legal nor moral. The leaders of the automotive industry should be more aware of this than any other single group. It should not be necessary to document for the automotive industry the great inroads made by America's professional liberals on our freedom as individuals and as citizens of sovereign states in a federal government. And yet we have accommodated ourselves to political beliefs we could not have abided in braver years. We are men who are afraid to say the word capitalism out loud. We have succumbed, ourselves, to the blandishments of the protective superstate.

"I hear them say, 'David, you're behind the times.' Because I believe in freedom? They say, 'Relax and make the best of it.' Men who say that fill me with sorrow and with emotions stronger than sorrow. I indict the business leaders of Detroit. Surrender? Just because the going is tough, we should surrender? That's when you fight. You fight. You win.

"I think there has been created in America a new race of men, the corporate managers, men who wear blinders, one blinder marked *National,* and the other blinder marked *Motors,* men who see nothing but Chrysler Corporation, and Ford, and General Motors, men who live in a warm bath of conformity. I think there are men in this Corporation of ours who haven't stuck their heads out and looked at the real world in twenty years. This attention to duty does wonders for dividends and stock options. It will also be destructive of us in our time. While we're hewing to our line, the professional liberals are indeed busy remaking our world."

Tony Campbell said silently: Tough, Davey. Really lay it on.

"I'll go one step further in my indictment. Our corporation executives have not only failed to give strength to those who believe as they believe, they have actually been unwittingly in the forefront of the raiding party. I'm talking about men who have brought on the evils of the big union. We may be able to convince outsiders that the Government installed big unions, but we won't convince ourselves. For the sake of convenience in bargaining, the Big Four put the unions in business to stay. That is typical of our surrender to expediency. Our automotive executives have rationalized themselves into careers of expediency. They view themselves strictly as hired managers, not leaders. They will do what is expedient for the corporation, not what is in the grand sense right. They do what is comfortable. The average automotive executive today is like a tooth from which a dentist has pulled the nerve. 'There is prosperity. Don't move. It might go away.' "

Tony Campbell looked for reaction in the impassive faces at the table.

"What do I want you to do about it? Gather your saliva and spit against this wind? Indeed I do. How do I reconcile my distemper with my cosmic sense of humor and perspective? Mr. Dankworth, a million years from now, nobody will know what we have done, but the man who fights for his beliefs here and now is a man who has

580

done much with himself. He will have won the greatest of prizes. He will have won self-esteem and the esteem of his Creator.

"I believe in the immutable virtues which built our country. I believe in the Golden Rule. I think it is time to return to these basic, eternal precepts for judgments on puzzling social problems in our modern complex, as our burgeoning knowledge gets further and further out of the grasp of the puny men in government. Things change. We must adapt our existence to the changes. We must be modern in our view of the world, as we are modern in our Corporation. But truth does not change. The words of the Bible were true when they were written, are true now, and will be true tomorrow when men can accomplish wonders now undreamed. Americans do believe in unalterable morality. You can't invent new moralities just to meet new exigencies.

"I believe that our great strength in America has been in the dignity and initiative of individual man. I believe that those who subvert individual man to collectivism in any form are destroying our great strength, and that if they are not checked, there will inevitably come a day when we are no longer the greatest nation on earth. I don't want freedom to come back in another place. I want it here. I am an American.

"Mr. Dankworth, I want our automotive leaders to stand up and tell this country that government is not God, government is men. I want them to stand up and tell the men in government to stop directing us, and stop intimidating us. I have no patience with our weeping, and wailing, and gnashing of teeth. Do you agree with my beliefs? When was the last time the people in this room did anything about it?

"We're an anomaly. We're against big government, and yet we are big business, and our people have become bureaucrats. Corporate responsibility? That is correct, our first duty is to the stockholders, that's what we're paid for. That's our first duty as businessmen. But as American citizens, our first duty is to our moralities. We have the United Fund, and the Boy Scouts, and all the formalized ways of fulfilling our responsibility to the public. But what about our responsibility of leading? The men in this industry are the leaders in the state of Michigan. We run the single most important industry in the world. We *can* make our views felt. If we do, we will be applauded by millions of people.

"I'm not suggesting that this Board of Directors get up on a soapbox. I'm not talking about rash action, or full-time action. We've got a business job to do. But we are leaders. We must lead.

"I believe in the fundamental morality of the American people. I believe that our basic virtues will never succumb, in the ultimate, and that the strength of individual man in America will let us survive as the greatest of nations. You *must* lead. You *are* the leaders. Men with your strength must preside at a rebirth of idealistic, Golden Rule America."

David Battle's square jaw set with his determination and his fervor. His brilliant blue eyes held the great men of the board enraptured.

Dankworth came to his feet. He applauded soundlessly with his hands raised high. He said softly, "Hear, hear."

Each of the men at the board table applauded. Ruggles rose, and Carideo, and Dana Albright. The last man to applaud was Carl Pearson. He was barely preceded by Tony Campbell.

The board settled back in their chairs.

Dana Albright said, "Well done, David, well done."

Carl Pearson said, "Well said." He didn't smile.

Avery Winston said, "Very enlightening, Mr. Battle. This has been a tour de force. We have occupied you for a full hour of our board meeting, a performance of virtuosity and versatility unprecedented in this room. I believe that we will have no further requirements of you at this meeting."

Tony Campbell leaned back in his director's chair. He put the eraser of his pencil to his lips. In his mingled emotions, he thought to himself: Too bad, Davey, boy. A great performance. A great speech. And you're dead, boy. You've killed yourself. Avery Winston and Carl Pearson don't want a radical like you running a company like this.

10

CARL PEARSON entered his forty-foot-square office on the seventh floor of the Glass Tower. David Battle waited for him. Carl waved his hand. "Sit still, David."

"You wanted to see me, Carl?"

Pearson sat at his desk. He lit a cigar. As he puffed, he said, "Yes. I've got some things to go over with you." He stopped puffing and leaned back in his chair. "David, we've become aware in the past weeks that Jim Parker wasn't doing all the things we thought he was doing."

David said earnestly, "If you mean that he knew how to delegate authority, you're right."

"We miss Jim, but he's not indispensable."

"He was indispensable as a man. No one is indispensable as a vice-president."

"You always say the right thing. One of these days, break down and make a mistake."

"Is that an order?"

Without changing expression or tone, Pearson said, "We've made you Group Vice-President Automotive."

David did not move a muscle.

Carl Pearson asked, "Did you hear me?"

"Yes. Effective when?"

"Effective immediately. You were also elected to the board."

"I'm prepared, Carl."

"I'm sure you are."

"I'm most appreciative. May I ask you—I assume Jim had said something to you about his intentions?"

"What intentions?"

"To give me the Group."

Pearson lied again. "No, I didn't know he had such an intention. I think you should know, Albright and Dankworth proposed you. Tell me something, David. Your big day at the board meeting, was it stage-managed?"

"If it was, I wasn't in on it."

"But you know what I'm talking about."

"Yes. Dana and Mr. Dankworth were doing their best to give me a chance to star."

"Do you think you starred, David?"

"Not every minute. And I'm sure my political opinions alienated a couple of people."

"I'm sure you're right. I think I'll go out of my way to deflate you a little bit. While you were there, you had the board in the palm of your hand, but I'm sure the second thoughts were somewhat less enthusiastic."

"They remain my views nonetheless."

"In the enthusiasm at the conclusion of your performance, you were nominated to be Group Vice-President Automotive. You were nominated by Dana Albright and seconded by Dankworth. I think I will withhold from you the comfort you would take from knowing the vote. But it was not unanimous. My own opinion was that the action was precipitate. All of us have suddenly become aware of the"—he almost hesitated—"catholicity of your interests. Albright said without equivocation that you have been running the Group for some time and that we should install you immediately to insure the continuity. I congratulate you, David. I also would like to ask you, What is there between you and Albright?"

David studied his superior. "There's nothing between us. We have had the contact you would expect on the seventh floor."

"I'll tell you what I think. I think Dana's making a move for the presidency." Carl Pearson stopped. He was appalled with himself. He had brought Corporation politics into discussion with a junior officer, one for whom he harbored distrust if not downright aversion. He said with some sarcasm, "I'm sure you'll have some ideas on that subject, too, David. That was quite a performance you put on. I think they'll be naming the cars Commando and National. And building a new building for Embassy. And locating the stamping plant in Bryan. You are our . . ." again he hesitated . . . "catholic expert."

David stood up. He said with a good smile, "I think I'll have to write a letter to Father Hesburgh. He'll be pleased to know that one of the boys finally made it so high in this heathen corporation."

Pearson didn't smile. David wondered how far to go. Pearson had revealed himself, apparently with intention.

David said, "I was prepared to drop the Knights of Columbus and join the Masons." He watched Pearson's face.

Pearson said, "I meant catholic universal, I'm sure you're aware. It is a fact, however, that in the fifty years, no Catholic has risen this high. That could be a matter of coincidence."

David said, "I'll choose to assume it's exactly that."

"You and I will be working quite closely until the new president is elected, and then of course you will work with him. I should remind you of the outside possibility that the new president will want to choose his own man for the Automotive Group. In the meantime it's yours."

"Carl, when will the new president be elected?"

"The deliberations of the nominating committee are secret. I will tell you that there has been discussion and no decision." He smiled just a little. "I'm sure you're entitled to that much information in your new eminence." The smile left. "Tell me about Dana Albright."

"Are you asking my opinion on his qualifications?"

Pearson hesitated. Then he said, "Yes, I'd like to have it."

"He's well qualified. Between Albright and Williams, Dana is the better qualified. He has the broader grasp. If you're telling me that Dana's putting a team together, and he's got me for his Group VP, it's news to me. As a matter of fact, until this minute I'd supposed that you were going all the way, that you weren't going to elect an interim president."

"Where do you get your information?"

"From the newspapers and the drinking fountain, like everybody else around here."

"Maybe you should root for Albright. It would cer-

585

tainly appear that he'd line you up as his successor."

"And if he doesn't get it?"

"You're ahead of the game. In the burst of enthusiasm for your abilities, you've gotten ahead of the game." The eyes narrowed. "Are you familiar with the new situation on Bud Volk?"

"I know of no situation involving Bud Volk."

"I imagine you will. In due time."

"I think I should ask, Carl. Did Bud expect to get the Group?"

"You'll have to ask him. I don't know just how high his ambitions have run. You will be pleased to know that he voted for you enthusiastically as the band wagon formed. I think we had better not discuss Bud Volk further until you know the situation."

"Carl, shall I take Jim's office?"

"Do you want it?"

"Yes. It's best situated to do the job."

"Yes. I'm sure you'll fill Jim's shoes and his office." Then he said with some weariness, "I'm sure you'll more than fill Jim's shoes and office."

Bud Volk stuck his head in David's new office. "Congratulations, old man. I see you've been given the news."

David said, "Thanks. Do you have a few minutes?"

"I may later. I'm on my way to see Dana. I'll try to drop by afterward. Do you have anything special in mind?"

David said evenly, "There are a couple of things I'd like to go over with you, Bud."

Bud Volk said airily, "Sure, David."

But he left in some agitation. Was Battle pulling rank on him? Didn't he know what had transpired in the Board Room? Didn't he know that it was Bud Volk who had supported him to the hilt? Didn't he understand the ramifications of it? All right, David Battle was the new Group Vice-President Automotive. The Cutlass Division manager reported directly to Battle. But didn't David understand the technicality of it? Surely Battle knew that Bud Volk would be the next president of National Motors. Surely he knew that Bud had backed him because he was delighted to have him as the key man. Who did Battle think he was, then, suggesting in that calm tone of voice that the next president of the Corporation stop by for a discussion? Bud Volk didn't like it.

Tony Campbell came to David's office. He waved his hand around. He said pleasantly, "Not bad for a broken-down football player."

David said, "Jim always went first-class. I hope you realize that this is not only the most modern office on the seventh floor, with the most expensive paneling and furniture, it's the biggest. Jim had the partition moved a few inches just so he could have a bigger office than Carl." He smiled. "Carl doesn't know this."

Tony draped himself into one of the handsome chairs before David's desk. "Things are moving fast."

"Like what?"

"I think the decisions are being made. That's the feeling I get."

David said, "Tony, sometime tomorrow I'd like half an hour with you. Would the morning be convenient?"

Tony smiled, "Enjoying yourself, David?"

David cocked his head.

Tony kept his smile. "On our way to Los Angeles, Jim Parker was going to give you the Automotive Group, and he's dead, but you got the Group anyhow. At that time we were both going to go on the board. I beat you to it."

"Yes."

"Would you like to know how I voted on you?"

"No."

"Then I won't say. Did Carl tell you what went on? When you left the board meeting, Dana made the pitch to put you in the spot. And old man Dankworth got in there with all four feet for you. It looked like a put-up job to me."

"And to Carl."

"Was it?"

"No."

"I'm not sure what Dana's up to. I've got the feeling he's making noises like the next president. Like he's already choosing the men around him. Do you think that's possible?"

"I don't have any way of knowing."

"I'll tell you the truth. I was convinced they'd already decided to go with a younger man. Now I'm not so sure.

587

Dana Albright is one savvy man. Maybe he knows something we don't know."

"Maybe he's just got the guts to step into the vacuum."

"That could be it. While the other candidates are standing around being too polite to do anything about it, the old hatchet man will do us all in. Have you seen Bud Volk? He's in the building."

"Yes, I saw him just before you came in."

"How did your new relationship come off?"

"You'll have to ask him that."

"I'm sure you don't need advice, but I'll give you some concerning Bud. When you're climbing the ladder of success, David, keep your feet clean, so you won't get your hands dirty climbing back down. Bud just may be your boss one of these days soon."

"And so might you?"

"So might I. David, we should probably be friends. The business fates are driving us into the closer relationship. We also have Palm Springs in common."

David Battle did not flinch at all. He said easily, "Yes, we do that. Even though you had me outnumbered two to one."

"David . . ."

"What?"

"I think I'm going to want to talk to you one of these days. I might even ask for some advice. In the meantime, I'm going to tell you straight out, I want the presidency. I think it's between Bud and me. But Albright does worry me."

Dana Albright said, "Bud, this is C. J. Kermit. I'm sure you're familiar with his column. Mr. Kermit, this is Mr. Volk, vice-president of the Corporation and general manager of the Cutlass Division."

The two men shook hands. Bud was puzzled. Were they leaking a story through Kermit? A story on the new president? That didn't seem likely. Kermit was a hot-tip columnist, a poison-pen columnist, a sensationalist. What did he have to do with National Motors?

Dana Albright said, "Mr. Kermit, I suggest you begin at the beginning. And without preliminaries."

Kermit asked abruptly, "Mr. Volk, do you know a Colonel Wickersham?"

Bud Volk felt a quick paralysis through his entire body.

588

He said softly, "Yes, I knew a Major Wickersham. I assume he's the same."

"He's a retired colonel. He's working in Washington as a general flunky for the Washington office of U.S. Machine & Foundry. A week ago he paid a call on our Washington tipster. He offered to sell a story on you for five hundred dollars."

Bud Volk said, "Go on, Mr. Kermit."

"Mr. Volk, rumors have it that you may be the next president of National Motors. That's what our inside men tell us. If this is true, you stand at this moment just a step from one of the most important jobs in this country, a job in which you will influence the lives of every American . . ."

Bud Volk said, "Spare us the flag-waving. Get to your point."

Kermit smiled an ameliorating smile. "We're not quite as heartless in our column as you might think. We've never been successfully sued for libel. We check our stories thoroughly. In addition, we do have some conscience, improbable as that may appear to you. We could have waited until you were elected president of National Motors and then printed the story on you. We thought it over and decided to print it while you are still general manager of Cutlass."

Bud said, "I know what you will print, of course."

Dana Albright said, "I'd like to hear it from you."

Bud Volk said, "Dana, during World War II, I lost my clearance because of past association with neighbors who turned out to be German sympathizers. Major Wickersham was the security officer involved. I was taken out of the Armed Forces, placed on inactive duty, and assigned as an engineer in the Embassy tank plant under Jim Parker." He almost sighed. "The allegation was not true."

Kermit asked, "Which allegation was not true, Mr. Volk?"

"There was never a hearing. Major Wickersham promised a full investigation, which would have cleared me, but they never got around to it. I was neither convicted nor cleared of the allegation of being a security risk."

Kermit said, "Colonel Wickersham points out that you accepted your disposition at the time the matter came up. You did not demand the hearing at that time."

"Yes. That was a mistake."

Dana Albright said, "Mr. Kermit, this whole affair is more than a little bit unsavory. How does an ex-colonel get five hundred dollars for selling such information? What kind of evidence is that to go on? You could be ruining Mr. Volk's life."

Kermit smiled again the ingratiating smile. "As far as we're concerned, we paid the colonel and have nothing more to do with him. You're welcome to any action you may take against him, Mr. Volk. Personally, I think you might have a case. But as far as our column is concerned, we didn't rely on the colonel's word. We went to the files."

Volk said, "I'm sure those files are confidential."

"We print confidential information every day. It's somebody else that designates things confidential, not us. If they can't keep it away from us, that's their problem."

Bud asked, "Are you really going to run this story, Mr. Kermit?"

"Yes, we are. I've decided, listening to you, that we've got the story we can print. If we print anything that isn't true, you can sue us."

"The net result will be an untruth. People will believe that I was in fact a security risk, when I was not."

Dana Albright said, "I'm Mr. Volk's superior in the Corporation. Naturally, I have the greatest confidence in him. I am making an official request of you not to run the story."

"We will run it nonetheless."

"Should we bring some pressure to bear?"

Kermit's eyes lighted up.

Albright said, "Obviously that's exactly what you want. I suspect the real reason you came out here was to bait us into threatening you. We will not threaten. We will ask you not to run it, and that's the best we can do."

Bud Volk surveyed Dana Albright. He said, "I think you're throwing me to the wolves. I think I had better have a talk with Carl."

Dana Albright said, "I've already discussed it with Carl. And with Mr. Winston." He nodded to the two incredulous men at his desk. "Colonel Wickersham. He sold us the information, too. He needs money. He's going to be indicted for a messy job he did in Washington. As a matter of fact, Mr. Kermit, you were only his second choice. He was going to sell it to a national magazine, but they must have turned him down."

Bud Volk lighted a cigarette. He said calmly, "Mr. Kermit, Dana Albright has a long-standing reputation as the Corporation hatchet man."

Albright said easily, "That's not quite fair, Bud. As a matter of fact, I've gone to bat for you with Pearson and Winston. You will remain as general manager of Cutlass, no matter what."

Bud Volk was drained white, but his disciplined voice was steady. "I will not be president, is that what you're telling me?"

"You will not be president. Not this time, not ever."

"You know it's not fair. How could such an important decision turn on something as ridiculous as this?"

"Bud, you know it's not ridiculous. Be objective. What if it was Tony Campbell? Do you think the Corporation could afford to have Tony's name smeared all over the front pages as an alleged security risk?"

Kermit said speculatively, "I assume you realize, Mr. Albright, that you're giving me the best story of all. The in-fighting of a corporation."

Albright shook his head. "No, not this time. We're going to make a bargain with you. If Mr. Volk had become president, we couldn't in good conscience ask you not to run your story. The president of National Motors is public property. But this is not true of the general manager of the Cutlass Division. He is not quite public property. On that basis, we are asking you not to run this story."

Kermit said, "Of course the story loses a lot of its impact and importance if he doesn't make president. Just what have you got in mind? I have the feeling you're going to offer me something else."

Bud Volk said, "Maybe he'll offer you Tony Campbell. Maybe he's got a dossier on Tony."

Dana Albright said, "I don't blame you for being bitter, Bud. I think you'll get over that. The breaks of the game? As for you, Mr. Kermit, I'm offering you nothing. Except maybe this time it really is a small threat."

Kermit's eyes glistened again. "Please do threaten me, Mr. Albright. That's why I did come here. The story would be that much more dramatic with the embellishment of your threat."

Dana Albright said, "Bud, I'm sorry it had to be this way. Rest assured, this is between us and will go no further in the Corporation. I thought it would be fairer to let you know the reason that you will not be promoted as you expected. You did get the opportunity to meet your accuser face to face."

Bud Volk stood. He looked from one to the other of the men. He said, "Thanks." He walked from the office, his head as high as he could manage.

Dana Albright said, "Now Mr. Kermit. Do you know a woman named Denning? Her maiden name was Anton. She goes by her maiden name as often as by her married name."

Kermit waited, stock-still, tense.

"We know you do. Let me see if I've got my facts straight. Wickersham functioned as procurer for the customers of U.S. Machine. He did all the jobs needed done by their Washington office. With another hat, he was bag man for Senator Court. He's up to his neck. Now, Miss Anton, she was one of the call girls on Wickersham's string. Nothing but the best for the best, that was Wickersham's motto. As I understand it, Miss Anton was born in Hungary, married a U.S. Army officer on occupation liaison duty, and has been in this country for three years. For the first two years nothing much was heard of her except that somebody in charge of assignments went a long way out of his way to see that Major Denning, and consequently Mrs. Denning, stayed on in Washington. For the past year Miss Anton has been spreading herself on a broader base, or how can I say that delicately? Obviously, she has had relationships with people high enough to know better than to have relationships of this kind with a woman from Hungary. And it would appear that in the very near future she and her husband will be accused of representing the interests of international communism and the Soviet Union. That's a messy situation. Do I have my facts right?"

Kermit said calmly, "I assume you know that my relationship with her was on a different basis. I'm a bachelor. I was free to date any girl I wanted to. I met her and dated her. When I found out she was a call girl, and particularly which call girl, I stopped seeing her."

"In the meantime, the Soviet Union must have thought your column could be useful to them."

"Mr. Albright, do you think that of me?"

"We're not concerned with truth, are we, Mr. Kermit? We never are."

"I congratulate you. You do know more than I do. I've just heard the rumors so far."

"My investigators are very good."

"Yes, they are. They've gotten rid of Mr. Volk. Are you now going to be president?"

"At this moment all we know is that Colonel Wickersham will be persuaded to cease and desist his efforts to sell information concerning Volk and will undoubtedly be most careful not to inject the name of innocent parties into the hearings on Miss Anton. We know that you will now forget about Mr. Volk and let us get back to our business here at NM."

Kermit smiled ruefully. "He who lives by the sword, dies by the sword. I'm surprised I lasted this long."

Dana Albright said, "Oh, I'm sure you'll last a lot longer. There's a place for people like you in this world. You fill a basic human need."

Kermit said, "Well, now, thank you, Mr. Albright. You're right, I will undoubtedly recover my equilibrium in a week or so. Then I will waste no time looking for a skeleton in your closet. I assume that I will find none and will end up with your hatchet in my back for my pains. Say hello to Colonel Wickersham when you see him, Mr. President. I'm not being presumptive, am I? You do know Colonel Wickersham fairly well by now? You are determined to be president of this Corporation?"

Bud Volk stopped back in the office of David Battle. His agitation was obvious.

David asked, "Something wrong, Bud?"

Volk sat in the couch against the near wall. "David, I assume you know."

"Know what?"

"I'm staying at Cutlass. I'm not moving up."

"No, I didn't know that."

"David, do you know why?"

"I told you, I don't know anything about this."

Volk rose and paced the office. "I'm sure you would tell me the truth. Well, if Albright wants to tell you the details, he can. In the meantime, I'm working for you."

David said, "I've had no other impression. The man-

593

agers of the divisions report to the Group Vice-President Automotive. If you had become president, then I would have reported to you."

Bud Volk drew a deep breath. "Well, you're calling the shots. I'll consider myself lucky to keep my three-hundred-thousand-dollar-a-year job."

"Bud, tomorrow at ten, if you're free. Plan to stay through lunch. We have a lot to get through."

Bud Volk said with a wry smile of bitterness and resignation, "I'll be free at ten. You just bet your life, Davey." Then he said, "David, watch out for Dana Albright. I won't explain. Just watch out."

Tony Campbell sauntered into the office. "I just met Bud in the hall. I assume you know by now."

"Do you, Tony?"

"Carl filled me in."

David digested that information. Carl Pearson had declined to tell David Battle what it was with Bud Volk, but had told Tony Campbell. That did have significance. Some of the ramifications must account for the special ease with which Tony Campbell now lounged in the office of his superior.

Carl Pearson phoned Avery Winston. He said, "Mr. Winston, I think we shouldn't prolong our decision. There's too much speculation going on around here, at every level, from the shop to the seventh floor. I think we should make an end of it."

"Has Dana had it out with Bud Volk?"

"Yes, sir, he has."

"What was Volk's reaction?"

"He didn't fight it. He's accepted it."

"That's too bad. I hoped he'd fight back. I've had my mind set on him." Then he said, "I assume Dana was able to squelch that columnist."

"Yes, sir."

"Do you know by what means?"

"No, sir. I didn't ask. Mr. Winston, I suggest a meeting of the nominating committee. Is it possible that you could come out this way tomorrow?"

"Yes. Please have your plane for me at La Guardia at ten o'clock. I'll be in Detroit for lunch with you."

Dana Albright phoned David at his home. "David? I thought I'd rather talk to you on the phone than in the office. I want to talk to you about the nominating committee meeting. They will meet on the seventh floor tomorrow."

"It must be important, if Mr. Winston is leaving New York. It must be urgent."

"Carl told me they would probably make the decision. David, are you aware of what transpired after you made your presentation to the board? Do you know the sequence of your nomination and election?"

"I understand that you and Mr. Dankworth proposed me. I appreciate your confidence."

"It wasn't as easy and simple as it sounds. I think you should know that. The timing was delicate. We caught them in the surge of approval of you, and at a time when they were concerned over the long wait for the election of new officers. I think you should also know that I made a personal recital of the areas in which you have been exercising at least some degree of executive control. We were successful, as you see."

"I appreciate your recommendation, Dana."

"David, Bud Volk will not be president."

"I know that."

"Do you know why?"

"I'm not sure I care to know why. There is apparently some mystery afoot."

"He reports to you, so I think you had better hear the story. Bud committed some indiscretions when he was a kid. He got himself involved, at least socially, with the German-American Bund. It caught up with him in World War II. As far as the Board of Directors is concerned, there was nothing to it. But he was never officially cleared. The information was given to C. J. Kermit, the columnist. You know what he could do with something like that."

"Dana, how strongly did the Corporation go to bat for Bud? It seems as though he gave up mighty quick. Just one conversation with you?"

"What would you have done, David?"

"My first instinct is certainly to go down the line for him."

"David, you have lessons to learn. Don't always go by your first instinct. Don't rush in where angels fear to tread. You've made a tremendous impression on the board. The

595

more they hear about you, the more pleased they are with your qualifications. But they are also a little bit leery of you. Your political views made some of them uneasy, to put it mildly. I'd suggest a little bit of circumspection all around, David."

"Do you mean I should change my views?"

"No. I happen to agree with them. The auto executives are doing less than they could do in the way of leadership. But you can scare people off when you talk about things. Take it easy. You won't build Rome in a day."

"That criticism I accept. But my viewpoint will not change."

"Well, we did get you in a key spot, David. I'm taking a proprietary pride in you. It was a good victory. When we proposed you, there were some raised eyebrows. And I think you should know, Carl Pearson opposed you. He said only that we should not be precipitate, but it was obvious that he was opposed to your promotion."

"Then how did I get it? I thought he could control it."

"I'll tell you exactly how. His resistance was half-hearted. David, his resistance to you is based on your religion. Does that shock you?"

"No."

"That is also true of Avery Winston. After fifty years of Protestants, they don't see any reason to change. David, I think they finally accepted you and made the vote unanimous with the realization that you are the best qualified for the job, by the obvious virtue of what you've been doing for the past two years. But also I think they now feel you are assigned your permanent spot and will not be considered for the presidency. In other words, why would they bother going through this motion, if they intended to consider you for president?"

David said, "I could give you an answer. If they wanted me to be a director at the time they elevated me to president, this interim move would make sense."

"But of course there's no point in speculation. That's not what the board had in mind. I'm sure it's not what the nominating committee has in mind."

"Do you know what the nominating committee has in mind, Dana?"

"No, I don't know. I'm sure of one thing. I'm sure Avery Winston was sold on Bud Volk. He'll be very disappointed that this scandal has ruled Bud out. Among the younger men, this leaves only Tony and Cleary."

David said, "And me."

"Yes. By now I think it's for sure Cleary won't get it. He's too colorless, and that's become painfully apparent with the scrutiny of the past weeks. That leaves Tony. And you. Carl and Mr. Winston will go for Tony. David, what is your opinion of Tony's qualifications?"

"I think I'll tell you straight out, Dana. On paper, he's qualified. In actuality, he is not in any degree qualified. It would be unfortunate for the Corporation if he were elected president."

"Are you referring to his peccadilloes? In what other way is he not qualified, David?"

"He is not philosophically or emotionally qualified. I don't intend to elaborate, but I think the Corporation should be prevented from making this mistake."

"David, I think they will be. Bud Volk was qualified. Not Tony. Never Tony. He won't make it."

"You sound very sure." Then David asked, "To what peccadilloes are you referring?"

Dana Albright said smoothly, "I misspoke. I meant the rumors of peccadilloes. Let's talk about the alternative left to the nominating committee. They can still elect an interim president."

"Since Marion is on the committee, that leaves you."

"Yes, that leaves me. My ambition still burns brightly. More brightly than Marion's ever did. I want this job. I've got a package deal to offer them. It will be presented by Mr. Dankworth. You're part of the package, David."

"I see."

"Dankworth will propose that I be elected president for the eighteen-month period until my retirement. He will propose a time-table that in one year you will be elevated to executive vice-president, and then you will succeed me on my retirement. Dankworth is sold on you. He couldn't be more impressed by you. And that includes your fire-eating political views. Do you have any comment, David?"

"No, I don't. I'm not sure just what I could say. Once more, I appreciate your confidence, Dana."

"I'm not telling you all this idly. I could have just waited until the decision was made. But I wanted you to know that your promotion was at my instigation. I want something in return. Tomorrow morning Mr. Dankworth wants to sit down with you for ten minutes. I think he will want your recommendations. I have been assuming that the admiration is mutual between us."

David said, "Yes, sir. Dana, I have high regard for you. Mr. Dankworth will know this. More than this, I can't say until I think it over."

Dana Albright said, "David, don't play this too cool. I don't expect you to be prostrate with gratitude that out of nowhere I've brought you to consideration to become president of this Corporation in eighteen months. But I don't expect you to play it quite this cool, either. David, don't louse it up for the two of us. I can't make it any plainer than that."

Sarajean Court Battle said, "I gather from the conversation that you are still climbing."

"It's possible."

"David, you won't make it. I'm guaranteeing you won't make it. I'm filing suit for divorce tomorrow. I already have the appointment with the attorneys."

He said stonily, "I think you should have made an appointment with a psychiatrist instead."

"Too bad, David. You did fool me. I never thought you had a chance. Then just when you get to prove I was wrong, I pull the rug out from under you. I'm going to splash this divorce right across the front pages and deliver the papers to Carl Pearson personally. You're dead, David. As a matter of fact, I'm thinking of claiming that you're impotent. Would you like that?"

"Go fix yourself a drink."

"I have the appointment tomorrow. Tomorrow it happens."

"Sarajean, I wish you wouldn't. But there's nothing I can do to stop you. So I don't want to discuss it."

"Oh, yes, there is. You can get that woman out of here. I'll make you a promise—if you'll send her packing tonight, I won't file the suit. I'll just stay with you and drink myself to death, while you're married to the Corporation."

"Sarajean, I will not be blackmailed. Do what you have to do."

"David, you won't discuss anything with me. Everything hangs in the balance, and you still won't discuss it."

"Because you don't make sense when you're drinking."

"I'll speak slowly and clearly. Discuss it this one time, David. I think you had better. Just tell me, do you keep your mother here because you love her? Is that why?"

"No."

"I knew that. If it was because you loved her, I could understand it. I was sure you couldn't love a woman who made such a cold potato out of you. Is it sense of duty?"

"Probably."

"No, that's not it, either. I could understand that, too. Do you know what it really is? It's guilt. You love the guilt feelings she gives you. There's something deep down inside you that makes you feel good when you detest yourself. And she's just the one that can make you do it, isn't that right?"

"That might have been true once, Sarajean. Not any more. Maybe by now it's just force of habit."

Ellen Battle said, "Well, you can break the habit starting right now. I'm leaving."

David said, "Mama, that's what you get for eavesdropping."

"Well, David, I knew it had to come to this. It doesn't matter how much you try to do, if there's something wrong in a man's make-up, it's going to come out. You're his son."

"Mama, just let us alone. Sarajean's right. We should make a try to talk out the problems."

"Well, I won't be one of your problems any more. I'll be gone in the morning. That's what she's wanted. She's been fighting for it ever since I got here. She's no different than that other one. No different. And you know what happened to that other one. This one will end up just the same way."

David Battle was forty-six years old. For one of the few times in his life he took the name of the Lord in vain. He said loudly, "Mama, for sweet God damn Christ's sake, will you shut up!"

"Don't you talk to me like that, young man."

"I'll talk to you anyway I God damn please. You listen to me, both of you. I've got problems. I don't expect you to help me with them. I'll take care of them by myself. But in the meantime, don't expect me to solve your problems. Right now I just haven't got the time, the energy, or the inclination left over. Now go do what you have to do, both of you—you do whatever you want to do, just leave me alone."

Sarajean Battle asked, "David, are you telling me that when you've solved your problems, you'll have time for mine?"

"I'm not telling you anything of the sort. I'm not at all sure I will. I might even have less time than I have now. If I make it, you'll be the wife of the president of National Motors. I won't have any time to wet-nurse you. You may have to wait until my retirement to get any attention from me, and that's so many years from now that none of us might even be here. You just better reconcile yourself, Sarajean—if you stay with me, you're going to have to fight your own battles."

"David, for God's sake, I'm an alcoholic!"

Ellen Battle said, "She drinks all the time when she thinks nobody's looking."

"Sarajean, do you think your problem is going to get any better if you divorce me? I don't see how that's going to help you any."

"David, I need to be needed. You've got to help me. David, please."

"Go talk to a priest. Talk to the doctor. Get somebody that knows how to help you. I don't know how. I can't help you."

"David, all I want is for you to pay some attention to me."

Ellen Battle said, "David, all she wants is for you to get rid of me. Let her go. She's no better than the other one. She doesn't fool me, with that Tony Campbell when you weren't here. She's a slut just like the other one."

A great, thundering silence fell over the room.

David Battle said calmly, "Mama, I will instruct Gladys to pack your things, all your things. In the morning my driver will be here at ten o'clock and will drive you to Sweet Water. He will have instructions to stow your gear away for you, and then he will leave you. There will be enough money in your account for you to do whatever you want. I will come to see you in six months, and I will stay two days. I will do the same every six months from then on, providing you still want to see me. Otherwise, I have no desire to see you again."

She said venomously, "It came out. It always comes out in you. He came out in you again." He turned his back on her. Her voice rose. She said in measured tones, "I hope you die just like he did!"

He turned to face her. "I already did, Mama. A long time ago. I died just as miserably as he did, and just as shamefully."

Ellen Battle said, "I didn't mean that. You know I didn't."

Sarajean Battle said, "David, I'll try. I'll really try."

David said, "I really don't give a damn what either of you do. It's too late for me to worry. I've already committed my emotions to National Motors. Sarajean, I will appreciate it if you hold off your suit until the decision is made. Other than that, I just don't give a damn any more."

"David, it was your fault! It wasn't mine!"

"Don't you understand? I just don't give a damn. You go ahead and convince yourself it was my fault, if that will make you feel any better."

He turned and left the room.

She called out, "David, you'll see, with her gone, things will be different. I'll really try, David! I will!"

He stopped just outside the door. He said, "That will be very nice, Sarajean." He resumed his way to his study.

11

Old Dankworth said, "Young man, I've been very much impressed by you. I like the way you do things. I like the way you think."

David waited.

"Do you know why I'm down here?"

"Yes, sir. The nominating committee is meeting."

"I suppose that that confidential news is all over the Corporation by now. It's been decided that we can't delay any longer. We have to make a decision. As of this moment, I can tell you how it will go."

David waited.

"Last week Mr. Bud Volk would have been elected president of this corporation. As of this moment, Mr. Volk is completely out of the picture. Do you know the circumstances?"

"Yes, I do."

"As of this moment Carl Pearson and Avery Winston will support young Mr. Tony Campbell. Williams will go along with Pearson and the old master."

David's mouth was dry. "Then Tony will be president?"

"I want your estimation of young Mr. Campbell?"

"Mr. Dankworth, it's most difficult to know when to keep quiet and when to speak up. This is a case where what I say could be considered self-serving. I've got to take that risk. Tony Campbell is not qualified to head this Corporation. If he becomes president, it will not be a good thing to happen to National Motors."

"Would you care to elaborate, young man?"

"No, sir. But I couldn't feel more strongly than I do. Bud Volk is qualified, even with that cloud over his head. But Tony Campbell is not qualified."

"If you were on the committee, Mr. Battle, what would your choice be?"

"I'd select Bud Volk."

"Is that only because you couldn't vote for yourself?"

David didn't answer.

"David, are you qualified to be president of National Motors?"

"Yes, sir, I am."

"I think you would make an outstanding president. We've come up with a way to skin that cat."

"You and Dana?"

"I assume that he's talked to you. David, I told him that I wanted you as president. He came up with the solution. Avery Winston and Carl Pearson have some distrust of you, to put it mildly. They're afraid you might be a little too impulsive. In Dana's plan, we'll have eighteen months to mend your fences for you, to reassure the board of your soundness, your stability and your good judgment in all situations, including political situations." Dankworth smiled with his lips only. "I don't know that we can convert those two Protestants to Catholicism in just eighteen months, but we might build the rudiments of tolerance in them. I have an ace up my sleeve. I know how to handle Avery Winston. I should. I've been on the board with him for more than forty years. Young man, in our first committee meeting Mr. Winston expressed some views on corporate responsibility that are rather close to your views. By the time I've twisted the untwistable Mr. Winston around my finger, he'll be viewing you as his disciple and champion. He'll pull Williams with him. The decision of the committee will be three to one for the compromise plan of Albright now and you in eighteen months. I'm sure that meets with your approval."

"No, sir, not entirely."

With an edge in his voice, Dankworth asked, "Just what would meet with your approval, Mr. Battle?"

"Mr. Dankworth, I have high regard for Dana Albright, but when Carl Pearson was selected over Albright and Williams, I'm sure it was for good and sufficient reasons. Those reasons could only be the greater after Albright and Williams have been on the shelf these years, riding their time out, to whatever degree they've inevitably done that."

"Yes, Avery pointed that out. Is it that significant?"

"It is. Albright no longer commands the complete respect of the operating people."

"Do you?"

"Yes."

"Do you want me to propose you as president?"

"Yes, sir, I do. I want you to propose Dana Albright as chairman of the board."

Old Dankworth did smile.

David said, "His would be a public relations post." He smiled, too. "He'll be able to take some of the fire out of my pronouncements. I would be president and chief executive officer. That's the key to it—I would run the show."

"I think you would run the show under any circumstances. Mr. Albright would make you executive vice-president almost immediately."

"Mr. Dankworth, I've given you my recommendations of a sounder arrangement. There's one thing I do want you to consider. If I am elected president, my first move would be to elevate Bud Volk to executive vice-president. I would expect to spend a considerable amount of time in what *I* consider the duties of the president of an automotive company. Bud Volk is the man best qualified to handle a great deal of the burden of the operations of the company."

"And Marion Williams?"

"He stays, of course, in his present capacity. There could be no other thought."

"And Tony Campbell?"

"I don't know. I'd have to do some thinking about Tony Campbell. I might want to consult with you, Mr. Dankworth."

"This is assuming that I make your proposal to the committee."

"I hope you will, Mr. Dankworth."

"Mr. Battle, concerning young Mr. Campbell and his lally-gagging, he's made himself extremely vulnerable. But

I will remind you that your own skirts are not entirely clean. I will presume to give you some advice."

David stared at the old man with a mixture of surprise and consternation.

Dankworth said, "This is a highly moral corporation. I can remember one administration when nobody got to the top who wasn't a regular whoremaster. That hasn't been true for some time. Our vice-presidents now are so thoroughly dedicated to the Corporation, and spend so much time at it, that they just don't seem to have the energy and inclination left over to chase women. There are two notable exceptions. There is young Mr. Campbell, and there is you."

David asked calmly, "Where do you get your information, Mr. Dankworth?"

"I'm sure you know. Don't let it worry you. The past will be past. You're not as vulnerable as young Tony. But in the future, I would advise you—circumspection, David. Be Caesar's wife, if the Corporation is as important to you as it should be."

David Battle strode purposefully past the secretary of Dana Albright and into the inner office. He said abruptly, "I want to know something, Dana."

"Sit down, David. What's on your mind?"

"In your Public Relations, what is it you have, a Gestapo?"

Dana Albright leaned back in his chair. Again he asked, "What's on your mind, David?"

"First, who blew the whistle on Bud Volk?"

"I'll answer your question, but I'll precede it with a statement. It doesn't matter who blew the whistle. The important fact is that Bud Volk could not become president of this Corporation with that cloud over him. He was too vulnerable. The important fact is that he has been removed from the competition. The important fact is that you will become president of National Motors, David, and you would not have had the remotest chance had Bud Volk not been forcibly ejected from the picture. To answer your question, I blew the whistle. When I got wind of Colonel Wickersham, I took him into my custody. If I hadn't, he'd have sent the thing sky-high, believe me. Either way, Volk would not be president. But my way, I got rid of Bud, all right, but he kept his job and his good name. What's your next question?"

"Mr. Dankworth questioned my propriety. And Tony Campbell's."

"I hope he commended caution to you. I suggested it. David, I know about you and Miss Brand. I know about Tony Campbell and a few dozen assorted women, including a Miss Leslie Templeton and a Miss Jeanie Templeton on your recent joint trip to Palm Springs."

"It was not a joint trip, if that has any importance."

"Your coincidental trip, then. I must confess, David, it was only coincident that you and Miss Brand were included in the surveillance. You were a bonus in our observation of Tony."

"You're flooring me. How can you say this so calmly?"

"I'm always calm. Let me tell you about Tony, David. He has led a charmed life. It's hard to believe that a man could know that many women and not run across one with the desire to cut him up in little pieces and feed his gizzard to the vultures. They like him. They all like him. Until now. Miss Leslie Templeton would like to see him drawn and quartered. I have her statement. Her affidavit, to be correct. It might not hold up. It's only her sworn word that Tony had sexual intercourse with the seventeen-year-old sister, but in any event, it's a damning testament. Seventeen, that's statutory rape. Isn't that fascinating? All those years you'd think he'd have gotten caught on the Mann Act, but when you finally do get him, it's even better. Statutory rape!"

David contemplated the older man. He thought he should be incensed, outraged. He was not. He was only incredulous. He said, "I know they've called you the hatchet man all these years. I thought it was a joke. You're remarkable, Dana, remarkable. Do you have something on every executive in the Corporation?"

"No, because most of them have kept their skirts fairly clean, once they got the scent of the roses. Just on those who fall off the track on a regular basis. Just on some who have business investments they wouldn't want shouted to the world. Or the Tony Campbells and Bud Volks. I'll tell you this, when you're president, you'll be on a good footing with certain of our competition. We have some fairly bulky reports on some of our friends at Chrysler, Ford and GM. I'm a handy man to have around."

606

"And what do you have on me, would you care to tell me?"

"Miss Kelly Brand, and our investigation revealing that you have met her a number of times in Palm Springs, staying usually at Jim Parker's place."

"How on earth can you find out things like that?"

"It is amazing what trained investigators can do. David, I sent the investigators to Sweet Water. It seemed appropriate."

David Battle's jaw clenched. He said, "I assume you discovered that Jim Parker's mother was part Indian."

Dana Albright smiled again, "Is that a question? Are you asking me if I discovered that you are a Dankowski?"

"Is it an important discovery?"

"I'm not quite sure how important. I know one thing. I don't intend to tell the board. It would solidify the opposition of Carl Pearson and Avery Winston."

"But you have something to hold over my head. That it? Is there anything else?"

"David, you and I are on the same team. Mr. Dankworth is in there right now, doing a job for us."

"I want to know more about you. Would you stoop to using that young girl against Tony?"

"I might, in the last ditch. Would you?"

After a moment David said, "I'm surprising myself. That temptation comes sweeping in, when I think of Tony getting this spot he doesn't deserve. When I think of the harm he can do the Corporation. I just might use it. I don't know."

"David, let me show you my good faith and put you on an equal basis. I had my own affair. It lasted for fifteen years."

"And her name?"

"I'm not ready for quite that equal a basis. Not just yet. But we are on the same team."

"I'm sure it won't shock you or displease you if I say I have a healthy respect for you. I will not turn my back on you. Dana, I've decided. Public Relations no longer reports to you. We'll have it report directly to the president."

"That is me, David, remember?"

"No, I made a separate proposal to Dankworth."

Albright narrowed his eyes. "Where do I fit into this proposal?"

David smiled just a little. "All honor will be yours, Dana."

"Are you thinking of bucking me?"

"Heavens, no! I'm blackmailable, remember?"

Albright said calmly, "I haven't told you the rest."

David asked uneasily, "The rest of what, Dana?"

"What my people learned in Sweet Water."

David Battle was hollow. He said, "I'll listen."

"There is a rumor you're part Jew."

"Is that all?"

"It sounds like a lot to me. You want to be president of this Calvinistic, fundamentalist corporation, and you're a Catholic Polack Jew named Dankowski."

"Dana, what shame would you say would make a man most susceptible to blackmail?"

"I haven't finished, David. We know about your father. About his death."

There was, in the office of the executive vice-president, a long, long silence. David Battle said, "I was hoping you would not discover that."

"I have the distinct impression that I have finally found your breaking point."

"How did you find out? Who else knows?"

"I couldn't say how many know. My men found the husband."

After another moment David asked, "What husband?"

"The husband of the nigger prostitute."

"Oh."

"It is quite a story. But of course I'll never use it. We're on the same team."

David Battle said woodenly, "Yes, we are."

"Now as to your plans for becoming president immediately, I won't say I won't go along with it, but I want to hear more."

"Tell me what happened to my father."

"I thought you know."

"I do know. But not the details. I think I want to know."

"Did you go to the funeral?"

"Yes. It was during summer vacation from Notre Dame. I got home the day after he was killed."

"Killed? That's a strange word for it."

After a moment David said, "All right, I didn't want to say murdered."

Dana Albright said with interest, "I don't know anything about murder. Maybe we haven't got the right story after all."

"Tell me what you know."

"Yes, I'll do that. You correct me. There was Green Billy's. You know Green Billy's?"

"Yes, I know it. I know about the colored prostitute. I know she became a regular thing with my father."

"From what I hear, it was no wonder. She was a beautiful woman. Do you know about her husband?"

"No."

"She got married. But that didn't stop your father and her. Only now the husband was privy to the situation, and he got money from your father. Apparently a lot of money."

"My father didn't have a lot of money."

"But the union did."

David's jaw clenched again. He didn't speak.

Albright said, "It would appear your father took a very sizable amount of money from the union treasury to buy off the husband. The auditors caught up with him the day he killed himself."

Another wait. David echoed, "Killed himself."

"David, apparently you don't really know. Killed himself, I'm using the wrong word myself. Died maybe semi-accidentally."

David said sharply, "Tell me."

"They were at the prostitute's shack over in the town of Shawnee. Your father had been there for two days and nights. There were four of them, your father and the nigger girl, and then there was a white woman for the husband. They ran out of white lightning, and the husband went out and got some more. That's when they got the bad batch. Wood alcohol. It killed the nigger girl and your father. The husband says your father drank a quart of it all by himself. The white woman, she didn't have any. She was already passed out. She's gone, nobody knows where. The husband, he drank enough to go blind. He's in a sanatorium. That's where my men found him."

David Battle stared at Dana Albright. A slow smile spread on his face. Albright raised his eyebrows. David said, "Dana, by God, I thank you!"

"What on earth for, David?"

"I thought she murdered him!"

"The nigger girl?"

"My mother."

"You can't be serious."

"All these years, I thought she murdered him. Nobody told me enough. All these years, I thought she caught him with the colored girl and murdered him. Dana, you have no idea how relieved I am."

"Don't the actual facts distress you?"

"I don't think so. It makes sense. How else could he die? It had to be from drinking rotgut whiskey in complete degradation. Utter debauchery, nothing else would be fitting. Nothing else would be messy enough, gruesome enough." His grin was broad. "Dana, you have no idea what a lousy thing it is to go through some years thinking it was your mother that murdered your father. You have no idea how relieved I am. My name? It's Dankowski. I'm a Catholic Polack Jew, if you say so. I couldn't care less. Nor could you. You won't do a damn thing about it. My father's unsavory death? It's a relief to me, a bloody relief. This I can face with absolute equanimity, after what I've been through. Do you realize that I finally feel absolved of all responsibility for her? It's great, just great. And this grisly tale, you won't tell, either. I'll ask you the question I was going to ask before, only this time with even greater confidence. What shame would you say would make a man most susceptible to blackmail?"

After a moment Albright said with curiosity, "I would have said a reflection on his manhood."

"Possibly. How about the shame of being a blackmailer for business and personal advantage? A man who would do that would be vulnerable, I'd think, to another man with the courage to call him at his own game. Dana, you and I are going to be on the same team, but I'm calling the shots. If ever it comes to exposure, it is I who will expose you as a professional blackmailer. Are we, indeed, still on the same team?"

Dana Albright said smoothly, "Of course, David. There was never any doubt."

Tony Campbell came once more into David's office. David said, "You're nervous as a cat, Tony."

610

"Yes. I don't know why I should be."

"Because something could always come along to up-set your apple cart, right?"

"Davey, I'll ask you the question straight out. Do you consider yourself a candidate?"

"Can you *be* a candidate to be president of National Motors? It had been my impression that you stood modestly waiting to be called."

"This is different. This is an emergency situation. The best and worst in people are bound to come out at a time like this, and this place is fairly seething with intrigue. I'll rephrase my question. Do you think the nominating committee will consider you as a possibility?"

"Yes. Don't you?"

"I didn't. I was concentrating on Bud Volk. But it's beginning to sink in, they must think of you as one possibility."

"I trust more readily than did you."

"David, I think you're qualified. I've been thinking about that. Probably you're best qualified." He smiled just a lit-tle. "One thing sure, you'd be the people's choice, the rank-and-file choice." The smile left. "I don't know how you do that. I'm not sure how your popularity comes about. They picture you as an easygoing, friendly sort of modest football player with blue eyes. I don't. As far as I know you, you're hard as nails. They picture you as the all-American boy. I don't. I see just another smart guy with his share of faults and problems. As you can see, I'm curious about you. I'm not sure you might not be the best choice the board could make."

"Would you like to so inform them?"

"No. I want the job."

"Do you?"

"Can you show me a man in his right mind who wouldn't want it?"

"I can show you a couple hundred thousand men in their right minds that work for this Corporation that wouldn't want to be president. It's too hard a job. It takes too much away from a man. You have to be out of your mind to want it."

"I'm out of my mind. I want it. Do you?"

"Yes, I do want it. Do you—really?"

"Now you're playing games. Explain yourself."

"I suspect you know me better than most people,

Tony. I've got ambitions. I think they're as strong as Jim Parker's were. I've also got pride. I'm no modest, silent knight. For whatever technical deficiencies I have, I think I have some qualities of attitude that more than compensate. Tony, I must tell you, there is a very good chance that I will be made president of the Corporation. If I get it, I'll take it in stride. That's because I really want it. But if you were elected, I'm not at all sure you would take it in stride. I think you'd sit down and suddenly do the soul-searching you should have been doing all along. I think if you didn't make it, you'd heave a sigh of relief. I think you have things you're much more interested in doing than running this Corporation."

"Like what?"

"Like Palm Springs." David smiled. "I didn't know you'd seen me, Tony."

"And the only difference between you and me?" Tony grinned broadly. "I guess the difference is that my two girls added up in age to your one." The grin changed to a friendly smile. "I trust you take that as a crack at myself, rather than you and your girl. Don't I know her? Isn't she the one that used to go with you when you were playing ball?"

"The difference, Tony, between you and me, is that the girl is my avocation."

"And it's a full-time job with me? Do you really think that?"

"I think I've had the revelation, Tony. It's been a long time since sex was even in the same league with business."

"I haven't had that problem. I'll let you know when I want to borrow your Geritol."

"It's not old age, Tony. It's a matter of dissipating your sexual drive, like ballplayers do. I don't mean sexual vigor, either, I mean sexual drive. And I mean getting over the kid stuff of always chasing after something new."

"Chasing is kid stuff?"

"Wouldn't you say so?"

"No, by God, I wouldn't. Non-conformism, maybe. You're not supposed to keep on loving the world every morning, but I do. Did you see them, David, my girls, how beautiful?"

"Her name is Jeanie Templeton. The older one is Leslie."

"How do you know that?"

"The hatchet man knows about us, both of us. I wasn't going to tell you, but I think I should."

"What does he know?"

"He knows that Leslie Templeton has sworn in an affidavit that you had relations with her seventeen-year-old sister."

"Good God in heaven."

"You don't look as startled as I thought you would."

"I'm startled, but not frightened."

"Dana has in his possession such an affidavit."

"I've got a letter of my own. From one of our Embassy salesmen out there. I decided that the older girl had cooked it up with him. She's sure whizzed off."

"Tony, I'd say you've got real trouble."

Tony shook his head negatively. "I'm not particularly concerned. The saleman presented no problem. I sent a couple of private detectives around to his apartment to ask him if he was contemplating extortion and blackmail, or just what it was he was after. They also promised to shadow him for the rest of his life if he opened his mouth about me. Do you realize what a threat that is, David? Every man contemplates with pleasure some evil deeds that he's going to commit sooner or later. The thought of being circumspect forever is more than a man could stand."

"But you won't handle the girl that easily, or Dana."

"Just as easy. Maybe I should tell you. Will it ease your mind, or will it disappoint you, to find that I can handle a situation like this?"

David just smiled.

Tony went on, "I should tell you some of what transpired in Palm Springs. She took her sister along to play me for a sucker. Girls do that kind of thing sometimes. They were just out for a free ride. But she changed her mind en route. I won't bother to guess why, except it's a combination of my money, which she discovered, and my charm, which gradually permeated her. You can blend those ingredients as you choose. So she was sorry she brought the young girl along, especially since I couldn't take my eyes off her. So that night I put them in their room, and about two hours later there came the tap on the door. Which one, David?"

"Tell me."

613

"The older one. Leslie. She'd made up her mind once and for all that our relationship should blossom. I'll tell you this much, I've never seen a better figure. I've never made love to a girl that knew how better. A man would have to be out of his mind not to get wound up in that girl. And the whole time I was thinking about the younger one. The young one had me mesmerized. And Leslie knew it. When she left to go back to her room, she was whizzed off. Well, you can guess. I smoked a pack of cigarettes, then I went out to take a swim in the pool, and at four o'clock in the morning I figured it was safe, so I went in skinny. That's when Jeanie showed up and said she'd been looking for me, so I told her to shush up before she waked up the hotel, so she slipped off her nightshirt and popped into the pool with me and gave me a hug, and so that was that, we went back up to my room, and I suppose Leslie woke up and found her sister gone."

David said, "And this isn't double trouble?"

"You don't understand. In the long run, a girl like Leslie Templeton would never get on a witness stand and tell the whole world that I preferred her kid sister."

"But the district attorney would. Man, he'd paint you as a slavering lecher with that seventeen-year-old girl."

"Relax. Those girls will never bring me to trial. I'm surprised Leslie went as far as she did. I'll make sure she doesn't go any further. As for Jeanie, she'd never say anything."

"Tony, you're vulnerable. Believe it. Dana believes it."

Again Tony shook his head. "Dana's over his head when it gets to sex. I'm not anywhere near as vulnerable as you. I'm just a sex maniac. Suppose it all came out. I'd be like the national debt, people couldn't comprehend me. If I ever told the world how many girls I've loved, men's minds would rebel, or even if they believed it, they'd be reduced to abject admiration. Now you, you apparently are having a full-fledged affair with just one girl. The average man and woman can understand that. That's something they all do, or would do if they had the opportunity and the nerve. Seeing themselves in you, they will hate you for it. You add that to an alcoholic wife and an oddball mother, and I think you're in worse shape than I am."

David Battle's eyes narrowed to slits.

Tony said, "Sorry, old man, but we seemed to be getting

614

down to brass tacks. I had the feeling you were beginning to work me over, test me out."

David said levelly, "Tony, I think it was a gesture of friendship when I told you what Dana knew."

"Then I apologize. I think I'm not used to friendship in this Corporation. My stock and people's admiration and lust for it get in the way of friendship. A newspaper feature called me the golden boy. That was wrong. I'm gilt-edged securities. I apologize, David."

"There's no need. I've thought about it—an alcoholic wife is scarcely newsworthy in Bloomfield. I'll just be expected to keep her under lock and key as much as possible and not let the public see her. If she filed suit for divorce, yes. But if I can get her to wait five to six years after I'm elected, then the eyebrows won't rise so high after all."

"You have another solution, you know. You could be as nice to Sarajean as you are to other people."

"Yes. Have you healed yourself, physician?"

"I'm going to. By amputation. I'm going to divorce Wendy and marry that young girl. That's the reason I'm really not the least bit concerned about what Dana knows."

"When are you going to get divorced?"

"Like you, at the appropriate time."

"Are you in love with her? Are you really, with a seventeen-year-old girl?"

"I'm head-over-heels infatuated, and since I haven't the remotest idea what love is, that will have to do. She's an obsession with me. I can't get her out of my mind. I'd be happier if she didn't exist, but she does exist, and I'm overwhelmed. It's got its ironies. I'm planning on doing with Jeanie Templeton a lot of the things I should have done with Wendy Barrett, and never got around to. I feel sorry for Wendy, I think. Not in an intensely personal way. Remotely. Too bad things didn't work out better for a girl as nice as that."

"Did you marry her as abstractly as that?"

"Yes."

David said, "Me, too."

"Conceivably you did marry for advantage. You are a detached scoundrel like me. I hope you don't meet a Jeanie Templeton. She's going to destroy me utterly. She's going to teach me emotions, and then destroy me, because she has none of her own."

After a long time David asked, "And you're in the right

frame of mind to be president of National Motors?"

Tony smiled with some bitterness. "Back to topic A. Are you concerned that I think of her all the time? The all the time I think about her is the all the time I'm thinking about girls. Most of the all the time I'm thinking about business, and I'm sure you know that, and I'm sure you know my ability to concentrate on the business at hand to the exclusion of all else."

David studied that thought. If he were to state his true belief, it would be to say that Tony Campbell did not devote half the time needed to be a successful, contributing executive at National Motors. Other observers might be beguiled by Tony, but not David Battle. The golden robot was not qualified. But why say that at this point? More than anything else that could be said, more than any castigation for bad conduct, disapproval of Tony's working habits and his abilities would serve to alienate him. This was a powerful young man. Why alienate him needlessly? There would be time for that, if it became the indicated course.

David said, "Everyone knows you're qualified. I do think you feel you can run roughshod over all adverse opinion if your personal life becomes known. I think you feel your money is all powerful."

"You're correct. It's proven to be just that so far. David, are you going to continue your own affair in the face of Dana and his NKVD?"

"Probably not."

"Can't it even excite a passionate decision on its disposition? Doesn't it have any more fire than that? Is it just a wishy-washy kind of thing at best?"

David smiled. He said, "You've gone to the heart of it. My mind is indeed much more on business than on Kelly Brand. I'll keep her if I can, for as long as I can. That's cruel. It doesn't even bother me that I'm cruel. It's remarkable. I think I burn with my cause for humanity, and yet the more I'm drawn into the great visions, the more remote the individual human beings become to me. I'm not sure either one of us is morally qualified to be president of National Motors."

"Who is, David? Nobody's yet elected Jesus Christ to run an automobile company. We're talking about human beings. All of them have their faults. They might not be so grueling as some of yours, or as unsavory as mine,

616

but they've got faults. But the public just gets to see the polished-up image standing out in front of the company. The president of an automotive company exists as a real person only to those who do know him intimately. Otherwise, he exists as a painting. And if the PR office can manage it, Dorian Gray. In real life, presidents of companies are ordinary people. We should know that better than anybody, sitting here with a chance to make it. No, I refuse to be abashed by my misdeeds. My misdeeds have been the best things I've done in my life. I refuse to be abashed."

"And if Dana sinks his hatchet?"

"I'd spend twenty-eight million dollars crucifying him, and he knows it. Don't be intimidated by him. He scares some people, but only scareable people. If I judge you right, he'll never push you around."

"No, he won't. Nor you?"

"Never me. He won't even try it. Dana can be useful. I'll keep him on. I'll even use him to scare some scareable people. But I'll never lose any sleep over him myself."

"Well, I'm glad to hear you say that. I was beginning to get the notion that something as important as selecting the next president of this Corporation could be managed by a man with the mentality and methods of the editor of *Confidential*."

"David, in our burst of confidences I'll include one more confession, one more comfort to you. The ideas you expressed in the board meeting, I'm in sympathy with them. I think you can only create them if you do indeed remove yourself from individuals and contemplate the world as a philosopher does. It's unfortunate that the people who get hurt by you in real life see you as some kind of heartless ogre, something less than humanly compassionate, when actually your compassion has gone on to a greater usefulness. Is that a comfort to you? In any event, when I'm president, you will have the opportunity to do those things in the area of corporate leadership that you are better qualified than I to do. We'll get along well, David."

"That's good," said David Battle.

Dankworth closed the door of David's office. He stood just inside. David jumped up. "Yes, sir?"

"Our committee meeting has concluded."

"Yes, sir?" David felt the tingling glow coming on him.

"The recommendation went three to one for Anthony Campbell."

David said calmly, "Yes, sir."

"I thought they would take to my presentation. One is frequently so enthusiastic over one's own incontrovertible logic, that it doesn't occur to suspect that the other man might not buy it. What will you do now?"

"I have no plans beyond doing what I'm doing now. I'm Group Vice-President Automotive. But I think I will closet myself with myself as soon as the shock passes."

"Millions of men have served under men for whom they had less than whole-hearted regard. Whether or not you are the better man is no longer important."

David didn't answer. He wasn't sure he could.

"I have not informed Mr. Campbell of the decision. If anyone does, it will be Carl Pearson. I'm sure you're very much aware of the complete impropriety and consequent confidential nature of our discussions."

"Yes, sir. Thank you, Mr. Dankworth."

"For what? I couldn't deliver. I'll see you at the board meeting, Mr. Battle."

"Yes, sir."

"By the way, they bought your basic idea. They're making Albright chairman and young Mr. Campbell president for eighteen months."

David said, "Yes, it was a good idea. It solved a lot of problems."

Dana Albright said, "It was an unexpected twist. I'm sorry it's him instead of you, David."

"Do you intend to go along with it, Dana?"

"Go along with it? I'm not sure what more can be done at this time. I think maybe we've shot our bolt."

"Do we now pull out the stops? Do we throw everything we've got at Tony?"

The hatchet man smiled. "We, Davey? David, we couldn't use what we have on Tony. We'd never get away with it. He's too powerful. He'd kill both of us in that kind of contest. We've both got bigger skeletons in our closet than he does."

"Just what is yours, Dana?"

"Find out, David. Hire yourself a team of investigators, spend several thousand dollars, and maybe you can find

618

out about me. I know Tony has enough money to do it. I'd hoped to find something worse than the girls. I couldn't do it."

"Dana, he's going to marry that seventeen-year-old girl."

"I'll cross that bridge when I get to it. When this election is over, I'll have a talk with him about corporate image and propriety. David, I wish it had worked out another way."

David Battle said, "You listen to me, and listen close, Albright. Tony Campbell is not qualified to be president of this Corporation. You know that as well as I. I now charge you, find a way to stop him. This is a threat on my part. I have not decided what I would do or could do, but I would find something to do which would give you nothing but regret if you do not see me through as president. At least this much you must realize, the two of you, Tony and you, will send this Corporation on its way down, if you end up in the two top spots. That should be incentive enough for you to start plotting all over again. You wanted to be at the top. I'm sure you want your administration to reflect credit on you. Just think about that."

Dana Albright said uneasily, "I'll give it some more thought."

"And when you have given it some more thought, do something about it."

David walked abruptly out of the office.

12

CARL PEARSON called to order the meeting of the National Motors Board of Directors.

He said, "Gentlemen, on November 22 I expected to resign my offices as chairman of the board and president of the Corporation. It was a tragic day for me. The impact of the deaths that day still has a profound effect on me.

"We had expected to name James Parker as president of the Corporation on that day. My term was extended to cover the emergency period until we were ready to select a man to take the place of Jim Parker.

"Gentlemen, these have been rich and full years for me. I leave them behind with regret. I leave them, unhappily, at the time of a tragedy. But I leave them with trust that my successor wilh be capable and diligent.

"Mr. Winston, if my resignation is accepted, I will step down from this chair and take my place with the other members of the Board of Directors."

Avery Winston rose from his chair. Carl Pearson moved over and seated himself. Winston stood behind the chairman's chair and said, "Mr. Pearson, the Board of Directors has accepted your resignation effective this date. We do so with an expression of unanimous and enthusiastic approval for the job of work you have done in your years in the post. Your shoes will be difficult to fill.

"Fill them, we must. Gentlemen, the chair will entertain nominations for president."

On the cue, Marion Williams, the chairman of the nominating committee, rose and said, "I nominate Dana N. Albright to be chairman of the board. When this vote is taken, I will nominate Anthony B. Campbell to be president."

Holmquist, from the brokerage house, said, "I second the nomination of Dana N. Albright as chairman of the board."

Avery Winston asked, "Are there any other nominations? There being none, the chair asks for a voice vote. All in favor of Dana N. Albright as chairman of the board say aye. The ayes have it. Mr. Dana N. Albright is elected chairman of the board of National Motors Corporation. Mr. Albright, the chair is yours."

Dana Albright said, "If you please, Mr. Winston, will you retain the chair until this voting is concluded?"

Winston said, "Nominations are now in order for president."

Marion Williams said, "I nominate Anthony B. Campbell."

Holmquist said, "I second the nomination."

Winston said, "Are there any other nominations? There being none, the . . ."

Werner Bud Volk said, "Mr. Chairman."

"Yes, Mr. Volk."

"I nominate David Battle."

Hankins, from the insurance firm, said immediately, "I second the nomination."

There was dead silence in the Board Room. All the eyes turned to David Battle. David looked at Dankworth, then to Dana Albright. Albright nodded his head slightly in the direction of Bud Volk.

Holmquist said, "Mr. Winston, I was given to understand that there would be only one nomination."

Winston said, "Apparently we were given to understand incorrectly. What is your wish, gentlemen? Shall we have a discussion, or shall we vote?"

Dankworth said, "I think a discussion is in order. I would suggest, if it meets with the chair's approval, that Mr. Campbell and Mr. Battle remove themselves temporarily from the room to permit complete freedom of expression."

Winston said, "You gentlemen may leave or remain, as you see fit."

David Battle and Tony Campbell surveyed one another. Almost simultaneously they rose from their chairs and walked from the room.

Winston said, "Gentlemen, for obvious reasons, it is preferable to have a unanimous nomination as well as election. I should now advise you that Mr. Dankworth dissented from the nominating committee's recommendation of Mr. Campbell. He held forth at that time for Mr. Battle. I believe I will call first on Mr. Williams."

Marion Williams rose and said, "In the committee we considered all the aspects. The qualifications of both men are beyond question. We decided in clear conscience that Mr. Campbell is the better choice. I cannot see that elaboration of our reasoning would serve a good purpose."

"Mr. Pearson?"

Carl Pearson said, "We have all been impressed with Mr. Battle's performance. I confess that I was not aware of the scope of his activities for Jim Parker. It is my opinion, however, that he needs seasoning, and Mr. Campbell, who is equally qualified, does not need seasoning."

"Mr. Dankworth?"

"It was my opinion that both Mr. Campbell and Mr. Battle needed seasoning. It was for this reason that I recommended the election of Mr. Albright as chairman of the board, to provide a steady hand while the new president got himself settled down. Having accomplished this much, I then felt that we should choose as president that man best qualified from an operational standpoint. There was little question in my mind that this was the remarkable young Mr. Battle. And need I add that the remarkable young Mr. Battle is two years older than the remarkable young Mr. Campbell?"

Holmquist, who had been selected to nominate Tony Campbell, said, "Mr. Chairman."

"Mr. Holmquist."

"As an item of curiosity, I should like to inquire if there has been a rump nominating committee. Mr. Dankworth, have you carried your dissent to members of the board?"

Bud Volk said, "Mr. Chairman, Mr. Holmquist, I would like to answer the question as it regards my actions. I have not had any consultation in any way with Mr. Dankworth. As a matter of fact, so far as I knew, he was perfectly satisfied with, and party to, the nominating committee's selection."

Holmquist said, "Then may I ask, Mr. Volk, why did you choose to make this independent action? With two separate supporting moves for Mr. Battle, I am concerned. We should surely hear what this is all about."

"Mr. Holmquist, we should be concerning ourselves only with direct qualifications for this position. I have never been impressed that Mr. Campbell's stock holdings had a bearing on his qualifications. As an operating man, I will tell you bluntly, I could not in good conscience work for Mr. Albright, nor for Mr. Campbell. I do not consider either of these gentlemen qualified to operate this company as has Mr. Pearson, or as Mr. Parker would have done. David Battle is qualified. I know this first-hand. I think I should tell you, I have known all along of his qualifications. At the time I considered myself a possibility for this office, I had no intention of broadcasting my estimations of Battle's ability. He is the only possible choice. Prior to this meeting I had communicated this belief only to Mr. Hankins. We agreed that it should be aired, and I am greatly pleased to see support from Mr. Dankworth."

Avery Winston said, "Mr. Cleary."

The Vice-President Engineering said, "I will vote for David Battle. There is just no question on this."

Winston said, "Gentlemen, we have heard opinions from the Corporation representatives. Who now wishes to address himself to the meeting?"

Dankworth said, "Mr. Winston, I suggest that you take a poll at this time. It should let us know whether further discussion is appropriate."

Avery Winston said, "Agreed. Mr. Pearson?"

Carl Pearson said, "Pass."

"Mr. Ruggles?"

The president of Columbia Steamship Lines said, "This has the earmarks of a dog fight. I'm delighted that this could occur. For the past twenty years I've had the impression that this board has been a rubber stamp for Mr. Winston and whoever happened to be president. Regarding Mr. Battle and Mr. Campbell, I am impressed with the fervent opinion of those men closest to the firing line. I will vote for David Battle."

"Mr. Williams?"

"Anthony Campbell."

"Mr. Volk?"

"David Battle."

"Mr. Hankins?"

The insurance man said, "David Battle."

"Mr. Carideo?"

The president of the Bank of the United States said, "David Battle."

"Mr. Wolgast?"

The chemical man said, "David Battle."

"Mr. Albright?"

The new chairman of the board of National Motors said, "Had Anthony Campbell been elected president, I would have insisted on immediate appointment of David Battle as executive vice-president with broader powers than have previously resided in that office. I am now delighted to be able to vote for the man I would have selected—David Battle."

Avery Winston said, "Gentlemen, it would appear that the nominating committee did not have the pulse of this Board of Directors. And that is the understatement of the year. Our Mr. Battle must indeed be a remarkable young man to excite such loyalty from those who work with him. If I recall his history, he was captain of each of the football teams for which he played. Sweet Water, Notre Dame and the Detroit Lions. He has just made captain again. Mr. Ruggles, the race is always to the swift and strong. This board has heeded me through the years because I have a record of success, and for no other reason. If a stronger man has now come on the board, the deference will find its way to him. Will the secretary please invite Mr. Battle and Mr. Campbell to rejoin the meeting?"

Carl Pearson said, "I would like to do the honors."

The retired head of National Motors opened the door to the anteroom, walked through, and closed the door behind himself. Anthony Campbell and David Battle looked up expectantly.

13

WILLY FUNMAKER, the half-breed Menominee Indian, greeted the second planeload of guests as they climbed from the station wagon at the main hunting lodge of the Blue River Ranch. Funmaker smashed his big hand heartily into David Battle's back.

"You Davey Battle?" He shook his head in wonder. "You sure a little bitty rascal. You mean tell me you got your little bitty ass out on that football field with growed men?"

He pulled David into the raftered and beamed central room of the hundred-foot lodge. The earlier arrivals turned their heads to the newcomers.

Funmaker said, "Reckon you know these folks, Davey. You don't know 'em like I know 'em, that I garn-tee. You take that Albright. He looks like the meanest man in town. But you kin bluff him out a pot every time. You believe that, Davey? Don't believe a word I tell you. That seedy-looking ole summabitch in the baggy trousers, that's the man usta have your job. We won't be astin' him back, now he can't do us any good. Sure hope you don't drink like him, Davey. I expect he's right dignified around the store, but up here, the summabitch make alcoholicists outen all of us."

Carl Pearson raised his glass of ginger ale in a sort of reluctant salute to his successor.

Funmaker said, "Next him is Ginril Hardesty. I think he's only a lieutenant ginril, but we make him feel good."

David stepped forward and held out his hand. "General Hardesty."

The SAC general said, "Congratulations, Mr. Battle, on your election. I'm glad to meet you. I saw your Irish team beat our good Army team. It seemed like every time I looked up, you were scoring."

"I wish we could get those glory days back again."

"Maybe Parseghian will do the job."

"I hope so. Praying gave out a long time ago. That's the trouble with de-emphasizing anything, including football. Once you start it, you can't stop it."

The general nodded sagely.

Tony Campbell thought to himself, amused: When you're president, even your ordinary comments ring like pronouncements. That's a magic mantle you put on, and it gives you that final burst of confidence and it exacts that final deference from the others of us.

Funmaker said, "This Tony Campbell, he got more good-looking sports clothes than Ambercrombie and Finch. Birds just drop swoonin' at his feet, he's so purty dressed. In case you don't know, Davey, this boy, he kin afford it. I heard it NM jist might merge with him, iffen he don't first merge with the U S of A. Who-eee, that boy's *rich*. But now, you take that gentleman next, that Mr. Dankworth, that is the man makes Tony Campbell a churchmouse."

Dankworth said to David, "Good to see you, young man."

Funmaker grinned, his mouth filling his big face, the gold in his teeth glittering. "I call him Mister, on account a man gets as old and rich as him, this is one half-breed going to treat him with ree-spect, on account he might give me some of what he got so much of."

Dankworth said, "I just might do that, Willy. I might just leave you a million."

"Fust thing I'll do, I'd bend over and inn-vite Mr. Jimmy Sidell to kiss my rusty Injun dusty." The big half-breed smiled fondly at his employer.

The president of Buckeye Stamping put his arm around his chief guide. "David, the Funmaker and me, we been together fifteen year, ever since I found him in a Georgia swamp talking like he was a Cracker. How a Menominee got there, I can't say."

Funmaker said, "Same way a Cracker name Sidell got hisself a Ohio factory called Buckeye, you think that makes sense? Davey, Jimmy's our big boss. He turns out all those good stampings you folks buy, and he'll turn out more, you just say the word. But it's these two here makes the money. You know the Dipper, he was the second best football player the Dee-troit Lions ever had, and the biggest pussy chaser, bar none, and ain't slowed a step in that dee-partment. And King, the white-haired summabitch, he's looked that dissting-geeshed for a hundred year, and he's got a real Yankee buck for every white hair in his head. I do all the selling for Buckeye, and Dipper and King, they divvy up the money just 'tween theirselves."

The two old adversaries of David Battle exchanged silent, quick nods with him, saying nothing. He was frustrated. Not even now? Not even in the flush of his triumph, would they relent? Even after all this time, they still held the grudge?

David said, "Well, I'm glad to be here."

Funmaker said, "I hope we wasn't too pointed, astin' you soon's you became the big boss. And I surely hope them Russians don't pick now to drop a atom bomb on us this weekend, or NM goes sky-high. Davey, we got 'em all up here to celebrate you and Dana's ee-lections. Now you jist make yourself to home. You want it, you ast me. Huxtable, that's my middle name, and the nickname for that is Hux, and you know what that rhymes with, and that's what I do best, so you jist treat me real nice, and I'll let you in on some. What you drinking, Davey? You jist name your anti-*dote*."

David said, "Pass."

Funmaker roared. "Pass! You a tee-totaler, Davey?"

"No, I'm an approver and a drinker, both." He moved on to Bud Volk, and the conversation in the room resumed.

Volk said, "Funmaker's my hero, David. He's as great a bird shot as you'll see, and most of these antlers, he shot. His irreverence tickles the daylights out of me. Why do you disapprove of him?"

"Was I that obvious?"

"To me."

"I'm not sure I disapprove. I'm taken aback. The rest of you are used to him." He looked around the room at the key men of National Motors. He listened to the hum of conversation and watched the smoke drifting up into the rafters. He said in ordinary conversational tones, "I'm sure you know I haven't been to many gatherings like this."

"Are you disapproving of us? Will the Blue River Ranch be out of bounds from now on? Are you going to out-Calvin the Calvinist?"

"When I came to the Lions, I couldn't make up my mind whether I disapproved of Dipper Coogan and his gang, or envied them. In the long run I decided I had no choice but to live and let live. That applies to the Blue River Ranch. This weekend I've got a lot on my mind, and I want to intrude on you. Do you think we can get a couple hours tomorrow?"

"We can. There's no better place. No secretaries, no phones."

"Women? How seriously do I take Funmaker?"

"No women at the lodge. If you think that's an equivocal answer, that's the best you get. We'll take a drive before supper tomorrow, that will be the best time to talk."

"Good. I'll get Tony with us. It concerns the three of us." David moved on. He came to Dipper Coogan and King Smith again. They looked him over. He passed on without saying a word. He came to Tony Campbell. He asked with confident politeness, "Can I have a word with you, Tony?"

Tony Campbell smiled just a little. "Sure, David. Do you know who you sound like?"

"Who?"

"Carl Pearson, Warren Court, Barrett, my father, Avery Winston. All of them."

David said soberly, "That's good."

They walked through the crowd of men to a library. David closed the door behind them, and they sat.

Tony asked, "What do you want, my resignation?"

"Not now."

"Does that mean you will later?"

"No, it means that I thought I might want it, but now I know better. The vice-presidents' union would picket me if I fired a man as high as you. I want you to take a bigger job, Tony. I've decided on a new alignment, a complete new organizational approach. Since you play a considerable part in my proposal, I want your opinion of it."

"Why do I get the feeling you're about to sell me the Brooklyn Bridge?"

"I've got no intention or time for buttering you or conning you, Tony. You should know by now I'm too seriousminded for that." He did smile. "I don't blame Sidell and the Funmaker for not inviting me before." The rare smile left as quickly as it came. "I'm going to ask permission of the board for a new executive vice-presidency. I want to be turned down, because that's just window trimming for the next move of inviting Marion Williams to move upstairs as first vice-president or vice-chairman of the board. I think he'll assent."

"Even if it takes thumbscrews, yes, he will."

"I'll use them if necessary. I won't be thwarted in this. One of my two executive vice-presidents will be Bud Volk. Under him will come all manufacturing operations. There will be no Group Vice-President Automotive. I'm retiring that jersey. Bud himself will perform that function, as he properly should. He will have all the operating vice-presidents, including Cleary, Vogel and the division general managers, reporting directly to him."

"Which leaves the usual assortment of cats and dogs for the other executive vice-president."

"In the realignment it leaves equal responsibility, perhaps greater. You would have all services, all staff functions, all the junk, but you would also have Sales, Finance, and the biggest plum, the reorganized policy function. You would have your own vice-presidents for each responsibility. Marion Williams would function as your adviser until his retirement. So this is the way it breaks down—Bud will do the things, but you will tell him the things to do. I'm offering this position to you. Will you take it?"

"What does Dana think of all this?"

"I haven't consulted him. He knows where we stand. I'm running the show. Tony, I sure want you to take this job. Will you take it?"

"I'm not sure."

"Resentment?"

"Only you would come right out and ask that. I don't think it's resentment, David. I got over that quicker than I thought I would. When Carl told us, I thought it was the end of the world, but ten seconds later I was feeling relieved. David, I like the idea of the reorganization. I agree, you've offered me what could be the prize spot. I'm pleased. But I don't know if I want it. I'd better tell you. I may resign. That's been going through my mind. It's been a time for soul-searching."

"For both of us. What have you discovered?"

With a pleasant smile, Tony said, "That I'm nobody."

David raised one black eyebrow, and his eyes lighted. "Not that harsh, Tony."

"I didn't say it was a harsh discovery. I'm really quite fascinated with it. I'm nobody. I'm a man with thirty million dollars, and it wasn't able to make me somebody. I'm a man with an excellent education and apparently a good mind, but I've spent my life being intentionally stupid. Do you believe that? It's true. I've tailored my vocabulary for the stupes that surround us, so that they'll feel comfortable. I've been pleasant, that's what I've been, a pleasantly stupid man accepted by one and all. Have you ever met anybody less controversial than me? Good old Tony Campbell, what a swell guy, his money didn't go to his head, he's a real regular fellow. David, it's a fascinating discovery. I've been molded into that perfect nonentity pattern that's poured out so many of the people we know. I'm a success in Bloomfield, hurray, hurray, I'm the perfect, rich, handsome nobody who can go to eight thousand parties and say eight hundred thousand things, and never say anything."

"And not bitter, Tony?"

"Do I sound it? I'm not the least bit bitter, just pleased that I discovered it. Have I ever told you about my clubs? Are you aware I belong to both Country Club of Detroit and Bloomfield Hills, isn't that a remarkable accomplishment?"

David said, "Well, it is. Me, my ambition is to be elected to the Yondontaga Club and never go."

"Now you take Palm Springs. I belong to El Dorado and Thunderbird both, and to both the Racquet Club and the Tennis Club. Did you know I belong to Cypress Point, up Bing Crosby way at Monterey? Before leaving California, don't forget the Los Angeles Country Club. Now, down in Florida there's just naturally Seminole and Everglades and the Country Club, because with your winter home in Palm Beach, where all your free-loading friends

come, you've got to have places for them to play golf snob-
bishly. And over in Naples on the Gulf, Hole in the
Wall. And then there's Fred Waring's Shawnee on the
Delaware. Am I leaving some out? Do you realize that I
have been accepted for club memberships that cost me
about fifteen hundred dollars a month just in dues? Do
you know the main thing it's gotten me? I've met lots of
famous people and played golf in lots of famous invita-
tional and celebrity tournaments. I'll tell you about celeb-
rities. When I get all done rubbing butts with them, I find
out that famous people are just ordinary people who got
famous, and that's exactly what they are, and that's all
they are, and some of them have a lot to offer, some are
brilliant men, some are fine gentlemen, and some are
stinkers, and some are absolute boors, and some of the
women are witty, intelligent, graceful and attractive, and
some are hard, and really rather ugly, and certainly most
unattractive and stupid, and I know all this—they're just
ordinary people that got famous, and I spend a lot of time
convincing people and convincing myself that I'm somehow a kind of big shot because I know these big shots.
Are you beginning to get the picture of Tony Campbell?
But I like it. I do like it."

"Tony, I sure wouldn't presume to give you advice. I
can only invite you to be important with National Motors."

"No, don't make the mistake of offering me advice. I
can accept your being president, David, but I couldn't
accept any condescension."

"Then be forbearing on your own part, Tony. I think
this job fits me like a glove, but I'm going to have to take
some time smoothing out and adjusting."

Tony cocked his head in his characteristic manner. "Yes,
that's true. Your new presidential personality takes a little
cut and try, but so far you're bringing it off just fine. I'm
very much impressed with you. I think we will be friends.
Have you got one?"

David smiled just a little and hesitated a moment to
show that he was studying the question. "No, I do not
have a friend. I have had some people who considered
themselves friends."

"I think we're remarkably alike."

"Do you? In most ways I couldn't think of two people
more unalike."

631

"We're unalike in details. I'm scarcely as pristine as you. You're certainly not as much fun at a party as I am. But I think we're remarkably alike in the essential fact that we've both made our way through to the ripe, old middle forties without acquiring a capacity for emotion. I know that's true of me. I surely suspect it's true of you. Will you argue the question?"

"At the moment I can't think of a good argument."

"Then we should be friends. I can't think of a better basis for friendship than that we will provide one another with a completely impersonal, completely unemotional sounding board."

"I think your new introspection is considerably more bitter than you're admitting. In any event, I accept the relationship. Will you accept the job I'm offering you?"

"I'll consider it." Tony Campbell lit a cigarette. "I'm considering a lot of things. I'm considering giving up smoking, because they finally got to me, how stupid it is. I'm considering divorcing my wife and going off with a seventeen-year-old girl. In this case, I'm not sure which is stupid, staying or going. If I go, I think I'll have to resign the Corporation. I don't think I give a damn for public opinion, but you, Davey boy, you have to give a damn for it. The people around here will forgive me for getting divorced, what the hell, but the middle-aged wives will never forgive me for marrying a beautiful seventeen-year-old girl."

"Well, let me do some thinking out loud. The Corporation wouldn't like it, that's for sure. It could turn the tide against you at some crucial point. But you've got some things going for you. You've got *me* going for you. I'm sure not going to be personally distressed if you decide to get divorced. The fact is, for the president of the Corporation, it would probably be nation-wide news, but as vice-president, it would not be, particularly if we make strenuous efforts to hold it down. You can name a lot of vice-presidents who have gotten divorced with little or no fanfare. On the other hand, your money does always demand publicity, so you'd get more than most, but I don't think enough to be a real problem. It's not as though you were Liz and Richard. As for the young girl, we do have precedent. There was some initial eyebrow-raising about Justice Douglas, but that passed in a hurry, and from the beginning I assume every man in the country

632

was like me and admired the son of a gun. No, I don't think it's going to be a corporate problem. It would just be neater if you stayed with Wendy and me with Sarajean."

"Christ, David, I've thought it over and thought it over. I keep coming to this, it's too bad, but it's also too late. There's no retracing. You don't make up for things. It's only in romantic stories that you pick up a thread of love and life after letting it alone for this many years. I'm committed to Jeanie Templeton. Do you want to hear a strange thing? I feel as though I'm going to live vicariously in her, the way a mother lives in her glamorous daughter. I want her to do all the things with emotion and feeling that I did the first time around only as an existence and a way of life. That sounds as though I have almost a noble concept of it. That's not quite accurate. I'll feel I have made my*self* live, if I can make this carbon copy of me live. I assure you, if I marry her, she does indeed have a lot to look forward to." The smile flashed. "I'm just awfully rich, David." He smiled again. "I can hear the wives of Bloomfield now. *What does he want with that young girl? They have nothing in common. They won't even be able to carry on a decent conversation.* Well, they're kidding themselves, David, Jeanie and me have a lot in common. Sex. The love of sex, we have that in common, and that whiles away a lot of Sunday afternoons. And if you want me to be quite serious, we have in common a very happy thing—the love of the world, we're both in love with the world. No matter what else, we'll have a wonderful, beautiful life, Jeanie Templeton and me. I guess I won't really last long with my program of rehabilitating her. When I picture myself going off with her into a brave new world of emotion, that's tomfoolery. Jeanie Templeton is exactly the same as I was at her age, and with her I'll ride off, hand in hand, into the beautiful sunset of many-splendored un-caring. I was created, and I've been cradled all my life, in the warm, unknowing, so very pleasant womb of sex. With Jeanie Templeton, I will go on the rest of my life, secure from all the buffeting of censure or conscience, because in the womb of sex, there is nothing but the safe, secure warmth of sex."

David Battle felt sorry for Tony Campbell. He didn't want to feel sorry for him. Emotion would interfere with his planning for Tony Campbell. What should he say now? What would be best calculated to carry the mood to the right conclusion? He decided on the truth as he saw it. "Tony, I hate to disillusion you, but you just may be the man of compassion of the two of us. As for me, I'll keep Kelly Brand as long as I can, whether it's for old times' sake or just the convenience of having somebody tried and true. If I lose her, I'll find another, if I need another. My job just may be entirely sufficient. We're not alike. Not yet. We'll be alike in one important regard when you put your talents to bigger use."

"The decisions are killing me. Do you know how I'm going to decide this whole question between Wendy Barrett and Jeanie Templeton? I'm going to flip a coin."

"When?"

"How long will you give me?"

"One year."

"That surprises me. I thought you might say a week."

"If you've got the guts to go through with being a nobody for the sake of a beautiful young girl, you've got the guts to go through with being somebody for the sake of a lot of people. I'll wait if I have to."

"David, I admire you. You do have that deep, abiding purpose that I don't have. Galahad. On the surface you're getting colder every day. Underneath, the fire of the quest is hotter than ever. Pursue your Grail. I'll continue to admire you for it."

"But you think I won't find it?"

"The true grails are simpler, I think, than you look for. The true grails are more personal, I think, than you look for. I don't think a man can possibly find more than his own salvation, if that. Jesus Christ, Buddha, Mohammed, they found their own grails, but they never have swept mankind to drink with full fervor and belief. Do you think you can do what they couldn't do? David, listening to you that day at the board meeting, I wished you well, all the time I was hoping you'd fall on your face. I wished you well because you were so full of the belief, the earnestness busting out of you, but doomed, oh, boy, doomed. You think you'll do all these things for mankind? Mankind will crucify you. Do you really think you can do more than all the automotive giants have done in the past? Do you really think you can stand up all holy-eyed in the world and lead men to that glory you envision? The professionals will cut you up and feed you to

634

the rats. Not a chance in the world. The tides of time are running against you. Do you really think you can stand there, one lone man, and hold up your hands with your Cross of Golden Rule and Morality and stop the oceans of greed and sloth and defeat and anger that are engulfing us? Never, David, never, because of people like me who won't help. I really am going to decide my future by flipping a coin. What kind of man is it that you're going to help? But I'll tell you, if I come up tails and leave the Corporation, I'll be sorry I didn't really quite get to know you. I congratulate you, David, you're one hell of a man. Well, those men in there don't understand you. They don't even understand me, and I'm as clear as the noses on their faces. I'd been thinking that the only difference between you and me was that your emotionless, assumptive drive was channeled into productive things, and mine into nothingness. Lord, here is the discovery, David, that is disconcerting. I'm likely to say that at least I'm poetic. My love of life is poetic. But not compared to you. The remote detachment, that is the real poetry. David, I sure hope I throw that coin right and go off with my beautiful young girl and my money and don't have to stay here and watch you get torn apart. I just want to take that girl's hand and go running off somewhere and think about you as little as I can."

Tony Campbell took a quarter from his pocket.

David Battle said, "I need Bud Volk to run the Corporation for me. I need Dana Albright to give me temperance when I'm intemperate, caution when I'm too bold, wisdom when I'm too young. I think I'm sure going to need you to go chasing the Grail with me."

"Then you see me wrong. You haven't listened. I'm too narrow. I'm shallow. Find yourself another acolyte."

"Get in the barrel, Tony, and listen for a minute. I'll tell you, when Carl Pearson came in that room and told me I was president of National Motors, I could feel the power of it go right through me. It's a great thing, for a man with ambition to have all that power. You start thinking about all the great things you can do with this company, all the money you can make for the stockholders, all the cars you can sell, the big hero you'll be. That's what happens to all of them. The realization of the great responsibility and the great power. I must not jeopardize the life of this Corporation. I have a job to do. By God, it's a sacred trust, that's what it is, to make this Corporation prosper. I told Jim Parker, so many years ago it doesn't seem possible, that he would forget his ideals before he became president of National Motors. He did. He forgot along the way. The job became the end instead of the means. They forget. Those hard-driving men with the great ideals, how few of them keep the ideals to the end! The United Fund, the Symphony, the Birmingham Arts Association, the Cinderella Ball, the Boy Scouts, and all the host of worth-while things that are beyond criticism, the civic things they do that will offend no man. Where are the ones that will stand up and fight now for the issues in which they believed so fervently as they approached the top? Well, they've acquired judgment, that's what. The judgment not to jeopardize their careers, or jeopardize the comfortable public image of the Corporation. I don't think they've really acquired judgment, I think they've just acquired the faculty for accommodation. I think they've acquired laziness, because they just plain won't do those things that cost them real energy and dedication. I indict our business leaders. I indict you, Tony. You've got no business thinking about that young girl if she diverts you in any degree from doing the things of importance for mankind. And I indict myself, because I've felt myself slipping into it, because it's so easy to go into that warm bath of comfort and adulation, where my needs are amply filled, and where men admire me for my great accomplishments in this great industry, and where men defer to me because I am mighty and they want something from me. The warm bath, I began slipping into it the moment I stood before that board and knew I had it all in my hands—the power, the responsibility, the adulation of Detroit. Tony, I'm pleased that we will be friends. We've exchanged confidences that have been shared I'm sure with no one else. Well, maybe you can see that I'm asking you to come in and help me look for the Grail because that's the kind of man I see in you, and because if I don't get some support, I'm going to succumb to the blandishments."

Tony Campbell smiled. He held out his hand. He shook David's hand firmly. He said, "We will indeed be friends. But, David, I think I will not be able to help you, and that we will both succumb to ourselves."

636

He took the quarter between his thumb and forefinger.

"Do you remember the joke about phrenology? Heads I stay with you and Wendy."

"Would you really decide it this way, Tony?" The honest-to-God grin spread on the face of David Battle.

"Sure I would. I'm superstitious. I think the coin will turn the way it's meant to."

"You're fascinating. You're fabulous. You're ridiculous."

Tony flipped the coin in the air and let it fall on the deerskin at their feet. They bent over it.

Tony said, "Tails. Jeanie Templeton. I'm sorry, David." He walked from the room.

David said to himself, "Lord God, I want to try. I can't promise You. I don't think I'll do for Sarajean the things I should do to help her. If You have to, punish me for my shortcomings with her, and with Kelly, and with Mama and poor Pete. I'm so wise and have no wisdom at all, to do for them the things I should have done. But help me in that search for which I do have wisdom. I pray, merciful Father, that You will now let a man who could not live his own life well, help other men to live their lives well."

Dipper Coogan walked into the room. David was disconcerted and felt for a moment that he had been caught on his knees praying. When the Dipper saw David, he would have retreated.

David said, "Dipper, I'd like to say something."

Dipper Coogan waited.

"I've made every apology I could. Isn't it enough?"

Dipper Coogan said in his high rasp, "If you don't like our attitude toward you, you're high enough to do something about it. You're calling the shots, Battle."

"You know that's not true. I'm too high to do you any good or any harm, either one."

"Then we've got nothing to talk about."

"Does King feel the same way?"

"Ask him."

"I'm asking you."

"He feels the same way."

"For God's sake, what do you want me to do?" For a moment he had betrayed emotion. Then he said more calmly, "Dipper, I think it's time I explained to you. I was not part of the plot. I just plain wasn't in on it. I'll tell you exactly what I did do. I was an accessory after the fact. I let my greed get the better of me and I joined up with the crooks. All right, it was wrong. But apparently you don't know the lengths I've gone to to make it up. For all these years I've been steering business to you. I took it away from them and gave it to you at every opportunity. Don't you know this? You must. Everybody else seems to know it. So just what else do you want me to do?"

Dipper Coogan said, "Battle, what you were going to do, you did it a long time ago. What do you think, that you can make up for it? What do you want to tell us, that you made a mistake? People don't make that kind of mistake. Not people that I want to have anything to do with. Battle, I remember you in that locker room. You stood up and put it to me. Well, now I'll tell you something. It wasn't necessary. You always were going to get a fair fight. You got it and you won. You did win. You beat me fair and square. Well, I hated your guts because you beat me, but I treated you like a white man. But you were a nigger all along, and I don't care if it only came out once, it came out, and King and I have got no use for you then, now, or any time. Do you have something else to say?"

"No. Yes. One thing. I've got no ill will toward you. By God, you are consistent, I'll give you credit. I think if you really opened your mind to the whole story, or . . ."

Coogan opened his mouth to interrupt.

David said sharply, "I'm talking, Coogan. I could just plain ask you to give me one more chance to be a white man. But that's not how we get the chance, not by asking. All of us, us black ones and us white ones, that have something worth-while to offer, and have got so many short-comings and faults, and have to live with some people that don't believe in mistakes, I think we should be glad you're there. You're the ones that make us fight back instead of sitting there waiting for something to come to us. For that I thank you."

"You through?"

"I will never have another word to say to you."

David Battle rose and walked from the room. He walked close to Dana Albright, the chairman of the board, and said, "You were right. The friendship approach and the

638

call to duty, I think it's reaching him. I'm sure we've got Tony."

Albright said, "You mean we've got his stock. His vote, that's what we want. I don't care where he goes or what he does, as long as you get his vote in your hip pocket."

David said flatly, "Yes, I did say that wrong. I think we've got his stock, his vote. I'm playing it very well."

"What about the girl?"

"I think he'll marry her."

Dana Albright said, "Well, I don't suppose that makes any difference, either. Does it to you?"

David said, "No, not to me, as long as we get his vote."

David walked on across the room. He passed by Tony Campbell. Tony raised his glass in salute, a solemn expression on his face. Looking at him, David was consumed with sudden curiosity. Had Tony Campbell made love to Sarajean Court Battle? David smiled at Tony. If this had happened, he hoped that she had not been made unhappier by it, because she had enough unhappiness. David handed Tony a quarter.

Tony said, "You want me to make it two out of three? I've thrown."

David said, "Straight Nose Billy Turner wrote me a letter saying we get another chance. I think what he meant was that as long as we were alive, we still did have a chance to start making things right, but you shouldn't wait too long, because you might get dead."

"David, I've already tossed the coin. I really am going to go through with it. I'm going to divorce Wendy and marry that Jeanie Templeton just as soon as possible. As a matter of fact, now that I know it, I'm looking forward to it."

"But there was never anything said that I couldn't overlook your lecherous conduct. At the next board meeting, I want to have you elected executive vice-president. I need your talents." To himself, he said, smiling grimly inside, "Your stock, Tony boy, we need it. Add it to the vote old Dankworth will give us, I've got this Corporation in the palm of my hand." He said aloud, "Throw the coin, Tony. Heads you marry that girl and resign. Tails, you marry her but stay and give me a chance to work you so hard you won't have time for any woman besides her, if that."

Tony Campbell cocked his head, the smile spreading

across his face. He flipped the coin high, and it came loudly to the wooden floor, spinning, and all the heads in the room turned as they bent intently over it as it wobbled and finally flopped flat.